Jeffery W. Olsen was born in 1954 in Salt Lake City, has six siblings, and enjoys a rich and varied heritage. After a botched Ulpanim trip to Israel in 1972, underestimating the effects of the Munich Olympics, he served a mission for the Church of Jesus Christ of Latter-day Saints for two years in Rio Grande do Sul, Brazil. He returned home and married Sylvia Lee Rost, a native of Nevada, in 1976, and they are the parents of five children. Most of his life has been spent in western Nevada, where he graduated from UNR, then at times ranged through the deserts and mountains, the benefactor of celestial tolerance and erudition.

Dedicated to Barbara June Jackson, Kenneth Lee Rost, Maxwell Bernard Olsen Jr., and Elma Marie Anderson, the ultimate in parenting and inclusion. This book is also dedicated to our dear friends, Brent and Joyce Wadsworth, who have blessed our relationship with inspiration, instruction, and joy.

Jeffery W. Olsen

DESERET: A DEFENSE AND A REFUGE

AUSTIN MACAULEY PUBLISHERS™

LONDON ★ CAMBRIDGE ★ NEW YORK ★ SHARJAH

Ordering Information
Quantity sales: Special discounts are available on quantity purchases by corporations, associations, and others. For details, contact the publisher at the address below.

Publisher's Cataloging-in-Publication data
Olsen, Jeffery W.
Deseret: A Defense and a Refuge

ISBN 9781685621940 (Paperback)
ISBN 9781685621957 (Hardback)
ISBN 9781685621964 (ePub e-book)

Library of Congress Control Number: 2022918238

www.austinmacauley.com/us

First Published 2023
Austin Macauley Publishers LLC
40 Wall Street, 33rd Floor, Suite 3302
New York, NY 10005
USA

mail-usa@austinmacauley.com
+1 (646) 5125767

Preface

"…that the gathering together…may be for a defense and a refuge from the storm…" Doctrine and Covenants

"Deseret," the feisty 52-year-old Dr. John Bernhisel muttered as he stepped back from the heavily curtained window in his congressional Washington DC office. The rains were miserable and cold in the middle of March. Low clouds darkened the landscape, bringing on an early evening. A heavy sigh helped the man reorient himself. He lit a lantern, raising the wick high enough to give off the maximum light. Whale oil worked well enough but it gave off an unpleasant odor. Coal oil seemed better, at least easier to obtain but caused a lot of smoke, making its use primarily out of doors.

Continuing to shake his head, he dropped into the leather padded chair before his dark wooden desk. The hardwood was ornately carved. Looking over the disorganized pile of papers before him, he collected and shuffled, then pushed them to one side. It was then that he saw the old map, half-covered by legal correspondence. Drawing it out, he unfolded and gazed upon the fading drawings.

The map was 100 years old and of Spanish origin. The edges were worn and tattered and the ink drawings and writings were dimming. His fingers traced to the left and the mountain symbols so carefully copied by an old, foreign cartographer. He decided that it was a real work of art, if not drawn to scale. Someone, years ago, had attempted to map a distant and isolated area of the continent. He did it confidently, believing it could guide future explorers and even protect them.

The map had been given to Bernhisel by Almon Babbitt, a compatriot politician from the newly formed Utah Territory, only days before. The well-traveled man had a knack for obtaining information. That was one of the things that made him so valuable. Babbitt had received the document from Judge William Drummond. Brigham Young had aggressively pushed his representatives in the nation's capital to get the application into Congress for the organization and formation of the State of Deseret when the 1850 Compromise was being solidified the previous September. A brief window had been opened on the legislative floor when the clever, and some suggested, subversive, Mormon leader was hoping to take advantage of bypassing the territory stage of the country's growth and move straight to statehood. The plan didn't work. It was California that was granted statehood. New Mexico and Utah were both given territory status.

The Mormon contingent was curious as to why their petition for the territory being called Deseret was denied and instead switched to an unknown name: Utah. The Mormons had never heard of the title. One crusty Congressman finally snapped after considering their pestering questions as a form of badgering. "Because the damned word, Deseret, isn't in the dictionary!" he hollered. "That's why! And don't bother us about it anymore!" the man huffed angrily. "Brigham doesn't run a fiefdom! He can't conjure up any word he wants and expect the Congress of the United States to kowtow to his wishes! We have our ethics. And when it comes down to it, we have the clout!"

It seemed to be the demise of Deseret. "Or, maybe not," the doctor mumbled to himself.

It was a little piece of the puzzle for the balding Dr. Bernhisel. The rag-tag Mormon refugees living for the past three years in the Great Basin were well aware that their ideas were not embraced by most of the citizens of the country. They felt that the name of Deseret was a small request. It also signaled a connection with their Book of Mormon. It reminded one and all that there was still a substantial difference existing between them, known as Gentiles, and the followers of Joseph Smith and Brigham Young and God, couched in the doctrines proclaimed by this text, a book the adherents claimed was a companion scripture to the Bible. This belief had infuriated their unbelieving neighbors since the publication of the book in 1830.

The sect's history had been wracked with misunderstanding and violence. Members of the Church of Jesus Christ of Latter-day Saints, known informally and derisively as Mormons, had finally been driven from Nauvoo, Illinois, on the shores of the Mississippi, and the confines of the United States in 1846. The outcasts fled west into Mexican territory, into the Rocky Mountains and beyond, into the valleys of the Great Basin, where they found a modicum of peace and began farming, and building. New colonies were sprouting monthly. Redress of their constitutional rights denied them as citizens of the fledgling republic, the United States of America, was never considered by the politicians. These same representatives felt overburdened by the acquisition of more land after the war with Mexico, as well as with the deep and divisive principle of slavery.

This occurrence didn't take place in a vacuum. War with Mexico was imminent in 1846 as the Mormons poised to set off on their westward trek. That summer the government of the United States drafted, then scooped up a Mormon battalion, consisting of 500 of their strongest young men from the ranks of the downtrodden Saints, to fight in the war. After mustering at Fort Leavenworth in August, the infantry marched 1900 miles across the deserts of the southwest, arriving in San Diego in January 1847, all without needing to fire a single shot in anger. Five months later, the battalion was discharged.

The men worked their way north to Sacramento in preparation for the crossing of the mighty Sierra Nevadas and making their way eastward to the valley of the Great Salt Lake, where Brigham Young had stopped the westward migration of their families. While working in anticipation for their upcoming trip, Battalion member, Henry Bigler, noted in his diary that gold was discovered near Sutter's Mill on 24 January 1848, which news was soon trumpeted in the national press, causing the tremendous California Gold Rush, changing the face of the relatively new country. The men of the Mormon Battalion crossed the towering Sierra Nevadas and then the wide Great Basin, joining their new desert home with a welcome $17,000 in gold for their destitute families and friends.

It was a detail that was not lost on the weary Dr. Bernhisel. He had watched it unfold before his eyes. Brigham Young had promised his tired, worn followers that if they would be patient, the Lord would come to their aid. An abundance of food and resources would soon be coming their way. Prices of these life-preserving necessities, which for them were rare, would be minimal. The Saints would be blessed beyond their abilities to comprehend. That's what they were told by their president. Brigham Young, a glazier and dynamic convert of 20 years to the fledgling church, was the successor of Joseph Smith. And even though the people sustained him as a prophet, seer, and revelator, he was quite different from their founding Prophet.

In the valleys of the Rocky Mountains, pioneer patience was tested early on and severely as they struggled to feed themselves on stored or scoured food while constructing houses and barns. The first week in the valley, the pioneers plowed and sowed crops in 53 acres of the hard earth. 2000 immigrants arrived in the valley the first year, with another 2400 arriving in 1848. Thankfully, the winter temperatures were mild. The ground was plowed and crops put in as early as the spring would allow. In May, as the promising green of the vegetation was beginning to sprout, the pioneers were faced with yet another devastation. Hordes of crickets descended on their fields and began devouring anything edible.

"They come up the valley looking like a gray ground covering from hell!"

The voracious insects were as large as a man's thumb. Small wings did not give them the ability to fly but they climbed and ran with swiftness, consuming everything green in sight. Companies of frantic farmers tried beating the swarms with pans and blankets but they were ineffectual. Panic gripped their hearts as they watched the attacks on the food that was to sustain them through the coming year. All appeared doomed. Then, in the second week of June, seagulls from the vast, saltwater lake to their northwest, arrived and began eating the crickets. The crickets were an easy game. They carried no diseases. Squadrons of seagulls dived onto the seething swarms. They ate until they were full, then drank water from the ditches and creeks, regurgitated their mucousy meals, then started their gorging orgies over again.

After three weeks, the nightmare threat had disappeared and the gulls returned to their normal haunts. To the uninitiated perhaps, it was the cycle of life. It was the normal way of the arid mountain valleys. But for the tormented Saints, it was the hand of the Lord in their preservation.

With the siren call of gold coming from the west, from the Promised Land of California, thousands of anxious prospectors and merchants began streaming across the plains and then mountain canyons, and through the camps of the Saints. The hopeful miners divested themselves of anything that wasn't necessary, looking to lighten their loads. Excess food, clothing, musical instruments, weapons, engineering instruments, all were discarded at rock bottom prices or just given away to help lighten the loads for the horses, oxen, and mules pulling the wagons. This took place before the disbelieving eyes of their religious hosts. Except for prayers of thanksgiving, they were quietly dumbfounded.

For Dr. John Bernhisel, these were days of awe. He saw the omnipotent hand of the Lord moving among his people. The rutted wagon trails in the dusty sagebrush of this new mountain home were far different from the vaunted halls of his University of Pennsylvania or even the quiet, broad, evenly placed streets of Nauvoo. But God was there nonetheless, among the outcasts. Even though their numbers remained insignificant on a national scale, the religious refugees were confident that God was with them.

The doctor smiled when he recalled the words of the simple pioneer leader remarking about the exodus from the United States. "Of course we left the country of our own free will because they made us!" With this unexpected change of prosperity, hearts were lightened. Hands that hung down were lifted. Feeble knees were strengthened. Gladsome music erupted from the trained throats of both men and women, soaring beyond parched lips, out across the arid valleys of their new Zion. Industry was taking place. In small increments, prophecy was being fulfilled. As noted by Isaiah, the desert was beginning to blossom as a rose. Dr. Bernhisel could not dismiss the wonders taking place among his comrades.

Years earlier, in Nauvoo, he had attended to the health concerns of Joseph Smith's family. He had even lived with them for a time. In June 1844, he had accompanied the Prophet Joseph from his home on the Mississippi to the Hancock County seat of Carthage, where he was incarcerated on trumped-up charges of treason, then murdered by an angry, lawless mob. Bernhisel had been at the Prophet's side a few days earlier as they left the Mormon Mecca on the Father of Waters and had heard the sobering words that Joseph prophesied, "I am going like a lamb to the slaughter."

He sensed the future storm clouds. And it had all come true. But a flourishing had also come about not many years after the persecutions and drivings and trekking. The Saints were constructing a bulwark in the mountains and deserts of the west in fulfillment of the prophetic words of English poet and Latter-day Saint, William Clayton:

We'll find the place which God for us prepared,
Far away in the West,
Where none shall come to hurt or make afraid.
There the Saints will be blessed.

However, God's blessings for the moment seemed distant from the physician-turned-politician. The burnished halls of Congress echoed coldly to his ears. He remained unimpressed, unmoved by the vitriol and rhetoric echoing among the corridors and chambers. Few were his friends and associates. He felt isolated among the teeming rush of national businessmen and their interests. Happily, for him, it seemed that the fast-vanishing day, coupled with the rain and growing gusts of wind spoke solace to his soul. Someone greater than politicians, judges, or even the president of the nation, was at the helm, ensconced on a throne above and beyond the towering storm clouds. He was watching over and blessing the events unfolding before the doctor. And this care was not contingent upon the numbers in the congregation.

Bernhisel's musings were interrupted by a sharp knock at his office door. He was pleased to be greeted by the smiling face of Colonel Thomas Kane, one of the few people in Washington the Mormons could claim as a friend. And contrary to his immediate appearance, he could be powerful, having appropriate connections and relationships. He was an attorney and had studied extensively in Europe. That he was fluent in French also helped solidify his stature in the budding capital. The Mormons had called upon this association extensively in the past and it would no doubt be needed in the future.

"Colonel! So good to see you. Please come in."

"Doctor." Kane entered, walking with a ramrod posture befitting a military man. The man wasn't tall and referred to himself in deprecating fashion, as a jockey or invalid. But he had serious strength residing beneath his uniform. Removing his soaking hat, he crossed the room to the large chair that Dr. Bernhisel proffered. "Damn cold outside," he commented as he shook the beaded rain from his cloak, then hung it on a peg. The polished black boots reached nearly to his knees but the dull, wet, muddy soles below bespoke miles of walking and wear. His uniform was a nondescript gray, although the somewhat shiny brass buttons added a variety of life to his clothing.

The bearded, dark-haired man was about thirty years old. He was confident, well connected, and came from money. For years his father, being a high-ranking judge in Pennsylvania, had been active in political and judicial endeavors. The colonel's older brother, Elisha, was an internationally famed explorer and adventurer. The Kanes were constantly involved in helping the poor, underprivileged members of society. They were abolitionists and supported women's suffrage. The Kanes were like a heavenly-gifted family. Five years earlier, this same Tom Kane had been pulled into the influence of Brigham Young and the Mormons fleeing Nauvoo.

From a distance, the colonel had also witnessed the demise of Nauvoo, the City of Joseph, as the remaining Latter-day Saints were driven across the river to the Iowa Territory. He had assisted in their safe departure from the United States and had also been involved with the selection and top dollar payment for the Mormon Battalion, which forthcoming money proved invaluable in helping with the head-pounding logistics of their relocation to the west.

God always seemed to raise men of ability for the help of his people. The well-placed and educated attorney, Alexander Doniphan in Missouri, had stepped up and protected the Mormons in numerous situations during the troubles of the 1830s. The gentleman did so kindly, freely, and without prejudice. Colonel Kane was another such gifted man, who anxiously offered help and counsel and resources to these miserable, nearly friendless vagabonds half a dozen years later. It was greatly appreciated. In 1850, Colonel Kane had delivered an impassioned speech before the Congress, detailing the myriad of wrongs heaped upon the Church of Jesus Christ of Latter-day Saints, the drivings, the murders, the thefts, and the shunnings they had experienced at the hands of their neighbors. The address was widely reported causing no small stir in the populous east, leaving some to wonder why people of such industrious bent had been chased from the country.

Even though unsuccessful, the Mormon cohort in the capital led by Babbitt and Bernhisel, appreciated Kane's efforts, as they wound their way through the halls of Congress seeking statehood for Deseret. The friendly nods and handshakes were more plentiful than before the speech was delivered.

"Oh, I see you found the map," Kane said with a pleased face, pointing to the document sitting on top of the desk.

Bernhisel nodded, pleased to have successfully come through with Kane's petition of several days earlier. "Judge Drummond sent it over."

Mention of Drummond's name brought a scowl to Kane's face. "He's still a sonofabitch," he replied. "What's he doing here? It's a long way from Illinois. Never cared much for him. Never will. He's a sycophant of Stephen Douglas."

"Still, it's just as he said." The doctor pushed the map across the desk, then got up and lighted another lamp to help with the viewing of the aged paper.

The two leaned over the map, each one bringing his background into its interpretation.

"It's right there," Bernhisel said, finally pointing to some finely etched characters.

Kane nodded. "Yutta. But you say your Indians don't have the word in their language?"

"Nope. That's what I'm told. I think the Spanish took the word from the Apaches or Navajos, then changed it around as only they can. It's supposed to refer to people who live higher in the mountains. Leastways that's why the author placed it there, signifying the native peoples who live here around the valley of the Great Salt Lake, or mostly south and east of there."

"So that's where Utah comes from?"

"I guess so. The tribe calls themselves Timpanogos. I think they're a branch of the Snake or Shoshone, more related to them than the Utes. The Utes are farther east, more in the main Rockies."

Colonel Kane nodded his comprehension. "Brigham's got his work cut out for him." He continued studying the map, then turned it in a couple of times to get a different look. "Drummond's fairly certain his cronies won't budge?"

"Quite certain. And Douglas. He says the southern states don't want any more free state senators and Senator Benton says Deseret sounds too much like a desert."

Kane heaved a deep sigh, then ran his hands over his beard. "I see it, I suppose. I don't think there's much we can do about it. Not at present. You can always keep at it. Tell Brigham there's always tomorrow, but for now, I'm afraid this Utah name is going to stick. Can he deal with it?"

"It's not the end of the world. Yet."

Kane chuckled at the doctor's words. "Not yet." Then he pointed to the oversized Bible Bernhisel kept near the window. "You mind?"

"Not at all." The doctor retrieved the heavy volume and handed it to him.

"Didn't you tell me that Young's planning on building another temple?"

"One of the first things he did when they got to the valley was to stick his cane into a spot and announce that was where a new temple would be built. Woodruff marched right over and drove a stake into the spot."

"How was the announcement received?"

Bernhisel shrugged. "Not great at first. We seem to have a bad record when it comes to temples. It seems that whenever we build one or even try, we get booted out. Some folks saw Brigham's statement as meaning we would be booted again." Bernhisel smiled at Kane. "The covenants we make there are the most sacred things we can do. Very important. God wants us to be a temple-building people."

Kane nodded solemnly. He remembered the beautiful edifice in Nauvoo. It was the biggest, most substantial building west of Cincinnati. "But you left. Nauvoo's temple still stands desolate and deserted and desecrated. Even though it's been looted and is falling into disrepair, it is an imposing structure."

"We left but not before most of our people were able to receive their endowment. The promises we make to God and one another are what have fueled the fire within us over these past years. I never would have made it across those rocky stretches without such blessings."

"So you'll give it another go?"

"And we won't stop with one. Brigham wants to build several temples." Dr. Bernhisel chuckled with the idea. "I recall him responding to some of his critics, worried about yet another temple. Brigham told us that every temple weakens Satan's power here on the earth. That the bells in hell ring an alarm whenever one is built. President Young then went on to say, 'And I want to hear those bells ring!'"

The words brought another smile to the military man. "So you're planning on staying a while?" he asked half-jokingly.

"'Fraid so. We're putting down roots. Brigham has been sending settlement companies throughout the territory. Most struggle for a bit but it's the best way for us to show God and the rest of the world what we're made of."

13

"So this endowment, what about the new members of the Church, those who missed any opportunity in Nauvoo? They now await the completion of this new temple?"

"Perhaps. The building will take years to finish. Brigham has taken some candidates to a small knoll north of the city called Ensign Peak, where the ordinances have been performed. More recently the ceremonies have been taken care of in the Council House. Brigham intends to construct an Endowment House for precisely this purpose. It won't be as nice and ornate or as complete as a temple, but it will do for the time being."

"A special lodge?"

"In a way, I guess. The endowment borrows some teaching methods from Free Masonry but our view of the Plan of Salvation, the meaning of life and our responsibilities are much broader than what the sons of the widow experience. And these supernal blessings are also extended to women. It's not a fraternity."

"Of course." Thomas Kane had heard the explanation several times.

"Are you still thinking about what President Fillmore has asked?"

"Nope. Not in the slightest. I told him that Brigham would be a much better fit as governor for the territory than I could ever hope to be. So that's what Brig will be doing for the next four years, along with being the commander of the militia and the superintendent of Indian Affairs. It will keep him busy but the people love him. They listen to him, generally."

"Generally, is the word," the doctor quipped.

"By the way, President Fillmore appreciates your gift. Have you given other presidents a copy of the Book of Mormon?"

Bernhisel sighed with regret and shook his head. "This is our first attempt."

Kane's hands ran down the cover of the Bible with reverence. From his childhood, he had been taught to respect the words found inside. He opened the book carefully, then began leafing through the pages. He found what he was searching for and handed the book back to Dr. Bernhisel. "There in Isaiah. Chapter two, verse two."

John Bernhisel was familiar with the passage.

Kane continued. "Maybe you can point this out to Brigham. Perhaps there's a reason you are camped up there in the top of the mountains. Sharing the top of the mountains with the Timpanogos. This might put the whole name thing into perspective, making it easier for him to swallow."

And it shall come to pass in the last days, that the mountain of the Lord's house shall be established in the top of the mountains, and shall be exalted above the hills; and all nations shall flow unto it.

Dr. Bernhisel knew the church members were steeped in the words of Isaiah.

And he shall set up an ensign for the nations, and shall assemble the outcasts of Israel, and gather together the dispersed of Judah from the four corners of the earth.

After being in the valley for two days, the pioneer leaders had climbed the hill they had dubbed Ensign Peak, and waving their flags to the wind-swept valleys, shouted to the Lord their intentions of taking their message to the people of the earth. At times he thought it comical, these few, stalwart people, were intent on converting the world, sending missionaries to the four quarters of the earth. The determination was married to the people's preparation. As their strength and stamina increased, so would their efforts to keep the commandments and spread the good news. Time and again the Church of Jesus Christ of Latter-day Saints had taught the foundational importance of preparation.

The Lord told the Prophet Joseph, *If ye are prepared, ye shall not fear.* Bernhisel knew the determination of these sunburned folks. He was proud of their example. He was also aware that many who followed the church saw that polygamy was becoming a tenet of the group, although not yet officially announced. The doctor also knew that this was not a favorite subject of the colonel's. He decided not to mention it. Not at that time.

In the quaint words of Joel Johnson and written in the early 1850, it was soon given a melody by Ebenezer Beesley and became a favorite in the territory.

High on the mountain top, a banner is unfurled.
Ye nations now look up; it waves to all the world.
In Deseret's sweet, peaceful land-
On Zion's mount behold it stand!

Chapter 1

"And they did also carry with them deseret, which, by interpretation, is a honey bee…" Ether

"Deseret," the middle-aged man chuckled to himself. His face was burned and worn, looking very unlike his pasty-skinned British forebears, as he guided the oxen with his weathered, wrinkled hands, pulling the wagon reins with the deftness of a veteran wagonmaster. Several days' worth of whiskers protruded from his cheeks. "What the hell damned kind of name is that? More like a damned desert."

"What?" his wife asked, sitting next to him on the buckboard, suddenly aware that her husband's mumblings were rising in crescendo, leaving the personal mutterings that were meant just for himself. The woman was equally weathered by the sun and long days spent traveling by wagon across rock, sand, and sagebrush.

"Nothing. I was just thinking about that damned Deseret. Is it still a territory or what? Where the hell did the name even come from?" He wiped the dirt from around his mouth and leaned over to spit. "That's the damnedest thing."

Agnes thought for a bit, then shrugged. "Bees. It's a Book of Mormon name for bees. That's what I heard." Through cracked lips, she smiled at her husband who was finally showing life and interest in something besides the faint trail stretching before them or their livestock or the others trailing behind in the small wagon train.

"Ridiculous. How did it go from bees to this damned desert?"

Agnes shook her head wearily. "Don't know."

"And hills. Mountains. Gawd, have you ever seen so many in your life? Not that they're so tall but there are scads. And they're barren. Just rocks and scrub. We've spent weeks weaving around them. And now we're coming up on the damned Sierras."

Bill and Agnes Pickett shared the wagon box with their four children, who were also beginning to show an interest in the conversation. Anything that distracted from the wagon's monotonous creaking and jostling while traveling across brittle sagebrush and rocks was welcome.

"Isn't it the territory?" fifteen-year-old Charlotte queried. "I thought that's what Brigham called the area the Mormons were settling."

Bill chuckled again. "Deseret. Zion. Utah. Who the hell knows? The sun's burned their brains. And this is damned hard ground, by the way."

"I still think it's supposed to mean bees," Agnes insisted.

16

"Then why switch it to the Utah Territory? Why not just keep the name?" The chatter was becoming more involved. It was beginning to interest ten-year-old Ina and the four-year-old twin boys.

Agnes was originally from Connecticut and had been fairly well educated. "I guess folks in Congress didn't like taking orders from Brigham Young, especially Senator Douglas, so when they settled with Mexico after the war and set up the New Mexico Territory, they decided at the same time to call this the Utah Territory."

"Oh, because they think Utah is prettier?" Bill responded sarcastically. "That's a load of manure. Deseret suits desert just fine."

Agnes smiled a beautiful smile despite her aging appearance. She enjoyed her husband's mental alacrity. "Utah is the name of one of the Indian tribes' native to the area. It means mountain dwellers."

"You should be a schoolmarm," Bill commented. The others in the family were equally impressed with what she had taught them.

"Oh, and this river," Ina enjoined, suddenly wanting to become more of a part of the discussion. "It's the Truckee River?"

"That's what the map says," her step-father replied. "Some old Indian by that name helped a wagon train up and over the pass years ago. So they named it after him. Truckee or something like that."

"The Donners? They were the ones the Indian helped?"

"Nope. A couple years even before them."

The brief conversation and new ideas gave all of them something to think about and they settled back into their thoughts.

"What about other settlers?" Charlotte finally asked. "Are there any ahead or did they all go over into California?"

"Yep. Most went over into California after the gold, I reckon." Now Bill Pickett was feeling more in charge of the knowledge dissemination. He had studied the map and grilled several travelers. "I hear there's a fort about forty miles south of here called Mormon Station. It's down in the Carson Valley and sits up against the mountains and was started last year. It helps with trade and the mail but we won't be going anywhere near it. Not yet, anyway."

Ina's ten-year-old heart skipped and she heaved a sigh of relief as their wagon finally cleared the canyon walls and rolled into the broad, flat, and mostly burned brown expanse of the Truckee Meadows. The faint road was rough and uneven, shaking the wagon's six passengers constantly. Clouds of low-hanging dust from oxen feet and wagon wheels kicked up in their wake, engulfing a dozen wagons following in the train, as they crawled alongside the river.

The majestic Sierra Nevada Mountains stood as a snowless, bleak, gray mass before them, hiding the confluence of this largest river in the Great Basin, although, by the end of July, the volume of water coursing its banks was significantly diminished. They knew it was still a danger. Days before, as the emigrants had finished crossing the terrible Forty Mile Desert, the parched, thirsty oxen that were not yoked to the wagons, smelled the water and bolted madly towards the deceptively inviting waters. Rushing blindly into the river's flow, a number had stumbled, then became tangled, twisted, and swallowed in the roiling currents. The weary travelers watched impotently as the violent splashing of the animals subsided and some of their unfettered livestock helplessly drowned, and their carcasses began rolling slowly, lifeless, away from them, downstream.

"They're so big!" Ina exclaimed to her older sister, pointing west across the small valley to the looming elevations representing the final barriers standing between them and the goldfields of California. Pines could be seen higher up.

The Truckee Meadows was a relatively small valley. From the canyon mouth where they emerged to the far side where the Truckee River entered the Sierras was perhaps 15 miles, disected by the twisty river and decked on either side by narrow ribbons of trees and brush. Most of the vale had been burned brown by the scorching summer sun. Everything smelled of sage.

The girls' stepfather, William Pickett, a printer and budding lawyer, had married their mother, Agnes Coolbrith in St. Louis 5 years earlier. The following year, their union was blessed with the birth of twin boys, Billy and Donny. Weeks after their birth, gold was discovered in northern California. It took months for the news to break across the young nation. The helter-skelter rush of would-be gold hunters was on. William and Agnes joined in the fervor. Missouri was much closer to the goal of California than were the eastern states, although few discounted the threat posed by crossing the wide deserts of the Basin. The preparation and planning took the Picketts several years. They felt lucky to have reached the final stretches separating them from the fertile valleys of California by the end of July 1851.

Their parents were pleased the girls were close socially. It relieved them of several burdens, not least of which was the care for the twins. They were cheerful girls despite the serious challenges and setbacks they had experienced in their short lifetimes. Illness had claimed both their father, Don, and sister, Sophronia. Then again, like most frontier families, they were hardy and bounced back readily from sorrows and disappointments. The Picketts leaned hard on one another. As long as William kept his distance from the liquor bottle, things were resolved with calm voices and clear heads.

The trail paralleled the river on its northside, staying several yards away from the embankment that was dense with willows and thick, verdant undergrowth. The foliage often hid steep embankments. A wagon careening into the river would easily cost a day or two to salvage.

Ina and Charlotte slowed their speaking, becoming intent on gazing into the shadows of the brush and willows. Doing so over the past several days had uncovered the hiding places of numerous creatures, winged and earthbound. The speed of the wagon was faster than usual and coming around a broad bend the Picketts spied a curious sight at the same time. Long branches, some of them quite thick, had been stacked in an orderly fashion, leaning against another severed, but horizontal bough. It was a crude but obvious lean-to. Like

18

his girls, Bill Pickett had seen the jumble. He tugged the oxen to a stop, waving his left land, then holding it up to signal the rest of the train to follow suit.

He hopped as nimbly as he could from the wagon, pulled his rifle from its rest in the wagon box, checked its charge, then started walking towards the shelter, closely followed by several of his male companions. Coming to the rough opening, they squatted and peered into the darkened interior, waiting for their eyes to become accustomed to the gloom.

"What is it, Pa?" Charlotte asked. Both girls were crowding closely behind, trying to get a look.

Pickett shook his head and gave the girls a warning wave to stay back, then stepped in closer.

There on the ground, covered with a pile of rags and buffalo rugs, lay the form of a large man. Buzzing flies were ever-present. There was a definite human odor but not so intense as to signal death.

"Hey. You there. You all right?"

Pickett had determined that the person had not died yet. Still, he was startled when the bunch of soiled cloth began to stir. After a few moments, a haggard man sat up and gazed back at him through narrowing eyes. "Just who the hell you be?" he snarled hoarsely.

****

James Pierson Beckwourth was born in Frederick County, Virginia, before the turn of the century, to Sir Jennings Beckwith, a descendent of Irish and English nobility, and his African-American wife, who was also his slave. Jim was the third of thirteen children. In 1809, Sir Beckwith took his family to St. Louis and enrolled the children in school. He also had Jim work as an apprentice blacksmith for several years. Although he claimed his wife and children as his slaves, Beckwith freed them through manumission by deed of emancipation in a Missouri court at that time.

Not caring to stay put for long, young Jim joined General William Ashley's Rocky Mountain Fur Company in 1824, curiously changing his last name to Beckwourth. He became a prominent trapper, scout, and Indian fighter. Jim fell in with the Crow Nation and lived with them for several seasons. They accepted the large, curly-haired mountain man wholeheartedly. Many whites thought he was Indian because of his dark skin and his facility with languages. He spent years ranging up and down the prairies and mountains and to California and back, trading and raiding. He was given the name, Bloody Arms, because of his skill at fighting. He was married to at least two Indian women and a slave woman.

In the late 1830s and then in 1840, Jim fell in with another American trapper named Pegleg Smith. The two were involved in a series of escapades against the Mexicans living in southern California. The greatest coup came when they joined up with Wakara, a hard-living Timpanogos Indian chief who ranged far south from his mountain haunts. The chief had spent several years capturing slaves from other tribes and selling them to the Mexicans for horses and guns. In April 1840, Wakara had a large raiding party of his warriors wind into southern California intent on stealing horses. Smith and Beckwourth joined the Indians and began spying out the best places to raid.

All were shocked by the potential number of horses they could capture. The Mexicans had never been intent on chasing raiders. Besides being dangerous, it was hard work. The Timpanogos typically fled back up the Old Spanish Trail for their mountain home. Following the crusty Americans' plan, Wakara had his men split into smaller parties. Simultaneously they struck San Luis Obispo, the mission of San Miguel and San Gabriel, along with some lesser Mexican ranchos. Bringing the horses into one large herd, they drove their prizes to the Cajon Pass. They captured 5,000 horses and the herd kicked up a huge cloud of dust. This time the Mexicans were not about to let them get away and gave chase. The swift trip across the Mojave Desert was brutal. 1,500 horses perished. The Mexicans caught up with the tail end of the stringing drive and recaptured 500 more. Still, the raid netted 3,000 horses for the raiders.

After distancing themselves from their pursuers, the Indians drove the horses to southern Colorado where they netted Beckwourth, Smith, and Wakara $100,000. After this hair-raising attack against the southern Californian missions, Wakara was named Napoleon of the Desert. The Mexicans called his fearsome warriors Los Chaguanosos.

With the opening salvo of the Gold Rush, Americans began flooding into California, both north and south. Smith, Beckwourth, and their crew backed away from any more raids, seeing the stealing of American horses as unpatriotic. Beckwourth became a card sharp in Sacramento. From there he found an Indian path that led past the headwaters of the Feather River, down a ridge dividing the two main tributaries, into the northern valley above Sacramento, ending up in Marysville. He decided that if he could get the wagon trains to follow his safer trail it would add some miles but also avoid several steep grades and dangerous passes, from the traditional roads like Donner Pass. The mayor and founding fathers of Marysville promised Beckwourth a rich bounty if he could bring the emigrants their way first.

Jim hired several men to help him drag logs along the trail to better clear and mark it. His help quit as soon as they could collect their money, leaving Beckwourth alone and at the mercy of the elements around Truckee Meadows. That was when the half-breed mountain man became sick. His fever climbed as he made his way close to the river. No settlers were living anywhere near. He quickly chopped some willow poles and fashioned a shelter as best he could, then laid down, waiting to die, miserable with the idea of having never taken any wagons along his new road.

"Gawdam all my damned luck," he moaned, then rolled over and waited for the inevitable.

****

The Pickett wagon train was surprised to stumble upon the mountain man. By July 1851 Jim Beckwourth had become legendary in the west. Agnes Pickett was a natural nurse. Together with the other girls and women of the company, they bathed and soothed the man's aches, fed and watched over him, and fanned away the flies until his fever finally broke. They plied him with an abundance of water and tasty meals. He ate what he could tolerate. The other travelers cleaned and fixed up his hovel, while all were captivated by the endless stories of adventure, exploration, and warfare that began to pour from his lips. The tales of prowess and audacity grew in frequency as he began to heal. His audience was especially excited to hear about the somewhat longer but easier trail he had found leading into California.

Upon hearing of their original plan to follow the Donner Party up into the Sierras, crossing and crashing multiple times through swift and rocky streams, just to reach the summit, Beckwourth promised them a better route. His pass was much lower and kinder. The trip would be far less taxing, and easier on their oxen and wagons. The news made the idea of losing several weeks from their travels as they tended to the mountain man, more palatable.

After three weeks, Beckwourth was back on his feet and feeling like he had another chance at life. There was a serious but quick discussion among the travelers before they all voted to follow their newfound friend northwest and into the uncharted wilderness. His confidence was infectious. He certainly was more acquainted with the area than any they had met.

Striking due north from the river they met the top of the Meadow, then turned west and skirted some low hills, before another desert valley opened up, leading to the northwest and away from the steep mountain grades and threatening histories of earlier wagon trains. Twenty miles later they moved into a narrowing gorge.

"And there it is!" Beckwourth announced victoriously from astride his painted horse that was pacing next to the Pickett wagon. He pointed to his left and a low hill marked by a simple saddle pass. It didn't look like much. During the previous two days, as the train picked its way along, skirting a dry creek bed, the length and difficulty of the travel became a sore spot. Some wondered how far they might have pushed into the Sierras by then had they not chosen to follow Beckwourth. This had been a chore. None recalled wanting to trek to Oregon. How far north were they going?

Several times the men had quizzed Beckwourth but when he was mounted it was harder to get many words from him. Suddenly they seemed to find themselves at the end of a dusty road, with the promised pass rising to their west. It didn't appear too steep and Beckwourth had already dragged a series of tree trunks along the ground, clearing it of most of the sagebrush and rocks. This would not be a difficult climb.

The travelers decided to camp for the night in preparation for the next day's event. Wagons were lined up or scattered as the people chose, especially since there were no threats from Indians. Small, individual campfires sprang up as dinners were fixed. It was the end of August and close to the end of their journey. California lay just over the ridge where the sun had set minutes earlier. At a time like this, the emigrants were grateful to have chanced upon James Beckwourth, taking advantage of his knowledge of the land and the more unexplored routes into California.

Most evenings Beckwourth spent by himself, with his horse, or keeping a watch on the rest of the livestock. He knew what the best course of action was. A born leader, he was a sociable, humorous man, especially when he started drinking, but for now, he wanted everyone's faith in him. It was no time to make a spectacle of himself.

"With your permission," he began, "I would like to take Ina and Charlotte with me in the morning, on my horse, and ride up to the pass and give them the chance to see the country first." He stopped and thought for a minute before looking back into the faces of the Picketts. "They will be the first white girls to ever see the valley. It's the headwaters of the Feather River. I guarantee they'll never forget the experience."

The parents readily agreed, surprised that he would even ask.

Satisfied, Beckwourth retired to his bedroll but was up early before the dawn, washing and braiding his long black hair that was shot through with gray. He carefully applied paint to his face, donned a large, ornate buckskin shirt, then twisted a broad eagle feather into his hair that he had kept in his sacred pouch. Instead of wearing boots, he slipped his feet into a pair of brightly beaded moccasins. Now he was back in his element, properly attired. He checked and saddled his pony, then retrieved a long decorated lance few had seen during the trek. Everything needed to be perfect. He loved the little Pickett girls, who repeatedly told one and all that he was the most beautiful man they had ever laid eyes on.

As the sun rose, Jim Beckwourth faced east, took some deep breaths, and raised his hands to welcome the new day. He took the reins and led his mount to the wagon. People from the train were up and tending to their morning chores and preparing breakfasts. The Picketts were no exception.

Ina was dressed and ready with a dazzling smile framed by her braided blonde hair. Charlotte was not quite as enamored or prepared about the pending adventure.

Beckwourth kindly passed on their offer of breakfast.

"I need to be clean. Fasting is how I will approach this moment," he commented seriously.

"Oh, now you sound just like Ina," Agnes replied.

Ina didn't say anything, only smiled more radiantly, as Jim turned his eyes on her, nodding his approval.

Without ceremony, he lifted her into his saddle, followed by Charlotte. He climbed on behind and they set off at a quick lope towards the rising ridge. The pony slowed but maintained a quick walk through the sage and rocks and sand, climbing up the hill in the early morning sun. It was the beginning of a perfect late summer day.

Ina squirmed with glee. This was a dream come true. She could smell the horse as he worked his way higher. Faint glimpses of steam rose from his neck as he exerted himself over the final yards. Ina felt the presence of both Charlotte and Beckwourth. It was exciting that this powerful, wise, well-traveled man had taken a liking to them. Ina inhaled broadly several times as they reached the top of the ridge, cresting the pass. The anticipation made her toes tingle.

Stretching before them in the morning mist was the perfect mountain valley scene. Birds flew over the lush green grass, masking the headwaters of the Feather River, awaiting the sun's rays to burn off the fog to give them better hunting.

"There it is," Beckwourth said, stretching his arm past them and pointing to the trees on the far side of the valley. "There's your kingdom. California. This was God's country. Now it's yours."

Ina pondered his words. They sank deeply into her mind. She grasped Beckwourth's arm and hugged it close. After a few minutes, the three turned and started back down towards the wagons. All could make out Ina's cheerful waving. She knew the 1850s would swirl together, making a wonderful decade. The future was bright.

An hour later, all were hitched and ready to begin their climb to the Beckwourth Pass, entering the promised ground of fortune and fame.

The wagons descended, then plodded across the moist valley. Mud was suddenly gripping the wagon wheels. Over the next ten days, they followed the newly created road, going southwest, down the ridge above the river as it finally, gently dropped into the vast plains north of the sprouting town of Marysville, leaving far behind the memories of the broad, isolated, dusty stretches of Deseret.

Chapter 2

"Yea, all things which come of the earth, in the season thereof, are made for the benefit and the use of man, both to please the eye and to gladden the heart."
Doctrine and Covenants

Giuseppe Maria Garibaldi was a powerful name, connected to a powerful man. It conjured up memories from another young man's childhood. Memories of the desperate conflict. Brazil was a country in turmoil. The Italian hero had embarked on an effort to carve separate countries from the states of Rio Grande do Sul and Santa Catarina. The Ragamuffin War or War of the Farrapos-*Revolução Farroupilha* that lasted from 1835 to 1842 marked a time of excitement and expectation, as well as bringing the combined forces of the Brazilian Empire to bear on the *gaúchos* of the south. The defeated Giuseppe Garibaldi finally fled to Montevideo, where he put together his army calling them the Red Shirts because they wore shredded crimson blouses and black hats to give the appearance of the *gaúchos*.

It was a heyday for the poor stockmen of South America, putting Brazil on the international stage. The notorious Italian finally left the Americas and returned to his work in Europe against France and the disjointed Italians. But for a while, things in Brazil had been chaotic and glorious.

Mercedes Martins da Silva was a beautiful young woman living in Porto Alegre, Rio Grande do Sul. Caught by the romance of the fighting and dreams of liberty, Mercedes felt the brief flame in her life. But she had been born at the wrong time. She grew into a woman's body early, drawing unwanted attention from the young men of her *bairro*. By the advent of Giuseppe Garibaldi in 1835, Mercedes da Silva had a five-year-old son and no prospects for marriage. None of her lovers merited her continued attention nor deserved to be memorialized in her son's name.

Mercedes found meager work and toiled to help her parents maintain a humble home, earning a few *reais* each month by cleaning the nearby cathedral. She realized that her lot in life did not lie with Garibaldi's Reds Shirts. But she loved her son. Mercedes wanted only the best for him. When still a young boy, she had his name officially changed to Giuseppe Mercedes Martins da Silva. She prayed that it would serve him well.

Life was challenging for her little boy with the damaged right ankle. The *bairro* offered nothing to interest him. The winding cobblestone streets and the noisy *fazendas* did not fascinate him. He adored his aging grandparents and loved his mother, as only a boy of a single mother can. But the larger animals, the cows, and the horses on the town's outskirts held Giuseppe's interests.

Little Giuseppe left his *bairro*, crossing the rivers onto the Brazilian *campo* as a very young man where he began working with the grazing herds of cattle and horses. He had a special love for these beasts. They didn't tease him because of his gait.

His grandfather, *vô,* and grandmother, *avó,* both died while relatively young. The surprise for Giuseppe came when his mother contracted a lung disease and passed away only months later, leaving him an orphan. Hiding his loneliness, he shifted his fealty to his comrades, these *campo* beasts of burden. No longer needing or wanting the confined life in the city or *bairro*, he spoke endearingly into their ears, while sharing his most tender vegetables and fruits with them. They listened attentively. They did not argue, nor did they run away at his approach.

Like all *Riograndenses*, he enjoyed eating the fried meats of the *churrasco*, but he made it a point to thank God for his relationships with these marvelous beasts, who allowed their lives to be sacrificed to preserve his own or those of his *companheiros*. Even the chickens and pigs. These kind, pesky or large, mighty friends were happy to hear his voice. They enjoyed him stroking their ears or feathers. He liked all kinds of horses. He refused to lean specifically towards one color or another. Bays, blacks, grays, or dappled animals were all received gently, inclusively by him. They represented God's gifts. It mattered not where he lived, he had friends.

Giuseppe became a master horseman, able to ride fast and far. His mounts loved him. They jostled one another to be selected by him. His cattle were calm. He was able to milk them easily, raising large heads of foam in his buckets, obtaining abundant amounts of cream, because of his tender manners and techniques.

His employers noted this difference while he was yet a very young man. They chose to teach him their trade. Giuseppe became a breeder of renown. The foals and calves his stout comrades bore were strong and well-balanced. He saw procreation as an extension of God. It was holy, not something to be joked about or demeaned.

Giuseppe moved from dreams of prestige and glory equated to his name, choosing instead to listen to the words of another Italian man of merit, St. Francis of Assissi. This holy man knew God and His relationship with the beasts.

"*Que mais necessitamos?*" he repeatedly asked his voiceless friends.

And then his life changed. A great island king in the Pacific Ocean had gotten word of Giuseppe's talent and offered his employers a fortune for them to ship Giuseppe and a score of his prized animals to his island, where they would live and breed, where the young Brazilian could teach the people of the islands how to love and rear these impressive animals.

A great ship sailed into Porto Alegre, loaded the hand-picked beasts, and under Giuseppe's careful watch, they set sail, around the southern tip of South America and into the broad expanse of the blue Pacific. Warm memories of Brazil, the noisy streets and quiet *campo*, his friends and, images of his family were moved into his much older memories, *lembranças mais antigas* and guarded there.

Giuseppe did not have a geographical education. He only knew that after weeks at sea, he was pleased to watch as they glided into the Harbor of Honolulu on the island of Oahu. The name meant Fair Haven and it was pleasant-sounding. The Hawaiian people were charming and animated and simple, but they did not speak Portuguese. He felt a sense of pride, being associated with his homeland, but now felt greatly outnumbered. Brazil was an exotic name that conjured fanciful ideas of a Shangri-La. Da Silva knew differently.

"Que coisa?"

Giuseppe knew some Spanish and English and German curse words, thanks to the relative proximity of Montevideo, Pasos de los Libres, and Blumenau to his home in Brazil. But he did not feel cosmopolitan. His mother encouraged him to explore outside of the *bairro* and to embrace the diverse cultures of his region but because of his ankle, this was limited.

King Kamehameha III introduced himself to the 18-year-old Giuseppe. The Brazilian was treated like a celebrity with pomp and circumstance. The officials took Giuseppe to a well-groomed pasture where both the cattle and horses would live. The fences and outbuildings were well laid out and clean. The king and his court were surprised and pleased with Giuseppe's strength, regardless of his stature or his gimpy leg. They were also impressed with the dark pigment of his skin, and quite curious with the abundance of black hair that sprouted from his arms, face, and chest. The animals took readily to their new surroundings, not having problems with their new home. They too were relieved to have land beneath their feet.

Giuseppe was left alone to manage the animals. Three Hawaiians were assigned to assist him, but since none could speak Portuguese, he was mostly left to himself in the beginning. After the first frustrating weeks, the workers developed a crude series of hand gestures that eased the burdens of their work. The Hawaiians also began teaching him their language. He picked up enough words to allow him to communicate. Giuseppe also appreciated the strength and beauty of the native people.

King Kamehameha saw to it that Giuseppe was well compensated, as befitting a man of talent who left his homeland and traveled across the broad ocean to fortify the kingdom of Hawaii. Given to shyness, the Brazilian spent his time with the livestock and away from the villages and the port, places his money would be welcome and quickly spent. He had never been faced with having many resources, so he cautiously saved, thinking his resources might be needed in the future.

The young women of the island found Giuseppe intriguing. His comical accent and easy smile attracted them. Small groups of the women passed by his fields, wrapped in bright dresses and belts that accentuated small waists. The long black hair that cascaded around bare shoulders was not lost on him. Several times he was diverted away from his work by sleek arms and ample bosoms and the encouraging whispers that emanated from full lips. Giuseppe had never been initiated into the art of socializing. He stumbled and fell and was finally judged to be lacking in the more important aspects of relationships. The appeal of his novelty wore off and his would-be suitors returned to their more comfortable associates, leaving the foreigner alone.

Da Silva missed the interaction and began grilling his co-workers more about the people and their past. His assistants were pleased with this awakening from the heady rush provided by the lovely young women. They responded to his questions, telling him what they could and more especially sharing their myths and beliefs. They told him of their favorite god, Lono, to whom they attributed good things. The powerful god enjoyed varied mythology and was celebrated often and in many ways by the people of the islands.

The messages, the stories of the Hawaiians, were sincere and blended well with their work and the seasons. Another success for Giuseppe began a couple of years later when his assistants enlisted the help of two Mormon missionaries who were working in Honolulu. These bearded, middle-aged men were happy to meet the young Brazilian. The men had a variety of resources to share, not least of which was a charcoal slate. They spoke Hawaiian and being Americans, they also spoke and were anxious to teach him English.

This was a thrill for Giuseppe, happily breaking the monotony of his normal work schedule. He sensed the importance of what they might offer, especially their language. He began focusing his attention on English. It started slowly. English did not follow the normal pronunciation rules he had come to expect from Latin and Polynesian languages. There were a variety of sounds that needed to be inserted simply because of tradition. The two men also had the same first name of elder. Elder Sweeney was carefree. Elder Thompson was regimented and possessed a good background in the history of Europe and Britain, blaming the language troubles on the mixing of the French Normans with the Anglo-Saxons.

Giuseppe put the reasons on the back burner. *What did it matter how the language had come to be?* Da Silva also had a vague understanding of where Europe was to Portugal and Italy and Brazil. He focused on phonetics. He could return to the geography and history and reasons why, at a later time.

On their part, the missionaries lost no time fostering a relationship. They were happy to push his learning, combining it carefully with doses of their brand of Christianity, as was appropriate.

After a year of intense immersion, melding with a quick mind, Giuseppe was beginning to feel comfortable with the English idiom. He learned that 'elder' was merely a title both men used, having little to do with their first names or ages. He found it comical, the bantering between the rather tall, blonde Elder Robert Thompson, who was born and raised in Britain, and his erstwhile companion, Elder Mark Sweeney, shorter and darker complected, who claimed to be from the southern portion of the United States. When either spoke, they displayed their backgrounds, accents, and educations. Both had left their wives and family in order to preach the gospel of Jesus Christ as missionaries. Despite their differences, they loved the message and the people of Hawaii, although they appeared quite rejuvenated to have someone so different, like Giuseppe, tagging along after them, giving them a new diversion in their mission. Brazil remained unexplored and unimagined.

He found a myriad of attendant topics attached to his lessons, finding out more about America and the cultures that had joined to produce this interesting duo of friends. On a larger scale, he learned about how the backgrounds had combined to start the world's first serious experiment with a democratic republic.

Of course, he missed Rio Grande do Sul. He missed hearing the melodic, smooth sounds of Portuguese. And he preferred the lilting accents of his countrymen over the more formal and stiff manners of the European Portuguese. It didn't matter. He felt his memories of his mother were etched solidly into his mind, that they would never diminish. In his mind, he could still hear her scolding, singing, or expressing her tender love. And Portuguese would always be the language of his nativity. *Lembranças mais antigas ou lembranças dos ceus? Ancient memories or those from heaven?*

On the other hand, Giuseppe couldn't see how he could ever return. He had accumulated enough money for a return trip to Brazil, but it was a part of his life on which the sun had set. His mother and grandparents were gone. Family relations didn't exist. Any connections he felt for his early employers or even the *gaúcho* culture, faded. Since his departure, he had met many important people. He was an accomplished stockman and assumed he would always be able to find employment among the islands, if not, then perhaps a trip to the United States of America. The latter dreams were fueled by both Thompson and Sweeney. To hear them weave their tales, the Latter-day Saints lived in a pristine wilderness, sparsely populated, but full of promise and joy.

Giuseppe loved the smell of the sea. Coupled with the heat, the humidity caused his curly black hair to ball into small, tight swirls. As the sun would go down, the stars thrilled him. He knew that these same celestial candles lit the skies in Rio Grande do Sul. He recalled a *gaúcho* folksong:

> *Quando a noite vêm descendo o luar,*
> *Com sua luz vai pelo ceu a brilhar,*
> *Sai o gaúcho so' cantando a toado,*
> *Segue doente e pensativo pela estrada.*

When the night comes down the moonlight
With your light goes through the sky to shine
The lonely gaucho leaves singing the ballad
Follows sick and thoughtful down the road
And the refrain:

> *Não ha, não ha noite mais azul,*
> *Do que as noites do Rio Grande do Sul.*

There are no nights bluer
Than those of Rio Grande do Sul

Giuseppe decided for himself that the song was correct. As beautiful as the skies over Hawaii were, for him, no nights were bluer than those of Rio Grande do Sul. He accepted that he would never be going back. He needed to love and learn to appreciate the beauties where he lived. These beauties charmed countless people and had done so for centuries.

"Would you mind telling me," Elder Thompson asked him one evening as they strolled to the house where they had incrementally brought Giuseppe to live, "What are those bands around your middle and ring fingers? Are they a sort of ring?"

The question caused the stubby Brazilian to come up short. He did not know. He shook his head slowly with consternation. "I don't know. No one has ever asked me before. I've seldom thought about it. When I was young, my mother had me wrap these fingers. She thought it was important. I thought they gave me strength. Maybe my mother thought it would protect me in my work. I never asked. I've done it my whole life, since working with the animals."

Both elders were impressed with the verbiage Giuseppe was able to string along.

"Could be a Brazilian thing," Sweeney drawled.

It was the first time in years that Giuseppe began thinking about his past. The memories of his family, especially his precious mother, Mercedes, were passing gently away. Another thing was his name. He had heard stories of Giuseppe Garibaldi and the Red Shirts, but he had no connection with the Italians, not directly, nor in his family's past. There were a variety of people in his homeland. Brazil had large colonies of Germans and Italians, let alone the Portuguese, the Indians and Africans. There was a huge African influence because of slavery, which affected the manner of speech, religion, and music throughout the nation. The Spanish and Dutch and English had all tried getting a toe-hold into their frontier colonies but had not been successful.

"And Giuseppe? Is your background Italian?" Thompson asked.

"I don't think so."

"It's the Italian way to say, Joseph," Elder Sweeney remarked.

"Portuguese is José" the young man replied.

"I think I'll call you Shep," Sweeney continued matter-of-factly, scratching his beard thoughtfully. "That's a strong name and goes with your work. What do you think?"

Both da Silva and Thompson shrugged.

"And you probably want to get rid of the 'da' in front of Silva. Silva is proper enough without it. Certainly in the States."

Shep Silva. *It was marvelous! What a wonderful change.* He felt reborn as if he had a new start on life. Almost a new identity. Shep sounded like it came from the American West. His Hawaiian laborers also seemed to appreciate the shorter title. The Brazilian wasn't sure, but he was certain that his horses and cattle nodded their approval.

The Americans shared broad interests. They were more experienced in life. They wrote regularly to their families, insisting that Shep join them. He wasn't illiterate but he noticed that his penmanship had more in common with the European scrip of Thompson's than Sweeney's, although the latter had more and older children than Thompson, meaning that Shep received several letters back from the Sweeneys. The children were excited about writing to a real *vaquero* from Brazil. He would need to teach them the proper word, *gaúcho*.

"It's not *gaúcho*?" Sweeney asked rather surprised with the revelation.

"That's the Spanish way of saying the word. *Gau-cho*. But in Portuguese, the true language of God, it's pronounced ga-OO-sho. That's what I am," he announced proudly. "I ride better than I walk," he said patting his right leg.

Both the Americans nodded in agreement. There was more to this Brazilian than they realized.

Religion had never been a focus for Shep, despite his *lembranças mais antigas*. He missed going to mass with his mother and the enchanting songs in Latin. There were some Protestant faiths on Oahu and their pastors and members were always pleased with him. It wasn't long after he started going with the Mormon missionaries that he began to see a difference between what the missionaries preached and that of the more orthodox Christianity. He heard of apostasy and revelation and scriptures. And then the singular token of his American friends' belief: The Book of Mormon.

It was a hefty volume and treated with respect by Sweeney and Thompson. They claimed it set them apart from other religions. Several times, Silva had glanced at the book. The wording was archaic, sounding like the Bible. Instinctively he became aware that those of other sects, especially the pastors, did not approve of this Book of Mormon. Countenances would darken and they would dismiss his questions with a swift motion of the hand. It was not a topic they cared to visit. He knew that Thompson and Sweeney had definite opinions about the subject. They didn't care to argue nor seem anxious to foist their beliefs onto the Hawaiians, who were still wrestling with Western ideas of Christianity.

"Why?" he asked one evening.

They had befriended the Brazilian, taught him English, shared him with the citizens of Honolulu, fed him, and finally invited him to share their house. Shep was comfortable and felt they respected him enough not to take advantage of the friendship or his naivete about life and the world. Religion was another story, something of which they felt quite convicted. Then again, they were confident in their message. It was the casual opening the Americans anticipated. They showed little anxiety about the length of time they had known him. Shep was introduced to their mission president and a number of their peers. None gave him the idea that they were trying to convert him. They spoke about the power of the Holy Ghost and figured this member of the Godhead would do the persuading or convincing, and at the proper timing.

"There's a lot of distaste towards your Book of Mormon."

Elder Thompson was ready and spoke with a measured tone. "It sets us apart from every other group. It testifies that Jesus Christ is the Savior of the whole world. He loves all people. He sacrificed his life for everyone, not just for those in the Old World. He spoke with prophets in other areas besides Palestine. And he speaks to us today from the heavens through prophets and apostles."

Shep pondered the ideas for a moment. "Okay, then if this book, this big revelation, is what sets you apart from all others, is that the belief that others don't have?"

Sweeney stepped close and patted Shep's back. "We believe in the gospel of Jesus Christ. This is the message that God has sent us to declare. It was preached to Adam and Noah and Abraham and Moses, all long before Jesus was born in Bethlehem. We believe the gospel of Christ started from the very beginning, not simply with the birth of Jesus. It is a very old and universal message."

"Are you telling me that all peoples have heard the Bible's message?"

"Far from it. That's why God calls missionaries. We do the best we can. But even Elder Thompson and I can't reach all the inhabitants of Oahu, let alone the rest of the islands. But God has a plan for all of us. The gospel will touch every heart."

"But there are millions in China who have never heard this message. And their dead grandparents? They haven't been baptized either. That is an important Christian belief, isn't it? So these folks from the past, who were isolated from Christ because they lived in China or on the islands. What about them? Do they just go to hell?"

"God doesn't see as we do. He knows every one of his children, even those who have died centuries ago and might have lived in China or the isles. The Book of Mormon tells us the dead go to a spirit world. That's where they can prepare for the resurrection. All will be found some time and taught somewhere and have the chance to accept the Savior before Judgment Day."

"It's the gospel," Sweeney added. "It's the good news. Friendships, families, associations, connections can all be cemented together and forever because of Christ's Atonement. That's exactly what it means: at-one-ment. We can all be at one again, husbands and wives, generations past and future. Jesus is our Redeemer. We simply need to love him and accept his covenants. The Savior and all who chose to follow him will wind up in heaven. Forever. That's eternal life."

"All of us come to earth where we experience good and evil. Some are born to prosperity while others have poverty or illness or maybe war or short lives. God makes sure that everyone ends up on equal footing. As long as we don't forget Him, He won't forget us. The Good Shepherd makes sure of it."

"And we all go to heaven?"

"God has prepared a place for each of us, more wonderful than we could ever hope for. His blessings far outstrip whatever we are called upon to deal with in mortality. It's a matter of faith. Do we trust the Lord enough to keep his commandments, to love him and our neighbors?"

Shep forced a smile. This was more than he had asked for. "I could use a Book of Mormon. It could help with my language study."

One of the bundles mixed among the other supplies that arrived with the sleek ships was a mailbag. Shep noticed how near to the docks the missionaries were whenever a ship was due to dock. They were also helpful with the dissemination of the mail, being willing to distribute it to the destinations. Doing this allowed them to be among the first to find if they had mail. Shep realized that the only letters he ever received came because of his relationship with the missionaries.

One particular evening after dinner, lanterns were lit and Shep settled down to peruse the book that was beginning to show signs of wear. The missionaries greedily hunched over the few epistles they had received. The pages were consumed over and over. It was during moments like this when Shep realized the sacrifices these men were making, leaving their families and homes, to spread their message. He knew some of the missionaries had even lost family members to disease and death during their absences. Faith in the fairness and love of God was apparent, as they then rounded their shoulders and prayed with even greater fervor.

"Got a note here for you," Elder Sweeney said to the Brazilian, flapping an envelope in his hand. "A while back I mentioned something to my wife about you and your knack with the animals. Well, she said something to Brother Lyman. He's a friend but also the mayor of our new settlement. He told her you'd be welcome in San Bernardino any time. There's plenty of work for a man with your skills." He paused for his announcement to sink in. "What of it?"

Shep was speechless. He couldn't believe that his existence was important enough to generate this communication. Folks in America knew his name and spoke of his abilities. Now they had stepped forward with a serious invitation.

"Uh-huh," was all he could mutter in stunned reply. Possibilities slammed into him, forcing him to close the book.

Two months later Shep skipped excitedly up the gangplank, boarding a fast-appearing ship named the Hallowed Wind. Thompson and Sweeney waved happily at him. Both of them would be following him to California and the territories before too many months. Kamehameha had been saddened by Shep's petition for dismissal, but the Brazilian had bequeathed all pertinent knowledge to his Hawaiian brothers. The livestock would be well taken care of. Silva's heart was light. He left behind no concerns or regrets. All of his obligations had been met. Adventure lay before him, across the darkening ocean. He expressed confidence in the decision as he turned and waved to a small group of his closest friends.

"*Aloha!*" the small group chimed, waving at Shep.

"*Tchau, amizades!*"

Chapter 3

"The wind did never cease to blow towards the promised land while they were upon the waters." Ether

The Book of Mormon told of an ancient story, how one Jared and his brother had led their family and friends into the wilderness after descending from the tower of Babel. The brother of Jared was the religious leader of the group, the high priest. His name was never given. It wasn't until 1834, four years after the publication of the volume, that Joseph Smith unveiled the man's name. In Kirtland, Ohio a member of the church named Reynolds Cahoon, petitioned the Prophet to bless their newborn baby boy. The jovial leader of the church had taken the child in his arms and gave him the charming name of Mahonri-Moriancumer Cahoon. Smiling broadly, the Prophet Joseph explained that it was the name of the enigmatic brother of Jared. Mahonri-Moriancumer. Shep chuckled to himself as he thought about the incident, facing into the sea wind. "No wonder the man was always referred to as the brother of Jared."

It was early in December 1851 as the Hallowed Wind headed due north. The captain wanted to get around the Pacific high that usually dominated the west coast of North America. After several hundred miles they would catch the westerly trade winds that would sling the ship with terrific force towards San Francisco. The 50-foot ship rode high in the water. They expected to make landfall by the New Year.

The second day at sea, Shep witnessed a curious exchange between a seaman and one of the other passengers as he stood gazing at the sea. The sailor was walking towards Shep carrying a sloshing bucket of water, along with a mop and when passing the other man, he slipped and almost fell. By his gait Shep was positive the sailor had been drinking more than his share of grog. To the Brazilian's surprise, the sailor quickly caught himself, then just as quickly, snarled at the tall, slender passenger, "Best get out o' my way, Jew boy!"

The victim of the verbal assault simply grinned, nodded, and stood aside. The sailor continued on his way, swearing under his breath. Not since leaving Brazil had he heard such a dressing down by one man. Shep thought he would have understood the vitriol even without his English classes.

The solitary passenger continued strolling towards him when Shep held up his hand for the man to stop. "Oh, you're the Jew boy?" he asked with a smile.

The other man's face lit up immediately and he responded with a toothy smile, revealing a silver cap in front. "That I be. Yessir!"

"Shep Silva," the Brazilian answered, extending his hand to shake. "Bound for San Francisco, US of A." He was suddenly quite pleased with his ability to communicate in English. At the same time, he was aware that due to a heavy accent, his newfound friend had also not been raised speaking the language.

"Likewise."

Silva guessed the man to be about ten years his senior. He was clean-shaven and well dressed. The Brazilian was thankful that he had shaved before coming up on deck, aware of how quickly his beard grew and knowing he'd need to be shaving again soon if he were to keep his clean-scrubbed look.

"I am from Brazil and probably Catholic. I work with livestock."

"Very pleased to meet you, Shep Silva." His speech was clear. Despite his accent, the man had no trouble speaking English. They shook hands warmly. "I am Aaron Rost, from Posnan, Prussia or else Danzig. I'm a merchant."

It was nice to have an acquaintance, especially since they had several weeks left before landfall. It was doubly pleasant to learn that Aaron was traveling by himself and Shep didn't need to worry about encroaching on his time with family or friends.

"You don't have trouble with being sick on the sea," Aaron commented one morning to his younger friend.

Shep shook his head. "But when I sailed to Hawaii from Brazil, oh that was terrible! There were stretches when I could barely get out of bed. And I lost weight. A lot of it." He smiled with the recollection. "I think the crew was ready to throw me over the side."

Aaron nodded. "You don't talk about your family in Brazil."

"I don't have any. My *mãe*, Mercedes. She's about all. She died when I was young."

"She took you to church?"

"Yes. She also cleaned the cathedral. So she wanted to do right."

"But you don't know about where your family originated? In Europe?"

Shep shrugged. "Portugal, I guess. That's where the name da Silva comes from. Does it matter?"

"Of course not," Aaron answered. "I have just been watching you these last few days and you do something that's interested me. You hold your middle fingers together, on both hands. Your hand seems to work well, but I haven't seen this many times, with both hands."

"Oh, I know. *Mãe* insisted that I bind my two inside fingers, especially when working. I always thought it was for strength or perhaps a superstition. It has become a habit. The fingers seem to stay together even when they're not tied. You're not the first to mention it to me."

"It's a curious thing."

"I guess."

"Have you ever heard of *Marranos*?"

"Pigs?"

Aaron chuckled. "That's one meaning of the word. Or 'forbidden'. But many years ago, Ferdinand and Isabella ruled, they conquered the Moors and expelled them and the Jews from Spain and Portugal. Many could not afford to leave. That's when the Spanish Inquisition started. Jews and Moors were forced to convert to Christianity or be banished. It was very difficult. I know that many Jews converted but secretly claimed the religion of their fathers. Hebrew was used behind closed doors. Festivals and rituals continued secretly. Of course, some were found out. Torture of suspected Jews became routine, driving many even further underground. They developed secret words and gestures to identify one another. They needed to be very careful. When the New World was discovered, many of the colonists from Spain and Portugal were these kinds of people. Jews. They were called '*Marranos*'. Their main goal was the fleeing of discovery by the Crown and the Inquisitors. The rulers branded them as evil and forbidden. The *Marranos*. It has different meanings for the Jews. It was easier for them to mingle in these new lands far from the Rome or Madrid or Lisbon. Anyway, the way you hold your fingers has long been suspected to be a secret *Marrano* hand gesture. Just thought I'd ask."

Shep allowed the new ideas to germinate for a while. It was unsettling. Later that afternoon he decided to bring the topic up again.

"You say that you're from Prussia. That's a distance from Spain, even from a Brazilian point of view. And you are aware of the Jews there?"

"It's true," Rost admitted. "The Jews who settled in northern Europe are quite removed from those who lived in northern Africa and Andalusia, the Iberian Peninsula, Spain. My family always referred to these Jews living south of us as Sepharadi. They are more closely woven into the Moors. Muslims. Arabs. My people moved into northern Europe centuries ago. We're the Ashkenazi. Our biggest influence has been German. We mixed our language with German. Today our language is called Yiddish. But even though we are separated by long distances from our southern brothers, we are somewhat aware of the troubles they've endured. I have noticed it in some paintings. The artists have captured some *Marranos* with the position of their fingers. Like yours. It's just a matter of curiosity for me. I don't mean to offend."

"Oh, no. But your thoughts make me think. And perhaps you could help me. There have been some things stirring in my head since I was a *menino*. My birthday is tomorrow. I was born 21 years ago. *Minha mãe* told me that it was a special day, and not just because of my birth. There was something in the way she told me, that seemed to mean more than what she said."

"Ah," Aaron said thoughtfully. And then he suddenly brightened. "Do you mind if I go to my locker for a few minutes?"

Aaron Rost returned after 15 minutes, beaming like a schoolboy with a discovery.

"I'm not sure," he began. "But I think we may have stumbled on something quite remarkable."

Shep was all ears.

"Your birthday is on the 11th of December? And it was 1830?"

Silva nodded.

"Jews use a different calendar. Ours is lunar and things shift when compared with the Latin calendar. That's why Easter never falls on the same day. It's in the springtime but determined by when Jews mark Passover. The same goes for *Hanukkah*. It's always late in the year but jumps around. But on December 11, 1830, started the first day of the Jewish holiday, *Hanukkah*! It's not a religious holiday, more like a national one. It commemorates the saving of the Second Temple from the Seleucid Greeks years before Christ. It's the Feast of Dedication.

"Our people were fighting a guerrilla war against the Greeks. They had captured the temple in Jerusalem, where the Greeks had desecrated it by sacrificing pigs to Zeus. Once they took the temple back, they washed and cleaned the altars and threw down the statue of Zeus, then dedicated the temple once again to God. The Eternal Light was lit, but they only had enough oil for the lamps to burn for a single day. The Greeks mounted a counterattack, cutting off the temple defenders. It took the Jews eight days before they could break the siege and chase the Greeks away and bring the needed olive oil to the temple. It was a miracle because, from the time of the lighting of the Eternal Flame, it lasted the eight days until new oil was brought in."

Aaron was pleased to relate the tale. It was obvious that it meant more than a little to the slender man. "That's the main reason I work with mercantile. Mostly, I sell lamp oils. Coal oil. Some whale oil. But even now, there are some acquaintances of mine in Prussia and America who are working with shale oil, refining it. It will burn longer, brighter, and with less smoke. And the price will be less. It will provide work for many of the poor and unemployed."

"And you think there might be a connection to my birthday and *Hanukkah*?"

"Maybe. Have you ever seen one of these?" Aaron withdrew a small four-sided top from his pocket. "This is a dreidel." He handed the wooden toy to Shep.

Shep inspected the little piece closely. There was a symbol painted on each of the four sides. "Never seen one. How does it work?"

"Jewish children play with these at *Hanukkah*. These characters are Hebrew letters. N, G, H, and Sh. They represent a short phrase in Hebrew: *Nes Gadol Hayah Sham*. It means: A Great Miracle Happened There—referring to the miracle of the dedication. I'm not sure if the Sephardi Jews play with dreidels, but we do. We've assigned the letters another meaning in Yiddish. It uses the same characters but the meanings are different, but it explains the way to play the game. Nichts, Ganz, Halb, Schtel. So, as you take turns spinning the top, there is a pot in the center of the table. Kids bet their candy, or *Hanukkah geld*, placing some into the pot. Then as they spin, if it lands on the N, they get nothing. The G means they take everything from the pot. H means they take half from the pot. Or if it's the Sh, they have to put candy into the pot. It's simple and the kids love it."

"Dreidels are that old?"

Aaron shrugged. "I don't know. Just thought I'd show you my dreidel to see if you had any memories of it from when you were little."

Shep shook his head. "Nope. And for sure, when I was small, I would have enjoyed playing with his kind of top."

"This year *Hanukkah* starts next week on the 19th."

The rest of the day was spent changing chores with other passengers and sailors. It fascinated Shep, how the sails could be tacked, keeping the ship moving in the direction they wanted, even if it was contrary to the wind's direction. Jibing remained a mystery to the *gaúcho*. The duties kept most of those on board busy and helped the time pass.

Climbing a gangway Shep ran into the ill-mannered sailor who had disparaged Aaron a few days earlier. He purposefully stepped into the man's path.

"Outta my way, boy," the man ordered tersely.

Shep stayed put.

"I said—"

"I heard you fine," Shep interrupted. "Since we're going to be on this boat for a while, some things need to be set straight. I don't like the way you talk, not to me or my friends. You change your ways or I will happily box your ears." Even though he was smiling, Shep's eyes flashed as he calmly rolled up his sleeves, exposing thick wrists and forearms.

The sailor thought for a moment then nodded. "Nuf said," and he stepped around the Brazilian.

In the evening, with chores done and lanterns lit, Shep found Aaron again for a brief meal and a chance to talk more.

"You know Jesus was a Jew?"

"I've been told that my whole life," Aaron admitted sarcastically. "I've yet to figure out why that gives Christians license to beat the hell out of us."

"Do you think he was a good Jew?"

"I hope so. Why?"

"I like thinking about him as the Shepherd. It makes me feel closer to him. Work stuff, you know. Anyway, I was looking through my Bible and found this in John."

"And it was at Jerusalem the feast of the dedication, and it was winter. And Jesus walked in the temple in Solomon's porch."

"Am I right? *Hanukkah* means dedication and it's winter."

Aaron smiled victoriously. He had found gold. "It sounds to me like Jesus was a good Jewish man. Among other things."

The Hallowed Wind sailed into the San Francisco harbor two weeks later before the festivities of the New Year.

Chapter 4

"Hear O Israel, the Lord our God is one." Deuteronomy 6:4

Life was going well for Sam Brannan at the beginning of 1852. Still a few years from crossing into his mid-thirties, he owned stores in San Francisco as well as Sacramento. He controlled several real estate investments, thanks to the sale of his printing press, one of the first in California. He had gotten in on the ground floor of the California Gold craze, selling pans and picks to the hordes of Forty-Niners who had begun flocking to the west. He had a knack for commercial affairs. State leaders listened intently to Brannan's opinions and moved the state capital from San Jose, which he considered too muddy, to the new settlement of Vallejo on the north side of the San Francisco Bay. The town was easy to be seen from the southern peninsula on a clear day.

Sam was a familiar figure in San Francisco as well as Sacramento. Men doffed their caps and women smiled prettily at him. The wharves were a promising hunting ground. Ships from the Orient docked regularly, carrying extraordinary cargo, that if approached then and purchased correctly, could bring great dividends.

The Hallowed Wind was a ship he readily recognized. He knew she was arriving from Honolulu. He pulled up short and watched the flurry of activity as sailors ordered their merchandise, before opening the gangways for the passengers to begin departure. *What an idyllic place, that Honolulu. Money could certainly be made there.* He made a mental note to investigate more seriously the real estate prices on Oahu.

Brannan spotted Shep's short stature as the young man hoisted his duffle bag and started down the plank. Sam made sure to intercept him at the bottom.

"Good morning to you, sir," Brannan said as cheerily as he could, stretching a hand out to Shep.

Silva was surprised and stopped. The man was addressing him and in a friendly fashion. And there was something familiar about him. Perhaps it was an American air.

"Thank you and to you, sir," he replied, taking the proffered hand.

"Whoa!" Brannan announced with a smile. "That has got to be one of the hairiest mitts I have ever seen!" he nodded at Shep's hand, causing the latter to blush with uncertainty. "A strong grip, too. I don't mean to be a bore, just glad to meet you up close."

Shep nodded, still with some confusion.

"I know you," Brannan continued. "At least of you. In Honolulu. The king took me out to his ranch one day and showed off some of the work you've done for him. Quite impressive, young man. That is you, right? The imported stockman?"

Relaxing a bit, Shep smiled. "Yes. Thank you."

"Now, your accent. You're dark like a Hawaiian but I've never seen an islander as hairy as you. Again, no offense intended."

"Brazil. I'm from Brazil." A romantic name and place few had heard of.

"Wonderful. Well, let me be one of the first to welcome you to San Francisco. You do nothing but make our city better. Thank you for coming. May I ask what brings you all this way? Stockman extraordinaire, from Brazil and Hawaii?"

"Excuse me, may I barge in?" Aaron asked, having recently walked up behind his partner. "I am Aaron Rost, from Prussia. Mercantilist. This is my good friend, Shep Silva. How may we assist you, sir?"

"Very, very good, my dear fellows! You can do me the favor of accompanying me for a short while. I will be pleased to pay for lunch. I have to say that I am intrigued and it would be my pleasure to get to know the both of you. Are my plans acceptable?"

The two travelers traded looks and nodded their agreement. This could be the providential opening they needed. They turned and walked a short distance to a series of tables spread for visitors along the dock and seated themselves. Brannan ordered three cups of coffee to begin their meal.

"I thought you looked familiar as well," Shep said. "You were with a small entourage from Honolulu. You came to the ranch. What? About 4 months ago?"

"Excellent memory! Yes, indeed. The middle of September. The king was rightfully proud of what you were doing with some of his most prized animals. I must say, I've never understood the connection between man and these beasts of burden. It must be a knack and you certainly possess it."

Shep appreciated the compliment.

"And what brings you here from Prussia?" Brannan asked Rost. "Not the goldfields. What type of mercantilism?"

"Oil. Lamp oil and not from whales."

Sam agreed. "Nasty business, that. And I don't care for the smell either. You have other products we could use in these parts?"

"Coal oil, mostly. But it's inexpensive and burns cleanly. I do have associates back on the Continent who are working to refine shale oil even more. It will burn longer, brighter, and cost less than expected. Thousands of jobs will be created. The streets and houses will no longer be dark. It promises to be a revolution."

"You have done your work in coming here, Mr. Rost. This is exactly the type of industry we are seeking. I, for one, will be glad to dismiss these bloody whalers and turn to something more beneficial."

"You've lived here long?" Silva asked, then thought it a poor question.

Brannan shook his head and waved off any concerns. "Not to worry. I came on the ship Brooklyn, in 1846. We sailed from New York City and came around the Horn as the war was breaking out against Mexico. This place was called Yerba Buena in those days. We wanted to capture the *pueblo* for the States but Commander Montgomery and the Portsmouth beat us. Still, when our company arrived, we more than tripled the population. We changed the name of the town to San Francisco. This has been my home since. They are even building a synagogue there," he said, nodding to Rost.

Aaron held up his hands in defeat. "Now how is it?" he asked. "Do I have a sign on my sleeve naming me a Jew? Perhaps I should have told you that my name is Maher-shalal-hash-baz."

The men were impressed with the facility the longest name in the Bible rolled off Aaron's tongue.

"Maybe it's your shiny tooth," Silva guessed with a wink at Brannan. All laughed good-naturedly. Their meals arrived and they enjoyed the diversion.

"We have two new synagogues here in this city." Brannan was proud of the achievement. "Both were finished last year. Temple Emanu-El was built for the German Jews and Temple Sherith Israel caters to the Polish Jews. I guess they couldn't agree on how to say their prayers. But you'd know more about that better than me."

Rost felt embarrassed. "I suppose," he said, holding out his hands in defeat. It was amazing just how much information Brannan possessed. He was a wealth of knowledge, especially as related to the city, the goldfields, and northern California.

"I think our timing is perfect, gentlemen," Brannan finally announced. He pointed to the northeast and the approach of a ferry. "Hopefully that will be my friend."

Rost and Silva exchanged glances once again, bringing a laugh from Brannan.

"Please don't worry. I consider you my friends and would appreciate your company for the afternoon. This evening I insist that you stay in my hotel at my expense."

The kindness and timing of Brannan were beyond fortuitous. And he could not be talked out of his generous offer. He certainly was the man of the hour.

"This friend from Vallejo is Mr. Lilburn Boggs, originally from Kentucky, but spent much of his life in Missouri. Matter of fact, he was the governor of the state in the 1830s. He emigrated to California in 1846. A number in his group separated for whatever reason and became known as the Donner Party that got stranded in the Sierras that winter, and resorted to cannibalism." Both Silva and Rost had heard the gruesome stories. "Boggs' party arrived peacefully enough and he settled in Sonoma, where he's the postmaster. His first wife died quite young, back east. His second wife, Panthea, is the granddaughter of a famous American frontiersman named Daniel Boone. Boggs is a good man. He is considering running for office in the California State Assembly this year."

They rose from their chairs and descended the slight slope to the waterfront and the dock where the ferry was being tied up.

There was much that was familiar to Shep with the Hispanic influence of the area. He enjoyed hearing and seeing Spanish. It held an emotional response in his heart. He had always considered the language as a pidgin Portuguese. It was easy for him to understand, making him feel quite at home. He knew there were many places where he would be accepted and not seen as a foreigner with an accent.

Boggs was a portly, powerfully built man. Low to the ground but still taller than Shep. The man's hair was white. He carried himself with confidence and waved at the trio as they drew closer. Brannan shared introductions quickly and succinctly. The four then flagged a coach to take them farther into the city. Sam explained that he and Boggs had official business regarding the election that needed to be addressed. The weary but pleased travelers were dropped at an elegant hotel a block from Brannan's office. Before continuing, he escorted the men inside and explained his intentions to the clerk, who jotted down all of Brannan's wishes on a pad of paper, seeing that they were given decent accommodations.

"And I will see the both of you next door for dinner at 6:00?" After they nodded, he exited quickly and climbed back into the stagecoach, leaving in a cloud of dust and the creaking sounds of iron wheels and springs and horses' hooves.

The following two weeks were a flurry of activity as the new year was welcomed. Despite Sam Brannan's assertion that the city had the world's best climate, January was wet and cold, especially for Shep who had grown accustomed to the tropical weather on Oahu. Even then the bustle of the streets and wharves was noisy and continuous.

Aaron Rost thought he had died and gone to heaven. With every turn, he met more and more potential clients who wanted to hear about his products. He fired off a stack of letters to Prussia, then chaffed at the slowness of ships and mail.

"I don't care if it's the other side of the world, I don't have the luxury of waiting."

Shep tagged along for a while but the passing of each day told him that this was not where he was meant to be. As friendly and enthusiastic as Brannan and even Rost were, he knew that he did not belong in San Francisco. Not at this time.

"I'll be going to San Bernardino," he told Aaron. "That's what I intended to do and that's where I told Elder Sweeney I'd be going. His family is awaiting me and I have some jobs set to work."

"When would you leave?"

"Soon. In the next couple of days."

Rost understood. He wanted to mount a protest but had already offered him work. It didn't hold the Brazilian's interest.

"I love the animals."

"Maybe I can ask you to do yet one more thing for me?" Rost queried. "Today is Friday. Tonight will start the Sabbath. Come with me and meet some of the folks. I haven't found anyone from Posnan yet. Most are from Bavaria. But, my friend, I can't help but think you are a Jew deep down inside."

Silva smiled. Rost hadn't given up. "Without a doubt, we're cousins," he chuckled.

The synagogue was small but sturdy. The congregation was building it out of stone. They had plans to extend in the future. It was set on Lake Street not far from Brannan's Sea Cliff properties on the north end of the peninsula.

Shep had never attended a Jewish service. The men wore mostly black coats and broad-brimmed hats. They outnumbered the women considerably but it was obvious that this was a growing congregation and there were more women proportionately here than throughout the city, in general.

As the sun was setting, all stood and turned to face the west. Shep patiently tried to follow Aaron's lead as the group began to chant the Shema.

Shema, Yisroel, Adonai elohenu, adonai echaaadd...

Shep felt a distinct shock run down his back.

Hear, O Israel, the Lord our God is One.

There was a glimmer of recognition. The words were familiar. He had been in the situation before. *Had it been a synagogue?* But the tender singing, the bowing, the dark clothing, the bearded men, the veiled women, the supplicating hands spoke to him.

Shep could feel the increased beating of his heart. There was something here, something too familiar. Back in his youth. *Lembranças mais antigas*? *When was it?* The word "*echad*" had been intoned by these pious people. They dragged it out to a close and yet as they did, he could hear the melodic voice of his mother, Mercedes, singing the phrase. And it was more than once. It was unnerving as if she had returned from the dead, a voice from the dust speaking in his ears.

Tears began to fill his eyes as he contemplated the connection. *Was Aaron right? Was he a secret Jew? A Marrano? Were they his people? Did they pray thusly in secret, behind closed doors, hiding from the Inquisitors?*

Aaron noticed the tears rolling down Shep's cheeks but kept his silence. He knew something was transpiring. The congregations held powerful sway in some Gentile communities. *Chazans* or cantors and rabbis were talented. They were touched by God with a special power. They helped bring the otherwise scattered people together into a community.

After the service, the two men begged off from participating in the *oneg* or post-Sabbath communal meal. Walking pensively, they wound their way back to the pension. The silence was amplified by their hearts. Upon reaching their destination, Shep pulled on Aaron's arm to stop.

"I have heard that before. That *Shema*," he confessed. "When I was a boy with my *mãe*. I could hear my mother's sweet voice. She sang those words. They were holy to her."

This revelation was more than even Aaron had hoped for. "Rabbi Akiva spoke them at the end of the Third Rebellion. As the Romans tortured him, as their flesh combs ripped the skin from his aging body, he looked out the window of his prison and said these sacred words, dying as he pronounced the last "*echad*"—one. That's why our people always prolong that part of the verse. We are trying to capture the heart and emotion of this great rabbi."

"It has changed my life, Aaron," he declared soberly.

Chapter 5

"Remember the worth of souls is great in the sight of God." Doctrine and Covenants

Shep purchased a ticket for passage to the port of San Pedro that serviced Los Angeles, on a coastal steamboat and left San Francisco two days later. He was pleased with his decision. The company of Brannan and more particularly that of Aaron Rost had been magnetic. Had he stayed any longer Shep doubted that he would have made his way to the southern portion of the state.

Most of the steamboats in California went to Benecia or Sacramento from San Francisco. Large herds of beef were raised in the south to support the swelling numbers of people in the north. There were herds in Monterey and Santa Barbara but the largest numbers were from Los Angeles, giving rise to the term of cow counties. Sometimes the cattle were driven north in herds. At other times, if the timing was prompt, some of the beef was slaughtered, aired, cut up, and shipped by steamboat.

El Pueblo de la Reina de Los Angeles began on September 4, 1781. The *pueblo* was named the Queen of the Cow Counties. It had remained a sleepy-eyed town until the Treaty of Guadalupe Hidalgo ended the war with Mexico. After that, Americans began flocking to the area. Vigilance Committees in the San Francisco and Sacramento areas chased away most of the gamblers, prostitutes, and criminals. They ended up in Los Angeles. It became bedlam and was termed the most lawless town west of Santa Fe. Los Angeles was incorporated as a city on April 4, 1850. Five months later the State of California was admitted into the Union.

There was a definite pecking order in the society of lower California. Anglos took advantage of every angle, quickly rising to the top. Mexicans were kicked to the side. Their language was disdained and ignored and belittled. The Indians were at the bottom of the pile, treated with disgust by the others. It was virtually impossible to bring an Anglo to trial for killing an Indian or forcing them from their land. That became the order of the day and the Indians in and around Los Angeles lived in constant dread of being victimized.

Some passengers on the side-wheel-driven steamboat were tough and hardened, standing at the railing, looking for the next port of call, when they could disembark, gamble, get drunk, and find loose women. The goal was to avoid getting shot or lynched or ending up in jail. It made for dicey conversations, mostly in low tones, punctuated by loud guffaws and snickers.

Bill Pickett regretted having brought Agnes and their five-year-old twins on the trip. He had serious doubts about moving the family back to the north.

Legal prospects were good around the goldfields but his talents had been spoken for in Los Angeles. As disappointing as the town was, he was able to make a respectable living. Between his work and Agnes and the children, he was kept away from the more troublesome elements of society.

"I think we're doing the right thing," he told his nervous wife. She could hardly wait to get back to their daughters, away from the mayhem offered by the likes of these steamboat passengers. "We make enough money, don't we? We could always move inland, to Rancho San Bernardino, if you want. It's quieter and much calmer. There should be plenty of chances for me to work. I hear it's growing."

"And filled with Mormons," she added. "Don't forget that."

"There's not any drinking or gambling. Hell, they don't even have a jail."

"We'll be fine in Los Angeles, for now," Agnes assured him.

Both noticed the short, dark-haired man standing close to them. He was alone and not given to participating in the antics of the other single men. When on deck, he tended to drift towards the few families who were also keeping close to one another.

After clearing the waters near San Luis Obispo, Bill decided to open a discussion with the silent stranger. "Going to Los Angeles?" he opened.

"Yessir."

"You from there?"

"No sir."

"What land are you from?"

"Brazil."

He had never heard of it. Bill was not given to speaking much and was running out of ideas. Agnes came to his aid.

"We live in Los Angeles. We have for several months. My husband, Bill Pickett, is an attorney. He also is a printer. These are our twin five-year-olds, Donny and Billy. My name is Agnes and we have two older girls, Charlotte and Ina who are keeping house for us in the city."

"My name is Shep Silva."

"You're coming from San Francisco," Bill stated.

Silva nodded. "I arrived a couple weeks ago. I'm going to San Bernardino and work with horses and cattle."

"We were thinking about moving back to the Bay, to northern California and San Francisco," Agnes explained. "But we don't know folks there. We tried a bit but we'll be better off in Los Angeles."

"My best friend is a merchant in San Francisco. Aaron Rost. I also got to know Sam Brannan in the city and a gentleman from Sonoma named Lilburn Boggs."

The news startled the Picketts. It did not go unnoticed by Silva. "Oh, you know either of them?"

They nodded together.

"Who in San Francisco doesn't know Samuel Brannan?" the woman asked. "And Bill and I both come from St. Louis, Missouri. Mr. Boggs was a governor of that state years ago. They are friends of yours?"

"Perhaps. Or acquaintances, at least." Silva could tell from the expressions on their faces that they weren't taken with them in the same way he had been. "What don't I know?"

Agnes sighed and apologized. "We don't know either of them very well. We do know that some of the trouble we are experiencing in Los Angeles is a direct result of some of Brannan's activities. Last year he and some others started up a group of fellows, calling themselves the San Francisco Committee of Vigilance. They became the police force and began rousting the undesirables from the city, even hanging some they thought were offenders. I guess it worked in San Francisco and Sacramento, at least for a while. It didn't help us much, in Los Angeles. Many of the undesirables fled south."

"So he leads the vigilantes?"

"And other worrisome things. When he arrived in the area, he was leading some Mormons who were intending to then travel east, cross the mountains and meet up with Brigham Young. Instead, he encouraged them to stay put and settle down. Mr. Brannan and a small party rode to meet Young before they reached the Great Salt Lake Valley and tried to convince him to bring his followers to California instead of staying by the Great Salt Lake. Brannan had also been a church leader in New York and was accused of keeping all the tithes from the Mormons on the ship. Some church leaders came to check last summer. Someone claimed that he would return the money to the church as soon as the Lord gave him a written receipt. I guess he was disfellowshipped from the Mormon Church because of his work with the Vigilance Committee. The church doesn't see these kinds of strong-arm tactics as anything they want their members involved with."

The information was instructive. There was always more to the story than initially presented. Shep still approved of the man. Brannan had been a bright and welcome light to him and Rost. Of course, there were things they didn't know about him, but that was always the case. Silva decided to file the accusations away for scrutiny at a later date. At present, he was pleased to have met and interacted with the Picketts.

Los Angeles was everything the Picketts had said. It began as a mission, then changed into a *pueblo* and finally a town. Silva got separated from the Picketts right off the steamboat. He figured they should get home without interference from him. They gave him their address and invited him to visit. The city was bustling, dusty, and noisy. The inhabitants were mostly Mexican and Indians. It was obvious that the Anglos enjoyed the upper crust prominence.

Shep found a room for the night, then picked up a stagecoach ticket to take him into San Bernardino. The 70-mile trip and would require two days. He understood that the road was fairly straight heading west. Indians were not a problem for the travelers at present.

The family of Jose del Carmen Lugo had established Rancho San Bernardino in the 1830s. It was a sub-mission of Mission San Gabriel. The family had developed strong relations with the mountain band of Cahuilla Indians. Chief Juan Antonio had joined with the Mexicans in grazing cattle, horses, sheep, and, pigs and they helped protect the livestock from marauding Indians coming from the south or east through the Yucaipa Valley below the San Gorgonio mountain. The most fearsome invader was Wakara who came from far to the north and east. He and his warriors frightened all of southern California. Over the years, especially during the Mexican-American War, there had been a series of battles with competing Indian neighbors, most memorably the massacres of Pauma and Temecula.

Life was proving difficult for the Lugos. They yearned for the stability and opportunities of Los Angeles. So when the Mormon settlers approached them about the sale of the Rancho, not only did they make a handsome profit, but they were able to leave the inland valleys and return to Los Angeles. On their part, the Mormons were happy to acquire the thousands of acres surrounding the *rancho*, as well as considerable numbers of livestock. The Mountain Band of Cahuilla accepted the newcomers easily.

After eating dinner in the communal hall of his pension, Shep made the youthful mistake of accepting an invitation to play a "friendly game" of cards. Most of the gamblers were Mexican and smoked and drank and cussed, but they were happy to welcome the Brazilian and begin taking his money with glee. It didn't take Shep long before he realized that he was outmatched. He excused himself to retire to bed. Several of the others followed suit, leaving the table almost empty.

"Oh no, *amigo*!" the remaining gambler pleaded with Shep. "Stay. Just one more hand. I think you will be sure to win this time."

Silva wasn't quite as sure. Effects from the liquor that the gambler had been nursing were not evident. He remained sharp and clear-eyed. The man implored Shep to sit back down in one of the empty chairs.

"Sorry, not tonight, Juanito."

"It will be quick, you will see." He smiled. "And if you want, I'll bet my horses. I also have three slaves. Healthy and strong. You can win everything. Please."

Silva looked around the room at the gambler's comrades. Even though they too were out of funds, they enjoyed watching the game. Each of them had hope etched on their faces. The possibility of picking up some horses is what swung Silva's decision.

"But just one game!" he added.

"Of course. Of course. Just one. *Solomente una vez.*"

Juanito's friends nodded in satisfied unison. Maybe the evening wasn't over.

The cards were dealt. The gamers jockeyed funds and took more cards, then eyed one another. Looking at his hand, Shep suddenly felt sick to his stomach. He could never win with such a mishmash of cards. Glancing up, he saw his friendly opponent chuckling merrily as he began arranging the newly received cards.

"Ah, *mi amigo*, it looks like God is watching over me." He pointed at the promissory note he had placed in the pot, representing the ownership of his horses. It was a steep bet. "You are indeed a brave man."

And then the earth shook. There was a low rumbling and the ground bounced violently, stiffly. Chairs and tables seemed to jump, as dust cascaded from the ceiling, covering everything below, including the men's hats and shoulders. Most stood frozen, not knowing what to do or where to go. There was a loud roar that then quickly receded into the darkness. The men looked wide-eyed at one another. Los Angeles was prone to these unnerving earthquakes. It lasted fifteen seconds and was gone. All breathed collective breaths of relief. Then there was an awful creaking as one end of a ceiling rafter broke from its mooring, dropping down heavily onto Juanito's head with a sickening thud, splaying the gambler out flat. The heavy log remained on top of the man.

The men scrambled to free their comrade, lifting the unwieldy rafter from Juanito. They were too late. Juanito was dead. He had sustained a solid, direct blow. The men looked at each other in disbelief. They shook their heads and began dusting off their hats and clothes. One of the men stooped down and picked up Juanito's promissory note from the floor, listing all his holdings. He looked at it closely, then handed it to Shep Silva.

"This is yours, *amigo*."

The others nodded in agreement.

"It's what Juanito would have wanted. It's what *Dios* wants."

Despite being a gambler, Juanito had a large amount of property. The previous evening's events substantially changed Shep's circumstances. The following morning, four handsome horses were delivered to him. Two browns and two dappled. They were short-legged cayuses but very strong, useful, and capable. He checked their teeth. One was only two years old. The other three were five. Juanito's friends arrived in a wagon drawn by two sturdy mules. Inside the wagon were some blankets, a saddle and reins, four halters, a lariat, and two buckets of grain. Shep was also quick to notice Juanito's .45 caliber Colt Dragoon pistol and belted holster that he wore on his hip was included, along with a Hawken rifle and a shotgun, small barrels of black powder, and lead. Silva was surprised that the latter items had also made it to him. Nothing had been pilfered. The supernatural feelings surrounding the previous night remained ensconced in everyone's memories.

Some arranging would be necessary. Silva continued to shake his head in disbelief. First, even winning the game. Second, getting such decent horses. And thirdly, that Juanito's comrades would come through with the delivery. Then again, it was an uncanny occurrence, the timing of the tremblor and the killing of the Mexican gambler. Juanito's *amigos* did not even consider shortchanging the Brazilian. He had contributed to their evening's enjoyment and then God stepped in and cleared the way for the short man who spoke their language with a funny accent. If they helped him, God would surely bless them.

Shep was thrilled to walk among his new mounts. They were brushed and well maintained. Their nearness was surreal. None were lame. He listened intently to their breathing and smelled their odor. None were wheezing from hay dust. Strong, agile horses, now belonging to him and ready to do his bidding. *God moves in mysterious ways, His wonders to perform.*

"Juanito doesn't have a family?"

They all shook their heads, no.

But this would interfere with his plans to travel by stagecoach. As he thanked the men, he began thinking of his next move in regards to the stagecoach, another of Juanito's friends appeared with three Indians in tow. He motioned them forward.

"These are yours. They are Juanito's slaves."

The three looked like teenagers and were clothed in nondescript cloaks of brown burlap.

Silva shook his head. "No. California is a free state. Slaves are not allowed here and I certainly don't need them."

"Then these are your servants. Call them what you will. And you must take them, *señor*. They cannot stay here in Los Angeles without you. It is too dangerous. They are Hopi. They will never fit in here."

"Do they have names?"

The Mexican shrugged. "*No sei.*"

Shep looked at them more closely, trying to size them up. The oldest was a girl and then two boys. He could see they were older teens. The girl, the young woman, was quite impressive. She was quite attractive. Her face and eyes were symmetrical. Her long black hair was combed and clean. Both boys had relatively scraggly black hair that was cropped just below their ears. The youths stood awkwardly, shifting from side to side on bare feet, looking first at their intermediary and then back at Shep, who was barely taller than them.

What a quandary.

Silva swallowed hard and nodded his agreement. He could take the Hopis with him to San Bernardino. Someone there was bound to know what to do with them. Maybe they could be sent back to the New Mexico Territory. Maybe they could find their family.

Shep nodded again at Juanito's friend. "*Esta' bien, amigo.* I will take them. *Gracias.*"

The other smiled happily and looked relieved to hand them over to their new owner. He turned and trotted after the rest of his associates.

Shep looked at his new "servants" more closely. As was his custom, he opened their mouths and gazed at their teeth. White and intact. Suddenly, he was repulsed by his actions. It felt too much like he was a slave owner.

"Okay. Do you speak English or Spanish," he asked the silent trio.

They traded looks uncertainly. They were shy.

Finally, the young woman stepped forward, then said haltingly, "We family. We to you." She gestured that they were now to follow Silva. They belonged to him.

"We to you," she said it with a heavy accent but it was clear what she meant. We to you. Silva was not anxious to assume ownership. Maybe he could use that as their surname. Wetoyou. It sounded all right and believable. Yes, Wetoyou.

"What are your names?" He was met with blank expressions. "Do you have names? What should I call you?"

Again he was met with silence.

Pointing to his chest, he said, "Shep Silva." Then repeated the gesture. "Shep Silva." The youths smiled but said nothing. This could be troublesome.

"Family?" he asked pointing at all three. "Family?"

"*Si*," the young woman responded.

Oh no, she speaks hybrid Spanish. Or perhaps more than a few words.

He looked at her carefully. She was a beautiful young woman. She did not appear to harbor anger or fear. And the other two deferred to her. Was she an older sister? He pointed again to his chest.

"Shep. Shep Silva."

He returned to the young woman and pointed at her expectantly. "*Su nombre?*" The quizzical expression on her face lightened and she smiled.

"*Puta*," she said pointing at herself.

That would never do. Shep shook his head, frowned, and gave her a definite, "*No! Nunca!*" He recollected himself.

Suddenly he began wondering what the young woman's life with Juanito might have been like or how long it might have been. Hopi were not the typical Indians who were sold into slavery, not in these parts. He had heard from Thompson and Sweeney that Timpanogos Chief Wakara was big in the slave trade, coming down from the north and raiding Navajos and lesser tribes for victims and then bringing them to sell in Los Angeles. Perhaps this is what happened to these three. He now had more of a reason to speak with them. He decided to try Spanish over the coming days. Something else might be forthcoming.

He sighed and thought for a few moments. Nothing.

"All right. You," he said, pointing to the young woman, "You are *linda de mais*. That is what I will call you, *Linda de mais*." The most beautiful. He used the familiar Portuguese case for "*de*" as it was pronounced "jee". "But I will just say Linda G. All right?" He nodded and pointed at her once more. "Linda G," and nodded.

The young woman smiled happily and nodded in response. "Leenda Jee," she said and pointed to herself. She then turned to the boy who looked the eldest. "*Hermano*," she said, and then the younger boy she called "*Hermanito*."

For a brief moment, he toyed with the idea of naming one of the brothers Mahonri and the other Moriancumer but quickly discarded it as frivolous.

A Spanish or Portuguese name might work. Shep smiled and pointed to the young woman. "Linda G." The youths repeated his words. Then he named the older boy, "*Irmão*," using the Portuguese word for brother. And the youngest, who was probably in his early teens, "*Irmãozinho*," for "little brother". The "h" in Portuguese often sounds like a double "l" in Spanish or a "y" in English. He was satisfied as they repeated the names. There was some bantering and chatting among themselves in their native tongue, then laughing. The names were twisted a bit and shortened, but Linda G kept her name. The name that stuck with the older brother was Herman and the youngest had his title abbreviated and came to be called Zeenyo. The names seemed to fit. Now if they chose to speak something, it would have a twinge of Portuguese. And they all looked pleased to now be Wetoyous and belong with "Shep".

After purchasing two wooden barrels, he loaded them onto the wagon, then filled the barrels with water from a local spring. He was ready for the trip.

The Brazilian was glad that it was still January. The temperature was cool. Shep was pleasantly surprised to find that the boys were familiar with yoking the mules and driving the small wagon. After being reimbursed for his stagecoach ticket to San Bernardino, Silva cornered a few of the drivers and got a decent lay of the land and direction to the *rancho*.

The weather remained clear, almost warm for winter. Some folks called the road Foothill because it ran along the base of the San Gabriel mountains and in an almost straight course to the east. Outside of Los Angeles, the scattering of houses became sparse immediately. After a couple of miles, they only saw the high desert. The road was rolling but nearly every time they moved down into a depression, there were signs of water seeping from the mountains. Shep was pleased to have the barrels, as were his animals.

That night when they made camp, he was further impressed with the Wetoyous. They knew how to kindle a fire, keeping the flames small for cooking and warmth, not large enough to attract undue attention. The activities reminded him of his youth on the *campo* in Brazil. Lower California was much drier and not nearly as green but there was something almost universal in the camp preparations and then eating their meager meals of dried pork and tortillas

Shep spent most of his time that evening going over the newly acquired firearms. They were marvels in engineering. He understood the basics but was happy to have some time to explore their intricacies. With Herman driving the mules and Linda G at his side, Shep had Zeenyo in the saddle and leading two of the other cayuses. This gave him ample time to ride ahead and zig-zag around the road to familiarize himself with the trail. He also began to practice with the pistol and rifle. The loading and priming were becoming easier, more familiar. He hadn't seen any Indians in the vicinity but thought that maybe all his discharging of firearms might keep them at bay.

At noon on the second day, he spotted the fort built around Rancho San Bernardino. It was still 10 miles ahead. Two score of adobe houses along with half as many tents, dotted the flats, the area where water flowed from the Cajon

Pass and into the open valley before proceeding down to the Santa Ana River during the wet season. This larger river ran to the southwest, finally emptying into the ocean.

Several substantial herds of cattle were also visible. Strings of smoke rose from the houses and as they drew nearer, people could be seen moving about. The walls of the fort were constructed by standing poles 10-foot tall. The gates of the fort were swung wide open. It was obvious that peace was the current climate.

Agricultural projects were also on display. Fields of alfalfa were interspersed by a potpourri of crops. Young fruit orchards could be seen in the distance, trees spaced evenly and in rows. Wagons, coaches, and buggies were moving on the streets that were also set out distinctly, running north-south and east-west, the gridwork making it much simpler to find directions and addresses than the haphazard layout of Los Angeles.

Shep's concern was how he and the Wetoyous might be accepted by the community. Drawing closer, he could see that most of the people working the fields or watching the animals were unarmed. That did not preclude him from noticing the several sharp-eyed sentinels who were armed and placed in a staggered manner, strategically at the edges of the community and its holdings.

Silva's approach had been observed. As they rode into the community, they were met first with looks trying to identify them and failing that, simple glances of curiosity. A few waved in a friendly fashion. Not knowing exactly where to go, Shep headed for the fort's main gate.

"Welcome, stranger," one of the sentries said. "Mind stating your business?"

"I'm Shep Silva. I come from Hawaii and am a friend of Mark Sweeney's. May I ask how to find his wife, Martha?"

The information satisfied the guard. "Go up three blocks north, then two blocks east. Can't miss the homestead. Just ask."

It was nice, this blooming settlement. Neat and orderly. The people all seemed busy and pleasant enough. The layout of the town was exactly as given and within a few minutes they reined up before an attractive yard with a low-hung adobe home. Chickens scampered about the fenced area. A handful of older children peered from the house and barn.

Shep swung from the back of his horse and approached the open-faced woman seated at the front door. She had been peeling potatoes. She stood and wiped her hands on her apron and smiled.

"Sister Sweeney. I am a friend of your husband's. Elder Mark Sweeney in Hawaii. My name is Shep Silva." The announcement, although spoken softly was heard by all and an eruption of excitement broke forth as even more children poured outside and ran to meet them, all jabbering and jumping to get a better view. The ten children ranged in ages from late teens to infants. This was the Brazilian *vaquero*, a friend of their pa's.

Elder Amasa Lyman was a busy man. He was the mayor of this newly organized settlement of San Bernardino. He also held ecclesiastical responsibilities with the Church of Jesus Christ of Latter-day Saints, not least of which, like those held by Elders Sweeny and Thompson, was the preaching of the gospel. Missionary work, spreading the good news. Lyman's duties were less concentrated than other missionaries. Still, he would go with his companion, Charles Rich and they would visit Los Angeles or head north into the valleys and preach among the ever-growing number of inhabitants there. But being gone, sometimes for weeks at a time, Lyman had the settlers marshaled into a tight-knit group. Responsibilities had been carefully parceled out. All was done with military precision. And yet there was a kindness and familiarity among the Saints as they kept an eye out for sickness, accidents, or anything that might get in people's way. The families stayed busy, focused on their plots or with their herds. Lyman and Rich were also apostles in the church.

Martha had been expecting Silva. Lyman left her with a variety of options to offer him, should he arrive before the town's administrators should return. Shep was pleased to see how well Martha matched up to his memories of Elder Sweeney. She was capable and organized. Mostly he was amazed to see how well she directed her children and then how well they responded. This kind of interaction made living in the desert much easier. Also, many of the children were in their later teens and held a variety of jobs within the family, about the neighborhood, with the livestock, or working in one of the several stores. There was plenty to be done.

The biggest concern for Shep had to do with the Wetoyous. The Sweeneys took care of that problem without him needing to ask. They swarmed around his charges and within minutes had paired up with them according to ages and sex, then split up to show off for their new friends and take them around the settlement. The fact that the Wetoyous didn't speak English posed no obstacle to the Sweeneys, as hand signals and pidgin Spanish mingled with smiles and facial expressions. With childhood exuberance, the children went their separate ways.

Martha Sweeney washed up and turned her duties over to a couple of the younger children who hadn't been selected for befriending the Wetoyous, then invited Shep around the back of the house where a buggy was parked.

"We're so pleased that you made it here," she said while taking an aging mare to be hitched. Shep stepped in and helped. "San Francisco has a lot to offer but we can really use your talents here."

Silva smiled in appreciation. Following her quick directions, he unhitched his mules and led them into a small outbuilding where there was water and provender, then settled his other horses. Within minutes they were in the buggy making their way back to the palisade.

"We arrived here a year ago," she said. "Mark had already left for the islands. We came with over 400 others to settle the area. Elder Rich had already purchased the Rancho from the Lugos. This is a delightful place. We are on the Old Spanish Trail that leads up to the Utah Territory or down to Los Angeles. Our livestock are thriving and we don't have problems with the

Indians. We were able to take over the orchards planted by the Lugos and have put in some other fruit trees. Our gardens are doing well and we don't have problems with locusts." It was clear that Martha was happy with their new home.

Reaching the fort, Martha stopped the buggy in front of a building that served as both a dry goods store and an office.

"Brother Bench, this is Brother Silva who has come from Hawaii. He's the one Elder Lyman has been waiting for. He's the one who works with the livestock."

"Yes, indeed," the smiling middle-aged man said, rising from his desk and limping slightly to shake the younger man's hand. "We have been expecting you." He politely dismissed Sister Sweeney, then took Shep in a wagon out of the palisade, to look at some of their herds. The sun was setting as he drove the wagon back to the Sweeneys' home. Bench had taken him by a small adobe structure next to the Sweeneys' that looked abandoned and told him that he and the Wetoyous could move in and set up their home in the morning.

It had been a whirlwind afternoon. Two lanterns were already burning as he entered the Sweeney house. Linda G and Herman and Zeenyo had eaten and were divided up for their bunks. The Sweeney children happily announced to Shep that their new friends were going to school with them in the morning as soon as the chores were done.

Shaking his head, Shep walked out back by the horses to start making his bed. The past couple of days had posed a series of highs and lows. Finally, things seemed to be settling down, taking shape as real possibilities for him and his Hopi charges.

The stars were crisp and sparkling as he tucked his blankets snuggly around him. The settlement of San Bernardino was not wracked with any of the boisterous howlings or gunshots that flavored the nights in Los Angeles. It was peaceful and quiet. He was happy to have taken the advice of Elder Mark Sweeney. This was quite different from Hawaii but the people were orderly and friendly. He could see himself staying for years.

Martha was up early in the morning with her children and smoke was rising from the chimney by the time Shep rolled from his bedroll. Sharp-eyed boys spotted his movements and invited him into their house. It was morning bedlam but quickly settled down as prayers were offered, breakfast was eaten and the rest of the chores were finished. Before Silva knew it, the six older Sweeney children had surrounded the Wetoyous and they marched out the door to go to school.

"I am so impressed," Silva said, "with all you have done and how well you have accepted me and the Wetoyous."

Martha waved off the compliment with a grin. "We've been waiting for you. But the Wetoyous have been an added blessing. We hope you feel at home."

After a hearty breakfast of porridge and eggs, Shep went to his lot and began assessing his plans and needs for the homestead. A few minutes later, two wagons and three men showed up and began unloading lumber and supplies. They introduced themselves as having been sent by Brother Bench, then started clearing away the brush and building a fence to encompass the lot. Two of the men went to the Sweeneys' and retrieved Shep's livestock and wagon. Not long after, Brother Bench pulled up in his buggy and took a rather confused Shep out to work with several contrary bulls.

"This will be your responsibility for a while," he explained. "These bulls are horny and it's past time they mated. We need to make sure they are isolated and tended to."

"What about this new place I've been given?"

"We'll do what we can. For now, just see what can be done with the bulls."

And it was a miracle. Upon returning in the evening, he saw the transformation that had taken place. The yard was raked, the house swept and the chinks in the house walls patched. A new door had been hung and the domicile was furnished with a table and several beds. The fireplace had been prepped, the wood had been cut and stacked. Pens for his horses and mules had been arranged, along with mangers and watering troughs.

Shep's mouth was propped open. "I don't know what to say."

Brother Bench slapped his back good-naturedly. "You do your part and we'll do ours."

The ranch was more extensive than the pastures of Oahu, not as lush, but Shep was able to cover most of the area on foot. When he wasn't mounted, he left his rifle with his saddle. He felt quite comfortable and safe with the heavy Dragoon six-shooter that sat on his hip. The settlement felt safe but Shep was also aware of the possibility of run-ins with the local Indians, many of whom longed to make off with their livestock.

Martha Sweeney invited Linda G to her house every afternoon after school, where she was taught to churn butter, bake, milk the cows, and do laundry. Martha and her eldest daughter, Julie, also began teaching Linda G some helpful songs. Before the first week was over the Wetoyous were learning to read and speak English, mostly through music. They also were given five chickens and mash. Herman and Zeenyo were kept busy at home or over at the Sweeneys'.

They embraced the mantra: Lifetime is working time.

Shep and the Wetoyous stayed busy from early morning until evening. The growing season was considerably longer than up north of Sacramento or the valleys around the Great Salt Lake, so Shep happily welcomed visitors to help him oversee the layout and planting of his garden. He also volunteered to work at keeping the irrigation system clear of weeds, rocks, and silt and assisted the water master in managing the use of the life-giving water. Weeding and watering now became another inescapable duty. There wasn't enough time in the day.

Sundays were a novelty. The community gathered under boweries to hear preaching from their leaders about the gospel. The sacrament was passed to the congregation. It was a time to rest from their hectic schedules and visit and get to know one another, to check on each other's welfare. Being together, they were able to see more of the community at once. One of the things that Shep noticed was other Indian youth, almost a dozen and not Hopi. They were younger than the Wetoyous. They were healthy and well-adjusted and sectioned off among some families. After that, he noticed the children working in the fields and going to school.

Elders Amasa Lyman and Charles Rich arrived in San Bernardino after Shep had been there two weeks. They came by his house to visit one night. Silva was pleased to make their acquaintance and invited them into his home. The Wetoyous were over at the Sweeneys'.

"Sorry I don't have a lantern yet," he apologized, ushering the men inside and inviting them to sit on a crude wooden bench near the fireplace. The evening was chill.

Both men wore beards and looked to be in their forties but Elder Rich was quite slender and tall and wasn't able to stand up straight in the low-ceilinged adobe house. They were soft-spoken and appreciated the hospitality.

"We have been well received and well treated. I can't thank you enough."

"We simply want to welcome you here to San Bernardino and hope you'll consider staying with us for a while."

"A man would be crazy not to."

A few minutes passed getting to know one another and then talking about the work in the Sandwich Islands. "We are expecting Elder Sweeney to return before summer," Rich said.

"I'm curious about these young Indian children you have with you," Lyman added.

The Brazilian gave them a brief sketch about how they had been acquired.

The elders nodded. Life on the frontier could be so complicated. "We appreciate you being willing to help them," Lyman continued. "They are most welcome here. They will find friends and protection."

"And will they return to their tribe?" Silva asked.

"Time will tell. We don't advise keeping them against their will. But as they get better a speaking English, as we find out more about them and what brought them here to southern California, then we can help them make decisions."

"I noticed other Indian children here."

The men nodded somberly. "Sometimes we find ourselves in terrible situations," Lyman said. "When we first arrived in the mountain valleys, some of the Indian tribes were quite involved with slavery, stealing women and children from other tribes and selling them to the Mexicans in the south for work in the mines. That was one of the first things we addressed with them, mostly Chief Wakara. He just changed his market and wanted to sell the people to us. I remember once telling him we couldn't do it. We didn't have the money or food. Wakara simply smiled and picked up a small child by her feet and then dashed her brains out on the frozen ground, then asked if we would be able to find the money soon. It was horrible, Brother Silva. And he's been extorting

56

us ever since. He knows we hate this kind of thing. The amount of slaves has shrunk but it's something we still have to deal with."

"That's why we have the children you've seen here," Rich said. "You see them in almost every settlement we have from here to Great Salt Lake City. President Young has tried to calm both the Indians and settlers. He says that it's easier to feed the Indians than to fight them, but I think there are plenty who would just as soon chase Wakara and his tribe out of the country. But because they have been doing this for a while, they have plenty of guns and horses and that's what they use to terrorize the smaller tribes and groups."

"Has this Wakara raided the Hopi?"

Lyman shrugged. "I haven't heard of it but who knows?"

"You are blessing the lives of your three stewards," Brother Rich assured. "As long as you can deal with them, we can too. We hope they will get some education and make friends and be productive members of the settlement. They seem to be clean and respectful."

"They certainly have been for me."

"No anger or running away?"

"I've only had them for less than a month. I think they have already made plenty of friends and there's a lot to keep them busy."

"Bless your heart, Brother Silva," Lyman said. "Without a doubt, God loves them every bit as much as he does you or me. It doesn't matter, this crazy time with abolitionists. We are all of one blood."

"You brethren know that I am not a member of the Church," Shep inserted.

Amasa nodded. "As I said. God loves his children. Every single one. That includes the Wetoyous as well as you and all the folks in Brazil. He is the Father of the whole earth and he's concerned about all. The least we can do is try and follow his lead."

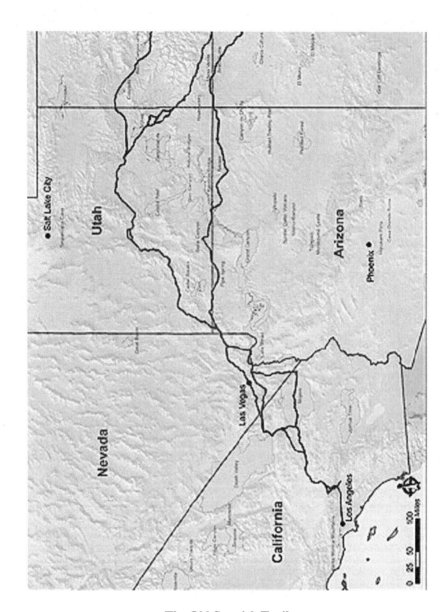

The Old Spanish Trail

Chapter 6

"You educate a man and you educate a man. Educate a woman and you educate a generation." Brigham Young

Spitting a large wad of tobacco towards a soiled can and missing, the grizzled 34-year-old steamboat captain swore and scratched his chin, then looked out of his wheelhouse at the teeming passengers below.

Captain Francis T. Belt was an energetic entrepreneur who had decided that he could make plenty of money ferrying emigrants up and down the main rivers of the inner US, the Ohio, the Mississippi, and the Missouri rivers. At present, the focus was on the western movement of settlers, mostly Mormons, wanting to make the trip to Florence, Nebraska. This week most of his cargo consisted of religious emigrants from England. Their timing was good. It was April 9, 1852, Good Friday. They should arrive in Florence or Council Bluffs early enough in the season to get outfitted and make the journey across the prairies of Nebraska and the high plains leading to South Pass, then drop down into the valley of the Great Salt Lake while it was still summer.

The *Saluda* was an excellent steamboat. It had carried hundreds of people to their destinations. It was well known along the waterways of the United States. To be named *Saluda*, elevating the importance of greetings or reunions, coming together after traveling, usually long distances, was such an honor and vitally memorable.

"If I can get enough power in this sonofabitchin' tin can to get us around the rapids," he moaned to himself. In the early morning light, he could see far enough forward to where the river, the Big Mo, came around a sharp corner with enough speed to have stopped Felt in his tracks twice before. He was tired of the impasse and ordered his boiler stokers to get as much steam generated as possible. They would build up the pressure, cast off and virtually fly past the obnoxious obstacle and reach Kansas City before the old river knew what had happened.

Lexington, Missouri was a nice town but Captain Belt was sick of it. And if he was sick of it, he was sure his passengers were as well. The townspeople had to be tiring of his steamboat.

Belt trotted from the wheelhouse and slid down the railing, dodging the smiling Saints. Their gold was worth as much as anyone else's. He reached the furnace room and entered. It was roaring hot. His stokers knew their orders. He ducked back out, away from the heat and into the refreshing air and, removed his cap to wipe away the perspiration that had suddenly beaded on his forehead, then he climbed back up the stairs.

Suddenly there was a sharp tearing sound as the boat's boiler burst and an explosion lifted the steamboat and its passengers completely out of the water, scattering debris and body parts into the air. Belt's lifeless remains were cast onto the grassy edge of the river. The explosion caught all by surprise, instantly killing more than 100 of the passengers, shredding bodies among the flotsam on the dock and shore or the pieces of wood spread across the width of the river. The fatally wounded derelict sputtered anemically, then slipped beneath the disturbing currents of the brown river. Many of the bodies of the dead were swept away by the unfeeling water and never found.

Two men on shore were also killed by flying debris. Stunned survivors stumbled incoherently trying to regain their hearing and stability while beginning a frantic search for lost loved ones or to help the wounded.

When Harriett Matthews regained consciousness, she was lying near the dock on the frozen ground. The ringing in her ears was all-consuming. As she tried to move, she discovered that her entire body was wracked with pain and stiffness, refusing her directions. After blinking furiously several times, she was able to take in some of the chaotic scenes. Smoke hung heavily on the shore, mingling with the running and shouts of the dark forms of people. Moving her head carefully downward, she could see her clothing had been torn away, leaving her in a semi-nude position, with a handful of tattered rags wrapped around her waist. Breathing was labored. Trying to inhale, she coughed violently. The spasms were excruciating. Within seconds, a series of hands touched her and she felt gentle words directed at her. Gently she was rolled onto a blanket, lifted from the icy, wet ground, and then the sensation of being whisked away. The words being spoken were faint, like a whisper, although through blurred eyes, it appeared that the men were yelling as forcefully as they could. Still, it remained as whispers and they seemed to fade away. She closed her eyes. *What had taken place?* She remembered the beautiful scents of the lilacs near her home in Preston, England. So precious. So memorable. Now so long ago, so far away…

Sleep is wonderful. Sleep is necessary. I love to sleep. Sometimes when I move in my sleep, I hurt. And the hurt is deep and pervading. Go back to sleep. The hurt will go away. Cherish the sleep.

It was two days later when Harriett's 18-year-old body gained sufficient strength and she awoke. Her face was puffy. She also felt warm, surrounded by fresh-smelling blankets. Opening her eyes, she didn't recognize the room. She turned her head slightly and saw a window and light coming from outside. Turning her body hurt immensely. Carefully she scooted herself up slightly, almost sitting.

What had happened? Everything was such a blur. Leaning back, she closed her eyes and tried to recall the incidents before the confusion and darkness. She caught a faint hint of nausea.

There had been a ground-swelling, noisy event beyond her ability to capture. Freedom. Floating or flying. Feeling crumpled and cold and unclothed.

But to awake. She decided that she had been asleep for at least a day. *So, was this Sunday? And on such a day as this. It was a wonderful day, was it not? Yes, it was Easter. Commemorating the resurrection of the Savior, the greatest miracle of all.* Church bells pealed, reminding one and all of Christ's victory over death. *"Death, where is thy sting?" He has saved us, the whole human family. Easter is what gives meaning to Christmas and every other holiday of the year. Renewal. Rebirth. Reunion. The completion of Christ's Atonement, the fruition of his life, giving us the gift of victory over the grave, to eventually be made at one with God and Christ and our loved ones, forever.*

"Good morning, Miss," a cherubic voice sang softly. Harriett's eyes shifted to a pleasant woman entering the room. She was busy, yet quiet. She walked nearer and began peering at Harriett, looking closely around her hair and ears. "You'll be just fine," she cooed confidently. Wringing a cloth from a nearby pan, she applied the soothing warmth to her face and neck. Drips of the liquid ran easily about her shoulders.

Harriett saw that she was wearing a soft cotton nightshirt. She opened her mouth to speak but nothing came out.

"Don't try to talk just yet. Things will come back soon enough."

The kind woman stood, smiled, and walked, floated from the room. Sleep returned graciously. She sighed quietly. *Answers will come soon enough.*

The next morning Harriet awoke with the rising sun. She hurt all over. It was even more intense than before. She also noticed that her hearing was returning. The swelling in her face was receding but it was sore. She sat up deliberately and realized that she was famished. Her lips were cracked and dry.

"Hello?" she called quietly. "Hello?"

There was an immediate shuffle of noise outside her door and a man poked his head inside. Without saying a word, he smiled and nodded, then left, closing the door slowly. In less than a minute the kind woman entered the room, smiling as before.

"How are you feeling, my dear?" she asked easily, sitting down and checking her over carefully.

"I feel very hungry," Harriet replied.

"No doubt. I will bring some breakfast momentarily." As the woman spoke, Harriett could suddenly smell the odors of cooking oats and she felt her mouth begin to water.

"What happened?" she asked with confusion still on her face.

"There was an explosion at the docks. The steamboat blew up. It was a horrible sight, my dear. But you are fine. You are here with us and we will care for you. The doctor will be along soon enough. But you are fine."

The woman left and returned with a steaming bowl of porridge and a small pitcher of cold cream. Harriett felt great hunger. Her hostess spooned the mush into her mouth carefully. It tasted wonderful. Her stomach reacted in anticipation. The smells of the food were heavenly and the cream was cool and coated her dry throat. She relaxed and soaked up the moment.

My family! Where's my family?

Harriett started up suddenly, spilling the bowl. "My family! Do you know my family?" she cried in desperation. "They were with me. We were together on the boat!"

The woman caught the jostling bowl and set it aside. "Not just now, my dear. There are still many things we don't know yet. They'll be found soon enough. God loves you my dear and I love you. You will be taken care of and we will answer any questions as soon as we're able."

Her words were comforting and she felt the racing of her heart begin to subside.

"They were up ahead on the boat. I was going to meet them," Harriett said.

"We'll find out soon enough, my dear." The woman patted her bandaged hand reassuringly.

Things did not roll out as easily and happily as Harriett felt she had been promised by Mrs. Winslow. The doctor arrived and checked her injuries, mild compared to other victims. Bandages were removed or changed and she was helped into new bed clothing. Her braids were slowly undone and her hair brushed gently.

With the passing of each hour, Harriett was becoming more concerned about her family. Her mother and father and three brothers. They had left England over a month before and crossed the wintry seas without a mishap. They wended their way up from New Orleans to St. Louis and then headed up the Missouri River on the *Saluda*. Most of the passengers were members of the Church of Jesus Christ of Latter-day Saints. Being on a tight budget, they had done all they could to hurry towards Florence, where they would acquire a wagon and a brace of oxen to take them to the valleys in the mountains, where they would join others in the establishment of Zion.

Captain Belt was a competent man. Despite his swearing and sometimes cross demeanor, all were confident he would get them to their destination quickly and safely.

It was Good Friday, the 9th of April. *And why was it called Good Friday? Why was anything called good to commemorate the crucifixion of a man? Or God? The Son of God? Perhaps, in the end, things got better. After the three days in the tomb, Jesus gathered his body and arose. There was now the hope of a resurrection. But crucifixion is such a ghastly manner of death.*

"Are you Harriett Matthews?" the man asked as he and two others came into her room.

"Yes sir."

The serious visitor held his hat humbly in his hands. "We have gone over and searched through the terrible accident on the *Saluda*. It just blew up. These things happen, but this one was extremely awful. More than 100 people were killed in the explosion. We have looked and looked and have not been able to find any trace of your family. We're sorry to say, but we believe your family perished in the explosion."

The news was devastating. Harriett's heart started racing again and she clutched at her throat as her breathing deepened and became labored.

"You have searched?"

The man nodded somberly. "For days. The citizens of Lexington have taken all the injured in. They are being cared for just as the Winslows have cared for you. But we have not found any of your family. We have checked everything against the passenger list and have not discovered any more Matthews. I am so sorry."

The news descended on her like a smothering, suffocating blanket. Harriett fought to orient herself. Her family? *All gone? Dead? No mother? No father? No brothers? But they were little brothers. They've been killed? They've all been taken from me?* She buried her face in her pillow and sobbed.

Oh God, how could this be possible? We were doing what was right. We were working to join with the other Saints. Life has forever changed.

Alone. Solitary. Tears came freely, abundantly. How could there be that much water left in her body?

"Miss Harriett?" It was Mrs. Winslow. She entered the room apologetically. "We have heard the news and we are so very sorry." Her sober-faced husband followed behind her and both sat gently beside her. "Can we offer a prayer with you?" she implored.

Harriett nodded gratefully. They each took her hands and bowed their heads.

"Our dear Father in heaven. Please, please be mindful of this dear young woman and help us all to understand thy will…"

The prayer, mingled with the following days, did much to quiet the confusion and fear in Harriett's heart. She got out of bed and started to explore the simple house. Mrs. Winslow's smile always greeted her. Several times they walked outside and enjoyed the spring showers and sunshine. Harriett was glad that the Winslow's lived several blocks away from the river and the dock. Most of the signs of the disaster had been cleaned up and life around Lexington was beginning to return to normal. The days were getting longer and warmer.

Harriett's healing continued. No mention was made regarding how long she would stay with the Winslows or what debts might be accumulating, gratefully.

A month after the explosion, the Winslows received another visitor. He was an attorney from across the river. He came from Richmond on the north side of the river. It was a town that lay 12 miles away. The middle-aged man identified himself as Alexander Doniphan, working to collect information about the victims and help them to get back on their feet. It was a charitable endeavor. No fees were assessed. A number, who had not been injured as severely had already gathered their things and continued up the Missouri. The citizens of Lexington had collected money from the community and surrounding farms to help the injured recoup some of their lives.

Doniphan was a pleasant, professional man whose ability to speak underscored his education. Harriett liked him immediately.

"You have come a long way, young lady," he intoned with a kindly grin.

Harriett nodded with a return smile and wondered about his visit. He didn't allow her to wonder long.

"You have been a blessing to the Winslows. This entire challenge has worked to strengthen the folks of this area. I'm certain the Winslows would adopt you in a minute should you desire."

Both the Winslows who were standing behind Doniphan nodded energetically.

"But some of us have wanted to know about any plans you might have. All at your own pace," he hurried to add.

She appreciated his measured words. He was a good attorney.

"I'm not sure," she said. "We were going to the Utah Territory. But now," she held up her hands. "I don't know. I don't have any family there. And I don't want to go. Not just now."

"What would you prefer to do?"

She sighed heavily. "I think I would like to return to England. That's what I would like, but I don't have any funds."

"And that's exactly why I'm here. The local citizens have collected enough money to get you back to your family and friends in Britain. The Mormons also have set up what they call a Perpetual Emigration Fund. You will also have access to that. Will you allow us this chance to act out our charity on your behalf?"

Such an unexpected opportunity. And yes, she still had plenty of family and friends in Preston, England.

"Oh yes, sir," she exclaimed happily. "That would be more than I could ever hope for."

"It's settled then," Doniphan announced. "When you are ready, we will make sure you return to your home."

The announcement shook Mrs. Winslow. Harriett suddenly found herself wondering about the make-up of the Winslow family. She had never asked about the family. She had been too concerned about her immediate problems.

The men shuffled out of the room and Mrs. Winslow glided to her side. She put her arms gently around Harriett and while hugging her tenderly, whispered into her ear, "God loves you, my dear. And I love you."

A week later Harriett waved a thankful goodbye to her benefactors at the dock, especially the Winslows. They had given her a suitcase and a few meager pieces of clothing. It was good to be leaving this portion of the earth, so far from the sights and sounds of England. And so sad and so lonely. And so memorable.

Chapter 7

"...as many of the Gentiles as will repent are the covenant people of the Lord; and as many of the Jews as will not repent shall be cast off; for the Lord covenanteth with none save it be with them that repent and believe in his Son, who is the Holy One of Israel." Nephi

Life in San Bernardino was good. It was busy and complete for Shep. The Wetoyous stayed busy as well. Silva had noted some differences in Zeenyo. He wasn't as sharp as Linda G and Herman but was still very social. He enjoyed playing and his friends. He smiled quickly and responded well with his chores. But he was still different than his siblings. Perhaps a little slower.

On their parts, Herman and Linda G were blossoming. School was what they needed. Both were chatting in English, even to one another. Their family was coming together swiftly. Their friendships broadened, keeping them engaged with various activities. All three of the children joined the choir and began learning to sing and harmonize. It was an uplifting experience.

One of the things becoming more apparent to Shep was the family make-up of the citizens. Mostly these were community leaders. They were involved with business and church. But what was interesting to Shep, was the size of their families. He thought that perhaps the extra women were sisters of the wives. This was a curiosity. At first, he just thought their wives were fertile but upon closer inspection, he realized that the men seemed to have multiple wives. Never had he experienced a family dynamic like this in Brazil. Hawaii was quite different, especially for the king and his family. But San Bernardino was different from the portion of the United States that he knew. He was aware of men visiting brothels or having mistresses, but that all seemed to be on the sly, not out in the open, certainly not keeping within the boundaries of morality. What he was beginning to notice was that these Mormon families belonged to one another. They were larger, sometimes considerably larger, and the men claimed their wives and the women seemed to accept one another as sister wives. It was very curious. The children referred to the women who were not their mothers as 'aunt'. In any event, the families were closely knit.

Elders Thompson and Sweeney had alluded to an idea of plural marriage, but this was mostly covered by the thoughts of eternal families and the life hereafter.

After being in the community for a decent time, Shep felt close enough to Charles Rich to breach the subject as they were riding in a wagon to check on some horses.

"You have more than one wife?" he asked. "And you all live under the same roof?"

The tall man smiled and nodded. "It's part of the restitution of all things the Bible speaks of. The blessings and covenants of God that he made with the ancient peoples are brought back. The family is the central object of the Lord's blessings. The relations between a man and his wife are holy. It's the conduit through which God sends his children to earth to be clothed with bodies of flesh and bones and blood. We are tried and tested and exposed to evil as well as the atonement of Jesus Christ. Some couples are called upon to have more than one wife to bring more children into the world. This is always done with the knowledge and permission of the first wife and it's done under the direction of the Prophet. We are married and we accept and love each other. This gives our men the ability to focus on their work and the women focus on theirs. For those who do not engage in it, it remains a mystery. For me and my family, we have found blessings from the Lord. And these blessings can only come about as we keep the commandments."

"But Elder Sweeney? He has one wife?"

Rich shrugged. "And he is a good man. And Martha is a good woman. Plural marriage is not for everyone. Some enter into it and fall flat on their faces. Others are never asked to participate. The Lord knows what's best. Some who have multiple wives think they are better, that they'll make it to heaven quicker than others, but it's not true. God has a plan. For some, this requires sickness and heartache or plural marriage, maybe the death of infants or children. Sometimes there's war or famine or scarcity. Regardless, this life is a gauntlet. It's a trying time, a time for us to lift and love one another despite the challenges placed in our way by Old Scratch."

"And Jesus? You claim to follow him. I don't remember reading that he was married and sure not having a harem."

"Plural marriage," Rich corrected. "Who knows? I don't. Some folks think the scriptures are clear, that the way is spelled out without question regarding the Savior's status and marriage and children and the like. I think they might be grasping at straws. Still, as members of the Church, we are given the gift of the Holy Ghost. He can and will lead us. For you, it might mean finding out that Joseph Smith was God's prophet and that the Book of Mormon is true. For me, maybe it's whether or not I need to tan one of my boy's hide or if I should encourage a daughter to court. Maybe I need to be more careful with a wife's feelings or what is being taught or said in our family. See?"

Things were a bit clearer. Shep felt glad to have opened the door with his questions. It would make things easier in the future.

Riding north, they were intercepted by two swiftly mounted men, whose horses were lathered and breathing hard. The men skidded to a stop.

"Got some trouble, Brother Rich," one said nervously. "Looks like some Indians have made off with some horses."

"How many?"

"Dunno. Ten or a dozen, I reckon."

"Dammit."

"We've been watching them the past couple of days. They've been staying far enough away but it's sure they've been spying on our cayuses."

"Juan Antonio's boys?"

"Your guess is as good as mine. Never had trouble with them before."

"They headed for the Cajon Pass?"

"Probably."

Charles Rich nodded. "Go and let Amasa know. Shep and I will see what we can find out. If you don't hear from us soon, get a posse out to help."

"Yessirree."

It was the first such interaction Shep had experienced since arriving. The Cahuilla Indians were the main tribe in the area. Juan Antonio, and had been friendly with the Mexicans and Americans. Several times he had protected the settlers from Wakara and his raiders when they moved south or through the San Gorgonio Pass. Marauders stealing horses often headed into the Cajon Pass for protection or to hide out. Years before there had been a flourishing band of thieves in the Big Box Pass. The Mexicans had employed trapper, frontiersman, and entrepreneur Jim Beckwourth and companion Pegleg Smith to ferret out the predators, with no success. Shep was reminded of a hawk keeping an eye on the chickens. Still, they never had trouble with the American trappers, regardless of the tales spun by the Mexicans.

Rich and Silva continued with the wagon. Several miles later they started into the mouth of the canyon and then up the creek bed. The Old Spanish Trail led across the southern portion of the Mojave Desert, then bending north towards the springs at Las Vegas, and finally on up and into the territory of the Timpanogos. The road was faint but used enough to keep it visible most of the time. Silva had been told about Captain Andrew Lytle, the man for whom the creek was named. In the early summer, the creek flowed heavily, out into the valley and to the southeast joining the Santa Ana River, then southwest where it emptied into the ocean. Lytle Creek was a refreshing source of food and water for the local tribes. The Cahuilla moved about in the San Bernardino Mountains to the east of the creek and the Cajon Pass. It was disconcerting for the two men not to see any signs of the Indians, not even a glimpse.

Rich finally tugged the mules to a halt and applied the brake.

"Why don't we split up and take a look," he suggested, removing his rifle and checking its charge.

Silva agreed and followed suit, looking to his supply of powder and percussion caps. The two men separated with Rich leaving the old road and walking up the east side of the canyon and Silva the west. All his life Shep had worked on strengthening his gimpy right leg. It wasn't as strong or mobile as he wanted but he was capable of walking, and he could do so for long periods. The biggest problem he faced was a sore leg the next day. The brush grew thicker and small ravines interrupted Silva's travel. He found a game trail and followed it. The game usually stuck to the surest, densest cover. It was quiet and had the best view, although the way was not always the quickest.

After a quarter of a mile, Silva had lost all track of Elder Rich. He kept climbing, ever vigilant, listening and watching for any tell-tale signs of Indians, horses, or game. Staying on the trail gave him instances where he came upon animals unawares. They spooked and fled but not in large numbers. Silva's presence was known to a limited number of mountain denizens.

Skirting a hillside, he looked across the canyon for any signs of his companion. All remained quiet and still.

He stopped and listened intently with his mouth half-open. Nothing. He continued onward, cautiously now. He wondered what would happen if he should come across the robbers. *Would Rich know and be able to help?* He sidestepped a rattlesnake slithering along the trail. He was quiet enough that he didn't disturb the serpent or set him to rattling.

Then he spotted a movement. Across the narrow canyon, covered by underbrush. He determined that it was a large animal movement. He paused and watched. A minute later he saw a string of ponies walking carefully up the far side of the hill. There were minders, or robbers, on either side, about half a dozen. They were making their way towards a low-slung ridge. The men were lightly armed with bows and arrows. Rifles were not visible. They appeared to be Cahuilla.

Now what? If they climbed the hill and got into the trees they could be gone for good.

He looked up and down the canyon for any signs of Rich. He felt completely alone. Taking a couple of deep breaths, he set off, still skirting his hillside. The climbing Indians' backs were towards him. He decided to race as quickly as he could, heading north. After assuring himself that he was beyond the Indians and had not been detected, he dropped into the bottoms, crossed the old road and creek, and started running up the far side, paralleling the Indians and the horses. It was a tough climb but he was motivated to distance them, then perhaps surprise them before they could vanish into the dark pine forest crowning the heights. He was happy that he was younger and stronger than a middle-aged man, despite his bum ankle. He doubted the long-legged Charles Rich could have kept up.

The sun climbed to its zenith. It was hot and Silva was perspiring and breathing hard. Reaching the ridge, he turned to the right and ran towards the location he thought would intersect the horse thieves. And he saw them. Just where he had envisioned. He had gotten ahead of them. A few more steps and they would walk right into him.

Stepping from the shadows, he raised his Hawken rifle, pointing it at the first man, and shouted, "*Pare!*" The Indians were startled by his sudden appearance. They stopped immediately and began looking around for others. The ropes about the horses' necks were dropped as the men slowly moved into a group, talking in low tones. Angry, furtive glances were cast at him. It was clear they were deciding what course of action to take.

"*Silencio!*" he yelled, confident that at least some understood Spanish. "*Los caballos aqui!*" he said, pointing at the ground before them.

He was the same size as them. Short. But he was well armed and appeared better prepared should it come to a fight.

The Indians stopped milling around. Some unslung bows and began nocking black flint-tipped arrows. Silva's heart was beating fast. The Hawken rifle was deadly but he was outnumbered by six. And then he sensed the weight on his hip. It was the Colt Dragoon. He regretted not having spent more time with it in practice. He lowered the rifle, holding it in his left hand, then drew out the lethal pistol and cocked the hammer menacingly. His opponents knew what they were facing. They didn't know how experienced he was. They opted not to find out. They shrugged and crossed in front of him, leaving the horses, then keeping them as a buffer between them. Reaching the tall pines, they started running, silently, and were out of his sight within a few seconds. Shep sighed with relief. He returned the pistol to its holster, which no longer felt heavy or uncomfortable.

Gathering up the tether ropes that held the horses, he stepped next to them and spoke individually to them in low tones, gently patting their noses and rubbing their backs. *Ah yes, they remembered him.* Together they started down the way they had come.

An hour later they emerged from the mouth of the canyon. Charles Rich was sitting in the wagon, nervously checking the position of the sun. He smiled broadly to see Shep with the horses. They waved, then shook hands vigorously as they met, relieved that they were experiencing a reunion rather than something more serious, more lasting, more sorrowful.

"I am glad to see you," Rich confessed. "I was starting to get worried. I was afraid we might have lost you. No matter how many showed up in the posse I was thinking these robbers might have gotten clean away. And you might have got the worst end of the stick. So? Any trouble talking the guys into letting you have these mounts back? I didn't hear any shots."

Shep shook his head. "Nope. Everything worked out just right, I guess." He tied the lead horse to the wagon, then climbed up to take his seat next to Rich, while at the same time determining to get some serious practice in with his firearms.

Arriving home, Silva was relieved to see the Wetoyous and then hear the good news that Elder Mark Sweeney was set to arrive home within a week from his mission. And when Mark returned, the town turned out with his family to welcome and congratulate him. The next day work and school and chores returned to normal. There were no extended festivities. Shep noted the curiosity.

Zeenyo was a sweet young man. His companionship was natural, very easy to accept. His English lessons were coming along. His problem with it was simply that he didn't choose to practice. He was content to be quiet. It was difficult for Shep to keep Linda G and Herman from chattering. At times they would revert to their native Hopi but only for seconds. They seemed to understand the importance of the language classes. Both of these youngsters were social, with no end in sight to their friends and the activities they pursued.

Zeenyo liked spending time in the yard, talking with the chickens. He was always first to volunteer for the chore of collecting eggs or feeding the birds. He enjoyed washing and buffing the eggs while talking to his feathered friends in a soft voice. They instinctively drew near to him, curiously wanting to hop into his lap or peck at the dirt around his shoes. It made him smile. Before long he seemed to graduate to the larger animals. He was a wonder with the sheep and goats, milking both breeds swiftly and with ease. The cows enjoyed his singing or chanting. And the horses were drawn to him as well. Shep soon identified Zeenyo's strengths and invited him to work as long as it didn't interfere with his studies or practice.

For months Shep had thought about practicing with his firearms but especially after the affair up the Cajon Pass, he decided to be more proactive. Having Zeenyo with him helped alleviate any worries he had regarding the time he spent with the Wetoyous. Linda G and Herrman were constantly on the go. Zeenyo held back. He hung by Shep, waiting for him to visit the horses or the cattle and maybe invite him along. Shep found it freeing, being able to turn Zeenyo loose on the animals, allowing him to find a corner where he could shoot at targets. The difficulty in setting and priming his charges lightened as he became more familiar with the workings of the arms. He also began to appreciate more the power of the weapons. They did much more than kick and make a loud sound and leave a huge plume of blue smoke. He began to hone his skills, tighten his aim and work his ability to draw the pistol, not fast, but fast enough. He tied the lower portion of the holster around his thigh. The six-inch barrel helped him to become quite accurate within twenty yards.

Meanwhile, Zeenyo began naming all his pets and there were scores. They soon began responding to his calls or whistles.

"Why?" Shep finally asked as they strolled home together late one summer evening.

"They like me," he replied. "They don't care how dark my skin is."

Zeenyo's declaration shocked and surprised Shep. First, he was surprised to see how well Zeenyo expressed himself using only English words. There were no Spanish or Hopi words used to help with his feelings. More importantly, was his statement about his feelings and his skin color. The Wetoyous were not the only Indians in San Bernardino nor the only ones with whom the people came in contact. The Wetoyous had not been baptized but they were reading the Book of Mormon and moving in that direction. They understood some of the ideas relating to tribes and the keeping of covenants.

Shep smiled and messed up the boy's hair. "You bless my life, Zeenyo." There were times when Shep felt like the Wetoyous' father but he was sorely mismatched and too close in age. He could act as their brother, although he felt a special sense to guard them, not like their owner.

A week later Shep took Herman with him on a fast trip into Los Angeles. Leaving Zeenyo with the care of the animals, he knew all would be well. He and Herman made it to the city with no trouble. It was interesting to see Herman's reactions to the place where he and his siblings had spent time. He was pleased that they didn't remain. After picking up some rock salt, they started back.

That night they camped by a small spring. The water had nearly dried up by that time. Shep quickly dammed the spring and dug a sufficient area that would allow them to bathe once it filled.

Like every young man, Herman couldn't wait and waded into the pool and started splashing as soon as he could. He was the image of joy and freedom. Shep started a small fire and began fixing dinner. The small pool provided Herman with an extended time to whoop and holler. He immersed himself as much as possible, spitting and sputtering and laughing as he arose. Brazil had never been as dry as California, and the water was deeper, darker, and more dangerous, but Shep also remembered the fascination he had with the life-giving water.

Their dinner was simple. As the embers began to fade, the two had time to discuss their lives and choices. Herman loved the Sweeneys and other friends. Life was good. He was proud of Linda G and her openness with her peers and how well she was doing with her reading and English class. She was also showing some interest in the opposite sex. Several community dances had been held. During the most recent Linda G seemed to have emerged from any previous shyness. She was a popular young woman and enjoyed a multitude of friends, male and female.

Herman was equally complimentary of Zeenyo. It pleased Shep to see how easily the children had taken to the names given them. Zeenyo was growing in responsibility with the animals. He appeared happy and content.

"None of you want to run away?"

The smile faded from Herman's face. "Where would we go? Our family is dead."

This was the first time Shep had heard. "The Timpanogos?"

Herman nodded. "Wakara." He spat in the sand with disgust.

"Zeenyo said he was unhappy with the darkness of his skin. You?"

Herman shrugged. "I don't know. My life has been happy knowing I have the color of my parents. But then there is you and our friends in San Bernardino. You are kind of white but hairy. The Book of Mormon speaks of God cursing the Lamanites with a dark skin. Then as they repented, they became whiter." He looked up at Shep from the coals, his dark eyes shining. "I am lighter than Linda G and Zeenyo. I know that I am not as light as you, but do you think that if I keep the commandments and work hard to please God, do you think I might turn as light as you after a few more years?"

The thought struck Shep hard. He knew some of what the Book of Mormon said but he had never been as steeped in it as the Wetoyous. He had no clear answer. This was an answer that needed to come from a father.

"I believe that God loves your family and he made you as he did for a reason."

The balance of their trip the next day was covered in silence. Shep was ashamed at not having a better response for this young man. *And what was the answer?*

That night after arriving home, he went to Mark Sweeney's home and knocked on the door.

"I think I have a real problem, *amizade*."

"The Wetoyous are all fine?"

"Maybe. Maybe not. At the first of the year, I thought I was ready to help these Hopi kids. I even thought that I could be their father, even though I'm only a couple years older than Linda G. But they are beginning to have some real questions. I don't know how to answer. They are every bit as smart me. Martha has been such a helper with Linda G, especially in the art of becoming a woman. But now the boys are giving me questions I don't know how to answer."

Shep quickly blurted out his concerns and the problems his young man had posed to him. Mark patted Shep's shoulder. "Let's go and have a talk. I can't say that I have all the answers either, but maybe some."

Relief washed over Shep like a splash of refreshing water. Entering the home, Shep was satisfied to see that both their lanterns were lighted. The evening chores were finished and while Zeenyo worked on a school assignment, Linda G and Herman were taking turns reading their Book of Mormon. Coming from absolutely nothing, Shep felt a sense of pride watching the scene.

Mark smiled. "Shep has asked me over for a discussion." The seriousness in his tone alerted the children. They instantly gave him their attention. "Shep loves you and wants your happiness. The Wetoyous flavor our town. We want to make sure we are adding the right flavor to you."

Chairs were scooted to the table where the best lamp stood and they all sat around it, looking expectantly at Mark Sweeney.

"I don't have all the answers. Neither does Shep. And you might have the answers we have not even considered." He looked into the faces of the youths. None were anxious to begin. "How about the color of your skin?"

An embarrassed pallor spread over the three faces. They looked down at the table. "Have your teachers said anything about it?"

Linda G was the oldest and bravest. "They don't talk about it. They hurry past it when we read the Book of Mormon."

Elder Sweeney nodded. "It can be a hard issue. But let me just say right here that I was a missionary in the Hawaiian Islands for more than three years. The Saints there are as good and righteous as any on earth. I watched as they sang and prayed and sacrificed. And, know what? Many of them were darker than any of you. It's true. The Hawaiians are wonderful people and God blesses them. God blesses their families. God blessed us to even be near them. I miss them all, terribly. God knows I missed Martha and the kids, but if it wasn't for them, I would still be in the islands as happy as could be."

The information began distilling upon the Wetoyous.

Mark continued. "Some might think that the color of our skin is what signals our righteousness. Right?"

The three Wetoyous nodded.

"I guess we see it here in America. Indians are not respected much by Americans, let alone each other. And black folks, slaves brought here from Africa. Slaves! Imagine that? Because of their color? Don't we all come from God, belong to the same family?"

Shep watched his charges. Mark was saying exactly what they needed to hear. He applauded himself silently for the wisdom to ask for Sweeney's assistance.

Elder Sweeney stopped for a few moments, waiting for a comment or a question. Silence.

"So the Book of Mormon talks about skin color? It speaks of a curse and a mark. The curse comes upon people who turn away from God. They lose his spirit, his presence. The mark is supposed to be a dark skin. But is it? Do we believe that God changed these people's race? They come from the same family. And how can some of the best people in the world have dark skins? I don't see the Hawaiians getting lighter. I know a man named Elijah Abels, a member of the church, easily one of the best men ever on God's green earth. He's treated second class because his ancestors are African."

Sweeney pulled the book from Herman and began flipping through its pages. "What about this? '*And he*—that's God—*inviteth them all to come unto him, black and white, bond and free, male and female; and he remembereth the heathen; and all are alike unto God, both Jew and Gentile.*'"

The final phrase struck Shep hard and he wondered why he had never heard it before.

"But the good people always seem to be white," Herman said.

Mark disagreed. "The Ammonites had been Lamanites. After their conversion, they became the best folks ever. Lots of times the Lamanites were more righteous than the Nephites, remember? But did they turn white? And besides that, how white are we talking about?" Sweeney answered. "White like a European? Some Europeans I've known have the blackest hearts of all. They can be evil to the core and their skin's white. A white skin can also be a sign of leprosy." He pointed to a peg on the wall where Shep's white Sunday shirt hung. "Or white like that? No matter how light a person might be, they're far from this color of white." He opened the book again. "*They saw a Man descending out of heaven; and he was clothed in a white robe.*" They were familiar with the verse. "So, was Jesus as white as his robe? Maybe. Maybe not." Sweeney turned a few pages. "Remember when Jesus was praying with the folks? It says that he got shiny. Is that white? Let me read this, '*and his countenance did smile upon them, and the light of his countenance did shine upon them, and behold they were as white as the countenance and also the garments of Jesus; and behold the whiteness thereof did exceed all the whiteness, yea, even there could be nothing upon earth so white as the whiteness thereof.*'" He closed the book. "Now that's white. Not just pale-skinned. When Moses came down off the mountain, his face was shining, so he needed to cover his face with a veil. I don't think it has anything to do with race or skin color or anything like that."

They were quiet for a few minutes, pondering their thoughts.

"So Jesus came to the Nephites?" Shep asked, feeling caught up in the lesson. "I thought he loved all his children."

Sweeney shrugged again. "You're as smart as me. You tell me. But this is the only book I know of that talks about it. It also says that the Savior went along to visit others, not just the Nephites. He visited others who belonged to the lost sheep of the House of Israel. Not just here. But we don't have the records, yet. What do you remember about Lono?"

The question surprised Shep. He remembered having spoken with some of his Hawaiian friends about their beliefs. "He was one of the Hawaiians' gods," he stammered. "He was good. And he was tall and yes, fair-skinned, and had blue eyes. That's one of the reasons they thought Captain Cook was Lono, returning as he promised."

"That's the way I remember it," Sweeney said. "I don't know if he was like a European or maybe shiny like Jesus in the Book of Mormon or maybe just dressed in white. There are plenty of legends among the people of this continent about some white god who appeared and blessed them and left, promising to return one day."

Another memory leaped up into Shep's mind. "Some of my Peruvians friends told a story about Viracocha, his name means Sea Foam, a bearded god who dressed in white and walking on water, performing miracles, teaching peace and, promising to return one day."

"The Indians in Mexico talk of Quetzalcoatl along the same lines," Mark added.

The Wetoyous suddenly became animated. They quickly said a few things among themselves in their native language. The conversation struck a nerve.

"What?" Shep asked them.

"Pahana," Linda G answered. The two boys nodded, their eyes now wide with anticipation. "Pahana is the name our parents told us. Pahana is the name of a white god who visited our people many years ago. He taught us to live in peace and how to plant maize. He stayed with the Hopi for a while and when he left, telling our people that he would come back. Years ago when the Spanish first came to our *mesa,* our people were happy. They thought Señor Tovar was the returning Pahana. The clan leader held out his hand in the sacred *nachwach* position. If it was Pahana, he would take the hand in a special handshake, the *nachwach.* But Señor Tovar just thought the Hopi wanted gifts and he told his soldiers to give them beads. That's what he thought they were asking for. Señor Tovar and his group did not know *nachwach.* Since then we have been careful around these people and the Mexicans after them. Even the Americans. But we have the legends."

Carefully, Zeenyo reached for the Book of Mormon and began looking through its pages towards the end of the volume. Everyone around the table stopped talking and watched the younger brother search. He was looking carefully at the words, then suddenly found his quest. Pointing to a verse, he asked, "Isn't this what we have been talking about?" He handed the book to Mark.

"Cry mightily unto the Father in the name of Jesus, that perhaps ye may be found spotless, pure, fair, and white, having been cleansed by the blood of the Lamb, at that great and last day."

"Exactly!" Mark said with a smile, clapping his hands. "There are lots of these stories. Don't ever fret the wondrous color God has given us. Let's just be as good as we can."

For several days Shep Silva wondered if the conversation had an impact on the Wetoyous. He left that aside as he watched the Wetoyous return to their studies and chores. They seemed infused with satisfaction.

A week later as they were riding to check on their grazing animals, Zeenyo commented to Shep, "It doesn't matter what Jesus looks like and if we'll recognize him when he comes, does it? I guess what matters is whether or not he recognizes us."

Smiling and nodding, Shep said quietly, "God bless you, Elder Mark Sweeney."

Chapter 8

"For I, the Lord God, delight in the chastity of women. And whoredoms are an abomination before me." Jacob, son of Lehi

"You're quite sure about this?" Thomas Kane asked the portly Mormon sitting in the ornately stuffed chair in the Kane parlor.

"Quite sure," Almon Babbit replied. He was a quintessential politician. Washington DC was becoming his first home. That he represented the scattered and destitute religious refugees in the Great Basin was a matter of secondary import to him. "A messenger delivered the information this week. It came directly from the West."

"Orson Pratt. That's quite a coup. Brig's sending him this way?"

Babbitt nodded affirmatively. "He'll be setting up a printing press and putting out a series of papers to augment the missionaries' work along the seaboard."

"Smart public relations move."

"Yes, sir." Babbitt bent over and started shuffling through the papers in his leather valise. Removing a large handful of documents, he handed them to the attorney. "You will find these interesting."

Kane thumbed through the pages thoughtfully. "It could work, Mr. Babbitt. The problem I see your people dealing with is that every time ground is made, something new sprouts before the dust has even settled. You might suggest that Brig take a breath before issuing new directives."

"He feels that God is urging him forward."

"Be that as it may, even God must understand the wisdom in moving forward with caution. Checking the winds and water. There has been a warming towards the Mormon people. Leastways, that's what I have felt here in Philadelphia these past months. But this continual ramming of religious ideas down the throats of normally secular politicians doesn't appear to be in your best interests."

"Agreed, but Governor Young doesn't seek my advice."

Kane smiled knowingly. "I thank you for your time and effort to keep me apprised. I will go over this information and any ideas I have will be forthcoming to you as soon as possible. You are headed back to the capital?"

"My coach awaits."

No sooner had Kane closed the door after his visitor and listened to the clopping of his shoes on the stone pavement descending to the street, than Kane's father, the Honorable John K. Kane strolled into the parlor.

"Any good news?" the affable judge asked.

Thomas held his hands up. "Just when I think we're making ground that damned Brigham Young pulls another rabbit out of the hat."

"Is this going to cause trouble?"

"Hopefully not. The Mormons are sending Orson Pratt out here to start up a printing press, to augment their missionary work."

"You know him?"

Kane nodded. "He's a sharp man. He'll be an asset. He's well-spoken and knows what he talking about. Generally." As an afterthought, he added, "He doesn't always see eye to eye with Brigham."

"They butt heads?"

"More than once, I understand."

Thomas' father smiled and chuckled. Something was invigorating when observing relationships. It was the spice of life. Even when people are two thousand miles away and sequestered in the Rocky Mountains, the clashing of personalities could be felt.

John Kintzing Kane was the 21st Attorney General of Pennsylvania and a United States District Judge of the United States District Court for the Eastern District of Pennsylvania. He was almost sixty years old. He and his wife, Jane, made a perfect power couple and were much sought after in the circles of people to know.

"It has long been a curiosity to your mother and me, the friends you choose. Tell your Mormon associates that it would be easier for us to help if they lived here in Pennsylvania."

Thomas smiled at the kindly jab. "Of course."

"You're leaving today for New York? To see Bessie?"

"As soon as I look over a few of these papers. Yes. Is there anything I can do for you while there?"

"Just give your sweet fiancé our love. Will Bessie be returning with you this time?"

"We both hope. She seems to be running out of patience."

"Ah, youth," the judge added.

The trip to New York took three days. Kane was aware of the Baltimore, and Ohio railroad system that was being used in some areas and contemplated in others. A rail system between Philadelphia and New York City would facilitate and quicken the travel. He knew that serious minds were debating the possibilities in Congress. The South used rails extensively for the transportation of goods. The North was looking at it more as a mode of transportation for people between the larger cities and eventually a transcontinental system that would make the trip to California much easier, less dangerous, and far swifter than travel by wagon or horse. All in good time and when money could be found.

With the prospect of an extended trip to New York City, Tom Kane was grateful to have the added papers provided by Almon Babbitt. It would give him plenty to read as well as a better insight into the thoughts and plans of his friends in the Utah Territory.

His luggage was situated on top of the coach and secured by a series of ropes. Kissing his mother and shaking his father's hand, Kane climbed into the coach and started the trip, crossing the Delaware River into New Jersey and towards New York City. He scrounged anxiously through the papers.

He found what he wanted. A treatise on what the Mormons called Celestial Marriage. Like many citizens of the US, he was recently aware of the Mormon idea regarding polygamy. Leaders of the religion saw it as a Biblical imperative and they intended it to be implemented, leaving a bad taste in Kane's mouth. There were a series of issues he did not understand. He was hoping Pratt could clear them up with his writings. The proposed newspaper was to be called "*The Seer*" referring to the martyred Mormon prophet, Joseph Smith, who had been murdered in Illinois in 1844.

He glanced through several pages and decided that he approved of Pratt's syntax.

Food for thought. Kane settled back and watched the passing of the country.

Three days later he was deposited at the tidy home of William Wood. Wood's daughter, Elizabeth, Kane's fiancé, had been anxiously awaiting Kane's arrival and didn't allow him time to offload his luggage, before urging him into the family carriage and they started for Manhattan.

"I've missed you so much!" the lovely, petit, dark-complexioned woman exclaimed. "I don't know how much longer I can stay here."

"Is Margaret still a bother?"

"I don't think my father ever considered his children when choosing a stepmother for us," she complained.

"I brought you a newspaper from home and thought you might like reading the headline story." He quickly scanned the article.

It had taken more than a month for the news from Utah to reach Philadelphia and get printed in the newspaper. Kane realized better than most, how isolated the Territory was. The story's headline was dated August 28, 1852, from the Great Salt Lake City. Its author had extensive quotes from none other than Brigham Young, governor of the territory.

Kane chuckled softly and handed the paper over to Elizabeth Wood, his charming companion. At sixteen years old, she was already outspoken in her views, well-read, and spoke French and Swedish fluently. She was currently studying Spanish. She was a good writer and a defiant proponent of women's suffrage. It was her turn to scan the article.

"And this is news?" she asked. "Mormons have been promoting harems for a decade. On the backs of women, or should I say, with women on their backs? Really? And Brigham thinks he'll be promoted to become a god!"

"Or angel. I think that would be a better word to use. I guess Brig felt he was far away enough and safe enough to announce the doctrine publicly."

Elizabeth frowned. "How you could ever support the likes of him or any who see things the same way is beyond me. It doesn't rise to the level of topics among civilized peoples."

"And slavery?"

"The Union still has a long way to go," she admitted. "But polygamy is nothing more or less than the enslavement of women."

"Mormon women are free to exercise their agency. They are not cowed or beaten into the practice. And Sweetheart, the Mormon women I have met all appear to be quite aware of what they are doing. This is not a foreign idea. It has been around for years. It has been ten years since the murder of Joseph Smith. The people on the whole are adamant. They want to be left alone to practice their religion as their god prescribes."

"Preposterous," she said with finality.

Kane looked at his fiancé approvingly. Even at her young age, she was capable to draw her own opinions and they did not rest on his ideas nor those of her father, William, who had brought his family from Liverpool ten years earlier. New York City was a good fit for the businessman, turned book publisher. His first wife, Harriett, had died while delivering their seventh child when Elizabeth was ten years old. He married the widow of his cousin, but Elizabeth had never grown close to her. As a consequence, she matured quickly and thought constantly about the freedom marriage would bring her. The dashing Thomas was a relative to the British-born woman. Her mother, Harriett Kane, was a cousin to Thomas' father, John. Although he was somewhat older than Elizabeth, fourteen years made little difference to Elizabeth. Thomas was an accomplished attorney who was adept in the halls of politics or military encampments. She anticipated a secure future with this man from a well-positioned family. His mind was open, and his actions were supportive of the under trodden: women, slaves, and even Mormons. Thomas was affectionate. He loved children. He was not defensive about his manhood, and he was open to political discussions. She knew that he could be swayed. She also knew theirs would be a wonderful relationship.

"We'll see what your father has to say."

"Oh please, Thomas, don't bring this up to him. He's already quite concerned about our relationship. He's worried we'll get married before I'm seventeen."

"I promised him that we'd wait. May isn't that far away."

"And he believes you. But I don't know that I do. You can get quite worked up."

"I blame you and your wiles."

"I'm just saying that May might be farther away than you think."

Thomas Kane knew she had a point.

"Who is this woman we are meeting?" Elizabeth asked.

"A friend of Doniphan's."

"From Missouri?"

"Yes. That's where he met her. But actually, she's British. From Preston."

"What's she doing way over here? Or in Missouri?"

"She was emigrating with her family to the West. There was a horrible accident with their steamboat on the Missouri River. It blew to pieces and killed all of her family. That's how Alex got to know her. You know that he is a first-rate philanthropist. Anyway, the folks in the area raised enough money to send her back home. That's where she still has family and friends."

"So how does Mr. Doniphan think you can help?"

Kane shrugged. "He's aware that I know a nurse working in the hospital in Middlesex. She is doing some excellent work there, gaining quite a following with her work on the wards. I understand she is a real stickler about cleanliness and the food the patients eat. They have seen some good results because of her. Anyway, the last time I was over there, I heard that she was looking for volunteers to train. This woman friend of Alex's seems to be a perfect fit."

"Because her family was killed?"

"Because she doesn't have peripheral worries and the work would allow her to immerse herself in helping the infirm."

"What's her name?"

"Harriett Matthews. She's 18 or 19."

"I certainly approve of the name," she said, referring to her mother's first name. "And the woman you're sending her to work with?"

"From a well-to-do British family and in her early thirties. She hasn't married yet, but she was born in Italy. Her folks named her after the town of her nativity. It's Florence. Florence Nightingale."

As she was preparing to leave Lexington, Harriett had given much thought to her future activities, even vocation. She was more than impressed with the sweetness of Mrs. Winslow. She was certain that the care she received from her hands had helped generate the healing she experienced. That was the direction she felt would be best for her. Nursing. She also knew that many women chose the path. They became probationers, where they worked long hours for little pay. After six weeks of instruction with bandage sterilization and enemas, she would be turned loose to earn a wage. She would be required to do everything prescribed by the physicians, who were all male, and if there were problems, the nurse would be blamed. It sounded like long, hard work. She also knew the situation of many people in England. Most were poor and had little access to the country's resources.

Before finally sailing down river, she swallowed her fears and took a ferry across the Missouri River, then rode the 12 miles to Richmond where she had made an appointment to see her benefactor, Mr. Alexander Doniphan.

He was very understanding. "We'll see that the ship you catch in New Orleans will take you to New York. I will write a referral and get it to you in Lexington by tomorrow, in plenty of time before you sail. You just need to post it once you arrive in New York. I think there's a fellow there who can be of assistance. He lives in Philadelphia but has family in the city. His fiancé's family is there so I'm quite certain he'll be close by. Anyway, I think he might have some ideas you could use going back to Britain."

A couple weeks later Harriett was sitting in a chair on the boardwalk outside of her hotel in New York City when she spotted Thomas Kane and Elizabeth Wood. She learned that they preferred to be called Tom and Bessie.

Neither was very tall but both were well dressed, standing out among the people on the street. Tom had set the time well by messenger, something that Harriett appreciated.

"Miss Matthews, I presume."

Harriett smiled. She noticed that Elizabeth was quite young and now that she was standing so close, also a bit possessive of her fiancé.

"Thank you so much for meeting me," she said. "And Miss Wood. It's a pleasure to meet you."

Bessie returned her smile, feeling slightly more comfortable.

"I was happy when Mr. Doniphan mentioned you and a possible connection you might have for me in England. Thank you so much for helping me."

Tom nodded and handed her a large envelope. "I have written all the pertinent information here. It's everything I am aware of and trust it will be of use."

Harriett received the envelope gratefully.

"When does your ship depart?" Bessie asked and immediately regretted sounding immature and impatient.

"This afternoon," Harriett replied, acting as if she didn't pick up on the queue. "Your timing is impeccable."

"Tom says you're from Preston? I'm from Liverpool."

"Lovely. Would you care for a seat and maybe some coffee?"

"Thank you, no," Tom said politely. "We are on a stroll around the city and will be doing a lot of sitting over the next few days when we travel back to Philadelphia."

"Oh yes, your family is there."

Looking around at the sights and smells of the street, all three were suddenly quite relieved they would be moving on, not staying in the ever-darkening squalor.

"Terrible accident with your steamboat and the deaths of your family. We are so sorry for your loss."

Harriett's smile faded slightly as she nodded.

"May I ask what brought you here from England? You were going west. To California?"

"No. We joined the Mormon Church and were traveling to Great Salt Lake City. That seems to be what converts from England do. Of course, we didn't have much money. That's what the Perpetual Emigration Fund is for. And it came in handy for us. We weren't destitute, mind you, but we appreciated the assistance."

"Do you have family in the Utah Territory?"

"No. It seemed to be an adventure for our family."

"I see."

"Your religion," Bessie interjected. "Do you like it?"

"I suppose. Not as much as my parents but it has answered some deep questions."

81

"What about polygamy?" Bessie pretended not to see the disapproving glance of her future husband.

"I haven't heard a lot and now with me going back home maybe it will be a while before I do." She shrugged and flashed them a pretty smile. "I liked hearing about the prophets and apostles. I like knowing that God still cares about us and that he continues to speak through revelation. I have read large portions of the Book of Mormon and it spoke to my heart. There are lots of things I am still learning. I'm sure that polygamy and harems and the like will turn out to be much less than is made out by the tabloids."

"You found some of the plain and precious things that were excised from orthodox Christianity?" Tom asked. "By translators or folks who didn't agree with some of the tenets they came across?"

"Exactly." She was impressed by the nuance in his conversation, showing that he was at least partially aware of some Book of Mormon phrasing. "How and when baptisms should be performed. The importance of priesthood. How the sacrament should be administered. And especially the duration of love and families. I think that has helped me a lot with the deaths of my parents and brothers." There was still noticeable sorrow in her voice at the mention of her family.

"So then, are you packed and ready for your voyage?"

"There are still a few remaining items to take care of."

"Very good. Then we will leave and let you be about your business. Thank you for your time and conversation."

"Please be well," Bessie added.

As she watched her new acquaintances depart, Harriett sighed deeply. She wished that she was as settled in her life as Bessie and Tom. There remained a lot before her. She suddenly remembered the envelope and opened it hungrily and began scouring the pages. Yes, this is what was needed. God was looking after her.

Chapter 9

"To accomplish this work there will have to be not one temple but thousands of them." Brigham Young

Mark Sweeney answered the knock on his door promptly. "Brother Silva. It's getting late. We didn't expect any visitors at this hour but please come in."

The short Brazilian entered while removing his hat. "Brother Mark Sweeney, may I introduce to you a friend of mine who just got in from Los Angeles? This is Aaron Rost, most recently from San Francisco." The lanky blonde Rost followed, stepping into the busy parlor. "Mr. Rost is a merchant and has been working this past year in northern California. He finally woke up and decided to come down here where life is calmer to check things in these parts."

Most of the Sweeney children were lined up in the kitchen waiting their turn at the washbasin. The two eldest boys stepped back to get a better look at Shep's friend. Their motion was discovered and they smiled and bowed carefully.

"Please come in, brethren, and make yourselves comfortable," Mark said, gesturing to the two parlor chairs set in the corner. He then turned the lantern up to get maximum light. A slightly flustered Martha appeared, quickly checking the pins in her hair, then turned and left after Shep shook his head to indicate they did not need any refreshments.

"Ah," Aaron replied with a smile. "Brethren. It makes me feel as if I'm in a lodge."

"Better than that," Sweeney replied. He was proud of his family and the lengths they had gone to fix up their home. Doilies adorned every chair. Festive wallpaper reflected the lamp's light. All was clean and swept. If one checked close enough, rough outlines could be made out in the ceiling, but even it had been plastered over, sealing out the cold night air, and keeping the warmth from the pot-bellied stove in.

"I met Aaron on the ship after leaving Honolulu," Shep continued. "He hails from Prussia and was a great friend to me when I left the islands and came to America."

"And Jewish? I remember Shep talking about you."

"Yes. Aaron the Jew," he confessed. "It's a better title than Aaron the Yid, I suppose." The silver of his front tooth flashed as he grinned. The other two nodded their agreement. "Although, I will tell you that I spent some time among the Mormons near Sacramento. Fine folks, but they referred to everyone other than themselves as Gentiles, including me."

The announcement made Mark and Shep chuckle.

"Imagine. Me, a goy. Not to worry. I spent several weeks among them and when I left, I felt no ill effects because of the title."

"I introduced Mr. Rost to Brother Lyman and Brother Rich. He is working at getting us some top-notch oil for our lamps that will help them burn brighter and longer and for a lot less money. Both were quite taken with his products. There's a chance that San Bernardino might buy some barrels in the future. It could go a long way in keeping the streets lit after dark. They'll be meeting in counsel in a couple of days and come up with a decision."

"That sounds perfect. And they think the settlement can afford it?"

Shep nodded enthusiastically. "And the citizens too. It's refined and very light and quite affordable. And it doesn't stink or send off much smoke. The houses would be brighter, cleaner, and smell better."

This was good news. It was another blessing people received simply because they lived during the last days. It was the Dispensation of the Fulness of Times.

The next half hour was taken up by the men in small talk. Mark was called away briefly to join the family in prayer, then Martha bundled her protesting children off to their beds, promising that they could visit with Shep and Mr. Rost later. Visitors always seemed to bring such fun news and stories.

"So what are your plans?" Mark asked Aaron.

The merchant smiled and shrugged. "I don't rightly know yet. Your town has a lot of promise for me. A month. Maybe more."

"And then?"

Aaron smiled, seeing his plot had slipped out. "Great Salt Lake City. I plan to go up there and lay my wares out before Governor Young. I understand that the whole territory is booming. There's lots of folks coming in all the time. And every town wants to outshine their neighbors."

It was a good plan. It sounded solid. It could be a real benefit if there were only a way the oil could be shipped and received on time. Rost assured them that refineries could be easily built, oil could be extracted, people trained. They did not need to depend on shipments from Europe, certainly not after finding out how valuable the commodity was, easy to find and refine and, how universally useful for virtually all walks of life.

"It will be a challenge. Especially in the beginning. But it's a new industry and there's plenty of money to be made by all. We just need to find some investors but that shouldn't be hard, not after seeing for themselves."

"Sure," Mark agreed. "But everyone is looking for money. Investors are being chased from pillar to post by locomotive or telegraph enthusiasts. The military wants newer and better guns. Some roads are even being resurfaced with gravel between towns. Not just inside the towns but outside, just to help with travel."

The competition wasn't news to Aaron Rost. "We'll just do what we can, gleaning whatever might be leftover. At any rate, lives will be improved as will education and safety."

"The whalers might not be happy," Shep noted somberly.

"There will always be a downside to innovation," Rost countered. "This is something that can be seen, sniffed, and carried about. Of course, it isn't free but once its advantages are weighed against other articles, I think we will win out."

The possibilities were obvious. Lives, communities, and even nations could be swayed by the introduction of this oil. Kerosene. If it performed as well as Rost promised, San Bernardino could become a dazzling jewel in the desert.

Sweeney filled three cups with ice-cold water. It was clear and sparkling. It even had its fresh flavor. "Can't beat well water," he said. "Will Mr. Rost be staying with you?"

Shep nodded. "He'll be our guest for the time being. We have stayed busy swapping stories."

"Has there been a winner?"

The men guffawed and drank more water.

Mark Sweeney looked intently at Shep. "Do I dare bring up the subject?"

The Brazilian smiled. "I've already talked it over some with Aaron. Brother Sweeney's talking about the Wetoyous."

"Ah, yes."

"They are getting old enough to start out on their own. I've spoken to Martha about it and she would love to invite them to stay with us. We are expanding the house. The kids all know each other and get along great. We would love to have them join us."

"Haven't you had them since you first got to Los Angeles?"

Shep nodded. "It's been more than a year."

"Are they tying you down?"

"I don't think so. They haven't been any trouble. They are respectful kids. They do their chores well. They all seem to be doing good in school. Even Zeenyo, who I was the most worried about, seems to be growing into a fine young man. All three are fitting in well in the settlement. Folks know them and they are honest. The problem I'm feeling is that they need a real family. A ma and a pa. Brothers and sisters. People they could latch on to for the rest of their lives."

"And you don't fill the slot?"

"Come on, Aaron. They speak English better than me. The animals love Zeenyo more than me. Linda G is blossoming into a beautiful young lady. She has several suitors and some are quite serious about their intentions."

"It's a serious matter," Sweeney admitted. "It's what we've been talking about for a while. Shep is unselfish. He has worked hard and is setting a great example for the kids. But he is just like an older brother. Now, don't get me wrong. Martha and I both know you could keep going and raise the kids as your own. But we have some extra areas where you might be lacking. We can't help but think that the Lord has brought you all here for the blessing of our family. Perhaps we could take some pressure off you, Shep, and allow you to do some socializing or even traveling some. This is your home. You can always spend time with the Wetoyous. We don't plan on taking them away or replacing you. Just adding a little more to their lives. That's all. Plus, they'll be up and out before any of us are ready."

The deal was set between Silva and the Sweeneys. Nothing would be imminent or sudden. Martha simply began calling more upon Linda G and Mark started weaving Herman and Zeenyo more and more into their chore routine. Mark was surprised at how fast Zeenyo was at milking, yet gentle. The cows all seemed to prefer him. Also, with Aaron taking up space in their small cottage, the Wetoyous started finding reasons to spend more nights with the Sweeneys. Friendships solidified. Shep began feeling more like a brother or guardian than the father, relieving everyone somewhat.

Aaron was pleased with the way things were going, not just with his work but also around the house. He claimed responsibility, thinking that he was the catalyst for the shift in the family dynamics. All felt like things were developing as they should. It wasn't a frantic or haphazard shift, but more natural and easy. And Martha Sweeney was in heaven. She had always wanted more children and the sudden influx of the Wetoyous was a perfect answer to her heavenly pleas.

"You realize why all of this is working out so well, don't you?" Rost asked Silva one morning as they were walking out to check on the horses. "It's because you and I are of the House of Israel. We are direct descendants. No adoptions here. We are naturally endowed with the understanding and know-how because it came with our births."

Shep looked sideways at his friend to make sure he understood that he was only suggesting a half-truth. "You been thinking about this for a while?"

"Long enough. I mean, face it. All these other fine folks around here are needing to learn how to become the House of Israel. You and I have been in place all along. You ever wonder why you have been so accepting of the Wetoyous? It's who you are. You are accepting. You see everyone as children of God. Now these fine folks in San Bernardino, are learning to get to know one another and start accepting things, like the Wetoyous or other Indians or even the slaves. It's true. We have all come from God only with different capacities and in different times and places. Everyone has their responsibilities but ours is to be examples. We are the lights. We set the pattern or mark the path. I'm not saying that we are better or anything like that. But we have been chosen. We are the chosen. God has chosen us for a reason and placed us where he has for a reason. And that's to act as beacons."

"You just keep up with your thinking, Aaron. No use wasting such a fine mind."

"Don't I know it."

****

86

On March 4, 1853, President Fillmore left office and was replaced by President Franklin Pierce, a Northern Democrat, as the 14th president of the still relatively young nation. People in the Utah Territory began to wonder about the future of the town of Fillmore. It had been started in 1851 to become the capital of the territory but it was being far outshone by the emigrants choosing to stay in the north of the territory, in the Great Salt Lake City, or areas close by.

Brigham Young was also quickly tiring of the slave trade in Utah, among the Indians. He had befriended Wakara, and the chief was baptized into the Church several years earlier. It did not mean that the Timpanogos started adhering to the wishes of the incoming Mormons. On January 31, 1852, the Utah Territorial Legislature passed a law prohibiting the whole slavery business. Its preamble read: *From time immemorial the practice of purchasing women and children of the Utah tribes of Indians by Mexican traders has been indulged and carried on by those respective people until the Indians consider it an allowable traffic and frequently offer their prisoners or children for sale.* Young began systematic harassment of Mexican traders in the territory. He thought they were in place to buy slaves and wanted to disrupt the business. Young gave orders for 30 Utah militiamen "to go south through the settlements, warn the people and apprehend all such strolling Mexicans and keep them in custody until further advised." The Mormon leader was no longer going to tolerate slave trading in his territory.

This was the same time Aaron Rost decided to leave San Bernardino and travel to the Great Salt Lake City. He posed the suggestion that Shep accompany him.

"That's a big step for me," Silva answered. "I don't know how the Wetoyous would like it."

"That's exactly why it's a good idea. Right now, they are still waffling between your house and Mark's. It's easy and comfortable but maybe they need to see that it's time for a break. They need to move completely in with the Sweeneys and understand that you have done your part. Now it's up to them to keep going forward, for themselves as well as all the rest of the town."

It made sense. As Shep began mulling over the thoughts, he tried listing the reasons he had to stay in San Bernardino versus the benefits of moving on and going to the Great Salt Lake City, at least for a visit. The idea became more pronounced as time went by. He could see that Aaron was running low on funds and needed to move on, sooner rather than later. Silva enjoyed San Bernardino. The people, the work, and even the climate. Until Aaron had arrived, he had never considered relocating. He was confident he could find more work and meeting new people was a delightful activity. People were good wherever they were. He realized the only thing keeping him back was his relationship with the Wetoyous. He suddenly missed them and began to mourn a separation. A Portuguese word kept returning to his mind, describing his feelings. It was *saudades*. It meant a longing for or regard. It meant there was emotion involved, a connection. *Saudades* is what he felt toward the Wetoyous

Aaron and Mark both sensed the struggles their friend was facing. "It doesn't need to be forever," Rost assured him. "It will be an adventure for you and them."

"Their feelings for you are set," Sweeney added. "Those feelings won't go away. They will always remember you as the one God gave them for their liberation."

These were new feelings for the Brazilian. He had never confronted such a loss in his life before this. And really, wasn't that what the gospel meant? The good news. Friends and family are not ever gone. Not for good. Even in the worst-case scenarios, the Savior will bring all back into one.

He felt an impression to begin a serious study of the subject.

"I'll be ready," he announced soberly.

Wednesday, April 6th, was a beautiful, clear day. Alexander Williams was prepared to take a small party of seven people and two wagons and head up the Old Spanish Trail for the Great Salt Lake. Aaron Rost and Shep Silva had signed on.

Linda G, Herman, and Zeenyo had cried all the night before, thinking about Shep's departure. They knew the decision was right. It would be the best for all involved, including them. Most of the town also turned out to see these popular friends depart.

Holding his right hand over his heart, Shep mouthed the word "*saudades*" to these loved ones, then stepped forward and embraced them endearingly. He didn't want it to end. Tears flowed freely among all, including the spectators.

"*Tchau*," Shep Silva said. "We will meet again. I promise."

All nodded their agreement.

****

April 6th was a significant day. It was also the twenty-third birthday of the Church of Jesus Christ of Latter-day Saints. The meaning of the anniversary rippled throughout the few Saints scattered the world over. Brigham Young and his followers gathered at the spot in the Great Salt Lake City that had been marked nearly six years earlier, the spot where he had announced a temple would be built. They prepared to break ground for the edifice.

Brigham recounted the importance of the temple. Succinctly, he gave all the definitions of the temple endowment: "Let me give you the definition in brief. Your endowment is to receive all those ordinances in the House of the Lord, which are necessary for you, after you have departed this life, to enable you to walk back to the presence of the Father, passing the angels who stand as sentinels, being enabled to give them the keys words, the signs, and tokens pertaining to the Holy Priesthood, and gain your eternal exaltation in spite of earth and hell."

The valley of the Great Salt Lake would never be the same.

****

The trip northward started hard and remained that way. Shep had a difficult time understanding what motivated Wakara and his warriors to make the trip multiple times over the past fifteen years. There had to be more in their lives than the capturing of slaves or the stealing of horses. Then again, perhaps not. The distance was long, dry, and arduous but there was the ability to make a name for oneself, to spread fear into the hearts of others who had never encountered the ferocity or cunning of the Timpanogos and come away with a fortune could be quite appealing.

Shep sat on the buckboard next to Aaron. They traded turns driving the mules. It gave them time to discuss their thoughts. Sometimes it even made the miles seem to pass away easier.

"I'm thinking about getting baptized," Aaron opened up one morning.

The news took Shep totally by surprise. "I didn't know you were even thinking about such a move."

"For quite some time now. Even before I came to San Bernardino."

"I thought you already considered yourself belonging to the House of Israel."

"Still do. But there have been a number of things whacking my mind, giving me things to think over. The Wetoyous were a great insight. And the settlement in San Bernardino. Lyman and Rich and Sweeney. Mostly I guess it's the personalities. Sam Brannan gave me plenty to ponder. Remember Boggs? He was good friends with Mariano and Benicia Vallejo and lived in Rancho Petaluma. Very interesting fellow. And he was governor in Missouri back in the 1830s when they had the Mormon War there. He wanted the Mormons out of the state. He even wrote an order that they be exterminated or kicked out in 1838. Anyway, the whole mess has followed him ever since. He lives in fear that the Mormons are going to sneak up on him and kill him."

"And these kinds of tales make you want to join the religion?"

"Not just that, although it goes a long way to explain why Boggs works as the postmaster in Sonoma. Keeps his head down."

"I thought Brannan was wanting him to get into politics."

"And he is. I think it's all just a bunch of tripe. Still, Boggs' relationship with the Mormons has gone a long way into identifying who he is." He thought for a minute. "That always seems to happen to people when they get wrapped up with the Church. No getting around that they take their feelings seriously. And the Mormons love their Bible, especially the Torah, and Isaiah. It tends to color who they are and the direction they are heading."

"What if you decide you don't care for it, down the road?"

Rost shrugged. "Mormons aren't like Jews or Indians or slaves. They can always change, kind of like using the *Kol Nidre* at *Yom Kippur*. We can always invoke that if we stumble, right? But blacks and Indians can't change the color of their skin. They go to sleep and wake up the same person. I'm a Jewish man. I've been circumcised. That's something I can't just walk away from."

"Me too."

"What?"

"*Minha mãe* had me circumcised when I was a kid."

"Aha! I knew it! *Marrano*, if ever I met one. See, that's just it. We don't just walk away from things like this. If you're baptized you can always step away if things get too crazy or hot. That's what makes it so convenient."

"Or not. The faithful don't have outward signs or marks that keep them in line. They are faced with their God-given agency every day to keep the commandments, to be upright in the covenants. It makes for a more serious commitment."

"Exactly. I find it appealing. I want to look closer. I want to feel the difference of being given the gift of the Holy Ghost. I already feel quite interesting things when reading the Book of Mormon. It is an experiment of sorts. But even that book suggests we give it a try. Plant the word of God in our hearts, nourish and watch over it, water it and see what happens. I have seen some interesting things surrounding some of these people. They stand out more than a little."

Shep looked over at Alex Williams. He was a solid man. He lived his religion without receiving commendations or accolades. He worked hard. He did his best. And all of this within a very dangerous milieu. *What was his payoff? What was Mark's or Martha's? Or any of his friends in San Bernardino? What made Thompson and Sweeney give up their time with their loved ones, just to sail far away and preach to the folks in the Sandwich Islands?* They spoke frequently about the gathering of Israel. His name Giuseppe or Yosep or Joseph meant to gather, collect. Once upon a time, God had seen to it that Israel was scattered far and wide. Over the generations, they had become lost, mixed with others, and forgot their initial beginnings. So now these Latter-day Saints felt that was one of their main responsibilities before the Second Coming of the Savior, the gathering of Israel. The missionaries didn't go over the earth looking for people living in certain areas or with a specific pigmentation to their skin, nor did they check for circumcisions of the boys. It was simple. The people who belonged to the House of Israel, the lost sheep, were those who heard their message and brought it into their hearts. The message rang true in their minds and hearts and they changed the course of their lives because of these messengers. Some even named their children after those who brought such insights to them.

But where was the payoff? What were the results of such an investment of time and effort? There had to be something, something that encouraged so many men to step up and accept the responsibilities placed upon their shoulders as holders of the priesthood, to forsake hearth and home, just to alert one and all of the Restoration of the gospel of Jesus Christ in these latter-days. That God spoke again to his children on the earth, through prophets, just as he had in earlier times. That the world was being prepared for the final conflict of good and evil, light and darkness, in preparation for the cosmic return of the Son of God, for the inauguration of the millennium, for the thousand years of peace, when Christ would reign personally on the earth. No more wars, sickness, destruction, or fear. When every tear would be wiped away from all eyes. Both Isaiah and John made the Biblical promise. And Silva knew that meant lots of tears and lots of sorrows.

Rost pulled out a copy of the Book of Mormon. It was well worn, obviously used a lot. He opened to a part toward the front of the book. "The Book of Mormon says that the words of Isaiah are great. It also says this, and this was years before the coming of Jesus to Mary in Bethlehem. The idea of witnesses was important to Nephi. He thought it quite important to mention that not only he, but his brother Jacob were witnesses of the Savior. They had seen him in vision. He then goes on to say that the prophet, Isaiah was also a witness, making three. Three witnesses of Jesus in the small plates of Nephi. Pretty important. And Isaiah wrote to everyone who repents, which should mean to all the rest of us. Important stuff, don't you know."

"And now, I write some of the words of Isaiah, that whoso of my people which shall see these words, may lift up their hearts and rejoice for all men. Now, these are the words; and ye may liken them unto you, and unto all men."

Shep thought for a moment and nodded before saying, "And there you have it. You have become a Mormonized Jew."

Shep had toyed with the idea of conversion more than once. He knew it would have pleased his friends in Hawaii. But once he put the decision on the back of the burner plate, it became easier to avoid. He had promised to revisit the option but never seemed to reach that point. That Aaron was considering the idea was unsettling and brought it back to the front portion of the stove.

Chapter 10

"Marriage is ordained of God unto man. Wherefore, it is lawful that he should have one wife, and they twain shall be one flesh, and all this that the earth might answer the end of its creation." Doctrine and Covenants

Isaac Platt was a prosperous pastor within Presbyterianism. He had studied in the seminary and since had worked to build and boost the members of the congregations around New York City. A real feather in his cap was the fetching Elizabeth Wood. Although still quite young, she was mature in her conduct and thought processes. He was pleased to have been asked by her father to preside over Elizabeth's nuptials in April. It was three weeks before the young woman's seventeenth birthday, but Platt had no qualms about the lady's intentions. Thomas Kane, her fiancé, on the other hand, posed a different story. He was a professional man but cared little for the church. He attended services as a boon to Elizabeth and her family. And there was uncomfortable talk about his championing the likes of Brigham Young and the Mormons living in the far western reaches of the nation.

Kane had written extensively about the Mormons, seeming to side with them in almost every instance. Platt noticed that until recently, Kane had not mentioned polygamy and when the subject finally surfaced, Thomas was reticent in directing his shock and horror towards the benighted souls, especially in light of his approaching wedding.

The relationship had given Platt pause to consider the position of the Mormons. He didn't spend long on the subject, dismissing them outright. "Damned fools who claim such intimate knowledge of apostles and prophets, yet having never attended seminary!"

Thomas Leiper Kane and Elizabeth Dennistoun Wood arrived at the attractive and well-groomed Presbyterian chapel in the morning, dressed in their finery. It was a Thursday, April 21st. Family and friends gathered to witness the nuptials and wish the newlyweds well.

Thomas remained somewhat aloof, not convinced of the Christian path but keeping his opinions to himself, especially at this time. Elizabeth had been confirmed in the church a year earlier. To her, religion meant everything. It was a connection with her dearly departed mother, who had died ten years earlier, as well as with a host of other British predecessors. The pomp was nice and exciting but she saw the real value of the sacrament as laying in the traditions and sanctity of following the word of God to the best of their abilities. God had seen to it that the Bible had been preserved and protected, then translated into modern vernacular so that the righteous, humble followers of the Holy Spirit might more closely adhere to providential expectations.

It was a day to contemplate the life they would be sharing. Thomas was years older than Elizabeth. He enjoyed the benefits of a successful, secure family. He was a capable attorney in his own right and for years had studied overseas. Thomas spoke French. He was also philanthropic and would divest himself of earthly wealth if someone else in the family didn't rein him in now and then. The man exhibited abolitionist attitudes and supported women's suffrage but retained a few rough corners. Sometimes he would be condescending to Elizabeth or as her self-appointed mentor, push her overtly into schools or the writing and publishing of her views.

From her point of view, Elizabeth was confident in her native ability to steer Thomas. The time would come when he would see the error of his understandings surrounding Christianity. Being married, having children, building their own nest at Fern Rock, north of Philadelphia, Thomas would see the virtue of her life's path and easily side with her. He was more experienced with worldly affairs, while she was young and pure but still strong and resolute. Their lives were bound to be filled with joy and unexpected rewards.

Guests entered the ornate chapel, awed by the colorful stained-glass windows, portraying a variety of canonical stories. The creeping vines that covered the outside portion of the building were beginning to turn green. The foliage also gave the building the appearance of being much older than it was.

The congregants took their seats as directed by Pastor Platt, who would be today's Celebrant. He was in his glory. There was a reason God had called him to this lofty position. Platt's voice was clear and measured. He had practiced this ceremony many times over the years. And what a charming couple. The well-being of the church was in good hands, having such admirable people as these to represent the moving forth and establishment of the gospel. Roots ran deep around their foundation. God was at the helm. The ship was in good hands. The winds were prosperous and the waters forgiving, as the vessel drove forward through the years, decades, and ages.

The homily began pleasingly. There were no terse directives nor rote prayers. The Presbyterians disdained the reading of prayers, preferring instead to allow the Holy Spirit to guide the preacher. This was manifest as the congregation felt lifted and sang the hymns of God.

Following the introductory services, Thomas listened intently to the words of their pastor as he referred to the ancient Book of Common Prayer, signaling the beginning of their lives together. The English was somewhat archaic but he had no problem understanding its meaning.

"Thomas Leiper Kane and Elizabeth Dennistoun Wood, you have come here today to seek the blessing of God and of His Church upon your marriage. As the Celebrant, I require, therefore, that you promise, with the help of God, to fulfill the obligations which Christian Marriage demands."

The function of the church was plain, causing smiles to erupt on faces throughout the audience. This was proper. This was institutional. This encompassed tradition. This blessed lives and generations.

Isaac Platt stretched forth his hands. "Do you, Thomas Leiper Kane, take this woman, Elizabeth Dennistoun Wood, as your wife, to have and to hold from this day forward, for better or for worse, till death you part?"

The verbiage cleverly avoided any messy remarks that might suggest alternate paths such as polygamy. Why had so much time passed before he was apprised of this Mormon doctrine? Platt's words also left a foul taste in Kane's mouth regarding the duration of the marriage. Was Bessie to be his solely as long as he should live? *What will happen in the next life? Will she still remember me? Will our love remain? Will a bond continue to exist between us because of the children we sire? How long should this love be expected to endure? Is it powerful enough to burst the gates of death?*

"I do," Tom affirmed seriously.

The Celebrant then turned his focus onto Bessie. "And do you, Elizabeth Dennistoun Wood, take this man, Thomas Leiper Kane, as your husband, to have and to hold from this day forward, for better, or for worse, till death do you part?"

The simpleness of the request was perfect. God had made Adam and Eve and given them one to another. That is the way heaven intended marriage. One man and one woman. Talk about divergent ways was sponsored by the devil. It was apostasy and undermined the sanctity of the family and home. Certainly, there were questions left to be answered but that would happen in God's own time. Meanwhile, faith needs to be maintained in the Savior. That's who he is and that's the work he would perform.

"I do." Bessie turned towards the crowd and flashed a beautiful smile at her father.

"Then as an authorized minister of the Lord Jesus Christ, I pronounce you, Thomas Leiper Kane, and Elizabeth Dennistoun Wood, husband, and wife for the duration of your earthly lives. May God have mercy on you and bless you with the abundant life you both so richly deserve. In the name of the Father and of the Son and of the Holy Ghost. Amen."

They bowed meekly under the beaming smile of Isaac Platt and reflected his approval as they were introduced to the congregation as the newly married Mister and Missus Thomas L. Kane.

****

The small wagon train from San Bernardino had left the springs of Las Vegas a week earlier. The area had been named more than twenty years earlier but besides Indians, an official settlement had yet to be built there. It was an important stop on the Old Spanish Trail. The small group had continued moving north and east, finally climbing the plateau and entering more temperate areas where trees flourished and water was more plentiful.

After covering a decent distance for the day, Alex Williams had them stop and prepare for the evening. Aaron watched as Shep removed his Hawken rifle from the wagon bed and inspect it carefully.

"You like your plain's rifle?"

"It's a great shooter," Shep commented. "It reaches out quite a distance. And it's accurate." He signaled Williams his intention to leave camp for target practice. Aaron chose to accompany him. The two friends weaved around some sagebrush and descended a slight rise. After getting far enough away from the animals, not wanting to spook them with the rifle reports, Shep set up a series of branches as targets. Sitting down, he cradled the rifle, aimed, and squeezed the trigger. The sharp crack was foreign to the silence of the surrounding valley. The intended branch jumped, breaking into pieces. "What did I tell you?"

Aaron nodded his approval as Shep withdrew the ramrod and began to load another round. Rost watched closely as he measured a small portion of black gunpowder from his horn and poured it into the rifle barrel. He then took a small piece of cloth and set it over the bore. The Brazilian then took a ball from his ammunition pouch, placed it on top of the cloth, and pushed it slightly into the barrel, then cut off the excess fabric. With the rod, he jammed the ball and cloth deep down into the barrel until it came to a stop. He pushed the rod on top of the ball several more times then took it out and smiled. He next removed the spent percussion cap from the nipple, replacing it with another live cap and, cocked the hammer back.

"Not bad, huh? And it's all ready to go again."

"I'm impressed," the Prussian admitted.

"Then all I do is select another target," he said as he stood and leveled the rifle once again, finding a promising branch, held his breath, set the trigger, then squeezed. The Hawken rifle leaped again with the falling of the hammer, belching a plume of blue smoke. The branch was no match for the .50 caliber ball that shattered it into bits.

"How far would you say your targets are?"

"Dunno. Fifty yards."

"How far can it shoot?"

"Accurately? Depends on the size of the target. Man size, easily a couple of hundred yards. But even farther away than that, the ball still has plenty of knock-down power. This is a powerful weapon. The riflings improve its accuracy and distance."

"Mahonri-Moriancumer long? But it takes longer to load."

"A guy has to decide what's most important, I guess. At first, I didn't worry too much about it but after a while, I am more and more impressed. With this, a person could pick off game well before needing to sneak upon them. Before they're even aware of being stalked. And the ball knocks things down. It gives a guy plenty of time to catch up and finish the job before the game can get away."

"How about war? How would it handle in battle?"

Silva shook his head. "I'd hate to find out. This kind of rifle has been in many scrapes from what I hear. Trappers love it. The old Brown Bess musket has made Britain quite powerful. The army is used to formation and drill. They can lay down some terrible fire. But the musket balls just don't travel far and they really don't have a reason to sight. It's just a flat-out barrage. With one of these, a guy could sit back and plunk soldiers for quite a while before they could ever reach him with their muskets. And if the trapper or Indian knows what he's doing, he could be out of the way, long gone before anything bad could catch up to him."

"Your style of rifle has been around for long? Maher-shalal-hash-baz long?"

Aaron was full of his quips, making Shep grin. "More than twenty years, I understand. But before that, it was the Kentucky long rifle. There isn't much comparison between a rifle and a musket."

"Except speed in loading."

"A guy gets better with time and practice."

"And your pistol?"

"My friend Juanito knew what he was doing when it came to his firearms. The pistol takes a while to load as well, but when it's set, a guy has six shots and that's a terrible problem for enemies who are close by. That's about it. It's mostly to scare folks away and is used for close range. No hunting with a pistol like this."

"You still practice with it?"

"As often as I can. I don't want to waste the tool. That's all it is. A tool. It can be used for a couple of things but here in America, in these days, this kind of tool can come in quite handily."

"You know, the Prussians are good at conducting war. Like the British and the French, they are always experimenting, looking for better weapons. Unfortunately for the military, there hasn't been any good, knockdown, drag-out wars since Napoleon."

"Hopefully things will stay that way."

Aaron shook his head seriously. "Maybe not for long. When I was leaving San Francisco, I heard about rumblings coming from the Turks and the Russians. There could be a blowout over there."

"Thank goodness we're in America."

The two men spent the next hour in target practice. Shep instructed Aaron in the use of the Hawken and his Colt Dragoon. It was an eye-opening experience for the Jew and he grew to understand better why so many of his countrymen chose the army as a vocation. At least the use of the ordnance was diverting.

Returning to camp as the sky was beginning to darken, they sought out Alex Williams. The man was naturally quiet, not given much to speak. He didn't mind sharing his information but people needed to be direct with their questions. After some small talk and thinking they had warmed Williams up some, Silva and Rost asked again how much longer before they reached the Great Salt Lake City.

"It's still more than 300 miles," he admitted thoughtfully. "And both you know how rough the road is. It will probably take us well over a week. I still think it should be the middle of May. That's just my guess."

"Still no trouble with the Indians?"

"None so far. None that I've heard. Hope it stays that way. We should be getting into Cedar City tomorrow. They always have plenty to say."

****

The mixture of Native American tribes in the valleys of the Great Basin that Brigham Young and his followers found upon their arrival in 1847 was confusing and dangerous. The numbers were not as extensive as those of the tribes on the plains or the Indians who had inhabited eastern and southern areas of the nation. Vast numbers of these peoples had been killed by European diseases or driven from their homelands, forced on to the Trail of Tears, relocated to reservations, lands that had nothing in common with their ancestral haunts. Presently the mountains and valleys around the Great Basin claimed about 20,000 inhabitants.

The Shoshone used tepees like the plains tribes and hunted buffalo when they could. They lived to the north of the valley of the Great Salt Lake, extending to the Snake River, from there west into Oregon Territory. On their western borders, they mingled with Paiutes and moved south into the Carson Valley, butting up against the Washoe Indians and the Sierra Nevada mountains.

Small groups of loosely organized bands of Goshutes were scattered throughout the desert valleys of the Basin. These posed little threat to the settlers moving across the arid region unless they let their guard down. The Goshutes were good at taking advantage of weakness and would kill or steal horses and cattle if the opportunity became open. Sometimes settlers fell victim to depredations. These groups of Goshutes were seen as nuisances by the Forty-Niners and often shot at, considering them vagabonds.

The southern Paiutes lived precariously on the Kaibab Plateau, bounded on the south by the Grand Canyon, broad deserts, and the much larger tribes of Navajos and Apaches. Paiutes were pressured by the raiding Timpanogos from the north, who stole their women and children to sell to as slaves, for use in the mines or ranchos.

The Hopi were reserved and not nomadic. They kept to themselves, living on three isolated *mesas* and surrounded by the Navajos.

Deep in the south, large numbers of Navajos and Apaches protected their lands and possessions fiercely. Claiming warrior traditions, they watched with suspicion as pioneers trekked through their lands. Few outsiders stopped to put down roots but they noted the springs and rivers carefully. This did not bode well for the natives.

The main body of Utes was related to the Shoshone and Comanche tribes, living in the fastness of the Rocky Mountains. Settlers preferred to move through their lands without stopping. The idea of gold and silver and the crazy looks they put in miners' eyes was not lost on the tribes. They knew those hunting for the metals would be returning in greater numbers soon enough.

The Pahvants were loosely connected with the stronger tribes to their east, like the Timpanogos. Living in the mountain canyons that bordered the broad desert valleys to the west, they were opportunists. The Old Spanish Trail ran close to their lands and they watched immigrants carefully, picking off livestock whenever it could be done quietly and safely.

The Timpanogos interacted the most frequently with the incoming Mormons. Because they had been called Utah Indians by the Spanish, many assumed they were Utes. This wasn't the case. They were tied to the Shoshone to the north and often clashed with them in the Valley of the Great Salt Lake. Their traditional lands were south of where the Mormons first entered. They fished in Utah Lake and the creeks surrounding its valley. They were hunters who enjoyed the aspen and pine forests of the Wasatch Range.

They had powerful chiefs who were wise and careful with their interactions and the newly arriving Latter-day Saints. Kanosh, San-Pete, Sowiette, and Arapeen led their bands through the canyons and mountain valleys of the western Rockies. The most notorious chief of the Timpanogos was Wakara. His birth was shrouded in mystery but he appeared to be about 40 years old when the Mormons arrived. In the Timpanogos idiom, his name meant Hawk. Natively clever, he ranged far and wide, raiding, stealing, kidnapping, trading, and threatening all who got in his way. He was related to the other chiefs but instead of preying on them, he rode far to the south, using the Old Spanish Trail to invade the southern areas of California. He developed relationships with other tribes but especially with the Mexicans with whom he traded horses and slaves for guns, ammunition, and other items that increased his wealth and strength. He had some close dealings with trappers and mountain men, most notably Pegleg Smith and Jim Beckwourth while stealing horses below the Cajon Pass. Wakara saw the advent of Mormon settlers as a chance to add to his coffers. His wealth shifted and moved according to the seasons. He pushed his understanding of the economy at the Mormons but hit a wall. The newcomers did not approve of his raiding techniques and the selling of slaves. They were not impressed with his physical strength or stamina. Theirs was a new perspective. The numbers behind their invasion kept multiplying. The driving force behind these English Americans was quite different from the Spanish. This would impact his garnering wealth.

At first, he tried to understand the Mormons. He was fluent in English and Spanish and a shrewd businessman, but these settlers were foreign to anything he had previously experienced. They were not like other tribesmen, Mexicans, or trappers. He quickly grasped the idea of conversion into their faith as a bargaining chip. He got to know Brigham Young and was finally baptized as a member of the church on May 13, 1850. Wakara became aware of the settlers' desire and determination to establish forts and towns. They did not set up encampments, hunt the game and fish, and then move on. They built solid houses, permanent structures. They fenced the land. They intended to stay. This caused consternation among the Timpanogos.

Wakara enjoyed complete sovereignty over his people. He had power over life and death. He was adored and feared by his tribe and those who knew him. His influence was felt far and wide. He had spent his life extending his power. But this authority did not translate over to the newcomers.

As a people, the Mormons were quite different from the Timpanogos. They followed their own set of laws. These were codified and not arbitrary. If depredation was committed against the settlers by an Indian, Wakara exercised complete control. He could demand property returned or payment to be made immediately in the case of lost livestock. The life of his tribal members lay within his control. From a transverse position, if there was an infraction committed against the Timpanogos by the Mormons, a series of steps would then follow. The perpetrator was never turned over to the Timpanogos for justice to be requited. Instead, the Mormons would have an investigation, which invariably lasted much longer than the Timpanogos wanted, and generally ended up leaving Wakara and his people with a foul taste in their mouths.

The passing of directives outlawing the selling of slaves and then arresting or chasing Mexican traders from the territory, greatly impacted Wakara's income. It came as a personal affront. He had tried working with the settlers but they continued to take and not give. Brigham Young counseled his people against fighting the Indians, telling them it was better to feed them and to share, but the number of settlers was swelling. Ancestral homes and the ways of life of the Timpanogos were diminishing rapidly.

Despite friendships with Brigham Young and Isaac Morely, Wakara felt he had been taken advantage of. The life he had been raised with and grown to love was being pushed aside. His people were not respected. Their understanding of land ownership was fluid and easy. The newcomers were different. What they took they did not give back. Easy access to tribal fishing areas around the lake was blocked. Game from the mountains was becoming scarcer. During the cold winters, famine was stalking his people. Whenever the Timpanogos took a cow to help stave off starvation, punishment, and retribution followed. They didn't feel the same way about the harvesting of their game. The Mormons made roads wherever they chose. They started building fences to keep their livestock in and the Timpanogos out.

Frustrations were building. Snares were being laid by members from both sides. Life could not go on as usual.

Chapter 11

"Action may not always bring happiness, but there is no happiness without action." Benjamin Disraeli

"Miss Nightingale, your appointment has arrived."

The thirty-three-year-old woman administrator was expecting to be made superintendent of the Hospital for Gentlewomen in London. Her facility was also known as the Institute for the Care of Sick Gentlewomen in Upper Harley Street. The pleasant woman smiled at her secretary. "Thank you, Miss Robins. Please show her in."

Nightingale had a busy stack of paperwork before her. She hoped this would be a quick visit. Worries were beginning to pile up. She was working with a first-class group of women nurses in the hospital. The pay was minimal but they studied and worked for altruistic reasons. Florence loved her calling, feeling that it came as a gift from God. Nursing was a blessing. She had conscientiously turned down a well-positioned suitor who wanted marriage, to travel to Germany's Institution of Kaiserswerth on the Rhine, for the Practical Training of Deaconesses, also known as the Lutheran Hospital of Pastor Fliedner, studying in the most updated nursing institution. It was a wonderful experience. She had found her life-long dream. Bringing education back with her to Britain, she had worked at several positions, trying out the theories of cleanliness and good nutrition. Her efforts gained her high acclaim and she was quickly moved into her current position as superintendent pro-tem of the most prestigious women's hospital in Middlesex.

Miss Robins opened her office door again. "This is Miss Matthews," she said, motioning the woman to enter and take a chair across the desk from Miss Nightingale.

"Thank you, Miss Robins. That will be all."

Florence glanced up from the paper she had been studying into the face of Harriett Matthews. The latter looked to be about twenty and nervous. She tried her best to smile back at the administrator.

"It's a pleasure to make your acquaintance, Miss Nightingale."

Florence sighed quietly and nodded. *How many women had she seen this week?* All were looking for employment, hoping to make the move into London.

"Did you bring your references?" she asked unemotionally.

Harriett nodded, then pulled her purse from the floor and began rummaging among the papers kept there. "It's here somewhere," she promised.

"Please take your time," she replied just as Harriett found the document and victoriously handed it across the desk.

Florence received the papers and scanned their contents swiftly. "You spent some time in Manchester?"

"I'm from Preston. I have family in the city and I thought it would be a good place to start my training."

"You worked there about a year?"

"Yes, mum."

"What did you think of the courses offered there?" Florence asked while continuing to look through Matthews' papers.

"It was sufficient but I want to be the best, Miss Nightingale. I have heard that you offer the best training."

Ah, yes, the correct answer. She looked young enough, eager enough, educated enough but was she capable enough? There were limited openings in the hospital for incoming nurses. She was an attractive girl. Her fingernails were clean. Very important. Her clothing was immaculate and ironed. Florence stood as if to collect some other papers from a shelf on the opposite wall but she was looking for an opportunity to walk around the side of her desk and look at Harriet's shoes. They appeared comfortable, clean, and useful. This was turning out to be a more pleasant interview than expected.

"This all looks in order, Miss Matthews," she said, returning to her desk and sitting down. "We appreciate your interest in our institution and your willingness to come here. I am not sure when an opening will be forthcoming and when exactly we could find a place for you. Are you currently staying in the city?"

"Yes, mum."

"Do you have the funds to be here a while?"

The strained smile on the girl's face lagged. "I believe so, mum." Their eyes met briefly. "Oh, and I have this for your consideration as well," she said, withdrawing a used envelope from her purse. She handed it to Florence carefully.

Florence Nightingale took the envelope and opened it. It was the personal missive addressed to her, from Colonel Thomas L. Kane, Esquire. Now that was an intriguing development. She immediately began to wonder about the young woman's connection to the American lawyer. How long had it even been since she last saw the military gentleman from Philadelphia?

"Thank you for delivering this," she told Harriett and continued reading the proper letter.

Florence read the words slowly, getting a feel for the man's tone. After a few minutes, she looked up at Harriett. "This is a wonderful letter, Miss Matthews. I consider it very important. May I ask why you didn't start with it?"

Harriet had been holding her breath and she exhaled softly. "I wanted you to meet me on my own merits, mum. I wanted to present myself in the best manner I could. I wanted to pass your inspection without needing to call upon

101

the assistance of Mr. Kane. I would have given you the letter in any event. It is addressed to you. But, well, he speaks so highly of you and all I have heard about your work since arriving back in Britain is marvelous. I knew that meeting you would be of utmost importance. Should I even been considered for selection to work here would be gravy, mum."

Very well thought out and delivered, Miss Nightingale thought to herself. She smiled sincerely and asked, "Why don't you tell me how you came to know Mr. Kane and when you arrived from America?"

Harriett took another deep breath and exhaled, then wiped her palms on her dress. They were beginning to sweat.

"A few years back my family was converted into the Mormon religion. My parents wanted us to follow the Saints and go to America, to Zion, to the Utah Territory in the west."

Nightingale nodded. She was aware of the phenomenon being caused by the Mormon missionaries around Manchester and Liverpool. They were moving up into Scotland as well. She had heard some rumblings caused by the religionists in Birmingham and even in London, but it seemed the American missionaries had more success with the displaced English commoners around Manchester. Florence was also aware that numbers of her countrymen had joined the religion, emigrated across the Atlantic, trekked across the American hinterland, and were establishing a home in the Rocky Mountains.

"Well, it was during our travels that we were overtaken by extreme tragedy. We were traveling up the Missouri River to Florence-" she stopped as Miss Nightingale's eyes looked at her quickly. "It's the name of a fairly new town. It used to be called Winter Quarters and had been settled by the Mormons as they were moving west. Anyway, as our steamboat was working its way up the river, it exploded, killing many people. My family was among its victims." The tale was still emotional. Harriett paused for a few seconds and Miss Nightingale waited patiently. "I was injured and well cared for by the nicest family. The Winslows of Lexington, Missouri. It was during my convalescence that I decided that I wanted to be a nurse. I wanted to be the one who cared for the injured, the dazed or confused. I wanted to be the one offering strength and encouragement to my brothers and sisters in need."

The story was engaging. It had merit. It also told her about Harriett's reason for choosing nursing.

"When did this unfortunate accident happen?"

"Just over a year ago."

Florence was paying rapt attention. "And you met Colonel Kane in Missouri?"

"An acquaintance of his, Mr. Alexander Doniphan, Esquire of Richmond, Missouri referred me to him as I traveled back to New York City."

"I see. And so you met the Colonel in New York City? And how is he faring?"

"Well enough. He is set to be married to a very pretty young thing."

"Good for them. And you didn't continue to be with the Mormons in their Zion? Your conversion isn't as solid as your parents?"

Harriett smiled cautiously. "I think it is, mum. But, well, I just didn't have as strong an urge to take me there. We still have some family in England and I thought it better for me to come back. Mr. Doniphan and his neighbors saw to it that I had the money necessary to return here after I healed up. Home. And I'm glad that I did, mum."

"And me, as well," Florence said with satisfaction. "And I thank you for delivering this post. It is always good to hear from associates and friends."

Florence Nightingale called Miss Robins back into her office and gave her a series of orders meant to line Harriett up with an apartment and requisitions for food and her nursing uniforms.

Harriet was hired. She had achieved her goal. Her peers were supportive and surrounded her with warmth and curiosity. It was exactly what Harriett had been looking and longing for. Some of the young women were from Wales or Scotland, but most were from England proper and of those, a majority hailed from London. After working their shifts, they plied her with questions about America and crossing the ocean. They also wanted to know about Mormon missionaries. Most had seen them and wondered what it was that drove them to leave their homes to preach to the British, especially since they felt themselves to be quite civilized.

Medical classes were organized and followed a curriculum set by Florence. The topics covered areas that Miss Nightingale had determined were the most important in hospitals and would best help the sick and injured return to their prior state of health.

Ventilation- with the free flow of fresh air from outside, when not too cold

Health in houses- this was especially important for the nurses since it was an area they controlled the easiest

Petty management (how things are done by others when you must be away)- this turned the nurses into educators, elevating them to a position of respected professionals

Noise- this was seen as an irritant that impeded rest and healing

Variety (environment)- the ill needed to be moved and given diverse opportunities to view rooms and flora; socializing was still to be kept to a minimum.

Taking food and what kinds of food- nutritious foods stoked the body's engines for recovery, generating the power and strength necessary

Bed and bedding- sleep was tantamount for healing and having fresh linen and supportive mattresses were very beneficial

Light- natural sunlight was empowering- lamps during the night gave orientation and identified the nurses to the ill

Cleanliness of rooms- terrible illnesses were associated with filthy rooms, inviting vermin as well as depression

Personal cleanliness- always lifted the sick, keeping them free from soiling through dysentery or vomit, mouths fresh, faces washed, and hair combed

Chattering hopes and advice (the false assurances and recommendations of family and friends to the sick) what they were about dealt with life and death, they offered hope but not undue promises

Observation- copious notes were taken during the care, giving the health professionals recourse to others as well as their thoughts, feelings, and understandings related to their charges

One of the ideas that united the women was their profound belief that theirs was a calling handed them by Deity. This understanding drove them in their studies and during the long stretches of night with patients. It was also a characteristic owned by Florence Nightingale herself. The sisterhood was strong. Very little fraternization was taking place outside of the institution. There simply wasn't time nor was there interest, not at that time. Competition was encouraged but it was lighthearted. There were no cut-throat approaches to the work. The nurses stood by one another and did not arbitrarily allow the male physicians to run roughshod over the sisterhood, without whose work the list of casualties would spike.

The nurses were acquainted with Miss Nightingale's friend, Sidney Herbert, the 1st Barron Herbert of Lea. He was an attractive and educated man, a politician, and currently serving as the British Secretary of War. The man had a reputation with ladies but his relationship with Florence and the nurses at the hospital were always above board. He sensed the value of women's work. One of the issues Florence had with the government was the insistence that women nurses not be used with the Empire's soldiers. Of course, there was the understandable temptation of there being less than professional relations among the young men and women. But Florence consistently hammered their education and preparation and abilities. Up to this point, it was a hopeless dream. Florence bided her time. She was confident the time would arrive when all the resources of the Empire would be needed and when it came, she would see to it that she and her colleagues were standing in order and at attention.

Chapter 12

"A good man, is a good man, whether in this church, or out of it." Brigham Young

Great Salt Lake City was a marvel for Shep and Aaron. San Bernardino was a Mormon settlement and it was laid out with a clean north-south, east-west grid, but it was tiny in comparison to this swelling city in the north. The streets were clean and broad, allowing for a wagon and its team to turn around. Ruts and garbage were controlled. Boardwalks were measured and free from holes.

The one thing that delighted Aaron was that the streets were also dark at night. This was a real opportunity for his business. Another thing that pleased the two travelers was their ability to gain access to an audience with Governor Brigham Young. He was an active man who was well aware of his people and the needs they were facing. He was anxious to see they were well provided for. His involvement spread beyond the city limits and the interests of the local members of the church. Young kept up with the emigrant trains that passed through the city. He kept his ear to the ground, especially where relations with the Indians were concerned. Several groups of federal workers were working in the territory. Most of these were surveying, mapping the desolate interior, trying to find the best routes for roads, telegraph poles, and one day, the railroads.

Brigham was delighted to hear of Aaron's interest in street lighting. "There's a market for your expertise here," he told him. "You can see how dark the streets are at night. That's good for some, encouraging folks to stay indoors and at home with their families. But others need to be out and about after the sun sets. And I'm afraid the darkness might tempt highwaymen to steal from the unwary. Streetlights would be a huge asset."

"Believe me, sir, I'll do my best to get things going here."

"Have you boys decided where you'll be living?"

"I've heard about some land in Tooele," Shep said. "Prices are good and I could have plenty of room for horses and cattle."

The governor nodded in agreement. "Ezra Benson's building a grist mill over that way and it will make things even better. What about you?" he asked Aaron.

"I think I'll do better where there's more folks. Probably the city. I've been thinking about setting up a store not just for oil but I've been thinking there's plenty of need for all kinds of merchandise."

"That's true. We can always use honest store owners."

"And Aaron's thinking about baptism."

The news surprised Brigham. Shep didn't know if it was because he had assumed they were already members.

"Can't go wrong there," he said.

"There's always *Kol Nidre*," Rost intoned causing Young to give a hearty laugh.

"Yep. There's always *Kol Nidre*," he chuckled. "I haven't heard that phrase since Britain. But you don't even need to wait for *Yom Kippur*. You get sick of us or the gospel and you're free to move on. I can tell you that we need good people. Folks of substance. You get baptized and all it will do is make us better. Jew or Gentile, we're looking for the lost sheep of the House of Israel. What about you Silva? You already a member of the Church? I know you spent a while with Lyman and Rich in San Bernardino."

"Not yet," the Brazilian admitted. "I have been reading the Book of Mormon. And rather seriously."

"Like I said, you'd just make us better. And you can't go wrong reading the Book of Mormon. The first time I laid my eyes on it I figured it was either from the devil or God and I was bound to find out which. Guess you can see which direction I chose."

After their interview with Brigham, the men decided to take him up on an offer since they were still untethered and take a wagon and some livestock south to Manti for Isaac Morley. They skirted the Utah Lake on the east side then wound their way into the Spanish Fork Canyon. Several encampments of Timpanogos were visible as the Indians fished the lake and creeks, doing their best to give space to the incoming settlers. Twenty-five miles later they crested the top of the San Pete Valley, named after a brother of Wakara. It sloped away to the south. The settlement of Manti was barely discernible. They made it into Manti a day later.

Despite the Spartan existence, the colonists were a cheerful, hard-working lot. Silva and Rost found Morley's cabin and introductions were made. Two of the men present, Orson Hyde and Parley Pratt, were members of the church's Twelve Apostles. They seemed normal enough, maybe a bit too gregarious. Aaron breached the topic of his baptism.

Hyde was quick to jump at the chance. "I'd be happy to baptize you, Brother Rost. Brigham thinks that I'm the next best thing to a Jew because I've been to Palestine." Orson Hyde was also a territorial judge and a man of no small reputation among the Mormons. He had a home in a small town just north of Manti called Spring City. He also had legal responsibilities to care for far away in the west next to California, in Carson Valley, where the Mormons had established the town of Genoa, once called Mormon Station. Franktown was another of the colonies north of Genoa. It had been named after the first white baby born in the area, Frank Bentley.

Parley Pratt was in constant motion as a missionary. Serving as a mission president in Britain more than ten years earlier, he was also aware of the Continent. He had circumvented South America and was especially interested in visiting with Shep Silva. He was slightly disappointed to find the Brazilian did not remember a lot about his homeland. Shep more than made up for it by recalling his friendship with Elders Thompson and Sweeney and could provide more up-to-date information about what was happening in the Sandwich Islands as well as San Francisco, Los Angeles, and San Bernardino.

The people of the community lost no time readjusting the dam on the city creek. Before long it was filled with water. Elder Hyde led Aaron Rost into the pool and baptized him. There were no trumpets, no pomp, and no circumstance. It was a simple ordinance. Elder Pratt then laid his hands on Rost's head and confirmed him a member of the church and officially blessed him with the gift of the Holy Ghost.

"This is the most sublime of gifts," Pratt later explained. "It will act like your conscience. It will lead you and protect you and help to answer questions most uniquely. Thoughts and ideas will cascade into your mind, as you continue to study and draw as close to our Maker as you can." He smiled. "Never underestimate both the gift and power of the Holy Ghost. Most sublime."

Aaron Rost admitted that he felt differently. He felt that he had been cleansed of past indiscretions. "This is exactly where I should be. I've repented and I'm doing exactly what God wants me to do," he explained to Shep.

The statement pleased and mystified Silva at the same time. He had known Rost for several months. They had discussed religion many times. For him to take such a significant step was interesting. But could he have already resolved his identity, shed his Jewishness with this simple immersion in the icy cold waters of the creek and then the promise of a heavenly gift, the presence of a member of the godhead?

"Not at all," Aaron replied after hearing his questions. "I am exactly the same person I was. All I have done is added to what has been given me. The message of the Book of Mormon has whispered to my soul. I knew this was the step I needed to take. It doesn't mean that I have surrendered my identity. I am not merely a Mormonized Jew. The power of the Holy Ghost has manifest itself within my heart. I love the message of the gospel. I truly believe that Christ is the Messiah. I believe that these Mormon emigrants are being collected by the God of Israel. From these mountains, their missionaries will go forth and proclaim the Restoration to all who will hear, regardless of their currently pathetic numbers." He patted Shep's shoulder. "I heard and I intend to move forward and make a difference." He smiled at his younger traveling companion. "So what are in your plans now? I saw you chatting with Morley. The two of you seemed quite interested in some kinds of plans."

Shep shrugged nonchalantly. "Like I told Brigham, I'd like to settle in Tooele. Problem is, I don't have a lot of expendable money at present. I really can't afford horses or cattle, let alone much land for their pasture. Isaac told me about a company that's expected to come through these parts soon enough. They are surveying for the government. He says they are always looking for roustabouts. He thinks I could get on with them for a couple months. It would give me a good lay of the land and I would be drawing pay as well."

"So you are going to stay here? I was planning on heading back north to the Great Salt Lake City in a few days. Pratt wants to help take some other livestock back."

"Yeah. I think I'll check out this survey job. In the meantime, Morley says there is plenty to do with the horses and cattle around here. Probably just building fences but it will keep me fed."

Two days later as he watched his friend and Elder Pratt ride the wagon back north, Shep felt the growing lump in his throat. It was not an unexpected sensation. He had experienced it several times before. When he sailed from Brazil, when he left Oahu, when he bid Rost goodbye in San Francisco, and then as he said goodbye to the Wetoyous and San Bernardino. Goodbyes were not what he looked forward to. Then again, life was filled with them. He expected he would have plenty more in his future. He did not know when he would get back to southern California, but he did believe he would see the Wetoyous, the Sweeneys, and Aaron Rost again. Life was a treasure chest of surprises.

****

In 1853, July 17th fell on Sunday, the Sabbath for members of the church. Most of the people in Springville, immediately south of Provo, had attended their religious services. The singing was a mixture of talent and mumbling. Some of the Welsh Saints, who prided themselves with their choirs and singing abilities, continued to be surprised at how poorly most of their neighbors sang, barely holding a note. They distributed the Lord's sacrament and then listened to some well-intentioned preaching by several men who had been called upon to speak. The homilies were interspersed with scripture and homespun wisdom.

When the services broke, Brother and Sister Ivie started for their home several blocks away. Three Timpanogos natives were awaiting them when they arrived, two men and a woman. Jim Ivie smiled at the men and invited them into his barn to view some blankets and a saddle, while Sister Ivie and the Indian woman began to bargain in their way. The Indian woman soon appeared in the barn, happily displaying three jars of flour to the men of her tribe. Her husband's face darkened quickly and he demanded what she had traded for the flour. When she replied that she had given Sister Ivie three fish in the exchange, the man struck her in the face, knocking her to the ground, then grabbing her by the hair, dragged her back to the cabin.

Jim jumped to intervene and broke the man's hold on his wife's hair. The incensed Indian raised his rifle and began to point it at Ivie. The farmer grabbed the barrel of the rifle and a struggle for the weapon started. Yelling and shrieks filled the peaceful air. With both men tugging on the rifle, the stock broke, with

Ivie retaining the barrel. Before the Indian could recover, Ivie swung the barrel as hard as he could, striking the Indian on the head, felling him immediately.

The other Indian man had strung his bow and shot an arrow at Ivie. The missile pierced his buckskin shirt. Before the brave could nock and shoot another arrow, Ivie clubbed him with the rifle barrel. The second Indian dropped in a heap on top of his companion. By that time, the Indian woman had retrieved a large branch from the woodpile and struck Jim across the face. Blood spurted from a deep wound above his mouth. He struck back with the metal barrel, hitting the woman on the head. She too dropped to the ground.

The fracas was noisy and the combatants scattered clouds of dust into the air, bringing neighbors running. It didn't take long for them to see what had happened. The first Indian man was recognized as a relative of the dangerous Wakara. The neighbors encouraged Ivie to take his family to the fort for protection against the depredations that were sure to follow, while they tended to the wounded Indians.

The Indian woman and the man with the bow were finally revived and their wounds cleaned and bound. The first man never regained consciousness and died several hours later.

Chief Wakara was furious, demanding that Ivie be handed over to him for execution. His demands went unfilled. Wakara saw this as blatant disrespect. The Timpanogos chieftain ordered his clansmen to break their camps and follow him into the canyons.

This was the beginning of a ten-month conflict known as the Wakara or Walker War. Settlements were attacked and burned, livestock was killed or stolen. Mormon militiamen were mobilized and rode after the Indians. Skirmishes were fought in several locations throughout the territory. Twelve men were killed on both sides of the conflict before it was subdued by a conference between Brigham Young and Chief Wakara the following May. More than 100 members of Wakara's tribe were baptized into the church in the city creek at Manti. Peace was declared between the leaders. Feelings mellowed but trouble continued to percolate below the surface of the waters for years to come.

****

Captain John Williams Gunnison of the US Army's Topographical Engineers corps was assigned to survey portions of the western United States, between the 38th and 39th parallels, looking for possible routes for a National Transcontinental Railroad. He had worked several years before with Captain Howard Stansbury, mapping the Great Salt Lake and writing a book entitled *The Mormons*, which gave a positive and objective view of the Latter-day Saints living at that time in the West. Gunnison was also well acquainted with Dr. John Bernhisel as well as Albert Carrington, a member of the Quorum of the Twelve, and with whom he corresponded frequently. Captain Gunnison and his party of twenty men left St. Louis in June 1853, where the officer had been promoted to captain and began working their way through the Rocky Mountains and then into the Utah Territory, arriving in Manti in the middle of October.

The day before riding into Manti, Gunnison had taken the papers written by Captain Stansbury from his trunk. It reminded him of their work and who some of the main players were in the region. It also recounted their exploits from several years earlier, leaving pleasant memories.

Gunnison put his papers down long enough to call a private. "You sure Captain Morris is already set up in Fillmore?"

"Yes sir. That's what his rider said."

"Very good. That's all." He returned to his readings, suddenly impressed with the facility Stansbury had with writing.

Isaac Morley greeted the surveying officials with all the pomp the town could muster. Gunnison was pleasantly surprised.

"For some reason, I was under the impression that Brigham Young wished to be left alone. That he didn't care for the telegraph or railroad coming through the territory. I understood he wanted to be left alone and keep his people from the influences of the United States."

"On the contrary," Morley replied. "The Utah Legislature has made applications for such inroads. Isolation has its merits but keeping far away from the heartbeat of the nation has even more distractions. The distance separating us from St. Joe and Sacramento is daunting. We want to be included. If possible."

"Of course. And I can only imagine how difficult carrying on business with Washington can be. Again, trying to cover such large distances."

"I will be glad to introduce you to the Honorable Almon Babbitt or the Honorable John Bernhisel. They each make the trip once a year, trying to keep our needs forefront with Congress. Sometimes they make the trip twice a year. It's hard for a young man and they are both aging."

"I can appreciate that," Gunnison nodded. "Now we have just lost a couple of our men while in the mountains. You mentioned something about having a volunteer here who would be willing to work with us?"

"He's standing right there," he said, pointing to a short, stocky young man who was listening to some of the soldiers' stories. "His name is Shep Silva. From Brazil, originally. He's a hard worker and speaks Spanish quite well."

"Excellent. I will make sure Lt. Beckwith is introduced and have him work with his party as a roustabout."

Both Gunnison and Beckwith were graduates from West Point, with Beckwith being six years younger than the captain. Both felt the importance of their assignment. Both were pleased with the reception they received in Manti. The town was thriving despite the threats of war with the Timpanogos. Streets were lined out properly, fences cordoned yards and lots. Cattle, horses, and sheep were omnipresent in their pastures. The Mormons didn't look to be short-timers.

Silva was happy to be offered a position with Gunnison's group. Time in Manti had dragged slowly and he was looking for a new venue. He was also happy to be involved with surveying. The men understood their roles and allowed him to join in whenever possible. None made fun of his accent. All were relieved to know how proficient he was with his firearms. He was a capable defender, should they need support. Silva also had a wealth of knowledge regarding the Indian tribes in the region. Like his thirst to know more about surveying, he had been devouring information about the local natives during the previous six months. Isaac Morley was a personal friend of Chief Wakara. The latter insisted on keeping his distance during the hostilities, but the Mormon elder made sure to leave signs of peace wherever and whenever he could, knowing the chief would be made aware.

Journals noted the cold, raw weather as the survey party set off from Manti. Leaving the San Pete Valley, the surveyors headed west, circumventing several rough mountain ranges, and finally descending into the flats leading to the north of Sevier, a desert lake, 35 miles northwest of the current Utah Territory capital of Fillmore.

The party made a side trip to Fillmore for supplies. Captain Gunnison calmed the natives of the area who were upset because one of their leaders had been shot by emigrants passing through on the Old Spanish Trail several days earlier.

Silva had been in the desert area a month before scouting for a winter range for their sheep. The lake was fed by two small creeks. The creek water was now being used more and more for irrigation by the settlers. Effects of this usage were apparent as the lake became shallower.

Silva pointed to the inflowing river. "The lake has been given many names by the trappers and Escalante's explorers. The Spanish called this one *Rio Severo* and it's the name that has stuck. Severo or Sevier."

Gunnison was content having Shep in his company. He was relatively new to the region but was more familiar with the area than any others in their group except another Mormon guide named William Potter.

After leaving Fillmore, Beckwith and Gunnison decided to split their company for a couple of days. They wouldn't be far apart but doing so would speed up their surveying assignments. Silva was assigned to go with the lieutenant.

Both parties were in the flats and as evening fires were started and food was being prepared, the distance between them appeared close. The Pahvant Indians who lived in the mountains and canyons to the east were also aware of the surveyors. They did not approve of the encroachment of the American soldiers. Neither did they appreciate their people being targeted by the passing emigrant wagon train. These people were not Mormon. There had also been a series of challenges regarding the usage of the water by the settlers' livestock. The Pahvants were aware of the war that had broken out between the Mormons and the Timpanogos. The larger tribe was an erstwhile ally of the poorer Pahvants. These events combined at the close of October. Angry braves decided that an attack on Gunnison's party was warranted. A resentful council of the Pahvant tribe's younger warriors was convened separate from their chief, Kanosh, and they solidified their plans.

That evening a war party of thirty braves filed out of the canyons, dressed in their warm winter clothing, and began trotting across the broad sagebrush flats, whitened by the snow flurries that had drifted through the area, towards the diminishing glow of the soldiers' fires. Discovering that there were two groups separated by 11 miles, the painted warriors decided to focus on the northern group led by Captain Gunnison.

No voices were raised during the single-file march. Communication was made with hand and arm gestures. Before daybreak the men had secreted themselves in the willows along the river, surrounding the surveyors' encampment. Their stealthy arrival and positioning were affected. The lethal attack was launched in the early morning of Wednesday, October 26th, as the sleepy soldiers were beginning to get their breakfast. The Pahvants burst from the willows that lay twenty yards from the encampment. They attacked with a deadly rush, screaming war cries. A few had firearms but most were armed with bows, knives, and tomahawks. Hearing the screams, Gunnison stepped from his tent and raised his hand in a sign of peace. He was instantly cut down. Four of the frightened soldiers sprinted after their fleeing horses and mounting them, escaped the attack. Within a few steps, one of the horses fell, throwing his rider into the willows, where the man scrambled for concealment, then lay quietly until the massacre was finished. The victorious Pahvants killed all who were left then sifted through the papers and surveying instruments, finally abandoning the camp. The sun had climbed high by the time the lone soldier arose from his cover and ran the distance to Beckwith's camp. The other three had reached Beckwith's group hours earlier.

Brevet Captain Morris arrived at Beckwith's camp from Fillmore. He collected a party of 12 riflemen and rode to the assistance of their brothers. They were accompanied by Silva and Potter's brother from Fillmore. Dr. Schiel, the group's surgeon, also followed.

Eight of the captain's twelve men were killed: Captain John Gunnison, Richard Kern, the botanist, Creuzfeldt, Bill Potter, Private Caulfield, Private Liptoote, Private Mehreens, and John Bellows, the camp roustabout. Beckwith's men rode hard to reach Gunnison's camp, hoping to find more survivors. The dead had been mutilated. The Pahvants did not have good access to guns, so Gunnison and his men had been killed with arrows and tomahawks.

Thinking his mission would not require much time, Morris left the bodies exposed in the open and rode after the culprits. Their search was in vain. Riding through the rugged canyons of the bitterly cold mountains, they were unsuccessful in finding the perpetrators. When Morris finally returned to the scene of the tragedy several days later, his company found that wolves had been among the dead and eaten or carried off the bodies. A thigh bone thought to belong to Gunnison and Potter's skull were all that could be found.

A week later, the despondent Beckwith and the remainder of the surveying party returned to Great Salt Lake City to spend the balance of the winter.

News of the massacre stirred emotions. Gentile residents clamored that Brigham had succumbed to his animosity towards the government and ordered an attack on the soldiers, using the Danites, a mythical band of Mormon vigilantes sworn to carry out the desires of their Prophet, ordering that they dress as Indians to commit the massacre, notwithstanding that Bill Potter, one of the victims, was a fellow Saint.

Lt. Beckwith's report noted the *"statement which has from time to time appeared (or been copied) in various newspapers and charging the Mormons or Mormon authorities with instigating the Indians, if not aiding them, to the murder of Captain Gunnison and his associates, is, I believe, not only entirely false, but there is no accidental circumstance connected with it affording the slightest foundation for such a charge."*

Chapter 13

"Ye hear of wars in foreign lands; but, behold, I say unto you, they are nigh, even at your doors, and not many years hence ye shall hear of wars in your own lands." Doctrine and Covenants

"Mahonri, it's so good to see you in one piece!" Aaron Rost announced cheerily, using a nickname he had chosen for his friend. He jumped from the wagon and embraced Shep on South Temple Street's boardwalk in Great Salt Lake City. It was a heartfelt, friendly hug.

"*Obrigado, amigo.* It was a nerve-wracking experience." *Obrigado* was the Portuguese form of saying thank you. It means 'I am obligated.' Shep felt it was much more expressive than Spanish.

"Without a doubt." The taller man stepped back and sized up his friend. "So now what?"

"The lieutenant has plenty of book-work for us, even for me. I'll probably be around here for a couple months."

"Then what? Tooele?"

"Things could be worse. Benson's grist mill is attracting a number of folks. And there will always be the need for someone to look after livestock, I guess." Silva looked while the wagon that had deposited Rost continued down the street. "That's for you?"

"Yep. It's got the mail. I hitched a ride and will be leaving tomorrow for the States. I need to look after some business with the oil, and it should keep me busy for a while. Lots of opportunities for the likes of me. But you don't need to worry. This place is like a gold mine. There's lots to do and plenty of chances to make a living. Speaking of that, what's new with your Hawken?"

Silva shrugged and pointed to the hotel door, suggesting they enter to get away from the cold. "Good enough, I suppose. It's a good thing the Pahvants didn't attack our group because I'd have only been good for one shot. I'm still no good with the pistol. From there on about all I could do would have been to use my rifle as a club. The Indians would have had plenty of time to feather me up. The rifle might be better than a tomahawk, but maybe not. Why?"

The two entered the hotel foyer and headed straight for the potbellied stove to warm up.

"There's new stuff coming out about rifles," Rost continued. He sounded excited. "The French have come up with a new kind of bullet. It's in a cone shape and has a hollowed-out base. Anyway, it's as fast and easy to load as a regular musket, but when it's fired the base of the bullet expands just enough to engage the rifling of the barrel, kind of changing the musket into a rifle. It

114

makes it more accurate and effective over a longer distance. It's like your Hawken but lots faster to load."

"That's news to me." Having warmed up, Shep took Rost by the arm. "Come on with me. Beckwith knows all kinds of stuff about new rifles." They went into a side room that acted as the lieutenant's temporary office. The officer was sitting behind a desk with stacks of maps and drawings. He was trying to make sense of the documents.

"You remember my friend Aaron Rost from your Manti visit?" Shep asked.

"Of course. Very pleasant to see you again, sir" he said, shaking Rost's hand vigorously.

"Aaron's leaving the city tomorrow and going back to the States. He's got a line on some new-fangled type of rifle, and I thought he should run his ideas past you."

"Uh-huh. What's up?"

"The mini-ball," Aaron replied.

Beckwith was immediately alert, and he nodded his head. "That's fine technology," he said. "The government is buying a number of the P1853s as we speak. From Britain."

"Is it as good as they say?"

"Yes, sir. I believe so. Care needs to be followed when loading so you don't foul the barrel. You need to burn the powder completely, but yes, it seems to be as good as everyone is saying. The government wants to buy a bunch more. The War Department's concern is that soldiers will fire through more ammunition than they'll be able to make. About two or three shots per minute."

The news surprised Silva. "And it fires accurately?"

Beckwith nodded confidently. "That's what I hear. Every bit as good as your rifle. Much better than the muskets our men have been dealing with. A company armed with P1853s could do damage. Safely and from a distance. Another thing about this mini-ball. It's not like a regular musket ball that bounces around. They're so slow you can almost watch them take off. These mini-balls are fierce. They're fast and they tear through muscle and bone. The wounds are devastating. Lots of amputations after being hit."

"Too bad there are no wars going on now to try it out," Aaron said. "Where's Napoleon when you need him?"

The trio chuckled.

"Well, for now," Beckwith added knowingly. "The Russians and the Ottomans have been sparing for a while. We might be seeing some real knock-down, drag-outs over there before too long."

"But do they have these P1853s?" Aaron asked.

"Nope. But the British and French do. They're the ones that need to be watched. All these weapons engineers are itching for a war."

Aaron smiled. "What was it Marx said about these two? 'There they are, the French doing nothing, and the British helping them as fast as possible.'" The three laughed again as Rost continued. "What about the regular use of the rifles? Do you see a need for them, say out here in Utah?"

115

Beckwith smiled. "There would be no problem with Indians if Brigham had P1853s for his Nauvoo Legion. But what always happens is that as soon as we come up with something to help out with our efforts, like with a six-shooter or the mini-ball, the Indians or the Mexicans or whoever gets their hands on the things, quick as Crockett, leveling the playing field."

"But you see a market here in the valleys?"

"No doubt."

"And just where are these rifles stored? Are they even for sale?"

"I don't know how many you could get your hands on, but it seems to me the government would be willing to sell a bunch, just to get some of their money back. They're kept in an armory not far from Washington. At Harper's Ferry."

"Excellent, lieutenant!" Aaron said. "You've been a wealth of information. My journey will doubtless be much more productive than I had imagined."

"Glad to be of some use," Beckwith replied, then turned back to his piles of papers.

Rost and Silva left the hotel, crossed the street, and started for where the mail wagon was parked. The driver was nowhere in sight.

"You should go with us, Shep. If you don't have anything that needs to be done immediately. We could always use another pair of sharp eyes."

Shep shook his head and declined. "I have been away from my life for too long. I think I need to get my feet back under me. How long you planning to be gone?"

"Dunno. Couple or three months. I'll take a steamboat from St. Joe's and go to Pittsburgh and then the capital. I think I have enough to place some orders. At least to get started."

"And the oil?"

Rost clapped his hands and smiled. "It's all coming together quicker than I expected. By this time next year, things should be better. The streets of the city will be lighted. It will be a city that is lighted, that will not be put under a bushel but will shine for the rest of the nation to see."

"*Adeus*, Mahonri-Moriancumer."

"*Shalom*, Maher-shalal-hash-baz."

Aaron Rost was pleased to find that Almon Babbitt chose to go with them on their cross-country journey. He was the secretary and treasurer of the Territory of Utah. As a veteran politician from the territory, he had made the trip to and from Washington many times. Even though he did not see eye to eye with Governor Young on many counts, he was brave, well-armed, and enjoyed interacting with Indians along the way. Rost liked his home-spun wisdom and observations. Babbitt was also well placed. He had a finger on the pulse, not only of the territory but on the country overall. With a limited cargo and a lively chance to share ideas, the trip moved along quickly. It was also a blessing that the snow stayed at minimal levels.

Chapter 14

"Silence may be golden, but can you think of a better way to entertain someone than to listen to him?" Brigham Young

"We trust that your holidays have been pleasant," Heber Kimball said to Shep as he was carrying a huge bag of mash into the grist mill.

"Pleasant enough," he replied, dropping the bag and walking to Kimball's wagon. The wagon also carried George Smith and Ezra Benson. They had come from Great Salt Lake City to check on the construction of Benson's mill in Tooele. There was also a strapping boy sitting sullenly in the back of the wagon. Silva knew Kimball and Benson but only knew Smith by sight.

"We're just checking on the building," Kimball continued. "You finding things okay over here?"

"Nice and quiet."

"You still staying with the Hansens?"

"Long as they can tolerate me."

"We've got some business that needs tending, but we'd like to visit with you before heading back. Would that be okay if we dropped by?"

"Suits me." The brief exchange gave Shep plenty to think about. He liked the folks he had met in Utah. Hardworking and sincere. He had been warned that others were underhanded and mean but he had yet to come across them. Kimball was a close associate of Brigham's and always had his hand on the wheel. Shep had yet to join the church officially through baptism but he felt a part of the community, nonetheless. Because he wasn't a member, he didn't think they would be calling him on a mission, although stranger things had happened.

He stayed busy the rest of the day. He had found employment at the growing mill. It gave him the resources necessary to begin his work and he was ready to buy a parcel of land for a cabin and some animals. Tooele was a thriving community on the west side of the Oquirrh Mountains, separating it from the valley and the Great Salt Lake City. The name of the mountains came from the Goshutes, meaning "wooded". The range ran north and south and formed the western boundary of the Great Salt Lake Valley.

Shep Silva caught glimpses of the visitors' wagon several times during the day but forgot all about them by the time he headed back to the Hansens'. Kimball and Company were awaiting his return. He suddenly felt uneasy.

"Not to worry, my boy," Kimball told him with a laugh, throwing an arm around his shoulders. "Let's take a walk."

They strolled back down the lane, the way he had just come.

"What about the others?"

Kimball waved the question off. "Visiting with the Hansens. We'll be just a minute, Brother Silva."

The use of "brother" did not lessen Silva's worry. Kimball chuckled again.

"You noticed the young man in the back of our wagon?"

Shep nodded.

"That's Joseph F. He's my stepson, more or less. He's a great young man but has been dealt a series of blows lately. His mom died of pneumonia last summer, leaving him and Martha Ann orphans. He has been acting the part of a man for years. His dad was murdered 10 years ago, and he has tried filling his spot since then, driving the teams across the plains and working as hard as he can. You know?"

Shep had come across similar stories and nodded.

"But Joseph is struggling, especially these past months. I'm afraid he might even have started to drink and try tobacco. This doesn't sit well with me or Brigham. We'd like to get him out of town for a bit until another plan can be found. We're hoping you might take him under your wing for a bit. Keep an eye on him. Be his friend. Bring him into town to see his sister now and then. Does that sound all right?"

It sounded easier than what had been worrying him. He was relieved. This would be a pleasure.

"Yep."

"Good. Let's head back. I think the Hansens have already given their approval that the two of you can bunk together in your room. And Brother Benson has some work set aside for him at the mill. Or he could help you."

Silva was impressed with the willingness of these men to help the lad.

"How old is he?"

"Just turned fifteen a couple months back."

The next few weeks were busy, but Shep enjoyed having Joseph by his side. The timidity of the young man wore off soon enough. Then Shep found him to be sharp and humorous. And he was strong, always willing to do more than his share. He was obedient. Shep found himself questioning what might have started the brethren worrying. Then again, they were away from the city. And Joseph F was not attending school.

Joseph was pleased to learn that Shep's name was Giuseppe and that it meant Joseph in Italian. He was also excited when Shep announced they would be making a trip into the city and that he could see his sister. Joseph had been willing to talk about work and the gospel and life in general, but it wasn't until they were riding the 40 miles into the Great Salt Lake City that he decided to open up to his new friend and mentor.

"I got kicked out of school," he said.

Shep did not show any emotion. "That kind of stuff happens."

"Our teacher, Mr. Merrick, had been mean to me. But mostly Martha Ann. One day he decided that she didn't answer quick enough or proper enough or something and he told her to come up to the front of the class and he took out his leather strap and was going to whip her."

Shep knew that schoolmasters could be corporal but that he wanted to punish this little girl surprised him. He waited for the rest of the tale.

"Well, what could I do? I'm her big brother. She doesn't have a ma or a pa. I wasn't going to let that happen and told Mr. Merrick so. I ended up having to lick him good and plenty. He made me so angry. To think he wanted to hurt Martha Ann or poke fun at her. No, sir."

Shep nodded, allowing several minutes to pass before speaking. "Serious business, you needing to be Martha's ma and pa."

"Don't get me wrong. Brother Kimball and Brother Young and others have tried their best to step in and make things better. I just can't stand some things. It's like I exploded or something. I felt hot, like a comet or a volcano. I just won't truck with Mr. Merrick threatening my sister. Know what I mean?"

"Can't say whipping Merrick was the best thing. Still, you have a man's responsibilities and matter of fact, you are acting like a man. That all?"

Joseph's face fell a little more. "Nope. I tried some liquor and tobacco."

"How was that?"

"It chased all the good from me. It made me feel rotten."

"You didn't like it?"

"Not even a little. They both tasted awful."

"I haven't seen you using any of that stuff in town. Haven't even heard you mention it."

"Don't care for it. That's all. What about your mom?"

"My mom was named Mercedes. She died when I was young, too."

"You still miss her?"

"Sometimes it's powerful. Sometimes, not so much. But we'll see them again, right?"

Joseph F nodded. "What about your pa?"

"Never knew him. I don't even know his name. You?"

"Yeah, my pa was the best man ever. He was Hyrum and was murdered with his brother Joseph in Carthage, Illinois almost ten years ago."

Life in Tooele moved forward. Shep felt himself growing closer to Joseph. Shep needed a dictionary to find the word he wanted to use to describe Joseph. "He has integrity," he told Heber on one of their visits. It pleased the man greatly.

During the April Conference of 1854, Brigham Young called the fifteen-year-old Joseph F. Smith to serve a mission in the Sandwich Islands. The brethren of the church also asked Shep to accompany Joseph F to San Bernardino and see that he found the employment necessary to pay for his fare to get him to the islands.

Kimball pulled Shep aside and once more threw his arm around his shoulders. "You have done us great favors with Joseph. He loves you now more than any of us. That you would consider going with him is also a strong blessing to us. We will see to it that your holdings in Tooele are taken care of in your absence."

Silva smiled and nodded. "You know that I was in Oahu. That's where I met Elder Sweeney. That's where I spent some good years. I love the Hawaiians. I know they are struggling. I heard that smallpox has killed more than five thousand of the folks around Honolulu since the summer."

"700 of our church members," Kimball said soberly. "European carried diseases have killed 11,000 of the islanders in the recent years."

"You know that I really can't go back to the islands. Not just now. But for you to have this kind of foresight, to send a man of Joseph's caliber, there is sheer inspiration. It will bless him and them."

Kimball nodded enthusiastically. "Can't agree more."

It had been two years since Shep Silva had traveled the Old Spanish Trail from San Bernardino. He had traded a few letters with the Sweeneys and the Wetoyous over the months, but he noticed the time slipping past him without his stepping up and writing more frequently. He anticipated seeing his friends again. He realized more and more how profoundly they had impacted his life. Shep was also surprised by how well-used the road appeared from how it had been. Now it was well worn, wide and, rutted.

The 650-mile trip took the wagon train bound for southern California almost two months. Shep and Joseph F. had their wagon and spent most of the time on the buckboard discussing life and the gospel. Shep trained the young man how to shoot his rifle and his pistol, as well as how to clean and maintain them. Joseph F. noticed how well their oxen responded to Silva and paid stricter attention to the manner he worked with and cared for them. Shep taught him rudimentary Spanish and Portuguese but refrained from any Hawaiian words since much of what he knew was unsuited for a missionary of the Church of Jesus Christ of Latter-day Saints.

The more their train descended in elevation, the more heightened became his anticipation, from the Kaibab Plateau down into Las Vegas. The springs were dug about and prepared for the pioneers and their livestock. From there the road wound into the Mojave Desert and then the Cajon Pass before finally opening into the gentle valley created by the Santa Ana River. And San Bernardino had grown as well. It was not as sleepy and quiet, but the Sweeneys still lived in the same place.

"Shep Silva!" Mark Sweeney exploded that evening as he and Joseph entered the yard, having walked from where they tethered their animals and dropped off their wagon at the fort. He grabbed the younger man into a back-crunching embrace. "We've been expecting you. Just didn't know when." He bellowed loud enough to be heard throughout the block, telling one and all to come as quickly as possible. The Sweeney children, all of varying heights, sexes, and hair color, came running, excited to see their Uncle Shep. The three Wetoyous showed up soon after, more careful in their appearance, smiling shyly. Now it was Shep's turn to grab and hug them.

"I love reunions!" Zeenyo chimed, after finally extricating himself from Silva's firm embrace.

Church administrators in San Bernardino had lined up work for the handful of incoming missionaries. A couple of months would be needed to earn money for passage to the islands, but it looked probable that Joseph F would be able to reach the Sandwich Islands by September.

Linda G was happy to meet someone who also had a middle initial in his name. She and Herman and Joseph F wandered off by themselves to explore as the day began to die.

"The town has grown so much," Shep remarked to Martha and Mark Sweeney.

"There's lots of growth," Mark added. "Most are members of the church who come from the north. Some Anglos are moving in from Los Angeles. So far, we've been quite lucky. Not many problems. Folks all seem to be getting along."

"What about the Cahuilla?"

"That's a sad one. I think Juan Antonio has seen the writing on the wall with all the emigrants. His tribe is running out of land. They have no space. They certainly don't have the numbers to start a fight. They seem to have moved farther and farther back into the mountains. We don't come into contact much."

"Still no need for jails?"

"Not right now," Martha said.

"It's not Zion yet," her husband added. "We've been lucky not to have much liquor around. The stuff folks bring from Los Angeles is usually all drunk by the time they get here. That cuts down on a lot of the troubles. Brother Rich runs a tight ship. He doesn't allow for funny business. Folks know it and I think they support him."

"There is that Carsley fellow."

Mark nodded. "Martha knows a young man from Los Angeles. Nice enough fellow. Came from the New England, working on fishing boats. He wants to be an actor, to work on stage. In the meantime, he's a metal worker. He has suggested to Brother Rich that he be allowed to build a work or a jail around here. It's something the town fathers are mulling over."

"Just hope you never have the need for a jail," Shep said. "I know it's something that bothers the brethren in the Great Salt Lake City. Whenever emigrant trains come to the city there seems to be trouble. Fights and disorderly conduct. Sometimes it's the soldiers who act up. It doesn't make for good relations."

"Brigham's built jails?"

"We could use more. Then again, Porter Rockwell is the Territory Marshal. He doesn't put up with much horseplay. He's a real scrapper and has busted several heads or simply chased the bad eggs out of town."

"He still as fast with his guns as his fists?"

"'Fraid so. That's what I hear. He doesn't use a holster. He prefers to carry his pistols in his coat pocket. Anyway, he does a lot of riding through the territory, tamping down rough elements. You see him down this way?"

Mark shook his head. "I think he spends most of his time in Carson Valley or the high plains around Fort Bridger if he's not in Great Salt Lake City. Rich and Lyman and their lawmen are capable enough. Not Texas Rangers but not vigilantes, either."

Small talk took up the next fifteen minutes when Joseph F and his new friends returned. He motioned for Shep to follow him outside. "I could use your help," he said after he and Silva had gotten away from the house.

"You're not looking to get out of work already, are you?"

The banter made Smith chuckle. "I should be so lucky."

"What's up?"

"Didn't you tell me once that when you left San Francisco to San Pedro you met a family from Missouri? The Picketts?"

"Good memory. I'm impressed. What of it?"

"I think they're here, Shep. And I think I know them."

"Don't remember you ever saying anything like that before."

"It wasn't a big deal then. Maybe it is now."

"What's up?"

"Maybe nothing. But I'd like to meet them and see if they aren't the same folks. I think it's important. Would you mind going with me over to their house?"

"Sure. Okay. When?"

"Tonight okay with you?"

Shep felt there was something more to the story that he wasn't being told. "Light's wasting. You know where they live?"

"Pretty sure." Joseph F led the Brazilian directly to the nondescript yard a few blocks away. "I'll let you do the introductions."

Agnes Pickett answered the door and instantly recognized Shep before he could utter half a dozen words. "Oh, Mr. Silva. Please come in. It is so nice to see you again." Her happiness and sincerity were welcome. "And this young man…" She stopped suddenly and stared. A shadow crossed her countenance as her smile faded. She couldn't hide the fact that she recognized the young man standing behind Silva. She sighed and nodded. "Joseph."

The young man shuffled awkwardly and looked down at the soiled hat in his hands. "Sister Agnes."

Instant silence enveloped the small cabin. Shep's mind raced as he tried to place the pieces into the proper frame. "Ummm…Joseph asked me to accompany him here. You have a history, things I know nothing about."

Agnes collected her wits quick enough. "Yes. Quite right, Mr. Silva. I apologize. Our families knew each other years ago in Missouri and Illinois. Those were dark days. A lot has changed, and I can see that you have grown up plenty, Joseph."

"Thank you, ma'am."

The statements piqued Shep's curiosity. More would be forthcoming, but he figured the flood gates were now open. It wouldn't be long before the balance of the story was uncovered. If that's what he wanted.

Shep stepped quickly to the rescue. "Joseph F's been called to serve a mission in the Sandwich Islands."

Agnes was appropriately impressed. "But you are still quite young."

Joseph F blushed. "I was getting in too much trouble, I reckon," he confessed.

"Missionary work as punishment? Lordy sakes."

Again, Shep rescued his friend. "Maybe that's so but he also knows a lot about the scriptures and he's a hard worker. His mom passed away a couple of years ago." He shot a glance at Joseph F who shrugged his shoulders, permitting him to continue. "She got pneumonia. Heber Kimball's family is keeping an eye on Martha Ann, so Brigham felt it was a good time for Joseph F to serve a mission." Shep felt a distinct chill in the room when he mentioned Brigham's name. More information was needed.

Agnes reacted smoothly, scarcely missing a beat. "Please sit down. Charlotte and Ina are gathering eggs in the hen house with the twins." She realized that this information might be lacking for Joseph F. "My husband Bill and I had twin boys about seven years ago. Bill is a printer but lately has been doing a lot of legal work in Los Angeles. He should be home here in a few days. He will be glad to see you boys," she said, trying to gather all the feelings of her heart. "Bill and I were hoping to run into you, Mr. Silva, when we came to San Bernardino. Folks remember you quite well, but they told us you had gone up to Great Salt Lake City for more work."

"I suppose that's why. I haven't really settled on much lately."

A slight scraping sound came from the cabin's back door as Agnes' children entered, carrying a bucket of eggs. They were surprised to see the visitors. Donny and Billy recognized Shep but the older boy's presence kept them and their antics in check. Charlotte and Ina instantly recognized Joseph F and smiled happily.

"Maybe after you girls clean the eggs you could take Brother Joseph here for a walk and let him know what has been going on in your lives. Or ask him what he's been up to."

The plan sounded perfect. Joseph jumped to help with the chores and then the three giggling teenagers left the house, hand in hand, chattering like long-lost friends. Shep wished he could have gone along but felt it better to stay and visit with Agnes Pickett.

"You have work lined up for Joseph so he can get to the islands?" Agnes led.

Shep nodded. "Some manual farm work just north of Santa Barbara. We should probably be leaving tomorrow or the next day to get him settled."

"Then you'll be headed back to Great Salt Lake City?"

"Brother Lyman asked me to take some horses up to Carson Valley. I've never been there but don't think I have the time. Mostly I want to visit with the Wetoyous."

Agnes knew the youths. "They are the ones you rescued?"

It made him feel important. Maybe that's exactly what he did. "I guess. I'd like to see Bill again."

The thought was kind and made Agnes smile. She was happy that Shep seemed unaware of their previous history. California seemed so far away from the States, like a hideaway. "I'm sure he'd be pleased to see you as well. Maybe before you leave."

An hour later, Joseph F. and the two Coolbrith girls returned. They were still holding hands and smiling and appeared quite refreshed and happy.

"I'm ready to go," the jubilant Joseph F announced to Shep. He held a folded piece of paper like a treasure that he quickly stuffed into his trouser pocket.

"Home to get some sleep or to get back to your mission?"

"Both!" There was a definite lift to his attitude and personality, which was not lost on either Agnes or Shep.

> *As grows the rose*
> *The thistle grows-*
> *Each to its purpose*
> *God He knows:*
> *But who may deem*
> *The lordlier scheme-*
> *The weed unsung,*
> *Or the poet's theme?*
> by Ina Coolbrith

Chapter 15

"I cannot remember a night so dark as to have hindered the coming day." John Brown

The previous six months were a whirlwind of travel and activity for Aaron Rost. He rode more miles on a buckboard than he thought possible. The endless horizons didn't seem to bother Almon Babbitt. Then again, the politician made the trip at least once every year. Babbitt's endless yarns helped the time pass. Still, Rost could not imagine the size of this new country. It was vast, yet young and raw. The eagerness he felt as they left the Rocky Mountains and headed across the plains dissipated, despite the endless herds of buffalo or the huge rivers they needed to ferry. Fortunately, they avoided contact with large groups of Indians until they reached Iowa. The roads improved the farther east they traveled. Broad expanses of forests were still omnipresent, contrary to the growing efforts of saws and plows wielded by the encroaching settlers.

After crossing the Mississippi, they reached the Ohio River and were soon in Pittsburgh and then Washington DC. Any hopes Rost had of finishing up his business activities evaporated as Babbitt dragged him around the burgeoning town, introducing him to his peers. The dream of democracy and a federal republic of this size boggled the Prussian's mind. Aaron was kept busy jotting down all the names, numbers, and addresses he could. These people were excited to hear about the new kinds of oils and how they could be used. Aaron liked the feeling of closeness to Europe he had while on the East Coast. He scribbled a series of messages and sent them to his associates in Danzig. The Americans were capitalists and there was money to be made in this young country.

"This is a teeming city," Babbitt admitted. "But just you wait and see. New York City will astound you. I'll see that you get there shortly and by the time you return, I should be ready to return to Utah. I trust you will be ready as well."

"I'm almost ready now."

Babbitt smirked. Could it be possible the Prussian was tired of the travel? "I will pay for your coach trip to New York, but I must ask you to stop by some friends of ours in Philadelphia first. Would that be possible?"

"You seem to have nice friends."

"And these are the best," Babbitt exclaimed. "Tom Kane is a real mover and shaker, plus he has done a lot for the Utah Territory. He doesn't care much for polygamy, but he has a good relationship with Brigham and Heber and scores of others in the territory."

The trip to Philadelphia was short in comparison to distances he had already covered. The road wound through broad-leafed forests. Rost knew some of the city's history and was surprised when he saw it. There were other reasons that the nation's capital had been given over to Washington DC that were not quite as apparent to him.

The Kanes welcomed Rost into their home readily and insisted that he stay for days.

"My father will pump you with every question possible," Tom guaranteed, "whether it be about Europe, your oils, or the Utah Territory."

Aaron was enchanted by Kane's young wife, Bessie. He learned they had been married for a year. Bessie lost their first child. The tragedy sent her into a depressive spin, thinking that perhaps God was punishing her or wanting to teach her more about the road her mother had trod. Happily, Bessie was young and strong and possessed a powerful constitution. Tom frequently took her with him on his trips. He also encouraged her writing. She was pleased to announce that she had just been accepted into the Female Medical College of Pennsylvania as one of its first female students.

One of the issues that was very pronounced around the Kane household was their aversion to slavery. They all wore their passions proudly. Certainly, a case could be made for the agricultural needs of the South but they felt the wealth of the land should be equally distributed among the inhabitants and not segregated into slaves and masters. These were issues that he had seen and heard debated strenuously in the governmental halls of power. Dark clouds were lowering on the horizon, and yet what could ever become of such a vibrant society as the United States? The country was blessed by Providence with wealth, strength, diversity, and opportunity. All seemed to be able to find a niche in this land: Europeans, mercantilists, soldiers, inventors, religionists, explorers, even Mexicans, and Indians were able to strike a balance, or so he thought.

But being a Mormon?

"Do you know Dr. Bernhisel?" Tom asked him nonchalantly.

"I think I met him once in the Great Salt Lake City. He works closely with Almon Babbitt and the Governor."

"I understand he just sent a letter to Brigham about Major Steptoe. Jeff Davis has just sent him and about 175 soldiers out that way. He wants them to end up in California and boost the numbers of military horses there. But first, he wants them to investigate the murders of Gunnison and his party. Then I guess they'll look for a better, easier route between Salt Lake and California."

"175 soldiers? Infantry? Horses?"

"800 horses and maybe some dragoons to augment the herds in California. Of course, there will be about the same number of camp followers."

"Compliments of the Secretary of War. Sounds sinister."

"That's what I'm thinking. How do you think Brigham and the church leaders will handle the news?"

"It would have been better if President Pierce had been the one writing the letter. This sounds more like there's something underhanded going on. It's not like Governor Young is hiding things but sending armed troops to the territory is a sure-fire way to scare folks. They were upset when Stansbury and his surveyors first got there. Communication can be bad, especially when talking about Utah but getting the news from your guys in the capital first doesn't quite cut it."

"It sounds like a big deal."

"Pierce is also sending a federal judge, Judge Kinney, to preside over the territory's supreme court."

"Just keeps getting worse. Do you think President Pierce is planning on swapping out the governor?"

"Certainly sounds like he's keeping his options open."

Rost enjoyed his visit with the Kanes. They were a source of intense knowledge. One thing they told him before he set off for New York City was the news that both France and Great Britain had declared war on Russia, March 28th, opting to join the Ottomans in their war against their traditional enemy, Russia. All agreed this would be an interesting conflict. Many military officials were anxious to see how their modern armies and tactics performed. Photographers were also on the front, ready to record events. Probably the greatest insertion into warfare was the telegraph technology. Poles and wires crisscrossed the continent. Leaders in London and Paris and Moscow would be made aware of the battles' outcomes almost instantly. The soldiers were also shadowed by numerous journalists representing a score of newspapers. These newsmen were also anxious to report their observations. If mistakes were made, regardless of the nation, these people were bound to tell their tales. No one felt safe. Not the combatants, not the military leaders, not the politicians, not the doctors, not the inventors of war machines or communications, and certainly not the people around whom the battles would whirl. But like all other conflicts of the past, there would be vast numbers of casualties found in dead and dying soldiers, horses, and livestock. Scorched earth was a practice engaged in by both sides. Huge acres of crops were burned, limiting abilities to provide life-saving foods for the dumb masses who were too slow or too poor to avoid the disastrous wakes of war.

The topic weighed heavily on Aaron as he entered the coach that would carry him to New York. He was pleased to find that only one other gentleman would be accompanying him. The man looked like a farmer about twenty years older than him. And the man was pleased to strike up a conversation with Rost. The conversation would help the time and miles pass more easily.

"Yesirree, I've heard," the man who introduced himself as Mr. Brown from Pennsylvania, replied to Rost's comment about the looming European war. "Nations seem quite capable of stumbling into wars. Lots of unnecessary deaths."

"Maybe we could learn something from their tactics or their weapons."

"What? For our war?" Brown chuckled and cleared his throat. "We have enough trouble on our shores. We don't need to go looking to the Continent for more insight into human suffering."

Rost pondered his words for several minutes, the quiet suddenly becoming uncomfortable. "Forgive me, sir. I am not a citizen of this fair country. I was born and raised in Prussia. America certainly has its growing pains but I do not know exactly what trouble you might be referring to."

"Where should I start? We treat the Indians like hell and have chased them all off their natural lands to settle in God-forsaken Kansas. And our officials have broken every treaty we've ever entered into with them. Our diseases, European diseases, have attacked them and killed off huge numbers. Now we're moving farther West. We're continuing to displace the tribes out there. And where should they be sent? Farther west? Into the Pacific?"

"There's no doubt America could do a better job."

"And that's not all," he continued as the coach did the same. "This is supposed to be a land of religious freedom? Well, how do we treat the Catholics or the Shakers, or the Mormons? Anyone a bit different. How plain and simple is my name? John Brown. Look at Joe Smith. Very plain and simple. And he was murdered."

"Joseph."

"What?"

"He preferred being called Joseph."

"You telling me you're a Mormon? I had you pegged as a Jew."

Aaron smiled. It was obvious this man had a pile of grievances and was happy to vent. It might be better to allow the man a chance to talk.

Brown collected his thoughts and started again. "That's not even all of it. What about slavery? It's the worst of all. One man thinking he can own another. That's like thinking we can own the ocean or the air. It's God's creation. We don't own anything like that. And man is his creation. Created in his image. We don't own miniature gods. We don't make them do our work and control what they do. It's not right. It's the height of evil to enslave people. It's not that they have done something terribly wrong. They haven't broken laws. The only thing they have done is to be born. They are colored by God's own hand and some folks think that gives them the right to put them into chains, to breed them like horses, and sell them like parcels of land. This is crazy and God will not allow this to continue. We will be judged. This whole nation is on the brink of God's judgment and the price will be much higher to pay than we even consider."

Aaron Rost had come into contact with abolitionists before. And many were quite animated about the subject. But this man, this John Brown, he seemed to be consumed by the issue.

"You know many slaves?"

"Nope. Mostly I just see them out a working. Their masters sure don't care for me to talk with them much. But they're good folks. Hard-working. They just want to live their lives the way God meant for them." He paused for a

128

moment. "I've come across Fred Douglass," he said. "He's born a black slave in Maryland but got away. He's an abolitionist if there ever was one. He's a big talker and very smart and has traveled all over, including Britain and the Continent. When he was in Britain the folks there raised the money for his emancipation. He thinks photographs are important in telling the story of slavery. That's why you never see any photographs of him smiling. He never smiles in front of a photograph machine. He doesn't want anyone thinking he's a happy-go-lucky slave. Slavery's as serious as death."

"And you, Mr. Brown?"

"Me? I talk a lot but I'm more of a doer. I want to walk the walk not talk the talk. It's time for freedom. For liberty. If ever there was a time and a place, it's here and now. Slaves, women, and their rights to suffrage, Indians. There are so many under the oppressive rule of ignorance and tradition."

"Isn't America the land of the free?"

Brown laughed. "You just hit the nail, my friend. That is what we have always been crowing about. It's also what Douglass meant when he said the Fourth of July means something different to a slave than to a white man. Freer for some than for others, I suppose. But it won't be for long."

The seriousness in Brown's voice told Rost that he meant exactly that.

"So you have business in the city?"

"Nothing big. Just farming stuff. I might find a chance to spout my feelings."

"No doubt you'll find something."

Brown smiled again. "And what about you, Jew boy? Are you selling more than oil?"

"Mostly oil for street lamps." He stopped and measured Brown for several moments. "Maybe guns. I have some friends back west who are interested in some of the more recent developments."

Now he was talking Brown's language. "You looking for mini-balls?"

"P1853s. I heard some about a breechloading carbine made by Sharp. You know anything about that?"

"Enough," John Brown said, nodding solemnly. "They're supposed to be just coming online. Folks in the know are pretty excited. As good as the musket-rifle P1853s are, the Sharps are faster, cleaner, and more accurate for longer distance. And it's breech-loading." Now it was Brown's turn to seriously measure Rost. He scratched the rough stubble on his face. "You want to take some west?"

"Don't know if I have enough money."

"I know the government is worried this kind of rifle would eat through a soldier's ammunition quick. A trained shooter could probably fire six to eight shots in a minute."

Rost whistled. Impressive. "Does it foul a lot?"

"Depends on the powder and how carefully the shooter is taking care of it and his carbine. Loading from the breach is so much quicker. And it uses a mini ball. 475 grains. .52 caliber. It's accurate up to 500 yards."

"Big bugger."

"And it tears hell out of anything it hits."

"Does it cost a lot?"

"Depends. Even one of these could really make a difference when facing Indians or militia who only have muskets. I have family in Kansas. The Territory is trying to become a state but Washington says it'll be a matter of sovereign rule. They have plenty of abolitionists but there are also plenty of pro-slavery folks just across the border in Missouri. And these guys are always wanting to stir the pot."

"There's a lot on the line?"

"You said it." Brown turned to a worn saddle bag that was lying on the floor. In a couple of seconds, he withdrew a book and handed it to Rost. "I've read this sometimes. You'll like it, especially since you're not a full-fledged American. It does a good job explaining some of the issues we've been talking over."

Aaron looked at the book. It was a novel written by Harriett Beecher Stowe and named *Uncle Tom's Cabin; or Life Among the Lowly*. He opened the book. It was printed in 1852. "I've heard a little about this. It's been quite popular in the States. That's what I understand."

"And the Beechers are probably the most active abolitionist family in the North. They spend their time speaking and raising money to help with problems just like those we're facing in Kansas."

"I thought you live in Pennsylvania."

"A bunch of my kids are in Kansas. I go out there now and then. But I'm watched and have a reputation that gets in the way. I can't get a hold of some stuff as easy as you."

"So you're thinking maybe I should be a gun runner?"

Brown shrugged. "You're not being watched right now. I guarantee you could make a bigger difference in folks' lives than selling street lamp oil. America is at a crossroads. There's plenty of resolve but not so much when it comes to time and money. You know where you're staying in New York?" He waved his hands. "No matter. I'll find you. I can get you a couple names of folks in the armory. It's in Maryland. I think I can get you some money for some carbines. You can accompany the shipment to my son Fred in Osawatomie. It wouldn't be much out of your way, if you're going through Kansas City. Then you could even take a couple of the rifles for yourself. To where? Oregon or California? Or perhaps the Utah Territory?"

"It sounds like a good plan. This time."

John Brown smiled and chuckled. "About all we need. This time."

For God remembers still His promise made of old
That He on Zion's hill truth's standard would unfold!
Her light should there attract the gaze
Of all the world in latter days.

Chapter 16

"Rather, ten times, die in the surf, heralding the way to a new world than stand idly on the shore." Florence Nightingale

"Please come in."

Harriett Matthews stepped into the superintendent's office and smiled. Florence Nightingale had treated her extremely well over the past year. She saw to it that her studies were integrated into her work, applying the principles she was learning. Her text, although not long, was dog-eared and well-used. Nightingale appreciated her honesty and willingness to work hard and then to stand as a witness to the articles she preached. And why not? They worked very well. Misery was relieved as was suffering. Healing took place and the nurses were proud of the rise they were receiving from the professional journals in London. They were even being singled out by the royals.

"Yes, mum?"

"The work on your floor is going well?"

"Yes, mum."

"Exceptional. The new hires are attending to their studies?"

"Quite well, mum."

Florence stood up from her desk and walked to the window behind her. The clear glass beckoned the summer sunlight into her office. It was a beautiful day with no smoke hanging above the rooftops. A recent rain seemed to have awakened the flowers in the window pots as well as greened-up leaves and grass. Gazing at the peaceful scene could successfully hide the worries of the woman's heart.

"Are you following the news?"

"When I can find the time. Is there a concern, mum?"

Leave it to Harriett to see into her heart. "The war with Russia."

"The newspapers are doing well in their reporting. I think the British people are pleased with the coverage. Maybe not as pleased with the Ottomans' ability to fight. I'm hoping the peace talks will wrap up the matter before too long."

"You and I both, my dear." Florence fidgeted with the drapes for a moment. "You are aware that I know Baron Herbert of Lea?"

"Yes, mum. Of course."

"Our friendship is nothing untoward but he is a man of prominence and maintains high regard in the government."

"The Secretary of State for War, if I'm not mistaken."

"Very good, my dear. I'm sure that I have chosen wisely."

"Mum?"

"Mr. Benjamin Disraeli. You also know of him?"

"Indeed."

Nightingale smiled. She could see her plan coming to fruition. "He frequently butted heads with Sir Robert Peel. The two could not seem to agree on anything. Well, Sidney, Baron Herbert of Lea was always working and siding with Sir Robert. This did not endear him to Mr. Disraeli, who frequently referred to him as Mr. Peel's valet."

The description made Harriett smile. There had always been something that intrigued her about British politics.

"So, Sidney, Mr. Herbert, returned the epithet by referring to Mr. Disraeli as Benjamin the Jew."

The information made Harriett laugh quietly. "I have always assumed he was Jewish."

"Sephardic Jew. Both sides of his family came from Italy and were steeped in their religion. Once here, however, his father stepped away from the synagogue. Benjamin followed suit and later converted to the Anglican religion. For political reasons, I'm confident, causing constant headaches between him and the Scottish Presbyterians."

"You're certain he's not a *Marrano*?"

The question caught Florence by surprise. She knew that Harriett was religious and precocious but she wasn't aware that she was as familiar as she seemed to be with the intricacies of Judaism in southern Europe. "Fairly certain," she replied. "With the war coming upon us, I was wondering if you might accept another assignment. This would need to be kept quiet. We don't need any publicity. The Baron Herbert has consented to give us, as nurses, a greater forum."

"He's consented to you," Harriett corrected.

"Yes. Well, this is quite the opportunity for nurses as well as women. We have never had such power, access to the ears of power. Even the Queen is aware of our comings and goings. But what we need from you, my dear, is someone who would be willing to insert herself into the activities of Mr. Disraeli, as an ally, as a set of ears for him. I see you acting as a go-between for him and our nurses here at the hospital and British women in general. It could be as innocent as simply introducing yourself, letting him know of your background and interests. From there, a timely missive now and then would keep the forefront of our interests in his mind. Right now political infighting has abated because of the war. This could prove very helpful to us. What are your thoughts?"

It was a heavy request and Harriett wisely chose to take some time in her considerations. "I am pleased with your confidence, mum. You make a series of very important points. I hope that I might be up to the task. May I think it over?"

"Certainly, my dear. But time is also of the essence."

"One more thing, mum."

"Yes?"

"Suffrage and the rights of women. Are we trying to insinuate ourselves into the male world? It doesn't sound like a worthy goal. Heaven knows the men haven't been able to handle things well over the millennia."

Florence Nightingale smiled knowingly. "Of course, you are right. We don't need to mimic the faults of the past or those of men. My hope is that women are treated with respect and honor, and not just the Queen. If we have the right to vote, the men of necessity will listen to us, at least pay us some attention. The things that are important to us as a sex, will then move into a higher priority. You are certainly right, my dear. We do not want to merely trade places with the infidels. But with females holding a higher priority, our wants and needs will receive greater attention." She sighed. "But Miss Matthews, this will be a long time coming. What little we can do at present will germinate and blossom, perhaps years down the path. In the end, we will be better off. We will also do the world justice by setting a proper example. Does that make sense?"

"Taking direction and lessons from you has only raised me, mum."

"Well, first things first, Harriett. My biggest goal is to get the British government to allow women nurses to assist the soldiers. It would do all involved a world of good. We could help immensely with the wounded and alleviate suffering. The surgeons could use our assistance. We could ensure our soldiers were afforded decent care and lodging. On the other hand, our skills would elevate us in the eyes of the government as well as the people. I know we can do this, Miss Harriett. It's our time to step forward. Do you agree?"

The next day Harriett delivered her written acceptance of the job to Florence Nightingale.

Chapter 17

"All happy families resemble one another, each unhappy family is unhappy in its own way." Leo Tolstoy

"Welcome home, Brother Silva. How are things in San Bernardino?" Brother Kimball was a pleasant man and kind of a step-father to Joseph F, as well as a church and community leader. Shep knew that his concern for Joseph F was sincere. "How were your travels?"

"All good, Brother Heber. The trip down and back wasn't as long as I had anticipated. But going, I was entertained by Joseph F. Coming back I had some time to target practice. Can't be too prepared, I reckon." He looked around the office of Brigham's first counselor. "I heard you wanted to see me as soon as I got back."

"And I appreciate your punctuality. Joseph F. got off all right?"

"He had some good employment with a handful of other missionaries. I suspect he has finished up his labors on the farm and should be getting to the islands any day. He will do his family and the church proud."

"Your willingness to go with him is immeasurable. We can never thank you enough."

"It was my pleasure. Anyway, I also have friends in the colony and it was good to renew our acquaintances."

"Oh?"

"Brother Mark Sweeney and his wife Martha and children."

"Yes indeed." Heber got a gleam in his eye. "Brother Mark's not ready to serve another mission just yet, is he?"

Shep laughed at the thought. "You've got him by the short hairs, Brother Kimball. You know the Sweeneys will do anything you ask of them."

Kimball knew his answer was correct. "Well, all in good time, I suppose. Did you have a chance to meet with Elder Lyman or Rich down there?"

"I did, as a matter of fact."

"Did they have anything of value they wanted you to pass our way?"

"You get their letters very often?"

"They are good men. They do their best to keep us posted."

"They told me a number of the Saints are leaving the territory up here and going to California to get away from Brigham. They think some of his tactics are a bit heavy-handed. The changes keep them on their toes. I have noticed that besides the growing numbers, San Bernardino is not the sleepy-eyed town I encountered a couple of years back."

"Nope. I hear change is good—but not always. I'd wager some of those fleeing might also be wanting to dodge me too."

Shep shrugged. "Maybe. I'm sure I'd see things differently if I joined the Church, too."

"I don't see you running away, Brother Shep." Elder Kimball cleared his throat. "Brigham calls California the strainer. It sifts folks. Hopefully, we won't lose them."

"It's a beautiful land and still quite cheap. But I think some are getting more concerned about feathering their nests rather than the community at large."

"We ask a lot of our people."

"Speaking of people, the Picketts? You know much about Bill and Agnes Pickett?"

Heber Kimball let out a long whistle and nodded. "Maybe too much for their liking. Have they left Los Angeles for San Bernardino?"

"'Fraid so."

"Good folks. I think they left from St. Louis. They both spent some time around the Mississippi. Friendly. We wish them no ill. Is Bill finding things to his liking there?"

"I think so. Practicing law and getting rich."

"The kids?"

"All fine. The twins are growing like weeds. Ina has a real talent with her poetry writing. I think Joseph F has taken a shine to her."

"Easy to do with such beautiful girls. They're talented as all get out if I recall. But it has been years since I saw them when they came through on their way to California." Heber Kimball had been a member of the Church for years. He had been through a series of scrapes and was tried and true in his testimony. He had been holding back, something more than the welfare of the Saints in San Bernardino. He didn't give Shep much time to wonder about it. "We have a situation on the horizon. Might be nothing or it might be. The Prophet has asked for your help."

"Okay."

"Dr. Bernhisel sent us a letter while you were away to let us know that President Pierce is sending some soldiers to the territory. He didn't want to alarm us but thought we should know. The column is supposed to be finding a better route from Salt Lake City to California, as well as taking some horses over there. But I think the real reason they're coming is to investigate the murder of Captain Gunnison and his men last year."

Shep sobered quickly. "I remember it well."

"Some of our very own discontents have suggested the Prophet ordered the execution. The thought makes me sick. President Pierce wants to make sure the massacre was only done by the Indians with no involvement by us and to see that the perpetrators are caught and justice is carried out."

"How can I help?"

"My intelligence tells me the column is about a week's distance out. They're being led by a Major Edward Steptoe. Bernhisel and Tom Kane both think he is a fair man, well-chosen. Steptoe is also bringing a federal judge along with him to make sure we're abiding by the law. Judge John Kinney. Anyway, we think it might be a good thing if you could ride out and meet them. It would show good faith on our part, especially since you were with the surveying expedition and have a better vision of the happenings."

"I'll leave first thing in the morning."

"Again, Brother Silva, we are in your debt."

Three days later a sentry spied Shep riding hard for their encampment and ran to the tent of his commander, Major Steptoe. He saluted and apologized for interrupting his evening meal. "A rider is coming," he announced. "Not an Indian."

"Have him come see me as soon as he arrives."

"Sir!" The sentry saluted and ran back the way he had come.

A few minutes later Shep Silva dismounted and was escorted to the tent of Major Steptoe. The officer was congenial and shook his hand warmly. Still, there was an air of authority about the man. Shep assumed he had graduated from the military academy at West Point as well.

Silva quickly explained his reason for coming.

"Excellent," Steptoe nodded approvingly. "With help like this, we will no doubt have our business wrapped up before long. You know these Indians we're after?"

Shep nodded. "The Pahvants."

"You think they're the ones responsible for Captain Gunnison's murder."

"I do."

"You sound certain."

"I was with the survey party. But when the massacre took place, I was with Lt. Beckwith and his men. I think that's a reason Brigham sent me to meet you. To give you a chance to meet me and ask questions before reaching the Great Salt Lake City."

"Very appropriate. I thank you for your assistance, sir." Steptoe summoned one of his soldiers. "Tell our guest that his friend has arrived and bring him here."

"Sir."

Five minutes later Shep's curiosity was answered as he saw the slender form of Aaron Rost enter the tent. The men shook hands and hugged. Steptoe smiled, knowing he had done a good job with the surprise reunion of the friends.

"Mr. Rost, why don't you show our visitor to his quarters. We will talk more tomorrow."

A heavy white canvas tent had been erected, complete with cots, blankets, and a table for the two men. Shep was tired after his ride but seeing his old friend gave him a new surge of strength.

"Mahonri! Here I thought you would be gone for only a couple months."

Aaron smiled. "My plans changed and in a big way. I have come across some of the most interesting folks. I got some substantial work done regarding kerosene in Washington and New York. I was able to place good orders. The business will only grow. Some capitalists want to build refineries in the States and bring the technology here from Europe. But that's not all, my friend. I spent some productive time with Dr. Bernhisel and Babbitt in the capital, as well as the Kane family in Philadelphia. But probably the most interesting of the people I came across were the abolitionists, starting with John Brown."

Silva smiled. "A rather common name."

"He said the same thing about Joseph Smith. Anyway, he got me in touch with the Beecher family in Massachusetts and they coughed up a stack of money to buy weapons for the cause. Abolitionism. You are now looking at a bona fide arms merchant."

Shep shook his head in amazement. "You always are on the lookout for this kind of work. People flock to you just to give you more chances to make money."

"What can I say? God loves me."

"So you used this Beecher money to buy arms and then what?"

"It was too exciting. There was a lot of intrigues, me running to and fro, trying to keep away from the federal police and shipping agents. They are on guard trying to keep weapons out of the hands of reactionary folks like the abolitionists. I must say that it was exciting. It got my heart pumping."

"So what did you buy and just where is this stockpile of arms?"

"That's the best part. I went to the armory in Harper's Ferry, Maryland, and paid for some P1853s but spent most of the money on Sharp's carbines. I even got you one. I had the rifles crated up and shipped to Osawatomie, Kansas, to Brown's son, Frederick. The rifles will be used to defend the settlers in the territory against the attacks of the pro-slavery forces who are constantly encroaching on their land from Missouri."

"How many did you end up with?"

"A couple score."

"And how about getting the crates through the customs officials? I trust you shipped it along the waterways?"

"That was the best part. We just had the crates stenciled with the words 'Beecher's Bibles'." Rost guffawed at his wit. "The stuff sailed straight through without a single glitch."

"You've managed to impress me. What about the guys in Bloody Kansas?"

"Very pleased. They always seem to be outnumbered, isolated on their farms when the pro-slavery mobs cross over from Missouri. But these rifles are a Godsend, especially these Sharps. They are amazing. I'm impressed that I already know as much about them as I do. Look here." Rost pulled a duffle bag from beneath his cot and withdrew a single Sharp's Carbine. "This is the only one I could get away with. I know I said I was going to get you a P1853, but Shep when you see what this can do, you'll be amazed." He handed the carbine to his friend. "It's every bit as good, no, I take that back. It's much better than any muzzle-loading rifle."

Shep's eyes and fingers went immediately to the breech-loading portion. The machinery was well crafted. It represented a huge jump in engineering. "And it still shoots as far?" he asked.

Rost nodded enthusiastically. "And it's accurate and it fires a mini-ball like the P1853s."

This was a surprise indeed. Silva had barely heard whispers of such advancements with rifles. The breech-loading capability made it quicker to load and fire. "Amazing," he said. "And you're sure you want me to have this, Maher-shalal-hash-baz?"

"Yep. Course if you want any more, you'll be paying through the nose."

The next couple of days were spent riding to the Great Salt Lake Valley. Silva was looked upon with curiosity. Even though he wasn't a member of Young's church, he had come from the settlement. Rost was a member of the church but he had joined them in Nebraska and had been with their column for several weeks. The real novelty came when Silva unsheathed his new carbine. This was a weapon to be appreciated. And the soldiers appreciated weapons. News of the carbine spread through the ranks and before long everyone from Steptoe to the lowliest private was keeping close to Silva, hoping to be invited to shoot it whenever they stopped to set up camp. The Major was treated with respect and access to the carbine. He was awed by the possibilities and the heavy bullets that tore huge limbs from trees at great distances.

"So you think you'll be in the territory for a short time?" Shep asked Steptoe one morning as they were descending Echo Canyon.

"That's my plan."

"Have you looked over your livestock?"

"That's why we've got bullwhackers," the major replied. "You see any problems?"

"Your horses aren't going to make it," Shep said, knowingly. He spoke with the confidence of someone who knew the animals as well as the land. "Not any time soon. It's a long way to California and the forage across the desert is none too good."

"You're thinking we should winter in Utah?"

Shep shrugged. "Suit yourself. Plus I don't know what Brigham would think of having a passel of horny soldiers and camp followers hanging around his people for a stretch. I just think your horses look beat. Where'd they come from anyway?"

"Leavenworth. I was told they were fine and ready for the trip. And yeah, I thought different. They were looking pretty poor from the outset. My bullwhackers haven't said much about it but then again, I don't think they realize how far California is, either."

"They'll be loads better if we can pasture them over the winter. They'll regain their strength and be a lot healthier for it. And folks won't think you're just showing up in California with some skin and bones nags."

138

"I'll ask Governor Young for his advice."

"Another good plan, *amigo*."

The column Major Edward Jenner Steptoe was commanding arrived in Great Salt Lake City on Thursday, August 31, 1854, amid cheers from the enthusiastic and stares from the gawking curious. Steptoe arrived as the military commander and potential governor of the territory. He didn't want to raise suspicion and carefully acquiesced to Brigham Young. On the other hand, Young was happy to finally be able to bring the Wakara War to a close and was looking for a moment of respite.

The US soldiers and their camp followers were equally impressed with the size of the city. More particularly with the idea of relaxation and especially the attractive gazes of the women. Polygamous women had to be easy pickings for the virile young soldiers from the States.

President Young was anxious to be helpful. He had time to process the news from Dr. Bernhisel and knew his best course of action was to support Steptoe on his mission and see to it that the soldiers were able to continue to California. Brigham did his best to hide his surprise when Major Steptoe asked for permission to winter the column in Utah. Shep Silva suggested the company move to Rush Valley just south of Tooele. There was plenty of open space to establish the encampment. Forage was plentiful and angry Indians were not close. The plan would be implemented as soon as Steptoe returned from his initial foray south to find the perpetrators of the Gunnison massacre. For the leaders of the church, the best thing was that the outsiders, the visiting guests would be staying more than 40 miles away from Great Salt Lake City. This was the fourth and the largest detachment of the US Army to visit Utah since 1847. It was a two-edged sword. The settlers would benefit from the influx of currency into their economy from the encampment. There was also the threat of inserting too many Gentiles into a heretofore quiet society. Liquor and tobacco would be introduced on a much grander scale.

While Aaron Rost began looking through the real estate along the broad avenues for a store to begin his merchandising efforts, Shep Silva was selected to go with Steptoe and a hand-picked number of his soldiers and head south, looking for the Pahvant murderers of Captain Gunnison. The leader of the Pahvant band was Chief Kanosh and his hunting grounds were south of the territorial capital of Fillmore. The company set off in search of him first. The small settlement of Fillmore, named after the preceding president of the US, boasted barely 150 structures, mostly cabins, and barns. A sizeable stone legislative and judicial courthouse was under construction and promised to be impressive when finished.

"The chiefs are all pretty upset with Chief Wakara," Silva explained. "They didn't like him starting the war and the bad feelings sort of rippled through the territory. I'll introduce you to Chief Tinic when we get back. He's the closest to us in Tooele. But Uinta, Sowiette, Sanpete and Kanosh are all mad at Wakara. I'm hoping things will settle down soon."

"Who does Governor Young have working with the Indians?"

"He uses Porter Rockwell plenty up north. Then John Lee and Jacob Hamblin down south where we're heading. They work mostly with Paiutes. Isaac Morley is another good friend of the Timpanogos, especially Wakara."

"You think we'll run into any trouble?"

"I doubt it. Your men look serious and there's enough of them to scare off any hunting bands. There has been plenty of trouble in the past. That was the whole reason for the attack on Captain Gunnison. An emigrant party from Missouri was heading south on the Old Spanish Trail a year ago and they decided to shoot at a couple Pahvants."

"Why?"

"No reason. Sometimes folks just see the Indians in these parts like varmints, wild animals that are free to be shot. Most are not mounted and they're quite poor. They live digging roots and eating rabbits, mostly. It would be another matter if they were the Cheyenne or Sioux or Arapaho. It's a touchy problem."

10 miles south of Fillmore they came to Corn Creek, the traditional home of the Pahvants. A creek wound down from the mountains to the east and watered a lush pasture area. Unlike the other native tribes, the Pahvants had accepted the agricultural education offered by the Mormons and set up farms and raised crops like potatoes, beans, maize, and pumpkins.

Chief Kanosh was in his mid-thirties and was instantly suspicious of the mounted soldiers. He was greatly relieved to see Shep Silva. The two had begun a friendly relationship the year before. Without much ado, the leaders gathered for a conference, while the soldiers dismounted outside of the village and let their horses graze. Kanosh spoke passable English. He was glad to show his abilities. His Spanish was quite good and that was how he and Shep usually visited. Kanosh appreciated the concern felt by the settlers and especially the soldiers over the murders of the Gunnison party. That someone with the standing and importance of Major Steptoe should come from such a distance to visit with him did not go unnoticed, either by Kanosh or his tribe. He glibly blamed the massacre on several of his hot-headed younger braves, who were conveniently not close by.

When Major Steptoe left the Great Salt Lake City, he took another officer with him and left the rest of his command under the watchful eyes of Lt. Mowry and Lt. Livingston. It was the former who was the most excited by the prospects of having access to the women.

Wanting to assure the good graces of the officers, the local population organized several balls and dinners for the soldiers. The food and music were festive. Alcoholic beverages were also smuggled into the halls. It wasn't long before the soldiers' tongues were loosened. The nearness of the coy women was intoxicating. Hands reached and groped and grabbed in a fashion that shocked and infuriated the church leaders, and titillated the women upon whom the attention was being lavished. The prey was as young as teenaged girls and as old as matronly polygamous wives. The novelty of these men's affections was blatant. Much to the dismay, embarrassment, and chagrin of Brigham

Young, illicit couples would break away from the groups, seeking darkness and privacy. Scandals were rampant and only grew more infectious over time.

Letters and kisses were traded. Promises were made. The willing were offered free transit to California with their newfound lovers. Or perhaps a life of leisure back in the States. A glamor and ease were assured. The austere life provided by the harsh desert would be left behind.

A nervous Brigham Young was relieved by the return of Major Steptoe. It took little for the officer to realize the disastrous situation. He lost no time barking orders, packing their supplies, gathering their livestock, and relocating his post to Rush Valley, giving one and all a manageable distance from the allures and temptations of their frustrated female companions.

Chapter 18

"When the nations have for years turned their attention to manufacturing instruments of death, they have sooner or later used those instruments...From the authority of all history, the deadly weapons now stored up and being manufactured will be used until the people are wasted away, and there is no help for it." Brigham Young

Events leading to the Crimean War were a kaleidoscope of intrigue. Geopolitical maneuvering laid dangerous trip-wires all across Eastern Europe, the Balkans, and the Middle East. The Ottoman Empire was in recession while Russia was growing and gobbling up possible toe-holds. The British, the French, the Austrians, and the Prussians watched with interest from the sidelines. Much had changed since the days of Napoleon. Railroads were crisscrossing the continent, as were telegraph wires. Photography was reaching a zenith. Stories could be collected and recorded, then distributed within hours across the continent. Military officers ached for a chance to wield new-found power and technology. The Ottoman's neighbors had all decided that the empire was decaying and would fall, leaving a tasty vacuum for the bystanders to carve up.

Russia was at the peak of land acquisition and boasted an army of one million men. A warm-water port in Sevastopol, having access to the Mediterranean Sea, would answer centuries of dreams. Austria and Prussia were jealous of the Danube River, its territorial neighbors and claims. Greece watched impatiently as a small-time power broker, seeing a conflict as an opportunity for expansion. France was still licking its wounds after the Napoleonic Wars. They had grown and expanded their colonies throughout the globe. Britain was the world's foremost naval power. They did not want the Russians moving into the Mediterranean, threatening shipping to India and the Far East. Negotiations were being set for the building of a canal across the Straits of Suez. Once completed it would allow ships to bypass traveling around the continent of Africa to reach these lucrative markets.

Biblical lands of the Middle East were governed by the Ottoman Empire. For the most part, Christians had been allowed to make pilgrimages for centuries. The Muslims expected them to continue playing the game by the generations-old rules. The Roman Catholics came into contact with the Eastern Orthodox believers over security issues of the sacred shrines. The Ottomans tried unsuccessfully to settle the differences. The French felt they had a vested interest in the conflict. Russia had long been the savior of the Orthodox

Church, stating that members of the religion, whether living in Palestine or not, were Russian subjects and would be protected from incursions and threats.

Ukrainian Cossacks and the Tartars of Crimea had been rolled over by the Russian Bear, but with these conquests also came the dissolution of buffering areas between them and the Ottomans, making conflict much simpler and more probable.

Tsar Nicholas I had reigned from the end of 1825 and oversaw Russia's expansion, the growth of the country to more than 7 million square miles. The earlier Russo-Turkish War was brought to a successful conclusion by him in 1828. He came to represent autocracy personified: infinitely majestic, determined and powerful, hard as stone, and relentless as fate.

Sultan Abdulmejid I was the 31st Sultan of the Ottoman Empire, taking the throne in 1839 as a young man of 16 years. He was the first sultan to speak French fluently. Samuel Morse received his first patent for the telegraph in 1847 from the Empire and Sultan Abdulmejid personally tested the new invention. The Sultan restored the ancient Hagia Sofia to its former glory between 1847 and 1849 and he initiated the first French Theater in Constantinople. The city controlled the Silk Road as well as railroads that ran to the Middle East. It being also the only port to control all traffic from the Black Sea into the Mediterranean, a problem for Russia since their main naval warm-water base was in the Black Sea at Sevastopol.

The Tsar and the Sultan finally tired of the exercises and declared war on one another on October 4, 1853. The Turks immediately attacked with two battle lines, one along the banks of the Danube, because the Russians had occupied the Danubian states of Wallachia and Moldavia. Another line was in the Caucasus Mountains.

On November 30, 1853, a Russian squadron of ships attacked the Turkish harbor of Sinop, destroying all but one ship. The battle proved the superiority of the exploding shells over the older, smoothbore cannonballs against wooden hulls.

The populations of France and Britain were kept aware of the conflict. It wasn't long before the people demanded their governments join the Ottomans in defeating the Russian threat. On March 28, 1854, France and Britain joined the fray, declaring war. The French sent the most soldiers to the arena, with half a million men and 50,000 horses. British warships filed through the Bosporus and into the Black Sea amid the cheers of support from their Turkish brothers in Constantinople.

Wanting to avoid an escalation of the fighting, the Russians pulled their forces out of the Danubian provinces. These were immediately replaced by Austrian soldiers, who put down roots, letting all know that they were in place for an extended duration.

On the afternoon of September 13th, the troop transports arrived at Eupatoria on the western side of the Crimean Peninsula, 35 miles north of Sevastopol. The French movements were methodical and orderly, whereas the British efforts were slow. Horses shied away from the ferries and many fell into the water. It was easier to offload 100 men than a single horse. The choppy waters increased. The rivalries between the French and the British were compounded by the infighting between the British sailors, Welsh Fusiliers, the Guardsmen, and the Scottish Highlanders.

The desperately sick were collected and placed on the hospital ship, Kangaroo, designed to carry three hundred sick. More than four times that number were crammed onto the decks and then transported hundreds of nautical miles to the military hospital of Scutari, on the Asian side of Constantinople. Their hopes of encountering dry, warm, clean facilities where they could rest and receive strengthening nourishment were dashed against the reality of misery, illness, and disorganization.

As things continued to fall apart for the British in Crimea, Florence Nightingale was put on alert by Sidney Herbert. He met with a cacophony of military and political men where he plead the need for female nurses at the war theater. There was considerable opposition but as the turmoil from the Black Sea continued to mount, the importance of a nursing presence became more important.

The Allies pressed eastward on the peninsula, marching towards the surprised Russians who had expected they would simply move south and attack Sevastopol. The Russians scrambled to dig in on the bluffs overlooking the Alma River.

On September 20th, the first battle of the Crimean War was fought above the river. The French ascended the left and steepest side, again surprising the Russians, who were not expecting them. The British went up the right side and using their rifles, cleared the way before the Russians were able to bring their cannons to bear. 3,300 Allied troops were killed, while the Russians lost 6,000. The Allies thought attacking the city from the north would prove too costly and decided to march southeast and encircle the city from the south, after first establishing port facilities at Balaklava for the British and at Kamiesch for the French.

"Please come in, Harriett," Florence called from behind her desk. As the nurse entered and sat in the proffered chair, the new superintendent waved a folded letter at her excitedly. "We got it," she announced victoriously. "We got the go-ahead from the War Department. We have permission to gather a group of our nurses and head for Constantinople."

Harriett beamed. She knew this was a long-sought dream of Florence's. "Who's the letter from?"

"Liz Herbert. She's been writing to let me know of her husband's progress in government. He has been pushing hard and it seems the administration is finally seeing things our way. I need you to call a meeting so we can let everyone know, then see who might be able to accompany us."

"I'll post a notice right now. Any special time you want to hold the mtg?"

"I think first thing tomorrow morning would be appropriate," she replied.

The nurses were energized and patriotic. 38 volunteered to travel to Constantinople, leaving on September 21st. They crossed the English Channel, traveled south through France to Marseilles where they were picked up by a mail ship that then carried them to Constantinople, arriving at the makeshift military hospital of Scutari, November 5, 1854. The hospital was 295 miles across the Black Sea from Balaklava on the Crimean Peninsula.

"Thoughts?" Florence asked Harriett as they peered across the broad gray Mediterranean Sea. The weather reflected autumn. It was cool and windy, making the waves choppy as they steamed to the east.

"Oh, I don't know. I'm just hoping the war comes to an end soon and that our soldiers are well and protected."

"Me too."

Harriett was glad to be working with Miss Nightingale. She was a well-placed woman of resolve and ability. Her personality rubbed off on the other 37 women. All were anxious to finish their trip and start work in Scutari.

"Have you heard any new reports?"

"Not really. Not since the Battle of the Alma. We lost a considerable number. I am sure our services will be needed."

"Do we have all the supplies we'll need?"

"No. One of the first things we need to do is contact our ambassador and sue for money and support from the government and maybe even the wives of the soldiers. With some coordination, I think we will be able to successfully gather the needed things. But then with winter coming on and cholera ravaging our troops, there might never be enough."

"That doesn't sound much like nursing."

Florence laughed. "It's what we have signed up for. Working on the floors and wards and then switching over to the conference rooms. We will be involved with the complete care of our men and if that means twisting the arms of government or officers, well, that's what we'll do."

The boat continued chugging eastward while affairs of the war continued to rage.

The invading armies marched on September 25th and faced few problems surrounding Sevastopol. Trenches were built and batteries brought ashore beginning October 10th. A week later the bombardment of the city began from the land and the sea. The exploding shells caused great damage in the city but the earthen set cannons of the Russians played havoc with the Allied fleet, which suffered great casualties.

The British were anxious to attack the city but the French wanted to wait. A couple of days later the Russians had moved some heavier guns to the south side of the city, outgunning the Allies. Reinforcements also began arriving, strengthening the Russian forces and bolstering their courage. The French were positioned on the west and the British on the east had more worries because of the large nine-mile wing that stretched to their supply base in the small port of Balaklava. At the same time, the Allies were losing large numbers of soldiers to a cholera outbreak that began in September. A large Russian assault was then made against the British supply base at the southeast of Balaklava on October 25th.

The Battle of Balaklava began at 6:00 a.m. as the Russians attacked the redoubts on the southern hills, manned by Turks. After chasing them from the fortifications, the Russians placed some batteries on the ridge overlooking the narrow valley that stretched to the east where another series of Russian batteries were stationed. There were also Russian cannons on the ridge opposing the redoubts. These guns, like those in the redoubts, were obscured from the valley below by the hills.

An arm of the Russian cavalry swept down from the northwest to attack the British. The 93rd Highlanders Heavy Infantry were all that stood between them and the town of Balaklava and the British stockpile of supplies. Instead of forming his men into the traditional rectangle formation used to confront cavalry charges, Colin Campbell, 1st Baron Clyde, chose to set his troops into two lines. They were armed with the Pattern 1853 mini-ball rifles. Spectators termed the 93rd Highlanders, the thin red line, a famous phrase that was used to describe the British warriors in numerous battles thereafter. The British opened fire when the Russians were 800 yards away and again when they were 500 yards distant. The withering bullets tore into the advancing cavalry, stopping them well before they could engage the infantry. It was an encouraging development, especially after the rout of the Turks from their redoubts.

A systemic failure inbred into the British, not only in Parliament and landed gentry, but also in the military, was the archaic structure of hierarchy. Brave soldiers were commandeered by professional officers, many of whom knew nothing about warfare besides the most fashionable way to dress. Many were granted their positions simply because of birth and pedigree. The multi-tiered organization was also plagued by rampant jealousy. Leaders wanted to be seen as paramount in their fields, a very difficult thing to do when being observed by more objective civilian journalists who were not slow to critique the poor decisions that led to debacles as well as the deaths of their countrymen.

FitzRoy James Henry Somerset, 1st Baron Raglan was born in 1788 and was in charge of the British expeditionary forces. He preferred to stay on his yacht, offshore. He was apprised of the beginning of the battle for Balaklava when awakened in his stateroom by the sound of gunshots. He scrambled to get ashore to obtain a clear view of the conflict, then clamored for intelligence. In the excitement of the conflict, he gave the confusing order to his next in command to "try to prevent the enemy from carrying away the guns." Turning to his aide-de-camp, Louis Nolan, he scribbled out his orders for George Charles Bingham, 3rd Earl of Lucan to have his cavalry attack the batteries, not being at all clear which batteries he meant.

Lucan was puzzled and couldn't make any sense of the orders. Nolan repeated that he was to attack immediately. Lucan then sent Nolan to pass the orders along to James Brudenell, 7th Earl of Cardigan who was in charge of the Light Brigade.

These men all wanted to impress and collect glory. They were arrogant and extravagant in their comportment, trying to demonstrate the superiority of the aristocracy. Advancement and commendation fueled their activities, often at the expense of their loyal soldiers.

Nolan was an impatient cavalryman. Much of his life had been spent studying tactics for mounted warfare. He was an accomplished rider and yearned for the attention he knew he merited. This was a prime opportunity. He had an audience. And he was impatient with the bumbling cascade of demands and orders. He forcefully repeated what he remembered being told.

"Attack, sir!"

"Attack what? What guns, sir?" Lucan couldn't believe his ears. Was he being told to commit his Light Brigade against the batteries at the far east end of the valley? He couldn't see the other Russian guns on the ridges to his left and right.

"There, my Lord, is your enemy!" Nolan was indignant, vaguely waving his arms eastwards. "There are your guns!"

It seemed obvious what he was being told and Nolan did not elaborate or explain any of Raglan's intentions. Lucan also didn't care for Nolan's insolence. He forwarded his orders along to Cardigan who commented tersely to Nolan, "Allow me to point out to you that there is a battery in front, battery on each flank, and the ground is covered with Russian riflemen."

"You have your orders, sir."

At 11:10 a.m. Cardigan formed up his brigade and they started their advance towards the batteries over a mile away to the east. They began their trot, moving directly towards the cannons, not inclining towards the redoubts on the right but onward towards Obolensky's battery. The confusion was instantly and horrifyingly apparent to Raglan. And Lucan, who had started leading his Heavy Brigade behind Cardigan, but then, seeing the problem, pulled them back. "They have sacrificed the Light Brigade, they shall not have the Heavy, if I can help it," he remarked, leaving Cardigan without support from the rear, letting his brigade charge forward alone into the horrid gauntlet.

The Russian batteries on the ridge of the Causeway opened up on the brigade at 11:15 and then the guns in the redoubts and finally the cannons in front of the cavalry, 250 yards away. Cardigan started the horses to gallop and finally, the order was given to the Light Brigade to break into a full charge.

Nolan was the first to be killed by shrapnel from a shell, as he was dashing ahead of Cardigan, either to force the pace or else, realizing the mistake, to change direction. He did not live to explain himself.

"And so we went through this scene of carnage wondering each moment which would be our last. It required a deal of closing in by this time, to fill up the vacant gaps."

By 11:17, half of the original cavalrymen reached the artillery, swords flying, and hacking. Some Russians foolishly fled, opening themselves up to the arcing strokes of the brigade. The decimated horsemen fought furiously to scatter the defenders of the artillery. A Russian cavalry unit then closed in behind the Light Brigade, trying to cut them off from any chance to retreat. Instead, the brigade wheeled and sliced their way back through their attackers, trying to make their way home. The whole, frantic assault lasted twenty minutes. Confusion surrounded the fate of Cardigan, whether he accompanied the brigade all the way or not, he found his way back on the path he had come and returned solitary to his camp, sometimes walking his horse or at others, galloping.

"It was not unlike leaving the forlorn hope, after storming a town, to fight their way out again instead of pushing on the supports. We cut their army completely in two, taking their principal battery, driving their calvary far to the rear. What more could 670 men do?"

The engagement was finished by noon. The British Light Brigade suffered a 40% loss of their manpower, 110 dead, 130 wounded, 58 captured or missing.

News of the battle, together with the conflicting events that lead to the futile charge of the Light Brigade was transmitted instantaneously to London, where the British poet laureate for the year, Alfred Tennyson, wrote his famous verses a month later:

> *Half a league, half a league,*
> *Half a league onward,*
> *All in the valley of Death*
> *Rode the six hundred.*
> *"Forward, the Light Brigade!*
> *Charge for the guns!" he said.*
> *Into the valley of Death*
> *Rode the six hundred.*

> *"Forward, the Light Brigade!"*
> *Was there a man dismayed?*
> *Not though the soldier knew*
> *Someone had blundered.*
> *Theirs not to make reply,*
> *Theirs not to reason why,*
> *Theirs but to do and die.*
> *Into the valley of Death*
> *Rode the six hundred.*

> *Cannon to right of them,*
> *Cannon to left of them,*
> *Cannon in front of them*
> *Volleyed and thundered;*
> *Stormed at with shot and shell,*
> *Boldly they rode and well,*

Into the jaws of Death,
Into the mouth of hell
Rode the six hundred.

Flashed all their sabers bare,
Flashed as they turned in air
Sabering the gunners there,
Charging an army, while
All the world wondered.
Plunged in the battery-smoke
Right through the line they broke;
Cossack and Russian
Reeled from the saber stroke
Shattered and sundered.
Then they rode back, but not
Not the six hundred.

Cannon to right of them,
Cannon to left of them,
Cannon behind them
Volleyed and thundered;
Stormed at with shot and shell,
While horse and hero fell.
They that had fought so well
Came through the jaws of Death,
Back from the mouth of hell,
All that was left of them,
Left of six hundred.

When can their glory fade?
O the wild charge they made!
All the world wondered.
Honor the charge they made!
Honor the Light Brigade,
Noble six hundred!

The Battle of Balaklava was termed a stalemate, although the Light Brigade did exactly what a cavalry unit should, by scattering the opposing forces and causing them to flee, despite their horrendous casualties. The British and French failure to decisively beat the Russians set the stage for the yet bloodier Battle at Inkerman fought less than two weeks later, when a much larger Russian force attacked the Allies and was soundly beaten, bringing all

Russian hopes of defeating the Allies in the open field to an end for the balance of the war.

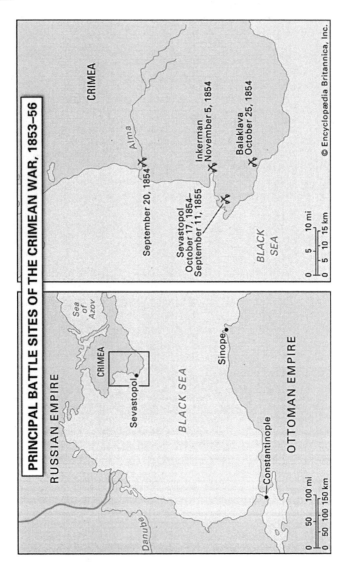

Chapter 19

"For after much tribulation come the blessings." Doctrine and Covenants

September 1854, Sandwich Islands

My dearest Ina,

Please forgive me when I tell you how lonely I am. These islands are green and lush but oh, so very far across the sea from our country. I would trade in an instant the beaches and the coconut trees for the rocks and sagebrush of our West. Water is in abundant supply here. It rains daily. The wet grass washes the mud from my shoes. It also keeps me wringing wet, like my socks. My feet are wrinkled.

The work is very hard. I have never struggled speaking with people. But these Hawaiians speak a whole other language. I have been trying to shadow the other missionaries. I am trying to learn this dialect. It is difficult for me.

About the only thing I can do that's of use is to study. I have been reading my scriptures every day. They remind me of where I have come from and bring memories of my mom and Martha Ann and why I have been called to labor here.

Please pray for me. Please write. Please tell Charlotte and everyone to write. I am lonely and the boats bringing the mail are few and far between. Besides that, not many folks remember to write me. Please don't be like them. I want to hear from you so bad. Please think to write me some of your poetry. You are a gifted poetess. Your words would lift me easily.

I think I'm in the right place. Maybe laboring in the Eastern States would be better for me. I believe Brigham is a prophet. I am concerned that he might not have heard the Lord correctly when calling me to labor here. The food tastes like paste. My ribs are starting to show. I itch a lot.

Please forgive me. I miss you and your family very much. I remember you in my prayers. California is a beautiful state and that is only how it should be since you live there. If you need money for postage you can ask Elder Lyman. I know he would help.

Some might think this place looks like the Garden of Eden. I think it's more like the lone and dreary world. I do miss you, dearest Ina. I miss San Bernardino. I even miss the dust.

I will persevere as best I can. Please write and tell me that you remember me.

I send you all my love, sincerely,
Joseph F. Smith

It's almost November

Dearest Joseph,

Thank you for your letter. Please be assured that I miss you, also. By just being in the islands you are blessing its people. Surely they love you. Surely they recognize the sacrifices you are making. Surely they pray for your health and success, as do I and our family.

I will continue to write you. I was so excited to receive your letter from Hawaii. It came from such a long distance. It found me well and hearty. It found me missing you and your silly ways. I miss your voice. I miss your smile. I am jealous of the people who even now are able to see you each day.

I laughed to hear about the food you eat. I am certain they also eat food that tastes better than paste.

We are well. Pa is spending more time here instead of going to Los Angeles. He is building a good reputation. Ma works hard. She sends her love. Charlotte is flirting with every boy she sees. The twins are good. They help around the house and keep the chickens alert.

I know I told you about Bob Carsley. He is an older boy that I like. He has worked a lot in Los Angeles. He is an ironmonger. He wants to spend more time on the stage. He is hoping to come here and help build a jail. It would require someone who knows what they are doing. I'm not sure Mr. Lyman wants one here in town yet. It would be nice to see Bob more frequently. I know you would like him as well.

I enjoyed your thoughts about Eden and Hawaii. I am sending you a poem I have worked on for a long time. Writing for the newspaper in Los Angeles makes me feel quite grown-up. I hope you like my words. Remember that I was thinking of you as I wrote them.

O foolish wisdom sought in books!
O aimless fret of household tasks!
O chains that bind the hand and mind—
A fuller life my spirit asks!
For there the grand hills, summer-crowned,
Slope greenly downward to the seas;
One hour of rest upon their breast
Were worth a year of days like these.
Their cool, soft green to ease the pain
Of eyes that ache o'er printed words;
This weary noise – the city's voice,
Lulled in the sound of bees and birds.
For Eden's life within me stirs,
And scorns the shackles that I wear;
The man-life grand – pure soul, strong hand,
The limb of steel, the heart of air!

And I could kiss, with longing wild,
Earth's dear brown bosom, loved so much,
A grass-blade fanned across my hand,
Would thrill me like a lover's touch.
The trees would talk with me; the flowers
Their hidden meanings each make known—
The olden lore revived once more,
When man's and nature's heart were one!
And as the pardoned pair might come
Back to the garden God first framed,
And hear Him call at even-fall,
And answer, 'Here am I,' unshamed—
So I, from out these toils, wherein
The Eden-faith grows stained and dim,
Would walk, a child, through nature's wild,
And hear His voice and answer Him.

Yes, dearest Joseph, I remember you, oh so fondly. I pray for your safety.
I long to hold your hand and go again for our walks. Please write me again,
soon. Your happiness is important to me.
I will cherish you, always.

Sincerely,
Ina

****

The mailboat stopped first at the landing in front of Scutari. It was late in the afternoon. The sun was setting in the west, its light illuminating the historic city of Constantinople, on both sides of the strait. The military appearance of the facility belied what was transpiring inside. As the tired, ship-worn nurses gathered their luggage and started up the long, narrow walkway leading to the expansive building, no one came to welcome or help them. Florence Nightingale shook it off, rounded her shoulders, and after giving several short phrases to strengthen the nurses, she marched ahead of the rejuvenated nursing vanguard.

Upon entering the weathered doors, the women were violently slapped by the stench of feces and vomit. The poorly lit interior partially revealed a cluttered hallway, stacked with garbage and hopeless men, moaning in desperation. The sight shocked the voyagers. They believed they were being summoned to help but they had no idea of the squalor the wounded soldiers of the British Expeditionary Forces were facing.

The few visible physicians ducked and scattered before the surprise arrival of the nurses. Miss Nightingale immediately collared a poorly dressed intern who was trying to avoid detection and demanded to be taken to the medical officer in charge of Scutari. The man attempted to wiggle his way free from her grip but was not successful.

"Right this minute!" she snapped.

The man nodded ashamedly. As she was led away, Nightingale ordered her nurses to drop their luggage and begin cleaning and washing as quickly as they could. A miracle started. Buckets were found. Water was procured from an outside pump. Doors and blinds were opened to allow fresher air to replace the stagnant odor. The women rolled up their sleeves, displaying not only clean but strong and talented forearms, wrists, and hands. The nearest sick and wounded were checked, then placed carefully in order along a wall as it became clear. Nurses did not leave them for long. The British women's voices were low but firm as they divided into disciplined squads whose sharp movements caught the attention of even the sickest. Their steps were every bit as martial as those of any military corps. Compassion was shown on their smooth feminine faces but they instantly recognized the difficulties their unfortunate countrymen were facing.

Like the other nurses, Harriett fought back the urge to wretch. Gripping a mop, she shoved garbage out of the way, uncovering a filthy floor, caked in layers of dirt that had been hardened by repeated doses of blood or urine. Discarding the mop, she picked up a hoe that had been left outside by the hodge-podge of headstones, marking the growing graveyard. The lack of order throughout the compound was disturbing to these women of the Empire who had stalwartly believed their soldiers were receiving the optimum care. *What else will be discovered?* Small pieces of candles were lit as darkness descended, the faint glimmering augmented the horror all about. The snide critiques offered by the non-military journalists began to gather more sure footing. *Could it be that the war is being lorded over by egocentric pseudo-officers? Is there a superiority in British ranks, weaponry, and leadership? Or is one British soldier simply equal to one Russian or Cossack or Tartar? And the Brits are not fighting on home turf. Patriotism and the concept of Fatherland play into the mix. Does that favor Russia? The French sent more troops to the arena than Britain but are the descendants of Napoleon's battalions as dedicated?* It had been bantered about the pubs that the strength of the Ottoman Empire had evaporated over the years.

Florence Nightingale returned shortly. Her face was red. The nurses interpreted that she had a confrontation with the hospital's overseer. The nurses had arrived unexpectedly. Nightingale would not accept that as an excuse for the deplorable condition of the hospital and its patients. She spoke her mind freely, not mincing any words. Within a couple of minutes, she had a desk set up close to the front door where she quickly wrote a series of letters, then had them posted that evening. One letter was sent to the British ambassador to the Ottoman Empire, Stratford Canning, 1st Viscount Stratford de Redcliffe, one went to the telegraph office directly connected to the British Secretary of War and put to the attention of her friend Sidney Herbert. The last two were sent to the offices of the London Times and the Manchester Guardian. The epistles were short and to the point. She demanded instant changes and the needed resources.

Shifts had hurriedly been organized among the nurses, allowing around-the-clock care. The job before them felt insurmountable. They had barely stepped into the hellish nightmare. Floors, corridors, and rooms stretched into the darkness which was not able to silence the moans and screams emitting from the as yet unexplored portions of the haphazard barracks.

As dusk turned to the darkness of night, Florence Nightingale retrieved a lamp and after lighting it, began her rounds among the destitute warriors. It was the symbol she would come to be identified with for the balance of her career.

Henry Wadsworth Longfellow wrote:

> *The wounded from the battle-plain*
> *In dreary hospitals of pain,*
> *The cheerless corridors,*
> *The cold and stony floors.*
> *Lo! in that house of misery*
> *A lady with a lamp I see*
> *Pass through the glimmering of gloom*
> *And flit from room to room.*
> *And slow, as in a dream of bliss,*
> *The speechless sufferer turns to kiss*
> *Her shadow, as it falls*
> *Upon the darkening walls.*

She was the embodiment of each of her nurses who resolutely stepped into place, to clean, protect, feed, and support these miserable souls. One of the things these stalwart nurses confronted from the very first day was death. It had become commonplace at Scutari and the interns quickly identified the dying, then carried them outside to be buried a couple of times each day. Death to disease and infestation was vastly more prevalent than the deaths due to wounds received in battle. Cholera was devastating the soldiers and winter was coming on.

It required three days of hard work before the hospital began to take on a semblance of order. The nurses scrubbed and washed and cooked, besides looking after their patients. The women's Spartan cots were lined up in the main hallway, across from the front doors where they had first entered. Privacy was accessed in their single lavatory and restroom. The nurses worked themselves beyond expectations, seventeen and eighteen hours a day, until they collapsed, exhausted onto their cots. They took no rest but felt they were serving their brethren as well as their country, making substantial inroads into the perceptions of women's abilities and capabilities.

After the first nervous few days, interns and doctors began to reappear, even speaking to some of the women. They were jealous of their wards but acquiesced to the women's persistence. They witnessed more work being accomplished within hours by the women than the men had done during previous weeks. They noticed a marked change in the patients' demeanor. The shrieks softened to moans or disappeared. Crusty bandages were changed and filth was washed carefully from wounds. Emaciated men were gently spoon-fed nourishing broth. They were looked after, given the attention they craved. One and all responded to the dedication provided by the efforts and training of Florence Nightingale and her company.

Besides the gentle light provided by the nurses during the nights, men recognized, then embraced the softness of Harriett Matthews. Her signature phrase was: "God loves you, my dear. And I love you." The quiet verbal prescription did more good for the suffering than a cohort of interns or doctors. Men looked forward to the nightly visits of this earthly angel, a nurse of authority, who all knew was sent to them from God. Like all the other women, she carried a clean, polished lamp, whose wick was lowered, keeping the light down, not wanting to disturb sleeping victims.

"I'm impressed that you always find time to read." Florence Nightingale set her lamp quietly next to the small table belonging to Harriett's cot. It was the end of another marathon day.

"It helps me sleep. Settles me down a bit," Harriett replied with her tired smile.

"May I see?"

Harriett handed over the worn newspaper. It was simple with no color.

"Millennial Star?"

"It's a church publication. It's mostly to help us keep track of one another and what is happening in the church."

Florence nodded easily. "I'm glad you have something to divert you slightly from this Kingdom of Hell. Anything that might interest me?"

"I was surprised to see a number of our church members listed who are currently serving in the Expeditionary Forces. The army, mostly."

"The poor souls."

"It gives me something to focus my prayers on."

"Are there many? Mormons, I mean, in the service?"

"About a score. He calls them the valiant little band."

"Who does? The writer, this Franklin Richards?"

Harriet nodded gracefully, a gesture Florence had seen more frequently among her nurses. "He's the president of the British Mission. It's his duty to try and keep track of us, besides the proselytizing and emigration."

"Do you know him?"

"I do and I like him."

"And he's from America?"

"Yes."

"Is he a polygamist?"

"He is."

Florence took a deep breath and exhaled. "This is something I don't understand. Not even a little." She patted Harriett's hand. "Well, one day we will talk. I have some questions I'm certain you would answer for me with more care and understanding than whatever I have heard as an aside from my pastor. In any event, it would be a relief to hear about religion from anyone other than a smug Anglican or a fuming Presbyterian."

"As you wish."

Five days after the nurses' arrival in Scutari, a line of hospital ships began docking before the facility in Scutari. The war in Crimea was the first to utilize railcars to transport the sick and injured from the battlefront to the port to be loaded into hospital ships. They were loaded with casualties from the battles at Balaklava and Inkerman and later from the siege of Sevastopol and the number of smaller battles that erupted in the immediate theater. The transport ships were built to carry a finite number of injured but invariably more were stacked into the ships, sometimes as many as 1500, as they began their journey to Constantinople.

The nurses were only beginning to see results from their initial efforts as this wave of new casualties arrived. With military precision, the men were off-loaded and worked through triage. The clipboards in every nurse's hand were filled with reams of paper, identifying the soldier and detailing the severity of the injuries or illness.

Nightingale ran constantly, petitioning for supplies, food, fuel, and whatever else she could think of. Instantly she made enemies with Ambassador Canning. He viewed her as an unnecessary tart, seeking validation through headlines. He did not like her meddling with British public opinion through the newspapers and he especially detested her relationship with Sidney Herbert, a long-time political rival. Florence wisely sidestepped any tripwires set by the ambassador, focusing instead on the well-being of the men rehabilitating at Scutari.

Being a fish of a much smaller status and after the settling of the first surge of patients, Harriett continued her clandestine correspondence with Benjamin Disraeli. The women at Scutari could not have enough support in Parliament.

Two things happened in December that encouraged Harriett. First was the knowledge of Mary Seacole, a Jamaican-born woman and holistic nurse who paid for her way to the Crimean Peninsula, where she established a field hospital. Receiving no remuneration for her work, she single-handedly organized an efficient location close to the front lines where she was able to treat men in a timely fashion, offering them a female role and expertise to help alleviate suffering and worry. Her humble influence was maintained throughout the war and her work was monumental.

The second came as a gift from Florence.

"You seem to be getting things in order on this floor. Despite the pain these men are going through, all want to thank me for you and your work."

"I appreciate the compliment, mum. I am mostly following in the footsteps of the other nurses."

"You are undoubtedly learning from one another. These are things that cannot be taught in class. It also speaks to your manner of interaction. You all work together, trading shifts and responsibilities when necessary. I am a blessed woman to have friends and associates such as yourselves."

"Mum."

"I am wanting to extend your work. I am not taking anything away. I want you to continue on your way, filling the shifts the best you can. But another area that needs our attention is the kitchen. The food we prepare for the men is sub-par and as the colder weather moves in, we need to pay even more attention to the menu. As you know, we are on a limited budget. There is only so much that we can purchase. That's where I need your help."

"Mum?" she answered with a quizzical look.

"We need to get out into the city, to the bazaars, and find better food, more food for the men and at a better price and more consistently."

What was being asked of her sounded overwhelming, and on top of her normal responsibilities. Disappointment clutched at her heart. She did not want to turn down Florence. She also realized that no one worked harder than Miss Nightingale. But to leave the hospital several times a week to shop for groceries? She did not speak Turkish.

"I…How?"

Florence quickly waved away her concerns. She could read her friend's thoughts. "A young woman has just come to Scutari, the result of many of our prayers, I'm sure." She lifted her arm and waved across the hallway. A young Turkish-looking woman immediately appeared at her side.

"This, my dear Harriett, is Yasmin bint Manara. She is an Arab but speaks Turkish well. She is aware of the foods that are available through the seasons and how they should be prepared. She is a quick study and wants to learn more about nursing. She could help in numerous ways, especially with our Turkish patients. She also speaks French like a native."

The charming Yasmin blushed at her compliments and averted her eyes downwards. It was obvious that the dark-haired woman also understood English

"It will be great fun!" Florence chimed. "It will be an adventure and get you out of this hell hole once in a while. Don't worry about the food preparation. Yasmin will help there. I am mostly concerned about our budget. I have watched you for more than a year and would quickly think you to be from Scotland, the way you pinch your pennies. That's what we need in the marketplace, someone who knows the value of our money. Can I count on you?"

"You say that I can use Yasmin on my rounds, as well?" Harriett queried.

"Absolutely, my dear." This time both Florence and the shy, self-conscious Yasmin beamed.

Chapter 20

"Love the giver more than the gift." Brigham Young

Crack! The carbine kicked back against Shep's shoulder, belching out a huge plume of blue smoke. He peered carefully downrange at the target and smiled.

"Still shoots like it's supposed to?" Aaron asked slyly. It was a dry December morning with blue skies but still, some snow was on the ground.

"Never better." Shep dropped the lever, checked the opening, then inserted another round. "These paper cartridges are a Godsend. I can crank through a series of shots in no time. The only problem is me trying to see through the smoke."

"I'm glad you spend as much time as you do, practicing. Makes me feel like I did the right thing bringing this back."

"Can't ever practice too much. Being able to shoot comes in handy out here."

"The carbine's still better than the P1853s?"

"Not even close. A lot of the soldiers out here have Enfields. It's certainly a sweet shooter, but come on, nothing compared to this carbine. The boys are always crowding me to give it a try. I usually let them take a shot now and then because it kicks the hell out of them."

"They doing okay? The troops keeping the wolves and the Indians away from the herds?"

"This is a great place, Aaron. Not many problems yet. Maybe once the wolves find out we're here but the boys are loaded and looking for any chance to shoot predators."

"Any plans for Christmas?"

"We were just hoping you'd come by and spend some time. For some reason, the Hansens think you're the cat's meow."

"But not thinking about going into town?"

Shep thought a moment while looking for another target, then spat on the ground. "I hoped to have a quiet couple of days. Brother Wells is expecting some trouble between the soldiers and the rowdies. He might call out the Legion to help police the streets. If he does that, then I'm toast, I figure."

Aaron held out his hands. "Mind if I try?"

Silva handed the precious carbine over to the man who procured it for him. Aaron looked it over again, marveling at its construction. "Who'd a thought?" He raised the rifle and sighted onto a clump of sagebrush 200 yards away.

Crack! The short rifle jumped. Flames could be seen erupting from the barrel. "Yep. That's still got quite the kick," he admitted.

Shep agreed, taking the Sharps carbine back and reloaded it.

"What about the women?"

Shep chuckled. "You don't mean the regular, run-of-the-mill, decent womenfolk, do you? Or are you referring to the soldiers' and the camp followers' favorites? What was it Kimball called them? Skitty wits?"

"I think he meant, whores."

"There doesn't seem to be a shortage of them. They come out of the woodwork whenever the Gentiles show up to the city in force. When there's the promise of whiskey, dancing, romance, and roughhousing."

"Steptoe's men are planning on taking a slew of them on to California."

"Where they rightly belong, I suppose."

"It makes Brigham mad."

"Rightly so, I suppose. Polygamy might work some of the time, but these are some of its rotten fruit. The troops are taking advantage."

"Everyone can't live the principle."

"And everyone isn't asked to."

"Is Major Steptoe doing anything about it?"

"He does his best to keep the hot-heads like Mowry out here, away from the city. It goes a long way, but I don't know that he'll be able to control everything at Christmas."

"Brigham's term as governor is running out. You heard anything about it?"

Shep nodded. "I guess President Pierce is tired of him and wants to appoint someone new. I even heard that he wants Steptoe to take over in the new year."

"Think that will work?"

"Nope. The Saints are happy enough with Governor Young. I don't see any replacement getting as much support from folks as the Governor. It would be a scary proposition for anyone to come into the territory and expect to take over and have things run as smoothly as they are right now."

"And the Indian Agent?"

"That's another burr under Pierce's saddle. He doesn't care for Governor Young wearing multiple hats. Pierce thinks he's been treating the Indians too easily. He wants heads to roll. He wants to put the fear of God into the tribes. That's why he sent Steptoe here in the first place, to make sure the culprits of the Gunnison murders are caught, tried, and punished severely. Pierce doesn't want the Indians meddling with anyone on their way to California, either along the Old Spanish Trail to the south or the northern Humbolt Trail."

Aaron scanned the valley and the hills that surrounded them. "Kinda quiet out this way. Don't you miss the people? Is it still okay that I call you Mahonri? Moriancumer?"

Shep shrugged. "If I can call you Maher-shalal-hash-baz. Tooele's big enough for me. I can always ride into town if I want to see more folks. Besides, the territory is filling up. Somebody's doing their job."

"Got plenty of water?"

"Sure ain't Hawaii. It's been a dry fall and if things don't pick up and get a lot more snow, we could be looking at some problems come the spring and summer."

"Steptoe's force notwithstanding?"

"I think Brother Wells said something about it. He said they have brought us about $400 thousand in commerce. It's money and supplies we can use. But nope, it's not enough, especially if Steptoe and his men are planning on leaving in the spring. The territory would be left high and dry."

Christmas Day 1854 in the downtown section of Great Salt Lake City landed as expected. Crowds of soldiers, along with others from their camp in Rush Valley, stalked the streets looking to cause trouble. There also were some local rowdies who chose to oblige them. A full-fledged riot ensued. Some shots were fired but no one was injured. General Daniel Wells, the commander of the Nauvoo Legion, had expected the melee. He turned his troops loose and they quickly rounded up the instigators, throwing them in jail, and hustled all the rest out of town. Fortunately, no one was injured despite the heights of emotion.

On December 27th, Lt. Livingston wrote to inform his father that he had spent Christmas day not festively but in rough-and-tumble riot control duty:

On Christmas day the Citizens and soldiers came in collision and the consequence was a general riot in the streets. This probably all grew out of some difficulties two or three days previous at the Theater. We had a row there in which I got my face scratched and hand lamed in trying to quell the disturbance...Some shots were fired on both sides, but no one hurt by that means. The stones and clubs did better execution. If the thing occurs again the Col. says he will move us all into the field again at a distance from the city ...Very friendly feeling exists between the Army Officers and Civil officers, and it is only some rowdies about town and drunken soldiers that give us trouble. The Governor ordered out the Nauvoo Legion and will keep them organized as a Police till after New Year...

On December 30th, more than forty leading citizens of Salt Lake City's non-Mormon community, including Major Steptoe and his officers, signed a petition to President Pierce that tracked a similar one that had just been adopted by Utah's legislative assembly. Both petitions urged Brigham Young's reappointment as governor on grounds that he was the man best qualified for the position. It was a strange turn of events, for among the signers were some of Young's most severe critics. All seemed to think he was best left alone.

Ever after Mormon leaders pointed to this petition as proof positive of Governor Young's effectiveness, loyalty, and broad local support across religious lines.

Why did the officers of the Steptoe Expedition and even Young's critics sign it? Multiple reasons were advanced, but perhaps as a courtesy, recognizing that the governor would be their host at a lavish party the following day. Four months later Steptoe had severe misgivings about his participation, repented, and privately told President Pierce, "You will probably remind me that I wrote differently once and recommended the reappointment of Governor Young: It is true, but I was not so well informed then as now, and have already explained to you why that recommendation was made."

Unknown to anyone in Utah, two weeks before this petition circulated, President Pierce had nominated Edward Steptoe to be Utah's governor, and the Senate had confirmed his appointment on December 21st. Young himself had written to Pierce shortly after his March 1853 inauguration to note that no non-Mormon, a non-resident, would accept a federal appointment in Utah, an assertion that prompted Young to then self-nominate for his reappointment. Among Pierce's alternatives to Young, Steptoe was not an obvious or early gubernatorial prospect.

Nonvoting delegate Dr. John Bernhisel later told Brigham Young, "I suppose the appointment will be entirely unexpected to Major Steptoe, and I have reason to believe that the President had never thought of appointing him until he received the letter from him in which he spoke in flattering terms of you and the people of our Alpine home."

In any event, President Pierce had enough problems of his own, especially those dealing with Kansas and Nebraska, and he decided to push the issue to the back of the stove and allow his successor to handle the mess in a couple of years.

Another problem for the Utah Territory and Governor Young was the total lack of sufficient snow or rainfall during the winter, leading them into drought conditions. This would affect all those living in the Great Basin, especially the farmers, as they sought to more firmly establish their hold on the land.

"A fine mess we find ourselves in, eh Mahonri?"

"You said it, Maher."

Chapter 21

"If ye are prepared ye shall not fear." Doctrine and Covenants

Dear Ina,

By the time you get this, it should be 1855. This past year has been a whirlwind for me. A lot of good things. Prob one of the best was the chance I had to see you and spend some time with your family in California. Of course, this mission call has been a blessing. I think Pres Young knew exactly what was best for me. I think the Lord's blessings to me are a testimony of it. My sister, Martha Ann, is doing well in her schooling.

The work here is going well. The elders treat me almost as a grown-up. One of the sweet families here has taken it upon themselves to teach me to speak Hawaiian. It is hard but it is also something to do after I get tired of preaching.

I don't think I have ever seen so much rain in all my life as we have had here so far. I must say that it keeps everything green.

Tell your ma and pa that I went to see the king's horses. They are the ones that Shep Silva worked with. They sure are beautiful animals. The people here still remember him fondly.

I miss you a lot. Thank you for your poetry. When I read it I really can't believe it was written by a woman as young as you are. It sounds very mature. You have a wonderful way with words.

Also, I don't know how you can write so well for so long. I try and write as many letters as I can because that means I should get some back. By the time I finish, my hand is getting crampy.

I hope you can still decipher my writing. It is important that you know how I love you.

Please tell our friends hello. Please tell them that I think about them. Please tell them to write to me.

I am feeling better and I am sleeping better and I am doing better.

All my love,
Joseph Fielding Smith

Dear Joseph,

You were right. It is 1855! Isn't it exciting how time goes by? Before you are aware, it will be time for your return. We all miss you terribly. I am sure that Martha Ann feels the same.

Your weather sounds heavenly. I love the rain. Not only does it make everything green but it keeps the ground soft. That is something I miss about the northern part of California. It is very green and lush. Right now we are having some very strong winds that blow from the mountains clear down to the sea. The winds are hot and the fires they fan get to be quite large.

I enjoy hearing about the native peoples helping you learn the language. The Indian people who have lived close to San Bernardino seem almost to have vanished away. There was a long time when the men here were always worried about them stealing our livestock. I also was happy to hear that you could see the horses Mr. Silva worked with. It came as pleasant news for Ma and Pa, as well. I think it pleased them for you to remember them in this way.

The Sweeneys are well, as are their new children the Wetoyous. I really like Linda G. She is easily one of my best friends. Charlotte's as well.

San Bernardino has started a small theater group. Bob likes it a lot because it gives him a chance to hone his skills. I have seen several of his plays. I think he is getting better all the time. I think you would appreciate his efforts as well. Bob enjoys my writing, almost as much as you. Pa sees to it that my poetry is printed in the Los Angeles Star every week. I receive quite a few letters regarding my prose from all over the state and that makes me feel quite special.

He walks with God upon the hills!
And sees, each morn, the world arise
New-bathed in light of paradise.
He hears the laughter of her rills,
Her melodies of many voices,
And greets her while his heart rejoices.
She to his spirit undefiled,
Makes answer as a little child;
Unveiled before his eyes she stands,
And gives her secrets to his hands.

I love writing to you. You inspire me. I hope you always continue to enjoy my writing. I do it mostly for you. I pray constantly for you, dear Joseph, and may the Lord God always holding you close to his breast, keeping you safe from the troubles of this aging and wrinkled world, and always knowing that you are important to so very many of His children.

Thank you for your words and thoughts.

Always yours,

Ina Coolbrith

Settlers from the east continued to spill into Nebraska. Farms were being set up and towns organized. The influx of these pioneers also demanded an increase in protection from the US Army. Leavenworth, Laramie, and Kearney provided additional strongholds. The Indians were wise enough not to attempt attacking these solid locations. They were more successful ambushing solitary parties traveling between the stations. With the clear skies and cold temperatures, there was an increase in traffic as people took advantage and push further into the west. Prices for acres of the Nebraska black earth beckoned, promising a comfortable living, getting the settlers away from the congested hubs of cities east of the Missouri River.

Far to the west, in the Great Basin, just north of Tooelethe wagon bounced easily behind the two mules. The young animals were happy to be away from their barn, the enclosure where they spent most of the winter. This was a bright January morning. It was cold. The wheels were lubricated and turned well. The Hansens and three of their children were loaded into the wooden box. Brother and Sister Hansen were escorted by Shep Silva as they made their way along the west side of the Oquirrh Mountains. Upon reaching the northernmost point of the rocky range, almost touching the huge salty lake, they would turn east and head for the next 20 miles to Great Salt Lake City. What an adventure. Some money and flour had been set aside to make necessary purchases. The children were excited to see the city. Some of the decorations were still in place, waiting to be taken down after Christmas and the New Year.

Small patches of snow lay along the road. It continued to be a dry winter. The ruts in the road were frozen solid. The mules did their best to pull the wagon across the dips with frequency, hearing the screams and giggles coming from the blanket-covered children. They were riding in the shadows of the mountains, still waiting for the sun to rise high enough to peer over the ridges and begin warming their valley.

Brother and Sister Hansen and Shep were sitting on the buckboard, their bodies swayed to the wagon's movements. The onward motion of the wagon did little to interrupt the conversation of the older trio. This was a much-anticipated excursion. Shep traveled to the city once a week but for the Hansens, this was a long time coming.

"The plains are still open for trade?" Sister Hansen asked Shep another time. "No snow has covered the roads yet?" Sister Hansen was a charming woman from Denmark. Her accent was a giveaway. She had waited for weeks to buy fabric that had been ordered from the States. It had not made it in time for Christmas. She had to make do with the cloth she had on hand to fashion some shirts and dresses. The new materiel would liven up not only their family but the whole town of Tooele.

"I believe the roads remain open."

"And the Indians? They remain nice?"

"Nice enough, I figure."

"You are certain that we will be welcome to stay with Brother Rost?" she continued.

"He would be upset if we didn't spend the night," Shep assured the woman, making her smile with anticipation.

"And he is not married, why?"

Shep sighed to hear the topic brought up again. "I promise that I don't know the reason. I will ask him."

"There are beautiful girls who are unmarried in Tooele. I'm certain there are also girls available in the city. They would make his life happier."

"I'm sure that you're right."

"And you, too, Mr. Silva."

"No doubt." He smiled, trying to keep his head low and away from the prying questions of this good, middle-aged woman. Ole and Georgina Hansen were pillars in Tooele. They were hard working. Their presence in the town attracted even more Scandinavian settlers. The incoming families were replete with hard-working young men and gorgeous, blue-eyed blonde women. With the passage of short spaces of time, these attractive young people found one another, paired off, and were soon married. Crude cabins were interspersed by rough dugout homes, sporting slender plumes of smoke from hearth fires. As yet Shep had kept too busy and away from home to think about starting a family, even though it was a topic of great interest among folks in the village.

Sister Georgina Hansen took the responsibility upon herself to make all potential single men aware of the desirability and willingness of the upcoming young women. Remnants of the Relief Society made sure the girls were trained, prepared for marriage and motherhood. It was a pinnacle of life.

"I have a question for you, Brother Hansen" Shep piped up, wanting to change the subject. "I've come across a word lately, one I don't quite understand. I don't know what it means."

The aging farmer knew he was caught and being used for camouflage. "You are a bright young man. I really don't know that I can help you."

"If not, we can ask the children."

The youngsters behind them heard they were being discussed, and suddenly sharpened their ears. It would be a coup if they could provide an acceptable answer.

"I've heard people, Saints, mostly from down south, use the word when frustrated or upset with something. They refer to it as a potlicker. Or do they mean pot liquor?" Shep spelled the different words. "What is it? What does it mean? How should it be used?" The question stumped those in the wagon as they started gearing up their minds and understanding of English to respond.

After a long time, Sister Hansen finally spoke up. "Does this really make a difference, Mr. Silva?"

Shep shrugged. "I don't rightly know. That's why I asked. Depending on what it means, maybe it could make a big difference."

The Hansens reverted to their silence. The kids exchanged looks, that morphed into making faces at one another. Laughter erupted.

The travelers heard a noise coming from behind them. Turning, they saw an approaching file of US dragoons or cavalrymen. They were riding two abreast and appeared to be heading for the same destination as they. The cantering horses were moving the men quickly toward the northern spur of the mountains. They soon caught up with the slower wagon. They were led by Lt. Mowry.

Mowry was an 1852 graduate of the military academy of West Point. He enjoyed his reputation and status as an officer. He was a dark-haired, handsome man who thought of himself as quite the ladies' man. He was the main reason discipline had disappeared when Major Steptoe left Great Salt Lake City the previous summer, looking for the Pahvant murderers of Captain Gunnison. The Major had left Mowry in charge of the troops and camp followers who did not ride south with him. Mowry took advantage of the goodwill being shown by the people of the city. Social decorum quickly descended into chaos as women, single or married, young and old, were suddenly being courted. Affairs sprouted. Church officials did their best to quench the flaming libidos demonstrated by women as well as men.

With the return of Steptoe's column, Governor Young made his displeasure known. The embarrassed major commanded his men to take their livestock and supplies and remove them to Rush Valley, miles south and west of the city. Being thus isolated, Mowry and his minions resorted to writing letters to maintain their new relationships. The physical separation had the desired effect. Mowry chaffed at being disciplined. He pushed to get to the city every chance he could. He was also a frequent denizen of the bars that sprang up with the advent of Steptoe's column the previous summer.

Shep interacted with Steptoe's men because of their horses. He also gained a following because of his firearms practice. Most of the soldiers enjoyed his hospitality. It was something that grated on Mowry's nerves, unbeknownst to Silva. It was obvious as the mounted soldiers passed Hansens' wagon. Shep was guiding the mules at the time.

"Get your damned wagon out of our way, Brazil boy!" Mowry snapped as his men filed around the creaking wagon. Mowry pulled his horse out of the column to observe the passing of his troops. He scowled at the Hansens, then glared menacingly at Silva and spit into the dirt. "Stay out of our way, if you know what's best," he warned, then turned his horse and whipped it up to speed, to regain the front.

"He's a potlicker," Ole said quietly to Shep and his wife.

Shep nodded his agreement. "And I always thought the stink around this area came from the lake."

It was evening by the time the Hansens and Shep stopped in front of Aaron Rost's house on the eastern side of Great Salt Lake City. The festive decorations had done their job, exciting the three young Hansens. By the time they arrived, they were tired and ready to nod off. Aaron was happy to see the travelers and invited them into his home.

"I'm having a couple new rooms built on," he apologized, pointing to the clutter of boards and bricks stacked in a far corner. "But the five Hansens should fit well enough into my bed. Shep and I will be fine on the floor by the stove."

167

The two Hansen girls and the one boy scampered under the covers, then waited expectantly for their parents to come and offer prayers. Aaron showed Georgina and Ole around, then he and Shep excused themselves and stepped outside onto the boardwalk. It was getting dark.

"Streetlamps would go a long way in this city," Aaron said.

"Any news yet?"

"We could get a shipment by summer," he said hopefully. "I have some folks who are waiting rather anxiously."

"We're not doing any stuff like that tonight. Correct?"

"Dan Wells wants to see us for a little bit."

"Legion stuff?"

"That should be about all. I think he's got Rockwell and Lot Smith over as well."

"Is he planning on attacking the boys at Rush Valley?"

Aaron pretended not to hear the sarcastic remark. "Some of Steptoe's plans. Brigham just wants us all on the same page. You living in Tooele doesn't facilitate things."

"I'm doing exactly what the Governor wants, keeping an eye on the encampment. Actually, Ed Steptoe and I are becoming pals. Can't say as much about his lieutenants."

"Mowry's still being an ass?"

"I don't really have much business with him. But yeah, he's a potlicker."

Rost looked at him curiously. Shep used plenty of American vernacular but this? He thought it over for a few moments and decided it didn't require any follow-up conversation.

The temperatures dropped precipitously with the setting of the sun. Their breath was changed into frost but they couldn't see it until they arrived at Wells' home. Light from the windows lit up their breath. They knocked on the door.

Daniel Wells opened the door and ushered them inside. The warmth from his stove was welcome. Porter Rockell was the marshal of the Utah Territory. He was sitting comfortably in a rocker, flanked by the younger Lot Smith. A conflict between the Legion and Steptoe's soldiers would result in the Mormons' defeat. They were outgunned. It was the topic Wells wanted to discuss first.

"Steptoe tells us that they will be leaving in May. Splitting their force, some will go north to the Snake River, then drop down to the Humbolt. The other group will be going more directly across the territory, more or less following the mail route to Carson Valley. They have asked for some guides to help. I'm thinking we could parlay our help into a trade for some firepower. Thoughts?"

The visitors remained quiet.

"Brother Silva, we are hoping you'd go with the major to the north."

"You know I still haven't joined the church."

168

Wells acted like he didn't hear. "Can we count on you? They will certainly need your help with their horses. I want you to meet up with Porter once you get to California."

"So you want me to take the other half to Carson Valley?" Rockwell asked.

"I have some others in mind for that. I'd like you to take a small group across the route a month or so early. Steptoe wants to take some wagons across the salt desert if it's dry enough by then. You can mark it and alert the tribes of the soldiers' coming. I'm hoping things should be fine by then. Judge Hyde should be in Genoa about that time. He can help if you need him. Mostly we need the armaments. Brother Rost thinks he can get us some rifles by the summer."

Shep's mouth dropped open and he looked at his friend. "You're going back east again? To get rifles? How do you propose to pay for them?"

Aaron smiled and returned the questioning looks of the men. Rost smiled victoriously and winked at Wells. "I have some interesting connections in the Kansas Territory, connections who are well healed. We should be able to skim off enough funding to keep the abolitionists happy while still having enough to buy some decent rifles for the Legion."

"And this is all above board?" Shep asked.

"Above board enough, I suppose."

The men nodded in unison. The plan would form up.

The next morning was a cold day for the Salt Lake Valley. The cold air caused an inversion layer, keeping the smoke from the stoves throughout the valley low over the houses, giving it a sooty appearance and the smell of burning wood and coal.

The Hansen children were happy to be free from Rost's house, able to run around and see all the buildings in the daylight. Georgina had prepared breakfast, then cleaned up. The three men who watched her, after she chased them from what she considered her chores, could also see that she was anxious to get outside. The sun would soon warm up the air. Without snow, the streets would be dry. There would be no jumping to avoid mud puddles.

South Temple Street was the main thoroughfare and only a block from Rost's house. The quartet strolled west on the wide avenue, commenting on the new buildings. Salt Lake City was a growing concern. The word 'great' was left off from the name more frequently. It wouldn't be long before it was forgotten.

Brigham Young had a beautiful house just east of the temple square, called the Beehive House. It was there he housed his growing family. It was also where his office was and where he entertained visitors. The spacious home had been completed a year earlier. West of it was the Lion House, a large, gabled structure that would be finished the following year. It was meant for the lodging of most of his wives.

"Brigham is doing well enough," Ole said.

Aaron agreed. "He's a shrewd businessman. He works hard and believes in bargaining for everything. He's also quite fortunate in that he knows most of the folks around, the best glaziers and craftsmen, and contracts with them for work. They all understand that the Beehive House is a major draw. People notice what is being done and then ask after the architect or the laborers. I think all benefit from the work."

"It is impressive," Shep noted.

"We could use these kinds of talents in Tooele," Georgina said, to which they all agreed.

They continued walking west, now and then catching glimpses of their children racing along the boardwalks, stopping long enough to gaze into a store window. They were joined by half a dozen local youth who wanted to join in their activities.

Temple Square was a foreboding block. Huge trenches had been dug for the placing of sizeable blocks of stone for the temple's foundation. Young told the members that it was to be built well enough to be able to stand through the Millennium. Its size promised to be enormous. The ground had been broken for its construction two years earlier. Large pieces of stone cluttered the block with no apparent order. For all the work being done by the men as a form of paying their tithing, the foundation remained unseen, still below ground level.

The crowning achievement on the block sat on the northwest corner. It looked like a large house under construction, appearing almost complete.

"The Endowment House," Aaron said pointing to the cleanly set structure.

Georgina and Ole stopped and took in a deep breath. They were emotional as they watched a couple of men carrying lumber into the building.

"We will come here, my dear," Ole said, pulling his wife closely to his side.

Georgina smiled and sighed. "Do we know when it will be finished?"

"Heber Kimball will dedicate it in May."

"Oooh. So very soon," Ole's wife and the mother of their children cooed.

"We will come here," her husband said. "We will make our promises to God and He will seal us as a couple for eternity." The matter-of-fact statement brought a smile to Georgina's face. She relaxed against him for several moments.

The Hansens stopped in their westward stroll, deciding to turn around and visit several stores they had passed, not least of which was the fabric store where Georgina was positive she would find what had been ordered. Shep and Aaron continued across West Temple Street. It was also where the lumberyards and stockyards flourished. The quality of animals was astounding. The Saints were efficient in gathering the best sheep and cows and horses and goats. There was also a flurry of chickens. The area would provide well for the entire territory. The two men spent time looking over the animals, prices, introducing themselves to the owners, and dreaming of what could be done, given the right amounts of money and time.

It was also a harder area of the city. Several brothels and bars were located nearby, providing for the soldiers, camp followers, emigrants, and disaffected members of the church. Shoddy hotels sheltered the visitors as well and barns were in place to feed and keep their animals overnight.

Aaron and Shep had wandered farther south and west than anticipated. It was late in the afternoon when they started heading back to South Temple. Shep did not remember there being as many bars as they passed. The denizens indoors were becoming rowdy after drinking for the day. Doors were left open to allow the cigarette and cigar smoke to find its way out. It also allowed those indoors to comment on and mock passers-by.

"Looky! There's the midget man!"

Shep's worries were suddenly bourne out. He knew Mowry and his crowd would be in the vicinity, yet he had hoped to avoid them, especially if the lieutenant had been drinking. And he knew that would be the case. He scowled his disappointment while Aaron looked over at him questioningly.

"Hey boy, I'm talking to you!" Mowry yelled, stepping to the door and spitting after the two men. "Where you high-tailing it? I want to talk with you!"

Shep stopped mid-step, nodded and turned around, and started back towards Mowry. The change surprised both Aaron and Mowry. The former tried unsuccessfully to grab his friend's arm, while the latter sneered at the challenge.

Sylvester Mowry was in a foul mood. He had intended on rousting several young Mormon women and bedding them to his content but watchful patriarchs had intervened, keeping their daughters from the predator's grasp. Mowry was forced to patronize a whorehouse. There the selection of women was limited. Substantial amounts of alcohol were needed to deaden his brain and turn him into the lover he knew himself to be. The transformation did not impress his female escorts.

A simple breakfast had prepared him for another day of imbibing and gambling, so that by the time Silva and Rost passed his bar, Mowry was feeling ugly. And now this damned stockman was challenging him.

"I'll wipe that smug look off your face!" he yelled as he charged the smaller man. "You damned little monkey!"

Shep did not stand idly awaiting his assailant. Instead, he charged at the lieutenant, ruining Mowry's timing, spearing the man in the stomach with his head and, knocking the air from Mowry's lungs. As the startled man tried to stand up, Shep pounded his fist into the man's crotch, sending a cloud of dust from his trousers.

Mowry dropped to the ground, his eyes squinting in pain and disorientation. Shep jumped onto his upper torso, pinning him solidly. A right hook landed with a solid smack on Mowry's left ear, knocking the man senseless and causing his eyelids to flutter.

Shep stood up, breathing hard, and looked at the small crowd that had rushed to the door to watch the altercation. Most were soldiers and most knew the Brazilian. They nodded approvingly at Shep then moved back inside, while two of the bartenders picked Mowry up under his arms and dragged him back into the bar.

Aaron was rightly impressed. He had never seen this side of the Brazilian.

"I never pegged you for a fighter, Mr. Moriancumer." he admitted as they started walking north.

"I got teased a lot as a kid because of my ankle. It gave me plenty of experience." Shep shook his hands and checked for abrasions. "Thanks, Mr. Mahel."

"Well, good for you, Mahonri. You think Mowry'll be all right?"

Shep shrugged. "He's a potlicker."

Chapter 22

"The secret of success is constancy to purpose." Benjamin Disraeli

A great advancement in the Western Hemisphere occurred on January 28th, when the Panama Railroad was completed. The 47 miles of track through the malaria-infested jungle would simplify travel from the east coast of the US to California. Most of the travel across the plains, mountains, and deserts combined with battling the native inhabitants could be traded for a quick voyage, divided by a relatively comfortable rail trip across the isthmus.

On January 26th, the Sardinians sent 10,000 troops to aid the Allies. The manpower was much appreciated by the French, who then threw their support behind the movement to unify Italy. It was for this reason that the Sardinians supported the Allies in Crimea. The Italian forces stepped forward and showed their courage and determination during the Battle of Chernaya.

Despite the steady influx of casualties resulting from the siege of Sevastopol, life in the military hospital of Scutari continued to improve, both for the patients as well as the medical personnel. Using the teachings of Florence Nightingale, the number of deaths resulting from disease plummeted, proving to the military as well as the British government, the usefulness, and viability of her nursing staff and practices. Resources began to arrive consistently. Her nurses knew how to utilize them. And letters of appreciation were returned to their homeland, accompanied by lists of what else was most needed. The secondary hospital of Kuolali was started close to Scutari, hoping to take some of the pressure off the main facility.

To Harriett, Florence looked frustrated and overly tired. The nurse came into the small cubicle used by the head of nursing in Scutari.

"We are making wonderful progress," she told her boss. "Our numbers tell us of the improvements daily."

Nightingale flashed an appreciative smile. She knew that she must look a sight for Harriett to try such a tact. Still, it was a kind effort. Indeed, she was tired, almost to exhaustion. She hoped the rest of the nurses were finding time to relax as they conquered the trying challenges among the suffering.

"A brilliant tribute to all of your efforts."

"And yours," Harriett added. "May I ask what keeps you tied to this desk? The only time you leave is when you attend to your rounds. It seems you are constantly writing. I would think folks are fairly well caught up on our situation here. At least by now."

"Our efforts are marvelous, my dear. I believe one and all can see the difference that is being made. Unfortunately, from my perspective, we live in a pluralistic society. Everyone wants to share in the victory. Accolades should be scattered hither and yon." She pulled a letter from beneath a pile of the papers cluttering her desktop and handed it to Harriett. "This is from Liz Herbert. She has been our most stalwart supporter. Now, she is suggesting we move over and make room for Mary Stanley and her pro-Catholic, Irish women. She calls them nurses. She thinks they could also make a difference. And then there's the Presbyterian nurses wanting to get their feet in the door. I constantly hear about these women wanting to help, especially now, after all the heavy lifting has been done."

An intern stuck his head in the door and summoned Nightingale for a quick conference.

"Please stay here, my dear," Florence said. "I need to speak with you."

"Of course, mum."

After sitting for a minute, Harriett decided to look at some of the correspondence left on the desk. Florence worked magic with her statistics, clearly showing the improvements being made at Scutari, both with concise language as well as with enlightening graphics. Harriett could see that some of these were destined for Parliament and, Sidney Herbert, the Secretary of War. Glancing through the lines she was surprised to see a few candid, matter-of-fact remarks. Being so intimate, she decided it must be a letter to either Sidney or his wife, Liz. Florence was referring to their need for competent, trained, and capable nurses not "fat, drunken, old dames." The words caused Harriett to smile and she refocused as she heard Nightingale's approach.

Florence could see that Harriet had been perusing her letters. She held up her hands in defeat. "There's a lot on the plate," she said simply.

"Does this mean you've come to a conclusion about what to do with Mary Seacole?"

The look of defeat transferred from her hands into her face. "She is a wonderful woman. Her heart is true. She knows what it's like to run into so many blockades. But yes, I declined her offer to work here." Florence sighed and shrugged. "She has not been trained as our nurses. She has so many of her own ideas. As a matter of fact, some could prove to be very good, but I am not willing to chance it with our patients."

"It has nothing to do with her being from Jamaica?"

"Heavens, no. I love her accent and the bright colors she wears. That alone will infuse our men with hope from their current drudgery. I would prefer her assistance much quicker than from the likes of some of these religious bigots." She gave Harriett a knowing glance. "If you know what I mean?"

"Of course."

"In the end, I think Miss Seacole will be much better off carrying on with her own plans. She will not have to answer to me or the ambassador's wife or Sidney Herbert. She is going on to the Crimea. She wants to build a hotel for the officers, a place of refuge for them, where they can relax and take refreshment. I do think that having a woman of her capacity so near to the front lines will do nothing but buoy the troops. She will encourage and lift and speak to them with her charming accent. But, no, I consider what we are doing here to be on a much different path."

"I am pleased, after all is said and done, that there are so many talented women in the Empire, who are willing to place life and limb in danger, to support and strengthen our men and the positions we have selected."

Florence Nightingale sighed once more. "We are expecting Mary Stanley and her Irish nurses in a few weeks. She wants to integrate her women here among our nurses. She thinks they can add to our success."

"And you?"

"You being a Mormon should understand better than any, the role that religion can play in difficult places such as this. Our soldiers are at the mercy of their caretakers. If they are Catholic, the chances are that they could be susceptible to a form of indoctrination. I have watched you, Miss Matthews, closely. I have never heard for myself nor from your co-workers, of your desire or willingness to share your religious beliefs with these poor souls. There is a time and place for all of this, of course, but Scutari, during the height of war, isn't the best locale for such activities. Not by the Catholics or Presbyterians or Anglicans or the Mormons. Is that understandable?"

"I couldn't agree with you more, mum."

"I will suggest to Lord Stratford de Redcliffe that Miss Stanley and her nurses occupy the hospital at Koulali. There she will have free reign to run things as she wishes, without needing to account to me. Time will tell how best to manage these hospitals. I dislike using our casualties in this fashion. The only thing I can say is that Koulali will be a much smaller location than Scutari, so the impact will be lessened. Does the plan agree with you, Harriett?"

"Completely."

"I will present my ideas to our nurses in a couple days. I hope to have their support as well. This will require our united front."

"You have nothing to worry over as far as we're concerned, mum."

"One last thing, Miss Harriett."

"Mum?"

"The men and the staff have responded quite favorably to your improved menus. Is the budget-stretching well enough?"

Harriett nodded enthusiastically. It was an area that had become solely her responsibility. "We make do, mum. Miss Yasmin has been a Godsend. She is an active sort. She knows exactly where to go and when and with whom to speak. We are most fortunate to have her in our ranks."

Florence nodded approvingly. "My thoughts exactly."

****

"You look like a busy man."

Shep Silva dropped the horse's hoof and stared at Bill Black, sitting astride his tall bay. "You're a long way from home," he said, motioning to the two soldiers who had been watching him shoe the cayuse, that he was finished.

175

"We'll pick this up later." The men nodded and walked back towards their encampment.

Bill smiled at his friend. "I was hoping it was warmer up this way."

"Were you right?"

"Not by a damned sight."

Shep took his horse's reins and gave his hooves a quick once over, then throwing the reins over the mane, he stepped into his stirrup and mounted easily. "You coming to the house? Sister Hansen will be cooking dinner quick enough."

"Thanks. Don't mind if I do. Really I'm here on business. President Morely sent me up here to see Major Steptoe."

"Trouble with Kanosh?"

"Naw. He's good. It's his brother."

"Wakara wanting to fight some more?"

"I think he's dying, Shep."

"What's Kanosh thinking?"

"He's good. I think he's got the braves who killed Gunnison. They're ready to be turned over and are looking pretty sorry."

"They going to jail in Fillmore?"

"Or Nephi. I think that's where the court will be held."

Silva whistled, then spat onto a clump of frozen sagebrush. "Anybody itching for a fight?"

"All calm right now. That's why I'm here. I told the major about the bucks. He wants them taken into custody sooner rather than later. I can't do it alone. Both he and Morley thought I should grab you to help."

Shep shook his head pensively. "Dammit. I've got plenty of work around here. You guys all know, right?"

"Wouldn't ask if it wasn't necessary. 'Sides, your carbine scares the daylights outta the Pahvants. They've never seen so many bullets fly out of the same barrel so fast. It scares them. They sober up quick."

"I'll let you borrow it."

"Plus you know how to aim it. The Pahvants know as well." Bill smiled, knowing he had Shep backed into a corner.

"What about Porter?"

"His wife is expecting a baby pretty soon so he's off the table."

"Good thing Georgina is in love with you. Otherwise, I'd turn you out to fend for yourself tonight." He shook his head sadly. "But if I did something like that to you, she'd never talk to me again. She'd probably turn me out."

Black and Silva were mounted and riding south early the next morning. Their horses set an easy trot. It was still dark when they passed Steptoe's encampment at Rush Valley. The bugler was stirring in his tent. He had several minutes before he needed to leave his tent to blow reveille for the morning formation.

The horses picked up speed, galloping along the worn dirt road. When going to Salt Lake City, people from the encampment usually rode south, then went around the southern spur of the Oquirrh Mountains, and once beyond them, they would turn again, this time heading north for the last 25 miles to the city. As a result, the road was packed hard.

Bill and Shep did not turn at the spur but continued moving south. The sun was cresting the majestic mountains. The jagged Wasatch range towered high above the valley and the sparkling waters of Utah Lake and the traditional fishing waters of the Timpanogos.

"What's Wakara doing so far south? Isn't that Kanosh's land?"

"That's why we think he's in serious condition. He and Kanosh were born over in the Spanish Fork Canyon but they were raised around Meadow and Corn creeks. The hills there hold special memories for them. Kinda hidden and outta the way. His band is hunkering around, not doing much besides hunting and flaking arrowheads. I think they're all just waiting."

"No farming?"

"Just Kanosh's tribe. Matter of fact, they're already busting up the clods, getting ready to plow as soon as things warm up a little. I wish we could get all the tribes to follow suit. Arapeen and San Pete and Sowiette would all be doing a lot better. Kanosh's people don't spend many hungry days since they've been following Morley's lead. That's a success story, right there."

"No problem with their hunting grounds?"

"None. And it seems they are better hunters when they aren't so worried about feeding their families on only the meat they shoot. The women and the kids look lots better than their cousins. I tell you, farming is the answer. Our people keep coming and they go into the hills looking for game as well. It won't be long before the area's hunted out and then they'd better have some corn or potatoes. It would make life so much better."

They skirted Nephi and made camp on the west side of the Mormon Trail heading southwest. They made good time and covered plenty of territory. Shep knew they should be able to ride the next 60 miles the following day and get to Meadow Creek where Wakara and his band were camped.

"Your pal Kanosh staying with Wakara?"

"Yep. Most of the time."

"How did things go last spring with Wakara? I heard you were with him and Brigham when the war ended."

"We could've used you."

"Sorry. I was in California with Joseph F."

"You didn't miss much. Ol' Wakara was dull and sulky. He knew he was in trouble. He is outnumbered by far. He just laid in his tent and didn't want to come out and talk with me or Brig."

"In Manti?"

"Yep. We finally walked in. He looked bad enough. First thing he does is ask Brigham for a blessing. He said his spirit was gone away and he wanted the prophet to lay his hands on his head and bring it back. He said he was full of anger because of all the fighting. He didn't know if he should turn to the side of peace or war. He really looked like a sad, broken man, Shep. I felt bad for him. We laid hands on him and he felt better. Then he wanted us to sing some 'Mormon' songs."

"That should have killed him right there."

Black chuckled. "Normally it would have, but not this time. We leaned back and sang like there was no tomorrow. Anyway, he felt better and didn't care to injure anyone. Not us. Not anyone. Not one particle. From then on, he was full of kindness and love to God and all His works. We took care of the treaty on the spot and all his kin watched. From there he went with us clear to Iron County and he had some dreams that President Young called pure revelation. It was an experience, believe you me."

"Wakara. The Hawk?"

"I guess. He has a son who is quite the hothead. Maybe he's just like his pa was twenty years ago. Anyway, he goes by the moniker of Black Hawk. He will be someone to reckon with, mark my words."

"Too bad."

Shep Silva and Bill Black didn't stop in Fillmore but continued to Wakara's camp, several miles south of town, set on the Meadow Creek. Pioneers knew the creek as the fourth one south of the Sevier River. The mood of the Timpanogos was somber as the visitors rode into the small number of tents and the generations-old wikiups. Cooking fires were crackling both within and without the shelters. The men were recognized and pointed to the tent where Kanosh was staying.

"*Hermanos*," he said quietly in deference to Shep. "My brother, the great Chief Wakara died yesterday."

"*Sientimos, hermano.*"

The aging chief acknowledged his sentiments. "He had breathing sickness," Kanosh explained, as the men followed him into his tent. "We buried him today up at the top of the creek, in the canyon. I am happy that you were not here. He wanted a traditional burial. He was granted his wish. Two of his wives were sent with him and two young children."

Shep looked at Bill, who only nodded somberly.

"To heaven? They were sent with Wakara to God?" he asked quietly.

Chief Kanosh nodded and wiped tears from his eyes.

"We are your friends, Kanosh. We are here to support you," Bill said gently. "We are here to sustain you and your family. We want only the best for your people."

Kanosh tried to smile. "The ways of my people are vanishing. They are going away like the animals. We are being left alone. The land is changing. It no longer looks the same. The memories remain but life has changed. We need someone to understand us. We need protection and guidance from our brothers."

"We will never leave you, Kanosh," William Black promised his long-time friend, placing his hand firmly on the chief's shoulder.

Chapter 23

"Youth is a blunder; manhood is a struggle; old age a regret." Benjamin Disraeli

On Friday, March 2, 1855, Tsar Nicholas I died at the Winter Palace in St. Petersburg from pneumonia. The aging warrior was 58 years old. For decades he had stood at the helm of the Russian Empire, overseeing the expansion of endless tracks of land, the enslavement of whole populations, and numerous conflicts. He had much more in common with his British, French, Austrian, and Prussian counterparts than the faceless serfs or the millions of poor he presided over. In 1827 he had written the edict, demanding the conscription of all Russian Jews 18 years of age, making them serve for 25 years. This was just one of the burdens he placed on Russia's 2.4 million Jews. The Cossacks and Tartars were similarly targeted.

Nicholas was succeeded by his son, Alexander II, Emperor of Russia, King of Poland, and Grand Duke of Finland.

****

The four soldiers crowded close around the back of Shep Silva while giving him space and light as he was working on his horse's back foot.

"Always keep an eye on your horse's hooves. They aren't indestructible. *Ne'*? You ride through some tough country. Rocks and creeks, snow, and brush all combine to hurt your animals. *Ne'*? You need healthy mounts to do your job, so pay attention. It will always help in the end. Plus, your horses will notice that they are important to you. They will act like your friends and do the best they can for you. Now you want to do the best you can for them. *Ne'*?" He lifted the hose's back foot again. "You want to make sure the hoof is as clean as possible before you start to rasp him or fit shoes on. You don't need to wash it off, just make sure there's not a lot of build-up. Check for sores and tenderness."

One of the soldiers bashfully held up his hand to ask a question.

"Yeah. What is it?"

"You keep saying *'ne'*. Just what the hell does that mean?"

Shep smiled and chuckled. "Sorry. It's habit. A shortened Brazilian term for *não é a verdade* that means, see or isn't that right? Like Spanish *verdad* or German *nicht wahr*. Get it?" The men all nodded and mumbled incoherently. Shep doubted they did and went back to his demonstration.

The men leaned in more closely to observe.

"Once you've cleaned off the bottom of the hoof, remove any of the old shoe that might still be attached. And be careful. You don't want to injure your horse. Sometimes throwing a shoe can hurt in several ways." Shep stood and walked around the horse to look at the other hooves, something he had already done. "But you can't be too careful. The horse is not just your tool. He is your friend, your companion. He bleeds and hurts like we do. But treat him right and he'll be as loyal as your dog."

"What if he's lame?"

"Then back off. Leave him alone for a while. Give him time to heal. After some rest, he could be back good as new." He retreated to his original hoof and positioned it between his knees. "Keep your backs straight. Sometimes your horse will think he wants to lean on you. Don't let him. He weighs too much. Now, take your rasp and smooth the hoof flat. Don't round things like a boat. Your horse isn't going to sea. He needs a stable, flat hoof and that's what you'll need to tack on the shoe." With a few strokes, Shep rasped the hoof and brushed it clean. "Check your shoe to make sure it'll fit. You might need to spread it some. You want a good fit. Now, when you start to nail it to the hoof, make sure you do it at an angle. Don't go too deep or he'll have sore feet for a long time. Just shallow. Then, where the nail comes out, bend it over and clip it off. Check it to make sure it's good before you move on to the next nail. Got it?"

The men shuffled unsurely.

"Jake," Shep said, singling out one of the men. "Come take my place. Let's see what you learned." Jake moved forward while the others grinned, relieved not to have been the one selected.

They all gathered to watch their comrade start his work. The horse merely stood and looked around with impatience. Jake carefully placed and tacked another nail into the shoe, clipped it off, and filed it smooth.

"Just like that," Shep commended the trainee, bringing smiles to all. Jake let out a huge sigh of relief. "All right, there's a number of horses the major wants looked after. Let's get to it."

They began milling around the corral where the horses were kept, searching for the one that promised to be easiest. Jake happily kept the first horse.

"Mr. Silva."

Shep looked up from his tools to see the nervous corporal standing at attention. A smug appearing Lt. Mowry was at his side.

"Mr. Silva," he repeated. "Major Steptoe would like a word."

Shep nodded, wondering what Mowry's role was in the request. He could see where the bandage had been removed from Mowry's head. His blow that had landed on the side of the officer's head days before had resulted in a seriously swollen ear that needed to be lanced or else Mowry would have had a terrible cauliflower ear. Shep stood and started to follow the corporal, who pivoted and began walking towards the commander's tent.

"Make it faster!" Mowry said and gave Silva a shove.

The Brazilian stopped and calmly faced the lieutenant. "You're about to have a real problem," he warned.

"Couldn't be happier," the officer snapped, then pushed Silva violently in the chest with both hands, sending the smaller man tumbling to the cold ground. Mowry stepped closer, towering over Shep. "Get up and get going!" he ordered.

Silva's foot swept quickly, knocking both of Mowry's feet out from under him, sending the officer crashing into the rocks and sagebrush. As he struggled to right himself, Shep pounced, slamming his head, face-first into the gravel. Shep leaned back far enough to get a clear stroke, then pounded Mowry's uncovered face with two hard jabs. Blood began coursing from his nose and mouth. Reminding the stunned onlookers of a raptor, Silva jumped onto Mowry's back then lifted him high enough to slam him back to the ground. A well-placed knee to Mowry's ribs drove the air from Mowry's lungs and made him groan forlornly. The altercation was finished within seconds. Mowry lay motionless. The surprised soldiers were pleased with the outcome. Few counted the lieutenant among their friends.

Shep stood up, grabbed his hat and dusted his clothes off, then leaned down and whispered something into Mowry's recently unbandaged ear, then arose and walked off towards Steptoe's tent.

An aching Sylvester Mowry rolled slowly over onto his back trying to orient himself. He spit dirt from his mouth, then bawled, "What the hell is a potlicker?"

The corporal had reached the major's tent a few seconds before Shep.

"So you've been harassing my troops again?" Steptoe asked with a broad smile.

"I don't think your Lt. Mowry cares much for me," he admitted.

"Don't think I would care too much for you either if you were always beating the hell outta me."

Silva smiled with a trace of embarrassment. "What can I do for you, Major?"

"Chief Kanosh is ready to turn over the men who murdered Captain Gunnison. Bill Black says he'll meet you in Nephi tomorrow. Would that work out for you?"

"I'll get going within the hour."

They met the next morning.

"So what's the difference between the Pahvants and the Timpanogos and the Shoshones and the Paiutes and the Utes?"

"Not an easy question to answer," Black replied. "Size of the band and where they live, I guess. They interact a lot."

"Their languages are the same?"

"Nope."

"They look a lot alike. At least to me."

"They also hate each other and fight and kidnap each other. Wakara was probably the most notorious."

"Now he's gone."

"Yep. Others, like his boy, Black Hawk, want to take his place, but it'll never work. Too many settlers filling up the valleys. Their way of life is going away."

"You wonder why they're angry?"

"Not a bit. But they lost and they'll be the ones who need to make the adjustments."

Arriving at Corn Creek a short time later they were surprised when Kanosh handed over eight Indians for trial. One was blind and another retarded. Only three were warriors. It was obvious that these were not the murderers of Captain Gunnison.

"This is the best I can do," Chief Kanosh said. "Your Major Steptoe might think this is a joke. I say that putting my people on trial for such an event during war, that is the joke."

The eight Pahvants were put into jail in Nephi to await their trial. It was a busy time for Shep as he shuttled back and forth between Salt Lake City and Nephi and Tooele. Major Edward Steptoe was trying to ready his men for the extended trek across the Great Basin, to set up shop in California. A serious worry that he was now facing, was the desire of 100 women who wanted to accompany the soldiers to the goldfields of California. Some claimed to have developed a relationship with a soldier and wanted to remain with him. Others simply wanted to leave the desert and move to a more refined location and get out from under the strenuous demands of Brigham Young and his religious adherents.

Once again, Aaron Rost hitched a ride to the east and the States with his associate, Almon Babbitt, trying to continue building his business. Shep continued being amazed at Rost's endurance and determination to spread his wares and ideas throughout the states and territories.

Trial for the murderers of Captain Gunnison was convened in Nephi at the first of May and presided over by the Honorable Judge John Fitch Kinney. A jury of twelve men was selected, all were members of the church. The trial lasted a week. Of the eight defendants, only three were convicted and then not of murder but manslaughter. They were sent to the local penitentiary to serve a three-year term but they escaped five days later and were never heard from again. Judge Kinney and Major Steptoe were incensed. One of the main reasons they had come to the territory the previous year was to catch and prosecute the murderers of Captain Gunnison. The attempt turned out to be a miserable failure. It was not a pleasing outcome for Major Steptoe. In his letter to President Franklin Pierce, he detailed the events of the trial. He also concluded that the church, contrary to the fiery newspaper assertions across the nation, had nothing to do with the attack. There was no collusion between the Mormons and the Pahvants and the massacre of Captain John Gunnison and his party.

A week later Major Edward Jenner Steptoe broke camp in the Rush Valley and headed north to intersect the Oregon Trail. He led his company of soldiers, together with their camp followers, teamsters, and a herd of 800 well-rested and shoed horses. They were joined by 100 women, seeking asylum from polygamy, the desert, and the austere overreach of Brigham Young or else had romantic relationships with the men.

Judge Kinney was left behind with his wife in the home they bought in Salt Lake City. He was a reminder of federal oversight. His job was to keep the Mormons in line and report eccentricities of Brigham Young's to President Pierce.

Shep Silva was pleased to have been chosen to go with Rockwell and Steptoe's troops to California. They set off moving north and going around the Great Salt Lake, then meeting up with the worn Oregon Trail. They continued west for several days before dropping south to meet the Humbolt River. This was the main trail followed by gold prospectors headed for California.

Major Steptoe was relieved to be leaving the Utah Territory. The camp followers and teamsters were necessary hangers-on. He wasn't as pleased to be escorting the gaggle of women wanting to spread their wings and seek more fertile pastures. He had wisely sent a smaller, rowdy group of men south along the Old Spanish Trail, including Lt. Sylvester Mowry, wanting to get them out of the territory as soon as possible and to Fort Tejon in California.

Rockwell and Silva paired up every day, riding before the column to check on the trail, springs, and opportunities for grazing. They also scouted for Indians, letting some know of their coming and keeping an eye on others.

Whatever his past or what made him as loyal to Brigham as Porter was, didn't concern Shep. He was more interested in the applicable traits he could learn from the Mormon lawman. On this trip, they spent ample time together. Before long, both were comfortable in the other's presence. A friendship developed. Porter also owned land close to Shep's by the Rush Valley giving them more in common. The men began looking for reasons to leave the column and ride off together. These forays were a chance to be away from the Gentile influences of the soldiers.

Shep pestered Porter about his use of his sidearm. The gunman spent the necessary time training the Brazilian about the use and care of his pistol. They practiced for hours on end. Porter also recognized the value of Shep's carbine and he took his turn sighting and firing the rifle.

"Whoa! That has quite a kick."

Shep smiled exultantly. "Told you. It can change a lot, fast."

"And it loads at the breech. What will they think of next?"

"Whatever it is, it'll be crazy."

"I heard the cannonballs they're using in Crimea explode. They blow up when they hit the ground or else a fuse is lit so they burst above the troops, showering them with splinters of iron. Quite deadly."

"Nothing I'd look forward to."

"You and me both, pard."

That was a milestone for Shep, to be referred to as Porter's 'pard' or partner.

"You have a friend who can get these?" Rockwell asked.

"Aaron Rost. He's turning into quite the arms dealer. You met him back at the first of the year at Wells' place."

"I remember."

"I'll see to it that he gets at least one for you."

Porter smiled in anticipation. "Much obliged."

Chapter 24

"To believe in the heroic makes heroes." Benjamin Disraeli

As spring continued to spread across the Bosporus Straits and into the Black Sea, then the countryside surrounding it, Harriett could tell that Florence was getting anxious to be out and about. The siege of Sevastopol continued to be a bloody event. Innumerable battles and skirmishes were pitched. Targets were selected by the military leaders on both sides of the conflict. Hills, redoubts, and places of strategic values were attacked and counterattacked. The Russians traded victories with the Allies. Cannons and mortars were constantly raining death and destruction. Men of strength and insight materialized from time to time, leading heroic clashes. At times they were successful. At times they floundered. Sometimes these personalities skyrocketed to prominence, only to be cut down the next day and forgotten in the jumble of trenches.

Because of these ceaseless battles, the casualties flowing into Scutari remained constant. The warming temperatures and the drying of the mud cut back on some types of illnesses. As trajectories merged into a lessening of the sick and wounded, and as the medical staff at Scutari continued to improve and strengthen their positions, Florence saw a chance to leave the main facility at Scutari and travel across the Black Sea to the port of Balaklava where she could get a first-hand look at the battlefields, perhaps collecting needed information regarding the Crimean War.

Harriett and Yasmin were selected to accompany Miss Nightingale. "I need some female travel companions," she told them matter-of-factly. "Both of you have proven yourselves invaluable in our efforts at Scutari. And Mr. Disraeli has commented several times to the Herberts how much he enjoys your correspondence and keeping him up to speed on the happenings at Scutari, for which I thank you. You have done a yeoman's job, Harriett."

"Thank you, mum."

"And I'm jealous of your companionship with Yasmin. The two of you have increased the well-being among our soldiers multiple times. I have spoken with the other nurses and they have promised to do their best during our absences. We really shouldn't be gone long."

"I have a question, mum. Does your traveling at this time have anything to do with Mary Seacole?"

Florence flashed her a brief smile. "I often forget how observant you are, my dear." She cleared her throat. "I would be less than honest if I denied there wasn't any desire on my part to see what the Jamaican Angel has been doing so close to the front. She has placed herself in extremely dangerous spots. She is a very brave woman. We can all learn from her spunk and hard work."

"I understand the hotel she has raised has been done mostly with her own funds."

"And the men respond to her willingness to serve and bless them. Memories of the time they spend in her lodge, eating her unique food, are quite long-lasting. I look forward to learning more from her."

Their ship landed in Balaklava on May 2nd. The women spent a few days making the rounds in the supply areas, introducing themselves to the British men who were manning their responsibilities several miles behind the siege lines and trenches that surrounded the bombed-out shell of Sevastopol.

Contrary to the hopes of Florence Nightingale, she came down with an illness shortly after docking. It was called the Crimea Fever and wracked her body for more than two weeks. After making sure that she was convalescing well, Harriett and Yasmin, following her orders, went on a tour of the battle areas, guided by grateful soldiers who made sure to keep them away from dangerous situations. It was a difficult task because the Russians seldom tipped off the opposition about their bombing schedule. And vice versa.

The two nurses were led through the British trenches where they were greeted with hurrahs and salutations. Seeing these vibrant young men against the shattered, smoking landscape was unnerving.

Most disturbing were the piles of dead, and dismembered, clothed in bloody or burned coats. Their guides did their best to keep them away from the gruesome scenes of battle but it wasn't always possible. The men apologized profusely. One day they were taken past a locale where the Russians had recently mounted a counterattack. The dead Russians were scattered about like so much refuse. Corpses of serfs, Cossacks, and Tartars moldered on top of the wet earth. Sulfa was thrown over the bodies to cut down on the stench.

At least by the time the soldiers reached the hospital at Scutari, their blood had staunched, or else they had died. The interns efficiently separated the dead from the dying before entering the military barracks. Despite their previous initiations into the horrors of war, they needed to pause now and again to wretch. Yasmin was especially affected when she saw what she perceived to be a corpse begin to move and sigh in agony.

Over and again the nurses were reminded that recently these casualties had been lively, active men, possessing dreams of family and friends. They laughed and cried. They felt the powerful pounding of their hearts as they charged or faced the bullets and bayonets of the legions of unknown enemies. A generation of European men had effectively been demolished and scared by the blood-chilling exposure of frantic fratricide.

After each tour, Harriett and Yasmin spent an hour scrubbing the gore from their boots and washing their hands over and over again, before putting on brave faces to greet Florence.

"You know, what you're doing, as awful as the nightmare is, still it lifts our men's spirits," Florence remarked one afternoon. "Having women witness the horror brings a semblance of humanity back into their hearts. I almost wish I could accompany you, but then seeing the looks on your faces when you return, or the reflections on our officer's faces, makes me feel that I'm really in the better place."

"We are grateful that you brought us along, mum, but the terror washes over me in waves. At times I think I am doing well and then I begin to shake and tremble. I feel the blood rush from my face. I must be quite the sight, not strengthening our boys at all, I'm afraid."

Yasmin laid her hand peacefully on her forearm. "I agree with Miss Nightingale. Our appearance startles the men but they don't want to flinch with fear. They want to keep up their façade of bravery. Bless their foolish hearts."

"Do you see an end to the siege?" Florence coughed weakly, trying to hide her discomfort.

Harriett shook her head. "The battles at Alma and here at Balaklava and Inkerman, as brutal as they were, were still over within several hours. The fighting around the city is every bit as ferocious, vicious as one of the pitched battles. They drag on and on and neither side seems to be winning. Day and night. It's just a slaughter ground."

"Thank you for your work. It really is needed."

A dirty white-coated doctor came into Florence's cubicle. He had heard some of the conversations. "What Miss Nightingale has said is as true as the sunlight. Our lads respond very positively to your presence."

"It is hell on earth," Harriet affirmed.

"Am I ever going to be released from this confinement, doctor?"

"This is a difficult illness, Miss Nightingale. I think you got it from drinking contaminated milk. It's an easy thing to do. Usually, it gets finished within a fortnight. That's what I'm hoping with your illness."

"Our scheduled departure will be after the 24th. I hope to be better by then."

"Hope is a good thing, as are prayers." He patted her head after checking her pupils. "You are on the mend, I trust."

The next day the intrepid duo went to see the British Hotel, built and maintained by Mary Seacole. Pastel colors covered its exterior. The woman imbued the place with her charms and her exquisite cooking.

Mary was flattered to have the visitors from Scutari. She was also concerned about Nightingale's illness, but at the same time, relieved not to have to dance around her expectations. "Don't get me wrong," she explained with her heavy Jamaican accent. "I love Miss Nightingale. She has always set such an example and high ideals. But, well, maybe I'm not her type of folk."

Harriett and Yasmin tried to wave off her concerns as imaginary, but at the same time were relieved Florence wasn't accompanying them. They both knew their boss could be critical. Mary took them on a quick tour of her facility, then turned them lose, encouraging them to explore and talk with as many as they could. She told them that they could learn more on their own. Then explaining that she was needed elsewhere, she kindly excused herself.

Harriett and Yasmin spent a couple of hours walking the halls and introducing themselves to a number of patients. They noted that a vast majority of the people in the hotel were British officers. They wished the facility were equally assessable to one and all but it was how society ran, even in Crimea.

For Florence Nightingale, the lingering effects of the disease never completely left, at times confining her to bed because of chronic pain. The illness did not deter Florence. She returned to the peninsula from Scutari several times more over the balance of 1855.

****

"We'll have the column and the horses turn south here?" Silva asked Rockwell. Steptoe's company was crossing the 40-mile desert, a dusty, rocky stretch and dry, even at that time of the year. The horses were anxious to get the desert behind them. They could almost smell the air getting wetter and feel the greener grass beneath their hooves.

"It'll get us to the Carson Valley a lot faster and keep us from having to cross the Truckee River several times more. We could turn west and ford the Truckee a bunch of times. Then we'd have to decide if we wanted to try the Donner Pass or turn north and take Beckwourth's Trail. It's gentler but a lot farther. Besides, don't you have business with Judge Hyde?"

"Yep, but not important enough to drag the column out of the way."

"Believe me, this is the best way."

The late spring temperatures were beginning to soar. The Sierra Nevada range could be seen in the distance. What couldn't be seen were patches of snow, a testament to the dry, protracted winter that was well in the past.

"And that river?"

"The Carson and it's a good deal slower and easier to cross than the Truckee. Plus we only need to cross it three times. From here on into Genoa the grazing will be good for the cayuses. If the column stays a bit, they'll be good and fat by the time we reach California."

"Genoa? Who thought that one up?"

"Orson Hyde. He didn't like the name Mormon Station. He thought the location at the foot of the mountains reminded him of some Italian city."

"But that city sits on the ocean."

Porter shrugged and smiled. "You'll have to take it up with Hyde."

They rode down into a steep draw where some tell-tale willows were growing. The ridge around them kept the sun's rays from the vegetation most of the year. They found the ground dark and muddy. Taking a few minutes, they began scraping and digging, going as deep and as fast as they could with their trenching tools. The two horses snorted and waited patiently. Before long the holes began filling with dirty, but cool water. The grateful horses descended to the pool and began slaking their thirst, not minding the soil still swirling in the water, while the scouts rested and surveyed their surroundings.

"It looks desolate now, but just give it another fifty years and I guarantee that even this place will be filled with settlers."

"Won't make the Paiutes very happy."

"Nope," Porter said. "And that's a damned shame. The settlers want to own pieces of ground. They want to fence it and irrigate it and then expand it as much as they can."

Silva had contemplated the problem several times. The topic depressed him. He decided to change the course of their discussion.

"I got a question for you."

"Shoot."

"Why do you wear your hair so long? It's got to be rough keeping it clean and braided. Why not just cut it off?"

"I keep it up. It don't get in the way, mostly just sits under my hat."

"It doesn't bother me, Port. I just thought your life could be simpler and cooler, especially in the summers, without all those locks stacked on top of your noggin."

When Rockwell and Silva reached the flats, Porter removed his hat and set it on his saddle horn. Silva's question about his hair touched a suggestion. The lawman pulled a few pins from his braids and let his hair drop down onto his shoulders. He shook his head. The thick braids were starting to be touched with shots of gray. He tugged on them, then looked at his partner.

"I'm trying to keep a promise," he said.

"What? With your hair?"

Rockwell nodded somberly. "Serious as death."

"You have a reason for growing it and keeping it long?"

Porter Rockwell nodded and sighed deeply. It had been years since he had told the story. "I was arrested back in St. Louis in the spring of 1843 and carted to jail in Independence, Jackson County. People there had bad memories of me and the church. They locked me up for months and treated me like buffalo chips."

"What about Joseph and the folks in Nauvoo?"

"That was the crooked plan. To draw the Prophet out, away from his city, out onto the prairie where he could be shot."

"So both sides just let you sit?"

"Folks did what they could, I reckon. Finally, the church ended up getting a hold of Doniphan and getting him to take my case. It wasn't a hard case and Doniphan jumped on it. He couldn't wait to stick his finger in the judge's eye and everybody else who was wanting to see me swing. He got me out of jail, just as the Prophet said he would. I wasn't tagged with breaking any laws or nothing."

"How'd you get back to Nauvoo?"

"That was the tricky part. No one wanted to give me a horse. I ended up hoofing it across the frozen state of Missouri. And it was damned cold. Somehow or other I got across the Mississippi and made my way to Nauvoo. I got there on Christmas Day, 1843. When I made it to Joseph's house, the people were all having a big party. I showed up looking like hell. I hadn't been cleaned up or had my hair cut in almost a year. Some of the Nauvoo lawmen mistook me for a drunk Missourian and wouldn't let me in. So we traded some blows. Joseph heard the ruckus and came outside. He recognized me right off and hugged me. I thought my bones would break. Anyway, he told everyone who I was and announced that I was a fulfillment of the prophecy he'd given, that I'd get clean away from Missouri without any serious stain and then he told me, loud enough for all to hear, that I had joined the ranks of Samson and other Nazarites. That my long hair was a badge and that as long as I didn't cut it, I would be like Samson. No blade or bullet would ever hurt me. So there you have it. I have taken the Prophet at face value and have never cut my hair since. It's been a dozen years. I've been in some awful scrapes. I've come close to losing my life, but the Prophet promised me that I'd be protected. That, my dear Brother Shep, is why I keep my hair long. It's better when it's braided. It doesn't get in my face. I keep it under my hat. It also scares hell out of my enemies."

Silva thought he did. It also gave him a new appreciation for the aging lawman, helping him to understand why Porter never showed fear.

Chapter 25

"The greatest good you can do for another is not just to share your riches but to reveal to him his own." Benjamin Disraeli

My Dear Ina, (May 1855)

Thank you for your prayers and tears in my behalf. I know that I am not alone in this labor. To know that you think about me now and again is a real blessing for me.

I can hardly believe that it's been a year since I last saw you. You, of course, are continuing to grow into a more beautiful young woman. I am so proud of you making such a name for yourself with your poetry that is published by the Los Angeles Star. That is no small feat.

Every day that passes finds me more in love with the Hawaiian people. I am beginning to understand the language better. The people are so kind and gentle and spiritual. They know that God loves them. They feel His closeness. When tragedy strikes them, they only pray harder. These people are not quitters. I wish you could know them as I do.

The time I have to write is short, so I will close, promising that I will write again, soon. Please give your family my regards.

All my love,
Joseph

My dear, sweet Joseph (June 1855),

I too must apologize about the time constraints I'm under. I have been writing a lot. I have even been traveling some.

I can almost smell the ocean and the beaches of your country. Without a doubt, God is blessing you as you labor to help the people of the Sandwich Islands.

My mother is planning to take me and Charlotte up to Santa Clara County in July to see some acquaintances. The Ousleys are friends of hers from back when we lived in the States. I am looking forward to seeing more greenery. Things around San Bernardino are livening up after the winter rains. Still, there is a great difference between the high desert here and the coastal valleys of northern California.

The twins are doing well, as is Ma and Pa.

I attempted a cameo on stage and totally flopped. I think Bob was mortified. He told me he wasn't but I think he really was. I think he dreams of us becoming some acting couple of renown.

Please know how much you are loved, not only by me but many people here in the town. I am also confident that others in the Great Salt Lake City are also aware of you and miss you. You bless my life, Joseph.

Thank you ever so much.

Love forever,
Ina

The Endowment House located on the northwestern corner of Temple Square was completed in May and dedicated by Heber Kimball. Still, it was no temple. There were some significant blessings, like the sealing of children to their parents, that could not be done outside of a temple. So while many were thrilled to be able to receive their endowments, to make and receive blessings with the Lord, they were clothed upon with power and started wearing the protective holy garment of the priesthood under their work-a-day clothing, they were not sealed beyond couples.

The beliefs of the church demanded that these holy locations where covenants were made with God needed to be sacred, set apart from the temporal and profane. Unlike public church meetings, where all are wanted and invited, entrance into the Endowment House required a recommend signed by ecclesiastical leaders, after an in-depth interview, thorough vetting of the candidate to be initiated.

Ole and Georgina Hansen strolled around the block designated for the temple. The deep trench that was dug in preparation for the temple's foundation, reminded them of how long they had yet to wait. They no longer lived in Denmark. They emigrated across the ocean and then trekked over a broad prairie. They now lived close to the Lord's apostles and prophets. Their steps were small, incremental. Sometimes it felt like they were moving backward. The Hansens persevered as did an anxious generation who responded to the call of chosen missionaries who were being scattered throughout the earth, seeking the lost sheep of Israel.

The next month hordes of grasshoppers descended on their fields once again, consuming every green thing. The people of Tooele, Salt Lake City, and the surrounding towns worked from sun up to sundown, beating the insect back, flushing them with water, or burning them, when possible. The summer of 1855 did not see a repeat of the miracle of the gulls.

Brigham called a series of councils to determine what could be done to help those wanting to come to Zion. Young's background and training were with the construction of windows, furniture, and wheels. He well understood the cost and feasibility of building wagons to cross the prairies and mountains of the West. The PEF had helped thousands from Britain and Scandinavia to emigrate to the Utah Territory. The one-two punch of the drought and the crickets hit the people in the territory hard in their pocketbooks. Young put out a plea for donations to help prop up the fund. Many people came forward, giving more than they were able. Brigham donated a $25000 home and land towards the effort. It looked like they would fall far short of their goals. This information needed to be passed along to the mission presidents, such as Franklin Richards, so they could give the disappointing news to their congregations, many of whom had waited years in line for the chance to emigrate.

Then Brigham Young came up with an idea surrounding what he called handcarts. Like wheelbarrows, the small wagons would be loaded with the necessary supplies, then instead of buying oxen or mules to pull them, they would use the strength of the emigrants themselves. They would push and pull their handcarts to Zion. It would cut costs immediately by a third. The President of the Church proposed his ideas to the councils. The specter of having emigrants caught on the plains or mountains by early snows could easily be avoided. Brigham wanted all handcart companies to leave the Missouri River by June 1, 1856. It would give them ample time to make the trek, even allowing for repairs and breakdowns.

A talented Irish member of the church quickly penned the inviting words describing how delightful the trek to the mountain valleys would be using the infinitely more economical handcarts.

> For some must push and some must pull
> As we go marching up the hill
> So merrily on our way we go
> Until we reach the Valley-O

****

FitzRoy Somerset, 1st Baron Raglan, had been the Field Marshal of the British Expeditionary forces, the first commander in chief of the British during the Crimean War. The short memories of the press and government had forgotten the victory on the Alma River and mauled him over the debacle at Balaklava. After Inkerman, Lord Raglan was made a full general. He was continually berated for the poor conditions and sufferings of the soldiers during the winter, owing to a shortage of food and clothing. This however was due in part to the home authorities who failed to provide adequate logistical support.

The siege of Sevastopol stagnated. Anemic charges and attacks were mounted, resulting in the slaughter of more men. Ground was not permanently captured. British warships bombarded the city back in October of 1854. Another series of sea-borne attacks were mounted by the British ships in April and then again on June 6th. Finally, the Allies decided to make a serious attack against the city on June 17th. Once again the warships steamed into the harbor and unleashed thousands of exploding shells against the defenders. At the same time, coordinated attacks were mounted by the British, French, Turks, and Sardinians. The Russians manfully absorbed the assaults, then repelled their enemies with ferocious counter-attacks, successfully throwing back the Allies. The Allies' piecemeal attack was another total failure.

It was more than the 67-year-old Lord FitzRoy Somerset could handle. The anxieties of the siege began to deleteriously undermine his health. He developed severe depression and contracted dysentery, then died unexpectedly on June 28th. His body was shipped back to England where he was interred at St. Michael and All Angels Church in Badminton.

He was replaced by General James Simpson, whose competence in the war theater was also criticized by his contemporaries.

Chapter 26

"The intent and not the deed is in our power; and therefore, who dares greatly, does greatly." John Brown

"It's Dr. Bernhisel if I'm not mistaken?"

The middle-aged politician stopped his steps to eye the man thus addressing him. They were both walking along the grass of the Washington DC mall. The summer afternoon was waning. A vibrant chorus of birds rose from the Potomac and the trees lining the mall.

He saw that the man addressing him was no threat. "You are correct sir. And who might you be?"

"I'm Aaron Rost. A merchant from Salt Lake City."

Bernhisel's brows furrowed for several seconds as the doctor waded through a series of memories. "Of course. I remember you. You are a friend of Shep Silva, the stockman."

"Yes, sir. He's from Brazil and living in Tooele. Out by Rush Valley."

"I remember the two of you being pointed out to me at Christmas."

"Exciting times, especially for Shep and Brother Wells."

The doctor chuckled. "I understand that Major Steptoe, has finally moved his people out of the territory and on to California. I also recall being told that he took a number of our women along with him."

"The city's better off, I reckon."

"And men are always looking for companionship." Dr. Bernhisel pointed in the direction he was heading and invited Rost to continue along with him. "So what brings you here, Mr. Rost? If my memory serves me correctly, you are working with lighting and heating oils."

Aaron was surprised by the doctor's memory. "This is a superb country with endless opportunities if the product is right."

"I can't agree with you more."

"I'm passing through the city, on my way back home. I had the pleasure of meeting Tom Kane in Philadelphia this time through. His wife is expecting a baby any day now."

"A great man, that Kane. One of our very best friends."

"I understand he is quite active in the cause of Zion."

"And to the discomfort of his sweet young wife," Bernhisel added. "I have never come across anyone better, Mr. Rost."

"Oh, you can call me Brother Rost."

"I understood Shep Silva isn't a Latter-day Saint. I thought that perhaps you had yet to join the church as well."

"I was baptized in Manti a couple years ago. Shep is just a dry dock Mormon. The time's coming if he keeps the same company."

"We should be so fortunate. So, Brother Rost, you are heading back home? What are your plans?"

"My business out this way is finishing up and I'm readying to head back to the territory and thought I'd check in with you to see if you might want a traveling companion? At least for part of the way?"

"What great fortune. As a matter of fact, yes, I am getting ready to leave soon. Congress is in recess. At the end of the week, I am taking a locomotive to Iowa City and will then continue overland. I will be traveling with a couple, also heading for the Great Salt Lake City. I am positive they would also welcome your company."

"Thank you so much, Dr. Bernhisel."

"Please call me John or Brother Bernhisel."

"Thank you, John. I will be pleased to travel with you to Iowa. From there I will need to make a detour down into the Kansas Territory. Until then it will be my pleasure. Who is this other couple?"

"Decent people, even though the judge is riding on the spoils system of the Democratic Party and President Pierce. He is the Honorable Judge William Drummond, a federally appointed officer who is looking forward to helping us out in the territory. I believe his wife's name is Ada. We can always use folks like them and the Kanes." Bernhisel took a deep breath. "I must say that I'll miss the scents of Washington and the humidity."

Aaron disagreed. "I think the heat gets oppressive when combined with the moisture. I do prefer the drier climate out west. Do you know if Almon Babbitt will be returning to the territory?"

"I'm not sure. Come by my office tomorrow and we can firm up our travel plans and we can also swing over to see Brother Babbitt and see what his plans are. He has been spending more and more time out here. I sometimes wonder if he even misses the territory or if he's using his address as an excuse to get appointed and move away." Bernhisel smiled but Aaron guessed there might be more to his statement than comedy.

"Anyway, come by tomorrow."

"You're too kind sir."

Three days later Aaron accompanied John Bernhisel to the railroad station.

"Brother Babbitt travels like a young man. He'll be leaving soon and perhaps even try and make it back before winter gets along."

The rail system was burgeoning. "This is simply amazing," Rost confessed. "Being able to travel so far and fast and without much effort. I understand Britain is becoming crisscrossed with the rail system."

"And where are you from, my boy? Your accent sounds European."

"Prussia."

"Of course. I wish we had legions of your countrymen here. Such diligent, hardworking people."

"Pennsylvania has plenty."

"Oh yes, the Pennsylvania Deutsch. I guess it's easier to call them Dutch, although that is quite the error. Yes indeed, folks there are a Godsend for this nation of ours."

"Judge Drummond is planning to meet us here?"

"Let's hop on board. I am sure the two of them will be along shortly."

The interior of the locomotive was uncluttered. The benches were simple. Some were padded. The windows allowed the passengers to watch the countryside as they moved but stayed shut to keep the soot out of the cars. Farmland, cities and towns, and unimproved stretches could be seen in a short time. And they were elevated, which also increased their vista.

"Here they are now," Bernhisel pointed to a couple entering their aisle, followed by a hulking black slave. Dr. Bernhisel waved to attract their attention.

Judge Drummond was a short, roly-poly man with long red hair. He smiled easily and often. Ada was quite the opposite. She had a disfigured hand and spoke with a slight lisp, but that's where the ordinary ceased. She was a stunning, full-buxom woman who wore the latest in clothing fashion. Her green eyes sparkled as she strolled with elegance and her hips swayed disconcertingly. The two Mormons averted their eyes. Drummond's slave was named Coffee Cato, because of the darkness of his skin, but was referred to as Cuffy.

"Dr. Bernhisel. And this must be Mr. Rost," Drummond said.

"My pleasure, sir."

The locomotive started, jerking roughly at first, but soon gained speed for the trip. Without saying a word, Cuffy walked to the back of the car and sat alone. Aaron found himself gazing out the window at the passing scenes. He watched as the wealth and variety of the country started unfolding before his eyes.

"I trust you haven't ridden the locomotive often," the judge said to him.

"This is really my first experience."

"I live in Illinois. The state is becoming well known for its rail system. It is so simple now to travel back and forth from Chicago to the Capital. It is almost mind-numbing. And the time will come, gentlemen, when we will be able to cross the entirety of this great country without trouble. The Indians, the buffalo, the snows, the troubles will be a thing of the past."

Drummond's positive statements were welcome. Some areas of the rails could be improved, especially the lack of smoothness when starting and stopping, but this remained a delight.

"I guess we'll see the comparisons as we change to our buggy in Iowa. But even then, the roads are much improved over the past five years, and riding in a light buggy is vastly superior to oxen pulling a Conestoga."

"Here, here," Dr. Bernhisel chimed.

"And you, Mrs. Drummond," Aaron said. "What are your ideas?"

"Give me a soft bed and a warm comforter. That's where I excel. I'm not worth much away from a bed." Ada cooed in a sultry voice, surprising Rost and Bernhisel. She winked at the men, who were desperately hoping that she was joking, while the judge grinned and nodded enthusiastically.

Another advantage of the locomotive was that it did not need to stop at night. It continued moving, eating up large sections of the country when dark. The railroad workmen stopped to replenish their water and coal but these were minimal. It was just as Drummond said. The 700 miles separating Chicago from Washington were covered in less than a day. Aaron had never seen so many scenery changes in such a short time. The dense greens of broad-leafed forests merged into plowed acreage. The overall verdant scenery was slowly replaced by a dark hue of brown.

In Chicago, they switched to the locomotive that would carry them to Iowa City, where the railroad tracks ended. From there it would be a comparatively short jaunt of 100 miles. Still, it would take them two days, to reach Des Moines. Rost was spending time recalling how long it had required to travel from the Salt Lake Valley, even when riding in a horse-drawn buggy. The blessings of modernity, living in the age of the locomotive.

"Will this be your first stay in the Utah Territory?" Rost asked the judge after they climbed into their buggy.

"Yes, sir. But I've had the pleasure of knowing quite a few Mormons, including Governor Young. That was clear back when they mostly lived in Illinois and I still lived in Kentucky. They have always treated me kindly. I am looking forward to spending time in a western city where most of the buildings are of stone and the first buildings seem to be schoolhouses. The Mormon people deserve great credit for their emphasis on education. The Utahns I know are among the best men and women. They are active in their work. They are among the most industrious. They are honest. And they want what's best not only for themselves but their communities as well."

Both Rost and Bernhisel smiled with satisfaction. Drummond could be a blow-hard. He spoke endlessly about his relationship with Stephen Douglas and his work for the Democratic Party. At least, for the moment, he was covering the important bases. Dr. Bernhisel was aware of Colonel Kane's impressions of the judge. And then there was the puzzle surrounding Ada. She seemed out of place with the judge and his political aspirations. Her interests lay more in the crowds, theaters, and larger cities. She enjoyed sophistication, fashion, and fine dining. Most of her life had been spent in Baltimore and Washington DC. The judge had recently acquired Cuffy in Virginia. The latter remained quiet during the trip.

The rails ended in Iowa City. They watched in amazement as the locomotive was changed around on the rail to begin its return east. Luggage was retrieved and the four made their way to a buggy they had rented near the station. Two porters assisted with the transfer of their belongings. The change was quick and simple and the four were soon sitting behind the driver and his guard, riding to the west. What they noticed immediately was how slow and bumpy the ride was when compared with the rail.

At night, the judge and Ada were discreet when retiring to their tent. She had remained quiet during the trip, smiling and nodding when she thought it proper. Cuffy slept on the ground outside the shelter. Aaron and John were thinking they had jumped the gun when judging the woman. She certainly was not the typical woman that folks would come across on the frontier.

Upon reaching Des Moines, Aaron was relieved that he had a reason to leave the company and head south. Dr. Bernhisel was sorry to see him leave but insisted that he visit when he reached Salt Lake City. The Drummonds were pleased to announce that Judge Kinney had extended an invitation for them to stay with him and his family until they decided where best to live.

The men shook hands as Aaron's coach left the station and headed south towards Kansas City. The other three paid for another buggy to take them on to the Missouri River. The driver and his guard were armed but did a good job keeping their weapons out of sight.

"I'll be back in the Great Salt Lake City before you know it," Rost said with a wave.

"Can't wait," Ada purred and batted her eyelashes. If the men heard her flirting, they pretended they hadn't.

Rost felt uncomfortable as his south-bound coach pulled away. He caught himself fantasizing over Ada's appearance as she disrobed. During their buggy trip, faint wisps of her perfume had wafted his way seductively through even the heaviest clouds of dust cast up by their buggy wheels. Rost had witnessed her ritual readying for the day. He knew that she kept a small bottle of perfume in her purse and placed drops of the scent on her neck and then down towards her exposed cleavage. Aaron Rost realized something was not right. He was relieved to be leaving the trio. During his adult life, he had resisted the siren call of the opposite sex. He wanted to be a man of character, not someone controlled by base instincts and desires.

This final leg of Rost's trip was 200 miles traveling directly south. There were times when he shared his bench with others but for most of the trip, he sat by himself. They passed several abandoned Indian villages, whose palisades had fallen to disrepair. Many of the posts that had once encircled happy, well-adjusted tribes of Indians, lay on the ground. Broad garden plots lay fallow. Clumps of weeds claimed the choicest plots of land. He learned that a number of the tribes from the area, the Pottawatomie, Sauk, and Fox, and their traditional enemies, the Osage, living farther south, had been decimated by new illnesses, slashing healthy populations and leaving bare vestiges in their wake. The dazed look on native faces spoke of uncertainty. Rost peered intently, trying to decide if he wasn't imagining their assumption into his apocalyptic paradigm. *Where were they to go? How would they live? Would their tribe remain intact? Would the government of the United States recognize them? Or would they be pushed aside and assigned to live the balance of their lives on worthless stretches of reservation land? Neighbors to unknown tribes with unknown languages?*

Kansas City sprang up overnight. Things had changed over the past year. From conversations on the street, he heard banter by pro-slavery men and then an equal amount of abolitionist jargon. Tripwires for violence were stretched across the beautiful plains.

Aaron hoped that he was doing the right thing. Getting involved with abolitionists was as dangerous as quicksand. But whenever he was around John Brown, he felt a magnetic draw coming from the man. His charisma penetrated beyond language. Brown was outspoken. Aaron knew the man would be a powerful influence, even in Prussia. This attraction not only infected Rost, but multitudes, including Brown's extensive family. They saw the Kansas Territory as the battleground over slavery. John Brown's sons moved to Kansas in the spring of 1855. They lost little time drawing the demarcation boundaries.

The year before, the US Congress passed the Kansas-Nebraska Act, which did away with the Missouri Compromise. The new act stated the territories would be governed by sovereign rule, the citizens would choose the direction of their territory, whether it be pro or anti-slavery. This opened up the land to a rush of settlers, as proponents on both sides flocked to the area. The resulting conflict created "Bleeding Kansas" because of the fighting that emerged.

Rost was treading on dangerous ground, buying and shipping rifles to the abolitionists in Kansas. The law was clear about the importation of weapons. But there were significant loopholes in the laws, allowing arms peddlers to proceed with clear consciences, although discretion was kept to a level of secrecy. Rost was won over by the arguments of John Brown. He agreed that slavery was a blight on the nation and needed to be excised. In the short time, he had spent in the United States, Aaron had witnessed a series of events that underscored the importance of the change.

There was a fine line between profiting from the sale of arms in the territory and the espousal of the abolitionist policies. The Prussian felt he was capable of walking the line successfully, perhaps helping his agenda in dealing arms for the Nauvoo Legion.

Rost showed up at the designated steamboat dock in Kansas City, flashed identifying documents, then was shown where his cases were stored. He had acquired a wagon with two mules to carry his supplies to Frederick Brown's place in Osawatomie, Kansas. On the outside of his crates were stenciled the words 'Beecher's Bibles'. It had worked before.

The customs agent scarcely looked up from his newspaper.

"Beecher's Bibles? For the savages, no doubt."

"I understand there is a revival planned. Lots of Bibles going out to help."

"If they can even read."

Aaron didn't care for the man's demeanor. "God will provide."

"Amen to that." The bill of lading was signed and Aaron headed out of town.

The rolling plains of the territory were promising to the new generation of settlers. The black soil was rich. Wheat and stocks of corn were growing in abundance along the road, thriving in the summer heat. Aaron found the time alone in the wagon valuable in his planning. He found himself putting his different accounts into mental boxes. The kerosene oil was arriving at the docks in New York and Baltimore. He hired some motivated agents to start receiving and storing the products. There were also American and Canadian entrepreneurs with deep pockets who were ready to get involved in the business. Rost's savings were depleted but he was confident they would rebound once the sales began in earnest.

The most dangerous, and most lucrative, of his endeavors was the peddling of the Sharp's carbines. The numbers remained low but provided the cash he needed to continue with his other projects. Abolitionist money from New England was plentiful. And so was the need for arms in the territory. The carbine was an easy sale. Its capabilities were demonstrated and understood. The Beecher's Bibles could be the tipping point abolitionist forces needed.

"I see you made it all right," Frederick Brown said. He had seen the wagon approaching on the road leading to his farm and had ridden out to meet him. "No problems, then?"

"Things are good. Your pa around yet?"

"Nope. I expect him in the next week or so. I told my brothers and they're excited about the shipment. They're up at the house."

A handful of men exited the house as Frederick and Aaron rode up closer. Rost could see similarities in the young men's features and that of their sire. Hard-working men had come with a fire in their hearts to do their part to abolish slavery from the nation. Kansas was a proving ground. Others in the area shared their feelings. But just across the border, in Missouri, a generation of slave owners resisted their influence. They wanted to expand their mode of farming and industry. They saw slavery as a necessary evil but one that would be tolerated for the foreseeable future. They did not like others, especially Yankees, dictating how to use their Constitutionally guaranteed rights to life and liberty.

Frederick dismounted while Aaron dragged the first heavy crate to the back of the wagon.

"Let's open them up," the youngest Brown named Salmon said excitedly.

"Hold up there," John Jr. said soberly. "We agreed not to do anything without prayer."

All remembered and removed their hats, while John Jr. started his heavenly petition. Aaron was struck by how devout these men were. They were not the typical religious fanatics he had encountered before. These men were simple, straight talkers, who let their actions speak for them.

The invocation ended and the men converged on the wagon. Aaron retrieved a bar and pried a crate open. The oily smell of metal preceded the vision of the weapons. The shiny carbines were lined up neatly, six in each crate. There were also two chests containing pre-formed bullets, gun powder, and the paper cartridges that would be used.

"Would ya looky there."

"We owe you anything for these?" Frederick asked.

"Your pa already took care of that," Rost answered.

Salmon removed one of the rifles and turned it over and over, looking at the dropping lever and the breech block while his brothers watched reverently. He then looked at Rost curiously. "You a Jew?"

"Shut your filthy mouth!" Owen snapped.

"Don't mean nothing by it," Salmon tried to explain. "Just that he talks like a foreigner. From Germany or someplace and pa said there are lots of Jews in Germany."

Rost waved off any concerns and smiled. "Matter of fact, that's what I was born. I just became a Mormon a couple years ago."

"Holy God!" one of the men exclaimed. "We're getting guns from a damned Mormon?"

"Now hold on, boys. We don't know nothing about nothing here." Frederick's words were true and were greeted with nods. "Lots of good folks could be Mormons. God knows they've got their problems with the government."

"Amen to that."

The Browns slowly began removing the weapons carefully from the crates. Thirty-six in total. "These will go a long way to scaring off the bushwhackers," Frederick commented pensively.

"Bushwhackers?" Rost asked.

Frederick shrugged. "It's what we called the pro-slavery boys, especially those from Missouri. Always stirring up trouble."

"So what does that make you?"

"They call us Jayhawkers. Don't make much difference. Folks just want to live their lives the way they see right. The problem we're facing is that we don't have a lot of people. Numbers is important. The majority wins."

Owen held up one of the rifles and smiled. "These should help our numbers quite a bit."

The crates were pulled from the wagon and two men each carried one into the house. They had seen or used a Sharp's carbine but Frederick insisted that Aaron spend time instructing them about the basics of the short rifle.

"So, the whole family's here in Kansas?"

"Well, like I said, Pa is coming for a visit. Our brother Watson is still in Pennsylvania. He might be coming later. Don't rightly know. Ma and the girls are probably staying put there in Pennsylvania. At least for now."

The next hour was spent in basic instruction. The men lined up and took turns shooting at targets. All were impressed with the accuracy and the range.

"So you're the Jayhawkers?"

"Don't really like that name," Frederick said. "We're just getting a number of us together in the next week or so and calling ourselves the Pottawatomie Rifles."

"Impressive."

"We getting more of these?"

202

"Not till next year but probably by springtime."

"Can't come too soon," Frederick added ominously.

Dr. Bernhisel and the Drummonds arrived in Salt Lake City at the end of July. It had been a long journey but they paced themselves enough not to be worn out. Bernhisel had half-heartedly offered Judge Drummond refuge in his home but Drummond followed through, accepting an offer from the Utah Territory Chief Supreme Court Justice, the Honorable John Fitch Kinney, another appointee of President Pierce.

John Bernhisel was tired and ready to relax for several months. It was good to be seen as an asset for the territory. It gave him a feeling of validation. He sent a message to Brigham Young, letting him know that he was back in town with the Drummonds and to find a time when he could bring Governor Young up to speed on the happenings in Washington.

The Honorable Judge John Kinney looked forward to having new roommates from the States, people with similar political backgrounds and ideals. He crafted a list of questions for the couple. Kinney was from Iowa, across the Mississippi from Illinois. The news would be interesting to him and his wife, Hannah.

The appearance of the Drummonds was not what he had hoped for. Their laughter was too quick and profane. Hannah was immediately put off and chose to stay as far away from the couple as possible. Judge Drummond insisted that Kinney refer to him as Bill. He claimed to be from a small town on the Mississippi called Oquawka, 12 miles northeast of Burlington. Originally he claimed to hail from Kentucky. It wasn't long before he was wearing out his guest with stories from Stephen Douglas, the Little Giant. The presence of Cuffy also concerned the Kinneys, who were staunch abolitionists, but the manservant of the Drummonds quietly took up residence in one of their outbuildings.

The disparity in ages and backgrounds of Ada and Bill told the Kinneys that the Drummonds had not been married long.

"Oh, no. I divorced my first wife. She was a shrew named Jemima. I have the papers to prove my marriage to Ada."

The remarks did little to convince the Kinneys. Hannah did not approve of Drummond's referring to his ex-wife as a shrew. Hannah began plotting a way to rid themselves of their guests, who were settling down for what she saw could be an extended stay.

The Drummonds flitted about the city, introducing themselves to Brigham Young and the town fathers. It felt good to stretch their legs. It was also a clever thing to meet the movers and shakers. A few days after walking around the city, taking in the sights and theater productions, Bill Drummond asked Judge Kinney for a private audience.

"How may I be of assistance?" Kinney asked his peer, after pouring them both a glass of whiskey.

Drummond paced in mock seriousness, then suddenly took a chair opposite his host's desk. "These Mormons are a gaggle of fools. How do you put up with them?" He didn't wait to hear from his surprised associate. "They are self-righteous prudes. Everyone kowtows to Brigham Young. Well, I'm here with strict orders from President Pierce. The hammer will strike the anvil. The president wants another hearing for the murderers of Gunnison. You did the best you could. What could you expect when Governor Young is dictating to the jury? The Mormons are too soft on the Indians. I've been sent here to shake things up. Now, can I expect your help?"

Kinney was taken aback. He assumed Drummond was waiting to get his own opinions of the people and especially Brigham Young. It had not taken long. Kinney suspected that Drummond had arrived with his preconceived ideas. Then again, Kinney was no ally of Young's. If cards were played correctly, something of value might be forthcoming with the arrival of the upstart judge. He wasn't sure what it might be but it would be worth his time not to burn any bridges. Not just yet.

"I will give you whatever assistance you might require," Kinney replied.

A travel-weary Aaron Rost arrived in Salt Lake City a week after the Drummonds and Dr. John Bernhisel. He was carrying a single crate in his buggy

Chapter 27

"The two most powerful warriors are patience and time." Leo Tolstoy

When Silva and Rockwell and the rest of Steptoe's company arrived in Genoa, Judge Orson Hyde was gone. Folks thought he had gone overland to Salt Lake City, but they expected him back soon. Being so close to their destination, Major Steptoe released his two scouts.

"I wish you were both in my permanent command," he told them as they shook hands. Steptoe had his soldiers set up their encampment where they would stay for five days before going over to California.

It felt like Silva was out from under a huge weight as he and Rockwell turned their horses up the mountain, heading for the south end of Lake Bigler. Being away from the column gave them the time they could once again speak of more personal matters.

"That is a beautiful lake," Shep noted, as they skirted its southern end and started picking their way across the rocky slopes to the west.

"Yep. Big and beautiful and I think it's deep. Not a shallow pond or salty like most in the Basin." The higher they climbed, the better the view.

"Plenty of trees."

"A piss poor bowl to get caught in if there was a fire." Porter turned back from his gazing. "You in a big hurry to get back to Tooele?"

"Not so much. Being here in California, I thought about going to see Brannan in the city. You?"

"About the same. I have some business just north of Sacramento. We can split up there. After a couple days I'll head for Brannan's. Just let him know where I can find you."

"Sounds good to me."

"I have a sister who lives with her family not far south of the city. You can go with me to see her before we head back. All right?"

They spent that night in Placerville and reached Sacramento the next day. The weather was clear and dry, helping them gain considerable time in their riding. After Porter headed off to handle his business, which sounded private, and the reason Shep had no qualms splitting up, the Brazilian reached San Francisco two days later.

"Shep Silva! You ornery bastard! How the hell have you been?" Sam Brannan was in rare form and his surprise and excitement seemed real.

"It's been a while," Shep said.

"What brings you this way? I thought you were going to be camped out in San Bernardino for a while yet."

"I moved up close to the Great Salt Lake City."

"Did you get baptized?"

"Not quite."

"Better be careful. Brigham will have you wrapped up before you know it."

"Don't I know it. He had me escort a military group over to Genoa. I think they'll be setting things up around Alcatraz before long."

Brannan sighed. "Like we need a bunch more soldiers."

"I'll be in the city for a while. I want to check the synagogue again. Think I can bunk down at your hotel for a night or two? I'm paying."

"No problem. We can work things out. Is it just you or are you with somebody?"

"I'm traveling with the marshal of the Utah Territory."

The announcement wiped the smile from Brannan's face. He became quite serious. "Rockwell. He's here with you?"

"He said he had business north of Sacramento. We'll meet up in a day or two."

"Oh, God. Hope we're not going to be jumping through more hoops."

"What you mean? You know what he's up to?"

"Boggs. Governor Boggs lives up there by Petaluma. I hope Port's not out on a hunting trip."

Life was going well for Lilburn Boggs. Moving to California was positive. He didn't make a fortune in the goldfields but he worked carefully and managed to accrue a substantial bank account. Politics were going well, keeping him busy, well-informed, and connected. The state capital was hopping and skipping about the countryside, trying to find a permanent location. The uncertainty about some things kept him in a more solid position. He was tightly bound to Mariano Vallejo and his wife Benicia. He and his second wife named their most recent child Mariano Guadalupe Vallejo Boggs, a move the Vallejos did not miss. Boggs' comfortable home was close to the former alcalde's *rancho*. Boggs patted himself on the back. Being the postmaster kept him and his family securely employed. It also let him know of people's comings and goings.

As he walked towards his house, Lilburn watched the effortless sailing of a flock of California gulls. So beautiful. On the sea or in the air. They withstood hurricane-force winds, appearing to relish the speed. On hot summer days like this, when the air was calm, the birds flapped their wings lazily, covering huge tracts of land with ease. They could be found on the beach or in the ocean, miles from shore. They even drifted inland. He heard some lived well in the Great Salt Lake.

Boggs stopped. He remembered hearing how the gulls had saved the Mormon settlers in 1848. *Was it a fluke or did Providence send them? Oh, God. Am I never going to be rid of this infestation? The Mormons blame all the ills they experienced in Missouri and Illinois on me when they were the instigators.*

The first of May 1842, years after the Mormons had been expelled from Missouri, an assassin had come to Independence and shot him while he was in his home, in his study, where he should have been safe. *It could have been one of my slaves. My own pistol was used and one of the boys ran away that day. Or could it have been Porter Rockell? He was seen in the area at the same time.* Porter quarreled with the ex-governor, blaming him for the Mormons' misfortune. He was Joseph Smith's friend. Some even referred to him as the Destroying Angel. Years later, Rockwell had followed Brigham Young to the valleys of the Great Basin. Brigham appointed Rockwell the territorial marshal. The newspapers were rife with stories of the lawman. No one had yet been able to kill him, although numbers had tried.

He stepped onto his porch and reached for the front door, when he caught a quick movement from the side of his eye, A thick burlap bag smelling like aged potatoes was thrown over his head, enveloping him in total darkness. At the same time, something hard smashed into his skull, dazing him. He dropped to the ground. A rope was tightened around his neck and the bag, then he was dragged roughly from the porch, across a drying garden that crunched at the passing, and slammed into a fence post.

A sinister voice whispered into his ear, "Just a reminder that you are not out of reach." The hissing was accompanied by a tightening of the rope around his throat, causing Boggs to gag and then cough.

The next thing Boggs knew, he was free from his assailant, lying in the dirt. He turned slowly and loosened the rope around his neck, then carefully pulled the bag off his head. The light of day made him squint as he slowly scanned the grounds nearby. No one was visible. Grunting, Boggs stood on shaky feet, then began shuffling back towards his house.

****

The two men rode their horses south along the ridge of the peninsula where San Francisco was built. They took turns looking to their right and the Pacific Ocean, while to the left lay the bay. They were quiet, riding in single file, both wrapped in their thoughts. Toward the end of the day, they dropped down into the valley and spent the night in San Jose.

"Everything all right?" Shep asked as they waited to place their horses into a waiting barn.

"Right as rain," Porter responded.

"Your business affairs good?"

"Yep."

That was all for the night. The next day Porter was far more animated.

"Brannan seems to be doing well."

"Seems to always land on his feet. The area is growing fast and he stays busy just trying to keep up."

Porter thought back. "He tried getting Brig to bring the Saints out this way clear back in '47. It might have done us some good. Or not. I think the Brig was right. Life in the desert has strengthened us. Growing crops and working with each other. Even the Indians have been a blessing."

"Steptoe thinks the Pahvants got off easy."

"Course he does. He doesn't know anything about these poor souls. They are being kicked out of every home they've known. A lot like us." Porter's point of view was a common one among members of the church.

Silva thought for a while. "Brannan was worried about you and his friend Lilburn Boggs."

"That so?"

"He says you have a history. He was worrying you might be hunting him."

"Lilburn's a sonofabitch, Shep. He caused our people plenty of trouble. The best thing he did was to leave Missouri. At least now he isn't butting up directly against us. Maybe it'll give him a better view of life. He can go to hell for all I care. I'm better off being rid of him."

"So your business didn't have anything to do with him?"

Porter stopped and looked Shep in the eye. "Now, what the hell do you think?"

Silva shrugged. "Don't make no never mind to me."

"You're sounding less and less like a Brazilian."

Shep was suddenly grateful for his horse, keeping him from walking such distances, going up and down the hills.

"Your sister came straight to California after Illinois?"

"More or less. Sam and Electa settled first in Placerville. They liked it but there was better land prices around here so they moved this way a couple years ago."

"They like it?"

Porter nodded. "A lot. They're probably the only folks in miles who speak English but they enjoy their neighbors. They have bought a bunch of land and put cattle on to graze. They've also been raising crops. Things grow here all year round. And there's good markets up in the city and Sacramento. They tell me they're doing well."

"Lots of kids?"

"Enough. The kids save them because they put them to work. They have about six or seven. I forget. They're hard workers. They're following their folks' example."

"Boys?"

"Mostly girls. They had a boy who died ten years ago or so. Since then they have John. He's about ten and some twins who are seven. Bryant and Porter. Guess who's my favorite?"

It was nice hearing Porter talk about his sister. He was usually quiet about his family.

"You miss your baby girl?"

"I've never been much of a father. But, yeah. God sees to it that I stay busy. I don't know that it'll be fine when judgment comes and I see God and he interviews me to see how I've used my days here on earth. I'm hoping that loyalty and hard work will work in my favor. I'm afraid it might not. I think Jesus will be more concerned with how I treat folks, especially my own kin. Keeping the law, enforcing the law is important. That's what I keep telling myself. But going to see my sister and her family, that is important too. I appreciate you going along with me. It's something I should have done way back."

"Electa and Sam are expecting us?"

"One of the things I did in Sacramento was drop them a post telling them our plans to drop in."

The seven-year-old twins, Porter and Bryant. were the first to spy the two riders. The barefoot boys with their worn overalls raced down the dirt road, jumping and yelling a series of yipees. Electa and four of her girls stepped out onto the porch and waved happily. Uncle Port had come a long distance. This was a treat.

"God love you, Port," Electa cried as he stepped from his horse and lifted her in an affectionate hug. "You look so good. The sun makes you look so healthy."

Porter beamed as the three boys attached themselves to his legs. "This here is Shep Silva. He's a good friend and has come clear out this way just to see you."

"Oh, Mr. Silva," Electa twittered with embarrassment and a smile. "You are welcome here."

"My pleasure, ma'am."

Porter dusted off his horse and saddle while looking around the homestead. "Sam's not home?"

Electa shook her head. "I expect him soon enough. He's been over helping Captain Angney set things up around his place."

"Good neighbor?"

"Pretty new, but yes, very good neighbors. Sam gets along well with them all."

"And you?"

Electa nodded once more, then blew air out of her lips that lifted a strand of hair hanging on her forehead. "Me too. I like them all, but right now I'm feeling tired. Some sick." She noticed Shep's sudden look of concern. "I'm expecting a baby," she explained quickly, lessening the Brazilian's worries.

John squeezed his uncle's leg. "Marshal Porter, you know my pa's a marshal too?"

Rockwell chuckled and patted the boy's hair. "I know that's Sam's middle name. Is that what you meant?"

That was exactly what he meant and he continued holding Porter's leg.

Shep dismounted and took the reins of both horses, then looked at the girls for directions. Two of them instantly skipped from the porch, braided pigtails bouncing in the afternoon sun. "Water's around here and we have some fodder in the barn." The change from riding was what he needed and stretched.

"You talk kinda funny," eleven-year-old Emma noted.

"Emma!" Caroline snapped.

"Well, he does," she insisted.

"That's what I've been told. I'm from another country away south of the United States of America."

"So, you're a foreigner? Do you like our country?" Emma continued.

"I do, Miss Emma. The best part of your country is the folks. Just like you. You make me want to stay."

"Away from your country?"

"My country is named Brazil. It's big, like America. And beautiful. But for right now I think God has brought me here. Mostly to meet you two lovely girls. Am I wrong?"

"Nope."

"Oh, Emma," Caroline said with exasperation.

After letting the horses drink, Shep removed their saddles and put them into their stalls for the evening. "We can turn them out to pasture in the morning," Caroline said.

"Where's your big sister?"

Caroline was surprised to be asked. "Oh, Sarah? She's playing with some of her friends who have come to visit. Clear from the south."

Emma chimed in with a knowing nod. "Their ma's here and sick."

Shep knocked some of the dust from his hat and shirt, then walked with the girls back to their house. He noticed a buggy parked out back and pointed to it.

"That's our visitors'," Emma answered.

The house had been started as a typical cabin but the active family had quickly added a handful of rooms. Sam was also putting in an attic. It all felt quite comfortable and lived in. Porter stepped from behind a door to the parent's bedroom. His face was serious.

"Sick visitor," he said, nodding his head back into the room. "Probably typhoid fever."

Shep glanced over at Electa. "She gonna be all right?"

"She will now. We'll have Porter and Sam give her a blessing when he gets back. Unless you hold the Priesthood too?"

"Sorry, ma'am. I haven't been baptized yet." By adding the word 'yet' both Caroline and Emma smiled contentedly.

"Shep Silva!"

Shep looked immediately to the doorway where Ina and Charlotte Coolbrith stood, with their mouths open in surprise.

Agnes Pickett had brought her two daughters with her to see her longtime friend Electa Ousley. The climate in Central California was perfect, causing the mother and her daughters to share their ideas about moving there. There wouldn't be the large swings in temperature they experienced in San Bernardino or Los Angeles. As pleasant as the idea sounded, Ina didn't think it would work for her.

"It's not Los Angeles," she said. "San Bernardino is far enough away from the *Star* that I barely get my things published as they are."

"But Sarah's here," Charlotte countered.

"Of course, because she's your friend. I would have to learn Spanish to find friends."

In the end, they decided they might bring it up with Bill. His work was what would be the most important. Right now, cattle and farming were the big draws for the area.

It was while they were traveling through the idyllic countryside that Agnes began developing a fever. By the time they reached the Ousleys', Agnes was quite sick. Electa and her daughters waited on her day and night. It was just as she was beginning to feel better when Porter and Shep arrived.

When Sam Ousley got home that evening, he was ready to join his brother-in-law, giving Agnes a priesthood blessing. The woman had been around enough Mormons to know about the ordinance.

"It can't hurt," Ina implored.

Fumbling nervously with a spoon of olive oil, Rockwell did his best to anoint Agnes' head. Laying his hands on her head, Porter could feel the warmth generated by the fever. He knew she was frail. He tried mightily to join what faith he had in the Savior with that of Sam's, as the man humbly petitioned God to open a conduit from heaven to bless his wife's friend.

After finishing the ordinance, the visitors filed quietly from the room to let Agnes snuggle under the comforter to get her rest.

"Well?" Porter asked Sam.

"I guess we'll see. I felt pretty good about it. You?"

Porter smiled weakly and looked at Shep and shrugged. "I guess." He looked down at his hands and saw a disturbing clump of Agnes' hair between his fingers. "Sam, you got a good nag I can take over to Monterey for a couple days? I got some business that needs tending."

"Sure."

Sam dragged Shep with him the next day to the *rancho* of Captain William Z. Angney where they spent the day splitting rails and building fences. It was hard work. The Captain preferred to be called W. Z. Angney was a proper host and plied them with lemonade and stories of the Mexican American War. He had studied law but for the present, he had a substantial herd of sheep. Both men showed an intense interest in Shep's memories of Brazil and the Sandwich Islands.

Charlotte and Sarah spent their time together as young women discussing potential suitors. Silva spent his evenings visiting with Ina. She was an encyclopedia of memories about the activities of San Bernardino, especially the Wetoyous. He felt tugs on his heartstrings, wanting to thank Deity for the happiness and well-being of those he considered his family. Ina also chatted on and on about Joseph F's escapades in the islands. She claimed he was over any feelings of homesickness and was delving deeply into the labor.

"Think he'll even want to return home in a couple years?"

Ina flashed him a coy smile. *Could there be more to this relationship?* He had pondered it several times. She certainly was growing into an enchanting young woman, very talented and charming. She enjoyed a connection to Joseph F that was undeniable.

A haggard Porter Rockwell rode up to the Ousley house on the third day. Shep was secretly happy, believing his friend's appearance meant their extended visit with the Ousley's was coming to an end. And he had seen a rather miraculous turn around in Agnes. She began leaving the bed more often, quizzing him about his activities. Shep was also aware of the large tufts of hair that were now falling from her head. It embarrassed her, so he pretended not to notice, trying to keep her head covered.

Rockwell was relieved to find Agnes feeling better. Visiting was so much better when health wasn't an issue. Asking if he could visit with Agnes in private, they entered the bedroom, with Porter carrying his saddlebag.

Curious. Shep stopped his talking, trying to overhear what might be said. The door muffled the low tones, but then he heard a sweet cry come from Agnes. Silva started wondering again about the relationship all these people shared.

Porter appeared at the door minutes later. It was obvious he had been crying, not something the marshal was often accused of.

Dinner was a quiet affair. The girls helped Electa set a wonderful spread. Porter announced after the meal that he and Shep would be leaving for their homes in the Utah Territory the following morning. Silva was surprised. He was also ready. The family attempted to talk them into staying, while the boys climbed onto their Uncle Porter's hat and shoulders. It was the first time Shep noticed the lawman wearing his hat at the dinner table. Little Porter grabbed his uncle's hat and stuck it on his crown.

And that was when all saw the change. Porter Rockwell was bald! The luxuriant locks, the braids he was so careful with, were gone.

"Where'd your hair go?" John hollered, wide-eyed in amazement.

The lawman shuffled uncomfortably.

"May I join you?"

The family turned to see the delicate Agnes standing at the doorway to her room. The tragically balding woman stood smiling, then gracefully floated to the table, wearing on her head a beautifully woven wig, compliments of her dear friend, Porter Rockwell.

Goodbyes were sweet the next morning, but not overextended. They knew that time and distance weren't in their favor of ever seeing one another again. Not in this lifetime. Shep didn't say much until they had been on the road for several hours.

"That was a nice gesture, Port. You have changed Agnes' life with your gift. The folks did a wonderful job with the wig. I noticed you have some knots and lumps on your head that can now be seen quite easily. And what about all that stuff you told me about Joseph Smith and Samson? On his very last Christmas Day, no less?"

Porter shrugged. "I think I'm already feeling its damned effects."

"How's that?"

"All I want to do now is cuss and go to a bar and get drunk!"

The announcement made Shep laugh harder than he had for a long time.

"You've known Agnes before?"

"For years."

"Still, that was quite the gift even if you've known her for your whole life."

Porter turned again and eyed Shep. "You don't even know the story, do you?"

Shep didn't but he was suddenly aware that he was about to learn some very important details to fill in the gaps.

"Agnes Pickett and Electa have been friends, seems like forever. But before she married Bill, she lived in Nauvoo and was married to Don Carlos Smith, Joseph Smith's little brother. Don Carlos died from consumption in 1841. Agnes later married Pickett. Both knew quite a bit about the violence that followed us around. They decided to stay away from the church. They even made the girls promise they would never tell folks about their connection to the church and especially the Prophet."

The news left Shep stunned. He tried to make sense of it. "Agnes was married to Joseph Smith's little brother? Don Carlos?"

Porter nodded.

"That means the girls are Joseph's nieces?"

"Yep."

"That's why Joseph F is so close to them and all the tense times I felt in San Bernardino. They're cousins?"

"Yep."

"So Ina's not secretly in love with Joseph F?"

"Hardly."

"So you didn't cut off your hair and make it into a wig and give it to Agnes just because she's a friend?"

Porter reined his horse back around. "Joseph was the best friend I've ever known. There's nothing I wouldn't do for his family. Agnes is his sister-in-law, whether she wants to remember it or not. It's the least I could do. If it means a lot to her, it means even more to me. If I have broken the Nazarite covenant that the Prophet spoke of, so be it, long as Agnes feels happy."

Shep shook his head. "Charlotte and Ina are Joseph's nieces."

Porter smiled. "Ina's real name, her full name, is Josephina Donna Smith."

The next couple of days, as they rode out of California's fertile valleys and into the Sierras, Shep caught himself staring at Porter's back. It was true. There were so many stories, relationships, things he had never considered. All these things were floating around him and he wasn't even aware of them. He thought back to some salient verses W.Z. had quoted him days earlier. They pertained to this intriguing man, his friend Porter Rockwell.

"We die not all, for our deeds remain

213

To crown with honor or mar with stain.
Through endless sequence of years to come,
Our lives shall speak, though our lips are dumb."

Chapter 28

"Let us seek for wisdom instead of power and we will have all the power we have wisdom to exercise." Eliza R. Snow

Dear Ina,

I am so proud of you. You are contributing to the conversation of the whole population of California, writing your poems, making folks feel happy, and thinking about beauty and love.

How are the twins? You said they were starting to shoot guns and like to go hunting. San Bernardino sounds like a real good place for them. Do they want to hunt rabbits or birds? Do they only want to go after the bigger animals? Do they like to fish? Maybe they could spend some time on the Santa Ana River or even go into the ocean. Folks around here fish a lot. For some of them that's about all they do and they do it quite well. I have started eating lots of fish. I really like most of it. I still have a hard time trying to eat octopus. Who knows but maybe I'll love eating it by the time I come home?

I hope you enjoy your trip to see Sam and Electa. Please give them my best and the kids too. I'm not expecting another letter from you soon because of your travels. When you get back home, write and tell me all the news.

Please remember me and write when you can.

All my love,
Joseph

Almost the end of September 1855

Dear Joseph,

I was happy and surprised to find your letter awaiting me when I got home. As always, I was pleased to hear from you. You sound so much better

The twins are still trouble. They do not stay around our house very much. As soon as Pa leaves they think they are free to roam the fields and hills. Yes, they love to hunt, mostly the little animals, so far. Pa is still spending a lot of time in Los Angeles but he promises to start taking them fishing. About all Pa knows about fishing is with catfish. It hurts me when they bring their trophies home. I ache for the animal families that are left destitute simply because of their want to destroy. I would state that they are just boys, but I do not remember you talking about such endeavors.

As soon as I read your epistle I began speaking with everyone. You are still remembered fondly here in San Bernardino. Everyone, including my family, knows that you are engaged in a man's work.

There seems to be trouble brewing here in the city (yes, I said city, because it continues to grow larger and larger). It is no longer the Mormon Mecca that you found several years ago. That would make plenty of folks in these parts quite happy. They appreciate being out from under the thumb of Brigham Young. I have heard some members of the church refer to the city as now being halfway between Carthage and Warsaw, Illinois.

I will tell you that Charlotte and Ma and I went to see Sam and Electa Ousley up in Santa Clara County. We had a delightful visit. Charlotte and Sarah still get along famously. We had a terrible dilemma when Ma caught typhoid just as we arrived. She was given good care and is now all on the mend. A bad thing happened, however. She began losing her beautiful hair. Then guess who came to visit? Electa's brother, OP Rockwell and he brought with him Shep Silva. It was a blessing to have them arrive at the right moment. Then Marshal Rockwell rode into Monterey and had his hair cut off and made into a wig for Ma. It is beautiful. The hair is thick and pleasing. Ma feels like it's her own hair.

Shep Silva looks fine. I think he was tired of the very long journey he has been on. I believe he will be happy to return to his home in the Utah Territory. He asked about you and is happy we are writing.

I understand the war in Crimea might be coming to a close. Oh that it were so. It seems to have engulfed the whole world. I leave you with a short stanza to contemplate.

Yet we sing of the splendor of battle,
"The pomp and glory of war!"
Oh, God could those battlefields open,
And show what their trophies are.
Be careful and be safe and write again to me, soon.

Love,
Ina

Chapter 29

"Truth, like gold, is to be obtained not by its growth, but by washing away from it all that isn't gold." Leo Tolstoy

Count Lev Nikolayevich Tolstoy, known by most as Leo, was born September 9, 1828, in Yasnaya Polyana. Now he was a young lieutenant in the Russian Army, stationed in Sevastopol. He had left his post in the Caucus region, fighting against the Ottoman Turks, to serve against the Allies in Crimea. He arrived after the initial battles of Alma, Balaklava, and Inkerman. He spent months in the trenches, participating in the ebb and flow of the siege. He saw the horrid results of battle up close and personal. He dealt with the depressing logistics of the war, clearing away the dead, putrefying refuse while attempting to acquire enough food to feed the city's decimated population.

Tsar Alexander II was growing impatient with the siege. Russia claimed a huge standing army, but as the rest of civilization was witnessing, sheer numbers did not translate into victory. The Sick Old Man of Turkey was being propped up by the perky British and the prickly French. The staunch Sardinians had thrown their weight behind the Allies. The Tsar was worried about facing an army that had received reinforcements. He fired off a letter to his general, commanding that they attack the Allies. The French and the Sardinians were camped along the Chernaya River running close by Sevastopol. The French were observing the Feast Day of the Emperor, while on the same day, the Sardinians were relaxed, commemorating their festival, Assumption Day. The Russians felt their attack should come on the heels of these holidays. They hoped to catch the Allies unprepared.

Prince Michael Gorchakov, the Russian general, ordered the attack to begin early in the morning of August 16th on the shores of the Black River, named Chernaya in Slavic. The Russians enjoyed a dominant number of 58,000 against 28,000 French and Sardinians. Unfortunately, because of the length and severity of the siege, the Russian forces were composed of militia and serfs.

General Gorchakov gave explicit orders to his two commanders, Generals Liprandi and Read, not to cross the river until they received specific orders. Under cover of the early morning fog, the Russians moved towards their enemy. Russian cannons had been positioned on the opposing hills, across the Chernaya and the Russian forces began crossing the river. But as happens so frequently in life and death situations, a miscommunication caused an early start. Prince Gorchakov was anxious that the preparations for the battle be deployed and move into place. He sent the order, "Let's start it." Both Read and Liprandi interpreted his order to mean they should begin the attack, even though reserve forces were still en route.

Russian forces charged against the French on the left and Sardinians on the right. The overwhelming numbers of the Russians pushed the French back up the hill. The Sardinian 16 pounder cannons, although difficult to move, were devastating once they were situated. And they were set when they began blasting the Russian flanks with deadly accuracy. The French countered by driving the Russians back down toward the river.

The Sardinians manfully withstood the right side of the Russian attack, led by General Read. When they were repulsed and driven downhill and General Read was killed, General Gorchakov took over the command. He attempted another anemic charge and feint but lost momentum. He ordered the retreat of his forces. It was a terrible day for General Gorchakov and Tsar Alexander II and the Russian Army and the city of Sevastopol.

And it was a terrible defeat for Lev Tolstoy. He had charged valiantly, again and again, trying to rally his men. His bravery on the field was noted by many. Finally, he was forced to retreat, to fall back, to return to his lines. Seeing so many of his comrades killed and wounded and then left to rot or be taken as prisoners, turned his stomach. It heightened his awareness of the social inequality that pervaded his country.

The Battle of Chernaya was a Russian loss. 5,000 Russians were either killed, wounded, or taken prisoner. The Allies lost 1,500.

In Crimea the battles were short-lived. The Battle of Chernaya was over by 10:00 a.m., despite the foggy morning mists, the surprise rush, and the counter-attacks. The correspondents were impressed by the strength and bravery, especially of the Sardinians. One of the men wrote: "Bravery in the soldiers and mediocrity in the generals are the chief characteristics, on both sides, of the present war."

The day after the engagement, British warships bombarded Sevastopol, destroying whatever targets held value. It was the fifth major sea attack during the 11-month siege. The ships returned two weeks later and for the sixth and final time, they pounded the suffering city and its inhabitants

The frustrated Lt. Leo Tolstoy wrote the only poetic verses of his career, detailing the debacle of the battle at Chernaya. After its publishing, it became a drinking hymn of the Russians, deploring their leadership.

> *The toppest brass*
> *Sat down to meet*
> *And pondered long;*
> *Topographers*
> *Lined paper black*
> *But all forgot*
> *The deep ravine*
> *They had to cross!*

On Saturday, September 8, 1855, French forces assaulted the fort of Malakoff, the Little Redan, and the Bastion du Mat, very important defenses inside the French sphere of influence. Ferocious fighting followed the attacks and counterattacks. Cannons were used by both sides with terrible consequences. The French were finally able to drive back the Russian forces and maintain the strategic locations. It was a time of jubilation. The French made strategic gains in Russia's defenses. The Frenchmen could sense a closing of the miserable conflict. This was a significant achievement in the 11-month siege.

On the same day, the British attacked the Great Redan. The Russians defended their positions manfully. Initially, the British were able to overrun the wall but once that happened there was no way to defend themselves against the counterattack. The British retreated. General James Simpson ordered that the Great Redan be assaulted the following morning, but at 2300 hours the Russians blew up their remaining arsenals, scuttling and sinking their remaining ships in the harbor, bringing an end to the great Russian Black Sea Fleet. Then they evacuated Sevastopol, crossing the bridges northward and into the peninsula. The Allies chose not to follow.

Sunday, September 9th, was Leo Tolstoy's 27th birthday.

Tuesday, September 11, 1855, the Siege of Sevastopol effectively came to an end, as the Allied forces entered the broken and smoking city and began the occupation.

The Victorians loudly proclaimed their victory at the end of the siege but Marx and Engels responded in their news columns that the British army consisted of lions led by donkeys.

By the time the Siege of Sevastopol ended, the nurses in Scutari were ready. During the summer months, they had received a steady number of casualties. It was a frightening crucible. Reading accounts from the front was disappointing. Nothing bespoke a quick end to the hostilities. When the news finally broke, speaking of the end of the siege, the nurses were numb. It was hard to believe that their efforts in Scutari might finally be coming to an end. The excitement of the anticipated cessation of the war had to be put on the back burner, as new waves of casualties began to arrive, reminding them that their work was not finished. The cries and moans of the wounded sounded every bit as drastic as the sounds made by their compatriots ten months earlier.

The Russians did not slink away into the night. On the south and east of the Black Sea, their forces attacked and besieged the Turkish city of Kars on the eastern edge of Anatolia. Armenians in the area had long memories of Turkish dominance and helped the Russians where they could. It was more of the same, only on a lesser scale, and this time Russia won. The Ottomans surrendered the castle. Their starving troops did not want to weather another winter at war.

Chapter 30

"If women could go into your Congress, I think justice would soon be done to the Indians." Sarah Winnemucca

Orson Hyde was happy to have Rockwell and Silva drop in to visit him. They told him they were heading back to Salt Lake City in a day or two.

"Meanwhile, the two of you bunk at my house and tell me what the news is. It's always nice to get someone else's point of view." The fifty-year-old judge enjoyed the notoriety he received living and presiding on the western skirts of the Utah Territory. Some Latter-day Saints farmed and ranched in the valley and vicinity. The land was filling with Gentile neighbors. All appreciated Hyde's education and willingness to help with their questions and disputes. Because of his missionary work, Hyde was also well-traveled, besides being a senior member of the church's Quorum of Twelve Apostles.

Others in the locale did not like the presence of the Mormon church president's hand-picked judge overseeing their activities. Some vied for independence from Salt Lake City, wanting to either join California or be given their statehood.

Most were content with the direction of their lives and the Carson Valley.

"I really want you to meet Numaga," he told the two dusty travelers. "He's coming to town with his niece today."

Porter's eyes lit up. "Is he the Paiute war chief from out by Pyramid Lake?"

"He is. I don't know that I'd call him a war chief though."

"I think we met him back when we were coming across the 40 Mile Desert with Steptoe. We came across a party of Paiutes who looked pretty nervous about having so many soldiers moving through their land. Numaga. Is he related to Winnemucca?"

"I think he's a nephew. The girl he's bringing with him is Winnemucca's daughter, Sarah"

"Why do you want us to meet?" Silva asked curiously.

"He is a great man. A real leader. He is trying to line his people up to work with the new settlers. They're trying to learn English and how to farm and raise cattle. He's a modern thinker. You knowing him might spread to the Shoshones and Timpanogos and Utes. It could be a good thing for everyone in the territory."

"He sounds like Kanosh," Shep said.

"Exactly! A lot like Kanosh. Given the chance, I think a lot of good could come about. But especially since you're the marshal, Port, knowing Numaga and the newer generation of Paiutes could really come in handy, for both sides."

Two hours later Orson pointed out the arrival of a small buggy carrying the two Paiutes.

"Numaga usually rides a horse but since he's bringing Sarah, I guess he decided to use a buggy. Also, he likes to be forward-looking. He likes the style of our clothes and hats, especially in the winter."

The judge welcomed the couple and invited them into his house, after sending one of his sons to take care of the horse and buggy. Numaga was twenty-five years old and wore buckskin leggings and a calico vest. His long black hair was tightly braided in two strands. Sarah was a lively girl of about eleven years. She politely, carefully examined whatever was close to her, being very curious. Being invited to join Numaga was an honor. She listened intently, choosing to save her practice of English for another time.

The men were introduced, followed by the customary handshakes. Numaga was pleased to know that Rockwell was also a man with authority throughout the area. He was a lawman and acted well on his part. Numaga and Sarah were also pleased to learn of Shep's relationship with the Hopi Wetoyous in San Bernardino.

"Life is changing," Numaga noted somberly. "My people are proud. They also must see the change coming and change to greet it." The man was wise beyond his years.

"You are the war chief?" Porter asked.

Numaga smiled. "I am strong. I am not afraid to fight. I do not wish to fight. Not with my people. Not with the Washoe or the Shoshone or your people. If there must be fighting, I can fight. I can lead my people. What I think the best medicine is peace. Living in peace. No war. No anger. No hatred. We can learn from you. We can teach you. My people have been here for many seasons. We can help. We can grow together."

Porter Rockwell was won over by the man's sincerity. He nodded at Hyde. "This is a good man, Orson. We should be so lucky to have him working with us."

The words also pleased Numaga, who then accepted Hyde's invitation to sit and prepare for the supper that was being cooked in the kitchen. With the table set, they followed Hyde's lead, bowing their heads and thanking God for their abundance and the peace in their lives.

Numaga breathed in the odors deeply. The volume and variety of food impressed him. "This is what I want for my people," he said plainly.

"We are your friends," Orson said. "What is ours also belongs to you."

"But you are different from other settlers. You are Mormonee. Not all white people treat us with the same respect."

"No, we are not all the same. But as long as Mormonee are here, you will always find friends."

The food was shared. Numaga and Sarah had been shown cutlery before and were aware of the table customs of these people. They were also satisfied when they were not corrected in their manner of eating. When the leisurely repast was over, the table was cleared and the friends stayed to visit more.

"Winnemucca is your father?" Shep asked Numaga.

"He is the father of my wife. He is a fine man. He wants the things we speak of."

"And he is your father also?"

Sarah was a precocious girl. She beamed to be noticed. She nodded. "Chief Winnemucca is my father. I am Sarah Winnemucca. My grandfather is Chief Truckee. My people are good people." She smiled proudly to be able to speak English. It was a chore she had been working on for several years.

"You honor us with your presence," Hyde said.

"Wuna Mucca means Giver of Spiritual Gifts," Numaga explained. "Some of the white people think his name means One Moccasin. His father, Truckee is also a holy man. He is a prophet."

All smiled and nodded. They appreciated being initiated with this little portion into Numaga's and Sarah's lives. There was simplicity combined with defined traditions.

"Mr. Rockwell and Mr. Silva, you will staying here?"

"Tonight," Shep replied. "Marshal Rockwell and I will be leaving tomorrow morning. We want to get back to our homes before it becomes winter."

The others at the table nodded their understanding.

"The land gets very cold at night. You will return to meet us again?" Numaga asked.

"God willing." He turned to Sarah. "Oh, that I had strong braids like yours," he remarked with a playful wink to Sarah and Numaga.

Shep and Porter were saddled and riding out of Genoa early the following morning. It was chilly enough to see their breath and that of their horses.

"Think it's going to work?"

"What's that?" Porter responded.

"This happiness. Living in peace with Numaga's people?"

"Not in a pig's eye."

His reply surprised Shep. "These are capable folks. They are hard workers. Don't you think they'll be able to line things up the way they want?"

Porter shook his head sadly. "Numaga might be able to work with the settlers for a while. But then what? What happens when he dies? What happens when there's no place left for the Paiutes to live? What happens if the Mormons are chased out of here? It's happened before."

"Not too uplifting, Rockwell."

"You asked, Shep." Porter shook his head. "I just want to get drunk and cuss."

Thirteen days later Shep climbed stiffly from his horse and tied him in front of Hansens' home in Tooele. Porter continued around the Oquirrh Mountain spur to the south and headed for the Millcreek portion of the Salt Lake Valley to see his wife and baby girl.

His house shall there be reared His glory to display
And people shall be heard in distant lands to say
We'll now go up and serve the Lord,
Obey His truth and learn His word.

Chapter 31

"Once you learn to read, you will be forever free." Frederick Douglass

Aaron Rost enjoyed reading. It was an eyeglass into a culture. He appreciated the books he had consumed, almost as much as the time and desire to read. Numerous people had given resources, education, opinions to be placed onto paper to influence or spread understanding. How did this affect him, Aaron Rost, Prussian Jew, merchant, and a worldwide wanderer? What were his responsibilities? Why was the belief in a oneness of all so important? Why did talk of abolition strike such a respondent chord within him?

Some of his peers, like Parley Pratt and Daniel Wells who had a previous foundation of scripture to build on, claimed this sublime gift of the Spirit, guided, directed, and enlightened them, giving them a rock-solid reason for living the way they did, and leaving their families to preach the gospel.

While some of these thoughts were ruminating in his head, Dr. Bernhisel presented Aaron with an interesting article that had been published in the Millennial Star in 1846. It read: *that the Jews among all nations are ...commanded, in the name of the Messiah, to prepare to return to Jerusalem in Palestine, and to rebuild that city and temple to the Lord. And also to organize and establish their own political government, under their own rulers, judges, and governors, in that country. For be it known unto them that we now hold the keys of the priesthood and kingdom which are soon to be restored unto them. Therefore let them also repent, and prepare to obey the ordinances of God.*

This kind of talk diminished his plans to grow his mercantile business. The building and refining of oil dug from the earth, took second chair when compared with such eternal, everlasting directives.

Aaron resorted to a series of prayers. As humbly as he could, he kneeled and bowed his head, praying for help. He stood in the form of the time-honored *Amidah* and plead with God for mercy. He draped his prayer shawl over his shoulders and wrapped his left arm in *tefillin* and laid his *phylactery* upon his forehead. He had been raised from youth to understand that God hears the cries of his children. These outward symbols were not relics or amulets but donning them made him feel close to his predecessors who revered such ornaments.

And he felt the draw of the Endowment House. He watched as people entered. They were making covenants with the Lord and as a condition of their faithfulness, He promised them increased blessings, strength, and power to confront the Adversary. Aaron knew that after receiving one's endowment, the candidates left the sanctuary of the Endowment House, wearing sacred vestments, underclothing meant to protect from spiritual darkness and assault. Things that took place within the Endowment House were not spoken of outside its walls. The silence increased Aaron's interest and curiosity. Sealed lips could not hide the smiles and satisfaction that adorned the faces of those who chose to enter the sanctuary, whether singly to receive their endowment of power from God, or as a couple, to be sealed together forever.

Aaron wished Shep Silva was home. He would be a good person to bounce his thoughts against. He was young but well-traveled enough to have some profound thoughts regarding issues like these. Silva's hesitancy to be baptized was a curiosity and concern for Rost. Could there be something he was aware of and hadn't shared with Aaron? Could he be cautious about making such a commitment, especially in light of the discovery that he was descended from Marranos? These were complicated issues.

"Thank you for seeing me, President Young."

The aging governor smiled and welcomed Aaron into his study. "To what do I owe such a privilege, my friend?" His sincerity helped Aaron relax.

"Being baptized has helped me grow, President. But more than that, it has stirred more questions. I have a lot to learn. I want to grow, to be a better servant of the Lord. I have read the Book of Mormon, twice. I feel the whisperings of the Spirit, telling me that there is more."

Young motioned Rost to sit in the chair opposite his chair. The drapes were partway opened, allowing sunlight to enter the room. It shined directly in Aaron's face. Aaron didn't like the light. It blocked Young's face. But the more they talked, the less he thought about Brigham and concentrated more on why he had come.

"I continue reading the Book of Mormon and other revelations. I read the Bible. I trust the Lord's timing. I know there is such a thing as the Lord's own due time. I don't want to be overly anxious. On the other hand, I don't want blessings to pass me by simply because I am cautious."

"Are you thinking of anything specific?"

"I want further light and knowledge. Perhaps a patriarchal blessing? Perhaps I should receive my endowment?"

Brigham thought for a moment. Through the sunlight, Aaron could see the Prophet's hand move to his chin in thought.

After another minute, Aaron spoke up. "Am I being too direct? Seeking for too much or aspiring for something I shouldn't?"

"Oh, no, Aaron. You are perfectly within your rights. You know, Brother Rost, I am a common judge in Israel. None of us has the right or claim that what we say will be binding on another. When the Savior said we shouldn't judge lest we also be judged, he wasn't saying we shouldn't make choices or decisions. Agency is a gift God has given us here on the earth. But if I were to say that you or someone else was going to hell, I'd be wasting my breath. I have no authority to say such a thing. Neither do you or your bishop or anyone. That is solely Jesus' domain. As a common judge though, I can visit with my people and decide who should be baptized or sign a recommend for those whom I feel are keeping the commandments and worthy to receive their endowments. From there it's up to all of us the keep the covenants we make with God, allowing Him to bless us with an increase in understanding, His Spirit, protection, and joy. What I really wish Brother Aaron is that more members of the church were as sensitive to the whisperings of the Holy Spirit as you and wanting to receive their endowment."

Young's words made sense. They were kind, non-judgmental. He found himself wondering how some people could detest such a man.

"I know that you are a maturing member of the church, Brother Aaron. I also know that you are aware of who your ancestors are and where you come from. I am expecting Isaac Morley to come by this evening. He's up from Manti. He is also an ordained patriarch in the church. May I suggest you visit with him and let him to give you a patriarchal blessing? These inspired words through the Lord's servant will come to you directly from heaven and give you some much-needed light on some of your concerns. Then after you have had some time to ponder your blessing, you come back and see me about this recommend for your endowment."

The prescription was what Aaron needed to hear. Life was glorious.

****

A knock sounded on Rost's door. Aaron was shocked to see the comely figure and attractive face of Ada Carroll. She was by herself. His surprised look caused her to smile.

"Yes, Mrs. Drummond. Is everything all right?"

She nodded. "Bill is at the courthouse working on some business. I have just been walking around the city and thought I would come over and pay you a visit."

"Oh, yes. Certainly. Would you like to come in?"

"Thank you, yes. It's starting to get cool."

Aaron held the door open and stood aside to allow her to enter, suddenly self-conscientious about her presence. He looked quickly up and down the street to see if anyone had noticed. He also smelled Ada's perfume.

"Could I get you some water?"

"Don't you have anything a little stronger?" Her smile seemed out of place.

Alarms sounded in his head. He didn't know how to respond.

"I'm just out for a quick stroll," she said. "I've always considered you a friend and wanted to drop by and renew our acquaintance."

Aaron was at a loss. As far as he knew, they had very little in common. Earlier, he judged her to be forward in her demeanor. He was not focusing on her lisp nor her two slightly tilted fingers. She was well-dressed and confident as if nothing whatever was wrong with her, a married woman stopping in to see an older bachelor.

"Am I making you nervous?" she asked.

"No," he lied, too quickly.

Ada nodded and stood. "My goal is not to make you uncomfortable, Aaron. I should be leaving. I merely wanted to see you. I think you are an accomplished man. Without a doubt, you will make a mark in life." She walked to the door then turned to face him as he was reaching to open it. She intercepted his hand and quickly, gently guided it to her breast. Her eyes met his as she sighed. "I am accomplished in my own way, Aaron. It would please me to get to know you better." She lowered his hand, then opened the door and left.

The experience dominated Aaron's thoughts for the balance of the evening. He tried to erase the sensation of her breast in his hand. *What was that about?* He didn't need to ask himself the question again. It was obvious to him what had happened. He had traveled to many places in the world. He knew how some women earned a living. There were times he had succumbed to their wiles, actually believing the flattering words. His money was quickly accepted by these escorts, some more charming than others. He had thought about them, the depths they had to sink to sell themselves to the equally, morally bankrupt men. The women would find other avenues for work if the men weren't willing to part with their money for such companionship.

He dipped a cup of cold water from his barrel, then sat down to think. The water helped him refocus, taking his thoughts from Ada's form and the intoxicating, subtle smell of her perfume. He drained the cup then retreated to his bedroom, trying not to think about his simple bed, where he might be, had he been accepting of her advances. He dragged a beat-up trunk from beneath the bed and began rummaging through its contents, mostly clothing. At the bottom, he discovered his aged prayer shawl. Despite their ages, the item was folded carefully.

He pulled the shawl around his shoulders. "Maybe I should put a *mezuzah* on my door."

Just as he said the day before, Isaac Morley showed up at Brigham Young's office. Rost followed suit. Morley had fond memories of Aaron and needed little encouragement to give him a blessing.

Brigham dismissed himself, giving the two his office for the ordinance. Shortly, one of Brigham's older sons appeared and sitting at his father's desk, found a sheet of paper and a pen. "I'm ready to record," he said.

"This blessing will stay with you long after today, Aaron," Morley noted. "It comes to you from God and will act as a spiritual map throughout the remainder of your days."

The aging patriarch placed his hands on Aaron Rost's head. As the blessing commenced, Aaron found himself thinking about the places the hands had been and the people whose hands they had shaken. Isaac pronounced a thoughtful blessing, encouraging Aaron to be faithful, to work hard, to listen to his leaders and friends. Isaac blessed him with success in finding a wife, just the right person who would be his helpmeet. Together they would grow to be a power in the Lord's hands. Isaac reinforced Aaron's understanding that he was descended from the tribe of Judah in the House of Israel and that the responsibilities of this house rested upon his shoulders. Aaron wondered when he might have disclosed his lineage to Brother Morley. It was a tender blessing. He was happy to have known Isaac since his baptism. Brother Morley closed the blessing, telling Aaron that he would come forth in the morning of the first resurrection and take his place with the righteous children of the Lord and go forth to claim all the blessings due them. The blessing was closed in the name of Jesus Christ.

"Thank you, Brother Morley," he said rising from the chair and embracing the older man. The man's power was impressive.

"I wrote it all down," the young man announced. "I will copy it for our records and then send it to you for your records and personal use."

"This is a sacred document, my friend," Isaac added. "Please take care of it. Share it carefully and only with those you hold most dear. Then use it as your own Urim and Thumim, or interpreter, your own Liahona or compass to guide you through life."

A couple of mornings later, a hell-raiser of a boy ran by Aaron's house with a message that the merchant stop by the Governor's office at his convenience. Brigham used the talents of such scrappy boys, paying them to be his messengers, wanting to give them alternatives for their unused time.

It was a beautiful crisp autumn morning. The reds and yellows of the turning oak leaves splashed on the sides of the mountains. It felt good to be outside, to breathe the fresh air and stretch his legs. Aaron started for the Beehive House, knowing that Young was an early riser. He was escorted into the Governor's office where he noticed the chairs had been arranged, so the interviewee would be facing the sun.

"And? Did I not tell you?" Brigham began with an exultant smile. "Was your patriarchal blessing not everything I had said?"

"That and more," Rost confessed, seating himself in the proffered chair. "I appreciate you sending my copy to my house."

"You've had the chance to read it over then?"

"Yes. Several times as a matter of fact. Brother Morely performed a marvelous service for me. I appreciate the closeness he has with the Lord to be able to summon such wonderful words and ideas pertaining to my life."

"He's a good one, that Isaac Morley. We have a number of great souls right here in the valleys. Men and women of stature and ability. God loves them. He pours inspiration into their hearts. I could never do my job without them."

"Agreed."

"Then again, we have some of the most nefarious characters on earth, right here in these valleys. We have charlatans, liars, thieves, and adulterers. The Adversary hasn't decided to leave us alone. He has sent some of his best to counter everything we do."

"Will he ever win?"

"Not against the Lord. That is a done deal. It's us, you and me, against Satan. That's where the challenge lies. Old Scratch has never been able to confront God. Now us, that's another matter. He is after us all the time. I guarantee that he hates the youngest child as vehemently as he does me, being the president of the church. Our challenge is to show him that we will choose God every step of the way. We follow Jesus despite the siren calls the devil sends our way. Do you believe that Brother Rost?"

"I do, President Young. I only wish I had a promise that I would never come short of what's expected of me."

"Oh, you will, my friend. You will. We all do. That's the beauty of this work. Christ has already paid for our mistakes. Then, it's up to us to turn to Him for forgiveness, to repent, to break away from evil and become Saints, always willing to be humble and meek, wanting the Lord's glory above all else."

"And just what is His glory, may I ask?"

"God's glory is to bring about the immortality and eternal life of man. It is our joy and happiness, our exaltation and purity. It is the good news of the gospel, to always live in the presence of the Father and Son, together with our loved ones." Brigham opened a drawer and removed a piece of paper and handed it to Aaron. "Now you take this, and you go and present it to the tyler of the Endowment House, then you go in and make your covenants with the Lord, those special promises he asks of us and you will be endowed with power from on high. The blessings of God will accompany you all your days."

A knock came onto his office door and Mary Young opened it carefully. "Your next appointment has arrived, dear."

Brigham stood and clapped his hands on Rost's shoulders, then shook his hands manfully. "After that, then you return and tell me what you have found."

Aaron was as light as a feather returning to his store. He opened and wrote a note to put in the door, saying he had other business and would return on the next day. As he closed the door to leave, he was surprised to see the approach of Ada Drummond. She was accompanied by her manservant, Cuffy Cato.

"You seem to be a man in a hurry," she called pleasantly.

Aaron wanted to dodge any interaction. "I actually do have business that needs my attention."

"Well, I'm not about to stand in your way, Mr. Rost." She reached out her white-gloved hand and gave him a folded note. "I appreciate your attention," she said merrily, then winked at him as they turned and strolled away.

Everything had been pleasant until the wink. It suggested more than friendship. Aaron opened the note and read: *Please come by the house, anytime during the day. I would love to know you better.*

The Drummonds' house was a couple of blocks away. The Judge and Ada had moved into the stone structure after staying with the Kinneys for a week. The impressive house was built for the federal officials who came to the territory. It was well located as far as access to the courthouse and other government buildings. The Drummonds had hosted several parties in their house. Most of the citizens of the city kept their distance.

Judge Drummond let it be known that he was not in favor of the current practice in the territory of using probate judges and juries. To him, it smacked too much of sovereignty and self-will. He wanted the federal jurisdiction to be pervasive and universal. These ideas did not sit well with the local population that had been functioning quite well before any interference from Washington. It allowed leeway for attitudes to be addressed and not diminished. Because the majority of residents were members of the church, if an issue became toxic or unassailable, it was handed over to ecclesiastical authorities for resolution. The practice had worked well for ten years. Judge Stiles, a federally appointed judge and Mormon in name only, and Judge John Kinney did not condone the practice. It side-stepped their authority. Judge W.W. Drummond detested the whole idea. He made his opinions known loudly and frequently. Folks in the city were holding their breath, waiting for him to travel the 150 miles south to Fillmore to hold his sessions of court, starting in November. His absence would allow the business to return to normal for a month or two.

As the time for his departure drew near, the judge became irate and impatient with those about him. He was anxious to leave the Great Salt Lake City. He had several cases to present. First and foremost was the capture and trial of the murderers of Captain John Gunnison. He complained that Steptoe had done a miserable job and then Judge Kinney allowed Brigham and the Mormons to walk all over his role and authority. Drummond promised that it would never happen again. Young's policy of appeasement towards the Indians would never do. The thought that it was better to feed the natives than to fight them was ludicrous, despite the track record of successes they could trot out.

****

From the outside, the Endowment House was a nondescript building, not overly ornate but large, and built with the universal adobe bricks. It was situated on the northwest corner of the temple block, far enough away to keep from hearing the workers as they continued to dig the deep and wide trench and begin chiseling the sandstone for the foundation of the temple.

Nervously, Aaron knocked on the portal. He felt alone and wished he had more and closer friends in the city. Shep should be returning from California soon enough, but then again, he was not even baptized. He couldn't enter the sanctuary. One thing Aaron did know, Shep was a good person to speak with. He was thoughtful and not too quick to draw a judgment on the subject they were discussing. Aaron also knew that he was a convicted believer. He only had yet to pull the trigger and get baptized.

The door opened and a clean-shaven man appeared and welcomed him inside. After checking his recommend, Aaron was directed to ascend the double-wide stairs leading to the second floor, where he would begin his journey through the esoteric instructions of the endowment. As he started his journey, he noted that nothing was earth-shaking or new to his understanding of the gospel. Things had been rearranged, situated to better illustrate man's walk through the plan of salvation, designed and executed by Jesus Christ. The centrality for the premortal council and the creation of the earth was presented, as was the role of Christ throughout the history of man. Several covenants were presented for his consideration. All seemed very natural, very normal. He saw his place in the all-encompassing designs of God. A progression through the cosmos was represented, with him finally ending up in a beautiful room that represented the culmination of his experience. It was called the celestial room and was to imitate the splendor, peace, and serenity one achieves once the return back into the presence of God is complete. Aaron was also shown a small side room with chairs for witnesses and an altar where couples were sealed to one another forever, meaning that as they kept their promises, the priesthood of God would join them through the ages, as man and wife.

Following this transformative experience, Aaron was allowed time to sit on an ornate couch in the celestial room, to think over the things he had been shown. The lightly draped windows allowed the daylight into the room and thickly woven rugs muffled the steps of people as they walked into the room. If visitors spoke, it was only in whispers, magnifying the sanctity of this unusual house.

The feelings of peace that Aaron felt were unique. They entered deeply into his heart. He wished that everyone could experience such a sensation of joy and contemplation. The world would be a different place. The fear of loss, of separation, of confusion, disappeared.

Rost remained in the room an hour until the tyler entered to ensure that all was well. When he replied that things were fine, the man invited him to return as a witness with his friends and associates who had not yet received their endowments. "And you can come back into this room," he was told. "This isn't fully the House of the Lord. Perhaps a preliminary edifice. There are many here in Deseret who have yet to take out their endowments. Just know the Lord loves you and is anxious to bestow the most glorious blessings upon you, dear brother."

As Aaron left the Endowment House, it was late afternoon. Evening was approaching. How much nicer the city would appear with lamps lit by his oil. They would burn late into the night, giving light to one and all, without the soot or smell. The thought encouraged him to push forward with his business plans.

Under his arm, he carried a cloth packet containing several white union suits. These represented the garments of the holy priesthood and were to be worn under his clothing at all times. They would be a protection to him. They had curious markings sewn in them, reminding the wearer of the covenants entered into with the Lord. In a way, the garment acted almost like a wedding ring, letting one and all but especially himself, know of his status before the Lord.

Returning to his home, Aaron lit his lamps and sat in his rocking chair, opening his scriptures and began recounting the things he had learned. *Oh, that*

Shep was near. He was too excited to sleep. He remained awake through much of the night, enveloped in his thoughts and wonders, trying to project his place in the universe.

Chapter 32

"The wounds of a friend are better than the kisses of an enemy." Parley P. Pratt

A sharp knock on his door startled Aaron from his slumbers. He had fallen asleep in his rocking chair. The Book of Mormon was in his lap. Stiffly he stood from his reclining position and walking to the door, opened it.

The Drummonds' slave, Cuffy, was outside.

"How may I help you, Mr. Cato?"

"Your presence is requested at the Drummonds."

"Is the Judge all right?" he asked rubbing his eyes.

"Just come. And the sooner the better."

Aaron nodded. "Soon as I can," he said and closed the door. That was a curious request. It had never been made before. He dressed and left his house, his mind still whirling around ideas that had been presented to him the day before.

Cuffy was sitting in his usual place on the Drummond porch, watching the passers-by. Aaron wondered if that might be one of the reasons the Drummonds didn't have many visitors. Cuffy was young and strong and intimidating.

The man stood from his perch and opened the front door, motioning Aaron to enter.

"Mr. Rost is here," he called, then stepped back outside and closed the door. The house was spacious, and the parlor had a high, vaulted ceiling. No one was visible, although he thought he might have caught a flash of movement on the landing at the top of the stairs.

"I'll be right down," Ada called from her room. "Please make yourself at home."

A feeling of discomfort gripped his stomach. *What was happening?* Had he been trapped? He shook the thoughts away. Quite presumptuous, the idea that Ada would be so overt with any sordid plans, the plans had haunted him during moments of spiritual clarity. He remained standing by the door, holding his hat and glancing around for clues. The judge was absent. Cuffy remained outside.

"Thank you for coming so promptly," Ada said moving to the top of the stairs.

He looked up to see that she was dressed in her bathrobe. It appeared that she was preparing to attend a dinner or the theater, but then she started down the stairs. Her blonde hair was curled, and she was wearing her make-up lightly. Her blue eyes were remarkably beautiful, and her white teeth shone nicely as she smiled.

"Please sit and make yourself comfortable," she repeated, walking directly up to him. She took his hat and pointed to the couch, then walked to a rack by the door where she hung his hat, then returned and sat on the couch opposite him.

Aaron sat nervously on the couch, looking down at his shoes, suddenly aware of how dirty they were.

"My God, Mr. Rost, it is like pulling eye teeth just to get you over here." Her smile was unoffensive. She was happy enough, not devious or plotting, although as she had descended the stairs, one leg was exposed, long and smooth, clear up to her mid-thigh, causing Aaron's attention to rivet.

"I just wanted you to come over, to give us a chance to visit, to get to know one another better."

"I thought we had spoken plenty during our trip from Washington."

"Certainly. But not about the proper things. I want to know more about you, Aaron. You intrigue me. From your accent to your curly hair. It's blonde like mine." She smiled again.

"I don't feel comfortable being here without Bill."

"He has his own agenda, Aaron. If he wanted to be here, he would be. But I need a social outlet. I love people. I am especially interested in you. You are an enigma here in the city. You work hard. You travel, I assume back to the States. You are always busy. Surely all of your needs are not being met. I mean, you have no wife. I rarely see you at the dances. Are you really fulfilled, Aaron? Are you certain that there are no things that I could do to add to your life? To your enjoyment?"

Aaron cleared his throat. "Mrs. Drummond…"

"Ada."

"I don't know exactly what you mean. I don't see how your presence in my life might contribute to its quality."

"Oh, come now, Aaron," she said, this time looking quite serious. She stood from the couch and opened her robe, revealing her nakedness. "Please don't push me away. Don't you like what you see? I am yours, Aaron. Come, let's go upstairs to my bed. You can have me for as long as you want."

Aaron stood up, feeling all the blood leave his face. "Ada, please. No."

She stepped close and insinuated her arms around his waist, pressing her breasts seductively against him. The aroma of her perfume filled his nostrils and her hair fell against his shoulders. Soft lips sought his neck, while one hand moved from his back and down from his waist.

"I've dreamed about seeing your circumcision," she moaned into his throat.

The dizzying events cascaded onto him. His heart was racing, and his breathing increased dramatically. Ada responded by groping him forcefully, her movements demanding more in return.

As clearly as the day outside, Aaron heard the voice of his papa from years gone by, recounting the memorable tale of Joseph who was sold into Egypt. It was one of his favorites. His master's wife had been attracted to the seventeen-year-old boy and insisted he sleep with her. Joseph, the Titan of the Bible, acted as a man of God. The scriptures said that he *"fled and got him out."* Joseph didn't stay around to lecture the woman or explain to her why her behavior was unacceptable. It simply related that he fled and got him out.

As if a cup of icy water had been dashed into his face, Aaron shook himself clear and gently pushed Ada away, then turned, grabbed his hat, and walked from the house as quickly as he could. He didn't think about the surprised look that rose on Ada's face nor how quickly she covered herself with the robe when he opened the door. He did not register the fury that imprinted itself on her face as he hurried down the street to the corner. With heart racing, he gulped air, wanting just to get as far away as he could. The experience was unbelievable. He couldn't fathom what had overcome Ada to assault him so blatantly, plying her wiles on him so openly.

Reaching his house, he decided to go to his store, thinking that interaction with people might help to calm his frazzled nerves. It didn't. He also didn't have many customers.

What had happened? Have I given her some kind of signal that I wanted to be a participant? On the contrary, if anything, he had been cold and standoffish. He was distant. He was not attracted to prostitutes. Not anymore. Not at this stage of his life. This type of relationship was not what he wanted. Ada was an attractive woman. But it seemed that she saw herself as a sexual being, willing to trade herself to get what she desired. As long as there were men vacuous enough to fall into her web, she would be successful or until her beauty faded. That did not matter to him. She was a fully grown woman, capable to live her life as she wanted.

The next day Aaron was starting to relax. The events of the previous day were fading. He had no interactions with the Drummonds. Perhaps they would disappear, a bad dream, an unfortunate occurrence. Worst case scenario, they might drag on for a while, but Drummond made no bones of the dislike he had for the Utah Territory and unless President Pierce was willing to make him the governor, he would be taking his luggage and Ada as soon as possible and return to Illinois where he would help with the election of Stephen Douglas. Memories of the nightmare were beginning to wane.

There was another knock on his front door. Aaron didn't recognize the visitor. The man identified himself as a deputy sheriff in the city and had Aaron step outside, then arrested him on charges of sexual assault. Chains were fastened onto his wrists, and he was led away to jail. When the stunned Rost asked what the reason was for the arrest, he was informed that it was under the direction of Judge William W. Drummond. The deputy wasn't a font of information.

"Judge says you attacked Mrs. Drummond."

"It never happened!"

"It's something you'll have to take up with him and a jury, I guess."

"And when will that be?"

"We're all going to Fillmore in the morning. I guess that's where you'll have your chance."

Aaron was taken to jail and locked away, alone with his thoughts and prayers. Late that night, cloaked in a dark blue shawl, Ada slipped into the holding area of the jail. Aaron was the only one incarcerated and he awoke to her whispered summons.

"I have come here under duress," she said quietly. "There is no reason for you to be in here. There's no reason for you to travel to Fillmore in the morning. My only reason for contacting you is because of your candor. The sweetness of your life. I want that. I want you. Oh please, Aaron. Is my asking that you sleep in my arms, between my breasts, such an awful request?"

"Maybe once upon a time, it wouldn't have been such a hard request. But now I'm afraid I cannot countenance such behavior."

Ada slipped her shawl down and undid her blouse then pulled it wide to expose her breasts in the dim light. "Am I so diabolical? So undeserving? Come closer to the bars and place your ear here. Listen to the beating of my heart. Oh Aaron, please don't turn this into a fiasco. I don't want a fight. I promise that I can make you happy. I will see to your release tonight. Then afterward we need not speak of this again. I will go to Fillmore and by the time we return you will be traveling in the States. Please, Aaron. I can't explain how desperately I ache for your touch, for your kisses."

She reached through the bars and fumbled with the buttons on his shirt. He stepped beyond her reach.

"No, Ada. This is wrong. I cannot and I will not."

The woman also took a step back and sized up her intended quarry. After pondering for a moment, she buttoned her blouse back and slipped the shawl up and over her shoulders and head. "Until tomorrow then," she commented quietly, then slipped noiselessly from the room.

Aaron looked down at his shirt where Ada had addressed his buttons. He slowly undid several more of the buttons, exposing the white cloth of his temple garment. He grasped a portion with his hand and wept. "Oh, thank you, dear Father, for preserving and protecting me in this dire hour of need."

The next morning Aaron was taken from the jail and put on a horse with the heavily armed deputy riding next to him. They headed south and within half an hour caught up with the brightly colored carriage carrying Ada and Judge Drummond, driven by Cuffy. The three in the carriage carried on a lively conversation.

Aaron kept quiet, following the example of the lawman. They passed the point of the mountain and the narrows of the Jordan River. According to watermarks, Utah Lake was still low, following the dry winter and summer. After a long day, they stopped for the evening in Provo. The town had been named after a French-Canadian fur trapper named Etienne Provost.

Drummond and Ada retired into a small hotel for dinner and to spend the night, while Aaron was given a brittle piece of smoked venison. He and the deputy and Cuffy slept in the barn.

The next day was more of the same. The road skirted the east side of the lake. At the southern end, they split off and headed more directly south. After traveling another 40 miles they spent the night in Nephi. It had originally been named Salt Creek because of the alkaline soil. The third day of their trip was the longest. They had debated the pros and cons of making the ride in a single day. Ada, who did not care to sleep under the stars, won out. The party arose early and set off at a decent clip, coming into Fillmore well after dark. They followed the deputy who had a lantern to light the road the last half dozen miles. After rousting tired inhabitants, room and board for the weary Drummonds were found. The other three men spent another night beneath their blankets in a barn.

The morning revealed the sorry state of the town. Two scores of cabins were scattered about the valley, riding up against the hills to the east. A broad desert stretched to their west. Glimmers of water in the distance could be seen, reflecting the mysterious, although diminishing, waters of Sevier Lake. The proximity to the site of the Gunnison Massacre, combined with the closeness to the Pahvant colony of Chief Kanosh were two of the reasons Drummond wanted to come south. Still, the biggest reason for wanting to distance himself from the population center of the Great Salt Lake City was the freedom he would have wielding his authority and whipping the locals into conformity.

Hosea Stout was an interesting man and a local celebrity. He had fought against Chief Black Hawk in the Sauk and Fox wars in Illinois in the 1830s, where he also learned of the church. He joined the religion in time to participate in the conflict with the mobs, then participated with the Saints when they were driven from Missouri. He was a close associate of Joseph Smith's and held responsible positions in the Nauvoo Legion as well as the city police force. Stout was an avid diarist and kept a daily log of his experiences starting in 1844. After studying the law, he was one of the first to pass the Utah bar, beginning a long career for him in law and politics. He was elected to the Utah Territory's House of Representatives in 1849 and was part of the delegation whose role was to write the constitution for the proposed State of Deseret. In 1852, Stout was called to preach the gospel in the church's first mission to China. Hosea was a tough, strong, opinionated man who carried two six-shooters and a Bowie knife in plain view. He had strong feelings towards the church. "I always feel that it is my duty to look to myself, for I am in as much danger of apostatizing as any in the Church. If I ever do get led astray and depart from the principles of the gospel of salvation, it will be because I led myself off from the path. It was not my brethren who led me away, it was my own doing."

Stout was one of the first to encounter Judge William W. Drummond and Ada. He did his best to put on a smiling face. He had heard tales of the judge's record in Salt Lake City and was determined to draw his own conclusions.

"This is the courthouse," he announced proudly, leading the couple to the large, half-finished stone structure. They climbed the front steps and entered. "We're working hard to get things finished up, for you to begin hearing your cases. When would you like to start your proceedings?"

"Today!" Drummond said curtly. "I didn't come all this way to sit on my hands."

Stout remained unflustered. "Should be finishing up soon enough. We can talk with the construction folks to get a better idea."

"Is this my office?" he asked, pointing to a large room off the courtroom.

"I believe so."

"Get some men to carry my baggage here and set the office up. I will be back this afternoon and begin my interviews."

Stout smiled good-naturedly. "I'm sure your Honor understands that I am not in your employ. I am here for both our convenience. I likewise have responsibilities that need tending. It doesn't matter if these responsibilities have to do with my chickens or horses, I will take care of them in the order they deserve. Should you require more express attention, I suggest that you begin introducing yourself about town and find who might be available to assist in your needs." He then turned and walked away, leaving the judge standing with his mouth open.

Aaron Rost was locked in the jail until the court was to open on Monday, November 12, 1855. Shep Silva had arrived in town the previous evening, carrying bail money that Brigham Young had sent to help with the trial.

"See what happens when I leave town?" Silva joked with his friend through the bars. "I step out for a paltry few months and you get all involved with the judge's wife, dragged to Fillmore, and put on trial."

Aaron didn't find his situation as comical, although he was relieved to see Shep arrive. He was also pleased that Governor Young had put up the money for his bail to keep him from languishing in jail. "At least mine is the first case."

"You got an attorney?"

"I think Stout is planning on representing me."

Silva chuckled again. "That'll be more fun than watching the sun come up."

"No real love lost between those two. The Judge and Stout."

"Mind telling me what this is all about?"

Aaron shrugged and shook his head. "It's just a thing with the judge's wife, Ada. I think she just took a shine to me, even back when we were coming in from Washington. I mean, she is a nice girl. Quite pretty. But she just got me into her sights. I didn't know if I was coming or going. She made a couple of passes, but come on, Shep. Do you think I'm such a catch?"

"No argument from me."

"So she starts coming around and winking and being chummy. I didn't know what was happening. I didn't for the life of me, think she was serious.

Plus I'd just got a patriarchal blessing from Brother Morley. I took out my endowment."

Shep nodded seriously. "Brigham told me."

"So Ada sends Cuffy over with an invitation to come to their house. It was during the day. I did. Drummond was at the courthouse and while we were alone inside, she showed up in a bathrobe and then dropped it in front of me."

"What did you do, Maher-shalal-hash-baz?" he asked jokingly

"It scared the hell out of me, Mahonri. I didn't know what to do. I don't even know if I could rightly recall my name. She is a beautiful girl, Shep. But I just ran out of the house and went home. I hoped this would all blow over. And then the deputy showed up a couple of days later and arrested me for assaulting her."

Shep held up his hand. "I should stop you there. The pa of some folks in Salt Lake City is serving his mission in Illinois. He happened to pass through Oquawka. That's where Drummond says he lives, and the man asked around. You know about the divorce and all. He was pointed to Jemima Drummond, a woman who claims she's his wife! That he never divorced her but just abandoned her and their five children. How's that for news?"

It didn't make Aaron happy but suddenly he was feeling better about his chances in front of a jury.

"And Ada?"

"Folks in Washington think she's a whore who worked there and in Baltimore. Her husband's a teacher there, but she goes by a different name. Ada Carroll."

"I know that Tom Kane's always been suspicious of Drummond. I didn't think he'd just go and get a prostitute to fill in for his wife, especially when coming to Utah."

"Maybe that's why he did it."

"Who knows? Anyway, I ran out of the house so fast, I almost forgot my hat. I guess she had Cuffy tell Judge Drummond that I'd been by. As a matter of fact, I don't think the three of us said more than a couple of sentences to each other the whole way here. Judge Bill wasn't too keen on me coming down here with him except I think he liked the fact that I was wearing chains."

"No doubt he wants his pound of flesh."

"You think he's such a fool and doesn't know what's going on with Ada?"

"Don't know. Maybe he's just pretending it's nothing." Silva smiled at his friend. "Well, I'm bunking in the barn by the courthouse. I'm sure I'll sleep sounder than you."

Aaron was awakened early, hearing the jail door creak open. As he was opening his eyes to see who was entering, he felt two powerful hands grab him and throw him against the bars. He was then pounded numerous times in his face and chest until he was senseless. His assailant was Cuffy Cato. Bending down, he picked Rost up and slung him over his shoulder like a bag of wheat, then carried him out of the building and threw him to the ground in the square in front of the courthouse. Without saying a word, Cuffy began unrolling a long, rawhide whip, then wound up and snapped it violently across Aaron's back and neck. The pain was searing. Cuffy was a strong, agile man and struck his victim two more times in quick succession. With the last stroke, Aaron was finally able to scream. He didn't know how loudly, but people heard the commotion and came running to view the spectacle. Aaron could feel blood beginning to run down his back.

"That's enough, Cuffy!"

Aaron recognized the Brazilian accent. But Cuffy was more than a match for Shep. Ignoring the command, Cuffy hauled off once again, striking another stinging blow onto the trembling prisoner.

"I said that's enough!" Shep's voice was booming and authoritative.

"You think you can handle me?" Cuffy sneered.

Shep smiled. "Listen here, Cuffy. God made men but Sam Colt has made us equal. I got a six-shooter right here that says you're not faster or tougher than a .45."

The beating ceased. Aaron sat up slowly and pushed back the blood from his face.

"You okay?" Shep asked, his eyes not leaving Cuffy.

"I reckon so."

With that, Hosea Stout crashed through the circle of humanity that had gathered around the square, still buttoning his pants. "Mind if I ask what this is all about!" he said angrily, looking at Cato.

The servant dropped his head and held out his hands, still holding the whip. "This piece of shit attacked Miss Ada. I just figured he had it coming."

"Just you? That's all?"

Cuffy looked around uncertainly. He didn't see many faces showing approval. "Well, me and the judge. We thought he should look the part when hauled into court."

"That's enough for me!" Shep announced loudly. He looked around until he spotted the deputy who had escorted Aaron from Salt Lake City. "I'm charging both Cuffy Cato and Judge Willian Drummond with assault with the intent to kill. I demand they be arrested, deputy. I will swear out and sign any documents necessary. Will the law be able to handle the case?" he asked Hosea.

The lawyer chuckled. "There shouldn't be a problem. Course, it will push the judge's calendar back a ways and he'll need to get a good attorney. Both him and Mr. Cato."

With that, the deputy walked over to the house sheltering Judge Drummond, knocked then invited the judge outside and placed him under arrest. He then brought the judge back to the square where he collected Cuffy and the two men were led to the jail. Drummond was furious.

Again, Hosea Stout followed. "You know, you're in trouble here. You're going to need bail and a good lawyer. I can suggest my services, although I'm usually a prosecutor. Without too much trouble you should be out of here in a day or so. Then you can get back to your work." Hosea decided to give them time to make up their minds and stepped out of the holding area

Drummond coughed and sputtered and stomped around inside the cell for several minutes, while Cuffy sat silently.

An hour later, Stout had another horse for Aaron saddled. "You're out on bail. I honestly don't think a hearing will be set, not from what I understand of the case. In any event, you might as well get along back to Salt Lake City and relax a bit if it's possible. I think I can handle things around here for a while."

Rost thanked him profusely.

Shep had another concern before riding off with his friend. "Kanosh. Is Drummond going to cause him grief?"

"I'm sure he wants to. He sees himself as a glorious crusader, come to right the wrongs with Captain Gunnison. I don't think he'll be able to. He'll drum up a couple of posses and that will cost him a lot of money. But from what I know, all the Pahvants that might have been involved in the attack have gone to the hills or out on the desert. They won't be found. Not while Bill Drummond is here."

"Governor Young wasn't happy with all this either. He told me he thinks the judge should be removed. He's a patsy for President Pierce because he transcended his authority and demeaned himself very much like a dog or wolf, vicious and brutal, whining and snappish, vain as a peacock and ignorant as a jackass."

"Sounds just like something Brig would say." Stout saw to it that the men were well-prepared with blankets and supplies. The return ride would be easier.

They rode to Payson the first day and put in at a hotel.

"We'll reach home tomorrow. That is if you don't want to stop and sightsee in Provo, Maher."

"I'm done with that, Mahonri. Thanks."

"There is something that I've been meaning to ask you for a long time. Have there been women in your life before? Serious women?"

Aaron nodded his head slowly. "I've had my run-ins with women around the ports. But it was not with any I wanted to make a relationship with. Before I left Prussia, I lived in a tiny village. It was called a *shtetl*. It was on the border with Poland and went back and forth. Just a Jewish village. I was a boy. Maybe a young man. I met Hadassah. She was the most perfect woman I had ever met. About my age. She lived in a *shtetl* close to mine. Our parents noticed and made the match. We were married with a lovely ceremony. I thought my life was complete. We lived simply. I was trying to work in the pharmacy. We didn't have any money." Aaron sighed and stopped momentarily while he gathered his thoughts. "My wife became pregnant. We were so happy. We had nothing and yet we were happy. And then the tsar's police told me I would be going into the army. But Hadassah sickened and died, and the baby died, and I was alone. I didn't want the army, so I went to Danzig and put to sea. That's my life. I miss my home. I miss my parents. Hadassah. You know her name means myrtle tree. She was so lovely." He stopped again and surveyed his friend. "So, no. I had a life with the best. She was funny and happy. She cooked and prepared for *Shabbas*. She raised me to a place of honor. An honor I had never experienced before until I entered the Endowment House."

Shep extinguished their lamp and laid down, studying the ceiling.

"You know," Aaron continued. "There's an old story about Joseph being sold into Egypt."

"I've heard it."

"Well, this other one says that the wife of Joseph's master was so in love with him, she couldn't think of anything else. She went by the jail, even after he'd been disgraced, and begged him to sleep with her. Every day. And she kept it up for years. Imagine that, being thrown into a dungeon when you are seventeen and this beautiful woman begging you to be with her, for which she would have him released. Well, he stayed true to his vow, his covenants with God, and remained in jail until he was thirty years old." Aaron cleared his throat. "I'm no Joseph, but I remembered the story, Shep, and for once I wanted to be good and righteous and holy. I didn't want to further ruin my memories of Hadassah. I know better now."

"God bless you, Aaron Rost or should I say Maher-shalal-hash-baz?"

Chapter 33

"Tis mean for empty praise of wit to write, as fopplings grin to show their teeth are white." John Brown

Dear Ina,

Thank you for your news about your travels. Sometimes I took it for granted how very big America is. Now that I am on this island it is easy to remember just how far away some things can be. California itself is a very big state. I recall how tall the mountains are. Also, the deserts are very big. The beaches that run along the coast seem to be endless. I remember the water around Los Angeles isn't too cold but up by San Francisco, the ocean waters are very chilly. The waters around these islands are very warm. Fish are all over. I have even seen some sharks but that has always been from a distance.

I can only do these kinds of activities when I'm not busy, which means not too often. I stay very busy. But these Hawaiian people are the kindest. They don't worry too much about the troubles in the world. Like you mentioned the war in Crimea. That is just not something these people know about. They know about war and they don't like it. I just think their lives are busy enough for them here. They love each other. They even love me. I have been invited to many community dinners. They call them luaus. I am grateful that I began to enjoy eating fish. That's about all they eat here. They catch and eat all kinds of fish. They also find all kinds of food on the island, especially roots, kind of like potatoes.

Hawaiians like to eat pork. They kill the pig and bury it in the earth and cook it with coals from a fire. It takes all day. We all look forward to taking it back out. It's quite greasy but it always tastes very good. I am happy with the food. I think I am starting to gain weight. I am also growing taller. Most of the missionaries are from the Utah Territory. Some of them are married and have left wives and children. They understand the importance of the Gospel of Christ. I have been invited by lots of them to visit them after my service here. I don't know when that might be.

Winter is coming but it is very different here. Maybe you do too. We get a lot of rain. From what I gather from folks back in the territory we haven't gotten much snow there either. That's the way it was last winter. This one might be different. I know people are praying for snow. It helps so much in the spring and summer when they have enough water to irrigate.

My hand is cramping. This means I need to stop soon. I am happy to hear about your ma. Will her hair ever grow back or does she need to wear her wig the rest of her life? I was happy to hear about Shep, too. I miss him.

I love you, Ina. I can't tell you how important you are to me. I look for your letters with the arrival of every ship from America.

Love,
Joseph

Dear Joseph F (that's the way Shep Silva refers to you),

I love your letters too. I also appreciate our ability to write. We simply use twenty-six letters, and we can share thoughts and hopes and ideas and send them clear across the earth. I am convinced that writing is a gift from God. I don't think I would enjoy just printing things at a newspaper. That is hard work and it's very necessary. On the other hand, I would like to be a writer, the one who crafts the stories or poems. I want to be able to capture what people want to hear, the things that will lift and please them. Still, the news can be so depressing, I want to write about the happy, good things in life. I want to write things that will inspire others. You probably think I'm crazy. Well, that's something we can discuss more when you come home.

I like hearing about Hawaii. There are many times when I think I'd like to travel. Then again, it was very difficult when we first came to California. I never thought that trip would end. Some investors are building railroads here in California. Pa even says there is talk of constructing a railroad that would extend clear across America. That would be a marvel. At the first of this year, a railroad was completed across Panama. This means that people wanting to come to the west from the States merely need to sail to Panama, then catch a train for a short ride and then catch another ship that will bring them to Los Angeles or San Francisco, instead of needing to sail clear around South America.

I have some bad news. Sister Ousley's (Electa's) husband, Sam (Samuel Marshall Ousley) was killed in a terrible accident while working in a well. A bucket dropped down and hit him in the head. It was a very sad thing. And then, just now, in December, Sister Ousley gave birth to their last baby, a girl they have named Clara. It is such a tragedy. I cried and cried. Ma helped me to know that Sister Ousley is a strong woman, and she has a good family. She also has good neighbors.

Older people remind me that time seems to speed by the older one gets. For me, the days continue to pass at a snail's pace. How is it for you? Does the time race away or does the sun seem to be stalled in the heavens? I question some truth, whether it is absolute or changing. I trust that you believe in God with all your heart. But have you wondered? Is the work you are involved with as all-important as you feel or could it be a way to appease your understanding? Please don't be offended. I know that we do not see eye to eye on some of these issues. I question the God who would allow his prophets, Joseph and Hyrum to be butchered in a jail in Illinois. I am curious about my own father and how much differently my life might be had he lived longer. These are just some things I have been pondering. I appreciate having you to write to. It gives me a chance to understand you better. It also gives me a more complete understanding to hear your responses. What you say and how you feel are quite important to me. There are so many times, Joseph, when I wish I had you here with me, to visit, and share ideas. I miss the yesterdays of our lives, the times we had to run and skip and play. Wasn't it so fun?

But a sorrow dwells in my young heart-
Its shade is on my brow,
And the memory of the past is all
That's left to cheer me now.

I wish I could tell you how much I enjoy writing to you and receiving your letters. It lifts my rather ho-hum life around here. Bob doesn't care about writing. I think I know more about your activities than his. I am also a little worried about some of his demonstrations of jealousy towards me. He doesn't want me socializing. Then again, he is a delightful man. Some things are becoming very clear in my mind's eye. This is another reason I wish you were here.

I love you Joseph Fielding. Every night I pray to the heavens that you are kept well and safe.

Always and always,

Ina

Aaron answered his front door, cautiously. It was Shep. Silva noticed the hesitancy.

"You've been home for better than a week and you're still spooked?"

Rost grinned and invited his visitor inside. "I guess it had a bigger impact on me than I thought. Any news?"

"Nope. I think it's as expected. Hosea has Bill Drummond jumping through the hoops. I heard that Stout got him off the case I swore out against him. Good thing too, or I'd be hoofing it back down south. He got him off the hook so Drummond's back on the bench, trying to run the show. He and Ada Carroll."

"How's that going?"

"Just as you'd expect. Folks in the county are not impressed with the judge having his paramour sit at his side when trying cases."

Aaron grinned and shook his head in mock disbelief. "Well, what would you expect from a handful of prudish Mormons?"

"Getting what they deserve, I reckon."

"You know when he's coming back this way?"

"Not for a while, I suspect. He's filled his calendar and pushing things way back. It doesn't make his juries happy. He still has assorted men riding around as his posse and that can't be cheap."

"Is Ada helping pay the bill?"

"I don't think so. Not here, anyway. I heard she wants to buy some horses to sell in California. She's no dummy."

"Did Hosea run up his tab?"

245

Shep chuckled. "You know, the man's notorious. By the time he got charges dropped, he had Drummond owing him everything he owned. I heard Hosea bartered for Drummond's law books." He nodded. "Yep. And he got every one of them. They're still new and hardbound. About 39 volumes. Stout will need an extra wagon just to haul his stuff back up here." Silva walked to the water barrel and got a cup to drink. "I don't mean to change the subject but how's business?"

"Tight. I'm starting to run out of money. It costs a fortune trying to have oil shipped overland. If the Great Salt Lake City were a port city, I'd be rich. As is, I'm having a tough time making ends meet. Any ideas?"

"I've got some hay. Maybe you can light it on fire."

Rost's face became more serious as he stood to retrieve a letter from between two books on his table. "I just got this," he said, handing the envelope over to his friend. "Could turn out to be pretty good. I just have to wait for a good thaw to allow me to get through South Pass and onto the plains."

"Who the hell is John Brown?"

"John Brown? My abolitionist friend?"

"Of course, yes, like Joseph Smith, your religious friend."

"Plain names and fame."

"Isn't he way back in Pennsylvania?"

"Was. He's staying with his children in Kansas nowadays. It's a hotbed."

"He after you to round up some more rifles?"

"Exactly. And he has plenty of backing. Lots of money still pouring into his coffers from Yankee abolitionists. I could get set without too much trouble, just a little footwork."

"Abolitionists are serious folks."

"So are the pro-slavery mobs."

"Are you going to get sucked in?"

"There's no doubt about that. They are definitely on God's errand. My problem is trying to fit everything into a day. There's lots of work. That's the nice thing about abolitionists. They're already on board, doing the heavy lifting."

"You're still thinking that way after Cuffy just beat the hell out of you with the whip?"

Rost shrugged. "Drummond put him up to it. Besides slaves are exactly like the rest of us. There are some good ones and some meaner than badgers. Give them a break, set them free, allow them education and a chance to work for decent wages and they'd be more than fine."

Shep's expression was somber as he thought on the subject. "It's a terrible quandary."

"All right now let me ask you, again changing the subject. What about women in your life? There was a time when I thought something might spark between you and Linda G."

Silva smiled. He was glad the subject hadn't been breached before but now saw that it was time. "And Linda G is a lovely young woman, but I've always felt more like a brother, there. I love women, Aaron. First my mother, *mãe,* and my grandmother, *avó.* I remember seeing their faces on paintings of the with Madonna. My mind just replaced the images. When they died, it left a huge hole in my life. It was a hole I knew could never be filled. For some time, I even considered becoming a Catholic priest. I thought that being celibate would show God how deeply they meant to me." This was a subject that he had chosen to leave buried for years. "But one of the real problems I continued to face was just as I had replaced the faces of the Madonna paintings with my mother's, I then started to do the same with other women. Even when I visited a brothel. I thought I was doing the manly thing. But these women seemed to change. I started seeing them as my ma or *avó.*" He shrugged. "After that, I have wanted to fill my life up with work. I love the nature God had put all around me. I love animals. They are so guileless. I never see anything devious in the way they act. They are simply trying to live their lives as God has intended."

"You are very deep, my friend."

Shep smiled, happy to have finally vocalized thoughts.

"So where are you going to end up?"

"Don't know. I have just sort of left that up to God. I believe He'll help me down the road. Maybe the time will come when I no longer see my mother's face imprinted on other women. Who knows? What I do know is I don't ever remember talking so much."

"It's a good exercise for you. It's been good for me to hear. It has given me a better insight into who you are. I, for one, am grateful the Lord allowed our paths to cross."

"I will admit there are times when I wish the Lord would hurry in his work and let me know how and where he wants me."

"In his own due time."

Shep nodded. "That's the trouble. The due time of the Lord seldom lines up with what I am wanting or expecting or hoping for."

"I'd wager it doesn't line up for the rest of us, either." Aaron was quiet for a long time.

"What?"

"This building Zion. Brigham says we should have the same heart and the same mind. We should dwell in righteousness and shouldn't countenance any poor among us. Instead of seeing your ma's face on women, how would it be if we saw the image of God on everyone? How could we kill or hate, if that were how things were for everybody?"

"I like being myself."

"And God does too. He's not wanting to throw away variety. He loves variety. Like you said, in nature and in people. We all have our favorites and our likes. But when we start to think of each other as brothers and sisters, children of the same Father in heaven, then it will be much harder to turn our backs and pretend we don't care."

"Tall order."

"God's up to the challenge. That's the way I feel after visiting the Endowment House.

"Brazilian, Prussian, Hopi, Timpanogos, Navajo, Mexican, Spanish, abolitionists, slaveholders, Indians, slaves, men, women, old, young, Easterners, Westerners, Southerners, Protestants, Catholics, Jews, Mormons, Irish, English. God has a plan for us to make it back home. To heaven."

Shep shook his head. "How? Life's too short." And he purposely dragged out the name, "Maher-shalal-hash-baz."

"Exactly. The life we see all around us, it's too short. Still, this is God's work. If we don't short-sheet Him, I think we'll see greater things than even these. If not in this lifetime maybe in the spirit world. It will be resolved before the resurrection."

Chapter 34

"The world is governed by very different personages from what is imagined by those who are not behind the scenes." Benjamin Disraeli

Crimea.

For the suffering, those who had been besieged, those who had escaped, the natives and the foreigners, the old and the young, men and women, the soldiers and the non-combatants, the winter dragged on for an eternity. Harsh winds whipped tents and coats, exposing flesh to the bitter cold. Sickness stalked the streets of the bombed-out city, leaving weak and crippled relics in its wake. Food and warmth were nowhere to be found. Strength of both horses and men succumbed to the elements. The only thing good about the fierce gales was that they carried away the stench of death and putrefaction. There was little let up for the cadres selected to pick up and dispose of the corpses.

News of peace talks filled hearts with anticipation that this hell on earth was coming to an end. And not just on the Crimean Peninsula. Selfish countries spewed hosts of diplomats, clothed in warmth and sporting distended stomachs, into the luxurious courts to debate the outcome of the conflict. These were momentous times, signaling the ending of the first war of modern times. Nobility postured for pictures, putting forth their best appearance, downplaying any display of engorged paunches. This was a tight-knit group, most claiming their position because of God-granted pedigrees. Cousins greeted each other in their mother tongues that frequently had nothing to do with the countries they represented or ruled. Color and fashion were on display, wigs and shoes and make-up highlighted the impressive talents of their regimes.

Russia was proud. The British demanded Russia's Black Sea Fleet be scuttled. This demand was met on January 15, 1856. The tsar was angry but when the Prussians threatened to join the Allies, he knew his ability to negotiate was gone. The terms demanded were unfavorable for the Russians.

On February 24, 1856, the Paris Peace Conference opened. There was intense blustering by all the parties involved. By February 29th, the Armistice in Crimea was put into effect. On March 30th the Treaty of Paris was signed, bringing to an end the uncivilized war fought by civilized nations.

The horrific losses were never completely tallied, although the more advanced nations trotted out accountants to declare the precise numbers for their citizens. Body counts became an important area of modern warfare. The Allies committed 603,132 soldiers to the war as opposed to the much larger Russian army of 889,000. The Russian army was composed of conscripted serfs and was far from professional. Russia lost 450,015 casualties but some accounts raised it as high as 1 million. The French contributed 309,268 troops and suffered 95,615 casualties. 10,240 were killed outright; 85,375 were wounded or diseased. The percent of deaths was 30.9%. The British contributed 97,864 soldiers. 2,755 were killed in action. 19, 427 died from wounds or illness. Their total deaths were 22,182. The percent of deaths was 22.7%. The Ottoman Turks lost 45,400 and the Sardinian casualty list contained 2,166.

Within weeks the seas were crowded with troop transports as victorious soldiers scrambled to return to their homes. Orderly departure was demanded. Return with honor and glory. Stories were spun in pubs and bars in Western Europe, recounting the victorious clashes their countrymen had experienced in the far-flung war. Exotic tales told of strange peoples and food and customs. Exultant tales were filled with dashing cavalry, flashing sabers and frenzied horses, booming cannons, and the sudden disappearance of gallant comrades as bombs exploded. Memories of the vicissitudes of disease, battle, and the duration of winter and adverse weather faded into the past. The armies of amputees, blind and otherwise wounded were carefully swept away to the nameless docks and the dead-end streets of London and Paris.

There were muddy roads in Russia clogged with the miserable and defeated and disheartened masses making their ways home slowly, leaving shattered commands and military structures that once required their loyalty and courage, now hoping that maybe some of the stings of loss could be made up by planting their spring crops.

Affairs in Scutari quieted immensely. Ships carrying the wounded and ill to her dock, slowed. As nurses continued their selfless work, an amazing sight met their eyes. The numbers in their wards began to shrink. Men were healing and becoming healthy and then they would leave, returning to Britain. And there were not nearly as many to take their places. Long-term invalids would remain, needing care, but numbers continued to diminish. As days grew longer and warming returned to the region, the sun passed the spring equinox, life again began to bloom from the ground and with the appearance of ducklings. Hope rose and the tired nurses of Scutari looked to the west and their island sweet.

Florence Nightingale called a meeting of her tireless heroines, to thank them for jobs well done.

The pervasive odors that consumed Scutari for the previous year and a half began to change, lessening in the stench. The fresh air invited into the hospital through open windows was not chased away by the smell exuded from wounded bodies.

As the frantic need for nursing services slowed and the facility continued to transform into a more manageable undertaking, the women found themselves with less and less to do. Following Nightingale's directives, they tightened their organizations and began contemplating their own leaving. And then, miracle of miracles, the nurses began to leaving Scutari, carrying their luggage and memories.

"Please, come in!"

Harriett walked into Florence's small cubicle. "I think my time is coming, Florence."

Florence pushed some papers aside from the top of her cluttered desk. "Sorry for the chaos," she said. She found a small calendar and studied it for several seconds. "My goodness, Harriett. You are correct." She scooted her chair back as far as she could before hitting the wall. "There were many days I thought this one would never arrive. You have plans set?"

"I do, mum."

"It's still Florence, dear. You have been such a great help. Your work has been an example for all the other nurses. The world, especially Scutari, is a much better place because of you."

"Thank you, Florence."

"So? Will I be seeing you around London or are your returning back north to Liverpool or Preston?"

"Preston will be first. And that's one of the reasons I wanted to speak with you. It's about Yasmin. She really has no home to return to. Would I be terrible to invite her to come with me?"

"Back to England?" Florence thought about the idea, then shook her head. "No. No. We have much to share with her. If she hasn't a home, we should be so fortunate to have a woman of her capabilities helping us."

"There's another thing, Florence. I might not be remaining in England. I have been toying with the idea of emigrating to America."

"Now this is news. Haven't you already given that plan a go?"

Harriett nodded. "This time it will be different. I am now a woman with training. I would be an asset wherever I chose to live. And having Yasmin for companionship would make the travel enjoyable."

"How does she feel about sailing across the Atlantic? It is still quite the feat."

"So far I haven't spoken much with her about it. First things first, I suppose. Being in the Ottoman Empire holds memories, mostly nightmares for her. She has worked so hard, I see it as the least the Queen can do, welcoming her to Britain."

"And there will be many men who will remember her, many families who will praise her selfless work. I see absolutely no trouble with you taking her to England. Now, crossing the broad ocean, that could be a whole other situation."

"I promise not to push her too hard or insist she follow, should that be the path I choose. But if she comes with me, I have no doubts that she would fit in. Her talent for languages is amazing. And her beauty is exotic. I believe most of my time will be spent beating her suitors back with my Bumbershoot."

Florence leaned back once more and sighed. "These past months have welded us together into a phenomenal sisterhood. Lord Herbert quakes with the thought of strong, independent women returning to the isle. Women's suffrage will not be far behind, I'll wager."

"Mr. Disraeli has mentioned his own concerns. There is nothing to worry ourselves over. All women will do for the Empire is to strengthen her, and give her resolve."

"Of course, my dear." Florence Nightingale realized this chapter in her life was coming to a close. "I will miss you, perhaps the most, Miss Harriett Matthews. Your plans certainly meet my approval. I would only ask that you, and Miss Yasmin, spend more time with me over the remaining weeks."

"Yes, mum. It will be our greatest pleasure."

At the close of the war, besides sending a personal letter to Florence, Queen Victoria instituted a new medal that was called the Victoria Cross and awarded to British soldiers who exhibited the utmost gallantry in battle.

The next two weeks sped by. Yasmin bint Manara trembled with excitement and anticipation to be asked to remain at Harriett's side and voyage to Britain. The idea of this wonderful realm had long played in her mind. A country where it rains so frequently. *How green would the countryside be?* This would be a world apart from Syria. One of the things that drew Yasmin especially close to Harriett was the similarities in their lives. She had lost her own family to the brutality of Ottoman forces years earlier. She felt a tugging on her heartstrings as she contemplated leaving the lands of the minarets, the beacons from whence came the calls to prayer. In Arabic, the *minaret* originated from her name Manara. It was a high place, cliffs in southern Lebanon. But Harriett loved her. She shared with her. She taught her and never in a condescending manner. She was a sister. Yasmin knew her life was almost complete. She needed now only to bear and raise children. When she was in Harriett's presence, she dreamed of more. Together they could embrace the diversity and challenges.

The bitter-sweet day arrived when they walked down the gangplank, heading toward their ship and looking to the west.

Florence followed them at a respectful distance. She waved her white kerchief with animation. "Goodbye, my dear hearts!" she called.

Harriett paused for a moment, placed her luggage on the ground, turned, and sprinted back up the hill to where Florence stood with large streams of tears rolling from her sparkling eyes. Harriett clasped her tightly in an embrace. "God loves you, my dear. And I love you."

As Harriett and Yasmin faced away from Scutari, they did so with the utmost confidence that their lives were never going to be the same. The past, the tiredness, the frustration, the horror, the impotency, the freezing rain, the universal coughing, blood and despair, endless amputations. Modern warfare could only bluster and buffer so much attempting to shield the warriors from the devil's playground. Eventually, they were all engulfed by the fire and brimstone.

The broad ship cast off from its moorings and lunged into the deeper water of the strait and headed towards the Dardenelles, spouting black columns of smoke into the air. The railing around the ship was tightly lined with British soldiers who were looking back at the outlines of Scutari as they grew smaller and fainter. Lights soon began to illuminate the windows of the scattered houses, growing fewer and farther apart.

"I have never seen so much water in all my life," Yasmin admitted.

"Do you feel all right?"

Yasmin smiled. "Camels roll and shake more than this ship. There were times when we traveled back and forth to Balaklava when the ships were smaller and the waves larger, that I felt sick indeed."

"I don't remember you saying anything about it."

The Syrian woman shook her head. "I would not have done that. I did not want to show my weakness. The suffering I experienced was so little when compared with the suffering of the soldiers." They looked down at the foam being cast by the ship's bow. "And you say the ocean is even bigger than this sea?"

"Yes."

"And dangerous?"

"Weather can make things very dangerous on the water, I suppose. There were times I felt very sick. Some people even died during the crossings."

"Were your travels worth it?"

Harriett nodded. "For me, they were worth it."

"Do you want to return to America?"

The question caught Harriett by surprise. "Why do you ask?"

"You are my friend. I have watched you for months. I have listened to you talk to the others. You are a balanced woman. I see much of that because of your travels. It gives strength to what you say. Most of the people we dealt with during the war had never been to America. It sounds like a very promised land."

Harriett agreed. "And it's very large. The people are as different as one would ever find in Europe or Asia or Africa. God has blessed the land with riches and the people have been protected by the oceans from invasions. They value education. America is still very young. It has many weaknesses because of its age. It also has many strengths brought by others who are fleeing the traditions of centuries."

"Like religion?"

"Exactly."

"Allah raises up countries to act as beacons, to be examples, to use their strength to forgive. Do you also believe that?"

"Yes, Yasmin. Allah has blessed me with a very wise friend in you. Thank you for traveling with me. You give me purpose and confidence."

Her words pleased Yasmin.

A week later, after sailing between the Straits of Gibraltar, circumventing the Iberian Peninsula and cutting directly across the Bay of Biscayne, the Plymouth Hope sighted the southern coast of England. It sailed around the lush greenery of Wales and headed to the busy port of Liverpool.

The month of May in England was most beautiful. The skies were clear and breezes were calm. The docks were busiest as the men carrying their duffle bags descended the gangways and began making their way through the streets, looking for transportation, mostly on the rails, taking them farther inland.

"The buildings are newer than those of Constantinople. And taller."

"England has been a port in the storm for many people. They have made her great. But just as you've seen some of the frustrations with the soldiers and Miss Nightingale and the failures to provide, there remains plenty to be done."

"There are no longer slaves here?"

"No slaves from Africa. Laws have been passed about that. Black people are still not accepted by the English as equals. But neither are people from Ireland or India. There are others who feel women now are the slaves of this country."

Yasmin remained silent for several minutes. "There is so much wealth."

"You would think. We'll see more about what you think after you have spent a while here."

True to form, as the days passed by Yasmin, she began seeing the underside of the country. There were problems with unemployment. Homeless Irish littered the streets and wharves in various degrees of inebriation. The constables were kept busy and tweeting from their whistles pierced the busy marketplaces.

The two women made their way to Manchester and then a skip over to Preston. The sights and smells were welcome to Harriett. Yasmin was a novelty. All were impressed with her abilities as her level of education. They universally decided that if Britain's involvement overseas was producing such quality of people, especially women, they were on the right track. The Matthews family and relations clamored for the chance to house and feed the two nurses. They were also anxious to show off their prizes to the villages nearby.

They all did their best to disguise their disappointment when Harriett announced that she needed to return to Liverpool. Yasmin was also ready to accompany her.

"Your family is very nice. The sun must not shine here much. They are so white and no one has black hair."

Harriett decided it was a fair observation.

President Franklin Richards was a busy man. Proselytizing had taken a back seat as converts to the Church of Jesus Christ of Latter-day Saints began lining up to emigrate to the United States and from there on to the Utah Territory. Excitement was high as was the anxiety. The greatest news was the amount of money needed for ocean passage and then the rail trip to Iowa City. The prices had dropped significantly because of the decision to begin using handcarts for the new arrivals. This change in cost made the possibility of travel much more accessible.

President Richards was a hard-working man, from a hard-working family. He was also well placed. His Uncle Willard had been a close friend of the

Prophet Joseph and had been present in the Carthage Jail when Joseph and Hyrum Smith were murdered. The family continued faithful, moving with the Saints from Illinois to the valleys of the mountains. It was now time for him to return to America. His stint as the mission president in Britain was coming to a close.

"Oh, Sister Harriett it is so good to see you again. Your letters were always welcome, but now to see you again, is wonderful beyond belief." The man had been visiting with a couple of his elders. He quietly ushered them from his office.

"Thank you, President Richards. And this is my good friend, and close nursing associate from Syria, Yasmin bint Manara."

Richards smiled pleasantly. "You have both accomplished wonders for the men in the war. God bless you for your willingness to serve."

The women smiled their appreciation.

"Now, to what do I owe this unexpected visit?"

Harriett flashed a quick look at Yasmin. "We have talked over the possibilities, President. We want to emigrate with the Saints. We want to go to America."

The news startled Richards but just as quickly he nodded. "This can easily be done. Do you know when you would like to go?"

"As soon as possible."

Yasmin nodded her agreement.

Richards clapped his hands happily. "This is exactly what we need. I am leaving this next week for New York. I know that the ship's staff is looking for some medical officers. Would that be acceptable?"

"Certainly. And what about the remainder of the cost to get us to Great Salt Lake City?"

"Very reasonable. You can travel with me and my family."

"Well, President Richards there are some people we would like to see on our way west through America. They won't be in your line of travel. We don't want to delay you any."

"That will be just fine. We can line things up once we arrive in America. And to you, Yasmin, may I extend my hand of welcome. We should be so lucky as to have a woman of your stature coming to the Utah Territory."

The next several days were a blur of activity, then suddenly Harriett and Yasmin were watching again as their ship cast off from the dock, this time moving towards the Irish Sea.

"This is indeed exciting, Harriett."

The Atlantic crossing was gentle. Winds and waves stayed low. It was hard not to be excited by the passengers as they realized their destination was drawing closer. Lifetimes of prayer and hopes paved the path before them. America was the land of their Prophet Joseph Smith. It had provided the security and freedoms necessary for the restoration of the gospel of Jesus Christ. As wonderful as the prospects were, none were unaware of the trials many of their people had been forced to endure. They had been expelled from the United States of America. As citizens, they were denied their constitutional rights. The dreary elements had caused a large number of them to perish. Yet they pushed forward and began settling in the fastness of the mountains and deserts of western North America. Letters to Britain from their predecessors informed them of the abundance of beauty and opportunities. There were challenges with the lack of water and the Indians and the long distances between settlements, as well as the States themselves. But they knew that the God of their fathers was watching over them.

"You have been remarkably quiet regarding religion," Harriett finally said as they were drawing closer to the East Coast of the United States.

"I have few questions at present."

"And yet you are willing to travel across the earth?"

Yasmin replied confidently. "It is similar to a *hajj*. I am going to a holy city. I am going to see these Children of Israel for myself. Afterward, I might have questions."

"The United States is so very far from Syria."

"Scutari was far from Syria. But there I was surrounded by need and I had you. I trust there will still be need in America and you are still close. I am complete."

New York City was the gateway to the country's hinterlands. Splitting off from the main group, the nurses bid farewell to President Richards and the Saints they had come to know during the month-long crossing. Most of the passengers would continue to Iowa City and from there they would be assigned a handcart company to travel with for the balance of the trek.

The excitable Latter-day Saint emigrants were met by specially trained facilitators who guided them away from the sketchier areas of town and got them boarded onto rail trains to carry them to Iowa and away from the confusion that engulfing everyone else.

Harriett used the no-nonsense skills she had developed in Liverpool and Constantinople to steer their way clear of danger and found a suitable coach to take them south to Philadelphia.

Chapter 35

"If you have a bad thought about yourself, tell it to go to hell because that is exactly where it came from." Brigham Young

Cuffy Cato answered the door and looked down on Shep, recognizing him instantly. "What do you want?"

"I'm here to talk with the judge. I heard he could use my help."

Cato glanced down at the six-shooter strapped around Silva's waist. "Still armed, I see."

"Wouldn't have it any other way."

"Lucky you."

"That's the way I see it."

"Give me a minute." Cato closed the door and went to call the judge.

The man Cuffy didn't come across as surly or brutish, yet whenever in his presence and because of their history, Shep felt it best to be armed. Shep looked the house over. It was good sized, well preserved while the Drummonds were in Fillmore.

While in Fillmore, the Drummonds had rented a house belonging to Hosea Stout, the man of many trades, and the man that was successful in bringing Drummond into financial bondage. The attorney had been elected to the House of Representatives for the territory. He was also elevated to be the speaker. Stout turned around and rented his place to the Drummonds as long as they would need to stay in Fillmore. Court had dragged on this year much longer than expected.

All things in this life come to an end, including the Drummonds' stay in Fillmore. They returned to Salt Lake City by the beginning of springtime. After nine months of dealing with the pompous federal judge, the residents of the territory knew how to avoid him and his oppressive court proceedings. Drummond had not intended to stay in Utah Territory for more than a year. He felt justified with his efforts. He had developed an intense dislike for Brigham Young and the theocratic form of government the people in the territory adopted, choosing it over a federal system. Judge Kinney wasn't much of an ally, either.

By the look of things, it had been a long day for Judge William Drummond. Cuffy invited the stockman into the parlor, then disappeared.

"Got any news?" the judge asked, his voice underscoring the tiredness that permeated his entire body.

"Brother Call has some men and half a dozen wagons set to meet you just above Bear River. You can go with them around to the Humbolt and then on to the Carson Valley."

"What would it cost me to have you go along with us?"

"You sure that's what you want?"

"I gotta get out of here. Clean. What's your cost?"

Shep counted the days in his head. "$200."

Drummond swiveled his chair around and called into the back portion of the house. A minute later Ada appeared, looking as fresh as ever. "You got $200 to pay this man for an escort to Carson Valley?"

"Will I get it back?" she asked with a hint of suspicion, then winked at Shep, reminding him of the crucible she had put Aaron through.

"Sure. We'll need to leave in a couple days." Drummond turned back to Shep. "Any luck with Kanosh?"

"'Fraid not. He says he hasn't seen the men. Let me ask you this, Bill. If he scrounged up the culprits, would it be enough to keep you here to see things through?"

Judge Drummond didn't like Shep calling him by his common name. Then again, he knew he was in the man's debt. He shook his head and held up his arms in defeat. "Not a chance in hell. Damned Indians will always get their way. Just between us, I can't stand this place any longer. Carson Valley belongs to the third district and it's close enough to California. I'll take care of business and then hop over the border and leave this God-forsaken land forever."

"President Pierce and his cronies okay with that?"

"They will be when they hear what I have to say."

Shep nodded as if he were paying attention. "I'm lighting out right now. You want me to have Brother Call wait up a couple days?"

"Sure. We might be a little late. What about you?"

"You're on the hook for $200, *amigo*. I'll wait for you."

Shep left the house and untied his horse.

"Do you have a minute, sir?"

He recognized Ada's voice and turned to see her lean casually against the banister.

"Ma'am?"

"What can you tell me about Mr. Rost?"

The question didn't surprise him. "He's out of town, ma'am."

"I see. He didn't go to California, did he?"

"The opposite direction, to the States, with Almon Babbitt. He's been gone a while."

****

A broad title of Beecher's Bibles ornamented the wooden boxes. The stenciling on Rost's crates always brought a smile to his lips. One customs agent had commented about the obvious need for Bibles to be distributed among the Indians. "Probably help the likes of those damned abolitionists, too," the man said.

Rost agreed, promising that he would take the crates to them first, remarking they would get the most use out of them.

"Damned straight."

Regardless of the recension of the Missouri Compromise, the state remained a slave holder's stronghold. Smuggling the rifles across the state was fraught with danger. The river was the safest and most direct way to Kansas City. Aaron's best trait was his accent. Few of the rough-looking characters hanging around the boat docks gave him a second glance.

Another thing that impressed Rost, was the swift manner the country implemented new modes of transportation. These days, the riverboats were much safer, having fewer explosions. Rail tracks were being laid, continually dividing the land, slowing and interfering with the migration of the buffalo herds across the Great Plains. Unfortunately, his trip to Osawatomie was still by buckboard.

When the Kansas-Nebraska Act was written in 1853, establishing the territories of Kansas and Nebraska, both Senator Douglas of Illinois and Atchison of Missouri thought the Free-Staters living in Illinois and Iowa would move into Nebraska, while Pro-Slavery people would go into Kansas. But Free Staters preferred Kansas. And the pro-slavery people were not as quick to move.

The Territory of Kansas was seething because of the conflict between the Free State forces and those of the Pro-Slavery stance. Lawrence had been founded in 1854 by abolitionists from Massachusetts. They were loathed by their pro-slavery neighbors. With Missouri so close and having been a slave state for so long, pro-slavery groups were larger. Forts Leavenworth and Achison housed soldiers who leaned heavily on the pro-slavery side. This proved a problem when the militias or when the military was called to settle a skirmish between factions.

With it appearing that Kansas was leaning towards becoming a Free-State, David Atchison viewed this as a breach of faith. Atchison led 5000 heavily armed Border Ruffians into Kansas, calling on pro-slavery Missourians to uphold slavery by force and "to kill every God-damned abolitionist in the district." They seized control of all polling places at gunpoint, cast tens of thousands of fraudulent votes for pro-slavery candidates, and elected a pro-slavery legislature.

Pro-slavery camps generally had most of the money and were able to control larger amounts of land. On July 2, 1855, they set up a territorial capital in Pawnee, Kansas. It lasted for five days, then moved on to Shawnee Mission. Abolitionists called the attempt bogus and tried setting up their version of a territorial capital in Topeka

In November and December 1855, a series of skirmishes broke out around Lawrence and the Wakarusa River valley. Pro-Slavery forces broke into the

US Arsenal at Liberty, Missouri, and stole weapons and munitions, including the Old Sacramento Cannon.

On April 23rd, Sam Jones, the sheriff of Douglas County, entered Lawrence attempting to arrest several Free State men. The incensed citizens fired at him, wounding him as he escaped. The federal marshal, Israel Donaldson, proclaimed that the failed assassination of Jones had interfered with the execution of warrants issued against the extra-legal Free State legislature. In consequence, Jones and Donaldson raised an 800-man mob from Missouri and attacked the town. On May 21st they destroyed the two anti-slavery newspapers and threw the type into the river. After ordering the evacuation of the Free State Hotel, a structure that was seen as a military building, the Border Ruffians knocked down the building, firing balls into it with the Old Sacramento Cannon They then burned it, while Jones shouted, "This is the happiest moment of my life." Only one man died during the sack. One of Jones' gang was struck in the head by falling debris as the hotel was coming down.

A fiery John Brown showed up in Kansas, spouting his opinions and doing everything he could to draw attention to the abolitionist point of view. "I don't think the people of the slave states will ever consider the subject of slavery in its true light till some other argument is resorted to other than moral persuasion," he thundered. "Now let us thank the eternal power, convinced that Heaven but tries our virtue by affliction: That oft the cloud that wraps the present hour serves but to brighten all our future days."

Rost again felt the blood coursing in his veins. John Brown had a way with words. And he did not possess an ounce of cowardice. He called the Free Staters cowards more than once, to buoy flagging spirits.

On May 19th and 20th, a Republican senator from Massachusetts, Charles Sumner, an ardent abolitionist, spent days giving a long diatribe against the Kansas-Nebraska Act, in Washington, calling it the Crime Against Kansas. Both sides of the debate sexualized the rhetoric. Abolitionists claimed that slaveholders wanted the slave women for their stables, while the slaveholders claimed the abolitionists only wanted to have black women accessible to marry and dilute the race.

Because of this argument, South Carolina Representative Preston Brooks, a pro-slavery Democrat, attacked Sumner on the floor of the capital with his cane, beating the older man senseless. News of the assault was spread via the telegraph. John Brown was apprised of it, infuriating him further. He insisted the Pottawatomie Rifles ride north to intervene where they could. On May 24th, after sundown, the abolitionists attacked several houses, dragging the pro-slavery men out and hacking them to death with sabers, killing five men. The incident was called the Pottawatomie Massacre. Frederick Douglass called it a terrible remedy for a terrible malady.

"Regardless of the evils of slavery, this form of mobocracy cannot be tolerated."

"The men made their beds," Brown argued. "This has gone too far. It is beyond debate or discussion. Look at what happened to Senator Sumner. A younger man takes offense at his cousin being dressed down by Senator Sumner, so he resorts to beating the man within an inch of his life. Talking has lost its purpose. Now is the time for action."

Aaron shook his head adamantly. "It can't be, John. This is craziness. A death here will result in a murder there. There will be no end to the bloodshed."

"Of course, I don't expect a foreigner to understand. These are terrible days, Aaron. We are indebted to you for the rifles you have brought. They will help even the field, but the war is moving forward. You are either with us or else you need to get out of the territory. We can't be spending our efforts defending someone not willing to fight."

"But this is not the way to prosecute the problem. You and I have both read the scripture. Let God be the judge."

"So far as I ever observed God's dealings with my soul, the flights of preachers sometimes entertained me, but it was scripture expressions which did penetrate my heart, and in a way peculiar to themselves. God sees it." He snorted indignantly. "I have only a short time to live, only one death to die, and I will die fighting for this cause. There will be no more peace in this land until slavery is done for. I will give them something else to do than extend slave territory."

Chapter 36

"I think every family should have a dog; it is like having a perpetual baby; it is the plaything and crony of the whole house. It keeps them all young." John Brown

The Winslows and the extended town of Lexington were thrilled to see Harriett again, to hear of her exploits and be introduced to Yasmin. They were proud to claim them. The visit was over too soon. Mrs. Winslow cried as they prepared to leave. Hugging Harriett and trembling in her embrace, Mrs. Winslow stepped back and wiped the tears from her cheeks. She started to speak but Harriett put her fingers to the older woman's lips and nodded.

"God loves you, my dear. And I love you."

From the office in his house, A.W. Doniphan watched the approach of the carriage carrying two women. They had come from the direction of the river. *Lexington, maybe?*

He checked the clock on the wall. It wasn't 10:00 a.m. yet. Too late for breakfast and too early for lunch. He started wondering about the visitors, then decided to sit back and allow them to come and present their needs.

A few minutes later, a knock came softly on his door. "Mr. Doniphan, two women to see you, sir," his servant girl announced.

He smiled pleasantly. "Please show them in, Jane."

A minute later the two young women were escorted into Doniphan's office and seated. They were both attractive women, quite different from one another in appearance. The lighter-skinned woman looked familiar. *Where have I crossed her path?*

"I am Mr. Doniphan at your service," he said after shaking their gloved hands briefly, then returning to his seat.

"Yes, of course, Mr. Doniphan. I met you four years ago. You assisted me after the deaths of my family, killed in the *Saluda* explosion on the river. You came to Lexington where I was convalescing."

The recollection returned immediately. *Yes, it was the same woman, now somewhat more mature and more traveled. Slightly weathered but not yet thirty years old.*

"Yes. Yes, of course...Miss Matthews?"

"Harriett Matthews."

"You were staying with the Winslows. Very fine family." With the return of his memories, Doniphan leaned back in his chair and began wondering about the visit. *Are things in order? Who was this darker-skinned woman? Was she Mexican?* "And how may I be of service to you, Miss Harriett?"

"First let me thank you for the referral to see Colonel Thomas Kane. He was more than prepared for me and gave me all the direction I was needing at the time."

"Yes. Kane. Another excellent man. I am pleased to hear he was helpful. But that was a number of years ago. What has transpired since, may I ask?"

"Certainly. But first, this is my companion, Miss Yasmin bint Manara."

The blood left Doniphan's face as the weight of Harriett's information sat ready to unfold. "Very pleased," he said quickly, nodding at Yasmin. "But just one minute. You are an English woman and wanted to return home and take up nursing. I trust that is what happened. Suddenly I am curious as to where your work led you. Were you by chance assigned to work with the British overseas, during the war?"

Harriett was happy to see how well-connected Mr. Doniphan had stayed. "I'm quite impressed with your understanding, Mr. Doniphan."

He waived the courtesy aside. "Please. Call me Alexander."

"I had the opportunity to work and study in a hospital in London with a brilliant nursing corps, taught and led by Miss Florence Nightingale."

"Yes! Yes! That's the name of the woman Tom, er, Colonel Kane, knew in Britain. She was a help, then?"

"If I could only choose her to be my sister," she glowed. "Florence was also well-connected with the government and when the war broke out in the Crimea, she was asked to take her nurses to the military barracks in Scutari and turn it into a hospital. I was selected with about 40 other women and that's exactly what we did. That's where I worked for the past two years. Yasmin was also a nurse there. She is from Syria and has a definite knack when it comes to medicine and languages."

Alexander nodded and pondered the information for several long minutes. "Such a terrible conflict, for both sides. I can only imagine how brutal it was and how important your role was to tend the wounded."

Harriett smiled again. Yasmin also nodded and followed her example.

"So, now you have returned to the United States. A diplomatic mission or education, perhaps?"

"No, sir. We are simply returning to continue the journey I was undertaking four years ago. We had the chance of stopping by the Kane household in Philadelphia first to thank him for his help. His sweet young wife, Bessie, is just expecting a new baby."

Doniphan smiled. "That's what I call my Elizabeth. She's Bessie too. Is this their first?"

"No. They lost their first baby but then had a little girl several years ago."

"And her name?"

"Harriett."

"Oh?"

"Named after Bessie's mother."

"Oh."

"They're hoping this new baby is a boy. She's expecting in November. They want to name him Elisha Kent after Thomas' big brother."

"Oh, yes. The explorer. The adventurer. Very famous."

"We also stopped in on the Winslows in Lexington before coming here. They are all well and send their best."

"This information is much appreciated." Then, as if struck by lightning, he added, "Oh, yes. You are a Mormon. Your family was traveling to the Utah Territory."

"We think our services may be needed in the mountains," Yasmin interjected. Both Alexander and Harriett were surprised and pleased to hear her voice, as well as sense her independence.

"Without a doubt, young lady. I'm sure Harriett has told you that I knew many of the Latter-day Saints years back. I even defended some of them."

"She has told me, sir. And we thank you, sir."

"I assure you it was my pleasure. I rather enjoyed sticking my finger in Governor Boggs' eye. Then a little later, Porter Rockwell was picked up and thrown in jail just across the river in Independence. We were successful there, as well. But when he got out, he looked like a starving scarecrow. Fortunately, he got back to Nauvoo safely. I haven't heard much from him or them since. Our newspapers continue to harangue the Mormons, accusing them of every dastardly happening that takes place in the West, what with making league with the Indians to murdering federal representatives to wanting to secede from the Union. For being so isolated from the States, Brigham seems quite adept at stirring the pot. And now all this talk about polygamy…" He stopped, suddenly concerned that he might have stumbled onto something where the two women were concerned.

Harriett jumped to his rescue. "Oh no, sir. We are not members of a harem. And we are not wandering blindly into Brigham Young's lair. This is just a direction we feel we should go."

"Yes. And thank you. I didn't mean to pry." He looked the women over quickly. Their clothing attested to their well-being. "And so then, Miss Harriett, may I inquire after the meaning of the visit?"

"I wanted to thank you, sir, for your help and concern after the devastating trial I was called to pass through. You were a Godsend. The help you offered financially as well as your professional services. You played a special role in helping me to right myself and get on with my life. I am also aware of some of the troubles you have here at home, with your dear wife. I merely wanted to stop and thank you for your help and wisdom. It has blessed my life."

Harriett's announcement was not what he had expected. It came as sweetly as fresh running water. "You are most kind," he said. He thought again for a moment. "I am reminded of a story I have heard. It comes from the Bible. Ten lepers sought the Savior for healing. When he helped them, they went on their way rejoicing, but one returned and thanked him. And he was a Samaritan. Now, I'm certainly not saying that you were a leper and of course not a Samaritan, nor am I the Savior, but your words today remind me of the sweet account. You are a remarkable woman, Harriett Matthews. You are a credit to your family and sex."

Harriett and Yasmin smiled and stood from their chairs and started for the door. "May I ask you one other thing, Alexander?"

"Of course."

"Your servant girl. She is black. Does that mean you are a slaveholder?"

The question hit like an accusation. "I am, my dear. Unfortunately." He shook his head while thinking. "It has been my lot in life for years. I have become used to the lifestyle. I do not approve of the institution. But I am at a loss as to how to settle the issue. Besides being a humanitarian problem, it is also an immediate financial quandary. What should happen to the slaves if they were emancipated? Do we allow them to wander through the country, homeless? Jobless? Or do we ship them back to Africa? I have followed some of the speeches of Frederick Douglass. At this moment there is trouble brewing not many miles west of here between the abolitionists and pro-slavery folks in Kansas. We have an active underground railroad going right through this state and up into Iowa." He stopped and noticed that both women were listening intently to what he was saying. "Please know that personally, I am in favor of northern leanings, despite living in Missouri. It is a serious matter that needs to be resolved but even in our Congress, people are infused with emotion over the subject, enough so as to come to blows."

"Would it be different if women and slaves could vote?"

Doniphan smiled. "Of course. We are working with a Constitution that has as many interpretations as people who read it. I pray to God that slavery will be resolved. And soon. And to everyone's satisfaction. We, in America, are aware of Britain's laws regarding slavery. I wish we were as progressive. Then again, we are a much different country. A much different society."

Harriett and Yasmin appreciated his willingness to give them some time. He walked them outside and saw that they were comfortably seated behind their driver. They waved and smiled pleasantly as they rode away, back towards the river. *Will they continue to their destination on a steamboat?*

Alexander absentmindedly stomped the dust from his boots and turned back into his house. Abolitionism and slavery. How he hated the topic. He knew storm clouds were forming on the horizon. *Could they be war clouds? What will happen to life in Richmond? The family? What about the people he had known and associated with for decades?* The seriousness began cascading onto his shoulders as he passed by Jane, and entered once again into his office. He could see his visitors as they crested a low rise then disappeared.

Doniphan flopped into his chair. It was good to be a public servant. He had done good things throughout his career, not least of which had been to assist this Harriett Matthews. He had helped Smith, and then Rockwell, all against the wishes of his friend David Rice Atchison. They had marched together during the Mormon War of 1838, and they had fought together against Mexico almost a decade later. Their careers were quite interrelated. Now Atchison was in Washington. He was also a staunch slaveholder. He was a proponent of the status quo. He had worked hard to get the Kansas-Nebraska Act passed. Now he was furious with the abolitionists in the Kansas Territory, stirring up such trouble, even committing murders. He knew too many residents of Missouri who were not about to let it go. The conflict aroused severe emotions. People on both sides of the argument quoted the same verses from the Bible to support their stance, only they interpreted them with diametric opposition.

Alexander shook the thoughts from his head. He had plenty to contend with. His law practice was busy, and his wife's health was an issue. He hoped to be excused for not being caught up in the conflict. One thing was certain. A resolution was in the offing and it would turn the world on its head, if not for a year, then for generations to come.

****

"How much longer is this damn trip?" a worn-out Bill Drummond asked Shep when he returned to the wagon after a short scouting jaunt.

"Come on now, Judge. You can see the Sierras as well as anyone."

Drummond rolled his eyes with exasperation. "I've been seeing the same mountains for a week," he whined. "Just tell me we're almost there."

"We're almost there."

"And mean it."

"We'll be in Carson Valley tomorrow."

Relief washed over Drummond's countenance. "Tomorrow."

"Late tomorrow."

Drummond sighed.

"Get control of yourself, Bill," Ada snapped. She was tired of his whining as well. "You knew this was going to be a long one."

"I don't think I can stand seeing another bean or piece of salted beef."

Ada shook her head. The travel had taken effect on her as well. Her hair wasn't curled. Her make-up was non-existent. The clothing she was wearing was rumpled and dusty. She had removed her jewelry and stored it away shortly after leaving Salt Lake City.

"I feel like one of the squaws," she said wearily.

Now it was Shep's turn to roll his eyes in disbelief. Cuffy caught his antics and chuckled.

There were five wagons in the party with four men sitting in each one. They were escorted by ten mounted soldiers. They liked being referred to as Dragoons. Silva looked at them like a mounted mob, uncouth in their demeanor. Since Ada was the only woman traveling with them, assorted men found a reason to stand around the Drummond wagon whenever she was getting up in the morning or getting ready for bed. She noticed the attention and casually bared a shoulder or allowed her slip to ride up higher on her hip than normal.

"What you thinking about, Shep?" Cuffy's low voice caught the Brazilian by surprise. He was beginning to like Drummond's servant. His presence drew the attention of every Indian with whom they came in contact. His stature frightened them as well. The tight curls in his hair also caused a stir among. They appreciated long black locks, but Cuffy's short, scrunchy hair instigated numerous conversations.

Some northern Paiutes braves had been hired by Ada and the mounted soldiers to collect any stray horses they could find. They had been successful during the trip, always seeming to return with five or six every time they left to scour for the animals. Shep wondered if they knew where the wild horses were grazing or perhaps, they would simply swoop into an isolated *rancho* and make off with their livestock. Although he chose not to look at the horses closely, Silva was certain a number sported their singular brands.

"I'm leaving early," Shep said to the Drummonds. "Going into Genoa and letting them know of our plans. I'll be back before you get too close."

Drummond began to argue but Shep held his hand up.

"Hales knows the way. Just keep behind him. You'll just keep following the Carson River. It'll get you there pretty close by the time I get back."

With the rising sun on his back, Shep nudged his horse into a gallop, watching for tell-tale potholes and rocks, making his way quickly towards the growing town of Genoa and Judge Orson Hyde's homestead. From a distance, he noticed some changes. There were more horses than he would have expected and a couple more wagons. The Hydes had visitors.

By the time he arrived and tied his horse to a hitching post, Shep noticed the slender string of smoke spiraling into the clear summer air. He had arrived just in time for breakfast. The Hydes were well regimented, having their children doing the morning cooking and gathering the eggs, allowing their mother to sleep.

"Shep Silva!" Orson bellowed as he saw the other man stroll into his house. "Didn't expect you so soon." He stood and shook hands forcefully.

"Drummond's driving me crazy. I was ready to ride day and night just to get him to stay quiet. The company will be here this evening."

Hyde sighed. "It'll be good to have him here and then go. His attitude tuckers me out."

"Who you got visiting?"

Orson perked up. "You noticed, did you? You'll never guess in a hundred years. They got in just last night. The Sweeneys!"

Shep was speechless. "Wait. My Sweeneys? From San Bernardino?"

"The very ones."

"What are they doing here in Genoa?"

"I'll let you ask them. I heard them up. Matter of fact, when you came inside, I was thinking it might have been Mark."

Signaling that he would return shortly, Orson Hyde trotted up the creaking stairs. A few muffled words were exchanged and there was a sudden rush of activity. The Sweeneys came bounding down the stairs, almost running over Hyde. All were happy to see the Brazilian, especially the Wetoyous. Hugs went all around. Smiles beamed. Shep took a minute gazing into each face, then squeezed each carefully.

He pointed knowingly at Linda G. "Just who is this beautiful woman?" he asked causing her to blush. "What is the matter with those blind men in San Berdo? How could they ever let someone this fine escape?" Linda G blushed again.

By this time the whole house was awake and crowding into the kitchen and front room. Everyone was talking and laughing. The boys were horsing around and showing off. The Hydes finally demanded that they quiet down long enough to say a prayer on the breakfast.

The quantity of food was impressive. Shep didn't remember so many pans being used to cook. He also didn't remember being so hungry. Fortunately, Sister Hyde knew how to stoke the fires and his stomach was filled quickly.

"Now Mark are you going to tell me why you're here?"

Sweeney sighed and burped. "It was time for us to get out of California," he said. "The place keeps growing and we're getting outnumbered, and the newcomers are mostly Gentiles. We did well enough for a while, but it just got to be a bit much. Brig's called Lyman and Rich back to the Great Salt Lake City and is sending them off on missions. It's leaving folks in San Bernardino slim on the leadership side."

"What about Bill Pickett? He's smart enough."

Mark shook his head. "Don't think so. And with most of his business coming from Los Angeles, he's spending more and more of his time over there."

"So, Genoa?"

Mark shrugged. "Not quite ready to go back to Salt Lake City yet. We just thought this might be where we're needed."

"You got that right," Orson chimed.

Shep stayed visiting longer than he had planned. By the time he climbed back onto his horse and thundered out of town to meet up with the Drummonds, they were an hour outside of town. If Judge Drummond was upset, he didn't say anything.

Drummond's party was happy to arrive in Genoa. The men hurriedly checked into the hotel, unpacked their belongings, stabled their animals, and turned Ada's horses into a well-fenced pasture. All this was accomplished in record time. From there, their trained lookouts directed them to the bars and brothel. By nightfall, most of the men were drunk, asleep, or in jail. It was just how they hoped it would be. The citizens had come to expect this type of behavior from soldiers. The settlers could endure such comportment, at least for a limited time. The visitors would be placed on notice before it got too out of hand.

"You staying long this time?" Hyde asked the Brazilian.

"A few more days, maybe."

"The Wetoyous are pretty happy to see you."

"Likewise."

As if reading his thoughts, Hyde added, "I think the Sweeneys will fit in just fine. I sent them to see a couple places in Franktown that are up for sale. There's some good places to garden and grazing is real good. Brother Sweeney has his eye on some cattle and horses."

"I appreciate you looking after them."

"Anything to keep me away from Drummond."

"What are your thoughts about Linda G?"

"She's a real keeper. Numaga and Sarah were here when they arrived. He sized her up quick-like."

"I don't want Little Winnemucca trying to corral her as another wife."

"She's too smart for that. I will say, however, that Sarah was also quite taken with her. I think she's adopted her as a sister. It was a good thing the Sweeneys had so many kids, otherwise, Sarah would have spent the night."

"Sorry for the trouble."

"What trouble? Sarah acts like Linda G is a goddess. Everything from the way she smiles speaks, walks, braids hair. Sarah is wanting to copy her."

"She is a good girl. I can't believe how much I've missed them."

"Zeenyo spends his time with the animals. All the little kids follow him, too. At first, it bothered him, but I think he's getting to like it."

"What can you tell me about Herman?"

"Ah. He's the berries. He takes his role as brother and priesthood holder very seriously. The church means everything to him. He's read the Book of Mormon several times. He doesn't see it as a fairytale. It has real meaning for him. That first night he stayed up talking with me till late. Being Hopi, he sees a lot of his people's stories as parallels. You named him Herman?"

Shep smiled at the memory. "Yep. They spoke Spanish, so I decided he would be Hermano. It's been shortened to Herman. Seems to suit him fine."

"You couldn't have come up with a better name. Back when I went to Palestine, I remember seeing Mount Hermon, away up in the north part of the country. It's tall and has snow much of the year on it. Some people even think it might have been where Jesus took Peter, James, and John when he was transfigured. Anyway, some say it means the table of God or his altar. It has the same root as Amen and that was certainly a title used for Jesus in John's book of Revelation. And Ammon is one of the Egyptian names for God."

"You told Herman all this?"

"He was quite impressed. He thinks you were inspired to give him that name."

"Wish I could claim it."

"In any event, it's an mn name, It's theophoric. It's using God's name in ours. Like Israel. The el stands for God. Or Isaiah. The iah stands for Jehovah. We have names like this all over in the Bible. Well, if mn is like that, a theophoric name, then there you have it. The reason it's used so much in the Book of Mormon."

"MN names, huh?"

"It's the most common name in the book. Amon, that's number one. So, you have Laman. Then Mormon. It's all over the place. And it certainly makes sense."

Shep smiled. "Whatever works, Orson. The thing is, I can't tell you how much I appreciate the help you and Mark and others are in raising the Wetoyous. Giving them a sense of their importance. Talking to them about scriptures."

"It's easy when it's true."

"Well, some folks think I deserve the credit. They couldn't be further from the truth. The Wetoyous are just good kids, listening to good instruction. Good as gold."

Shep couldn't sleep that night. Seeing the Wetoyous was an inspiration. He came upon the idea of inviting them to ride with him to Tooele. The next morning a bleary-eyed Shep Silva made his presentation to the Sweeneys. Both Mark and Martha had grown to love and cherish the youths, but Martha especially was concerned about losing Linda G.

"She's become my daughter, Shep. Just like Julie. I would rather go with her than to lose her. Especially at this time. She is such a blessing. I will give in to whatever she decides, but I'm letting you know that it would be extremely difficult for me. Also, don't even think about bringing the subject up to Sarah Winnemucca. Not until Linda G has decided to leave Carson Valley."

The Sweeneys' feelings helped Shep see things differently.

"What do you think?" he asked after positing the idea to the Wetoyous. Herman and Zeenyo lit up like firecrackers. They loved the Sweeneys but the thought of tagging along with Shep sounded like the adventure they were craving.

Linda G was more composed. "I love you, Shep," she said. "I just don't know that this would be the best for me and Martha and the Sweeny kids. Not now."

These were precisely the answers he was hoping to receive. It was like the Lord had read their thoughts and answered their prayers.

He nodded as wisely as he could. "And I am sure Sarah Winnemucca would agree with your decision," he told her, bringing a beautiful smile to her face.

A week later, following the advice of Orson Hyde, Shep stopped in at the courthouse prior to his leaving for Great Salt Lake City. "Judge Hyde wanted to make sure you didn't have anything for me to take back, messages or whatnot."

Judge William Drummond was rested from his travels and beginning to feel his oats, reverting to his smug ways and attitudes. He shook his head. "Not besides telling that sonofabitch Brigham Young to start counting his days, because they're numbered."

"He's heard that before."

"Damn you, Shep. You just put up with things. You need to take a stand, then stick to it."

"I'm going to join the church and become an abolitionist."

Drummond smiled at Silva's snide remarks. "I'd send Cuffy to get you."

"Not before I'd have him freed. He'll name his kids after me sooner than after you."

The thought made Drummond pause. Their verbal sparring was good-natured but what Shep said struck a chord. Perhaps he was telling the truth. "I'll be letting Cuffy go before long," he confessed.

"Write and let me know."

Drummond didn't understand the Brazilian. He never seemed to take himself seriously so he could never get under his skin. Shep was an independent man who was hard to read. Several times Drummond suspected that he had secretly joined the church. He was respectful of the leadership in Salt Lake City. He worked with and got along famously with the members, including Porter Rockwell and Bill Hickman. As a matter of another fact, Drummond saw Shep as being groomed for future leadership, if not in the church, then in the territory. His accent and background were endearing. The judge was also thankful that Ada hadn't cast her eyes upon Silva. That would have been an even more difficult row to hoe.

Shep's eyes scanned the letter lying on the desk that Drummond was writing. The latter was instantly disappointed it had been seen.

"You writing to Gunnison's widow?"

Judge Drummond had been caught. It was something he didn't want to get out until the timing was right. "No. Not really. Just some legal stuff."

"Doesn't sound too legal to me. You're still mad that you couldn't get Kanosh to cough up the murderers. It made you look lame so you're out to clear your name, make yourself not stink quite so much to folks back in the States."

"I warn you, Silva. You'd best mind your own damned business."

Shep chuckled. "Now you're mad because I read faster than you thought I could. Here, let me just finish it."

The judge snatched it from off the desk. "Go to hell, Shep."

"After you, Bill. I'm sure we'll be in good company."

"I got nothing more to say. I'll stay here long enough to catch up on the dockets, then we'll be going to California. I plan on heading back to Illinois in the springtime."

Shep nodded. "That's more than what I came with. Maybe you'll want to tamp down all the anti-Mormon speculation that's swirling around. President Pierce and Stephen Douglas already have their hands full with Bloody Kansas. Fomenting a bunch of other lies won't be helping them any. That's what I think."

"I think you're a sonofabitch."

Shep Silva checked his horse outside the courthouse, resaddled him, and noted his hooves. Both he and his mount were anxious to get on the trail. Nothing Drummond had shared was news. Drummond was finished with his stint in the territory. He wanted to return to the States with as much pomp and circumstance as he could muster. His political capital was draining by the day. He decided that stirring public opinion against the church was a sure-fire way to maintain a high profile. He had lived among the Saints. He claimed to know, how business was run and the secret intentions of the esoteric Mormon patriarchy.

Meeting up with the Wetoyou boys just outside of town, Shep Silva chose not to ride the Humbolt River trail, taking instead a more direct, southerly route. It was more difficult, more dangerous, but fewer miles.

Chapter 37

"Without knowing what I am and why I am here, life is impossible." Leo Tolstoy

The Republican Party was established in 1854 in opposition to the Kansas-Nebraska Act, in an attempt to keep slavery from expanding into western states.

John Charles Fremont was an iconic American. He was given the name: The Pathfinder. He was a native of Georgia but an outspoken abolitionist. He was well educated and spent a good amount of his life exploring the American West, finding and naming Pyramid Lake and the Carson Pass over the Sierra Nevada mountains. Because of the time he spent in the West, he came to know some famous explorers and trappers, especially Kit Carson. He helped solidify the US control over California during the Mexican-American War. After California was admitted into the United States, Fremont was one of the first two Senators elected.

The Republican Party held their first presidential convention June 17-19, 1856 in Philadelphia, Pennsylvania, and nominated John C. Fremont as their presidential nominee. They ran on the phrase, Free Soil, Free Men, and Fremont, looking to rid the country of those twin relics of barbarism, slavery, and polygamy, popular planks in northern states. Bloody Kansas and the position of John Brown threatened to ignite a civil war, something the Republican Party wanted to manage.

James Buchanan was chosen by the Democrats as their nominee and even though he was a northern politician. Millard Fillmore was the nominee for the Know-Nothing Party, which split the Republican vote, allowing Buchanan to be elected. None of the three presidential candidates spent any time stumping for the position.

****

The excitement was heightened by the Mormons in Britain wanting to emigrate to America and take advantage of the Perpetual Emigration Fund, together with the lowering of costs due to the use of handcarts.

Steamships could cross the Atlantic in 10 days but passages on these swift vessels were much more expensive. Sailing ships required between 38 and 42 days, when they were in good working order and enjoyed a decent wind. At this time, the turnaround for the sailing ships required lengthier stays in the docks.

Brigham Young had designated agents in New York, Philadelphia, Boston and St. Louis set to assist the Saints in their overland travels. John Taylor was a senior apostle in the church working with the Saints who arrived in New York City. His counterpart in Boston was Daniel Spencer. These men met the ships upon their arrivals and helped with the currency exchange and overland rail passage from New York City to Iowa City. The cost was $11 per individual.

The ships that were involved with the transportation of the Latter-day Saints in 1856 were the Enoch Train that left Liverpool on March 23rd and arrived in Boston on May 1st, carrying 551 passengers. Next was the Samuel Curling that left Liverpool on April 19th and arrived in Boston on May 22nd, carrying 734 passengers. These Saints were led by Dan Jones, a well-known Mormon missionary to Wales and friend of Joseph Smith's. The last two ships were the Thornton with 792 passengers, which left Liverpool May 4th and arrived in New York City, June 14th, and lastly, the Horizon carrying 946, left England on May 25th and arrived in Boston, June 30th. These Saints traveled to Iowa City on the railroad and once there began to assemble their handcarts in early June. From there they began the first leg of the walking experience, trekking 250 miles to Florence, Nebraska. It was a difficult, but important introduction for these people, who had been factory workers, farmers, cobblers, fishermen, businessmen, seamstresses, and aristocrats in the Old World. Only a handful had ever spent time on the plains and there were no trained pioneers. Unlike most other pioneers, these men were accompanied by their wives and children, greatly changing the make-up of the companies and priorities. Although most traveling this year were English, there were still representatives from Switzerland, Denmark, Scotland, Norway, Wales, and Germany.

From Florence, Nebraska, which had been first established by Mormon refugees from Nauvoo in 1846, and had been known as Winter Quarters. Then from the banks on the Missouri River into the Salt Lake Valley was a distance of 1030 grueling miles, through the plains of Nebraska, then the mountains, and passes and the high plains leading to South Pass, as well as needing to ford several rivers, multiple times, then the canyons leading into the valley.

President Brigham Young was emphatic that the handcart companies leave Florence before the start of June.

1856 lined up a series of challenges for the handcart pioneers. The most devastating was the domino effect of late starts. Leaving Liverpool on time was a trial, then crossing the Atlantic. From there they needed to travel in a timely fashion to Iowa City. Once there, they constructed their handcarts, a timely exercise. Because of the sudden influx of migrants, the handcarts were not made with seasoned wood. This caused a series of problems over the trek, splitting of the wood, and difficulty for the axles to turn. The pioneers were walking over higher altitudes than they expected. Mountain roads, rocks, and sand posed problems. The Platte River needed to be crossed multiple times, meaning the person pulling the handcart was chest-deep in the water at times.

There was an over-optimism on the part of Brigham Young, as well as on the part of the captains of the companies and those newly converted members of the church, on their way to Zion. Faith was strong, that God, who had brought them thus far, would not allow them to fail, but would make sure that the elements would combine to help them along. Threats of harm from Indians were a concern and the news of depredations by the Cheyenne was on the rise, impacting their planned route. There was a breakdown in communication between Europe and what was needed in Iowa City. And finally, there was the real threat of the early arrival of winter.

In 1856, the first handcart company to leave for the valleys was led by Edmund Ellsworth, a missionary who was familiar with the people and like most of the missionaries, he had traveled across the plains before. The company consisted of 274 individuals. They left Florence on July 20th. Already, it was much later in the season than Brigham wanted. It was a challenging journey. 13 members of the company died. Still, they forged ahead and arrived in Salt Lake City on September 26, 1856.

This was a new experiment in emigration. Cattle were lost, cutting down on their food stores as well as back-up draft animals for the few wagons accompanying them and carrying their extra supplies. With the loss of their wagons, men were forced to carry more weight on their handcarts, increasing the wear on the carts as well as those pulling them. As axels became increasingly stiff, fat from bacon was used for lubrication but this attracted more dust and sand, causing the axels to wear out quicker.

The second handcart company was led by Daniel McArthur. It had 221 individuals and left Florence four days later on July 24th and arrived in Salt Lake City on September 26th, the same day as the first company. 7 people in this company passed away during the trek.

The third handcart company was led by Edward Bunker and consisted of 320 Welsh converts. This group left Florence on July 30th and arrived in Salt Lake City on October 2, 1856. This company lost less than 7 individuals to death.

****

The road to Kansas City provided Aaron with time to ponder. John Brown and his family had taken a stand regarding slavery. They moved from Pennsylvania to the battleground of Kansas where they found folks with similar beliefs. They also encountered opponents who did not appreciate their presence or their desire to affect policy. The idea of slavery, was foreign to Rost but as he thought about his position, he saw similarities in Prussia and especially in Russia with the serfs, whose lives were akin to America's slaves. Kidnapped from traditional homes, they weren't segregated because of their skin color or their continent of origin. But they were denied education and work and access to resources. Serfs were despised and shunned by society.

They were forced to labor at the most menial of tasks. And these terrible circumstances had been endured for hundreds of years.

The fact that they couldn't be singled out if they were well dressed and didn't give away their background through speaking, thus alerting those around them to identify them as the underclass, was in and of itself a great boon. Also, there were multitudes of other lower-class peoples: Jews, Cossacks, Tartars, and the typical poor. All were able to select scapegoats when things became too unbearable, giving them a sense of relief.

American slaves had no such outlets. Even the free slaves had vast mountains to climb just to achieve a small semblance of equality. Poles, Russians, Cossacks, and Jews had been in the same regions for centuries. American slaves had been imported as lower-class workers. Otherwise progressive and liberal thinkers found reasons in the Bible to exclude Africans, justifying their lower caste. Intermarrying, while not condoned by some minorities, was abhorred where Africans were concerned in America. Some minorities were identified as having special gifts in finance or music or politics or the military. Africans were not only denied the chance to participate, but they were frequently and systematically denied the experience to prove themselves, to flourish, to place a stamp on their possibilities. The lower classes in America, the Irish, the Germans, the Mexicans claimed the few benefits they were granted, selfishly denying these hard-won privileges to others standing on lower rungs. Perhaps Indians had closer parity with the slaves.

One time, Aaron had suggested that Brown use a bit more caution in his approach to politics and was met with a scathing rejoinder. "Caution, Sir! I am eternally tired of hearing that word caution. It is nothing but the word of cowardice!"

Perhaps these powerful men, clothed with the most simple of names, had seen the need to overcome doubts as to their position, by choosing dynamic stances, then supporting them with all the soul's energy. Brown had repeatedly said that his anti-slavery activities in Kansas were in accordance with the Golden Rule. He claimed the most famous statement in the Declaration of Independence, all men are created equal, "meant the same thing!"

And what about religion? America was a Protestant haven. Catholics were loathed as were Jews. Few had even heard of Muslims. And Mormons? This religion had sprung up in the American heartland. Aaron had seen firsthand the persecution Latter-day Saints experienced as they emigrated from other countries. Upon arriving in the United States, they were quickly identified, castigated and belittled, by all degrees of inhabitants.

Rost was relieved to reach Kansas City and purchase steamboat passage to Florence. He was grateful to get such terrible thoughts and populations behind him. Life would prove more acceptable heading for the valley of the Saints. Slavery, Indians, federal intervention could all be left behind. He would relish the chance to be at ease in his mountain home.

The manner of dress made the two women look out of place traveling on the steamboat.

"This is quite a distance from New York," Aaron said with a mocking jibe. Harriett looked at the tall blonde stranger, then rolled her eyes. Yasmin responded quite differently. She felt empowered in the United States, quite a new sensation for her.

"We want to be presentable when we reach Florence," she replied.

"I am going there myself. My name is Aaron Rost. I am a merchant."

"Your accent suggests you are not an American."

"Prussian and a merchant."

"Harriett and I are nurses. We are hoping to be able to find employment. It is getting rather late in the year to travel far."

"So Florence is not your final destination?"

"It might be for this year. We are heading west."

"To California, perhaps?"

"Perhaps." Yasmin looked at Harriett to make sure she wasn't divulging too much. Harriett smiled and encouraged her to continue. "Or the Great Salt Lake City."

"That's where I live! Are you members of the church?"

"We're followers of the truth," Harriett interjected.

"Of course. So that is what brings two talented women here to the frontier? The search for truth? I noticed that neither of you are wearing wedding bands. You are both quite comely. To gaze at one of you means looking away from the other." Aaron watched to see if his flirtation landed on solid ground. More success with Yasmin than Harriett.

Harriett paused and sized up the man. He was friendly but she questioned his interest in wedding bands. He did not seem to be a masher. *Could he really be a citizen of the Utah Territory?* The Saints heading for the valley took the railroad to Iowa City, then traveled overland to Florence. They had encountered none traveling up the Missouri, not at this time of year. He claimed to be from Prussia, one of the European powers that had wisely remained out of the Crimean conflict. *Was he intending to stay in America or merely traveling through?* He smiled often enough, revealing a silver capped tooth. *Could he actually live in Salt Lake City?*

"Do you travel on the rivers frequently?" she asked.

"Usually not until I reach the Mississippi. I must admit that this is gentler on my aging frame."

He sounded inoffensive. *It might be good for Yasmin to hone her language and social skills with someone like this.* Harriett nodded and lowered her eyes, signaling that she had finished talking.

Yasmin picked up on the motion. "This is a very large land. The roads in this area are quite rough."

"And they get rougher the farther west you go, at least until you reach California."

"You have been back and forth several times?"

"Not as often as some. As a matter of fact, I am set to meet a friend of mine in Florence and continue on with him to Great Salt Lake City."

"He's also a merchant?"

Aaron shook his head. "Sometimes I believe he wishes he were. No, Almon Babbitt is a politician. He travels back and forth at least once a year, sometimes twice. At times I have traveled with him. He is an interesting man with many stories."

Harriett's brow furrowed at the mention of his name. "Does your friend know many people? Back in Washington?"

"More than his share."

"I seem to have heard the name before. From one Thomas Kane. His father is a judge in Pennsylvania. The Honorable John Kane."

"Yes, of course, I know Tom Kane!" He almost shouted. He smiled and clapped his hands. "I have known the colonel for a while. He takes care to watch over the happenings in the Utah Territory. He is a great friend of Brigham Young." Rost could almost feel both women relax. *This is a positive sign. Then again, the territory is still quite sparsely inhabited. It is easy to know many people and if not personally, then by reputation or association.*

Harriett wasn't sure she liked Rost's casual, almost intimate, reference to Mr. Kane's first name.

"You have traveled to New York City and Washington DC?" Yasmin asked.

"Several months ago. But I am returning from the Kansas Territory."

"Oh, you have business there?" Harriett's question had a tinge of suspicion.

"Only a small bit for now," he explained. "It could grow but I will need to wait and watch, I suppose."

"Are you an abolitionist?"

Rost was surprised at the question. Being a foreigner to the American shores, it wasn't one that he received often. Admitting to it could also be dangerous in some areas of the country. *And just how much do these women know?* He decided to lay his opinions out before them. *What is the worst that could happen? They could leave and not speak with me again. Then again, they seem to have a connection with the church and the members of the church are overwhelmingly abolitionists.*

He smiled and responded easily. "Yes, of course. I am an abolitionist." He didn't try to keep his voice low, not caring who might overhear. Usually, steamboats were safe from attacks as a result of political ideas.

For the next few days, Rost entertained Yasmin and Harriett with his tales from Europe, the high seas, and then America. It was fascinating for the women, who were looking forward more and more to their time in the young country. In their turn, they spoke to Rost about some of their experiences in Turkey and the Crimea, impressing him with the wealth of things they had learned. He concluded that the three of them had seen and done just about everything there was, short of raising a family.

"Do you think we'll arrive in Florence with enough time to travel overland to the Great Salt Lake City?" Yasmin queried. "Or is it too late in the season?"

"That's a good question. It is getting late in the year to make such a trip. I guess it depends on how quickly we can travel. Do either of you have plans already?"

"We were simply hoping we could catch a ride with a wagon train. Yasmin and I aren't anxious to spend a winter in Florence. Then again, this has been a very crowded year, with all the people coming and going, especially after the war in Crimea. We made a short side trip but didn't think it would be a problem. Elder Richards has been encouraging everyone simply to push onward. He thinks we'll all be able to reach the valley and maybe get in on the last harvest."

"I've come this way, late in the year like this once before. Again, I was with Brother Babbitt. He believes in traveling with all haste and thinks nothing of wearing out the mules or horses. He simply trades them at the forts. Anyway, we'll find out quick enough, I guess."

The steamboat docked in Florence on Wednesday, August 27, 1856, the same time a wagon train was arriving from Iowa City. It was named after its lead captain, William Hodgetts, consisting of 33 wagons and 160 individuals. They were planning on leaving Florence in a few days, after taking on supplies and tightening up their equipment. They intended to follow the two previous handcart companies that recently left from Cutler's Park, a few miles west-southwest of Florence. The Willie Handcart Company, whose captain was James Willie, was made up of 404 individuals and had left Florence, Saturday, August 16th. Before their departure, they had a spirited debate as to the wisdom of leaving so late in the year. The only people with the company familiar with the trail were the missionaries. One of them, named Levi Savage, argued against the idea. He had experienced a series of difficult travels in his missionary travels and was worried such a trip would jeopardize the group. Franklin Richards, who was traveling separately, promised the pioneers that they were early enough in the season. With missionary bravado, he assured them that he would eat every snowflake that fell on them during the trip. Most, including Levi Savage, chose to leave with the handcarts.

Levi Savage, a sub-captain in the Willie Company wrote in his journal that he warned the party before they left Florence of *"the hard Ships that we Should have to endure. I Said that we were liable to have to wade in Snow up to our knees, and Should at night rap ourselves in a thin blanket. and lye on the frozen ground without abed...the lateness of the Season was my only objection, of leaving this point for the mountains at this time."*

However, Savage's advice was ignored. He explained, *"Brother Willey Exhorted the Saints to go forward regardless of Suffering even to death,"* and Savage was later reprimanded for *"the wrong impression made by my expressing myself So freely."*

The fifth handcart company for the year, led by Edward Martin, consisting of the largest group of 576 individuals, left Florence earlier that day before the steamboat coming up the Missouri River had docked. The feelings throughout the community were of hope, although some had trepidation.

The final wagon train to follow the companies was led by John Alexander Hunt, recently taking over from Welsh missionary, Dan Jones, and was leaving Florence on Sunday, August 31st. It had 300 individuals and 56 wagons.

The trio, arriving on the steamboat, checked with Captain Hunt about the possibility of signing on with them for the trip. He would need a couple of days to go through his charts before granting them permission. They were instructed to be ready for a Sunday morning departure. Aaron promised he would check early and that they would be prepared.

"What did you find out?" Harriett and Yasmin were both anxiously awaiting the news Aaron was bringing. His face looked drawn and much more perplexed than they had seen before. He was carrying a copy of the Florence Weekly Bugle.

"Captain Hunt decided against us?" Harriett asked with astonishment.

"Oh, no. We're going all right."

"Then what is bothering you, Mr. Rost?" Yasmin asked.

He held up the paper, fresh off the press. "News is bad. The Cheyenne Indians have been doing a bunch of raiding between here and Fort Kearny. It shouldn't get in our way. Our party is just too big. Still, it's something to worry about. I think Dan Jones and Elder Richards and their group should also be fine. They're fast and armed and have plenty of people. I'm hoping that Almon Babbitt throws in with them. Of course, he doesn't like waiting around for anything or anyone. I'm just hoping he doesn't go off half-cocked."

"Is that all? Or do you have other news? In your newspaper, perhaps?" Harriett asked.

Aaron sighed with some resignation. "My friends in Kansas. Remember me telling you about John Brown and his family? The abolitionists? News says there has been a massacre down that way, in Osawatomie. The first person shot dead was John's son, Frederick. He was shot straight through the heart." He shook his head sorrowfully. "There's going to be more hell to pay in that direction."

On Sunday morning, Harriett, Yasmin, and Aaron found John Hunt and he pointed them to his final wagon. Well ladened, it looked sturdy and the oxen were both young and healthy. Things would move along fine. Then again, Rost knew a lot could happen while traveling a thousand miles overland.

****

"Well, don't that just beat all?" Shep said quietly as the three men rode up the dusty road to the Hansens' house on the southern outskirts of Tooele. It was late and the sun was setting. The previous twenty days had been filled with long rides, always keeping a sharp eye out for marauding Indians. Their evenings around the small campfire were spent sharing endless stories that had taken place over the previous three years. The Sweeneys were the star

280

attractions of the talk, making Shep happy he had chosen them to continue the rearing and raising of the Wetoyous.

The surprise for Shep came as they neared the Hansen home and saw a nearly completed house sitting to the south of the Hansens'. It was on Shep's land. He didn't know what to think. He did know who to ask. They dismounted and tied their horses to the railing in front of the Hansens. Lights in the house were not lit yet and he hoped someone would be at home.

"Hello?" he called, opening the door and looking inside. Herman and Zeenyo stood back a respectable distance. "Anybody home?"

There was a sudden rustling from inside the house and momentarily all the Hansen family was crowding the door, peering at Shep and his two companions. The Hansens looked anxious. Their faces were well-scrubbed and smiling. Some were holding their breath.

"We weren't sure when to expect you," Ole managed to say, while a beaming Georgina wiped her hands unconsciously on her apron. They were already dry.

"Mind telling me what all this is about?" Shep asked, pointing at the new house.

"It's yours, my friend," Ole exclaimed, no longer able to keep the news back. "The bishop thought you needed your own place. He rounded up some men and we all worked together and started building the house. It isn't finished yet but should only take a few more days."

The news shocked Shep. It was a wonderful gift. He agreed that he had been staying with the Hansens far too long and had thought about putting up some form of shelter. *But this?* This was a fine adobe brick and wood house. It had a fireplace and a well-measured porch. Glaziers had added several windows. The yard had also been fenced with split rails.

He had been concerned about lodging for Zeenyo and Herman, especially since the Hansens' family continued to grow. This new house would give them some independence. They could come and go as they pleased. Zeenyo could watch over his livestock and he had no doubts that the folks running Benson's grist mill would hire Herman.

"What do you think?" Ole asked.

"Don't you just love it?" Georgina squealed excitedly.

The Wetoyous were standing still, gawking at the house while holding their hats in their hands. The horses were bored and simply shifted from side to side.

"Okay, enough, I guess," Shep finally said. "But who the hell thought it should be set right there?"

Chapter 38

"It is against the law of our brethren, which was established by my father, that there should be any slaves among them." Ammon in the Book of Mormon

Secretary Almon Babbitt from the Utah Territory was anxious to get back home. He had been in Washington for 8 weeks. He ordered an ox team and wagons fitted out with books and stationery and carpet, things that would look good in the new statehouse. The approaching Legislative Assembly would see how useful he was, especially in transforming the country-bumpkin meetings into first-class affairs. He lined up four teamsters to ride west with the wagons, planning to catch up with the group by using a lightweight buggy when they were nearing Fort Kearny.

Arriving in Florence, he found the Martin Handcart Company scattered around Cutler's Park, working on shoring up their flimsy handcarts.

One of the members noted Babbitt's passing, as he came through the crowd, introducing himself and wishing them all Godspeed.

John Jacques wrote: *Almon Babbitt, dressed in corduroy pants, woolen overshirt and a felt hat, called as he was passing west. He seemed in high glee, his spirits seemed very elastic, almost mercurial. He had started with one carriage for Salt Lake, with the mail and a considerable amount of money. He was very confident that he should be in Salt Lake within fifteen days. He intended to push through vigorously and sleep on the wind, meaning an air-filled mattress.*

Babbitt and his shotgun-toting guard, Tom Sutherland, rode out of town in their smart little buggy but a couple of days later. A day's ride east of Fort Kearny they came across the remains of the little wagon train he hired. It had been attacked by the Cheyenne. Babbitt drove on to the fort where he discovered Orrin Parrish, one of his surviving teamsters. Parrish reported that two of the teamsters had been killed and one wounded. The men had taken a passenger named Mrs. Wilson and her child with them. The Cheyenne killed the child and kidnapped Mrs. Wilson. When she couldn't keep pace, she was killed as well.

At Fort Kearny, Babbitt also ran into Porter Rockwell who was trying to outfit transportation for President Richards and the rest of his party for Salt Lake City.

"Helluva mess," Porter noted somberly. He had heard Parrish's story earlier.

"Do you have time to ride back with me tomorrow?" Almon asked. "I really needed to scoot out of there. I didn't know if the Indians were still around. They burned the wagons and most of the stuff from what I could see. I left it in a mess."

Porter agreed. The next day they rode the 30 miles east to the site of the massacre and were surprised to find the Willie Handcart Company there. Babbitt and Rockwell arrived as the last rocks were piled onto the cairn of the two dead teamsters. It was sobering for the emigrants to come across the rubble so early on their trek. It alerted them to the dangerous business they had undertaken, walking through tribal lands. Most of the emigrants were unarmed.

Gathering what little could be salvaged, Porter and Babbitt rode back to the fort, where Rockwell offered to help the politician refit another wagon for his trip. Captain Wharton commanded the fort and together with Rockwell and the missionaries tried to talk Babbitt into waiting. Babbitt couldn't be swayed. Wharton offered him an armed escort of cavalry since he was a territorial executive. A larger wagon train could be put together, the more easily to carry his equipment. He waved off the offers, telling one and all that the extra men would only slow him down. He was a veteran traveler.

"I appreciate all the help and the warnings, and the Indians can all go to hell for all I care," he said, "but Porter, perhaps the next thing you will hear of me will be in my grave, but I must go on."

On the morning of September 6th, Babbitt left with his guards, Sutherland and Frank Rowland. He attempted to hire James Ferguson as an additional guard, but the man chose not to leave President Richards' group.

Babbitt's party made excellent time, being pulled by four mules. By the end of the following day, they had covered 120 miles. They decided to set up camp in Ash Hollow. What they were not aware of was the Cheyenne war party who had been watching them since leaving Fort Kearney. The natives were confident that they could successfully attack, free from worry that US soldiers would be close enough to intervene.

A dozen Cheyenne dog warriors rode to the crest of the ridge and looked down on the three men making camp. Screaming wildly, they raced their ponies down the hill towards the startled men.

Almon Babbitt knew what was happening. He grabbed his shotgun and fired both barrels at the Indians without noticeable effect. He then drew his revolver and began shooting at the whirling targets whizzing past, yipping and yelling, encouraging one another as they frightened their victims. Using the horses as shields, the native plainsmen fired volleys of arrows at the travelers.

Since they were hopelessly outnumbered, Tom Sutherland decided to run for his life. A Cheyenne warrior caught him after forty yards, thrusting his lance deep into his back.

Rowland screamed violently as he was struck with a volley of arrows, felling him instantly. The marauding warriors continued to shoot arrows into his quivering corpse until he looked like a porcupine.

Almon Babbitt emptied his revolver. He snatched his shotgun and began wielding it like a club, keeping the main body of warriors at bay. A stealthy Cheyenne leaped from his horse several yards behind Babbitt and sprinted towards the man. Swinging his tomahawk in a vicious arc, the warrior split Babbitt's head. The bloodied secretary toppled over, dead.

Almon Whiting Babbitt participated in a lifelong adventure in the western United States as a member of the Church of Jesus Christ of Latter-day Saints. In 1834 he had marched with Joseph Smith and Zion's Camp. Twelve years later, he joined two other men signing the surrender document of the city of Nauvoo. Almon Babbitt was an active, participating politician for the Utah Territory. He often battled Brigham Young over policy and interpretation, refusing to back down. He was killed on September 7, 1856, shy of 44 years old in Nebraska while traveling back to the Utah Territory.

****

"You see who's coming after us?" Aaron asked Harriett and Yasmin, sitting beside him in the wagon.

The women turned and scanned the sweeping plains behind them. The Hunt Company was the last of the Mormon pioneers heading across the plains for the year. It was noon on September 5th and they were 10 miles east of the Loup Fork, where it connected to the Platte River. The oncoming party was traveling much faster, the two wagons being drawn by teams of four mules. Clouds of dust were being kicked up behind them. The men in the seats looked comfortable and relaxed, watching as they drew closer, then finally sped by. They were hurrying up front to reach Captain Hunt.

Harriett and Yasmin noticed that one of the men was President Richards. He seemed to be in a good mood, chatting with his companions and holding onto his hat. They watched for several minutes as the lighter wagons gained on the front of their train. The dirt road that led west was wide and getting well-worn over the seasons.

Unlike the mules, the oxen pulling the Hunt wagons had two speeds: slow and stop. The dust clung to their coats. Snot from their noses and slobber from their tongues as they continuously licked to keep their nostrils open and also the flies away, kept their faces and mouths moist but the edges grew darker, where the dust dried, then tried to cake hard. The oxen's eyes continually ran tears and they were always shaking their heads to keep the flying insects at bay, at least from time to time.

"They're in a hurry." Aaron looked scornfully down at the oxen. "Wouldn't mind having these critters pick up the pace some."

"I think those gentlemen intend to set a new speed record."

"Something I would prefer to this boring, flat prairie." Aaron glanced over at Yasmin who seemed caught up in her thoughts. "I guess going this slow makes it easy for cartographers to draw extra good maps." He saw her smile, telling him that she was listening.

An hour later, Captain Hunt signaled the train to stop and begin preparing lunch. Harriett, Aaron, and Yasmin had not seen the express riders forge ahead. They assumed the men would be eating with members of the train. The small amounts of flour and salted pork were easy to prepare and the staple for the pioneers. The boring food was something Aaron determined to cast aside once he reached more civilized climes.

"Uh-oh," he said as he saw one of the express wagons, a mile ahead of them, turn around and head back towards their location was, bringing up the rear. The men were waving gaily as they passed the wagons. Lunch was over and folks were beginning to pack things up, ready to start again on the trail.

The light wagon carrying Franklin Richards slowed as it neared the trio's wagon and then stopped, as Richards waved enthusiastically at Harriett and the other two who were ready to climb back into their buckboard.

"You're just the person I wanted to see," he announced to Harriett. "I trust your trip is proceeding as planned."

"It is. Yes, sir."

Aaron leaned over and spoke quietly to Yasmin. "I knew there was a reason I said uh-oh." She smiled and nodded, then tried to hear what was being said.

"I have a proposition for you, Sister Matthews. There's an opening in the wagon carrying church supplies away up ahead in the Martin Company. I was wondering what you might think about going with us and taking over that ride?" He then looked at Aaron who was the current driver of the wagon.

"All three of us?"

"Yes, of course. Would your companions also agree?" he asked looking again at them. His eyes sparkled and he winked. The man was filled with positive thoughts. He was jovial and animated. It did a lot for the tired spirits of the folks who had been on the road for days and knew they had much longer to go. President Richards knew something the two women didn't. He had been over the road before. He knew its destination. Life wouldn't remain stagnant forever. It was the same thing Aaron had been saying for days but for some reason, the women believed President Richards more readily. "Well? What do you think?"

The three exchanged looks, shuffled slightly, and nodded.

"Does this mean we'll get better food?"

Richards laughed at Rost. "You three grab your things and throw them in our wagon. Captain Hunt has another driver coming to take your place."

After a few minutes, the three were sitting in the flexible wagon as comfortably as they could, while the mules trotted back towards the head of the train. There was a brief exchange with Captain Hunt and then the two light wagons set off at a pleasing clip, leaving the last wagon company in the rear.

"I have reasons for this change," Richards continued, speaking mostly to Harriett. "Of course, the Martin Handcart Company could always use the help of able-bodied nurses like you and Yasmin. And Brother Rost can fend off predators." He smiled and nodded at the Sharp's carbine at Aaron's side, where he was trying to keep it concealed. "And I know you know how to use that thing." Richards went back to his explanation. "You kept records in Scutari, am I right, Sister Matthews?"

"Patient records," she agreed.

"Well, I'm here to ask you to keep some more records for us. Records of the trip. Call it a journal or a diary or whatever you choose. It will be a great help for all concerned."

Harriett was suddenly concerned. "President, I have no problem being a nurse and tending to the weak and infirm but writing a diary? I'm not so certain. I have tried doing it before as a girl and never was able to keep up."

Richards laughed. "Of course. You're just like the rest of us. But I tell you, my dear, this will be a great blessing to you and for all the rest of us. We need a record of the trip, you know, times and dates, and places. But comments, your observations. It will memorialize these handcart companies. This is the first year we have ever attempted such an endeavor. We're learning every day but having such a record will help us in so many ways. Another thing, Sister Matthews. The Lord blesses us as we write things down. He knows they will not be forgotten. If he has some good things to share with two of his children, they being equal in just about everything except one keeps a journal and the other does not, who do you think the Lord will grant the experience or blessing to? I guarantee you this is true. You are literate. You are talented. You can capture moments, events, and thoughts during this trip. Will you assist us?" Richards' eyes were imploring, although the smile never left his face.

Harriett sighed. "Yes. I guess so."

"That's wonderful! We have quills and paper and ink just for you. We'll get things all set up."

"Okay. Fine."

Aaron and Yasmin looked on with amusement, happy not to have been asked.

"Oh," Richards said. "It might be a good idea to have your companions here help whenever they can. You aren't looking after children, so I'll leave the chore of making such a timely assignment up to you. Okay?"

This time Harriett smiled enthusiastically, while the smiles on the faces of both Aaron and Yasmin faded.

7 September 1856, Sunday- Martin Company- Thinking more about this assignment, I have decided to pepper the narrative with the writings of one of my favorite writers, beginning with Aeschylus. "Rumors voiced by women come to nothing."

Our fleet wagons caught up with the Martin Company and we were handed off to Captain Edward Martin and are in charge of the church wagon and supplies. The comparison between the mules we have been using and the oxen is quite marked. The large lumbering oxen are plodding and can barely keep up with the handcart people walking beside us.

A couple of days ago we came across some burned-out remains of a train that had been outfitted by Honorable Almon Babbitt. The Willie Company found them and buried the dead before we reached them. Two were teamsters and one woman and a child. One of the teamsters was wounded and he and another got away, presumably to Fort Laramie. We have been put on alert that the Cheyenne tribe is actively raiding in this area.

We also came across two men from the Willie Company who had doubled back and were looking for 30 head of their cattle who went missing. We have not seen them and that will be a tremendous loss should they not be recovered. It is also a dangerous undertaking for these men to be out alone and searching for the cattle.

Captain Martin says we are averaging about 100 miles a week. This is good because our people are not getting too fatigued, says he. We should be arriving in Fort Kearney before long. The weather has been clear and dry. It is a nice fall to be prosecuting such a trip.

I guess we are scattered out for many miles. This country is so much larger than Britain or the Crimea and even Turkey. Still, I am happy to be here rather than where we were just last year

As I begin this writing exercise, I would be remiss if I did not comment on the stature and heroism being shown before me by these handcart pioneers, men, women, and children. The task at hand is formidable. They are walking one thousand miles across rocky, hard ground. Food and clothing are sparse and yet they sing and exchange good conversation. I am proud to be an Englishwoman, from where so many of these good people hail. They are fired by testimonies much deeper than mine. In the face of such uncertainty, they forge forward. The only compensation they seek is the blessings of a satisfied, pleased Creator, the Father of us all.

Harriett Matthews

"Why shouldn't it happen to them?" Yasmin asked Aaron.

Rost shook his head. He didn't have the answer, not right then. He looked across the buckboard to where Harriett sat, driving the oxen, but she didn't seem to be paying the slightest attention to the conversation between him and Yasmin. "I'm just saying that it's a hard row to hoe. The people you were dealing with during the war. The devastation. The terrible inhumanity. As bad as you say the Turks are and as bad as I know the Russians to be, I think it was an awful price they paid."

"They weren't the only ones paying the price, Aaron."

He enjoyed hearing her use his name. He wondered how he could get her to do it more often. She was a charming young woman. Besides being a typical Middle Eastern beauty, she was more intelligent than everyone he knew. He was grateful for the time they had to share. He gleaned much more knowledge about her than she knew. Yasmin did not spend time talking about her life or family or what had brought her to America, but Aaron was shrewd enough to question carefully, then await the answers, which at times were not forthcoming for hours if not days.

"Of course, the women and children, the old folks…"

Yasmin sighed with a touch of exasperation. "Please, Aaron, there is more than enough suffering to go around and around. It's not just the war in Crimea. Look at the state of the world. Financially we are bankrupt. Huge populations are starving, right now, even as we speak. And they are not walking to Zion. No. They are dealing with malaria, corrupt regimes, dishonesty in the highest places." She shook her head with conviction. "The world is Satan's playground. He does what he wants. He has enough dupes to perform his will. Beyond the awful consequences of his machinations, this world, as beautiful and breathtaking as it can be, at times, continues to be a hard taskmaster. Hard things, terrible things are poured out upon peoples and individuals alike, indiscriminately."

"I grant you that, to an extent. But what then is the motivation for us to do good? Why do we continue to learn and obey the commandments?"

"Of course God blesses the righteous. But show me anyone of value. Point out to me any of the righteous that were spared these awful tribulations. It seems that the more righteous people are, the more serious the trials. Adam and Eve's son Cain murdered his brother. King David committed adultery with Bathsheba and then had Uriah murdered and that caused him a generation of the deepest sorrow. Joseph Smith languished in a frozen jail for five months and then he was murdered at such a young age, never even seeing the birth of his youngest child. Father Abraham was commanded to sacrifice his son, Isaac. God himself offered his Only Son as an offering to complete the Atonement. If these men were not spared then why should any resent tribulation?"

Aaron knew the arguments. He had made them before. *But did there not need to be refining? A grace? A sparing? A release?*

Aaron tried again. "And usually that's the case. I agree that we came here to earth to be tested, to see if we would develop faith in the Savior and love for each other. This is similar to a laboratory and we are students away from home, experimenting with elements we have before us. God gives us knowledge and curiosity and we attempt to solve the problems. But at what cost? This is so much greater than just a simple philosophical debate. We are talking about lives, millions of lives, and they are being lived out in the utmost squalor and without hope. It would be another story if the only ones who suffered were the chosen, the elect of God. But, no. So many are pulled into the cesspool, without knowing why or being told how long. And the women and children. Where is the mercy? Where is the love? I appreciate the work you did at Scutari with Miss Nightingale. The lives you saved and the misery you quelled is impossible to measure, but surely immense. My question deals with the severity and duration."

Yasmin thought for a few moments. "Should men suffer more than women? Just because we are termed the fairer sex?" she asked.

"That's my question. Women were the last of God's creation. As such, should not the crowning achievement of God's work be granted some saving dispensation?"

"Or could it be that Satan chooses to focus more on women because we are more blessed. Or because we are weaker physically and become prey to cads? Or because we are more nurturing, the Adversary chooses to destroy the family through the destruction of the wives and mothers?"

This was a more challenging dialogue than he had expected. He looked out over the great expanse of the prairie. Chimney Rock could be seen far to the west. He was thankful they had the responsibility for the church wagon, consequently, they brought up the rear. Their position gave them a better insight into the weak who were lagging. Many times it was the fathers whose strength was flagging, while their younger children were dancing and throwing rocks or racing through the long grass. Older children were more circumspect and tried to pitch in with pulling the carts to relieve their parents. Aaron Rost had been over this road several times. He was pleased with the progress being made. He also knew they had much, much farther to go. He knew the land remained fairly flat until they reached Fort Laramie. From there it became more rugged and rough. *If folks are starting to wear thin now, how will it be in another month?* Thus far they had been spared from Indian forays or encounters with the huge herds of buffalo. The ever-present threat of wolves also stayed at a distance, for now.

"You know, I enjoy these chats, Yasmin."

"You are dodging the subject, Aaron. Are women just not as strong? Should chivalry always win out and take over because of the damsel in distress?"

"Oh, that it was so."

"You and our brethren speak about fathers, of their position and wisdom. You raise them up, place them on pedestals of granite. We even pray to our Father in heaven. But where was there ever a father without the mother who made him one?"

Aaron gulped more loudly than he wanted.

She kept going. "I suggest that strength does not require muscles and bone or even priesthood. Strength comes through virtue and integrity. We seek guidance from the Holy Ghost, the greatest blessing of all. Perhaps the fault lies in our language. We choose to gloss over women and their place simply because they are not the ones carrying the lances or charging the heights. No, I think Satan has done his greatest work by diminishing women, not allowing us to participate in the government or education. We have been subjugated, devalued, bought, and traded. We are raped and beaten. We are underfed. We are robbed of the children who come from our wombs. You take a look at the women in our lives and histories. Mary or Miriam, Eve, Ruth, Sarah, Rebecca, and Rachel, Abigail, and Naomi. Esther or Hadassah..." She allowed the emphasis to rest on the last name. She looked closely at Aaron Rost and noticed an immediate reaction. Yasmin lowered her eyes. "I am sorry if I offended you."

"No. Please, Yasmin." He felt tears begin to run down his cheeks. Suddenly he felt quite exposed. He couldn't remember when he had ever brought up the name of his late wife. He wasn't the only one paying attention to the dialogue. Over the years he had heard her name only a few times, but the way Yasmin pronounced Hadassah was with reverence and an accent that mirrored his mother's and the women in his *shtetl*. "No, Yasmin, you are more than welcome to say her name."

Now the conversation had captured Harriett.

Yasmin gave him a knowing smile and she nodded. "Hadassah. You need not speak another word about her, Aaron. I know that she was a strong woman, capable in so many areas, not least of which was turning you into a good man, a proper husband."

The tears on his cheeks that had been slowing, started flowing again. Sacred memories were unlocked. Once again he gazed upon Hadassah's tender face and saw her soft lips move as she spoke to him, sweet words, endearing words. So long ago, so far away. The blur of his life flashed before him. His achievements, the things he had accomplished, the places he had visited, all dwindled to insignificance with the mention of her name. Her image appeared in his mind's eye. *Was she the beginning of my sorrows?* He couldn't remember any terrible events before her passing. His childhood had been carefree. There had been the occasional deaths and pogroms but the *shtetl* had protected him. Whenever he wandered beyond his village he was taunted and challenged and not always by *goyim*. But he had no memories more consistently happy and sweet and filled with promise than the times he spent with Hadassah. She was the helpmeet God had made for him. He knew that without a doubt. And now here he was. So far away from Prussia and his *shtetl*, so far removed from German and Yiddish. He had wandered far and wide. He had made many different acquaintances. He had even joined the Mormon Church. The latter was something that never bothered him. He felt the truth from its members and within the pages of the Book of Mormon. All of the people who mattered to him, especially those who saw to his raising, insisted that he follow the truth. Absolute truth was a gift from God and whenever it crossed his path, he felt a powerful jolt within his soul, as it did when he entered the Endowment House. Brigham Young and the apostles and other leaders of the church carried and displayed baggage they had adopted or kept from their youth. But there were times, luminous times when the words they spoke were definitely from God.

30 September 1856, Tuesday- Martin Company- I know that President Richards expects this journal to reflect the happenings among the pioneers. I have made an effort to walk among them. They are good people. I note that many of their shoes are becoming quite worn. The weather has been quite warm and pleasant. I am concerned that before we reach Salt Lake City much colder weather will arrive and I do not see very many heavy coats.

We passed Ash Hollow yesterday. We and our animals had a chance to drink very sweet water. We filled as many containers as we could with the clear, clean water. It has been an important stopping place for travelers in these parts for generations. We also learned to our dismay and great sadness that Secretary Almon Babbitt was killed here by Cheyenne Indians earlier in the month. That will be a deep loss felt among members of the church and people living in the Utah Territory for years to come.

Aaron Rost has been having both me and Yasmin drive our wagon lately. In the beginning, I thought he just didn't like us sitting back and sightseeing. Perhaps he has more insight than what I have granted. We have come to know the animals better. They also know us and respond to our commands much better than when we first started. Sometimes it comes in handy when we travel longer or later into the evenings. Brother Rost has taken it upon himself to walk around this end of the train, keeping his eye on things. Our people appreciate his willingness to converse. He has a good manner. He also shares many jokes. He owns a curious rifle of which he is quite proud. For several days we were being followed by a swift pack of wolves. They were very threatening, especially as far as the children are concerned or the weak who might be lagging. Brother Rost shot one of the wolves at quite a distance. This scared the others away. Since then we have only seen them late at night or far in the distance. They are wily and do not care to come within range of Brother Rost's rifle again.

Since leaving Florence, we three have had a good time visiting. I think we are coming to know one another much better than when we were on the steamboat. Both Brother Rost and I are grateful to Yasmin who has such a knack at cooking. She can turn the most simple ingredients into a sumptuous fare. A number of our fellow travelers have also noticed this ability of Yasmin's and seem to wander close to the wagon when it is meal time.

Yasmin and Brother Rost have started a rather in-depth discussion over the past few days. At first, I minded my own business. It has become more intense and sincere. They seem to be more than simple travel companions. I am sensing a closeness develop. At first, this worried me. I must say that I was jealous of anyone else claiming the attention of my long-time friend, Yasmin. She is a lovely creature and needs to hear about her charms from someone other than me. I don't think I would accuse Brother Rost of courting Yasmin yet, but the lines are diminishing.

Before he joined the church, Brother Rost was a practicing Jew. From some of the conversations between him and Yasmin, I gathered that today is Rosh Hashanah, the start of their High Holy Days. I also noted that he was more circumspect during the day. I am quite certain he was recalling memories from yesteryear. He is becoming a more important person for our company. Duties that once were forgotten are divulging more upon him. Captain Martin rides back here several times a day to confer with him. I think Brother Rost appreciates the attention. It certainly doesn't hurt with his estimation in the eyes of Yasmin

From the indomitable Aeschylus, cheering Yasmin from the sidelines: "Suffering brings experience."

Harriett Matthews

Chapter 39

"Holiness does not consist in mystic speculations, enthusiastic fervours, or uncommanded austerities; it consists in thinking as God thinks, and willing as God wills." Leo Tolstoy

President Richards reported that things were well with the handcart and other companies traveling to the Great Salt Lake City. They overtook the train of Captain James Hunt on September 5th, 10 miles east of the Loup Fork. They had 240 persons, 50 wagons, 297 oxen and cows, 7 horses and mules, and 4 church wagons. They had light loads and good teams.

On the evening of the 7th, they overtook Elder Edward Martin's company, 40 miles from the Loup Fork. Martin had 576 persons, 146 handcarts, 7 wagons, 6 mules and horses, and 50 cows and beef cattle. One wagon was loaded with church goods. This company had some feeble emigrants. Richards thought the Martin Company could average 100 miles a week without fatiguing the company.

10 miles beyond they came across William Hodgetts' camp, composed of 150 persons, 33 wagons, 84 yokes of oxen, 19 cows, and 250 heifers. They were heavily ladened but making good progress.

Visiting with Captain Wharton at Fort Kearney, Richards and his group were apprised of other Cheyenne depredations in the area.

On the 12th they overtook the Willie Company at North Bluff Creek, consisting of 404 persons, 6 wagons, 87 handcarts, 6 yokes of oxen, 32 cows, and 5 mules. They lost 30 head of cattle and spent several days looking for them in vain. The Willie Company was averaging 14-16 miles a day. When they found them, they were fording the North Platte River, one of many times.

On the 16th, Richards met with Porter Rockwell, driving 5 wagons and 11 yokes of oxen, with three families, the Grimshaws, Cooks, and Barnes. President Richards turned the families back, deeming them too weak to continue. From there, they rode to Fort Laramie, arriving on the morning of the 19th. All were kindly received by Colonel Huffman. Some buffalo robes for the Willie Company were bought, along with some mules and provisions.

They left on the 23rd at the Platte Bridge, arriving the next day at Independence Rock, meeting Elder Parley Pratt and several missionaries who were traveling in the opposite direction. Pratt was headed on a mission to the Eastern States, accompanied by his newest wife, Eleanor.

On September 27th, 15 miles east of the Pacific Springs, they met two brethren with 2 wagons carrying flour for the companies. Richards encouraged them to cache the flour and move forward to inform the Willie Company, which they did.

On the 28th, 3 miles east of Big Sandy Creek, President Richards met others taking provisions to the companies.

On September 29th they camped with Jacob Croft's company from Texas and the Cherokee land, 58 persons, 14 wagons, 80 yokes of oxen, 30 horses, and 130 loose cattle. It was the last company they passed on the road.

Arriving at Fort Bridger on October 1st, they were welcomed by Major Burton. The missionaries returning with Franklin Richards, Daniel Spencer, and other Perpetual Fund agents, arrived in Salt Lake City on October 4, 1856.

The report delivered to President Young detailing a large number of emigrants still on the plains, especially late in the season, worried the brethren, causing Brigham Young to issue the following plea:

"I will now give this people the subject and the text for the Elders who may speak today and during the Conference, it is this, on the 5th day of October 1856, many of our brethren and sisters are on the Plains with handcarts, and probably many are now seven hundred miles from this place, and they must be brought here, we must send assistance to them. The text will be—to get them here! I want the brethren who may speak to understand that their text is the people on the Plains, and the subject matter for this community is to send for them and bring them in before the winter sets in.

"That is my religion; that is the dictation of the Holy Ghost that I possess, it is to save the people. We must bring them in from the Plains, and when we get them here, we will try to keep the same spirit that we have had and teach them the way of life and salvation; tell them how they can be saved, and how they can save their friends. This is the salvation I am now seeking for, to save our brethren that would be apt to perish or suffer extremely, if we do not send them assistance.

"I shall call upon the Bishops this day, I shall not wait until tomorrow, nor until next day, for sixty good mule teams and twelve or fifteen wagons. I do not want to send oxen, I want good horses and mules. They are in this Territory, and we must have them; also twelve tons of flour and forty good teamsters, besides those that drive the teams. This is dividing my text into heads; first, forty good young men who know how to drive teams, to take charge of the teams that are now managed by men, women, and children who know nothing about driving them; second, sixty or sixty-five good spans of mules, or horses, with harness, whipple-trees, neck-yokes, stretchers, load chains; and thirdly, twenty-four thousand pounds of flour, which we have on hand.

"I will repeat the division; forty extra teamsters is number one; sixty spans of mules or horses is part of number two; twelve tons of flour, and wagons to take it, is number three; and, fourthly, I will allow the brethren to tell something about their missions, by way of exhortation to wind up with.

"I will tell you all that your faith, religion, and profession of religion, will never save one soul of you in the celestial kingdom of our God, unless you carry out just such principles as I am now teaching you. Go and bring in those people now on the Plains, and attend strictly to those things which we call temporal, or temporal duties, otherwise your faith will be in vain; the preaching you have heard will be in vain to you, and you will sink to hell, unless you attend to the things we tell you. Any man or woman can reason this out in their own minds, without trouble. The Gospel has been already preached to those brethren and sisters now on the Plains; they have believed and obeyed it, and are willing to do anything for salvation; they are doing all they can do, and the Lord has done all that is required of Him to do, and has given us power to bring them in from the Plains, and teach them the further things of the kingdom of God, and prepare them to enter into the celestial kingdom of their Father. First and foremost is to secure our own salvation and do right pertaining to ourselves, and then extend the hand of right to save others."

Chapter 40

"It is easier to build strong children than to repair broken men." Frederick Douglass

Shep felt pleased to be riding up Emigration Canyon with Herman and Zeenyo. Each led another horse loaded with blankets. The animals were healthy and well-shod. All seemed happy to leave the pasture and Tooele. Salt Lake City was growing ever larger and more complete.

"Does Brigham call for this kind of help for emigrants very often?" Herman asked.

"Often enough. It's not a new thing."

"Why aren't we bringing our wagons?" Zeenyo asked as they entered the canyon's mouth.

"Weren't asked to. Not this time. A bunch has already left the city. I'm hoping the handcart folks won't need the help."

"We've had dry winters. Maybe this will be the same."

"It would be nice for the people afoot."

"Are they going to run out of food soon?"

"Probably. That's why Brigham sent the wagons as soon as he did. He doesn't want folks hiking all over the hills with no food in their stomachs."

"Do you think they'll still be needing all the blankets?"

"Maybe. Maybe not. If they don't need them, we can just drop them off at Bridger and come back home."

It was nice to be out with the boys. Herman had found employment at Benson's grist mill and Zeenyo stayed busy with the cattle and the horses. They were hard-working, conscientious young men. The whole town recognized that. Having come from San Bernardino and having known Shep years earlier, the Wetoyous enjoyed special notoriety in Tooele. And the Hopi Indians were exotic to the local folks. The town fathers were also anxious to attract more and diverse settlers. They pestered Shep mercilessly about inviting the Sweeney family to join them from Carson Valley.

"We'll see," was all he could answer.

As happened every year, the fall colors in Emigration Canyon were gorgeous. The leaves on the scrub oaks were fiery red or brilliant yellow. As they climber higher into the quaking aspens the trees were replete with yellows and light greens. The pines remained dark and foreboding.

Deer and elk crossed the creeks. It was mating season and the bucks were dueling and the bulls bugling, while the does and cows watched from a respectable distance. Squirrels and marmots sunned themselves or else continued to gather food into their garners. Autumn was a tense time for the unprepared despite the breathtaking splendor.

"It's been a warm fall. Was President Young worried or do you think the Lord warned him about things?"

Shep shrugged again at Herman's query. "Don't rightly know. But he's a careful sort. He doesn't want any of the Saints to suffer. Not if he can help it."

"God does warn him, doesn't he?"

"God warns all of us, don't you think? It's up to us to do the listening."

Herman and Zeenyo were satisfied. Shep was a good man. Folks in town added to their conclusions. He worked hard. He was quick to help others in need. He liked doing things for others, especially before being asked. This willingness to go to the aid of the incoming handcarts companies was nothing that surprised them.

The Wetoyous were impressed with the things that Shep had acquired, in a rather short period, even though he had yet to join the Church. The fact that he spoke with an accent was nothing new. A majority of the people in the Utah Territory had come from other parts of the earth. For many, English was not their mother tongue, so almost all spoke with accents.

They hadn't been on the road long before they started catching and passing the rescue wagons. These were faster than most. Brigham Young had asked that the teamsters harness their wagons with the quicker, more versatile mules or horses. For the most part, the drivers were pleasant, although some seemed anxious. Crossing the high plains, no matter the time of year, presented its special set of problems. Some people died with every incoming company, either from fatigue or disease. The handcart companies were especially fragile in that they counted on the strength and endurance of those walking and pulling the carts.

The Shoshone Indian tribe that claimed the lands of northern Utah and into the high plains were led by a great chief named Washakie who did everything in his power to assure that peace reigned between his people and the Mormons. This allowed the drivers one less problem to worry about as they drove towards Fort Supply and Fort Bridger. The famous fur trapper and trader, mountain man, Jim Bridger, had established the fort named after him in 1842. The Latter-day Saints purchased Fort Bridger in 1855. It was 115 miles from Salt Lake City. In 1853 the Mormons also established Fort Supply, 12 miles southwest of Fort Bridger. These locations provided support for emigrants going to Salt Lake City or for those heading farther still towards California.

"Do you know the plan, Shep?"

"Nope. I figure the wagons will stage at Bridger. Some might go on to South Pass. Don't really know. I guess that's why they need us to go out and find them, then help them move forward."

"Who's heading it all up?"

"George Grant, I reckon."

"Didn't he just get home from his mission?"

"Earlier this month. He came in with Brother Richards, but I understand George has been in the States for six months in Iowa City helping folks get their handcarts put together."

"So, he gets home and turns right back around and heads out?"

"You both know as much about this as me. That's sometimes the way things need to be done. The Lord knows. He also knows who is on his side. They don't get better than George Grant."

It took them two days to reach Fort Supply. Shep was impressed with the men and oxen that were prepared to launch into the wilderness. The wagons also seemed to be in good condition and were being loaded with flour and clothing. Fortunately, there was no urgent need, at present.

George Grant didn't see things quite the same.

"I need you, Shep, and a couple more riders to head out and find the companies. I expect Willie's Company will be the first. But don't go beyond Devil's Gate if Martin's Company's not already there. I'll need you to wait there for a bit. Sound all right?"

"Yes, sir. What about the Wetoyous?"

"I want to pair them up with some teamsters. They'll be heading to Bridger and then on with some wagons after that in a couple days."

4 October 1856, Saturday- Martin Company- We reached Scott's Bluff today. Chimney Rock has been left away behind us. The weather continues to be good. We are starting to get worried. A rider arrived the other day and said he expected the Willie Company to be pulling in to Fort Laramie about now. The trouble they will be facing and the same trouble we'll be facing next week is that there do not appear to be many provisions to be bought at the fort. As bland as our diets have been, we at least have had food to be prepared. Physical exertion is taking its toll. Our speed has slowed down considerably.

Brother Aaron Rost has been more melancholy these past several days. I suspect he has been doing some serious pondering. This is the time of his High Holy Days. He and Yasmin continue speaking at times, but these episodes have also diminished some. There does not seem to be a problem there, but he remains quieter than I would expect.

Fort Laramie was named after a French fur trader named Jaques La Ramie, who died around these parts back in the 1820s. His name has been given to some different landmarks in this part of the country.

We press onward. The days do not slow down, certainly not like our pace. I am starting to feel more anxious about our situation. I have been thinking about the wisdom of canceling our journey and remaining in Fort Laramie for the winter. We should be getting there in a few more days, but if they also have no extra food for our needs, I guess the more prudent thing would be for us to keep going. Captain Edward Martin knows the trail well enough. I will leave such decisions in his hands.

From my Greek friend: "There is no avoidance in delay."

On the same day, the Willie Company had to cut the flour rations from 16 ounces per day per adult, down to 12 ounces. They forded the North Platte River for the final time and began crossing a bleak stretch to intersect the Sweetwater River. They had been losing emigrants to the elements and lack of food. These were buried next to the road. The exertions caused some to lose their orientation. One woman wandered away from the company. Desperate men searched after her, following her footprints until they decided she had been taken by Indians. Another party was sent after her, also following her footprints but they didn't think she had been taken by Indians. A few hours later they were surprised to find her, still quite confused but fine, even after more than 36 hours of being alone and away from the company with no food or water.

The Martin Company pulled up next to Fort Laramie on Wednesday, October 8th. As had been foreshadowed by express riders, the supplies at the fort were at a minimum. They stayed long enough to exchange whatever livestock they could and then started back on the trail. 40 miles to the east rose the towering Laramie Peak. Its snow-laden cap spoke a severe warning to the company, reminding them of the season.

"Why are you smiling at me?" Aaron asked Yasmin, seeing her watching him intently from her seat at his side. It was a clear, fine morning but cold enough to see everyone's breath. The oxen were breathing hard too and the three riders in the wagon dodged the pungent vapors as they floated back towards them. "Have I done something wrong or curious?"

"Why do you always see to it that you are clean-shaven?" she asked.

"Oh, that's a simple one. My whiskers are light and patchy. I have attempted growing a beard before but without much luck. And my hair is blonde and that doesn't help the matter either."

Yasmin smiled again. "I think you have a handsome face. Why try to cover it up?"

It was an interesting thought. Many men on the frontier grew beards. His friend, Shep Silva, had dark, almost black hair. He needed to shave twice a day if he wanted to be clean-shaven. Most of the time he would grow his whiskers for a couple of days before shaving, except in the winter he allowed his beard to grow. During his younger years, Aaron envied some in his community who were able to successfully grow beards. It was a sign of masculinity and wisdom. Hadassah was raven-haired and the men in her family easily grew whiskers. Aaron appeared too Teutonic. He looked German. When he finally left the *shtetl* and went to Danzig it helped him to blend in more easily. His Jewishness was pushed behind.

"If you prefer my face clean-shaven, then I will continue to keep it that way." He thought for a moment. "The men in your family, did they all have beards?"

"Of course," she admitted. "It was a sign of their age and sex. On the other hand, unlike the Jews I have known, my people believed in trimming their beards. It almost became a fashion statement. Some were quite hideous." Yasmin patted his knee. "There are many times when you appear to me to be British. We knew many soldiers whose whiskers were also blonde and perhaps not thick. Like yours."

"I hope that's all right."

"Of course, it is. Do you ever feel slighted by your lack of a beard? Do you believe a beard helps in your approach to Deity?"

Aaron thought for a few moments. "Maybe once upon a time, I did. The religious men in my life grew beards and combed them with their fingers as they pontificated on serious matters. But no, not anymore. It has become apparent to me that women have as much access to God as their male counterparts, if not more. If anything, I now wish my face were as smooth as yours." The statement came as a compliment, causing Yasmin to blush and she lowered her eyes once again.

"Today, this is still important to you?"

He nodded. "It doesn't seem to matter how long I am away from the synagogue, how long I am no longer pursuing Jewish lore or customs, how far I am from my *shtetl*, high holy days always return to me, reminding me, if nothing else, of my heritage and some of the things my people have been through because of their religion."

"Are you fasting for *Yom Kippur*?"

Aaron Rost chuckled. "I thought that's what all of us were doing on this trip. Fasting does come quite naturally out here on the trail, don't you think?"

"Does it bring you closer to God?"

Aaron sobered. "It does but Yasmin, being here on the trail, covered at night by the twinkling stars and listening to you breathe as you sleep, that is what brings God the closest to me." Yasmin blushed once more. The stalwart Aaron Rost was adamant in his pronouncement. Harriett was the silent observer.

The Willie Company had started from Florence and being smaller, managed to travel farther and faster than the more ponderous Martin Company. The latter also managed to slow both the Hodgetts and Hunt wagon companies. By Wednesday, October 15th the Willie Company passed Independence Rock and Devil's Gate. They were still more than 100 miles from South Pass and 225 miles away from Fort Bridger. Their stores of flour were meager and would not last long. Captain Willie decided the company needed to cut back further on their flour rations. The distance and effort were having a more severe effect on the pioneers, whose images were thinning by the hour. Generating warmth for one another beneath the nightly covers was less and less successful.

Levi Savage – October 15, 1856

"Today we traveled fifteen and a half miles. Last night Caroline Reeder,

aged seventeen years, died and was buried this morning. The people are getting weak and failing very fast. A great many are sick. Our teams are also failing fast, and it requires great exertion to make any progress.

"Our rations were reduced last night, one quarter, bringing the men to ten ounces and the women to nine ounces. Some of the children were reduced to six and others to three ounces each."

18 October, Saturday- Martin Company- We are getting close to the last of our crossings on the North Platte River. I must admit that this trip has proven quite difficult, especially these past weeks when we have had to deal with much rougher terrain. Our cattle have been perishing much swifter than I thought. They have been brought as a backup for our food but with so many dying, I have wondered how many we might end up with. Captain Martin runs a tight ship. He likes our tents set in order, almost like a small town. The tents house 15-20 people but as of yet, there hasn't been a serious need for them. Many times, we simply bundle up under our blankets, beneath our wagon, or pack ourselves close to others. The handcart pioneers use their carts for protection. It has worked so far.

"Happiness is a choice that requires effort at times."

Harriett Matthews

On Sunday morning the pioneers scattered across the rough, high plains, awoke to howling north winds and blowing, blinding sheets of snow. Temperatures dropped drastically. The wind made it even more desperate. Swirling white clouds danced low on the ground, disguising the horizons. The Saints were instantly miserable, not able to claim shelter. Few wanted to rise early and face the elements.

The Martin Company were on the banks of the wide North Platte River. Even though the waters weren't running fast, they now were clogged with slushy snow and chunks of ice. The people knew this was the last time they would need to cross this river, but it was small consolation when trying to see the landscape beyond the waters. The storm continued howling, giving no signs of letting up. After breaking camp, the emigrants began lining up along the bank. The icy waters looked treacherous. Horses and cattle were hesitant about entering. Finally, the stalwart people pushed forward into the freezing waters, pulling and dragging their carts. In some places, the water reached the men's chests. Frigid water turned their limbs numb as they pushed and pried to keep their belongings moving. After several minutes the first of the venturers began climbing the opposite banks. The wind was merciless. More and more began following, crowding into the freezing currents, catching their breaths, and striving to conquer the watery barrier. As they scrambled from the frigid waters, they were met by the fierce wind that quickly transformed their shirts or dresses into sheets of stiff ice. The pioneers cried and yelled, hopping up and down, trying desperately to force the blood back into their legs and feet. The miserable travelers on the east side of the river watched anxiously as more proceeded them and splashed into the formidable waters and then realized that their turns were approaching inevitably. The shock of the icy bath caused many to balk but all knew the only way to survive was to press onward, cross the river and start walking as crisply as possible, to break up the clinging ice from their clothes and begin generating a semblance of warmth before the wind could whisk it away. The complexions of men, women, and children took on a curious blue tint. Crying and coughing brought some color and feeling back into lips, although the breathing became raspy and painful.

The slow, confused crossing proved to be a life-altering experience. The terror and shock that was experienced by entering to frozen flow were remembered for the balance of their lives. For some, it proved too great a barrier. They began slowing and staggering. Hypothermia set in and disorientation seized their brains. They began babbling incoherently, instantly worrying the rest of their loved ones. Strength was immediately sapped. The vanguard was able to wobble only a few miles before stopping to attempt setting up a camp in preparation for those who continued straggling in. Frozen ground made driving tent stakes nearly impossible. The wind whipped flaps, catching some corners and flattening the shelters. Misery permeated the entire company. Frantic mothers pulled children close, trying to muffle the cries and sobs, while their half-frozen fathers pulled on the creaking handcarts. The camp became the immediate goal, a chance to crowd around a fire in an attempt to begin the process of thawing. Strong, young bodies shivered violently. Older, weaker, more fragile people were either helped along or they would sit in the snow and begin to freeze. Death was never far away.

The biting winds were ceaseless, pushing snow and ice and temperatures ever lower. The storm continued throughout the day, torturing the isolated, famished emigrants to the breaking point.

19 October, Sunday- Martin Company- The most awful Sabbath of my experience. We woke up to find several inches of snow blowing over the ground. Fighting against the blizzard, we prepared for the crossing, knowing this obstacle had to be overcome. By mid-morning, the first of our handcart families entered the frigid waters. The horrid scenes were repeated again and again as people were exposed to the icy baths. As they left the water and climbed the banks of the far side, they were exposed to gusting winds that froze their garments and consequently their bodies.

Our wagon was set at the rear, giving us a chance to watch almost all of our brethren and sisters be submerged and flounder their way to the other side.

Aaron and a number of the men could not sit idly by and watch, but rather ventured forward to help as they could. Invariably these men got pulled into the water and were immediately almost frozen to death. Still, several crossed back and forth to assist. Prayers were offered constantly, vocally, but the longer the crossing took, the louder. The moans and sobs grew in volume until the banks of the river were engulfed in the cries of these destitute vagabonds.

The only thing that saved our Aaron Rost was his being able to return to the wagon where he found some dry clothing and was able to change. This helped somewhat until we also needed to cross. Our oxen tried to find any way other than entering the cold water. I am confident they both would have succumbed had not Aaron jumped down to drag them across. The little drama we experienced was multiplied hundreds of times throughout the company. We pushed on to our makeshift camp that lay several miles away. They were the longest miles of my life. Yasmin hugged and warmed Aaron the best she could, while I drove our suffering oxen.

Our camp was a picture of varying degrees of suffering, from youngest to oldest, men and women. Several fires had been started. Few tents were erected. The wind and snow kept most of us as close together and as near the fires as possible. Our clothing began steaming. The side of our bodies facing the fire warmed while the opposite side ached with the cold. Most stayed as near as we could for as long as possible. Men were chosen to leave and find more wood. That too was a terrible crucible. I am not convinced that all of our brethren returned.

Death stalks our company. It has been most grievous with the aged and infirm. Even so, a number of our littlest children have succumbed to the dropping temperatures. This frozen nightmare shows no signs of lessening. For the first time in weeks, we have heard the approaching howls of wolves, and this despite Aaron's rifle.

The Hodgetts wagons crossed the river today, doing their best not to interfere. They were much more successful in their efforts. They allowed some of our emigrants a chance to ride on their wagons. But not many and then they were suddenly gone from our view, and we continued battling the fierce storm. Once the wagons exited the Platte, they continued, traveling farther away to set up their camp, farther than we were ever capable.

The Hunt wagons arrived later in the day and after witnessing the suffering we had passed through, decided not to cross today, perhaps waiting out the winter storm. I think that had we known we might have waited with them. Regardless, we are in this mess together. I am heartened by the resilience of these wonderful, yet famished, people. We remain quite a distance from the Great Salt Lake Valley. Still, Aaron assures us that Pres Brigham Young will not leave us out here alone.

At times, standing in the warmth of the fire, we feel somewhat better, but then again, our stomachs are empty. Our stores of food are minimal. I don't know how we will be able to persevere without a chance to eat as well as being in the presence of this horrible storm.

"It is easy when we are in prosperity to give advice to the afflicted."

Harriett Matthews

Josiah Rogerson

October 1856

"The crossing of the North Platte was fraught with more fatalities than any other incident of the entire journey...More than a score or two of the young female members waded the stream that in places was waist-deep. Blocks of mushy snow and ice had to be dodged. The result of wading of this stream by the female members was immediately followed by partial and temporary dementia from which several did not recover until the next spring."

Elizabeth Horrocks Jackson Kingsford

October 19, 1856

"Some of the men carried some of the women on their back or in their arms, but others of the women tied up their skirts and waded through, like the heroines that they were, and as they had gone through many other rivers and creeks. My husband (Aaron Jackson) attempted to ford the stream. He had only gone a short distance when he reached a sandbar in the river, on which he sank down through weakness and exhaustion."

Elizabeth Horrocks Jackson Kingsford

October 1856

"I was six or seven thousand miles from my native land, in a wild, rocky, mountain country, in a destitute condition, the ground covered with snow, the waters covered with ice, and I with three fatherless children with scarcely nothing to protect them from the merciless storms. I will not attempt to describe my feelings at finding myself thus left a widow with three children."

Chapter 41

"Life is too short to be little. Man is never so manly as when he feels deeply, acts boldly, and expresses himself with frankness and with fervor." Benjamin Disraeli

The Willie Company was 100 miles in front of the Martin Company. They were moving towards the Sixth Crossing of the Sweetwater. The small river looped wildly across the plains, starting near the heights of South Pass, finally running through Devil's Gate, past Independence Rock, and then finally merging with the North Platte River far to the south. Until the advent of the winter blast, the Willie Company had been making good time, although they were in desperate need of food. Knees were getting weaker. The grip on the handcarts was loosening. The freezing blast of the snow and north wind surprised one and all. The Willie Company became snowbound.

George Grant organized a series of wagons in Fort Bridger, then set out with the first of them, heading for South Pass, then down to the Sweetwater nine miles farther on. As the storm began arriving, the men turned off the road and headed three miles north towards a large stand of willows that would allow them a refuge from the elements. They spent the rest of the day solidifying their position. Redick Allred was in charge of staging the six wagons and setting up a protective camping area. Grant left during the blinding storm, leading three other mounted men, and set off to find the Willie Company. They crossed over the dangerous, wind-swept Rocky Ridge and when descending, saw the straggling line of Captain Willie's company moving toward the Sixth Crossing of the Sweetwater in the mid-afternoon.

It was on this day of white gloom that George Grant and Shep Silva and two of their mounted companions encountered the shivering company. The arrival of the healthy, positive-sounding men brightened all. The four distributed what little they could spare, promising that more rescuers were on their way behind them.

"Don't lose hope," Grant boomed out as loud as he could. "Wagons are coming within a few days. Hold out strong. The Lord lives and he loves you. You are not alone in this matter."

Captain Willie cornered Shep before they rode off farther to the east. "Should I go looking for the rescuers?"

"You're sitting in damned cold weather. It's up to you. And the Lord."

"Thanks for your help."

The four riders turned and started their horses back through the snow, heading for Devil's Gate. Their purpose was to reach Devil's Gate, looking for the other three companies but they weren't to go further. Some wondered whether the other companies might have decided to set up winter quarters and wait out the weather.

Not wanting to waste any time, Captain James Willie instructed Levi Savage to organize their camp and get the tents set. Then he and Joseph Elder rode off in search of the wagons Grant had described. The icy climb over the Rocky Ridge was treacherous. Several times their horses slipped, nearly dropping their mounts onto the frozen earth, or worse, down steep, icy chasms.

Finishing his chores, Harvey Cluff sought out Redick Allred to tell him his concerns.

"I've got a board here," he explained. "I can write a sign on it and take it back to the road, pointing to our encampment here. It's not much but it might help if others come looking for us."

"If the snow doesn't cover it or the wind blow it down."

"Still a good idea, or what?"

"God bless you, Harvey."

Cluff trudged back down the grade, helped by the howling wind until he found the road and a likely place to erect his makeshift sign. He wedged it as solidly as he could in the brush to prevent the wind from knocking it over. There wasn't much that could be done about the snow. He angled it away from the storm and prayed that it stay clear, then returned to their camp at the Willows.

It was less than an hour after Cluff's return to the camp that Captain James Willie and Joseph Elder rode their horses into the encampment, telling one and all how the Cluff sign had saved them from riding aimlessly into the swirling storm to the west and most certainly to their deaths.

Information was exchanged between the rescuers and Willie and Elder, then the two horsemen turned around and headed back over the miles to their handcart company, with the news of Allred's wagons and the aid that would be sent their way the following day.

On Tuesday, the six Allred wagons crested Rocky Ridge and made their way down to the Willie encampment. One of the rescuers said it looked like an Eskimo camp with trails through the snow running from tent to tent. The supplies carried by the wagons were not sufficient for the entire company but it went a long way towards clothing and feeding the emigrants. Most importantly, it raised flagging hopes.

Another series of wagons began arriving at Redick's camp from Fort Bridger. These were divided into those needed by the Willie Company and 10 other wagons were passed along and sent east to Devil's Gate, hoping to meet with the remaining three companies. Herman and Zeenyo were among these rescuers, anxious to catch up with Shep and help in the herculean rescue attempt.

After allowing themselves a few days to rest up, on Thursday the Willie Company broke their camp and headed for the Rocky Ridge. This posed a steep five-mile climb over some of the most jagged roads along the trip. The first two handcart companies that traveled during the summer had chosen the Seminoe Cutoff below the Rocky Ridge. This route was longer but not nearly as difficult. Willie Company decided to attack the height. The weather decided to snow again and it turned once more into a frosty blizzard, blinding and numbing. The small amounts of food provided by the rescue wagons were not enough for the pioneers as their stores of strength and stamina were called upon once again. Many of the men ascended, then returned to help others, making the trip several times during the day. They finally made camp late that night. The efforts proved too much for thirteen men who perished that day. These were buried in a common grave. Digging individual graves in the rock-hard frozen earth was asking far too much of the beleaguered travelers. Two more men died the following day, making it the deadliest 24 hours of the Willie Company's trek.

William Kimball had been assigned to collect the Willie Company and with the six more wagons just arriving from South Pass, to start bringing the emigrants to the pass and from there on to Fort Bridger.

Levi Savage

October 23, 1856
"We buried our dead, got up our teams and about nine o'clock a.m. commenced ascending the Rocky Ridge. This was a severe day. The wind blew hard and cold. The ascent was some five miles long and some places steep and covered with deep snow. We became weary, set down to rest, and some became chilled and commenced to freeze…

"About ten or eleven o'clock in the night we came to a creek [Strawberry Creek] that we did not like to attempt to cross without help, it being full of ice and freezing cold."

John Chislett, Willie Handcart Company

October 1856
"We had found a good camp among the willows, and after warming and partially drying ourselves before good fires, we ate our scanty fare, paid our usual devotions to the Deity and retired to rest with hopes of coming aid."

Jens Pederson

October 23, 1856
"When they were having such hard times with low rations and cold weather, one man decided he didn't want to put up with any more so just said he wasn't going another step. Different ones tried to talk to him and urge him to go on but had no effect upon his decision. Grandpa, Jens O. Pederson asked for permission to talk to the man."

John Chislett

October 1856

"Near South Pass we found more brethren from the Valley, with several quarters of good fat beef hanging frozen on the limbs of the trees where they were encamped. These quarters of beef were to us the handsomest pictures we ever saw. The statues of Michael Angelo, or the paintings of the ancient masters, would have been to us nothing in comparison to these life-giving pictures."

John Chislett

October 1856

"The Weather grew colder each day, and many got their feet so badly frozen that they could not walk and had to be lifted from place to place. Some got their fingers frozen; others their ears; and one woman lost her sight by the frost. These severities of the weather also increased our number of deaths, so that we buried several each day."

On Thursday, October 23rd, the Martin Company had struggled in their tattered clothes and without food for the ten miles that separated them from the Hodgetts Wagons camped at the Red Buttes. They did their best to set up camp, still, without much food, and two days later their rations needed to be cut once more, going down to 8 ounces per adult per day, and the children were allocated 4 ounces.

Wednesday 22nd. Camp rolled out. W.H. Kimball and others with 6 wagons went on to the Valley with us. G.D. Grant and others went on towards "Independence Rock" to meet Martin' s Handcart Company. Travelled 11 miles and camped on the Sweetwater. Roads good considering the snow on the ground. Eliza Philpot from Southampton, Hampshire, England, died, aged 36; also, John James from Whitbourne, Herefordshire, England, aged 61.

Thursday 23rd. Ascended a steep hill, travelled about 16 miles and camped on the Sweetwater. Crossed several creeks on the road, several men were near frozen through the day; two teams loaded with sick did not get to camp till very late. James Gibbs from Leith, East Lothian, Scotland, aged 67 died; also Chesterton J. Gilman from Yarmouth, Suffolk, England, aged 66 years died.

Friday, 24th. Redick N. Allred and others with 6 wagons came to camp this morning to assist the Handcart Company on our journey to the Valley. It was concluded to stay in camp today and bury the dead as there were 13 persons to inter. William James, from Pershore, Worcestershire, England, aged 46 died; Elizabeth Bailey, from Leigh, Worcestershire, England, aged 52 died; James Kirkwood from Glasgow, Scotland, aged 11 died Samuel Gadd, from Orwell, Cambridgeshire, England, aged 10 died; Lars Wendin [Venden], from Copenhagen, Denmark, aged 60 died; Anne Olsen, from Seeland, Denmark, aged 46 died; Ella Nilson, from Jutland, Denmark, aged 22 years, died; Jens Nilson, from Lolland, Denmark, aged 6 years died; Bodil Mortinsen from Lolland, Denmark, aged 9 years, died; Nils Anderson from Seeland, Denmark, aged 41 years died; Ole Madsen from Seeland, Denmark, aged 41 years died; Many of the Saints have their feet and hands frozen from the severity of the weather.

Saturday 25th. Rolled from camp in the morning. Thomas Gurdlestone from Great Melton, Norwich, aged 62 years died. William Groves, from Cranmoor, Somersetshire, England, aged 22 years died; Crossed the Sweetwater for the last time. Travelled about 15 miles and camped on the Sweetwater. Some brethren were stationed at this post on the river with supplies of flour and onions. John Watters from Bristol, Somerset, England, aged 65, William Smith from Eldersfield, Worcestershire, England, aged 48 years died.

Sunday 26th. Morning fine and pleasant. Samuel Wit from Bristol, Somerset, England, aged 66 years died; Mary Roberts from Eldersfield, Worcestershire, England, aged 44 years died. The camp rolled on, crossed the "South Pass" and Pacific Creek; travelled down Pacific creek and camped after travelling about 14 miles. Good place to camp for sagewood.

Shep looked strong and capable, facing the falling snow. The white flakes collected on his woolly black beard. The hair protruding from beneath his hat was curly and cut short. His horse was anxious and snorted, looking between the two rising pillars of granite through which the Sweetwater River ran. This was Devil's Gate. About a mile beyond the monument rose the turtle-shaped Independence Rock. Beyond that was a tundra, covered with snow. Again, the white clouds and white landscape masked any discerning landmarks besides hiding where the one ended and the other started.

George Grant joined him in gazing at the stark, lifeless expanse. He nodded thoughtfully. "We'll have the three of you ride out there. Make sure to follow the road the best you can. But don't go more than two days. Cover what ground you can and see if you can't find the companies. Let them know that we're here. We'll be fixing up camp around the bend in the cove, collecting firewood, and putting up what tents we can. Hopefully, we'll get more wagons before you get back and have something decent set up for them." Grant smiled. Doing hard things was so much easier when helped by men the likes of Shep Silva. "Not more than two days out. Got it?"

"Got it," Shep said stepping into his stirrup and swinging his right leg over the saddle. A couple of seconds later and Shep and Brigham's youngest son, Joseph, and Grant's eldest boy were thundering east into the growing fog, on their life-saving search.

Joseph Angell Young was a sincere, hard-working man. He had been serving a mission in England when Steptoe's company arrived in the Salt Lake Valley. It was Lt. Mowry who tried to seduce Joseph's wife. The outcome of his attempts as well as the drubbing Shep had given the soldier, cemented Silva and Young's friendship.

"You know the lay of the land better than me. Any ideas?" Shep asked Joseph.

"Who knows? Could be anywhere. I just wonder if they're not digging in for the winter."

"There enough water for that?"

Young shrugged. "Don't know. It's a pretty large number of folks. They'll be needing plenty of water."

"What we looking at?"

"Greasewood's first. About twenty miles out. From there, things are empty until Red Buttes. How far can we get?"

Now it was Shep's turn to shrug. "The horses look good. As long as we can help them find feed and water and rest up some, we should be able to cover 50 miles a day. A long day. And it's already getting late."

Grant's boy was just happy to be riding with these men. It made him feel important and he liked the fact that his father trusted him with such an important call.

Pulling their hats lower over their faces, they charged into the darkening white silence. Shep was protected by a tight leather coat that successfully kept the cold out. Later that night they reined up to a small stream. Dark forms against the white snow announced low lying clumps of the greasewood plants. They checked for a hundred yards but didn't come up with any signs of travelers. Yet.

"Greasewood," Joseph nodded. "I was hoping they'd be here. Doesn't look like anyone's been here since Willie's group."

"Long jaunt to the Buttes?"

"Long enough."

"And if they're not there?"

"I'll leave that up to you, Shep. Grant wants us back no later than two or three more days. Then again, I'm not out here to fail. My intentions are to find them. No disrespect to Brother Grant, but I plan on going till my horse gives out."

Silva appreciated the idea. "You're a good man, Joseph. Care for company?"

"Couldn't ask for anyone better."

The Grant boy held up his hands in mock defeat. "I'm just along for the ride."

They spent a cold night beneath their trail blankets, glad that they were riding horses rather than plodding the distance on foot. They arose early in the morning. Coals from their fire were still warm and easy enough to fan again into flames. A quick pot of Mormon tea was brewed. A couple of swallows of the bitter drink was enough to satiate the men. The horses were sturdy and free from saddle sores. Saddles were frozen stiff but the blanket protected the horses' backs. They climbed back into the creaking leather seats and headed again into the storm. Thankfully, the warmth of their bodies soon made the saddles easier to tolerate.

Looking ahead at Joseph, Shep found himself wondering what it would be like to have this man as a mission companion. He was bright and intelligent. His sense of humor was delightful. On the other hand, he was dead serious when it came to the gospel of Jesus Christ. Dealing with the salvation of men's souls was a serious business. President Young was proud of his son. It was a definite stamp of validation having this young man out with him in the fastness of the prairie. There was no room for doubt as to the importance of the lives and well-being of these emigrants in the heart and mind of Brigham Young.

Red Buttes William Binder

October 1856
"During our sojourn at this camp we were placed under very trying circumstances; being reduced to very low rations of flour; a scanty supply of clothing and in addition to these evils, it became our painful duty to bury very many of our friends and traveling companions also to see our cattle vanish from our view through starvation every day."

The pace kept by the horses was fast as if they expected to find feed and shelter at the end of the trip. The wind was blowing from the north but also moving across the prairie at such a clip increased the gusting. Being away from any substantial rivers kept the humidity low so the temperature wasn't as low as it could be. Riding in silence gave Shep time to think. One thought that kept returning was from his boyhood in Brazil. *The winters there could be brutal with the minuano winds flying up from the Antarctic. There were no mountains to slow their arrival. They were biting and cold and they came across the ocean bringing plenty of humidity. Even though the temps dipped, they seldom went below freezing. Whenever they did, the place turned into a winter wonderland, with frost covering all the trees and sparkling flecks of ice dancing in the air. It was cold. It was beautiful. It was also quite dangerous because the floating pieces of ice if inhaled could quickly cause pneumonia. Many people died as a result of the infections, despite the glorious appearance. Many winter days were spent next to his grandparent's stove. A similar thing would take place in the North American West with the frost. The Indians called it pogonip, a quaint word that accompanied the winter phenomenon. Its definition was quite removed from the harmless appearance. Pogonip meant white death.* From there, he began thinking about the Sierra Nevada Mountains. The misnomer created unrealistic thoughts in the minds of most Brazilians and Hawaiians. Both peoples had little concept of snow, but for them, the thought of the airborne fluffy, white substance was the thing dreams were made of. Presently, thoughts of the cool, cold snow, blowing in the face, stinging unprotected skin, covering the ground, causing man and animal to slip and slide, masking the surrounding countryside were anything but pleasant and magical. Snow combined with other winter elements bringing death and misery.

The continuous canter of the horses impressed Shep. The animals were strong and willing to allow the men to ride on their backs, all the while warming them.

Joseph pulled his horse to a stop, holding up his hand. Shep followed suit, then tried to follow where Young was pointing.

"Down there, in the bottom of the swell. I think I saw a flicker of light. Maybe a campfire?"

Shep strained to see through the tiny specs of snow that kept blowing into his eyes. The target was still several hundred yards away, but it was just after mid-day. If it was the company, and he didn't have any information of others being out on the prairie at that time, they were wisely staying put, not trying to march through the unmarked wilderness. *Then again, did they have access to any food stores?* Willie's Company was running out and the Martin Company was larger.

"I see it."

"Indians?"

Shep shook his head. "I think they'd do a better job of finding shelter. They wouldn't stay out in the open like this."

"All right then. Let's go and introduce ourselves."

News of the three men's arrival spread like fire through the Martin Company and then flashed over to the Hodgetts train. The two groups were sheltering together beyond the Red Buttes and not far from the North Platte River. And then the three riders were able to see the emigrants, the handcart pioneers. The destitute, the frozen, the disoriented, the tired and worn out.

The riders, in turn, were seen as delivering angels. The blue-coated Joseph Angell Young received the moniker that would remain with him for the rest of his life. Albert Jones said "The white animal Young was riding was lost sight of on the white background of snow, and Joseph A. with his big blue soldier's overcoat, its large cape and capacious skirts rising and falling with the motion of the horse, gave the appearance of a big blue-winged angel flying to our rescue. The scene that presented itself on his arrival I shall never forget; women and men surrounded him, weeping and crying aloud; on their knees, holding to the skirts of his coat, as though afraid he would escape from their grasp and fly away."

"Many declared we were angels," mused the down-to-earth young man, George Grant. "I told them I thought we were better than angels for this occasion, as we were good strong men come to help them into the valley, and that our company, and wagons loaded with provisions, were not far away."

Though the express riders brought no supplies with them, they provided life-saving hope by announcing that 10 wagons with food and clothing awaited them at Devil's Gate. The express riders then hurried on to find John Hunt's wagon camp.

Patience Loader was among those who received clothing. "I was thankful to get a nice warm quilted hood, which was very warm and comfortable. I also got a pair of slippers as I was nearly barefoot."

Hands were shaken and hugs exchanged. Smiles were on every face the riders could see. Listless people were energized, and children began racing between the tents whooping excitedly. The joy expressed made a knot develop in Silva's throat. They had ridden for two days from Devil's Gate. These poor souls would still need to pack up and head out again through the frozen wilderness, looking for the rescue wagons still two score miles away.

"We have ten wagons waiting at Devil's Gate," Joseph told a group of the company's leaders. "There is food and clothing. Tents are being set up and firewood gathered. Our only request is that you load up and follow after us as quickly as you're able. It will be your salvation."

The men nodded in unison. It was a daunting plan. But it was either that or await a winter death, stranded in the austere wasteland. After a sincere group prayer, the Martin Company decided to start in the morning. Looking their horses over and making sure they had some time to rest and feed, Young and Shep wanted to saddle up and return to Devil's Gate as soon as they could.

"A moment, please," Captain Martin urged before they mounted. "We'll send runners back to inform the wagon train. One of our men here has been attending to burial duty, keeping him busy for the last hour or so. I know he would like to have some words with you, Shep."

Silva nodded and looked into the faces of the folks surrounding them. His quick scanning was quickly stopped as his eyes fell onto the friendly face of Aaron Rost.

"Rost! I had no idea you were with the company!"

The slender blonde stepped forward and accepted the heartfelt hug, who then pounded his back and shoulders happily. Aaron simply smiled and held on to his friend.

Shep finally stepped back and looked Rost over, then nodded. "You're skinny but really don't look half bad."

Aaron smiled. "You're still quite ugly, Silva."

The Brazilian burst out with a loud laugh. "Wouldn't have it any other way, *amigo*. You'd never recognize me."

"Got just a minute? There's some folks I'd like you to meet."

Shep handed his reins over to Young and walked quickly after Aaron. "You've been digging burial plots?"

"Just a large one. It's too hard trying to do it for each person."

"Losing plenty of folks?"

Aaron nodded. "I think we're well under 500 emigrants by now. It has been a rough one."

"You still look healthy."

"I haven't been doing the walking and dragging the handcarts. I have a wagon to ride in. Consequently, my boots are still in one piece and I'm not using all my rations to fuel my march."

Shep pointed at Aaron's carbine. "You ever learn how to use that?"

"And thank goodness. The damned wolves are shadowing us like ghosts. They're vicious but smart. They stay far enough away that I haven't been able to knock many down. Their eyes reflect the firelight, always warning us of their presence. And they're big. Like swift monsters. And they howl. Enough to curdle your blood."

"I don't envy you."

"We stack as many rocks as we can find over the graves, hoping to keep these killers away from our loved ones. We don't want them dragging bodies across the prairie."

"These the people you want me to meet?"

Aaron smiled and nodded. "They're nurses, from England. Two of the most wonderful women you'd ever care to meet. Singlehandedly they have tended to scores of the sick and infirm. They're stronger than most men. They know what they're doing. Their smiles and faith have boosted the company more than I can say."

The outlines of the worn wagon told Shep they were reaching their destination. He also spied two dark forms, cloaked in blankets moving through the jumbled bags packed in the wagon box, guessing they were Aaron's friends.

"Yasmin. Harriett. This is my friend, Shep Silva. He and Joseph Young and George Grant's boy just arrived from Devil's Gate. A rescue party awaits us there. Plenty of wagons with food and supplies. We'll be starting for the place in the morning."

Both women approached carefully, wrapped tightly in their blankets with only their faces exposed. They had to be young women, although the wind and cold gave them a much older appearance.

Silva bowed gracefully. "It's an honor. Aaron tells me that you have held the company together with your skills, wit, and courage."

The two feminine countenances smiled slowly. They appreciated the attention. Both women's eyebrows were dark, telling Shep that they both had dark hair. He noticed tears beginning to run down the cheeks of the woman named Yasmin.

"I wish I could say the gauntlet is over," he added. "There is still quite a way to Devil's Gate. And there should be more food and a chance to dry yourselves out and get warmed up. The people of the valleys have sent some wagons to help. And there are more coming. Our prayer is that no one gives up. Even though the end is still a way off, you'll all be able to see it soon."

The two-woman audience appreciated his efforts to sustain them.

"It really is my pleasure to meet you and I say, God bless you for your resolve." He patted the hands that suddenly appeared from beneath the blankets.

Harriett's calloused hand gripped his for a brief minute and she looked into his eyes.

"God loves you, Shep Silva, and I love you," she said simply.

Although it seemed like a basic phrase, her words stirred deep within his heart. A spark ignited and he straightened up. "This will all be over soon enough," he assured them, "and because of you, future generations will rise up and bless your memories. I know this to be true."

The two men turned and walked back to the horses and Joseph Young and little Grant.

"He looks warm enough," Aaron said, gesturing at Young's heavy blue coat. "Better get you out of here before some of our company decide that he doesn't need it as much as they do."

Shep received his reins back and waved a hopeful hand at the men. "*Adeus, meus amigos.*"

Before he could step into his stirrup, Shep felt Aaron's strong arm reach out and pull him into a powerful embrace. "*Um abraço forte de teu irmão.*"

Silva waited several seconds for the emotion to pass, then mounted his horse. He didn't remember Aaron having ever spoken more than a word of Portuguese. The way he said it came so naturally and for a moment, Shep didn't realize that he had switched languages. Nodding assertively to their brethren, the riders turned and galloped back the way they had come just an hour before. Neither Young nor Silva nor Grant turned to watch the diminishing encampment. The snow was still coming down, but now the wind had ceased.

Behind them, someone shouted, "Let us go to the Valley! Let us go to Zion!"

"You think they'll be okay?"

"God is with them."

28 October, Tuesday- Martin Company- Red Buttes. The day started as bleak and disheartening as the others this week. The snow and cold are everywhere. I counted ten dead this morning. The tears and cries seem to be ebbing, as many of us see this as the same direction we are all headed. Quietness envelopes the camp, only broken now and again by soft sobs. The small fires that have been kindled also seem to be quiet, as emaciated forms gather around in an attempt to warm themselves.

Then, this afternoon, wonder of wonders, as three individual riders arrived. They had been sent from Devil's Gate where there are a number of rescue wagons awaiting their report, as they search for us. One of the riders is Shep Silva, a close friend of Aaron's. Another was Brigham's son, Joseph Angell Young. I have forgotten how strong men can appear when they are not walking long distances with little nutrition.

Also, most of the men in our company are surrounded by their families. These are people they love. These are who they continue to sacrifice their all to support and assist. We have long been taught that the family is the bedrock of society. It certainly is in the plan of God, but here we are seeing the drama play out, as men, women, and children combine to help and encourage one another.

314

Yasmin and I needed to amputate two more legs from men just before we encountered the riders. It has been very difficult. Aaron has been burying the corpses. The two amputees were simple and did not bleed much and were easy to bandage. However, they obviously cannot walk. We are taking one into our wagon and the other is being loaded into another. The added weight will also be hard on our livestock. As we head out tomorrow morning, young men will be taken from the driving of the cattle to help with the handcarts, and they will be replaced by either younger boys or young women. All are stepping up to do their parts.

Brother Silva was complimentary to Yasmin and me about our nursing work. His kindness reminded me of still other words from Aeschylus:

"I gave them hope, and so turned away their eyes from death."

Harriett Matthews

Late the next day, Shep and Joseph came skidding into the encampment of George Grant, west of Devil's Gate.

"Successful?" he asked, already noting the gleams in their eyes.

"Got 'em."

Whistling shrilly, Grant collected his men to announce the mission of Silva and Young. Within minutes the horses and mules were hitched to the ten wagons and the train started into the darkening prairie evening.

After turning his horse over to Joseph Young, Shep asked for permission to return with Herman and Zeenyo in their effort to bring help to the forlorn Martin Handcart Company. Both Wetoyous were anxious to leave the camp and go in search of the emigrants.

"This is what we came for," Herman said as he watched Shep nod and start to drift off to sleep. It had been a trying time. They felt they were on the cusp of completing something worthwhile. The wagons creaked through the night, the darkness slowing their progress, but men and animals sensed the urgency of the mission.

Mile after mile the column pushed into the frozen landscape, lookouts keeping a close eye on the distant horizon. It was Friday when the driver of the lead wagon stood and whooped loudly, pointing ahead at the distant cluster of greasewoods hugging the small stream. It was what they had been searching for. A quick look told them they had arrived before the handcarts. The drivers urged their horses and mules to a quicker pace, then pulled aside and set their brakes. The men piled out of their wagons and began clearing the area, setting up tents, and starting campfires.

"Think they'll be along before too late?" Herman asked.

"I do."

Zeenyo shivered as he dragged dead branches towards a growing stack of fuel. "See? This is why the Hopi lived so far to the south. They were smarter than wanting to spend the winters huddled against snowstorms."

315

Young and the other express riders left the Martin Company and arrived at Devil's Gate on October 31st. The camp sprang to life. Grant led the rescuers east that day, and they met the snowbound Martin company at Greasewood Creek. Although a welcome sight, Grant's supplies provided only about half of the pioneers with a good coat or a pair of stockings without holes.

The late morning sun was peeking through clouds but unable to generate warmth. It wasn't long before cries erupted from the camp, alerting the laborers of the handcarts' arrival. The tired people began pulling their carts into the cleared area and collapsed with exhaustion. It had been a strenuous hike. A few of the workers emerged from tents, as the emigrants continued to assemble, clapping and crying and hollering, raising hands to God with grateful hearts. Within minutes the first carts had entered the camp and the teamsters were swarmed with joyful shouts and glistening eyes. Food and water and clothing were dispersed, then thankful emigrants collected to pray and thank the Lord for this portion of their salvation. Several men ran off into the snow, looking to assist others struggling to reach camp.

Hours later the Hodgetts Train joined the Martin Company at the Greasewoods. All were able to partake of the increased bounty. It was not as much as they needed, but all were thankful for the respite. Riders were back towards Red Buttes, dozens of miles, to relay the news to the Hunt train.

It was a happy day for Aaron Rost as he rejoined the Wetoyous and Silva. Being professional nurses, Harriett and Yasmin remained more reserved but pleased with the appearance of the wagons. They were surprised to see that Shep had returned, not being content to send others to their relief.

After the hour needed to change clothes and eat, the company packed up and started again for the camp beyond Devil's Gate. With the added wagons, many of the aged and infirm were able to ride, speeding up their journey significantly.

Chapter 42

"The secret of success in life is for a man to be ready for his opportunity when it comes." Benjamin Disraeli

One hundred miles to their west, the Willie Company had been working all week and were finally able to cross South Pass on Sunday. They continued their labors and on Friday they met up with ten more supply wagons west of Green River. It didn't take them long to distribute the new supplies and food. The sorrows caused by the deaths, lack of food, physical exertion, and leagues of snow-covered terrain were starting to dissipate. Hope was springing within the warming bodies. The next day the Willie Company met up with another set of rescue wagons. By this time the majority of beleaguered handcart pioneers were able to ride in wagons. With the biting cold still encompassing them, most were able to snuggle against one another for warmth and enjoy the ride towards Fort Bridger.

1 November, Saturday- Martin Company- These continue to be trying times, regardless of the extra wagons. The food and the added clothing have been a blessing. Many feet had broken through their shoes and exposed toes were either frozen or bleeding. The added comfort cannot be measured adequately by me. As we draw closer to a more established camp, where food and warmth beckon, I must admit that I will not miss this portion of our trip. I am surprised that Aaron Rost has traveled over the trail time and again. Then again, as he continues to say, it was not through the snow.

One of the extra curiosities of the rescuers happens to be the presence of Shep Silva. He is a close friend of Aaron's. They have joined in some efforts to help pull many of the handcarts that become bogged down. Brother Silva is not a tall man, but his strength is formidable. He is also quite anxious to scare off the wolves and has shot at them regardless of the distance. His black beard appears very insulated against the cold. I have wondered as to his countenance that is so completely covered, whether it is as pleasant as his voice and the sparkle in his eyes. It seems that his hairy body is well adapted to this weather. But I am only guessing. Perhaps I should dwell on more appropriate thoughts.

"It's not the oath that makes us believe the man, but the man the oath"

Harriett Matthews

In 1852, French fur trader Charles Lajeunesse had established a trading post a stone's throw distance west of Devil's Gate. It was well situated on the

Oregon Trail, half the distance between Fort Laramie and Fort Bridger. It was called Seminoe after the Catholic baptismal name of Charles Simonot, or little Simon. It was small, having three cabins built around a series of corrals and outbuildings. Business was good for several years but in the fall of 1855, with war between the Sioux and the US Army looming, Lajeunesse abandoned the trading post. A year later it had fallen into disrepair.

For the handcart companies, it proved a valuable resting place. Captain Willie's company used it for several days before moving on to the west. It was now commandeered by George Grant. It sat on the south side of the small Sweetwater River. Across the creek, not far to the west lay the secluded cove the rescuers were setting up to house the emigrants.

Over the following days, the Martin Handcart Company began to arrive, followed by the Hodgetts Wagons and then, a week later, the Hunt Train, there being 1000 people in total. At first, some were housed in the Seminoe cabins, but this became too inefficient and isolated. Finally, all were brought around the corner and into the sheltering area that became known as Martin's Cove. Rock hills surrounded the flat, protecting it from the north wind and snow. Trees were cut as fuel and fires were quickly and efficiently built. It was a welcome relief for the bone-tired travelers. The men from Utah worked tirelessly to get the newcomers situated, warmed, and fed. It had been too long, trying to remember when they had been able to relax after being fed and clothed in warm, dry clothing. Socks were a forgotten novelty. Buffalo blankets were given to the travelers, helping them to push their concerns to the backs of their minds. For now, things were much calmer and happier. Like fresh air, or a stunning sunset, seeing these free, robust men from the Utah Territory, anxiously engaged in helping them, invigorated the pioneers. The rescuers didn't know their names. They didn't need to. It was an unimportant idea for the present. All they knew is that they were among like-minded brethren, men who accepted them regardless of accent, wealth, or homeland. They were the children of God, jointly framed together in the work of salvation. The worries that had plagued them, as to whether or not they would ever see the Salt Lake Valley, faded, grouping as families and friends in shelters and under blankets, drifting to sleep into the night. It fell onto other's shoulders this time to keep an eye out, to watch for predators, making sure that nothing interrupted the rest of these spent warriors.

On November 2nd, at Devil's Gate, George Grant penned an extensive letter to Brigham Young, detailing the situation they were facing and sent it by messengers.

3 November, Monday- Martin Company- I am amazed at the strength that seems to be rushing back into most of our bodies and limbs after receiving decent food and rest. The weather continues to be contrary, with bitter cold and winds. But we are being well provided for. Our food is prepared by able men who know their way around the fire. These are not people trained as

Yasmin, still, they make do and for every burned biscuit, they offer a humorous tale that seems to take away any offensive taste.

Brother Grant sent Joseph Young with a letter to Brigham Young advising him of our current situation. Even though we continue to suffer a good deal, I am pleased with the actions of the people in the Utah Territory. The crisis we are facing is made much easier with the help of these determined men.

"I know how men in exile feed on dreams."

Harriett Matthews

For many citizens, not black, Indian, or women, living in the States, Tuesday, November 4th was an auspicious day. It was when the voters chose James Buchanan of the Democrat Party to be the new president of the United States, beating out the first Republican candidate John C. Fremont. Neither candidate had stumped for the position but that didn't keep the winners from celebrating and anxiously looking forward to what the new year would bring.

The day posed a wholly different meaning for the handcart company being led by Edward Martin. After resting in Martin's Cove for two days, it was decided that the company needed to get back on the trail. Some strength had been recouped but just standing and walking reminded them that they had miles yet to cover. The weather continued to be horrendously cold. All knew that the sooner they started the sooner they would meet up with the other rescue wagons and finally make their way into the Salt Lake Valley. It was a continuous dream.

The real challenge was the thought of crossing the Sweetwater. The river was smaller than the North Platte that they had crossed two weeks earlier. But that crucible had sapped them so completely, the thought of stepping again into frigid waters jolted even the strongest of men. The night before the dreaded departure saw a meeting of the heartiest men. They surrounded Captain Martin, hoping to get a better idea as to how they would break camp and start-up their travels.

"We'll unload most of the wagons," Martin explained to his bearded and weary council. "We can store the stuff in the Seminoe cabins. Let's get after that first thing. We can also unload the handcarts. Some of the loads we can put in wagons. The unnecessary things can be stored in the cabins as well. We'll stack the handcarts against the rocks at the back of the cove."

"You think the belongings will be safe until spring when we can get back out and retrieve them?"

Martin didn't. "But I think we can get some of the young men we brought up with the wagons to stay behind and watch over the things. It's dangerous but something I think should be done. I hope we have enough food for them. They'll be here until spring. What are your thoughts?"

"There should be enough room to keep them dry and out of the weather."

"But the strength of the young men would sure come in handy helping the rest of us get out of here."

The gruff patriarchs pondered the idea. It was not an easy decision.

"Shep? I was hoping the Wetoyous would be up for hanging around, holding back, and helping keep an eye on things. I was especially thinking they would know how to provide for the group."

"Living off the land is nothing new to either of them," he replied.

Martin nodded soberly. "And if Indians come around, it could be extra good having men of their stature to step up and clear away any troubles."

"If they're Shoshone. Might be tricky, otherwise."

"If any other tribes come around it could be tricky. Shoshones are who we should be praying for."

"Of course, you're right, Brother Martin. I can ask the boys."

"A couple of the lads have six-shooters. They'll need at least one rifle."

Aaron waved at Martin. "If Herman and Zeenyo stay behind, I'll let them keep my carbine. They're trained. It's a straight shooter and I have enough cartridges to tide them over for a while. Unless they start a war with someone."

The idea of the young Hopi men getting into a shooting conflict with potential marauders caused all to chuckle. It also made the thought of asking the Wetoyous more palatable for Shep. He looked over and winked his appreciation at Aaron. Edward Martin accompanied Shep to ask the Wetoyous for their assistance. As expected, they gave their support for the idea, as did the other eighteen men who were selected.

The next morning, the camp was broken leisurely, and things packed as carefully as possible. Bundles were loaded onto wagons and taken across the Sweetwater, then unloaded into the cabins. Most of the bundles consisted of clothing and some books. This would make room for many of the sick, injured and infirm to ride inside the wagon boxes. The handcarts were stacked evenly against the far side of the cove. None regretted leaving these contraptions behind. They had come to be seen as instruments of torture.

"Are you going to be all right leaving these boys behind?" Aaron asked his friend good-naturedly.

"Sure hope so. I'm glad Linda G ain't anywhere close by. She'd have my skin for garters."

"They're level-headed boys. They'll be all right."

"Better up here keeping an eye on things than having Brigham send them off to some God-forsaken place to serve missions."

"Yeah. He'll wait until they get back before calling them as missionaries." Shep could see that Aaron was joking. Mostly.

The handcart emigrants began moving towards the ice-cold river. Echoes of the past reminded them of how they had approached the Platte, only this time, to one and all the consequences of their actions were very clear. They carefully looked around on each other's faces, wondering who might next be tapped to die. The wagons carrying the things to be cached in the cabins finished their work much sooner than expected. It would take too long to carry all across in wagons. Most of the emigrants would need to cross on foot.

Nervous people began to slowly work their way to the swift, narrow river, overflowing with ice. Beneath the shallow waters could be seen a floor of small, slippery rocks. A tumble into the icy waters could set the tone for the balance of the trip. All wanted to remain dry and avoid the river. They started lining up along the Sweetwater, wondering who might be the first to venture into the water or which wagon would come forward and offer safe passage.

Brother Grant's teenaged boy, George, stepped forward and held his hand out expectantly to a young woman. "Come with me, Miss, and you'll be the first to cross this silly river." She took a small breath, then confidently took his grip and he pulled her onto his back, then stepped manfully into the treacherous waters. Walking carefully, he climbed quickly out on the far side and deposited his cargo. "See? Nothing to it," he announced to the smiling young woman. The others on the opposite side felt they had seen a miracle.

With that example, Allen Huntington, David Kimball, and Stephen Taylor, all similar young men, followed his resolute suit, inviting others to climb onto their backs and they set out across the river. More and more of the men joined in the movement, most of them, those who would be staying behind. This was their chance to help once more before the company moved on, leaving them alone for the balance of the winter. Many people watched with fascination as these stalwart young men crossed and recrossed the flood. It was obvious that the freezing waters pained them, but they did not slow their efforts. Their long legs pumped with the strength of pistons. Their feet remained solidly planted. Before long, mothers were entrusting their babies and children into the sure-footed care of the young men. Few spoke, choosing simply to watch in awe as these brave souls continued to ferry the forlorn in preparation for their further trek.

The most popular telling, by Solomon Kimball, states:

"Three eighteen-year-old boys belonging to the relief party came to the rescue; and to the astonishment of all who saw, carried nearly every member of that ill-fated handcart company across the snow-bound stream. The strain was so terrible, and the exposure so great, that in later years all the boys died from the effects of it. When President Brigham Young heard of this heroic act, he wept like a child, and later declared publicly, "That act alone will ensure C. Allen Huntington, George W. Grant, and David P. Kimball an everlasting salvation in the Celestial Kingdom of God, worlds without end."

This was the first crossing of the Sweetwater. Staying on the road, it would need to be crossed nine more times before they reached South Pass. Contemplating the future crossings did not boost morale.

Aaron and Shep were both given wagons to drive. They loaded their precious, shivering cargo into the wagon boxes and started their horses across the winding river. Once they had successfully forded the water a great sigh erupted from those trekkers still on the river's north banks. The ease of the effort encouraged all and they too began crowding the shores, wanting to get on their way. Wagons carried many of the youngest, oldest, and most infirm.

The crossing proved easier and swifter than the Platte. Many of the emigrants were still required to walk but now it was without the burden of the handcarts. The snow remained deep and icy, but they were able to change into dry clothing and push on. Those they worried most over were being carried in wagons. Facing west on this afternoon was filled with more hope than they had felt for weeks.

And then Shep was facing Zeenyo and Herman as he prepared to leave them behind. *These young men, these servants of the living God, these few who were willing to sacrifice for others that perhaps things might be easier.*

"You'll be all right?"

"As long as you promise to pray for us," Herman answered.

The commitment was uncompromising. Shep knew the step needed to be made. "At least three times a day," he affirmed with determination, "I will formally petition God for your well-being. And I will pray for you constantly in my heart."

It was what the boys wanted to hear. "Then you don't need to do anything more," Herman continued. "The God of Israel will be here with us. We will be protected and kept in the hollow of his hand."

Zeenyo nodded his assent.

As he walked to the wagon, Shep turned several times to look back at the stripling young men, lined up and waving good-byes to the emigrants. Both groups were facing difficult days. The snow started to fall as the wind kicked up. It promised to be a severe and lengthy winter, lonely for some and desperate for others. Shep was happy that both Wetoyous had jet-black hair. It made them easy to pick out against the stark backdrop of snow. Like the others, the Wetoyous possessed the image of God in their countenances.

Aaron saw to it that Yasmin sat next to him in his wagon. He also made sure that Harriett was sitting next to Shep. This was a pleasant situation, giving them unexpected chances to visit. He decided the diversions would be welcome.

The wagons began the trip, mules and horses both snorting and ready for the journey. Only a few miles would be covered the first day. It was more of a symbol of their willingness to move than anything else.

Shep noticed the lamp at Harriett's side. Over the past few days, he had seen both Harriett and Yasmin use the lights as they tended to patients. The glow from the wicks illuminated both the nurse and whoever she was caring for. It also lit up the tents. It glowed warmly. Shadows were dispelled and created. Both women spoke in quiet tones. At times they worked together. At times, they were apart, following the teachings they embraced, watching for improvements or declines. These were two very strong women who addressed the infirm, mourned with the families when a loss of life was experienced and joined in the joy when new births were attended. There were many more of the latter than might have been expected. The mothers were focused and committed as were their determined spouses. Captain Edward Martin did his best to ensure proper nutrition and care were given to the new mothers.

Shep thought that they would have at least a couple of hours of travel before making camp. He decided to open up a discourse with Harriett. She was an astute young English woman, about whom he knew very little.

"Thank you for accompanying me in the wagon," he started.

"I know you have not been baptized but what are your feelings regarding the doctrine of plural marriage?" Harriett asked.

4 November, Tuesday- Martin Company- This was a full day crossing the Sweet Water River and getting back onto the trail. I am thankful that we are no longer proceeding with the handcarts. The change will definitely help in the health preservation of our people. We are already weak and diminished. I see a number of fellows who are already close to passing from this life. Riding in the wagons puts a greater burden on our animals but they seem up to the task. Also, riding close together with one another provides more warmth as well as companionship. Despite the larger numbers that are now able to rest and relax and ride in the wagon beds, there remain huge numbers of emigrants who are still walking. The snow crunches beneath their feet and they sink almost to their knees. I feel the crucible will continue to cull our ranks as well as strengthen our resolve. The Lord is among us. I heard a number of our handcart folks report to me that they experienced divine help as they were moving along the trail before arriving at Martin's Cove. There were times when the effort to pull the carts was almost nothing, causing the folks to glance around to see who might be helping with the load. No one was seen. So they determined that angels from heaven were in our midst, assisting with these considerable loads.

I am currently riding alongside Shep Silva. I found out from Aaron Rost that Brother Shep's name is in reality, Giuseppe da Silva, originally from Brazil. He has ties to Italy and Portugal. I immediately thought of our dear friend Giuseppe that we lost back in Balaklava. I am happy with the way the Lord seems to be directing my path. I tried speaking some with Brother Silva but he seems to be otherwise distracted.

"There is advantage in the wisdom won from pain."

Harriett Matthews

Willie Company

Monday 3rd. Several wagons came into our camp from the Valley to assist us on our journey this morning. We rolled out of camp about 11 a.m., passed Gilbert and Gerrish's merchant train going on slowly to the Valley. Crossed the "Basin Rim", forded Muddy Creek and camped on its banks. Some 10 ox teams with wagons were camped alongside us and were on their way to meet the rear companies. A meeting was held in the evening, the brethren from the

Valley attended. It was considered advisable to send on an express to the Valley and report the condition of things in the mountains in regard to the companies on the plains. W. H. Kimball said he would go as the express and he appointed Bro. Gould captain of the horse-teams and Bro. Wm. Hyde, captains of the ox-teams; travelled about 12 miles. Night cold.

Tuesday 4th. W. H. Kimball and Bro. Thomas went on to the Valley this morning. Camp rolled on to Bear River, forded the stream and camped on its banks. Bro. Blair with 3 ox wagons was camped on the opposite bank of the river. Met several teams during the day going to relieve the rear companies. Potatoes, onions and clothing was distributed among the different Hundreds in the evening. Franklin B. Woolley came on from A.O. Smoot's train informing the company that President B. Young had sent word that some freight still lying at "Fort Bridger" was to be brought in this season and that some teams and men of our company were needed to go on to "Bridger". Several teams and men were selected for the trip.

Friday 5th Wednesday Rolled on in the morning and crossed Yellow Creek, ascended a steep hill and then go down Echo Kanyon and camped; travelled about 23 miles and camped. Peter Madsen, from Copenhagen, Denmark, aged 66 years died during the day; Susannah Osborn from Norwich, Norfolk, England, aged 33 years died this day. A snowstorm came on this evening. The people are much exposed to cold from lying on the cold ground.

Nov. 6th. Archibald McPhiel, from Greenock, Argyleshire, Scotland, died about 2 a.m. aged 40 years. Much snow on the ground this morning and still more falling. Go down Echo Kanyon, roads very bad at the crossing of streams; forded Weber River and camped on its banks. It snowed most of the day. The camping ground presented a most dismal appearance, as we rolled on to it there being much snow on the ground and it being late at night. Rasmus P. Hansen, from Lango, Denmark, aged 16 years, died this evening.

Friday 7th. The camp rolled on, crossed a steep hill and came into East Kanyon; crossed East Kanyon Creek several times and camped in a cottonwood grove; good place to camp for wood. Maria S. Jorgen from Lango, Denmark, aged 8 years died; Theophilus Cox, from Bristol, Somersetshire, England, aged 25 years died; William Empey from Eaton Bray, Bedfordshire, England, aged 9 years died. During the night day we passed some teams going to relieve the rear companies.

Saturday 8th Travelled up the Kanyon about 3 miles, and then ascended the Big Mountain, which was difficult for teams to gain the top; go down the mountain and camp about a mile from the Little Mountain. Bro. Blair left us early this morning for the Valley. We travelled about 13 miles during the day. W.H. Kimball came to camp this evening; also, a load of provisions for the camp. W.H. Kimball and W. Woodward took an account of persons who had made engagements where they were going to stay in the mountains.

Sunday 9th Early this morning. The people were busy preparing to enter the Valley. Rhoda R. Oakey from Eldersfield, Worcestershire, England, aged 11 years died this morning. The teams after some difficulty ascended the Little

Mountain and rolled down Emigration Kanyon. Several of the wagons passed Captain Smoot's Church train in the Kanyon. The wagons formed in order on the bench at the mouth of the Kanyon and rolled on to the City. Captain Smoot's train went ahead. F.D. Richards, S.W. Richards and many others came to meet us on the Bench and went ahead of us into the City. As soon as the company arrived in the City of Great Salt Lake, the Bishops of the different wards took every person that was not provided for a home and put them into comfortable quarters. Hundreds of persons were round the wagons on our way through the city welcoming the company safely home.

68 people in the Willie Company had died.

During the next several nights, Shep and Aaron traded off accompanying the nurses on their calls, visiting the various family tents where suspected victims might be found and tended. Usually, the men poked their heads into the tent to make sure their presence wasn't needed, then stayed outside, keeping a watch out for predators. Shep's carbine was traded easily between Aaron and Shep. Cold and frost continued to plague the emigrants, especially as food rations were repeatedly reduced. Black fingers and toes required immediate attention. Generally, these gangrenous digits were simply snipped off using scissors. Blood was not usually in rich supply, making the bandaging easier. Always, prayer attended the operations, and sometimes priesthood holders were called to administer to the sick with an anointing of consecrated olive oil and a blessing.

There were times when the shock of an amputation pushed the person through the veil. Still, the people traveling with the Martin and Hodgetts companies appreciated the knowledge and willingness of Harriett and Yasmin to attend to their afflicted members. Prayers were offered on their behalf, with most of the people thinking the petitioning for heavenly support was infinitely more advantageous than money or medicine.

"Well?" Harriett asked Shep during a long jaunt of another day.

"What?"

"I never did receive an answer to my question. What are your thoughts regarding plural marriage?"

Shep shifted nervously. "I hoped you had forgotten."

"I don't mean to put you on the spot. And you don't have to answer if you don't want to. I just find the topic intriguing and especially with you not being a member of the church, I thought it would be enlightening to get some of your ideas."

Shep nodded with understanding, appreciating her giving him an out should he need it. He also wished that Harriett was not such an attractive young woman and never having been married. "I doubt I am much of an authority, having never been married myself."

"But you have lived among members of the church for years. Surely you have an opinion?" The woman was persistent.

Silva sighed deeply. "I have known a number of people who have entered into 'the principle'. For some, it works out just fine. For others, not so much."

"What do you think about its viability?"

"Do you mean why?" *She nodded, prettily*, he thought. "I think it sounds terrible for the sisters in the church. That's my first thought. I used to think it sounded good for the brethren. But not anymore. When love is involved, things become a lot messier. It's way different than a man's having a mistress. A physical relationship is much less work than coming out and marrying a woman, then having children, and trying to love and support all involved. And then there's the age thing. Younger, more nubile, or inexperienced wives seem to view it quite differently than women who are already mothers, perhaps widows."

Harriett was pleased to see that Shep had thought the issue through. And she was pleased that he had taken it seriously.

He continued. "There's no polygamy manual. Some families all live together. Some are very active in the religion. The families I know are close. The children especially. The good thing I see in all of it is that it is something that needs to be accepted by the women and then a call is made by the prophet. Brigham doesn't worry about a brother's libido."

"And do you think it's from God?"

"The revelations come to folks through the Spirit. I don't understand. Not as much as Aaron or Brigham or Brother Grant. These folks appreciate the inner workings of God. I have never committed appropriate time to study the scriptures or English."

"I think your English is lovely."

Harriett's statement brought him up short and he fumbled trying to get on track. "And, well, I understand that polygamy was something God had his prophets live years ago. Abraham, Jacob, and King David, and others. I really believe that Joseph Smith was a man of God. For Joseph to tell us that plural marriage is a law of God's, well, it needs to be considered." He stopped and looked at Harriett. "Is there a reason you are asking me so many questions?"

She shook her head. "I'm sorry, Giuseppe da Silva. I did not mean to pry. My lot at this time is to ride alongside you. I cannot think of anything more interesting to talk about at present than this idea. It certainly has set the church aside, causing untold numbers of tongues to wag, especially outside the church."

Shep didn't hear much of what she said after she invoked his Brazilian name. *What had gotten her to look into it and from whom? Doubtless, it was Aaron. And why was Harriett here? She obviously had her own feelings about the church and the subject.* He grasped the opening.

"What about you, Miss Harriett? You have come clear over here from England. You certainly have your own opinions about it. Is polygamy something you can accept?"

"I certainly have my questions. More questions than answers. I fit into your mold of younger more immature women. Maybe not quite so nubile." She allowed her face to look worried. "Sometimes when I am with these beautiful people, these emigrants, most of whom have come from my England, as I hear them pleading to God for help, as I see the love the parents have for each other and their children, out here on this frozen wasteland, that's when I start to really believe that this idea, this Zion, is not only a possibility but a living actuality. Not only is it attainable but it is probable. Whether we are polygamists or just refugees from the States, the Lord knows each of us. He will guide and protect and bless us as we seek his will. A real problem with polygamy is that men will never be able to spend enough time with their wives. Is there even enough time in monogamous marriages? Women will always be shorted of their husbands' time and attention. Only God can fix that one."

The conversation stopped while Shep mulled over her words. After a long minute, he finally turned towards her. "I happen to know Brigham. Better than most, I figure. I think he needs to know you, Sister Matthews. Before you know it, he'll have you giving addresses over the pulpit with the best of the brethren."

Harriett smiled again. *Prettily, again*, he noticed.

10 November, Monday- Martin Company- Captain Martin did not inform me that this journal writing should be limited solely to affairs of the Company, although that is what I expect of his wishes. On the other hand, I would be untrue to myself if I did not record some of the things that have been passing between me and Brother Shep Silva. He is an interesting man. He is kind and willing to work and even sacrifice his comfort for the other members of the company. Without having gotten to know him somewhat better, I would be cautious before attributing characteristics to him that might be possessed by all the other men in our group. I will say that I am quite taken with his manner. I feel that I can write these comments down without undue worry that he might snoop into my affairs. He is a busy man, serious with the calling of seeing that our choice people arrive in the Great Salt Lake City as easily as possible.

I will state that it is my intention to get to know more about this man, who has spent an inordinate amount of time pondering the depths of God's plan for our salvation. I have long enjoyed the friendship of Aaron Rost and it is apparent why the two men have become such fast friends. Also, from my perspective, I seem to be able to note a growing romantic interest building between Aaron and my sweet Yasmin. I cannot hope for anything more than that she finds love and purpose, even in this far-flung territory.

With the passing of each turn of the wagon wheel, with each step of our horse, yards, then miles, then leagues are being put behind us. There is a growing anxiety of our destiny, that we will reach the promised valley. Even though we continue to lose the weak and infirm to death, we will ultimately attain our goal and it will be long before we expend all the lives at hand.

I deny the following two statements by Aeschylus. I have seen firsthand the terrible fruits of war and despair. This is also what has spurred my testimony of the Book of Mormon forward, the explanation of the horrors of conflict, yet even there, righteousness is alive and vibrant within the hearts of the righteous.

Harriett Matthews

Chapter 43

"Live life when you have it. Life is a splendid gift—there is nothing small about it." Florence Nightingale

Elizabeth Sermon

November 1856
"Many cruel and painful things happening, the dying and dear ones all around us, poor souls, would sit down by the roadside and would never move again until carried into camp on handcarts by someone. It is a wonder any of us lived through it. My husband's health still failing, a young woman by the name of Caroline Marchant assisted me with the cart."

John Kirkman

11 November 1856
"Before we left Iowa, my dear Mother had given birth to a son, Peter. She was naturally weak with the care of a nursing baby and five other children. Father was weak from want of food, having denied himself for us..."

Elizabeth Sermon, Martin Company

November 1856
"My husband's health began to fail and his heart almost broken to see me falling in shafts. Myself and children hungry, almost naked, footsore and himself nearly done for. Many trials came after this. My oldest boy had the mountain fever, we had to haul him in the cart, there was not room in the wagon..."

Ephraim Hanks was happy. He had turned thirty years old six months earlier. He was a devout member of the church. In 1846 he had marched with the Mormon Battalion, hundreds of miles across the trackless desert to shore up flagging US forces. Receiving the blessings of the Lord, the Mormons were spared any confrontation with Mexican troops. He arrived in San Diego and was released. Shortly thereafter, he made his way to Sacramento and then over the Sierra Nevadas and across the Great Basin where he met up with Brigham Young and the Saints who were just entering the Great Salt Lake Valley. Hanks was a man who spent inordinate time on the prairies and plains scouting for Brigham Young, delivering mail, and protecting the emigrating Saints. After a dozen years, he was trying to settle down and use his talents to further the prospects of his family.

On Friday night, October 24th, after spending the day fishing in Utah Lake, Hanks stopped in with some friends living in Draper to spend the night. He was looking forward to getting back to his family in Salt Lake City. He settled down to sleep but was awakened by a voice, calling him by name. "The handcart people are in trouble. Will you go and help them?"

He turned to see where the voice was coming from and saw a man of average size, standing in his room. "Will you go and help them?"

"Yes, I will go if I am called."

The man remained and delivered the same message two more times. Sleep fled from his eyes. He got up shortly afterward, saddled his horse, and started for Salt Lake City arriving on Saturday. Brigham Young called again for more help to be taken to the stranded handcart emigrants. When some of the brethren said they would get their things together and start within a couple of days, Hanks announced, "I'm ready to go right now." The next morning, he was in his light buggy, wending up the canyon road by himself.

On November 2nd he came upon the Willie Company, nearing Fort Bridger. Always joyful and positive, he announced to the travelers that more wagons from the valley were on their way, with more help and supplies. The news eased worries. Hanks took two of his horses and left the buggy for the emigrants to use and he rode off towards South Pass.

Willie Company

Sunday 2nd. Camp rolled out. Ephraim Hanks passed our camp this morning, bringing news from the Valley of many teams being on the road, and that he was going on to the rear companies to meet them. Bros. Willie, Woodward, and Christiansen stayed behind to bring up the sick. This morning we had not teams enough to haul the feeble that were left behind. After a short time several teams came on from the Valley and picked up the sick. The brethren that stayed behind were late into camp. The company camped about half a mile west of Fort Bridger, travelled about 15 miles. James Cole of Fort Supply married Lucy Ward of the 4th Handcart Company at Fort Bridger in the evening. Bro. Willie' s feet were in such a bad condition from frost that he was unable to walk to the Camp; a wagon was sent for him. Peter Madsen, from Jutland, Denmark, aged 49 years died in the evening.

Ephraim Hanks

November 1856

"*The terrific storm which caused the immigrants so much suffering and loss overtook me near the South Pass, where I stopped about three days with Reddick N. Allred, who had come out with provisions for the immigrants. The storm during these three days was simply awful...*"

Just after crossing the broad divide, he was struck by a severe snowstorm. *"In all my travels in the Rocky Mountains, I have seen no worse. It lay on the ground so deep that for many days it was impossible for wagons to move through it."*

He continued his lonely journey on horseback and leading a packhorse. As he was preparing to make his bed in the snow, deep in a protective hollow, he asked the Lord for support and blessing, being a distinct believer in the power of prayer. *How nice would it be to have some buffalo meat? To have a decent place to sleep, warm and away from the snow.* He then looked and was surprised to see a lone buffalo, not 50 yards from his camp, standing in the snow on the hill above. He dropped the animal with a single shot, and it tumbled down the hill, coming to rest only yards from where he camped. Using his knife, Hanks quickly cut a gambol stick and hoisted the buffalo up high enough to allow him to dress it properly. It also made for a splendid meal. He sliced long strips of meat from the carcass. He skinned and dressed it out, cutting the meat into long strips. After removing the hide, he laid it on the snow and was able to make his bed on top of it and spent a very restful, warm night. The next morning, he loaded up his horses with the meat and his skin trophy. Both his horses were well ladened with the choice cuts of meat and buffalo hide. He then spotted another cow buffalo and took her down, skinned the animal and dressed the meat, then loaded it onto his horses, who by this time were close to buckling under the loads.

Ephraim Hanks spent 10 years delivering mail from the Territory of Utah to St. Louis, Missouri. He did it all year long and through the roughest conditions. He knew the terrain, and he knew how to survive it.

It was a Tuesday and that night as the sun was getting ready to set, Hanks saw the Martin Handcart Company in the snow, looking like a series of black streaks. By the time he reached them, they were just starting to make camp. Upon seeing his approach, the group started hollering and cheering, clapping at his arrival.

"The sufferers, as they moved about slowly, shivering with cold, to prepare their scanty evening meal was enough to touch the stoutest heart. When they saw me coming, they hailed me with joy inexpressible, and when they further beheld the supply of fresh meat I brought into camp, their gratitude knew no bounds. Flocking around me, one would say, 'Oh, please, give me a small piece of meat;' another would exclaim, 'My poor children are starving, do give me a little,' and children with tears in their eyes would call out, 'Give me some, give me some.' At first I tried to wait on them and handed out the meat as they called for it, but finally I told them to help themselves. Five minutes later both my horses had been released of their extra burden—the meat was all gone, and the next few hours found the people in camp busily engaged in cooking and eating it, with thankful hearts."

"A prophecy had been made by one of the brethren that the company should feast on buffalo meat when their provisions might run short; my arrival

in their camp, loaded with meat, was the beginning of the fulfillment of that prediction; but only the beginning, for them as we journeyed along."

Shep greeted Ephraim with a bear hug, clapping his back vigorously. "I never thought your face was much to look at, but sorry, Eph, I was wrong!"

"How do you know Brother Hanks?" Captain Martin asked.

"Dumb luck. He's always fishing in the lake. I think he was just looking for a place to sleep." Introductions were made all around. All felt a lessening in their dire condition after Hanks assured them that more wagons were on their way.

"The buffalo meat was great. How did you know that's exactly what we were needing?"

Hanks shrugged. "More dumb luck, I suppose. Tell you the truth, I have never seen as many buffalo out this way in all my years."

"You know where they are?" Martin quizzed.

"I just passed them this morning."

"You mind taking Shep and some of our boys out shooting in the morning?"

"We'll get you set with whatever you need," he promised. "I think the Lord knew it was just what you folks needed. These animals are here to meet our needs."

Shep nodded. He had heard himself saying almost those very words as a boy in Brazil twenty years earlier.

In an unexpected shift, Captain Martin decided to raise the flour rations to 8 ounces a day per adult and 4 ounces per child.

"A veritable feast!" Shep told Eph.

Two days later they met the first wagons that had been sent from Salt Lake City to help them back in the last days of October.

That evening Hanks surprised Shep and his friends, insisting that he be shown the families that were in the direst circumstances.

"Can't sleep," he explained. "I want to give blessings. That's what the Lord expects of me. I really need to get to it. We can sure use the nurses and Shep you bring your rifle and keep the wolves away while me and Aaron give blessings."

This was a new dimension of the trip. He apologized over and over for not having arrived weeks earlier. Under the watchful eye of Yasmin and Harriet, the men entered the chosen tent. Eph simply asked if the infirm person had faith in Christ. After a positive affirmation, he would rub his consecrated oil on the person, and then together with Rost, they would lay their hands gently on the person's head and with full confidence that he would be answered, Hanks would command the infirm to arise from their sickbed and get to work. The nurses were shocked as time after time, they witnessed a serious change come over the patients, and the injured or sick would stand and shake off any remaining signs of weakness. The lanterns of both women burned late into the night. Some of the wounded showed frozen limbs and Ephraim would gently

332

wash the area with water and castile soap long enough until the frozen part would simply fall away. Harriett and Yasmin would then bundle them with bandages. Many of the Saints had frozen limbs that were endangering their lives. Brother Hanks anointed these folks and prayed that amputation could be done without pain. Then he took out his great hunting knife, held it to the fire to cleanse it, and took off the dying limb with the keen blade. Many with tears in their eyes testified they hadn't felt a thing.

After spending the night administering to the ill, Hanks was ready for bed. Unrolling his saddle blanket, he settled into the snow and within minutes was snoring like a railroad train.

Aaron was exhausted. He helped both nurses into their bed in the wagon box. Warm blankets were welcome, and they both chatted excitedly as they snuggled under their covers. They too were soon asleep.

As he was closing off the wick to Harriett's lamp, Shep kept shaking his head. "Never in all my days," he said.

Aaron answered him. "You've seen what I've seen, Shep. There's no explaining it. Hanks' arrival was just what the doctor ordered. What the Lord ordered, I mean."

"I wish the doctor, or the Lord would have ordered a summer day. Amen."

First of October 1856

Dear Ina,

In all my days I haven't been so hot. The weather is oppressive. There is no wind or rain, just heat. Even during the nights, it doesn't cool off. I sweat so much I think my clothes are ruined. In the mornings I run into the ocean and cool down as much as possible. But the cool water is exactly what I need. Unfortunately, besides being very hot here, it is also very humid, so almost as soon as I get out of the ocean, I am sweating again. If there wasn't so much work to get done, I think I'd just live in the water.

Mosquitoes are also bad, especially at night. I can hear them in my sleep. I don't swell up nearly as much as at first and I try not to itch as much as I used to, but sometimes they get into my eyes and then I get all puffy and can't see too well. For all the beautiful plants and animals and people, the weather gets bad. Mostly because it's so much of the same, over and over, week after week. Some months it rains more than others but mostly it's a lot the same. Give me snow in the winter, flowers in the spring, heat in the summer and let the leaves fall in autumn. I enjoy planting crops, irrigating in the summer and then harvesting in the fall. It makes the winter such a nice, restful time. Don't you think?

Sorry for the short letter. Next one will be better, I promise.
Love,

Joseph

Dear Joseph,

Your letter got here rather quickly. I think communication is getting better all the time. I don't mean that ships are necessarily getting faster, although, I understand that the steamboats are exactly that, faster. More and more steamboats are being built, while the older sailing versions are being retired. I believe one is that they are definitely faster and probably even stronger and safer. They are not like the old steamboats on the Mississippi or the Missouri Rivers.

Here in California, we have lots of men putting up telegraph poles and then stringing wires, just like back in the States. People can communicate over hundreds of miles almost in a flash. I actually have heard that a number of investors are getting ready to lay wire clear across the Atlantic to Ireland where they will be able to communicate with people there. It is simply amazing, all the grand things that are being invented and brought to pass, right as we are watching. As things get better, I believe industrialists will also try and put up a transcontinental telegraph system. People San Francisco would be able to communicate with their friends in New York City in an instant. The need to send letters across the nation would not be necessary. Can you believe the times in which we live?

Thank you for telling us about your weather. Sometimes ours is quite flat as well. At least we are able to discern summers from winters. Ma and Pa sometimes talk of the way the weather was back in Missouri and Illinois. They enjoyed all four seasons. Still, Joseph, there are times when I hear them speak and even though they might miss some of the things about the weather, I think they also appreciate the blessings of this wonderful state. We too miss the variety of seasons, but California is a large state. We enjoy mountain splendor, ocean beaches, thick forests, seemingly endless deserts. Our population is growing daily. I think many are fleeing the cold of New York City and the Eastern seaboard. The gold started the influx of new settlers but now Americans are establishing themselves from Oregon down to San Diego. It is a blessing to belong to the United States. We also have rich fishing areas as well as very fertile farmlands. California is acting like a magnet and drawing many different factions to our shores. We also enjoy peace with the native tribes of the state. The Indians here are so much more peaceful than the Apache or Comanche or Kiowa or Cheyenne of Sioux.

My boyfriend, Bob Carsley, is working hard. He enjoys acting on the stage but the money he brings comes from his metalworking talents. New settlements are being started all the time. This keeps him busy. With so many of the new communities being built here in the southern portion of the state, Bob is able to find plenty of work close by. This means that we are able to spend much more time together. I can hardly wait for you to meet him. I know you'll be good friends. I even think Pa is warming up to him some. He is becoming a good friend of the twins.

My writing is coming along quite well. If I don't send something into the newspaper at least once every week, they start to write me, hoping that I am well and not looking for greener pastures or printing presses.

Light of the sun and stars of heaven,
The sweet warm air, and the green earth sod,
And birth and death, unto all are given,
Children alike of the selfsame God.
What matters the ebony locks or flaxen,
The skin of snow, or the skin of tan?
Indian, Afric, Mongol, Saxon,
Within are the heart and soul of Man.

I love you, dear, sweet Joseph.

Ina

13 November, Thursday- Martin Company- Today, finally, we met up with a number of wagons sent from the valley. These had started their journey in the last days of October when Brother Hanks also left. They brought us much-needed supplies. It is awful to see how very much we need in the form of supplies, but 1000 people, especially when ravenous, are able to consume very large amounts.

Brother Hanks has been going daily out to hunt, taking Shep with him. A day has not passed that they have not returned with at least one buffalo. The meat goes a long way to stave off the hunger we are feeling. We have a number of buffalo robes, those which were purchased in Fort Laramie and those we have gained during the trek. But even if we had 100, that is far too few to protect the others. We are grateful for the blessings of the Lord. I have not found a soul in this company who does not appreciate the bounty of the Lord, although we have all experienced greater bounty than we now have.

Our goal is to reach the valley before it becomes everlastingly too late for anymore in our group. The food has been more than welcome. It has strengthened us. I have seen the light in so many eyes more clearly than I have for weeks. With Brother Hanks and Brother Shep doing the hunting, we have more or less a continual source of meat. The rescue wagons have brought us bare essentials. The main problem we are now facing continues to be the weather. The snow really doesn't quit. Campfires help to warm our bodies, but that warmth dissipates almost as soon as we retire to our beds. Walking in deep snow is difficult. I think everyone would like to ride on a wagon. With the arrival of these new wagons, there is a little more room for the sick and the infirm.

If we pause to rest for a day, the snowstorms come in, making it even more difficult to get out. Also, the deep snow is keeping rescue wagons from us. We need to do our part to meet them. In the meantime, members of our company continue to pass away. We are losing half a dozen each day.

It has been a blessing to see Ephraim Hanks and his enthusiasm. He works hard. He has traveled these mountains before. He knows whereof he speaks. We listen to him and we learn from him, but even then, there are limits to his abilities. God alone will provide for us. God alone will protect us. And God alone will deliver us to our destination.

"There is no pain so great as the memory of joy in present grief."

Harriett Matthews

Three days later Captain Martin ordered the increase of rations to be 16 ounces per adult and 8 ounces per child. The news sparked a resurgence of faith and hope. The Martin Company reached and scaled the treacherous Rocky Ridge, the source of so much grief for their sister company being led by James Willie. The Martin Company was blessed to have access to some wagons to ride and even those who could not ride were spared from having to pull the handcarts. What was similar was the snow and the wind. Covering their faces, they moved up and over, slowly, with determination, wanting to meet their friends and neighbors, people with whom they had left their native countries, people they had crossed the ocean with, people of like minds, mirrors of themselves.

The tents provided a modicum of protection from the snow, but the winds seemed capable of finding every opening and whistling into their shelters, blew against the efforts to keep warm. The days seemed endless. The nights stretched on but without relief from the intense, bitter cold. The trail stood before them, open for miles with no visible landmark of significance.

On Tuesday, November 11th, Hosea Stout, the oldest member of the rescue teams, left Salt Lake with several other brethren to determine the fate of the previous teamsters. The next night they encountered some wagons heading back to the valley. They hadn't heard from the Martin handcart company and decided that they had either died on the trail or returned to Fort Laramie or been killed by Indians. Whatever, they thought they should return to the valley or they might also suffer starvation and death.

Brother Kimball reprimanded the men severely. All turned around and headed back toward Fort Bridger. They had covered only eight miles when they met Joseph Young and John Garr, who had been dispatched from the Martin Company at Devil's Gate and were hurrying with information from the group and seeking further assistance from Brigham Young.

On Saturday, they arrived again at Fort Bridger then started for the encampment at Green River with more than 77 wagons.

Stout wrote: *Tuesday, 18 November 1856. The weather which had been clear and pleasant ever since I left home began to be cloudy and after noon commenced to snow and blow hard from the North. We overtook another team at Pacific Creek. When traveling on fastly we arrived at the station on Sweet*

Water just before night, the rest of the teams coming in shortly afterward. Here we met the advance of the Hand cart Company who informed us that that the company would be here tonight. Several teams were dispatched to meet them and help them in. Soon they began to come in some in wagons, some on horses some on foot, while some had to be led or carried on the backs of men.

This presented a sad sight to see men, women, and children thinly clad, poor and worn out with hunger and fatigue trudging along in this dreary country, facing a severe snowstorm and the wind blowing hard in their face.

The wagons could not accommodate half of those not able to walk. Many were sick and many frosted and some severely. Grant when he met them left some 20 at the Devil's Gate at an abandoned station where he left a very great portion of the ox train besides wagons, handcarts, and worn-out cattle and horses, with provisions to winter them. The snowstorm increased all evening, but the tents were reared and the poor sick saints had many of them to be carried in.

Wednesday, 19 Nov 1856- Still snowing this morning all hands stirring for a start. With the addition of the teams which arrived last evening the entire company could be put in wagons as comfortably as the nature of the case would permit and travel at the rate of 25 miles a day. Some teams were sent back to the assistance of the ox train some eight miles below. GD Grant and WH Kimball tarried here to see and arrange matters with the ox train while all the rest proceeded facing the drifting falling snow and encamped on a dry ravine some 20 miles having no water for men or animals tonight. Sometime after night William and George arrived leaving the ox train at Pacific Springs.

This evening I went with Eph Hanks to visit and administer to the sick and had an opportunity of seeing the suffering and privations through which they passed. Some were merry and cheerful, some dull and stupid, some sick, some frosted, some lazy and mean but all seemed to be elated more or less with the idea of speedily arriving in the Valley.

The next morning Stout left with Grant and Kimball on an express trip to Salt Lake to inform Brigham Young of the Martin Company's current position, as well as the two ox-trains behind them led by Hodgetts and Hunt. Hodgetts' train was able to cross South Pass that day.

"I'm glad you didn't go with the others," Shep said to Hanks who was riding on his horse next to the church wagon manned by Silva and Harriett. "You invited?"

"Not really. Then again, how many men does it take to report to Brigham? I'm well enough off here. I want to help where I'm needed."

"You're needed plenty here. Don't you think he is?" he asked Harriett.

"You have been a breath of fresh air, Brother Hanks. We appreciate your strength and willingness."

Eph smiled and tipped his hat. "I could do without the cold."

"I think it was starting to drag on ol' Stout.

Hanks agreed. "He's a hero if there ever was one. He's probably the busiest guy I've ever seen. He loves his work. Loves doing things in court and helping folks get on the right track."

"He's not bad in the saddle, covering lots of ground, either." Shep checked the sky. "So, what do you think? I've only been over this road once. How long till we reach Fort Bridger?"

"We're still a ways out but I'd say three days. I think everyone in the company deserves a long bath and a hot supper." Hanks saluted them. "I've got some business with Captain Martin," he said and spurred his horse onward towards the head of the column.

"I've been a bit curious about something," Shep said to Harriett. "Neither you nor Yasmin have family in the Valley. Have you given it much thought where you'll settle down?"

She shook her head. "I haven't worried too much about it. Maybe it's time I started. We have just been too busy to talk much about it. When we started, President Richards assured us that a place would be provided. I'm sure things will work out as they should. And Brother Rost has invited us to stay with him in Salt Lake City should we need a room. At least for a short while. Why? Do you have any ideas?"

"Well, maybe. Salt Lake City's a going concern. A lot is happening. I think you will be pleasantly surprised. It doesn't look much like a town anymore. It is large and fairly attractive by the world's standards. On the other hand, Tooele is a nice place and not too far from the city."

"That's where you live? Tooele?"

He nodded. "Me and the Wetoyous. Mostly what I'm saying is that there are a number of very fine folks in Tooele. It isn't as big as San Bernardino but it is growing. My neighbors are the very best. You might want to look it over. Everyone would be happy to know you."

"Are there very many English?"

"I don't know much difference between the English and Welsh and Scots. But we have a number of Scandinavians. My next-door neighbors are from Denmark."

"The Hansens? Your neighbors?"

Shep was surprised that she was aware of them. "Yep." He took a few minutes to figure out where the information had come to her. Either from him or Aaron. He didn't recall mentioning them and wondered what might have come up to get Aaron to discuss them. "The family is a quick study. Having a medical person would go a long way to helping things out in Tooele."

The disappointing thing about this stage of their trip was the number of people who continued to die. They were getting so close to the valley. Everyone was now able to ride in wagons. There was no more walking, but the continued cold sapped the emigrants. Most who died were older or fragile. Some middle-aged men also passed away. Many of them had chosen to share their meager rations with their children rather than allow them to go hungry. As a result, the men weakened prematurely. With their passing, more worries were heaped upon the families. Uncertainty was a constant companion of the widows and fatherless.

"This is not the reason polygamy was instituted," Shep commented to Harriett. "It's not to provide for the weak and homeless. I'm not saying that it can't figure into the deal. But it would just be a happy coincidence."

"You sound pretty sure of yourself."

Shep had grown to enjoy the talks he had with Sister Matthews. "I noticed reading the Book of Mormon that having more than one wife isn't approved by God. Jacob tells the men that God loves the chastity of his daughters.

"He commanded the children of Israel not to kill but then sends them after the Canaanites. Just after reminding the Nephites how much God loves the chastity of women, he says that if the Lord wants to raise up seed unto his name, he will command his people, otherwise, no. If the Lord wants to change things around, he can. I know a man who has two wives. The first has fourteen children, and the second, fifteen."

The numbers shocked Harriett. "They almost sound like Irish Catholics."

"They take their responsibilities seriously."

Harriett continued shaking her head. "Thirty children with each one having three friends. Your friend would need a hotel."

He paused for a moment. "Anyway, King Limhi lost a large number of men in battle, leaving many widows and fatherless. A reason for polygamy? Nope. King Limhi simply told the men to be more charitable with their stuff."

"I always thought that one of the best arguments for the veracity of the Book of Mormon was the description of their wars. They are not depicted like Sir Walter Scott would write. There are no lances and banners and knights in shining armor. No maidens in distress. The wars in the Book of Mormon are very real, down-to-earth conflicts. They are awful and depressing, logistical, with prisoners of war."

"No quick fixes, like announcing polygamy to solve a problem."

Harriett smiled. "Why are you not yet baptized?"

A couple of days later the Martin Handcart Company met up with teamsters coming from Fort Bridger with scores of oxen for the Hodgetts train, which was still several days behind them, but they had just crossed the South Pass. The worn-out oxen would be exchanged for these fresh animals, helping the train move faster. As always, the sight of new faces, healthy, happy, yet concerned, lifted the spirits of the tired emigrants.

After the Martin Handcart Company crossed the South Pass, they noticed that they were beginning to descend. The trail was sloping downward. They no longer felt like they were walking upon the ceiling of the world. The depth of the snow also began to decrease, although it continued to be cold and Shep and Aaron continued burying the dead in mass graves. The wolves seemed to have given up on the wagon-assisted Saints.

The party reached the Green River, the final landmark before Fort Bridger. The man had chosen to keep this area for his haunts. In the summers Bridger moved to the south and took up residence in the Uinta Mountains. The tall mountains were the only ones in the Rocky Mountains whose range ran east and west, instead of the normal north-south direction. Folks who knew Bridger best, knew him to be contrary and would have expected nothing less. The obstinate mountains would be the best place for the obstinate mountain man's lair.

The fort was never needed to protect the newcomers from Indians. The local Shoshone were the most dominant in the area and they were always friendly with the pale-skinned settlers.

Bridger and Brigham did not see eye to eye, especially on the settlement of the Great Salt Lake Valley. In 1847 he offered gold to the Mormon leader for the first bushel of wheat that was ever successfully grown there. It was a bet that was never followed through. Because of the increase of emigrants and the need for a station, Brigham Young finally purchased the fort. They had also built another station 15 miles to the southwest, which they named Fort Supply. Both of these locations came in handy for the flood of settlers coming into the valleys of the west, not to mention how helpful they were for other pioneers, perhaps heading for southern California.

Arriving at Fort Bridger on November 23rd signaled to the handcart emigrants that they had reached the final leg of their journey. It was a roughly shod fort with not many amenities. The travelers were content to remain in their wagons.

Draft animals were traded out and the train resupplied. The trail continued to lower. The snow diminished but the freezing temperatures kept the ground hard, not allowing the mud to envelop the iron cast wagon wheels. Having teamsters to drive the wagons, the emigrants were able to cover much more ground than when they had been walking. The camp was often not set until almost midnight, the light of the moon and the reflecting white snow helping both man and beast to manage their direction.

27 November, Thursday- Martin Company- Today we moved into Echo Canyon. One of our dear sisters, Sister Squires, waited until today to give birth to a lovely baby girl, with long dark hair. Her wails notified the rest of the company, gladdening the hearts of most. The family named her Echo after this intriguing canyon, where sound echoes so easily.

We can almost see the valley from here. We have one more, large mountain to climb, called Big Mountain, appropriately. I understand that it still has some very deep snow and plenty of drifts. This will cause problems for the drivers and the oxen. As long as the wagons don't overturn or break down, we should be fine.

"Memory is the mother of all wisdom."

Harriett Matthews

29 November, Saturday- Martin Company- We have finally escaped the confines of Echo Canyon and are now set to begin our ascent of Big Mountain.

The pass we must go over is more than 7000 feet high. The snow here is quite deep, impeding our oxen. A number of the brethren, including Shep and Aaron, have decided to plow the snow themselves, locking arms and wading through the snow that is almost at their waist. This is very slow going. The men are working as hard and fast as they are able. Like most of the others in the company, Yasmin and I simply wait and hold our breath. As the men have moved forward, some of the wagons tried to follow but were unsuccessful and had to wait for the men to return for at least another pass. After leaving the canyon we have again climbed and are once again feeling the biting cold which is not restricted to the area before we reached Fort Bridger.

I find that I am finally beginning to wonder about my own future. To finally be knocking on the gates of the Great Salt Lake Valley, the reality of our position is setting in. I am comfortable with the education I have but also, I must confess that many of the English women I have met easily surpass my scholastic achievements. Thoughts of Tooele are becoming more attractive. On the other hand, Yasmin and Aaron seem to have struck up a very familiar relationship. They are being completely appropriate, although I now see them holding one another's hands. They speak in low tones so as not to be overheard by others. They smile often at one another. Their hearts seem to be lighter. I am happy that both are quite healthy. They have not had to worry about the serious effects brought on by ration reductions. I am happy for the two of them.

Harriett Matthews

Climbing through the last snow barrier covering Big Mountain was maddening. Progress was accomplished by the first teams yard by yard. The oxen lowed with exasperation, straining every fiber to pull the wagons. Many of the passengers got out of the wagons to lighten the load. Even then, the move forward was agonizingly slow. Some people got behind the wagon and pushed. The air was crisp, and some claimed they could smell the odor of the sage wafting up from the valleys, while others were sure they could smell the smoke coming from the chimneys or suppers on the stoves. Emigrants opened their mouths, trying to hear the slightest peep but knowing that the large mountain before them was mocking them. Passengers and teamsters and draft animals redoubled their efforts, forging through the snow, sensing it would have all been useless had not men already trudged through the drifts, clearing as wide a path as they could. Step by step they ascended. Breathing was labored. Birds could be seen high above them, flying effortlessly through the air and no doubt, seeing the valley of the Great Salt Lake in the distance. This encouraged the travelers. Then suddenly, as they neared the ridge, the depth of the snow lessened. The wind had done its job, keeping the snow from building too luxuriously in the thinning air. They crested the ridgeline, and a cry was let out by two of the teamsters, echoing back onto the others, who then scrambled forward to see a portion of the dazzling valley twenty miles to the west. The goal they had striven for, crossing miles of plains and prairies, fording countless streams and rivers, walking through blinding snow and stinging wind, growling stomachs aching for even a simple meal, frozen limbs fighting to maintain their circulation, loved ones succumbing to the unforgiving elements. And there it was, suddenly in plain view, almost near enough to touch.

The climb had been taxing but it proved to be less challenging than the terrifying descent. The steep trail colluded with gravity, bouncing the wagons dangerously, breaking wheels and axles of the uncareful, rendering their structures of no more use, putting the worn once more back onto their feet. Cautiously the oxen and the teamsters zig-zagged down the side of the mountain. Again, progress was measured in yards and feet. The gauntlet required the balance of the day but unlike the climb up the other side that was mostly accomplished by the first two or three wagons, rolling down the steep west side posed a severe challenge for each mode of transport. The breathtaking descent was finally accomplished. By late in the evening, the last wagons were rolling into camp, grateful in knowing the most severe trials were now behind them. Tiredness overcame the pioneers. Fires were started. Most were content to warm themselves and drink soup or porridge.

The next morning was the last day of November. It was Sunday. The bone-tired emigrants arose early and crossed the Little Mountain, from whose heights a greater amount of the valley could be seen. They descended the other side, the thinning snow now barely visible on the ground. Breaking out of the canyon, Edward Martin and the other leaders of the group formed up the wagons and moved towards the city.

Their arrival had been communicated and crowds thronged the streets of the surprisingly cosmopolitan city. Scores of well-constructed homes lined the broad avenues while cheering folks lined the street. Flags and banners waved in the warming forenoon air. Handkerchiefs fluttered, whistles sounded, cheers and calls crisscrossed the streets. Dogs barked and laughing kids ran alongside the weary but thankful travelers. They now saw their efforts as worthwhile. Relief settled in every heart. The terrible crucible was finished.

Martin's Company was the largest. 576 individuals had left Florence with the Company but more than 150 had died during the crossing. 104 wagons brought the beleaguered emigrants from Fort Bridger and into the city of the Great Salt Lake.

Sunday, November 30, 1856, Hosea Stout wrote: *The Handcart companies arrived today in the fore noon or rather the companies who went to the relief of the Hand Cart company brought them in wagons. The train of wagons was very large. The poor persons were sent to different parts of the Territory immediately to be taken care of until they could support themselves.*

Monday, 1 December 1856- This evening 20 minutes past 10, Jedediah M. Grant, Second Counselor to President Brigham Young died at his residence after a short but severe illness.

1 December, Monday- Martin Company- Praise be to the Lord, and we arrived yesterday in the forenoon, here in the Great Salt Lake City. We were enthusiastically greeted by throngs of well-wishers. Bishops and priesthood leaders mingled with our company, quickly ascertaining who among us had family or friends and who did not. The Company was quickly divided up among the citizens who happily took families into their homes to feed and care for them until they could be independent enough to care for themselves. Most stayed here in the city.

Yasmin and I were invited to stay in Aaron Rost's home. He had been gone for many mos. We found that his house had been occupied for the past month by two families from the Willie Company. They had cleaned and scrubbed it, leaving it immaculate for us, along with several loaves of bread, plenty of split wood for the stove, and some very necessary food stores. These people had then quietly moved on to other locations which were offered to them, leaving us quite alone and content.

Mr. Shep Silva rode on to his home in Tooele.

The Hodgetts and Hunt wagon trains should be arriving in Fort Bridger and are expected to finally make it here within a week or two. This has been the most extraordinary of journeys. We have suffered immense hardship. We have lost far too many of the company. The Lord had also stepped forward and blessed the rest of us with a burning testimony. How we love and appreciate the countless Saints who have forsaken all to come to our aid during this terrible crisis.

We are safe. We plan to rest and then explore this wonderful city and immediate locals. During our travels, I did have the occasion to visit with Brother Silva about the ill-fated Donner Party of ten years previous, who were caught in the bitter snows of the Sierra Nevada Mountains. These poor souls numbered 87 individuals—29 men, 15 women, and 43 children in a column of 23 wagons drawn by oxen. They were stranded in the severe weather conditions of the mountains for 5 mos. Nearly half of that time was after the people of California had been made aware of their location. 41 of their number died before rescuers were able to get them out.

While the number of our dead is much greater, we were spared the terrible consequences faced by the Donners because of the efforts and concerns of our fellow Latter-day Saints, who, at great cost and risk to themselves, mounted a tremendous rescue that saved our lives and resources, limiting the amount of time we spent in the frozen wasteland, as well as carrying us the hundreds of miles left on our journey and bringing most of us safely into the security of these mountain valleys, among our brothers and sisters.

I will now finish this record and commit it into the capable hands of Captain Edward Martin.

"Even in our sleep, pain which cannot forget
falls drop by drop upon the heart
until, in our own despair, against our will,

comes wisdom through the awful grace of God."

— Aeschylus
Harriet Matthews

    Lastly, these words of Bro John Daniel Thomas McAllister of Dublin, who wrote this handcart ditty earlier this year:

                For some must push and some must pull,
                   As we go marching up the hill;
                    So merrily on the way we go
                    Until we reach the Valley-O.

    As heartfelt and happy and longing as these words were as they fell from Bro McAllister's pen, they did not envision the terrible crucibles our people were forced to face over these past weeks.

    The next day 60 more wagons left Salt Lake City to assist the final trains of Hodgetts and Hunt, as these were beginning to arrive at Fort Bridger. The rescuers met on the 6th and all the wagon trains arrived safely in the city by December 15, 1856.

Chapter 44

"Time is a great restorer, and changes surely the greatest sorrow into a pleasing memory." Mary Seacole

A travel-weary Shep Silva made his way home, where he was greeted by heartfelt hugs and handshakes. His home had been further refurbished and his cupboards stocked. Georgina Hansen was a splendid cook, especially with Danish dishes but the first night he was back, the Hansens had him over for a tasty Brazilian dish of *linguiça* and black beans and rice, the tastes and smells taking him back to his childhood. Over the next weeks, the Hansens had him visit for multiple dinners, then sent him back to his home with additional food. He was content and pleased and wished he didn't worry so much about Zeenyo and Herman, who along with the other eighteen young men, were stranded hundreds of miles away near Devil's Gate.

Shep answered his door one evening, shortly after coming back to Tooele, expecting to see one of the blonde-haired Hansens. Instead, he was greeted by the familiar face of Eph Hanks.

"You're a long way from home."

"What's a few miles?" he asked. "Just wanted to make sure you got home okay."

Shep nodded. "It was longer than I'd expected but things turned out all right, I reckon."

"When you going after that travel companion of yours? Harriett?"

Shep should have guessed Eph would be getting right to the point. "Dunno, *amigo*."

"She's camped there at Rost's place and I'm not the only one who knows. You might want to get over there and touch bases, if you get my drift."

Shep shrugged his shoulders. "I've never been much for that sort of thing. I don't think I'm cut out of the right cloth."

"Maybe not but you can't just wait on the Lord for this one. He's already done his part. Now it's up to you. Come on, Shep. You're a healthy, happy man. All God wants is for you to be as happy. I'm here to tell you that Sister Matthews is a charming young woman. The two of you could go a long way to making each other happy."

"Can I get you something to eat?"

"Hell, no, Shep. Just saddle up and follow my advice. I'm not wrong here." With that Eph Hanks opened the door and stepped back into the night. His horse was pleased to see him so soon. "I got places to go. Just wanted you to know that you were on my mind." He stepped into his stirrup and was immediately in the saddle and riding down the lane.

"*Obrigado*," Silva called and was met with an easy salute.

"Come on in, Mahonri," Aaron Rost said loud enough to alert the two women sharing his house. "It's been a while. I was starting to think you had forgotten me." He peered more closely. "And your beard has magically disappeared."

"Not to worry."

"It's almost three weeks. Are things all right in Tooele?"

Shep nodded. "Here?"

"Business has picked up. It seems like folks have just been saving their money to give to me. I made an arrangement with a Canadian fellow, Abraham Gesner who has started the North American Kerosene Company. I got them to ship some barrels here in the spring and I'm just opening them up now. Look." He pointed to the lamps inside the house. "Brighter than ever, don't you think? And no smoke." Rost was pleased with himself.

"I'm here to see Harriett. Is she in?"

"I'm right here," she answered stepping into the room from behind a lace curtain. She was followed by Yasmin bint Manara who was looking downward but still smiling.

"Miss Harriett," he said, then stopped, feeling the swelling of a lump in his throat.

"Are you all right?" she asked.

"I am. *Obrigado*."

"You almost look like you've seen a ghost," Aaron added with a grin. "Maybe it can be blamed on your shaving."

I'm being baptized tomorrow. Will you join me at the dam up on the city creek. President Kimball will perform the ordinance."

The news surprised them. All chimed in their willingness, bringing a look of relief to Shep. "And then, if it's all right with you, Miss Harriett, I was wondering if you wouldn't mind taking a stroll with me?"

"Let me get a coat."

Rost and Yasmin smiled watching Shep shift his weight back and forth.

Harriett took only a few seconds before appearing and ready to leave the house. She turned to Aaron and said, "Brother Bench is planning to call. Would you please tell him not to wait?" She smiled and taking Shep's proffered arm, looked more closely at his uncovered face and the two departed.

"What has gotten into you deciding to be baptized? Was it the trip? I'm sure you could have found someone to take care of it for you in Tooele."

He sighed. "It's a special event. I wanted to share it with the Sweeneys and the Wetoyous. But they are not here. I don't want to use that for an excuse not to do what I should have done when in the islands."

"They will be pleased."

"As important as they are, I don't want them thinking that I am doing it for them or because of them. A couple of times I almost decided to have Aaron or Eph baptize me on the trip. But…" he let his words trail off.

"You didn't want me to think you were doing it for me?"

"This is my decision. I am the one who has come to this conclusion, as important as my family and friends are."

"Do you mind me asking, why now?"

"Can I ask you something first? This gift of the Holy Ghost. Have you felt it? Has it blessed your life?"

An interesting question that caused Harriett to think for a while. There were several other couples, most of them married, who had also chosen to take advantage of the warmer evening. Even though they were not dressed in the finery that might be exhibited on the streets of London, the couples strolled with contentment. It was a peaceful night. Both Harriett and Shep had noticed the lighting of the streetlamps. They were still few and far between, but they did a lot to dispel the darkness. Aaron Rost was making his presence felt in the city.

"I have felt quiet whisperings in my life, especially after the death of my family. I was led to the right people who cleared a path for me. I was guided to become a nurse and serve the Crown during an awful war. This whispering told me to look into the faces of the dead and dying, Allies and Russians. I saw the children of God following the dictates of the Adversary. After the conflict in Crimea ceased, I had the most compelling desire to return to the American West, to unite with the people here. And then, Shep, the people who have crossed our paths, men, and women of character, not least of whom is Yasmin. I have just felt my life increase. It has become better, more worthwhile."

"More challenging?"

She nodded. "I have never felt more like giving up than I have over the last two months. But amid the death and discouragement, I have been thanked. Folks have given me notice. My work has been of value."

"And the Holy Ghost?"

"It has led me. It has guided me. It has taught me, Shep."

"And you attribute that to this influence of the Holy Ghost?"

"The gift of the Holy Ghost. Where is all of this coming from?"

"I have known, for a long time, the truthfulness of the gospel. I have heard it from the lips of the missionaries. I have seen it in the lives of the Hawaiians. I have watched the Wetoyous. I was thinking that I needed a powerful confirmation, maybe the gift of the Holy Ghost but I knew this was something given after baptism. So then I thought, what about the power of the Holy Ghost? That is promised to one and all who are intent in their desire. Right? Well, that is what I was looking for, hoping for. A kind of manifestation."

"A sign from God?"

"It has never been anything I have sought for, Ett. Deep down inside, I knew the Lord would help me. And then, it was during our trip, when things were awful and cold and lonely and almost hopeless. It was while I was standing outside one of the tents and you and Yasmin were inside helping to some afflicted people and I heard you say those beautiful words, 'God loves you, my dear. And I love you.' It had a tremendous impact on me. And then, when you came out, it was the first time in my life that I saw you. I mean, really saw you. It is a long story Ett, but I no longer saw my mother's face. You emerged, like an angel and since then I have tried to push your image from my heart. The power of the Holy Ghost has etched you into my mind. I do not expect you to understand or agree, but your presence in my life has become the most important thing. It's why I want you there when I am baptized. It's why I want you to come to Tooele. I want to be as close to you as I can." He looked over at her to make sure she was still listening. She was. Maybe too intently. "Is that okay?"

She nodded. "When you showed up with Brother Grant and Joseph Young, I was pleased to finally meet this friend of Aaron's whom he had constantly spoken about. You were kind and shy and your beard acted as a sort of veil, not allowing me to see the person underneath. And yet, over the coming weeks, I was able to see you more clearly, even more clearly than if you had shaven. Again, Shep, I felt the whisperings of the Spirit. We had been given a special reunion. I hadn't a clue where we'd end up. I only knew that the Lord was pleased and introduced you as a token of his confidence."

Shep heaved a huge sigh of relief. "I was praying that I had not been deceived. For much of my life, my mother's image has protected me. When it lifted away, I felt vulnerable."

Harriett's heart felt light. "I remember hearing President Richards speak as we were on the trail. He said he was satisfied that we had journeyed thus far. He knew the handcarts would prove to be a salvation for the Saints. On the same conditions, he promised that though we might have trials to endure as proof to God that we had the true grit. I'm sure that has been shown clearly to God, at least to my mind's eye. He has blessed me with numerous relationships, not least of which is the experience of meeting you."

The next couple of hours the two spent walking closely, sharing the warmth of one another. They pondered shared expressions, what they meant and how they might develop.

The next morning, Aaron, Yasmin, Harriett, and Shep met Elder Heber C. Kimball at the banks of the small city creek. It had been dammed for just such occasions. It was a weekday. Few passers-by noticed as Shep walked into the frigid waters and took Brother Kimball's hand. The man lifted his right hand to heaven and pronounced the baptismal invocation over Giuseppe Mercedes da Silva, then immersed him under the water. When he emerged, Shep was shivering, and his lips had turned a light blue. A blanket was thrown about his shoulders as he stepped from the water. He was confirmed a member of the church and given the gift of the Holy Ghost by Aaron Rost, assisted by Brigham Young's First Counselor, Heber Kimball.

Congratulations were offered all around, along with hugs and handshakes. The clerk made sure he had the correct spellings and locations written down and the small party collected their things and returned to Aaron's house.

Shep was happy with his decision. It was a new day in his life. He felt prepared to face the future. "You may be next," he suggested quietly to Yasmin.

Aaron shook his head. "Haven't you noticed her glow? I baptized her two weeks ago."

****

"If I were to choose my favorite day of the year," Harriett said, "I think it would probably be the 21st or 22nd of December. That's the winter solstice. That's when the days stop getting shorter and things turn around and the days increase in length. It's not quite as apparent here but in England, believe you me, it's a big thing. What about you?"

Shep scratched his growing whiskers. "I guess I've never thought much about it. Of course, the holidays and birthdays, but for me, growing up in Brazil and then spending time in Hawaii, the length of days wasn't a big thing. It was warm most of the time."

"Well, especially in Britain, because it's so far north, there is a big difference in the seasons and the length of days. That's probably one of the reasons Christmas was tagged for the Savior's birthday. It had been an important time for centuries, I guess the Christian leaders thought they could kill two birds with one stone and tied Christmas to the solstice."

"Believing Jesus' birthday was in the spring has always made sense to me. I wondered about it in Brazil, of course, the seasons for lambing and calving are just the opposite in the southern hemisphere."

"But up here?"

"Yasmin?"

The Syrian woman was pleased to be included in the conversation. Aaron was puttering in the backrooms with some correspondence. "Well, normally, the shepherds keep their sheep and goats in a fold during the night. As a small fort, to keep out the predators. Then it only requires one or two shepherds to watch the door to the fold. In the mornings, the shepherds retrieve their sheep merely by calling or whistling. But when it is the season for the bearing of the lambs, the ewes do much better being away from other animals. That's why the story says that the shepherds were in the fields by night keeping watch over their sheep. The Jewish shepherds had the responsibility of marking the firstborn lamb, for service at the temple or other religious requirements. They were tagged with being witnesses. It was very appropriate then that the angels appeared to these men, who were generally poor and outcast, working away from the city, to go into Bethlehem and see Mary with her firstborn son, the Lamb of God."

Shep smiled. "Working with animals has always held a sweet sway in my life. I seem to sense God more nearly when I am with them, watching them, listening to them. God has given us dominion over the animals. I see them, especially the domestic ones, as servants of the Lord, always willing to fulfill his will, never upset with the outcome, even should it mean at the cost of their lives."

"And shepherds lead their flocks. They don't drive them."

Harriett had listened, contemplating the unfolding story. It made sense, at least for Shep and Yasmin. "I spent years in the border region between England and Scotland. We have a lot of sheep there. But these aren't small flocks of 100. These are quite large herds, and they depend on the herders to care for them, protect them and also keep them within the boundaries established. English herders are stricter with the sheep. They are sheepherders not shepherds. As a matter of fact, they have bred their own special dogs, called border collies, who specialize in herding or moving the sheep. These are wonderfully intelligent dogs who know how to move the sheep easily and peacefully without much barking or biting. They are also quick, surefooted and they know when to yap or nip at the sheep. They are a tremendous help for the herders."

The reality of a more modern way of life wasn't lost on Shep Silva. "I know that there's a romantic idea, in the scriptures, about the shepherds leading of their flocks, not driving them. But sometimes there might be a lot of animals and the best way to move them is to drive them. Sheep aren't always docile. I recall reading in the Book of Mormon when Ammon and the servants of King Lamoni were with his animals, it says that they were driving the flocks to the waters. There are times when the animals need to be driven, not led. The bigger the herd, the slimmer the chance the sheep will recognize a voice or whistle."

Yasmin nodded. "And in England, the raising of sheep is much more economical than in Syria. Wool is collected for clothing and the meat used for food. The larger populations have been moving into the cities. Manufacturing of clothing and the butchering of animals to sustain people has become a modern, industrial necessity."

"Doesn't this extend to fishing as well?"

Yasmin was happy to share her observations of Britain. "It really is a wonder to see how well the machinery works. People from all walks of life are employed. The implements of society stretch from the farmlands and pastures and coal mines and fishing beds throughout the Empire."

"And I love my England," Harriett said. "But contrary to the idealized models, there remains rampant unemployment. People are forced from ancestral homes. Children are forced to labor in mines and factories, where the pooling of wages from the whole family amounts to enough to buy some basic foods. We certainly have made some progress, but we remain far from the standard of Zion."

"I didn't mean to tout England's superiority, mum," Yasmin said.

"You are much too kind. And you are very observant, Yasmin. But we can do better. We must do better. Isn't that what God expects of us?"

"So, if you love the winter solstice," Shep added, "why does it remain important? If people are leaving the countryside and moving into the cities, why do you still see the solstice as an important time?"

"I don't know. Perhaps it reminds me of a simpler time. Or perhaps it reminds me that winter will not prevail. The sun will return to the north. Spring will return and with it, life and flowers and bees and warmer days. Crops will be planted. Fields will be worked. The glory of God will be showered once more upon the earth for all to witness."

"As long as there are no wars or famine or unemployment," Shep said.

Harriett nodded. "Yes, as long as…" She pondered a moment. "Like many folks, the Druids kept track of the rising sun, watching as it moved south. Then as it got to as far south as it could get, when they could no longer see any more movement south, that was when the miracle occurred. That was when the sun turned around and started its return to the north. Usually, it would take three days for them to be sure but by the 24th it was a certainty. Light was coming back into the world, and we could expect another year's cycle."

"The scriptures say that all things denote there is a God."

"Maybe that's why Joseph Smith was born on the 23rd to remind us that light is coming once more upon the earth."

A knock came on Aaron's front door, and he skipped from behind his curtain to answer, making the others think that he had been listening in to their conversation all the while.

"Brother Stout," he said happily. "Please come in."

The older jurist entered and nodded at everyone. "I've come here to speak with Shep. You got a minute?" he asked, then motioned for him to follow him back outside.

As Shep closed the door, he could hear a buzz of conversation erupt, but quietly, back inside. They didn't know the reason for the visit, either.

Hosea could read Shep's thoughts. "Not to worry, my friend," he said. "There's been some chatter regarding you and your talents. It's been going on for some time now. It didn't just start up with your baptism. Anyway, President Young wants you to be a deputy marshal. You'd be called on to assist Porter with some of his responsibilities. Mostly it would be to keep an eye on things around the courthouse when the legislature's in session but also to watch to comings and goings out west. If you don't mind me saying, you'd be a natural. We have a salary worked out for you and it should help cover whatever expenses you might run into."

"When do I start?"

Hosea wasn't able to mask his surprise. "You don't need any time to think this over? I mean, it would entail some doing."

Shep merely shook his head. "It's an answer to my prayers, Hosea. Tell Brigham, I'm ready and anxious to get started." Hosea acted as he had somewhere else to go. Shep shook his hand vigorously and smiled, "I'll let the folks inside know."

Stout winked. "You'll be hearing from us soon enough."

All eyes turned to look at him as Shep re-entered the house. He held up his hand to ward off the questions. "It's nothing big. Hosea's just up to his eyeballs at the state legislature and had some favors to ask."

The other relaxed, some, still slightly suspicious they weren't getting the whole story. Their suspicions were confirmed when Shep asked Harriett to once again take a stroll with him after supper.

"He does that all the time," Yasmin insisted, once the couple left the house.

"Trust me, Sweetheart, something's up."

Harriett enjoyed the walks around the city. She knew Shep could be a master of deceit, able to hide most things from the rest of the world. Harriett was a clever person. She knew just how to proceed.

"Longer days, huh?"

"I really look forward to them."

"More light and all?"

"And warmth and a restart of the seasons."

"And your thoughts about sheepherders?"

This was a surprise. "They are hardworking."

"But they drive the sheep?"

"With the help of their dogs."

"I love dogs. And those border collies, like you said, they are so smart. The Hansens have a couple and somehow or other they have decided the house really belongs to them and they just let the Hansens borrow it."

"Is everything okay, Shep?" Harriett asked suspiciously. "Where are you going with all this?"

Shep heaved a heavy sigh. "I believe in the gift of the Holy Ghost. It's like a looking glass. Whenever I look through it, things seem to be in a much better focus." He tugged her to a gentle stop. "I have seen you, Harriett Matthews, through this same looking glass. I am smitten by how smart you are. It's plain to me that you are sensitive to the whisperings of heaven. God is no stranger to you. He is the one who placed you in my path. He needed to do just that because I'm as dense as a fencepost. What I'm saying, sweet Harriett Matthews, is that I love you. From the moment you sat by me on the wagon, I have listened to your words. They have sounded calm and lyrical. They come from deep inside you."

"You didn't see my ogre side surfacing?"

"On the contrary. You are a beautiful person."

These words fell happily on her ears. These were the words she had dreamed of. She hoped they would reach her ears at the right time and come from the right man. "And just what is beauty to you, Giuseppe?"

The question brought him up short. What was his definition of beauty? *An eighteen-year-old at the peak of physical prowess? Light-colored hair or blue eyes? His mother had black hair and dark brown eyes. Smooth skin? Balance*

352

of face and teeth? Did height or weight and health play a significant role? The symmetry of features? Shifting positions, how about someone who is spiritually sensitive? Kind? Charitable? Forgiving? Literate? Gentle? Nurturing? Supportive? Happy and joyful? Comedic? Persevering? Strong? Constant? Obedient? Chaste? Virtuous? Diligent? Patient? All of these have their place. But it is also important that there be enough weakness added to the portrait that the foibles of mortality are also apparent. Not quite a total perfection. Not always beautiful the same way at the same time. There is something to be said about the way a person appears first thing in the morning, with disheveled hair and bad breath. Just what is beauty, Giuseppe?

He looked at her closely. "Beauty is progressive, Ett." He used a shortened form of her name with a familiarity that she embraced. It was a first for her. Her name had always been so proper, so complete. He had used this shortened term several times during their journey. It surprised her at first. She had attributed it to his accent, to his being Brazilian, to his habit of shortening things. "It is not stagnant. Beauty encompasses every stage of our lives, from infancy and toddler to toothless crone. Beauty is on display during every stage if a person is striving for progression, always working to improve even when the possibilities are quite limited. I am a stockman," he announced simply. "I know whereof I speak." His smile showed white teeth that stood out starkly against the darkening colors of his weathered face.

Harriett was impressed. "You are quite the thinker, Giuseppe da Silva. I am very pleased to have you in my life."

"And I, you, Harriett Matthews." The wind was starting up, causing the few flags and banners that still lined the streets to flap, reminding them just how far they had come from the wind-swept plains. He cleared his throat and while gazing deeply into her eyes, he asked, "May I be yours, forever?"

Tears welled up in the Englishwoman's eyes. "I have never in my sweetest dreams anticipated such a kind offer." Her gloved hand touched his mouth. "You may certainly be mine, forever, if I too may also belong to you."

President Brigham Young opened his office door to Harriett Matthews. His broad smile was warming, and he invited her into the room and offered her a chair opposite his desk. She noticed that the early sunlight shone directly on it. Brigham was in a good mood, in his element.

She took the chair, then looked at him curiously. "Do you have me sitting here, with the sun in my eyes, to give you a better view into my heart?"

"Ha! Sister Matthews I have been accused of a myriad of things but never that, at least not couched with your words. Would you feel more comfortable changing chairs or moving this one?"

"I'm happy to be here President Young."

"Please, my dear, in the office you can call me Brigham."

"As you wish."

"I have been aware of your coming here to the valley since President Richards arrived back in October. He was quite excited to learn that you and Yasmin had made the voyage from England and were on your way. I have also visited with Ed Martin, and he couldn't say enough good about the work both of you did among the handcart Saints. And if Ed and I are aware, believe me, so is the Lord."

Harriett looked closely at the man, this Lion of the Lord. He commanded the respect and fear of many frontier visitors. She watched for several moments and couldn't quite understand the phenomenon. He was kind, a perfect gentleman. He even kept several characteristics that he had gained from spending several years in England. They gave him a more polished manner, quite foreign with most Americans.

Harriett felt on the spot. "You know why I'm here?"

"Of course, my dear. And I don't mean to dodge your reasons. It's just such a pleasure to get to visit with you and learn some of your background. President Richards tells me that you wrote him regularly from Scutari, helping him keep a handle somewhat on our boys serving the Crown during the war."

"It was a blessing for me, President. Brigham," she quickly corrected herself.

He smiled. "Most of the time I want folks to respect my office, whether as governor or president of the Church. And as such, I encourage them to address me with the correct title. It means little to me. I remember too clearly where I come from. I am in this chair solely because of the grace of God. But you are someone I would like to count as a friend. I have gotten to know Shep and counted him a friend long before his baptism. He is a fine man and I know I can always count on him. He acts as my eyes and ears in Tooele or throughout the Territory."

"You're too kind, sir."

"So, you think your relationship with Shep Silva has progressed sufficiently to where you want to be wed, by the power of the priesthood in the Endowment House?"

Harriett sighed and smiled. "I feel it here in my heart. I am getting older and must confess that I have been concerned about my age and desirability. But there's more, Brigham." The somberness in her tone instantly drew Young's attention. "I love children. I love babies. I have wanted to be a mother from my earliest memories. I am somewhat aware of God's plan for his children and the importance of bringing them here, into a loving family, to be taught and loved. For years I have been aware of my fertility. I have gloried in it. And then there was that horrible day when my family was killed and I was seriously injured, when the *Saluda* exploded. And ever since then I seem to have lost my fertility. I doubt that I will be able to conceive. I know that Shep wants to be a father. He will make a wonderful father, but I don't think I'm the woman who will be able to make this dream of his into a reality."

Brigham thought seriously, then stood and retrieved another chair that he placed next to Harriett. He was very serious in his talk. "You are a chosen daughter of God, Harriett. He has placed you here for numberless reasons. You have served in so many capacities. Believe me, God knows the desires of your heart. You are doubtless destined to be a mother in Israel. I am so sorry to hear

354

about your injury and how it might impact your life. And I am sorry that this is something that has worried you. Your heavenly Father will see to it that you have a lifetime of service and love. Your value should never be measured simply by the number of children you bear. How do you think this news might affect Shep?"

"I'm afraid the poor man is hopelessly in love with me. It's nothing that I've done to woo him. It's just who he is."

"On the contrary, my dear, you, living your life, sharing your thoughts and ideas with him, being such an example. You are the one who has awakened the power of the Holy Ghost residing within him. As terrible and drawn out as the Martin Handcart journey has been, as devastating as the loss of life was, the Lord walked among you. Angels left the courts on high and came down to help with the pushing of the carts. As full of sorrow as those days were, they were also replete with the blessings of a grateful God. Neither you nor Shep have felt the need to strong-arm the other. You understand your roles and you press forward. You have come here, wanting to demonstrate to the Lord your willingness to be obedient, to sacrifice, and keep the law of the gospel. You understand the importance of virtue and chastity and as has been testified to me by countless others, you love your neighbors or fellow travelers, as you love yourself. Do you think, even for a minute that the Lord will withhold the choicest of blessings from you?" Brigham stood and walked back to his desk and chuckled. "Here's where we exercise faith in the Lord Jesus Christ. Here's where we allow Him to work things out with his own timing. Things will come to you. They will arrive in the own due time of the Lord, but still, they will be yours. Your calling will be to grasp the joys God has prepared for you, maybe in the form of Shep or the Hansens or the Wetoyous or whatever, and then never let go. Share your happiness with one and all. Make them thankful to have ever come across you. Use your considerable nursing skills to bring healing and recovery. It will allow others to smell the fresh air after spring showers or to see the colors of a glorious sunset, once again. You are perfectly positioned, Sister Harriett, to scatter joy and hope into an otherwise miserable world."

They looked at one another, then smiled, then looked away.

"I just thought of a scripture for you, Sister Harriett. And I want you to remember these words from Isaiah because they pertain to you as well. *'Sing, O barren, thou that didst not bear; break forth into singing and cry aloud, thou that didst not travail with child; for more are the children of the desolate than the children of the married wife, saith the Lord.'"*

The words entered into her heart, giving her hope and solace. Harriett cleared her voice. "Then, you approve of our wedding plans?"

"Sunday the 21st of December is the winter solstice. You have chosen your wedding day carefully. Making covenants with God on such an auspicious day will always stand as a testament to your goodness and the importance of Deity in your lives. There is no place I would rather be than with you and Shep in the Endowment House, to witness your sealing to one another forever and ever."

Brigham stood and walked around his desk again, this time taking Harriett's hand, he pulled her up. "Now please feel free to share your feelings with Shep. If I'm not mistaken, he will love you more intrepidly than ever. Then you watch and see if I'm not right. God will prove to you his love and commitment through numerous avenues. And Harriett, never forget, that He is a God of miracles."

Brigham ushered her back to the door of his office. Opening it she could see Shep and Aaron and Yasmin sitting in the chairs of the hallway. All were smiling. Harriett's appearance signaled that it was now Aaron's turn. As Shep enfolded Harriett in his arms, Aaron stepped into President Young's office. Brigham held up a finger to Yasmin and winked, then mouthed the words, asking for her patience. Before the door was closed, they heard Brigham say, "Monday, the 22nd of December. Isn't that the first day of *Hanukkah* this year?"

Chapter 45

"He who takes offense when no offense is intended is a fool, and he who takes offense when offense is intended is a greater fool." Brigham Young

After the Hodgetts and Hunt wagon trains left Devil's Gate and Fort Seminoe, the twenty young men were left to themselves, looking down the long conduit of winter for 1856-57. Several Shoshone hunting parties stopped in to visit. They were curious about what had been left behind and what the possibilities might be to make off with any wanted items. The number of young men easily deferred them. To show that there were no hard feelings, the Indians returned a couple of times to leave some antelope. They chose to keep the buffalo for their own families. The Shoshone were interested especially in Herman and Zeenyo, recognizing them as Native Americans.

Once they discovered that the boys weren't being held against their will, the warriors wanted to know about their tribe but couldn't imagine a land that far to the south. They were also curious as to why these two Indians weren't aware of some of the food sources that were sitting before them. Then again, they realized that a score of young men can easily consume much more than is easily accessible. The young men had been left with twenty days of rations, mostly flour but they were looking at five months of winter. They took turns thinking up nutritious meals that soon consisted of cowhide, moccasins, and an old buffalo robe that had been used as a doormat.

Their heartfelt prayers were that the Lord would bless their stomachs to gain the necessary nourishment from their poor food selections. Herman and Zeenyo began taking some of the men out to fish the Sweetwater, where they had some success now and then. Next, they turned to setting out trapping lines, catching several jackrabbits and squirrels. These were skinned, then the Wetoyous showed the others how to open them up to dry in the sun before pounding them into powder to be added to their soups. At first, it wasn't seen as the best option but then they began seeing it as far outdoing the boiled buffalo or cowhides.

As young men do, they devised several games to keep themselves busy and their minds active. They noticed that walking the trap lines or fishing or otherwise looking for game used up plenty of their energy, so they desisted unless it was necessary.

"So, when are we going to know when the passes open up? When might we expect to be rescued?" Herman asked Daniel Jones, their leader.

Hearing the question, a number of the other crowded closer to hear the answer. They all appreciated the amount of sleep they were getting but they were all smelling quite ripe and were grateful there were no corresponding girls nearby, knowing their chances of wooing were greatly diminished, given their lack of grooming.

"We'll probably be seeing the mail carriers coming through first. After that, we'll be seeing wagons. I'd expect President Young won't allow us to be out here any longer than needed. They'll round up some wagons and send them out to spring us and carry all this stuff back to the valley." Jones looked around at his companions. All were showing signs of malnutrition. Faces were much leaner. "I just want you all to know what a great source of pride I feel being here with you. This is tough. Tougher than harvesting or beating back crickets. You all make me proud. You show real grit. As funny as this might sound, there's no place I'd rather be. My ma cooks a lot better than the Wetoyous. Course she usually has a better selection of food. But, nope, there's no place on God's earth where I'd rather be than with the lot of you."

Jones' words comforted them. They also became closer with the passing of each day. All realized the challenges they faced and appreciated what each other was doing to make their stay more bearable.

A fur trapper wandered into the fort one day, unannounced, and was surprised to find the hungry platoon. He offered to swap them some hides for a deck of cards but was turned down.

"Salt? You got any salt?" Daniel asked him.

"Could be."

"Don't make us whoop you for it. Zeenyo's doing his best to make our meals bearable, but his onion roots are getting danged old. Salt would go a long ways."

The trapper took pity on the smelly youths, leaving them a couple of large nuggets of rock salt, along with some beaver carcasses.

"Make sure to tell us your name again, mister, cause I'm pretty sure every one of us is planning on naming our children after you."

The winter remained bitter cold. Storms blew in often, blanketing the landscape with the boring white covering.

"I remember the wind blowing sand on us down in my old home in the New Mexico Territory," Herman confessed. "I swore I hated that then but nothing's as bad as this horizontal snow. I guess we can at least melt it down and drink it. That's better than desert sand, I guess. And all you guys with your blonde hair can hide out well enough. Me and Zeenyo stand out like sore thumbs." His observations made everyone smile. They were glad the Wetoyous had such good personalities. Their comedic approaches also rubbed off on some of the others, especially when they were tired, hungry, or grouchy.

The choicest experiences for these young men came as the sun was setting, after eating their meager supper. That was when they would hold a devotional. They took turns explaining their lives and how they came to be at Fort Seminoe. Most already knew several of the others. Most were pleased to hear about the Wetoytous' conversion and their experiences and even though they were so young, they were quite well-traveled. Stories of the New Mexico

Territory, the evil Chief Wakara, Los Angeles and San Bernardino, and finally Carson Valley spurred many imaginations.

"All I know," Daniel said one time after they shared some stories, "is that I want to marry your sister."

"Get in line," another said.

Memories of Linda G made the cabins feel more like home. They all appreciated the thoughts of the Wetoyous. Before long, all were sharing stories of their families, going late into the night. God had blessed them to be where they were, doing what they could. He also blessed them with a desire to reunite with loved ones. These life-altering thoughts were ones to which they would always cling.

Some had known Judge Stiles, but mostly they remembered their interactions with Judge Drummond.

"And where did he get that wife?"

"There's no way he hooked her with his good looks."

The young men all snickered. They knew exactly what was meant.

"He showed up in Genoa just before we left," Herman added. "And he used to have her sit with him on the bench whenever trying a case. It made folks mad."

"Mormons?"

"Gentiles, too," Herman added. "Most women folk out that way are respected. Most Gentiles are okay with polygamy. Families are important. Everyone knows that. But Miss Ada caused a stir. I think she likes it. I know Judge Drummond does."

"And Judge Hyde puts up with it?"

"He doesn't have much choice. Drummond threatens to fine him for the smallest thing and he can do it because he's the federal guy. I think Judge Hyde's just hoping he gets out of town soon enough."

"And leave the Mormons alone?"

"I don't think that's ever going to happen soon. He hates President Young and Salt Lake City. He has been after the Gentiles to get the Carson Valley over into California. He says there's just too much distance between Carson and Salt Lake City. He gets plenty of support from the Gentiles with that one. They don't care much for sending their taxes and gold to the Great Salt Lake City."

Long nights and howling winds made such tales increase in interest.

"There's a man who now lives in Genoa, named John Thompson." Herman started the story. "He was born in Norway but came to the States when he was 10 years old and lived in Illinois. But in 1849, when the Gold Rush was peaking, he came to California, and then a couple years later he moved over the Sierras into Genoa."

Zeenyo picked it up. "Genoa used to be called Mormon Station and was the first white settlement in the Carson Valley. It was started by some members of the church in 1851 as a trading station up against the mountains where the Washoe tribe winters. They were successful and before long some ranchers and farmers began staking claim to the land. This meant they needed some law."

"In 1853, at the end of the year, the folks decided to have a dance over Spafford Hall's store. There were 150 ranchers and farmers but only nine females, including some little girls. I guess everyone still danced and had a good time."

"That was the same year some mill irons moved into the valley and began building a grist mill for Reese. Civilization started coming to Mormon Station in 1855 when Judge Orson Hyde arrived and began laying things out in a more orderly fashion, as Brigham had asked. First, he changed the name of the town to Genoa. Then he began laying out the town. It looks like the letter Y. River Road runs from the east and then branches off into the south and north sides of the town, with streets named Carson and Nixon, with one smack dab in the middle, called Mill Street. 1st Street is the farthest north, basically running east and west, then 2nd and so on until 10th Street. The streets that run north and south are named, going from the east and climbing towards the base of the mountains: Front Street, State Street, Main Street, Genoa Street, and finally Summit Street."

"It's a nice town. There's not too much trouble. I remember hearing that some Washoe Indians ran off with a bunch of horses. There's been a few robberies and lynching but mostly things are quiet. Judge Hyde got things set up just in time for an election in August of this year—just in time for the arrival of Judge Drummond. Houses are going up pretty fast. I think Judge Drummond is renting the Pink House on River Street." Herman looked at Zeenyo for confirmation, but his little brother wasn't certain either. "Mostly, I think he's just happy to have a courthouse to do his business. He likes swinging his gavel and thumping on the settlers."

"That's all he does?" one of the others asked.

"I think so. Miss Ada is working to build a good-sized herd of horses. She intends on taking them over the mountain to California where she can sell them. I hear she also wants to hire some lawmen to chase down escaped slaves. California is a free state, and a lot of slaves go there when they get away. It's pretty far from the southern States, so she thinks she can get a bunch of bounty money by rounding them up and sending them back in chains."

"You called her Miss Ada. I thought she was married to the Judge."

Herman was beginning to feel quite in the know. He was happy to have spent some time, however short, in Genoa. "That's what they like to tell everyone. But I know for a fact that one of our Elders was passing through Oquawka, Illinois. That's where the judge lived before coming to the Territory. Anyway, this guy says Judge Drummond left his wife, home with about 5 or 6 kids. Judge Drummond picked Miss Ada up somewhere around Washington and has brought her with him, along with his slave, Cuffy Cato."

The narrative was keeping all the young men in their cabin, awake.

"So, now what?"

"I hear he's disgusted with Judge Hyde and the way the court system works in Genoa. A couple juries let some guys go after the judge thought they should have been locked up. I think he's wanting to get away. He thinks he's been President Pierce's whipping boy long enough."

Zeenyo was anxious to add his two cents. "He's a potlicker. He likes politics and says he's friends with Stephen Douglas. He's a big Democrat and hopes to ride on the tails of the next president."

"Buchanan just got in."

Zeenyo shrugged. "Maybe him or whoever comes after. Could be the Little Giant," he said, referring to Douglas. "I didn't know him for very long, but I could tell he doesn't care a skitch for Brigham Young or the way the territory's run. He doesn't care for Indians either, and would just as soon ship us all off to a reservation."

"You think Judge Hyde will be able to put things back together once Judge Drummond and Miss Ada leave Carson County?"

Herman felt positive. "Judge Hyde is well enough respected. I heard Colonel Norton talk about him once, and he's not a Mormon. He said Hyde has a fine intellect and a kind and genial disposition and that he has it backed up with a fine liberal education. He claims that Hyde has a versatile mind and possesses great energy of character. He says that he's spent some nights sharing the same blanket with him, around the same campfire. He says that Mormon Elder Hyde has often preached when Norton was near and that his text is always taken from the Bible and it was always of that instructive character that would interest intelligent hearers."

"I'm getting tired guys but before I knock off, I want to hear about this Snowshoe Thompson."

"Me too."

A quick narrative followed about the most famous man in Genoa, the six-foot 180-pounder from Norway, who skied over the Sierras countless times to bring the mail.

"Judge Drummond likes him too?"

"I don't think there's anyone who doesn't."

"Is he a hunter and trapper?"

"I don't think so. He just eats salted and smoked meats when he's going over the mountains."

The talking ceased and the tired men began to drift off. "I'm just happy we don't need the lamp lit when we're telling stories."

****

"What is this?" an angry Judge Drummond growled as he rolled off the bed, fumbled to step into his pants, and then walked to answer the door of their hotel room, pulling up his suspenders. An anxious bellhop was waiting on the other side of the door, holding out a card. "What do you need?" the judge asked gruffly, then tried to lower his voice when he saw how nervous the boy was.

"I have a message here for you, sir," came the reply. The bellhop quickly handed the card to the judge, then turned and scampered away.

"Oh, nice," the judge said thoughtfully as he turned the ornate card over several times trying to discern its origin. It was well constructed of expensive and colored paper stock.

"Who's there?" a tired Ada Carroll asked, crawling from beneath the thick, down comforter.

Drummond and his courtesan had arrived in San Francisco the night before, after traveling several days over the snowy Sierras. It had been a cold and harrowing trip but what was to be expected in early January? Still, there were no storms and their drivers had made short work of the steep, treacherous road. It was a relief to finally descend into Placerville and from there, even further into the fragrant valleys of northern California, where the weather was so much more tolerable than the freezing temperatures of Carson Valley. They had reached the city and checked into the finest hotel they could find. Cuffy was relegated to spend his nights in the stables with the horses but even then, he was also pleased with the change of venue.

"What you got there?" Ada mumbled, keeping one eye shut while watching him through its bleary twin.

"Someone's sent us a card."

"What time is it?"

Drummond dragged his pocket watch out to check. "God. It's almost noon," he said, then turned his attention once more to the card and began to open it. By this time Ada's other eye had opened. Drummond scanned the writing. "Hmmm. We're invited to dinner this evening."

"Who's it from?"

The judge finished looking the missive over. "Oh. It's from Sam Brannan."

"Just who the hell is that?"

"A San Francisco fat-cat. He owns the hotel and several others if I'm not correct. He's a wealthy businessman."

"Well, that's a nice how-do-you-do."

William Drummond dropped back onto the bed next to Ada and handed the card over for her inspection, while he began groping at her beneath the comforter. She squealed slightly as he began to nuzzle her neck with his scruffy face.

"I guess this means we'll have to get cleaned up," she sighed, ever so grateful to be once more in a corner of civilization.

The hotel's dining room was well decorated, resembling European halls more than the American frontier. The carpet was thick and luxurious. At the far side of the room stood an imposing stage with heavy velvet curtains hiding the comings and goings of whatever entertainment might be planned for the evening. All the tables were covered with white linen and set with the finest porcelain and crystal and silver eating utensils. The maître d' escorted Judge Drummond and Ada to a pleasant table that stood not far from the front of the stage. The couple could tell that this was an envious locale, by all the envious looks being cast at them by other denizens of the room.

"Mr. Brannan begs your forgiveness," the maître d' said, bowing slightly, then helping seat Ada. This was a welcome change indeed. "Mr. Brannan is embroiled in some boring business but says that he will join you at his soonest. Please look over the menu and order whatever you want. Mr. Brannan also wanted me to make sure that you know that you are his special guests here and that he will not tolerate you spending one dollar of your own. He is more than happy to count you his friends and wants you to rest and relax during your stay."

"Do you know this man?" Ada queried after the man left.

Drummond shook his head. "Just heard about him some. He's a kingpin in the area. He made all his money during the Gold Rush, but he didn't dig or pan for a single nugget he just set up stores to cater to the miners' needs. Looks like it has paid off quite well."

"Quite posh. I don't remember anything in Baltimore or Chicago looking this nice. Perhaps New York or Washington, but darling, this is first-rate."

The food was delivered promptly and tasted even better now that Drummond knew he wasn't on the hook to pay the bill. A small orchestra was seated near the stage and played soft, current music while the room was filled with the equally soft chatter of voices and happy visitors.

Drummond looked around the room, staring several times at different diners, but wasn't able to place even one. "We are really a long way from the States," he proffered as he cut another piece from his stake and stuffed it into his mouth.

"Judge and Mrs. Drummond, I hope you are feeling welcome to the city." The judge and Ada turned to look at the man who had skillfully crept up behind them. His smile was disarming, and he was dressed in the city's finest. "Please let me introduce myself. I am Samuel Brannan the owner of this establishment." He shook Drummond's hand then took Ada's and raised it gently to his lips. "My God, what a beautiful woman," he noted, before placing a dry kiss on the back of her hand. Ada smiled and blushed. It was a reaction Drummond had not seen in months.

Brannan quickly dragged up a chair and seated himself between the two. "I trust the food and wine meet your standards?"

"Without a doubt, sir," Drummond assured him. Not able to keep his curiosity bottled up any longer, he blurted, "How do you know us?"

Brannan smiled slyly. "No one with your learning, sir, and bringing such beauty into the city as this," and he winked playfully at Ada, who by now was beginning to warm up, "can do so without my knowledge. Why I think I knew of you the minute you reached Placerville. I have certainly heard of your efforts to tame the wild west in Carson Valley and Genoa, although, for the life of me, I'll never understand how they ever allowed such a soft-pedaled rose, as your lovely companion here, escape over the mountains."

Ada blushed once more. She had not been exposed to this sort of silver-tongued attention for at least a year. And it was more than welcome.

The maître d' appeared at the table and Brannan ordered some wine, then turned his attention back to the couple. "You do us a great honor coming here. We should be so fortunate to have a judge of your caliber sitting on the bench in the city or anywhere here in California."

"That's quite the turn of affairs from over in Utah Territory," Drummond said. He held up his hands in mock defeat. "I did my best, considering what I had to work with. I dare say I would have gone stark raving mad had I not had Ada at my side."

"Ah," Brannan said with insight. "I have heard that as well. That you often seated this dainty woman at your side during your deliberations. And the cads did not appreciate the delicate turns of her cheek nor the fragrance of her perfume?"

"My God, I need to excuse myself and take a walk," Ada confessed nervously.

"Oh, please no," Brannan interjected. "My companion will be joining us soon and I want you to meet her."

Ada tried hard not to look disappointed at the mention of another woman.

"She is sweet. You both will love her. She is my special friend and has been here in the city for a few mos. She is a dancer, an entertainer and just arrived from Australia this past summer. She's originally from Europe and has traveled extensively there as well as in the eastern States."

"Perhaps we have heard of her?"

"Most decidedly. Her name is Lola Montez. She is multi-talented and has captured many hearts far and wide."

Drummond was thinking as hard as he could. Ada was less concerned. Brannan sipped his wine and smiled handsomely. His beard was trimmed immaculately, almost sensuously, Ada surmised.

Sam looked his guest's plates over, then signaled for a waiter to bring their desert, contrary to their bulging stomachs. He checked his pocket watch then looked around the room for several moments before he spotted Lola just entering. He stood and waved happily at the entertainer, who smiled as she saw Brannan, then walked towards their table.

"Ah, my dear, you look as lovely as ever," Brannan cooed, as he stood and gave her a welcome kiss on her cheek. "Please, I want you to meet the Honorable Judge William Drummond and his wife, Ada." They all exchanged smiles and greetings.

"Well, I don't know that we're married, yet," Ada said, starting to feel the effects of the wine.

William smiled at his hosts. "I did my best," he said with a tinge of embarrassment.

Lola Montez was a slender woman with an athletic build. She was a classic beauty with dark hair curled in Spanish style. Her painted lips were full and perfectly curved. The sparkling dress she wore was sculpted to display her charms in the most charming or alluring fashion, clinging to her desperately, as if almost ready to fall away, and answer the dreams of all the men in the room. All eyes in the room seemed to be on her small waist and her ample bosom. She was aware of her distraction but almost subconsciously continued to bend and sway to attract more intense looks.

Ada was not pleased to find herself suddenly upstaged. "Are the two of you married?" Ada finally asked, drawing a quick and knowing smile from Brannan and Montez.

"No. I have my wife," he announced. "She doesn't countenance my appetites, but she does a fine job raising the children, allowing me to manage my affairs." The look he traded with Lola did not go unnoticed by Ada, who also guessed the woman's age to be in her mid-thirties.

The foursome shared small talk for several minutes until there was a decidedly different turn in the music, alerting all to the approaching show. Lola stood and excused herself, blowing a kiss to Brannan, then she slipped away to one of the doors that would lead her back and up to the stage. There wasn't much of a pause, but the musicians raised the crescendo as the curtains rose carefully, exposing the diminutive Lola, still in her evening gown. From there, the music stepped up, lively and Lola instantly came alive, leaping and shaking and always smiling in a very come-hither manner. Her long skirt dropped as did her sleeves. The straps on her shoulders slipped easily low, exposing more of her breasts than the women in the audience were expecting, while the men watched raptly, intent, and hoping there might be some fault that would repay their focus. Lola was trained in the burlesque, bumping and grinding around the stage, mouthing the words to a foreign song that all the rest could only wonder at. Moving to the edge of the stage, she stretched and crouched, imitating a spider in its crawl. Her short skirt raised dangerously up her legs, threatening to uncover what all the men's eyes were longing to see. The house lights were above her, shining on her silken hair and well-placed cheekbones while shadowing what lay beneath her skimpy dress. The routine lasted longer than many expected, while the lecherous wondered if she might not be up for an encore. Lithe and limber, it was obvious to Drummond how she maintained such an exquisite physique.

And suddenly the show was over. The curtains lowered to a standing round of applause. Money and flowers were thrown onto the stage in appreciation. Whistles and shouts filled the room. A few wolf calls sounded but the perpetrators were silenced by disdainful looks. This was not the mining camps nor a bawdy house. Respect needed to be maintained. The hotel oozed class. The orchestra slowly began playing their regular fare and the rowdy calls were silenced and within a few minutes, everything was calm and peaceful once again. Some tables nearer the stage were quietly removed and a dance floor appeared. Couples happily moved in and began their waltzes, relishing the fact that they knew the steps as well as the music. This was San Francisco at its best.

A few minutes later a slightly disheveled Lola suddenly appeared at their table and sat down. Now she was covered with a dark, heavy cloak "How do you think that would go over in the Great Salt Lake City?" she asked with a wicked smile.

> For there we shall be taught the law that will go forth,
> With truth and wisdom fraught to govern all the earth;
> Forever there His ways we'll tread
> And save ourselves and all our dead.

Chapter 46

"Government is an association of men who do violence to the rest of us." Leo Tolstoy

After Judge Drummond told Brannan of their plans to take a steamer for New Orleans in a week, Sam insisted the couple go with him and Lola to Napa Valley. The judge was happy to suddenly have the next few days planned out for him. Ada was looking forward to seeing the countryside, not quite as enthused with Lola's presence but she did her best to disguise her disappointment.

Sam was talkative as they boarded the ferry and began paddling to the north side of the bay. "I'm looking at buying 2000 acres up around the Hot Springs. I want to turn it into a resort for those who would appreciate such things. There's a geyser that goes off prompting. You could set your watch to it. There's also excellent mud that some claim has wonderful healing effects. I want to build a spa, like the one in New York."

"Saratoga?" Ada asked.

"Yes!" Brannan clamored. "Exactly like that. Except this would be for the west. For California."

Ada was all in "You could call it Calistoga!"

The idea and name hit Brannan like a brick. "By Jove, that's exactly right! Calistoga! The name and reputation will draw all in the state who have money, who want to splash in the springs, try out the mud, and just enjoy the weather. It will be reminding one and all of Saratoga. Perfect!" He winked appreciatively at Ada, who was pleased with herself.

"So, we might meet this Governor Boggs?" Drummond asked, wanting the conversation to shift back to him.

"Of course, we will stop by his place in Santa Rosa. I'm afraid he might be in Sacramento doing political things." Brannan thought for a few moments. "Why don't you go there yourself, your honor? It's still a rather new state capital but it could serve you well. You're the one who claims to want to help Stephen Douglas. What could be better than having such a well-traveled, well-connected associate? What do you think?"

The thought was intriguing but a bit on the busy side. "Well, I have some other business to attend…"

"Nonsense! After we visit the hot springs, we'll just have you catch a carriage north with Lola. She has some business in Grass Valley. You could show up at the capital and make a big splash, introducing yourself. I guarantee that one and all will want to pester you about your time in the territory. You could even make a case for the redrawing of the Carson Valley boundaries, perhaps bringing them into California. That would surely cause some heads to turn. California would love to have the tax revenue instead of seeing it sent off to Salt Lake City."

It sounded tempting. "I'm not prepared. I need some different clothes."

"I have accounts with all the clothiers. Just put it on my tab."

This was almost too good to be true. And to have Lola as his traveling companion, at least for a while. "Where is Grass Valley?" he asked.

"Northeast of Sacramento. Not too far. I used to live there. One of my dance students has just moved back and I need to touch bases with her."

"A dance student?"

"Lotta Crabtree. A young student but very talented. She doesn't do the burlesque. Not yet, but she is amazing on stage. Audiences love her. She keeps in contact with me and honors me with her attention."

Drummond suddenly remembered his companion. "But Ada..."

"Please, your Honor, leave her to me," Brannan said slyly. "We have our own business to prosecute."

The idea suddenly sparked a curious interest in Ada Carroll.

"She tells me that she has almost a thousand horses still in Carson Valley. I have almost 30,000 in Napa and will happily buy Ada's mounts. The US government is always in search of more horses. I do my best to provide them. Also, Ada has spoken some of catching fugitive runaway slaves. We have a real problem here in the state. Some of my toughs have rounded up six of the vagrants and they're sitting in jail. For the right price, I can have them on the steamer with you when you return to New Orleans. They'll doubtless bring her a handsome bounty once you get back to the States. The Southern States."

The more he thought about it, the more excited Drummond became. This was turning into quite the adventure. And yes, after immersing himself substantially in the culture, he couldn't see how anyone like Douglas or the rest in Washington, could dismiss him. "I would be gone for...?"

"A couple of days at most, unless you find something else to your liking. Ada will be fine until you return." Sam withdrew a paper and pencil from his shirt pocket and leaning against the steamer railing, scrawled some few words and handed them over to the judge. "If you run into any problems, you can have the telegraph operator reach me at this number. It's amazing how fast business can be transacted using the wire."

It came together quickly, as Brannan was used to doing business. Lola had been a trifle resistant to traveling from Vallejo towards Sacramento with Drummond, but she realized his companionship could provide a pleasant diversion. Bill Drummond was content and immediately started planning out who he should see and why and what agreements could be crafted. He did not think about Ada, which was fine with her, as she started paying more attention to Brannan who continued to be talkative. He also resisted looking too longingly at her, although once he did and seeing her looking back, he flashed her a knowing grin and winked. It was not a simple gesture but one packed with innuendo. She sat back satisfied.

After docking, Brannan found a well-built carriage and arranged their travel to the hot springs 40 miles distant. Their time together was enjoyable. The judge and Ada quickly forgot the depressing business of dealing with Mormons and Gentiles and the distasteful temperatures of Carson Valley. Fleeing from the territory in such a drastic manner had left a bad taste in Drummond's mouth. Now he was enjoying the best vacation of his life. The company that had sought him out was wonderful. Brannan had more money than he knew what to do with. And that suited Drummond just fine. He couldn't remember having ever dined so well. And in California! Who would have thought?

They reached their cabins late in the afternoon and checked in. Brannan continued with his wealth of information, suggesting what he wanted to do and then asking for their opinions. The name Calistoga embedded itself in his mind. The two rooms they rented were rustic and smelled refreshingly of pine. This time their dinner was much more common, although still tasty. A runner returned to inform the company that Governor Boggs, was, in fact, in Sacramento.

"You need to look him up," Sam said. "He's from Kentucky."

"Me too!" Drummond said almost victoriously, as though he might have something to do with the relationship.

"He's married to Daniel Boone's granddaughter and has a passel of kids. He's a good one to have as your friend. Can't have too many. Boggs is well connected in these parts, especially among the Mexicans."

"I'll remember that. Did you say he was governor in Missouri?"

Brannan nodded. "During the nasty Mormon War. He's got plenty to say about that one."

"No doubt. You seem to know plenty about the Mormons. Any connection there?" With Drummond's question, Lola and Ada ceased their conversation to hear Brannan's response.

Brannan smiled. "Too much, I'm afraid. I came here in 1847 on a ship named the Brooklyn from New York. I was leading a party of 200 Mormons. We landed in Yerba Buena. It's what later was named San Francisco."

"And you were leading the Mormons? Or you were one?"

"Regrettably, I belonged to the sect at the time," he commented. "In those days California was open and unsettled. The people who emigrated with me were happy. They didn't want to leave. The land was plentiful and easy to buy and farm. I went with a group of men, up and over the mountains then we traveled across the Great Basin and up into the Rockies where we met Brigham Young and his party at Green River. I did the best I could to persuade him to keep coming with the Saints and to settle in California, but he would have none of it. Instead, he squatted there in that God-forsaken Great Salt Lake Valley."

Judge Drummond nodded knowingly. "The man hasn't changed a lick."

"I finally returned and haven't regretted it for a minute. There were some misunderstandings about my hanging onto the people's tithing. I didn't spend it but I didn't know what to do with it. Parley Pratt was one of the group's apostles, and he came by for a chat about the money. I turned over what I had and since have given the rest to Elders Lyman and Rich, so as far as the tithing is concerned, I'm fine."

"So, you're still a Mormon?"

"Not really. The Brethren in Great Salt Lake City didn't care for my involvement with the Vigilance Committee. They told me I needed to keep clear of the sort. But San Francisco is my city. Our police were nonexistent. Something had to be done with the ruffians who were collecting. So, we did. We haven't had much trouble since. Brigham didn't agree with my decision, and I was excommunicated. We haven't had much commerce between us since then."

"Good for you, says I. Brother Brigham will live to rue the day. You are a kind and charitable fellow. In all my life I have never met one so free with his substance. To tell the truth, sir, you are a captain of commerce. You could easily claim governorship of the state."

"Well, I'm happy to be who I am and doing what I enjoy. I have been quite fortunate. A number of my ventures have worked out beyond my wildest hopes. As far as politics are concerned, I am more than satisfied with my present position. Others would be so much better in the office but if I can help move the discussion in the right direction, what of it?"

"Exactly. You have certainly become a man of means."

"I don't care to brag, but I believe that I am the first bona fide millionaire in the state. It is a powerful position, one that carries many burdens. Then again, I wouldn't have it any other way."

"You tend your financial stewardship diligently, sir. You have relieved us of many worries and treated us as if we were royalty. We are more than fortunate to have run across the likes of you."

Brannan smiled. "From your lips to God's ears." Samuel Brannan finished his meal thoughtfully. "I remember something Elder Pratt told me once, as this empire was being built. He said something to the effect that I shall not die till I am in want for ten cents just to buy a loaf of bread."

"That goes to show how inspired the likes of Pratt are."

The foursome spent the following day relaxing in the warm waters of the springs and then playing in the thick, black mud. A cool breeze kept them close to the springs. It was still winter, they told one another. The next day, after a peaceful night, they rode back to Vallejo. Brannan expertly commandeered another carriage to take Drummond and Lola the 60 miles to Sacramento. W.W. Drummond was giddy with the prospects of riding the distance with such a beautiful and exotic woman. Lola was pleasant but made it obvious early on that she was not interested in pursuing a relationship. Drummond was deflated but upon reaching Sacramento, as she continued to Auburn and then Grass Valley, he worked his way into his element. Politics and law were his life. He had no problem convincing all in the hallowed halls of his importance and foresight. The trusted spies Brannan had employed in the state capital kept a close eye on the newcomer, reporting to their boss Drummond's contacts and conversations.

Ada Carroll was pleased to start her affair with the well-placed Brannan. During their strolls through the city, they were met with smiles, nods, and pleasant greetings. Ada was certain the women were jealous of her, making her cling more tightly to his arm. Sam helped arrange the steamer passage from San Francisco to San Pedro and then down to Panama where they would take the train across the Isthmus and pick up another steamer in the Caribbean that would carry them to New Orleans. And, as promised, Brannan discussed the passage of the six slaves who were being held for transport as well, with the captain. Details of the payment for Ada's horses and the slaves would be worked out at their leisure.

During dinner on their fourth night in the city, Brannan announced that Judge Drummond would be arriving late that night.

"That's too bad," Ada pouted and frowned.

"We still have a few hours to enjoy one another."

"We have been together for some days, but Sam, I have yet to meet your wife or know anything of your family."

"It's the price of doing business, my dear. I have explained the matter to my wife on numerous occasions. For now, she seems to be content. But believe me, having one wife is more work than I can handle. I have no clue how our Mormon brethren can juggle multiple women. When they call it a sacrifice, I tend to believe them. They know whereof they speak."

"Do you ever wish you were a polygamist?"

"Oh, God, no. It would be a nightmare. An affair. A mistress. It's so simple. No messy divorces. No confusion about children."

"Then why do they do it? The Mormons? Besides these problems, the sex would doubtless grow tiring for all concerned."

"Once I remember when Parley Pratt was here, he took out some ads in the newspapers, challenging one and all to debate him on the subject. He didn't have the slightest qualm. He said the idea of polygamy was sanctioned in the Bible and that no one could prove otherwise, not using the Old and the New Testament, the Constitution, or the laws of the Utah Territory. From what I recall, he handled himself quite expertly. But neither he nor any of his missionary peers seemed to be afraid of the subject. They see it as a hardship on their wives, dealing with other loves and families, while so many of their husbands are scouring the earth for more proselytes or else pulling up sagebrush and planting and irrigating. The life they have chosen is not easy. No siree."

Sam and Ada repaired to her room after dinner where once again they attempted to consume their lust with one another. Ada was pleased to find that Brannan had a very healthy sexual appetite. It required time and effort and all her wiles to satiate the land baron.

371

Late that night a soft knock sounded on the walls of the bedroom, waking Samuel Brannan instantly. He stepped from the bed and collected his well-folded clothes. After finding his hotel key, he unlocked and opened the door leading to an adjoining room, then stepped inside. It was unoccupied. He noticed that Ada was still asleep. He closed the door and lit the lamp at the side of the bed to dress and primp quickly in the mirror.

A few minutes later he heard the arrival of Judge Drummond. The man's clumsy and erratic footsteps informed Brannan that the judge had been drinking heavily. While he lowered the light in his room, Brannan noticed the light growing beneath the door as Drummond sought to gain his bearings. He heard the judge fumbling with his belt and suspenders, then heard as the trousers clanked loudly on the wooden floor. He was carrying coins. Brannan stepped to the door that led outside to a landing and steps leading into the night but not before he heard the rustling of the covers concealing the still sleeping Ada.

There was a muffled couple of words. Brannan recognized the question, "Nude?"

A groggy Ada turned and snapped, "You know I sleep best this way!"

Samuel Brannan closed the door behind him, then walked towards the stairs. The hotel was well built and creaked very little. Descending to the street, he started towards his house. Looking back at the hotel, he saw it as a monument to his work and personality. It provided him with an abundance of cash as well as lifted him in the eyes of all the community. And he claimed a number of the buildings, which also drew the ire and envy of many of his peers. *Tough luck, for them.* He chuckled as he remembered the dire prophecy of Pratt's, telling him that he wouldn't die till he needed ten cents to buy a loaf of bread.

Chapter 47

"I could not forego the idea of joining the church for aside from the disgrace which would follow I was fearful least I should not live up to its precepts."
Hosea Stout

The next couple of days, Brannan was conspicuously absent. But then, on the day of their departure from the city, the philanthropist businessman showed up as jovial as ever. After breakfast, he escorted them to the wharf.

"I trust your visit to Sacramento was productive?"

Drummond nodded. "I got plenty accomplished, including my official resignation letter. The men were all supportive and applauded my determination to pressure the Utah Territory."

It was a beautiful morning and the walk down to the wharf was short and pleasant. Gulls battled with seals for space along the boardwalk. If Drummond knew or suspected Brannan and Ada of their tryst, he certainly didn't pay it any heed. Cuffy walked respectfully behind.

"My mind keeps returning to this damned polygamy. I'm pleased that the new Republican Party has adopted one of its planks as moving against it. My God, we have Puritan ethics. We were founded by chaste and upright people and the Mormons, who claim to live with integrity, adhering to the strictest of morals, march blithely along this sordid path, collecting candidates for their harems, breaking hearts and breaking homes."

The judge was pleased to be allowed to pontificate, focusing on an issue that he couldn't comprehend but was equally sure the Saints in the desert could not either. He used the topic to berate and persecute the Mormons, calling their practice into the most vicious of questions. On the other hand, he chose to dismiss the social norms of the powerful and wealthy among the US society, of courting mistresses and wooing courtesans. Even the questionable mores expressed in San Francisco, where men flagrantly sought the companionship of prostitutes and elevated the skills of women such as Lola Montez, the practice of polygamy was soundly ridiculed. The irony of the paradox was never discussed. And Drummond was not alone. Throughout the State of California, men raised an outcry toward the Mormons, who were walking their streets and preaching against the inhumanity and sinfulness of adultery. *How dare these itinerant preachers mock them and the strength of their society?*

"So, this letter you crafted, telling the President of your plans to resign, it has already been posted?"

Drummond nodded enthusiastically. "Before I even left Sacramento. I figure Buchanan will receive it just after his inauguration. It will give him something to think."

"You mentioned the Mormon desire to secede from the Union?"

"They're a threat, Sam. These religious dupes want to play both sides of the fence. They pay taxes and claim to be honest, hardworking members of society, wanting nothing more than to be let into the Union as a state, while on the other hand, they worship Brigham and follow him blindly down whatever path he chooses."

"Serious allegations indeed, my friend. I am sure that your observations and words will go a long way towards righting this nuisance."

This was like music to Drummond's ears. To be noted as a man of talent and ability by the likes of Samuel Brannan was high praise indeed.

"They can't be trusted," he continued. "I also wrote a serious letter to my friend, the Honorable Stephen Douglas, and told him the only way I will ever come back out to the Utah Territory, is if President Buchanan were to award me governorship."

The nation's presses, including some in California, began demanding Mormon blood. The *San Francisco Bulletin* announced: *"Virtue, Christianity, and decency require that the blood of the incestuous miscreants who have perpetrated this atrocity be broken up and dispersed. Once the general detestation and hatred pervading the whole country is given legal countenance and direction, a crusade will start against Utah which will crush out this beastly heresy forever."*

Brannan had heard the ploy before and was suddenly tiring of the exercise with the increasingly pompous Judge William Drummond, although he did his best to hide his boredom. Now, Ada. There was a person he was sure to miss.

They arrived at the steamer. Their tickets were checked, and all were found to be in order. Brannan excused himself and quickly went below the deck to ascertain that his six slaves were in the hold. They were. He returned and announced his findings. "It doesn't matter if California is a free state or not," he said. "With all the fighting going in Washington about the Dred Scott case, I'm sure the slave owners will win out before long. No slaves should be allowed freedom and security simply because they escape and cross over some imaginary state line and into a free state. This is causing such heartache and allowing ruffians like John Brown to pillage and protest. It could seriously develop into a terrible conflict. The decision on the case will assert that there will be nowhere these escaped slaves or convicts can run, except maybe into Canada. The decision should be rendered soon, and it will change the discourse in the capital."

Cuffy Cato remained silent. He knew that if his opinion were wanted, he would be asked, otherwise, he was to stay quiet.

The call was made for passengers to board. Brannan shook hands with Judge Drummond and Ada gave him a lingering embrace. The gate to the railing was secured and the steamer slipped easily into the waters of the harbor, heading for San Pedro, then Panama. William and Ada, accompanied by his broad-shouldered slave, Cuffy, would be in New Orleans before two weeks were out.

****

"Well, well, I was wondering if we'd ever see you again," Aaron Rost said, opening his front door to let Harriett and Shep inside. Even though the outdoors were warming considerably, the inside of the house, by comparison, was almost toasty. "I should have known this would happen as soon as things started to warm up."

Shep nodded happily. "You guys ready?"

"The wagon is greased and ready. I just need to harness the mules."

The previous weeks had been excruciating for Brigham Young, who remembered all too well having left the 20 young men back in Fort Seminoe, keeping an eye on the emigrants' baggage. Keeping his ear close to the ground, as soon as the snows had dissipated enough, he sent a call out for more wagons to retrieve the men and the things that were left behind. Shep and Aaron were also anxious to return, this time Yasmin and Harriett were accompanying them as new brides, a far different setting than what they had finished at the end of November.

Now, the feelings were happy. Within minutes their two wagons merged onto the broad avenue and started for Emigration Canyon. Aaron and Shep took turns letting the women ride alongside them, trading now and again, all the while chatting about the news they were experiencing, not least of which was Yasmin's pregnancy. Fortunately, she had already passed the queasy stomach portion and was feeling quite exhilarated. The trading of seats on the wagons occurred frequently enough to keep both men in the loop, something they both appreciated.

With the snows melting, the roads were drying up considerably. There remained some mud that needed to be addressed but this was a far different version of their previous excursion. Excited birds flitted through tree branches and the warmth of the sun also colored the blue sky. Looking back, the city seemed to have grown even during the last few weeks. Commerce was active. Traffic on the streets was almost congested.

As a result of the shifting women, Shep learned that Aaron was again planning a trip to the States, this time in the early summer. There were some negotiations in New York City, surrounding the sale and distribution of kerosene that were set and would doubtless rocket the Rosts into an even wealthier stratum. It pleased Shep and Harriet, seeing how well the Rosts were getting along and the excitement they expressed to one and all regarding the coming of their first baby. It had been quite a distance for Yasmin to come. Syria and Turkey were now far in the past. She had embraced her new life in the valley, learning all she could about kerosene and bookkeeping. All seemed quite happy with their current occupations and responsibilities.

Harriett had also grasped onto the frontier life in Tooele, soon making herself an indispensable part of the town. The sisters were in awe, seeing how readily she applied her medical knowledge, whether it was the setting and binding of a broken arm, or helping a cow to deliver her calf. Blood and late hours did not bother her. She knew how to talk to the sick or injured, when to be gentle and understanding or when to be stern and direct. One of the results of her activities was the growing confidence the other women of the town had in her. They started coming by her house, always bringing an offering of food, wanting to put forth their myriad of questions. This was a great help to Harriett. It also allowed Shep the time he needed to spend with his horses and mend fences. But both felt the pressing need to go and bring Herman and Zeenyo home. By the time Brigham asked for volunteers, they were past ready and leaped for the chance. They were also happy to be joining Yasmin and Aaron. This type of rescue, as long as things turned out the way they expected, was much more restful than the previous one in the winter. The week had been anticipated and planned for.

Chapter 48

"A smile or a tear has no nationality; joy and sorrow speak alike to all nations, and they, above all the confusion of tongues, proclaim the brotherhood of man." Frederick Douglass

"A penny for your thoughts?" Bessie asked her husband.

Tom smiled. He was content. He knew he had made the right decision to marry this wonderful woman. "I'm just watching the way you are with Elisha. How you nurse him. The soft voice you use as you speak with him. We are a most fortunate family."

Elizabeth enjoyed hearing her husband's praise. He was a good and self-made man. Most of the time, he was spot on. And this was one time she hoped to fit into the same category. "He's handsome and strong just like his father."

"Do you ever regret naming him after my brother?"

"I have many regrets, dear, but giving him this name was the best thing we could have done."

Thomas nodded his agreement. "I wish he could have known his nephew."

"Well, he knows by now, Tom. And more importantly, your folks know. They know that you loved your big brother. He was a hero to all of us."

"He should have returned to Philadelphia to recuperate. We would have taken care of him."

"He was a Kane in every respect. He was independent. He did whatever he thought was best. And he lived by his decisions."

Thomas' older brother, Elisha Kent Kane was born in 1820, in Philadelphia to John Kintzing and Jane Duval Leiper Kane. He grew to become a famous American explorer.

On September 14, 1843, he became an assistant surgeon in the Navy. He served in the China Commercial Treaty mission under Caleb Cushing, in the Africa Squadron, and the United States Marine Corps during the Mexican–American War. One battle that Kane fought in was at Nopalucan on January 6, 1848. At Nopalucan, he captured, befriended, and saved the life of Mexican General Antonio Gaona and the general's wounded son.

Kane was appointed senior medical officer of the Grinnell Arctic expedition of 1850–1851 under the command of Edwin de Haven, which searched unsuccessfully for Sir John Franklin's lost expedition. During this expedition, the crew discovered Franklin's first winter camp.

In 1852, Kane met the Fox sisters, famous for their spirit rapping séances, and he became enamored with the middle sister, Margaret. Kane was convinced that the sisters were frauds and sought to reform Margaret. She would later claim that they were secretly married in 1856—she changed her name to Margaret Fox Kane—and engaged the family in lawsuits over his will. After Kane's death, Margaret converted to the Roman Catholic faith, but would eventually return to spiritualism.

Kane then organized and headed the Second Grinnell expedition which sailed from New York on May 31, 1853, and wintered in Rensselaer Bay. Though suffering from scurvy, and at times near death, he pushed on and charted the coasts of Smith Sound and the Kane Basin, penetrating farther north than any other explorer had done up to that time. At Cape Constitution he discovered the ice-free Kennedy Channel, later followed by Isaac Israel Hayes, Charles Francis Hall, Augustus Greely, and Robert E. Peary in turn as they drove toward the North Pole.

Kane finally abandoned the icebound brig *Advance* on May 20, 1855, and made an 83-day march of indomitable courage to Upernavik, a town in Greenland. The party, carrying the invalids, lost only one man. Kane and his men were saved by a sailing ship. Kane returned to New York on October 11, 1855, and the following year published his two-volume *Arctic Explorations*.

After visiting England to fulfill his promise to deliver his report personally to Lady Jane Franklin, he sailed to Havana in a vain attempt to recover his health, after being advised to do so by his doctor. He died there on February 16, 1857. His body was brought to New Orleans and carried by steamboat and a funeral train to Philadelphia; the train was met at nearly every platform by a memorial delegation, and was the longest funeral train of the century, surpassed only by that of Abraham Lincoln. After lying in state at Independence Hall, he was transported to Philadelphia's Laurel Hill Cemetery.

Tom's hands fluffed his beard. "It is wonderful having our son be his namesake. I am always reminded of him."

"I think you presented him with numerous opportunities to follow your lead or that of your father's."

"I wish he'd married."

"Then his wife would be a widow and his children fatherless."

"But what a husband and father."

"You are exactly who you should be, doing exactly what you need to do. The country is better off because of who you are. We are fortunate to have so many friends who know this same thing."

It was a pleasant conversation. Tom and Bessie had butted heads several times during their marriage, but they understood the importance of family and loyalty. These traits were magnified with the passing of time or the passing of acquaintances.

Bessie broke baby Elisha's suction on her breast, as he had drifted off to sleep. She rocked him tenderly, looking upon his face, trying to project where he would be in ten years or twenty. She looked at Tom, who was also deep in thought, and wrestled with the information she held. She finally acquiesced.

"A letter has been sent to you from Dr. John Bernhisel," she said quietly. The announcement awakened Tom. She could almost hear the gears turning in his head. "I left it on the bureau for you."

This was a surprise indeed. Tom walked to the desk and located the letter. He examined it briefly before opening it and scanning its contents.

"Drummond's resigned from the Utah Territory and seems intent on stirring up a hornet's nest. He'll be in New Orleans presently and plans to continue up the river, spreading as much rumor as possible until he lands in Douglas' camp."

Elizabeth appreciated hearing what the letter had to say but she wasn't pleased to note her husband's sudden interest. He just did not seem to have the power to extricate himself from the Mormons and their problems.

"What are you going to do?"

"I need to get to Washington and visit with Dr. Bernhisel. We'll need to come up with some sort of plan to lessen the impact Drummond might want to cause."

Elizabeth smiled slightly and nodded in resignation.

****

Life at Fort Seminoe for the twenty young Mormon men dragged through the winter. As young men do, they invented innumerable games to play. They took turns reading from a Bible and a Book of Mormon, then discussing the doctrinal messages. The fires of their faith burned hot and deep. All were prepared to serve missions, should President Young feel so inspired to call upon them. Under Herman's and Zeenyo's tutelage, they trapped and fished, trying to augment their food stores. They did not feel comfortable slaughtering the stock in their possession, seeing that as a form of stealing because they belonged to others. They usually got up early to see the sunrise, noting that it was slowly making its way back north and the days were getting longer and warmer. The snow was starting to thaw. The streams and creeks were running cold but faster. The last couple of weeks had them taking turns during the day, looking down the road for the arrival of the wagons sent to relieve and rescue them.

Early in March, Porter Rockwell arrived driving a wagon for the YX Company, the Young Express Company. Headed for Fort Laramie, he deposited 200 pounds of flour for the famished men, promising that he had passed a small group of wagons days earlier that was heading to Fort Seminoe for their relief. The food was a reminder of how exquisite meals could be when prepared with the proper ingredients.

True to his words, several days later the wagons arrived! The young men knew they had not been forgotten but there were times when faith was all they had to keep them going. A number of the first wagons in the lead were driven by fathers of the men. The fort erupted with shouts and tears and hugs.

"You two have grown a foot!" Shep exclaimed, pulling the smiling Herman and Zeenyo into his embrace and pounding their backs joyfully.

"But look how skinny they all are," Harriett noted with concern.

"They're healthy though," Aaron added.

The Wetoyous suddenly began looking closely at the four. Something had changed.

"Yes, we're married," Shep said suddenly, again bringing whoops of joy from their young men. "Sorry, but unlike you, I couldn't wait."

"Wait! Both you and Aaron too?"

Rost convinced them by showing his wedding band. Herman's and Zeenyo's teeth flashed whiter than ever.

"Good thing for you," Herman said. "I think everyone here has thought seriously about every woman who has ever come across their path and ordered them carefully, who they would propose to first."

The reunion was made even better as the rescuers insisted on cooking for the rescued. The food was delicious. A large bonfire was built that night and following the Wetoyous' lead, they danced and sang a series of Hopi dances taught to them by their comrades, accompanied by the steady beat of crudely constructed drums. The men wearing moccasins were light on their feet in contrast to the heavy booted others.

Snuggly contentedly beneath fresh blankets and next to Shep and Harriett, Zeenyo smiled but then paused. "With Sister Harriett living now in Tooele, does this mean we'll need to find someplace else?" His question was tinged with a touch of serious reflection.

"I would never countenance that," Harriett replied with finality. "You are our family. God has given you to us and we're not about to give you up."

Her answer was exactly what the Wetoyous needed to hear, and they all drifted off to sleep.

Some luggage and supplies were loaded onto the wagons the following day. The anxious folks made quick work of the chore and before it was afternoon the wagons began their homeward trek. A majority of the young men remained behind, awaiting their parents who were busy planting their crops.

A week later, some of the victorious guards from Fort Seminoe rode into the Great Salt Lake City, to the accompaniment of cheers and applause from a cheerful populace. Many of the healing handcart emigrants appeared to collect their belongings, grateful for the efforts made on their behalf. Many remembered these young men as having carried them across the freezing waters of the Sweetwater. Tears flowed again as heartfelt 'thank yous' were offered again in several different languages.

Brigham Young reveled in happiness and success. "Go with God," his voice boomed loudly as he waved and watched Shep and Harriett finally gather Herman and Zeenyo and begin their trip back to Tooele.

****

Reaching New Orleans was a goal William Drummond had dreamed of most, although the trip from San Francisco to Panama, across the isthmus and then the Caribbean took longer than anticipated. Mosquitoes and dysentery also took their toll, making the traveling judge angrier and more upset. He had an easy outlet. He blamed the Mormons and especially their leader Brigham Young for his discomfort. Landing again on US soil, he lost no time berating his enemies sequestered in the valleys of the Rocky Mountains. In his official letter of resignation, published in all the nation's leading newspapers, Drummond charged them with destroying court records and asserted that *"the Mormons look up to Brigham Young, and to him alone, for the law by which they are to be governed: therefore no law of Congress is by them considered binding in any manner."*

The press was anxious to hear the federal judge's accounts. Reporters flocked to capture every word. It became a feeding frenzy. From New Orleans the rumors spread quickly throughout the States, confirming what most already suspected of the Mormons secluded in their vast mountain hideaway. His public letter of resignation was filled with tales of the Danites, a Mormon vigilante group, that had been resurrected to perform the will of Brigham and the Holy Priesthood. A new governor must go to Utah "with sufficient military aid" to end the "withering curse which now rests upon this nation by virtue of the peculiar and heartrending institutions of the Territory of Utah." In his private missive to the government, Drummond assured the leaders that he could back up every allegation he made.

After spending a few days in the city, Drummond and his party were heading for the dock on the river, intent on working their way up the Mississippi to Illinois. Towns and cities along the waterway were clamoring to hear him speak. From there they would travel to Washington where Judge Drummond would be able to make his report personally to President James Buchanan.

Pausing momentarily at the dock, he looked out at the crowd. So many faceless individuals, but so powerful collectively. Then he spotted a familiar face, a woman who looked to be 40 years old, standing at the edge of the throng.

"Do you know her?" he asked quickly of Ada, pointing at the people. She had stepped back into the multitude before Ada could spot her. "I've seen her before. I know I have."

The incident continued to bother him for several hours after they started moving up the river. She could have been from Oquawka or Kentucky, but he seemed to have seen her more recently than that. It couldn't have been California. And then he remembered. Parley Pratt. *The Mormon Apostle. She was one of his wives!* He knew it. He then started working his memory to see what could be recalled. *Oh yes, she was a schoolteacher who worked for both Pratt and Brigham. She had lived in San Francisco. Brannan had commented about her and Pratt, accusing him of seducing her, encouraging her to leave her husband and follow him to Salt Lake City. That's right. But what was she doing here in New Orleans? If she was the woman, why was she in the Crescent City and not still in Deseret?*

Once he thought he'd uncovered the mystery, Drummond forgot about it and began readying himself for the next stop. Clinton, Louisiana.

Martha Gunnison, the widow of Captain John Gunnison, who had been massacred in Utah in 1853, was living in Grand Rapids, Michigan, and hearing some of the reports being made by Drummond and reviewing his letter of resignation, reached out to him through the mail, telling him of her conviction that her husband had been murdered by Mormons and asking him to weigh in with his evidence.

He replied with another public letter stating he did not doubt that the Captain and his party were murdered, victims of a deep and maturely laid plan of Brigham's. He proceeded to give a graphic account of the butchery, stating that while yet alive, Gunnison's heart was cut from his chest and bounded on the ground because of its blood. The Captain was then dismembered, limb from limb. "I also know that this dark and bloody picture will prostrate every nerve of your tender form," he continued but swore that it was his duty to make a full account.

It was exactly what the public was hungering for. A hue and cry arose from the readers, confident of the truthfulness of Drummond's claims. It elevated him and alerted all along the Mississippi of his arrival and what expectations he had now that he was back in. William Drummond then fired off a letter to the Buchanan Administration, telling them of his willingness to go as the newly appointed governor of the Utah Territory, but only if he had the proper military support, without which it would be sheer folly and madness.

Without making any attempt to confirm the reliability of Drummond's charges, President Buchanan decided to remove Brigham Young from his office as territorial governor and to send an army of twenty-five hundred men to assure the installation of a new governor. This force was as large as General Kearny's Army of the West during the Mexican War a decade earlier. At that same time, President or Governor Young vowed that no hostile army would drive the Saints from their homes again.

Chapter 49

"All violence consists in some people forcing others, under threat of suffering or death, to do what they do not want to." Leo Tolstoy

As the Latter-day Saints settled into their homes and settlements in the valleys, they became more and more proficient with their labors. Farms were irrigated, homes and barns were constructed, families were reared, education was pursued. From an outsider's point of view, everything looked as though it was flourishing. That's not what Brigham Young saw. Similar to every other group of Americans, the members of the church were beginning to fall into diverse temptations and troubles. President Young was determined to slow, if not reverse, this direction, and he began a serious effort to reform the Saints living in the Utah Valley. He began this ecclesiastical effort in 1854 and pushed it for the next several years.

A member of the Quorum of Twelve Apostles, Parley Parker Pratt was a talented and committed man. Born in 1807, Pratt was an early convert to the Church of Jesus Christ of Latter-day Saints, soon after coming upon a copy of the Book of Mormon in August 1830.

Pratt recounted: *"As I opened it with eagerness and read its title page. I then read the testimony of several witnesses in relation to the manner of its being found and translated. After this, I commenced its contents by course. I read all day; eating was a burden, I had no desire for food; sleep was a burden when the night came, for I preferred reading to sleep.*

"As I read, the spirit of the Lord was upon me, and I knew and comprehended that the book was true, as plainly and manifestly as a man comprehends and knows that he exists. My joy was now full, as it were, and I rejoiced sufficiently to more than pay me for all the sorrows, sacrifices, and toils of my life. I soon determined to see the young man who had been the instrument of its discovery and translation."

He visited the town of Palmyra, New York looking for Joseph Smith but found that he then lived in Pennsylvania, but the person who told him this happened to be Hyrum Smith, Joseph's brother. Parley spent the day visiting with him and then moved on. He later came across Oliver Cowdery, who baptized and confirmed him into the church. He was also ordained into the priesthood. The previous itinerant preacher was transformed into a missionary for the church.

Pratt became a powerful instrument for the expansion of the church. He served numerous missions, preaching the gospel, sharing his convictions with multitudes. Parley followed the Prophet Joseph Smith from New York to Ohio to Missouri and then to Illinois. He traveled across the Atlantic and preached in Britain and was a mission president there. After the death of Joseph in June 1844, Pratt and the other members of the Twelve left Nauvoo and crossed Iowa in preparation for their trek into the valley of the Great Salt Lake in 1847. Being the senior member of the quorum, Brigham Young was set apart as the president and prophet of the church that same year.

Life in the desolate wilderness was difficult but it did not distract men like Pratt, who felt the continuing need to spread the gospel to the four quarters of the earth. Missionary work grew and converts continued to follow the lead of the earlier pioneers and they flocked across the plains and through the canyons of the Rocky Mountains to find additional assignments with the Saints in Deseret.

With his wife, Parley embarked on a huge missionary voyage around South America, gathering information about the lands and peoples and languages that would serve the leadership of the church as the work progressed forward. When plural marriage was pronounced to the world in 1852, Pratt became one of its greatest defenders, looking for and delighting in the chance to spread its tenets to one and all through debate or over the pulpit or by the written word.

He never lost sight of the message of the Book of Mormon. "*I esteemed the book, or the information contained in it, more than all the riches of the world. Yes; I verily believe that I would not at that time have exchanged the knowledge I then possessed, for a legal title to all the beautiful farms, houses, villages, and property which passed in review before me, on my journey through one of the most flourishing settlements of western New York.*"

Pratt spent almost a year in San Francisco and Santa Clara in 1854, his second mission in the area, leaving for Salt Lake City in June 1855, crossing over the Sierras to Carson Valley. In California this final time, he had made the acquaintance of Eleanor McLean, the 37-year-old wife of Hector McLean. They had been married in 1841 and had three children but because of alcohol and his violence towards her, the marriage was extremely precarious. The family had relocated shortly before from Louisiana to the goldfields of California but the stress of work and the free access to the bottle did not help. Looking around for something different, they went to some meetings with the Mormons. Eleanor was convicted of the position, while her husband rejected everything they taught. After a long time of badgering, Hector gave in and presented her with his written approval to be baptized, May 24, 1854. She became an active member of the church. Sometime after his arrival, Pratt attempted to counsel Hector to mend the marriage, but McLean resented the efforts of a polygamist to help his relationship. McLean finally put their children onto a steamer and sent them to stay with their Presbyterian McComb grandparents in New Orleans, without informing Eleanor. He then threatened her to desist her activity with the church or he would have her committed to an insane asylum. Their marriage imploded and two weeks after the sailing of her children, Eleanor followed on another steamer to Nicaragua. A stagecoach ride took her to Lake Managua and from there, a boat along the San Juan River drained into the Caribbean, where she picked up another steamer. Her marriage to Hector was shattered. Arriving at her folks' place, she was happy to see her children but after unsuccessfully trying to find a way to extricate them from their grandparents, Eleanor left them there and traveled alone to Salt Lake City. She was married to Parley Pratt in November 1855 by Brigham Young.

After arriving home from California, Pratt served several small missions around the territory for President Young, encouraging the reformation of the members. He especially encouraged the young men and women to resort to the Endowment House to make their covenants with the Lord.

Parley was finally called on a mission to the Eastern States, leaving on September 11, 1856, with some other missionaries. He took Eleanor with him. On October 17th they reached Fort Kearney where they learned of the death of Almon Babbitt. After a long two-month journey, they arrived in St. Louis in the middle of November. From there, he took a rail to Cincinnati and on to Philadelphia, arriving December 24th and later to New York, arriving December 31st.

Eleanor returned to her home in New Orleans to be with her children and tried to work out a plan to take them with her to Deseret. She found there her two youngest, but her oldest son had been sent to a boarding school in Ohio. She was unable to convince her father to let them leave, but when he permitted them to go shopping, she disappeared with them.

Parley spent his time writing for *The Mormon* and preaching throughout the region with a fellow apostle, John Taylor. According to his writings, it was a melancholy trip for Parley. He missed his family greatly and wanted to return home soon. After welcoming a shipload of Saints to the States, Parley made his way to western Pennsylvania, where he stayed for a week with his youngest brother, Nelson, and family, not having seen them for 21 years. He then continued to St. Louis, arriving on February 25th. He was sick for a week but after he convalesced, he began working again with the Saints in the area.

Pratt had never had access to many resources and his constant traveling prevented him from acquiring much wealth. For the majority of his life, he depended on the charity of friends and hearers for his support. As a result, he was not well fed and dressed in tattered clothing. In his writings, he wished he had been blessed more abundantly. Other church leaders were much better off than he and his family, something he regretted at times. On the other hand, he exulted that he should be in the same company as many of the other disciples of Christ.

His brother Orson, another mendicant for the faith, was serving a mission in Liverpool, England.

"I feel lonesome, but I am reconciled to my fate—that of a poor wanderer. I have ceased to anticipate anything better in this life and I try to think of myself well off as I have any reason to expect."

In December 1856, the New Orleans Bulletin published a story called "Sad Story of Mormonism—The Mother and Children," and although it did not print names, it soon became widely known who the players were. Eleanor and her children were finally able to book passage from New Orleans and travel to Houston. From there, she made her way north, hoping to meet a wagon train of Saints bound for the territory.

Pratt's rejoinder was published in The Mormon, detailing his thoughts about his relationship with Eleanor and Hector. He titled the article "Sad Story of Presbyterianism: The Mother and Children". Rather than blaming the breakup of the family on Mormonism, he pointed to the religious intolerance of her family, coupled with abuse and alcohol.

Hector McLean was incensed by the idea of being turned into a cuckold by Parley Pratt and left California to follow Eleanor. He became a man obsessed with the destruction of Pratt, not to recoup his relationship with Eleanor, but merely to assert his manliness. Following leads printed by the newspapers, he ascertained that Pratt was in St. Louis. On his part, Parley did his best to put the relationship into context, to no avail. The national understanding was that the Mormon leaders were unscrupulous, seducers, hypnotists who took advantage of their simple flock. Despite her intellect, Eleanor was grouped into the latter. No one in their right mind would fall to the machinations of such an abominable cult, meaning she was ripe for the insane asylum. The police were alerted, along with soldiers and McLean's Masonic brethren and all began searching for the fugitive.

Pratt slipped out of St. Louis and headed south, having a letter of introduction for Erastus Snow in the city, he found a twenty-six-year-old missionary named George Higginson. Pratt sent Eleanor a letter informing her of a Texas wagon train that would be traveling to Deseret and that he wanted to meet up with her. The letter was intercepted by McLean and he sent lawmen after Pratt, claiming him to be an adulterer.

With US deputy marshal Shivers, McLean caught Eleanor in a wagon driven by non-Mormons, while in Creek territory, taking her to Nebraska. He grabbed twelve-year-old Albert and nine-year-old Ann and throwing them onto their horses in front of the saddles and galloped away. Three hours later Shivers returned and arrested Eleanor on the charge of stealing the children's clothing, valued at $10. McLean boasted that he had taken the children by force and that Eleanor would be taken to Van Buren the next day.

McLean persuaded an officer at Fort Gibson to follow two men who had been seen crossing the Arkansas River. The army patrol of eleven men headed by Captain Henry Little caught Pratt and Higginson, arrested them, and took them to Fort Gibson to be transported the following day to Van Buren.

The next morning the three prisoners, Eleanor, George Higginson, and Parley Pratt left the Indian Territory, crossed the Arkansas River, and continued the two-day, forty-mile trip to Van Buren. Eleanor was bruised and weak from her battle with Hector the previous day. She rode in a carriage driven by some soldiers, while Pratt and Higginson, walked being chained together.

Deputy Shivers told Eleanor, "McLean is determined to kill Pratt but will not do it while he is a prisoner! I told Captain Little and he reassured me that will not happen while Pratt is his prisoner."

Upon arriving in Van Buren, Shivers released Higginson, took Pratt to jail, and then escorted Eleanor to see Judge John Ogden, where he interviewed her in the presence of some lawyers. After his questions, Judge Ogden was convinced of Eleanor's innocence and incensed with the conduct of her husband, Hector McLean. Ogden detested the Scotsman's abusive behavior and his love of alcohol and the effects it had on the family. Afterward, the lawyers also were interested in the status of women in Utah.

"Are there not many discontented women there?" one asked.

She replied, "Yes, but I do not believe there are quite as many as there are here."

McLean ranted outside of the courthouse, demanding that Pratt be held responsible for the unraveling of his marriage and family, being cheered on by his supporters.

The district attorney wanted to drop the charges against Eleanor if she would be a witness for him against Pratt. She acknowledged that she was in their power and would be truthful in her answers.

The hearing was held the following morning. Like many such events on the frontier, this was a high point for many during their work-a-day lives. More than 500 spectators showed up to see the unfolding of the hearing. Not only were they excited to see McLean's wife, but she was also a living example of a polygamous wife from the Utah Territory.

Ogden dropped the charges against Eleanor and had her leave the courtroom. It was the final time she saw Parley. She described him as being weary but not sad. The judge postponed the hearing until the next day, wanting to give all the defense witnesses a chance to arrive.

That night, Judge Ogden called McLean into his office where he told him there would be no violence enacted upon Pratt, encouraging him and his supporters to leave the man alone.

McLean replied that he also didn't want anyone to touch Pratt. "That's a privilege I want to reserve for myself."

Ogden kept McLean in his office until 2:00 a.m., thinking that by the time he left, McLean would go to sleep. The judge then brought Pratt in secretly to release him very early in the morning. He also tried to give Pratt his revolver and knife for protection, which Parley refused. He believed God would be more than enough to protect him in his flight.

McLean's friends were keeping an all-night vigil on the courthouse and alerted McLean as soon as Parley mounted his horse. The race was on. At first, Pratt was able to elude some of his pursuers, but they soon caught up with him. McLean fired all the bullets from his pistol, hitting the saddle and five balls passing through Pratt's coat. McLean then chased him into a thicket of trees where he pulled the Mormon from his horse and stabbed him three times with his bowie knife, then left him to bleed out. Ten minutes later, Hector returned to check on his deed and found that Pratt was still alive, so he shot him point-blank in the neck with a derringer. From there McLean and his cohorts rode away while the people in the neighborhood began coming out of their houses to see what had happened. They found Parley still alive. He denied their desire to call for a doctor, telling them that he was through and asking for a drink of water. It was provided and he quietly closed his eyes as if going to sleep and passed away.

It did not take long for the news to blare across the region that Pratt had been killed by Hector McLean, but since there were no eyewitnesses, he was never charged, regardless of his bragging. The report was simply that Pratt had been killed by an unknown assailant. Jubilation erupted from the towns and cities nearby and these cheers grew slowly across the nation. The vaunted Mormon Apostle had met his Maker.

One paper exulted: *One Mormon Less! Nine More Widows! Alas for the Mormon Prophet! If thou hast power to raise the dead, Parley, raise thyself!*

Juxtaposed to this was what one observer of Pratt's death said the apostle stated at the very end of his life: "I die a firm believer in the Gospel of Jesus Christ as revealed through the Prophet Joseph Smith, and I wish you to carry this my dying testimony. I know that the Gospel is true and that Joseph Smith was a prophet of the Living God. I am dying a martyr to the faith."

The brutality of the attack and the finality of its effect on Eleanor numbed all in the area. The excitement of the day before was forgotten. The people regretted their role in the drama. Eleanor, the bereaved widow took the time to write a detailed account of what she had been through, illustrating to one and all how sharp her mind and intellect remained, not a candidate for any asylum.

Eleanor took the time to pen a thoughtful, literate cataloging and response to the tragedy, sending it to the Arkansas Intelligencer in Van Buren. It was dated 22 May 1857. Signing off:

E.J. McComb
Once E.J. McLean

Several days later Eleanor found some people who took her north to Independence, Missouri where she encountered Porter Rockwell carrying mail for the YX Carriers and he agreed to see that she was safely returned to the Salt Lake Valley.

Brigham Young wrote to Orson Pratt: "One more good man has gone to assist brothers Joseph and Hyrum…in another sphere."

Hosea Stout wrote: *Tuesday, 23 June 1857, Eastern mail came in today at 2 pm. All was peaceable on the road.*

The newspaper writers were louder against the Mormons than ever, whether the government will take notice of the excitement or not is not known.

Accounts are current in the papers that Elder Parley P. Pratt had been assassinated some eight miles from Van Buren, Arkansas by one Hector H. McLean, that he was shot and lived some two hrs. The truth is not known.

The Utah War

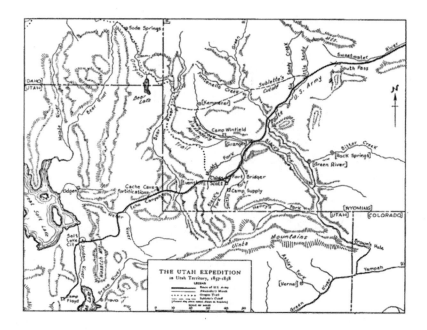

Chapter 50

"War is so unjust and ugly that all who wage it must try to stifle the voice of conscience within themselves." Leo Tolstoy

President James Buchanan was sworn into office, 3 March 1857. As a Democrat, he did not want his party upstaged by the Republicans whose platform included the destruction of those twin relics of barbarism, slavery, and polygamy. While his party was severely divided over slavery, including himself, polygamy was an easy scapegoat. Now with the resignation of the Honorable Judge W.W. Drummond and his insistence upon using the newspapers to hammer his anti-polygamy point home, President Buchanan thought this to be a safe and prudent position to assume at the beginning of his administration. He ordered General William S. Harney to leave Fort Leavenworth in a timely fashion and march to the Utah Territory, there to replace the renegade governor, Brigham Young, and then to quell any talk of secession from the Union by the Mormons.

His Attorney General, Jeremiah Black, wasn't as certain about the accusations. "I think more thought needs to go into this," he counseled. "There are always differing sides to an argument." Black was a self-educated man who was admitted to the bar when he was 21 years old.

Buchanan wouldn't budge. "You are listening to your friends from Pennsylvania. Judge Kane's boy, Tom, has long been an advocate for these religious miscreants. Has he been feeding you the story?"

"And what if he has? Would it be so foolish to collect all the information before sending an army off into the west to fight with the Mormons and drive them once again?"

"I have already issued the orders. General Harney will be on his way."

"Leading 2500 pro-slavery troops! This will not sit well with Brigham Young and his people. Have you at least warned Young, alerted him of your intentions?"

President James Buchanan was wearying of the debate. "I am a busy man. I have more than enough on my plate, thanks to President Pierce. This nation is tottering on the brink. A decisive show of force would not be a bad thing. Corralling that upstart Brigham Young would go a long way to settling some issues."

Black threw his hands in the air. "Yes, you are the president. Yes, you have several challenges to start your administration. Yes, John and Tom Kane are friends of mine and Tom has a well-known association with the Mormon people. He is sending me missives, almost daily, of Drummond's accusations and claims. My position is that it would be much better for you to investigate some of these claims further before committing men and money to stomp out a perceived threat, especially when the only information you possess has come from Bill Drummond."

Buchanan thought for a moment, then smacked his lips. "The troops are on their way, disorganized as usual. It should take them a while to get moving. General Harney has a mixed reputation for having beaten that slave woman to death with his cane."

"Hannah."

"Whatever. It was a long time ago. I'm also aware somewhat of his infidelities. Maybe these wouldn't be the premium traits wanted for the leader of the expedition." He paused to underscore his attempt at a serious reflection. "I'll have Harney return to Leavenworth and deal with Bloody Kansas. Maybe I'll replace him with General Lee or Colonel Johnston. Will that get you off my back?"

"They're both southerners."

"My God, Jeremiah! There's no pleasing you! That's as far as I'm going to go."

"As you wish, Jim. But I will also continue to make sure you are kept up to date with the rantings of Judge Drummond. His words are poisoning the waters. I would hate for you to be pulled into the same popular uproar without a decent explanation. The Mormons are good at collecting disparaging comments directed at them and they're sending them along to Dr. Bernhisel and Colonel Kane. He sends them to me. I will insist that the information at least makes its way onto your desk. From there, the ball will be in your court. But I never want you to think that I haven't had your best interests at heart."

Buchanan nodded his assent and dismissed his attorney general. A headache was coming on. It was barely the start of his term as president, and he was already battling a series of problems. Millard Fillmore had appointed Brigham Young the governor of the fledgling territory. The appointment had proceeded well over the next years. The Mormons listened to and obeyed the directives of their church president, a man they also believed to be a prophet. Management of the territory required little attention. Then Young's term had come to an end and President Pierce chose to kick the can down the street and allow the incoming administration of Buchanan's to handle the change. And just what was President Pierce thinking when he sent Judge Drummond to the Utah Territory? Drummond was no more than an unsympathetic, carpetbagging appointee. Didn't he know how volatile the place was becoming? Of course, he did. And that's why he followed through with his selection of Drummond, sending him, and then refusing to remove Brigham Young as the governor, leaving all of this to be handled by the incoming administration. It's no wonder Pierce didn't care for another term.

Delegates from the Utah Territory were energized about the possibility of the statehood of Deseret. With the Compromise of 1850 and the Nebraska-Kansas Act, sovereignty was elevated, and the Republican Party turned it into an issue. As one of the authors for the Act, Stephen Douglas saw the writing on the wall. He slammed the Mormons for pushing for statehood so they could use the new status as an invincible shield to protect their crime, debauchery, and infamy.

A politician from Illinois, Douglas was no stranger to the Mormons. He had a front-row seat in Springfield, watching the meteoric rise of the city of Nauvoo on the Mississippi and the national fascination with the personality of Joseph Smith in the early 1840s. Judge Douglas had a close association with the Mormons in Hancock County, the most populous in the state. It was also common knowledge that the members of the church tended to vote in blocks according to how the politicians treated the Mormons. It was a volatile time. Nauvoo turned into a boomtown because of the influx of members from the eastern states as well as Britain. Stephen Douglas was keeping a close eye on things, watching which way the wind was blowing.

In May 1843 he had a meeting with Joseph Smith when the charismatic leader made a well-publicized pronouncement concerning Stephen Douglas. He said: "Judge, you will aspire to the presidency of the United States; and if ever you turn your hand against me or the Latter-day Saints, you will feel the weight of the hand of the Almighty upon you; and you will live to see and know that I have testified the truth to you; for the conversation of this day will stick to you through life."

Smith's comments unnerved him and many more throughout the state. In 1844, after querying a number of the presidential candidates and not receiving any responses that he approved of, Joseph Smith threw his hat into the ring as a candidate for the presidency. He was killed by a mob in Carthage, Illinois that summer. His opponents were not worried about Smith's chances at the White House in 1844, but they knew things would look much different, his chances would be better should he decide to run again four years later.

Fortunately for the political structure wanting to maintain the status quo, he was killed, stopping the immediate threat. From there, the pressure was again exerted upon the Mormon people, once it was determined that they were not going quietly into the night. The vast majority of Saints coalesced behind Brigham Young and the rest of the Quorum of the Twelve. The Nauvoo Temple was completed and for six weeks they crowded into its sacred space, making covenants with God. The Saints in Nauvoo were allowed to be driven from the confines of the United States, denied of Constitutional redress, forced to cross the Mississippi and into the Iowa Territory where they made their way across its southern borders to the banks of the Missouri and Winter's Quarters.

The next ten years saw them trek across the plains and mountains to settle in the valley of the Great Salt Lake. They built up a powerful city and colonized many more towns throughout the Great Basin. Being so far away from the workings of Washington DC, they were granted little quarter, politically.

But Brigham Young was not through. He inserted his delegates into the capital. He used newspapers to raise their issues. He pounded the conscience of the American people for making the Mormons into refugees and promised that the nation would reap the whirlwind as a result of the multiple drivings of the Saints.

By this time, Stephen Douglas had matured. He well knew the intricacies of the workings in Washington. He had vested his life and reputation and he resented this rag-tag group of sectarian zealots living in the deserts of the west, for their threats and demeanor, their clamoring for attention and rights.

In June he addressed the folks in Springfield, Illinois about the trial and threats posed by numerous enemies. And he took particular delight slamming the Mormons and their bid for equality. *"The knife must be applied to this pestiferous, disgusting cancer which is gnawing into the very vitals of the body politic. It must be cut out by the roots and seared over by the red-hot iron of stern and unflinching law...Repeal the organic law of the Territory, on the ground that they are alien enemies and outlaws, unfit to be citizens of a Territory, much less to ever become citizens of one of the free and independent States of this confederacy."*

The Mormon publication in Salt Lake City, the Deseret News, reported the rant as well as the fourteen-year-old prophecy of Joseph Smith regarding Judge Douglas, causing many people to sit up and take notice. But it would require more than that to energize the halls of Washington on their behalf.

Rumors of the US Army contingent leaving Fort Leavenworth for the Utah Territory reached Porter Rockwell when he reached Fort Laramie. Leaving the main party to continue driving their livestock west, Rockwell and two other men hitched two of the fastest span of horses from the YX corrals to a light buggy and took off to warn Brigham of the threat. Salt Lake City lay 513 miles to the west, but Rockwell knew how best to handle the horses, pushing them to maintain an average of 100 miles per day. They drove in record time, arriving in Salt Lake on July 23rd but found the city empty. Most of the inhabitants had trekked up the Big Cottonwood Canyon to Silver Lake, where they were celebrating the tenth year of their arrival in the valley.

For the Silvas and the Wetoyous, this was a long-anticipated day. They had planned for the trip carefully. The Hansens were going to the celebration a day earlier but had allowed their two oldest boys to stay home to look after their animals and also those belonging to Shep Silva. For them, getting together with friends was always a treat but at their ages, the lure of money edged out the longing for immediate fun.

Aaron and Yasmin were awaiting their friends on the mountain top.

"You made it in good time," Aaron said, pleased to see Silva and his troop finally pull out of the long string of wagons.

"I'm glad you decided not to travel back to the States this year."

"Me too. It would have been bad timing," he said, pointing at Yasmin's distended stomach.

"How is she feeling?"

"Oh, much better now that she sees Harriett. Riding in a wagon nowadays doesn't make her feel very perky. Why don't you guys come to the city for a visit? It would please us all. And bring the Wetoyous."

Tables were quickly set up and covered with cloths. Blankets were also scattered around the grounds. It was a beautiful summer day, and all seemed happy to have made the effort to come. Church leaders had arrived and were busy threading through the throng, shaking hands and renewing acquaintances. Brigham's new second counselor after the death of Jedediah Grant was Daniel Wells, a well-known defender of the Saints. The party was a leisurely affair. Lunch was enjoyed and folks visited, and children raced around the oldsters in games of tag.

Impromptu speeches were made. The company was a close-knit group, with many having roots that extended far back into the past.

Brigham had the chance to welcome all. "We've come from near and far. This is a very important anniversary for us. Years ago, I made the promise that if our enemies would leave us alone for just ten years, we would never again be driven from our homes. Leaving New York, Ohio, Missouri, and Illinois was troubling and difficult. Old Scratch was happy to see us go. But now we have settled in these fair mountain valleys and are becoming a substantial people. We have grown and become strengthened. God has blessed us beyond our capacities. Even now, we are changing into a force to be reckoned with."

His remarks were met with cheers and applause. Other leaders confirmed Young's position as a prophet.

Shep noticed the arrival of another carriage, whose horses were drawn and tired. It moved quickly to Brigham's tent and the driver hopped out and invited President Young and his counselors inside.

"Did you see that?" he asked the other three. They hadn't. "It was Porter just got in. I heard he'd been out to collect mail from the East. Seems like he has some important information for the Prophet."

The information quieted their reveling. A minute later a breathless boy showed up at Shep's side. "President Young wants to see you right away."

Arriving at the tent door, Silva was immediately ushered inside.

Porter was sitting on a stool whittling. He looked up. "Deputy Silva," he said, "we got some serious troubles."

Brigham arose and walked to Shep, placing both hands upon his shoulders. "I need you to get back to your home and get two of your best horses, and ride to the Carson Valley and then down to San Bernardino. I have a couple letters for you to deliver, calling the folks back to Salt Lake, the sooner, the better, until we can figure out what we're going to do. President Buchanan has believed Judge Drummond's reports and he's sent an army out to quell any rebellion on our part. Can you do that for us?"

"Yes, sir. Quicker than Crockett could skin a raccoon."

Brigham smiled hearing the folksy phrase coming with the Brazilian accent. "The quicker, the better, my boy."

"Yes, sir."

Fifteen minutes later Shep had shared the news with Harriett and the Rosts, along with his calling. He borrowed a horse and was soon winding his way down the canyon, nonchalantly waving and smiling at the latecomers in their wagons, traveling the opposite direction. His heart was beating fast as he anticipated the long trip that lay before him.

Chapter 51

"Nurture your mind with great thoughts." Benjamin Disraeli

22 July 1857

My Dear Joseph,

I have heard from Elder Lyman that your mission may be coming to an end. I am so happy! It seems like it has been forever since you were here. I have been curious if you might be bringing home one of the native girls? I understand they are quite attractive. Certainly, the people of Hawaii will miss you tremendously once you come home.

Have you been called to do work other than preaching? Are you called upon to build houses or do landscaping or maybe even bookwork? I just think it would be a good experience for you to expand your abilities. My special friend Robert Carsley has made a name for himself as an ironmonger, although that really is not how he would like to spend his time. He's from the New England area and spent his time growing up on boats as a fisherman. Sometimes I think he misses the cold Atlantic and the rocky shores. He really is a good man, Joseph. He pays attention to me and the things I enjoy doing. He keeps himself clean, always washing up after work. I think he might be losing some of his hair.

Here on the mainland things are fine, maybe a little too hot. Charlotte has been traveling back and forth to San Francisco. There are good opportunities for her to work, either there or in Los Angeles, more than here in San Bernardino. As it gets so hot, I wonder how you are. Do the ocean currents keep you cool most of the time?

Ma and Pa are good. Business still keeps Pa away from home. The twins continue to grow. They keep very busy. It is a good thing they have one another.

As you prepare to come home, I am curious about your plans. I guess you will want to go back to Great Salt Lake City. I know there are many opportunities for hard-working young men here and in Los Angeles and San Francisco. You would be able to make decent money. There are not as many young women in California, but more are arriving daily. I know you would be able to find just the right person if you gave it a chance. Perhaps we could even be neighbors. I miss you very much. I know the church means a lot to you. How could it not, with you spending your whole lie teaching it? I love you and will do anything in my power to help you. My family will as well.

We Miss Thee at Home

We miss thee at home—we miss thee,

Through the long, weary hours of the day;
And wonder how long, as a pilgrim,
In a far distant land thou wilt stray.
How long, ere thy wanderings are ended—
How long art thou fated to roam—
To the land of thy birth a stranger,
Far away, from the loved ones at home?
We miss thee at home, when the shadows
Of evening are hovering nigh;
When the morn, in her majesty, rises
To her home in the star-spangled sky.

Then we dream of the loved ones departed;—
Of the friends we may never see more;—
And sigh o'er the pleasure now faded—
And the joys time can never restore.
We miss thee at home—we miss thee,
"At morning—at noon—and at night;"
And ever to thee, dearest cousin,
Fond memory taketh its flight.

Thy seat at the fire-side is vacant—
Oh! haste, o'er the oceans dark foam,
To the hearts that are mourning thy absence,
To the loved ones, who miss thee at home!

I love you with all my heart. Sometimes when I am visiting Los Angeles, I look out across the ocean and think about you, wishing and wondering the next ship might be bringing you home.

Love, always,
Ina

1 Sep 1857

Dear Ina,
   It's summer-time here on the islands. I believe that means it doesn't rain as often. I am doing better every day with the language. At least now the Hawaiians don't laugh at me as often. They never mean to be rude or hurtful, but I must admit that I have butchered their beautiful tongue more than I care to. My favorite is poi and laulau. I didn't like it at first but I have really grown to love it. They are also very good at cooking pig. They dig a deep pit and put the whole carcass of the animal in and them cover it up and build a fire on top. They know just when to put the fire out and they bring the pig out of the ground

397

and cut the meat into very tasty pieces. I have always liked pork but now it has become a real contest between some of the pork and some of the fish.

I think my time here in the Sandwich Islands is drawing to a close. That is what the mission pres says. The members here also think the same way. I have learned so much. I love it here and the people are easily the best on earth.

You have desisted in sharing your deepest concerns and worries until this past letter when you questioned my motives. I was surprised, to say the least. But I need to tell you that what I am involved in is the work of God. Do you not know that Mormonism is the foundation upon which I have built? The life of my soul, the sweetest morsel of my existence, the height of my pride and ambition? it is!...hear it ye worlds!—I KNOW IT IS TRUE!

I have seen the teachings of the gospel change people's lives.

I will do my best to alert you about my release from the mission and when I might expect to arrive in California. Because it will probably be winter, I think I will return to Deseret by traveling through San Bernardino. I want to see you and your family. I am so blessed to know you and to have the ties that bind us.

I love you too, sweet Ina.

Joseph

Chapter 52

"How very little can be done under the spirit of fear." Florence Nightingale

"There's no getting around the fact that the Mormons have done a good job here in Great Salt Lake City," Pleasant Tackitt said matter of factly as their train of wagons moved from the mouth of Emigration Canyon. "They really have made the desert blossom like a rose."

"It doesn't make things any easier for us," Captain Baker said.

The Fancher-Baker wagon train had left northern Arkansas in April. They had a hodge-podge organization. Some people joined the train wanting to permanently settle in California, while others were wanting to work the goldfields. Some people simply wanted to sell their livestock in the new state, while others were looking for adventure. The base of the wagon train was solid, financed carefully by the seasoned expedition, Alexander Fancher, and then managed by the leadership of 52-year-old Captain John Baker. Still, crossing the plains and then the mountains had diminished their supplies substantially, leaving them with only 800 head of cattle upon reaching the Great Salt Lake City the first of August 1857. Concerns regarding their direction and the lateness of the year raised doubts in many people's minds, with some opting to leave the train and instead of traveling on the Old Spanish Trail going south into California, others chose to take the northern route or even venture into Oregon Territory. These defections whittled the wagon train down substantially from more than 200 until they had fewer than 150 people.

Baker to thought things would be all right, contingent upon their being able to purchase supplies from the Mormons. Unfortunately, things were tense for the Mormons. The rumors had gotten out regarding US Army soldiers who were heading to the territory, intent upon removing Governor Young and replacing him with someone of President Buchanan's choosing. *With the uncertainty came the worry of how things would play out. Would there be a confrontation? Would blood be spilled? Would Governor Young go away quietly? Would the Mormon people stay put? And if they chose to leave, where would they go?*

Tensions between the Fancher emigrants and the settlers in the Utah Territory grew as needed supplies were not forthcoming. The emigrants offered to pay handsomely in an attempt to rebuild their depleted supplies. They were angered when the Mormons refused to help.

"We'll have plenty of water while we're around the city," Baker counseled his train leaders. "In the meantime, we will just have to keep asking for help to buy the things we need. I feel a lot of war hysteria right now among these people but maybe as we move farther south, we will be more successful."

"Folks are sure giving us the evil eye," one of the men said. "Not too trusting."

"How would you feel," Baker asked, "if the government sent troops to take over your land without any explanation? Regardless of our feelings towards the Mormons, we need to keep a tight rein on our tongues. Folks in these parts are worried and they're suspicious. Us speaking foolishly, threatening to bring more troops to attack them from California, to pay them back for the way we think they've mistreated us, won't do any of us any good."

His 7-year-old granddaughter, Mary, hopped from her wagon and scurried to find her older friends, Mary and Thomas Fancher. It had been determined that the two families would be following the same intentions once they reached California. Trading the broad-leafed forests of the Ozarks for the bleak desolation of the desert valleys did not seem to be a good choice. Not now. But the other members of the train promised that California was greener and more fertile than Arkansas ever was. And there was plenty of water where they were going.

Mary Fancher pulled the Baker girl into her lap and began to inspect the braids in her golden hair, while her 14-year-old brother Thomas was scoping out the city by looking through a hollow reed as if it were a telescope.

"Plenty of folks hereabouts," he said.

"I wish we could get some food," Mary added, noting how clean her little friend had kept her hair. "I'm tired of fried bread and salted beef."

"Ma tells me that in California, fruits of every kind grow. And they grow all year round!" The little Mary's excitement made the Fancher's smile. And what if it was true? How sweet would that be? Snow was never a problem along the beaches of the state, of course, if one missed the weather, the mountains were never too far away. The Indians sounded peaceful and the hunting was plentiful. No, California had been wisely selected by their families. It would do just fine.

Disappointment greeted the Fancher-Baker wagon train at every turn. Supplies were hard to find. The Mormons stayed tight-fisted as well as tight-lipped. Talk of an impending invasion did not please them in the slightest. Frustration was building in the Fancher train as well, watching their stores continue to dwindle. Then, if anything, the people living farther away from Salt Lake City and Provo were even more hostile with them.

The Indians began to steal their cattle. It was maddening because several times Indians had approached the train begging for food or wanting to trade. Both sides had precious little. Moving slowly south, they began to encounter Indians who were more brazen and threatening towards their herds of cattle and horses. They knew that a precarious balance between the Mormons and the Indians existed for several years. They didn't care to upset that balance. Then again, these Indians were poor. They didn't remind them of the stronger, bigger tribes of the plains. The Fancher-Baker party decided these could be quite deadly, as well.

"Now, I'm serious warning you about these Indians," Captain Baker remarked in the morning before several men left the encampment to take their turn driving the cattle. "We have no reason to be shooting at the Indians. Just because we can see them doesn't mean they are wanting to steal our cows. If you shoot them, it will only make things worse. And if you hit any with your bullets, or kill any, God forbid, our lives could be much harder before we ever get out of this territory."

Some of the men nodded in agreement, while others chose not to pay attention.

****

Crossing to the Carson Valley was rougher than usual for Shep. Both his horses took turns being obstinate. In the past, he had been able to trust his backup horse to follow without being led every step of the way. Not this time. Both animals refused to walk gently, insisting instead on tugging Shep's rope around their neck and wanting to take a different trail. Also, it was late in the year and the springs were dry. Water was harder to come by than normal. He was thankful he only had to worry about himself and the two horses. The grass and brush were burned brown by the sun, becoming crunchy under the hooves. The ground was hard and unforgiving.

He made the trip frequently enough to know what range of mountains were next, needing to be climbed or circumvented. Here again, they seemed higher and drier and less forgiving. Both his mounts took turns having sore feet. Shep did his best to cover as much ground as possible early in the morning or in the afternoon, taking time off during the heat of the day to shade up.

Constantly scanning the ridges and dry river beds, Shep kept an eye out for marauding natives. They were the last ones he needed to stand in his way, keeping him or diverting him from the most direct way he could survey across the dusty expanse.

Day after day he surged forward. Rattlesnakes were most bothersome during the mid-days. He avoided them deftly. Several times he came across herds of antelopes or even mountain sheep as he clambered up steep slopes.

His breathing became less labored when he finally caught sight of the distant Sierras. All the snow had melted. They stood as immovable barriers between him and the lush pastures of California on the far side. Now solitary cabins began to spring up more and more. Immigration was taking its toll on the barren vastness of the desert.

The Carson River had shrunken to a tickle, nevertheless one that both he and his horses were happy to encounter. Like most of the western rivers, this one snaked in erratic twists and turns. Shep took advantage of this, riding up and over the surrounding hills, avoiding the thickets of willows and treacherous stretches of mud.

Fences marked the settlers' claims to swaths of land, usually the most fertile and watered. Cows became more visible and numerous. They weren't as skinny and poor appearing as the couple he had come across during his trek. These were alert, watching him pass but strong and confident that they belonged in their pasture.

"Shep!" Orson Hyde yelled, waving at the tired, dusty rider as he approached the well-laid-out ranch at the end of a long lane. The trees planted along the roadside were now several years old and taking good hold in the soil, their trunks swelling with the seasons, their branches providing welcome shade with their abundant leaves. Silva had been spotted miles earlier as the dust from his horse's hooves announced his presence.

Hyde met him before his house and relieved him of his second horse and leading the way to a fresh trough of water.

"You're all by yourself?"

"Yep."

"In a hurry?"

"Yep."

Unsaddling the horses, they took them into the barn for grain and hay.

"I'll have the kids hang your stuff up. You come on in and let us get you something to eat and drink."

"Sounds just right," he answered with a smile, removing his hat and dusting himself off with a series of slaps.

Half an hour later he slowed his appetite and slaked his thirst with another cold cup of water. The drink was more welcome than he could remember.

"You left on the 25th? Damned fast, I say."

"Could have been faster if I wasn't fighting with the horses."

"So Buchanan's sending soldiers our way, huh?"

"Looks like it."

"How many? You know?"

"Not yet."

"Brigham wants us to pack up and head back? To fight or flee?"

"Dunno."

"Drummond's done his job well enough. Getting the whole nation up in arms. I'll call a meeting for tonight. I'll be ready to tell the folks what's going on if that's okay with you?"

Shep nodded.

"Just like Nauvoo all over again. We're getting kicked out and no one will be wanting to pay for our places. Guess we'll just be turning them over again. Has Rost been able to scare up some Sharps carbines for our men?"

"Some. Not enough."

"Cannons?"

"Nope."

"Has Dan Wells activated the Nauvoo Legion?"

This was a standing joke. Giving the militia the name of the Nauvoo Legion, made them sound more formidable. But they weren't. Numbers could be raised but the men and boys were not trained. Brigham threatened to get around to the training and arming of the Legion one day.

Shep smiled and chuckled. "For what it's worth." He snickered again, envisioning some of the antics of these farm boys and hayseeds.

"You'll want to be going to see the Sweeneys?"

"Sooner's better than later. You got a decent nag I can borrow? I'm sick of mine."

It was evening by the time Shep Silva had ridden north, crossing the Carson and Washoe Valleys and rode up to the Sweeney farm in Franktown. With a muffled cry of joy, Linda G hiked up her skirt and ran to him, laughing and crying. She dragged him from the saddle, smothering his face with kisses and tears. Shep smiled and sighed happily. This was more than worth the days spent in the saddle. Linda G looked good and was quite strong. The rest of the family appeared and gathered around the rider, shaking his hand and pounding his back, or shyly smiling and bowing. A beautiful family, indeed.

Shep decided to wait until he could discuss the situation alone with Mark after the family had tired of the novelty of his arrival and wandered back to their chores. Linda G Wetoyou was the last to leave.

"Holy smokes. Linda G gets prettier every time I see her."

Mark nodded. "She's got suitors all lined up. Mormons and Gentiles. She's a real catch. And she helps around here more than any of the other kids."

"Think she'll be ready to leave?"

"I'll tell you what. That little Sarah Winnemucca has adopted her as her big sister. She'll be the one that will have the real struggle."

"Wish it didn't have to be this way but you'll need to clear out."

"It's gonna come down to that, huh? We got time to sell our property?"

"Probably not. Hyde's holding a meeting in Genoa tonight. I left a letter with him from Brig. He's wanting folks back to the valley as soon as possible."

"Dammit."

The men sat quietly, mulling their thoughts. A movement at the corner of the parlor caught their eyes. It was Linda G.

"I just wanted to ask Shep about my brothers," she apologized.

The Brazilian smiled. "Both doing great. Missing you something awful."

Mark arose and offered his place to the young woman. "I'm going to talk with Martha. Why don't you two visit?"

"Just right, thanks," Shep replied, then stood to hug Linda G.

Brigham Young's request that the Saints return to the Great Salt Lake valley came as a surprise as well as at an inopportune time. Money was scarce and the Gentiles who had any were not too keen on separating themselves from it. Working closely together, the Mormons had built a series of well-designed farms and pastures. Their fences were solid and straight. They also constructed a sturdy grist mill that made a landmark and blessed the lives of all along the eastern side of the Sierras. True to Orson Hyde's predictions, the non-Mormons followed in the footsteps of their Illinois brethren and decided to wait for the Saints to leave the valley, then they quickly moved in and took possession of their abandoned holdings.

Before leaving, Judge Hyde somberly warned the Gentiles that if they didn't use the time wisely in raising the money necessary to buy out the Mormons, he would pronounce a devastating curse on the area, one the Lord would be sure to honor.

Two days after he arrived, Shep left Genoa, this time riding hard to the south to meet up with the Saints of the San Bernardino settlement, with a similar letter from Governor Young and the admonition to sell their things, pack up and leave for the Great Salt Lake Valley.

Chapter 53

"The same eye cannot look up to heaven and down to earth." John Brown

On 18 July 1857, soldiers left Fort Leavenworth to fulfill the command of President Buchanan. They were led by Colonel Edmund Alexander and accompanied by a host of teamsters and camp followers, anxious to join in on the spoils of the threatened war. They knew the bedraggled Mormons would be easy pickings. The newspapers were filled with stories of the poor and abused women of polygamy. The might of the US Army would liberate these benighted souls and the heroes would doubtless be showered with the appreciation commensurate to their efforts.

President Buchanan had searched for quite a while before finally settling on Alfred Cumming to be the new governor in the Utah Territory, replacing Brigham Young. He was a solid Democrat who had been the mayor of Atlanta. Cumming was not leaving at this time with the infantry, but planning on joining Lt. Colonel Philip St. George Cooke and his dragoons when they left the fort several weeks later. He would be traveling with his wife, Elizabeth. Also, three rabid federalist judges had thrown their hats into the ring, anxious to put the Mormons straight and get the Utah Territory into shape. Their names were Delana Eckels, John Cradlebaugh, and Charles Sinclair.

Colonel Alexander carried a letter for Brigham Young from General William Harney, demanding that he welcome the troops and accede to the demands of an irate President Buchanan. Harney had intended to march with his troops but violence in Bloody Kansas dissuaded him and the president. Harney also retained Colonel Albert Sydney Johnston with his dragoons, wanting them to control and protect Lecompton from threatened violence from an abolitionist group calling themselves the Army of the North. Once the danger was resolved, Johnston and his cavalry would be riding to join the other soldiers. Johnston would then relieve Alexander of the command.

Governor Brigham Young was incensed. "Twice in Missouri and once in Illinois they drove us from our homes at the point of a bayonet, and that, too, by aid of state authority. They murdered my dear friends Joseph and Hyrum Smith and many others. Mobs robbed and murdered us while the entire nation looked on without lifting one hand to help us. And now the U.S. Army is coming to our homes, a body of troops well-armed and equipped, evidently ordered to Utah by the president of the United States. They're coming without warning. Forgive me Father, if I'm wrong. But this time we will not turn the other cheek! This is our home, our Zion. This time we fight back!"

Brigham Young and the Mormon leaders invited several Indian chiefs to Great Salt Lake City to inform them of the growing storm and to hopefully engage the natives, if not as allies, then at least to keep them from joining the fray.

Seeing the Mormons as having come out in open rebellion against the country, President Buchanan wanted the formidable force to have enough supplies to last 20 months for 8000 men. He intended to establish three different army camps in the territory where they would bivouac about one-third of the nation's soldiers. The preliminary group would number almost 5000, including 2500 soldiers once Albert Johnston was able to quell any abolitionist troubles at Lecompton and follow up with his 1300 dragoons.

The infantry left Leavenworth marching, while their teamsters and herders pushed their livestock to accompany them. The US War Department dispatched Captain Stewart Van Vliet and a small thirty-man escort to chase after Alexander and get Harney's letter and carry it on to Governor Young with all haste. Priority was given to Harney's letter and ordered at the same time to proceed with all haste. Van Vliet's group was mounted or driving light wagons, covering a thousand miles as quickly as possible. Captain Van Vliet caught up with Alexander and his force 275 miles west of Fort Laramie. He explained his mission to Alexander, relieved him of Harney's letter to Young, then continued onward. Twenty miles up the Green River, while he was closing in on the Mormon-owned Fort Bridger, Van Vliet ran into several groups who were leaving the Salt Lake Valley and who warned him of the growing danger he and his men would be facing by riding further towards Salt Lake City. They told him that they were marked men. Also, that elements of the Nauvoo Legion were busy fortifying the long Echo Canyon, turning it into a shooting gallery should any troops try to enter from that direction. It would be a deadly gauntlet.

Jim Bridger was as scruffy and ornery as ever when he was discovered on the road and introduced to the captain. He listened to a quick explanation of Van Vliet's mission. He shook his head seriously. "Big mistake," he warned. "Brig and his boys are ready for what the hell you guys are planning to do. Just where did this order come from? Calling out the army?"

Captain Van Vliet was impressed to be talking to the aging man who was a legend in his own time. "President Buchanan thinks the territory is planning to secede from the Union."

"That's a pile of buffalo chips, my friend. Governor Young can be a turd but he's not out to fight the whole country. He's already got plenty on his plate and that's just not what he wants to do." He seemed to know what he was talking about. Besides that, they had been neighbors for ten years.

Van Vliet was at an impasse. "I've got my orders. What do you think should I do?"

The mountain man's eyes squinted as he grinned. "Go it alone, Captain. Leave your men here and you ride into the city by yourself. That will send a strong enough message to them that what you've got is important and besides that, you're not afraid of them."

406

The more Van Vliet thought it over, the more sense it made. He ordered his men to set up camp outside the thick stone walls of Fort Bridger. He checked to make sure his revolvers and rifle charged and that he was carrying plenty of ammunition, then mounted. He issued a few brief orders and reminded them that he would return shortly, then he left. He thought the 115-mile ride should take him 2 days. It was still late summer and the foliage was thick and green. The rivers were trickling.

Riding through Echo Canyon was eerie. Silent stone walls were pocked with caves. He could see signs of activity but never once saw another person, although he felt like he was being watched the whole way. He breathed much easier once he exited the canyon. It felt like an enclosed, smothering tunnel, a perfect defensive setup.

****

Shep rode the switchbacks from the southern Sierras down into the north end of the Owens Valley. He was relieved to see that the natives were still in the foothills and mountains harvesting pinion nuts, meaning he didn't have to worry about scrapping with them or keeping an extra close eye on his horses. The high desert was hot. Similar to traveling across the Great Basin, he moved mostly in the mornings or later in the afternoon.

The Mojave Desert was dangerous. Water was scarce. Desperate animals sought refuge in the shade of rocks or burrows, hiding from predators or seeking prey. The blue sky boasted no clouds, only the baking yellow sun.

It took him longer than imagined before he reached the upper portion of the Cajon Pass. Winding down into its depths brought cooler temperatures and even some trickles of clear water. The pass dumped him out onto the broad Santa Ana plains. San Bernardino looked like an oasis. Several farms had spread out from the town and their boundaries were carefully etched by straight fences. The vegetation guarded by the wooden barriers was slightly greener than the rest of the desert. Some methods of irrigation were being fairly well employed.

San Bernardino had sprouted, becoming more successful faster than anticipated. Silva figured there were at least 3000 people in the settlement. It had grown large enough and quickly enough to allow the creation of its county, splitting away from Los Angeles a couple of years earlier. He also noted several saloons as he rode into the town, a sure sign of a Gentile presence.

"Brother Lyman or Rich?" he asked a merchant who was sweeping his step. The man merely pointed to the city hall that was also used as a chapel.

He found both men in their cool, darkened office, busy with stacks of paperwork, clearly not the type they preferred.

"Brethren."

Shep's voice startled both but they instantly recognized the accent and his drawn face.

Lyman began nodding before any other words were exchanged. He pointed knowingly at the rider and spoke to his companion, Charles Rich. "Told you."

Elder Rich nodded back and smiled at Shep. "You know how lucky you are? We've both been gone for a while, just got back and now we're about to leave again. You got news from Brigham?"

"Yep. He says it's time to light out."

"Who?"

"Everyone we can get, I reckon."

"It'll be slim pickings," Rich said.

"The Gentiles will be happy with the news."

"Buchanan's got an army on the way into the territory."

The news didn't surprise either of the hardened men. The call to leave San Bernardino was slow in its coming, they thought. The Saints living in California were saturated by opposing philosophies, causing many of them to weaken in their resolve. The town was taking on more influence from the incoming Americans or Mexicans.

"Does Brother Brigham want us to fight?"

Shep smiled. "I think he's got enough young bucks to do that. I believe he's ready to send you both back out on missions."

There were times, not too many, but enough, when life seemed quite drawn out for Elders Lyman and Rich. "Whatever the Lord wants."

"Where from here, Brother Silva? You just come down from the Carson?"

"Yep. Las Vegas then back to the Great Salt Lake City."

"You be sure to give Bean and Bringhurst our best."

"Will do."

He had wanted to stay and rest for a while but the atmosphere of San Bernardino wasn't as conducive as he remembered. Besides, the sooner he got back on the trail, the sooner his labors would be done. It was over 220 miles to the springs, Las Vegas. It was a measly fort and mission. He was more than happy Brigham had not tapped him and Harriett to work the area. Too hot and desolate. They were the only ones who were happy to see the outlines of tired emigrant trains drawing near.

****

The wagons led by the Fanchers were not welcome. If anything, the farther they got away from the Great Salt Lake City, the more intense the feelings. Suspicions were rife. Angry settlers resented the jokes and tricks played on them by the emigrants. The antics were resorted to as a way to relieve some of their pent-up feelings. Many of their group had chosen to break away from the main train and took the northern route, going north around the Great Salt Lake and dropping down on the Humbolt River and from there heading to Carson Valley. They figured they could winter on the east side of the Sierras and then jump over into California with the spring. The rest of the beleaguered Fancher-Baker Party started south on the Old Spanish Trail.

The trip was long and telling on the emigrants from Arkansas. Contrary to their hopes, the Mormon settlements were not at all forthcoming with their goods, helping to rebuild their diminishing supplies. They remained uninterested in any kind of interaction. The men on both sides were quicker to anger and spout curses than the women and children. Indians remained a growing threat, staying out of range of their Kentucky long rifles but not out of sight. Their presence taunted patience and threatened their feelings of security. The emigrants knew the Indians probed their camp during the nights, stealing livestock or even blankets or unwatched firearms.

Corn Creek lay twelve miles south of Fillmore and looked like a good place for the Fancher Party to stop and rest. They had also picked up another group of emigrants from Missouri but since they didn't see eye to eye they generally kept apart. The men from Arkansas and Missouri took turns, seemingly, who could best the other with foul language and epithets aimed at each other, their animals, the Indians, or the Mormons.

That night an ox of the Fancher-Baker Party died. A smaller, lighter party of Mormons was traveling north at the same time and spending the night across the Corn Creek from the emigrants. The Fanchers asked them if the local Pahvants might want the carcass to eat. The Mormons said they were friendly Indians but usually fed well enough that they probably wouldn't want to eat anything that had died in such a manner. The Pahvants were a curious mixture of Utes from the north and Paiutes from the south. The Fanchers turned the animal over to the tribe. Some of the Indians ate the ox and then several of their people died. Suspicions immediately sprouted. They didn't understand how germs worked. A majority of the emigrants' cattle were Texas long-horns who had health problems the people in Utah were not familiar with. They were familiar with strychnine and arsenic and they knew how animals could be poisoned and that poison would pass along to whoever or whatever consumed it.

Rumors started about the emigrants having poisoned the Pahvants. These stories merged with the growing war hysteria that was building among the Mormon settlers in the southern settlements. Because of errant comments made by some of the emigrants, the Mormons began to look at them differently with jaundiced eyes, as real-life threats, promising to follow up with military groups from southern California to catch the Mormons in a pincher move. As unauthorized or off the cuff as the remarks may have been, they were not received as such by the Mormon militia leaders in Beaver, Parowan, and Cedar City. To them, the Fancher-Baker Party was morphing into a group of combatants, an extension of the enemy army.

In these southern settlements, plans began to unfold behind closed doors. How best to address these emigrants who could pose such a threat to the communities. Should they allow them to pass through peacefully or mount a preemptive strike? Would the Fancher hotheads be motivated enough to return and attack them once they were divested of their families and better armed?

Several men who specialized in Indian relations were brought in and questioned about the possibility of using the Indians as surrogate combatants. There was no love lost between the southern Paiutes and this newest emigrant train. The Indians were angry. The idea of striking for revenge sounded sweet. On the other hand, the natives did not want to make the venture on their own, to be tagged as the scapegoats in such a volatile exchange.

It was a relief for Alexander Fancher, as he watched their train roll into Cedar City. As usual, forthcoming supplies were meager at best. It was the final community along the way before they would move off the plateau and into the desert that separated them from California.

"Keep an eye on the hotheads," he cautioned John Baker. "We've come far enough without any blood being spilled."

Baker nodded affirmatively. Wisdom came with age. "How far away are we from the Mountain Meadows?"

"About twenty miles to the southwest. It's a nice valley ringed with hills and has a good spring on the south side that runs up north. The grass is thick and will do our animals good having some time to rest before crossing over the hill and going down into the desert for that long stretch."

The miles-long train snaked slowly through Cedar City, a community that didn't represent the people of Utah well at all. It boasted several scores of shacks and shanties scattered in uneven groups. The emigrants were not impressed. In the past, some of the men in the wagon train had called their oxen Brigham or Heber to anger the settlers, while others claimed to have participated in the drivings of the Mormons from Missouri in the 1830s. A Missourian claimed to have a pistol that was used to kill the Prophet Joseph Smith. These baseless words were meant to anger the local populace.

And they succeeded.

Things in Cedar City were tense without the use of caustic words or claims. Angry expressions were traded, while the tongues on both sides were controlled. The tripwires were drawn taut. The atmosphere seethed danger.

In all, the Fancher party was in Cedar City for one hour before making their way into the southwest, winding back towards the Old Spanish Trail and reaching the south end of Mountain Meadows on Saturday, September 5th. Because Jacob Hamblin was on business in Salt Lake City, the men herding the cattle checked with Rachel Hamblin, Jacob's wife, about the best place to pasture their animals. She thought south by the springs where the grass was thickest, as her cattle were grazing in the hills, thus keeping the herds apart. After speaking with the emigrants, she was relieved to have them move on a couple of miles away from her. She was also aware of the wicked rumors surrounding these people and their intentions as relating to the Mormons.

It took several hours for the balance of the wagons to reach the Meadows, unhitch their oxen and set up their encampment. Horses were staked close by, milk cows were tended to, lowing longhorns grazed in the thick grass close to the gurgling springs. Women and children gathered firewood as a cool wind blew quietly through the cedars and sage. It was an idyllic setting, one the emigrants had sought for some time.

Chapter 54

"To be 'in charge' is certainly not only to carry out the proper measures yourself but to see that everyone else does so too." Florence Nightingale

The ride across the Mojave Desert and then up to Fort Las Vegas was empty and quiet. It was hot and Shep didn't see any other emigrants on the trail. There were less than a score of people at the springs and Silva could easily understand why. Even the Indians avoided being in the valley during this time of year. Brother Bean and Brinbghurst both tried their best to hide their relief at being called back to the Great Salt Lake City. They did their best to listen to Brigham and then follow his direction, even when it was as challenging as it sometimes was. This time, it was a pleasant announcement. Of course, there was concern about the US Army troops and the uncertainty of where they might eventually end up, but at present, this was a pleasant opening. After a quick, informal council, they told Silva that they could have their things packed up and be on the road within a few days.

It was during the times he made long trips such as this that Shep was thankful that he wasn't a large man. His stature and weight didn't beat the horses down as much and the pounding and shaking on his own body were more tolerable.

"But I'm glad that I kind of fit in here," he told himself after taking a long, less than a satisfying draught of warm water from his canteen.

He was riding a sturdy, strong mountain horse that he had traded for in San Bernardino. The road from there to Cedar City tended to be softer because of the sand and didn't wear on the horse's hooves as quickly. Once he reached the southern settlements, he knew he could always get another mount should he require. In the meantime, the horse beneath him was as powerful and capable as any he had ever ridden.

Two days after leaving Las Vegas he was happy to spur his horse into climbing up and onto the plateau and leaving the suffocating heat of the valley. Cedar trees grew more thickly as he continued to follow the Old Spanish Trail. The trail also became harder and rockier. He finally crested the ridge that led into the Great Basin. All the drainage behind him flowed down and into the Colorado Basin. Before him, the small creeks ran into the oblivion of the broad sands and empty valleys of the northern desert basin.

Immediately he found himself at the southern end of the Mountain Meadows. This was like paradise when compared to where he had come from. The spring was active even though it was now the month of September. The grass was lush and thick and still green. He allowed his mount to slow and enjoy some mouthfuls of the grass and drank to his heart's content from the north running stream.

Shep also noticed the long-horned cattle that were beginning to fill the southern end of the narrow valley. Within several minutes he could see several wagons that were pulled off the trail. Camp was being made. These looked like typical emigrants headed for lower California, not caring to attempt crossing the treacherous Sierras this late in the season.

Shep Silva nudged his horse from the trail and entered the camp. He could see that most had observed his arrival and he was being watched closely, maybe too closely. He felt the hairs on the nape of his neck tingle. All was not right.

"You folks doing all right?" he asked with an open smile. The older man he addressed had approached him easily.

"Right enough," he replied. "Where you coming from?"

"Lower California."

"Alone?"

"For now, at least."

"Headed north?"

"Great Salt Lake City." Looking around Shep could see that suspicions were lessening. "Mind if I have supper with you?"

"You're more than welcome, sir."

"Much obliged," Shep said as he dismounted. He pulled some of his supplies from behind his saddle and found a fire that was less crowded and set up his cooking. "Long trip, huh?"

"Can't wait to clear these parts," a young man answered him. "How is it the rest of the way?"

"Dry and dusty. But California is a good choice. Good weather, good feed, and folks are decent. The ocean is amazing."

Talk of California drew listening ears. People slowed their eating and stepped a bit closer, leaning to hear better.

"San Bernardino or Los Angeles?"

"Los Angeles to start. After that, we'll have to see."

Shep nodded and stirred his warming mush and took a bite from a piece of salted beef.

"You care to share any of our food?" a woman asked, while two of her children peered curiously at the Brazilian from behind her skirt.

"Happy to give it a try," he answered. He was surprised to smell the rich aroma and the taste was as good as anything Harriett or Yasmin had ever put together. "Delicious." Not given to talking much, Shep forced himself to speak about the trip lying before the pioneers and then as much as he could remember about California. It seemed to raise spirits.

Accepting more of their kindness, Shep rolled out his blanket and slept close to his horse that he'd staked just beyond the wagons. His tired body sagged into a deep rest, awaking only when the eastern skies began to lighten. He ate a quick breakfast, then saddled up and readied to leave.

"It's the Sabbath, mister. You're more than welcome to stay and worship here with us."

"Thanks for everything but I gotta git," he said, scanning the quiet enclosure. This kind of people was the strength of the nation. Hard-working. Solid. Burned by the sun yet clean in their manner. Some were more calloused in their demeanor than he was used to. A couple of the young men openly commented on his thick black hair and the tufts of chest hair that sprouted from his shirt or that carpeted his arms. Shep was thankful to have chosen to keep his face fairly well-shaven. Being able to see his countenance seemed to give the folks more confidence in him.

The children were laughing, singing, skipping, and playing like children he had seen in every place he had visited during his life. Most of these had lighter hair and fairer eyes. Still, like children everywhere, they represented God's faith in the rising generation. Seeing their smiling faces and hearing their lyrical voices, he knew the world was in good hands.

He rode out of the Mountain Meadows encampment, rested, fed, and content. He would head for Great Salt Lake City after stopping to touch bases with Isaac Haight, the local stake president in Cedar City.

Sunday was a day of rest. A couple of Methodist preachers reminded the Arkansas travelers of their connection and commitment to God. It was good to hear sermons that sounded like those presented when they were in Arkansas.

Isaac Haight was the local stake president, corresponding to a Catholic diocese. He was also the local leader of the militia. Because of his military responsibilities he had spent more than a week in counsel with other leaders of the Mormon community trying to determine how real the threat was being posed by these emigrants. All in their settlements were gripped by the suffocating war hysteria, trying to deal with the realities of US troops being sent to their territory. Combined with the war hysteria and growing anger of the Paiutes, Haight finally decided to give in to John Lee's desire to attack the train. Having the Indians make the initial attack would provide them plausible deniability. The Paiutes weren't convinced but with each passing hour, the lure of cattle and wealth, combined with their ire urged them to join with the Mormons and decimate the enemy. It was the weightiest of decisions, eating at Haight's stomach and keeping him up late into the night.

Shep found Isaac Haight in his Cedar City office and made a brief report regarding his huge circular trip to Genoa, San Bernardino, and Las Vegas.

"Anything you want me to carry back to Brigham?"

Haight shook his head. "All should be fine," he lied, not caring to share his worries about John Lee, the Indians, and the frightful animosity that existed between the emigrants and the militia with this dark-haired foreigner. The Fancher Party was in Mountain Meadows. Once the wagon train moved on, things would settle down. Lee had drawn up some specific plans but they seemed too distant, too erratic, too improbable, too satanic. Nothing would come of them, he told himself. He had prepared a letter for Brigham that he handed to Shep in a sealed envelope and asked that he deliver it, then closed by saying, "Nope. All's good."

That Sunday afternoon, September 7, 1857, Shep Silva climbed back onto his horse and headed north. The three-day trip would finish his epic odyssey. He felt good about his contribution, having spread the word far and wide, preparing the Saints and Governor Young for the oncoming US Army.

Silva urged his mount onward, not noticing the gathering clouds, the foul odors that were being blown into the area, the clenched jaws, the hardened hearts, the murderous intentions that were growing in the lives and actions of men in the area. Sharpening knives and scythes, checking the pliability of saddle straps, assuring the preparation of their weapons, members of the militia looked down at the dirt where they stood in contemplation of their plans, failing to see the wafting, swirling diabolical grins peering at them from over the ridgeline, encouraging them onward to the precipice of no return.

Using anger and knowledge of the language, Indian agent John Lee whipped the Paiutes camped at Pinto into a frenzy, charging them to attack the emigrants early Monday morning while it was still dark. They balked at his insistence and instead waited until it was light and people were up and moving, starting their breakfast fires. The dogs began barking at the approaching warriors. The initial rush was surprising and horrid, interspersed with screams and shouts. Volleys of withering shots were fired, followed by waves of arrows. The melee was on. Seven of the emigrant men were killed with the first onslaught and sixteen others wounded before the painted Indians could be beaten back. Trenches were quickly dug and wagons lowered to provide adequate shelter for riflemen. The wagon wheels were chained together, forming a defensible circle.

Hearts were racing, as children huddled for protection, praying that the men would be able to ward off any further encroachments. Some claimed to have seen the Indian agent, John Lee riding in the rear of the natives, dashing their hopes of rescue by their Mormon brethren. Now bodies needed to be buried, wounds tended and wrapped, food fixed, shelter sought, and sanitary measures taken care of, all within the confines of a 100-foot diameter circle made by the wagons.

At the time of the attack, two emigrant men had been out of the encampment, beyond the reach of the sounds of shooting, looking for stray cattle and pine tar to grease their wagon axles. While watering their horses at the Pinto Springs, they were met by two Mormons who pretended not to know what was taking place in the meadows. They then shot and killed one of the young men and wounded the other who was able to escape and race the several miles back to the encampment.

The game was up. Word spread that the Mormons were in on the attack. The full-fledged plan needed to be put into action. All but the very youngest children were to be killed systematically and efficiently Those six years old and younger, were not a threat. They would not be able to testify to the attack and they were considered innocent blood.

SOUTHERN UTAH, 1857

N

Little Salt Lake

○ Parowan

Cedar
City ○

To Salt Lake City
Appx. 300 Miles

Spanish Trail to Los Angeles

Hamblin's Farm ○

Iron Mountains

Wasatch Mountains

Mountain
Meadow

Virgin River

Washington ○

Colorado River

○ Santa Clara

○ St. George

Mark Griffen
2004

Chapter 55

"It's better to die doing good than to live doing evil." Brigham Young

Captain Stewart Van Vliet rode solitary into Salt Lake City on Tuesday, September 8th. He was politely received and ushered to visit with Brigham Young at his office in the Beehive House. Dr. John Bernhisel was invited to join the counsel. Van Vliet delivered the letter of General Harney to the Governor, who read it with interest. It was the first correspondence he had received from the government regarding the military advancement. He read slowly then finally handed the missive over to Dr. Bernhisel who also scanned its words.

"There's nothing in General Harney's letter about the governance of the territory being changed to someone else," Governor Young said.

"An obvious oversight on the General's part," Van Vliet said. "Colonel Alexander is en route and he will be bringing the Honorable Alfred Cumming for the office appointment."

Brigham Young shook his head thoughtfully. "I am at an impasse, Captain. I don't know exactly how to proceed. I am the sworn protector of the people of this territory. I cannot roll over and give up on this responsibility through wish or rumor. I am bound to protect and that is what I plan to do. We are not rebelling against the nation. We are not criminals. We are a righteous remnant of the House of Israel. God has led us here I am the rightful governor of the people. I will not be removed willy-nilly not will we be casually removed from these valleys. I encourage you, sir, to enjoy our hospitality. Spend a few days here with us. Interact with our population. Talk with our people. Take note of our industry. See if our women are prisoners or if they are here among us of their own free will. We are happy. We are content. We wish no one ill. Then after your time among us, we encourage you to return and report to Colonel Alexander and if possible, go to Washington and let President Buchanan know of our heart and determination."

The idea fit precisely into Captain Van Vliet's itinerary. For the following six days he strolled the avenues and interviewed the inhabitants, focusing especially on the women in polygamous relationships. It was a worthy endeavor. Van Vliet was given an added respect for the accomplishments of the people and the religion they embraced. In the evenings, he was accompanied by Dr. John Bernhisel, who knew everyone and everything. He directed Van Vliet throughout the community, allowing him to see the corrals, the brickyards, the lumber factories, the houses, and buildings growing throughout the flourishing desert metropolis.

When Shep arrived in the city, he went straight to the Beehive House to present his report to President Young and deliver Haight's letter.

"We appreciate your willingness to cover so much ground in doing God's work, Brother Silva. The messages you have left will be a blessing to all. And I am grateful you chose to come here first instead of going to Tooele, especially because Sister Harriett is with the Rosts even as we speak. Yasmin is expecting her first baby any time." He stood and walked up next to the Brazilian and took his arm. "Brother Haight is doing well and our people in the south?"

It was a probing question. "I believe so, Brigham. As best I can tell. Why?"

"It's just that I am very concerned." Brigham sat back down into his office chair, stroking his beard thoughtfully. "I know you have spent days in the saddle but would I be asking too much of you to send you back to Cedar City with a letter from me? It is most urgent, my boy."

"Of course."

Brigham didn't expect any other answer. "You scoot on over to the Rosts' and see your wife, then get back here and I'll have the letter ready for you."

Upon his timely return, Brigham met Shep at the front door to the Beehive House and gave him the letter for Brother Haight. "Thanks for not dawdling. Get this to Haight as quickly as possible. Don't spare the horse."

****

The next several days at Mountain Meadows the beleaguered emigrants kept their heads low. Their enemies sniped at them during the day, whenever someone raised long enough to allow a bead to be drawn on them. After that, a series of shots were exchanged.

The tension was draining on the besieged emigrants and ammunition was running low. Three men dashed through the Indian lines and rode towards Cedar City for assistance but were summarily caught and killed.

On Friday morning, September 11th, three white men approached the wagons carrying a white flag. They were allowed inside. John Lee was the spokesman. He explained his role as the Indian agent, informing the emigrants that the Indians were geared up for battle. He also told them that if they would surrender to him and his militia forces, they would be peacefully escorted back to Cedar City.

The offer surprised the emigrants, who also noted the nervous exchanges of the visitors. Fancher and Baker called several of their captains together for a consult. Most were wary of the offer, thinking it to be a trap. The problem they were facing was how low their ammunition was, with only 20 balls remaining, leaving them with few other options. Whether they agreed with the Mormons or not, they felt they had more in common with them than the Paiutes. By the time they reached a consensus to accept Lee's offer and follow the militia, it was getting late in the morning.

A complicated arrangement was devised. After being completely disarmed, two wagons arrived. The first was to collect the wounded, along with necessary supplies. The second was for the smallest children and babies. The wagons led out, traveling north on the road to the north, through the meadows. After a short space, the wagons were followed by the women and children, walking in single file. These first two groups were lightly guarded. There was another break in the march, interspersed by mounted militia. Finally, the remaining thirty men and older boys brought up the rear, also walking in single file. Each of these had a militiaman walking at his side.

The procession moved out, silently except for the wailing of the babies. The cattle and horses were left behind. The emigrants were told that they would be gathered and delivered to them before long.

It was midafternoon when the wagons and the women and children crested a small rise and started down the far side, temporarily losing sight of their men. Militiaman, John Higbee, riding between the groups, reined his horse and holding up his hand, yelled, "Halt!" It was the signal for which the militia had waited. Sounding almost like a single volley, the militiamen escorting their captives, turned and shot their corresponding victims, killing most outright. The unarmed emigrant men were outnumbered and quickly cut down. Seeing the deceit, a few escaped, running into the sagebrush but this had been anticipated. Riders followed after and killed them.

At the same time, a few hundred yards in front of them, a wave of screaming Paiutes jumped from their hiding places in the brush and attacked the women and children, using rocks and arrows, guns, and tomahawks. Instinctively, the women turned and ran towards their men but were quickly cut off by their attackers and the vicious assault continued.

The wounded in the wagon were dispatched. The few scattered and fleeing children were cut down and dragged back to the road.

The bloody massacre took less than five minutes to finish. The air was filled with dense clouds of blue smoke from the pistols and rifles. The Indians were screaming victoriously, anxious to pillage what they could, beginning their frenzied grabbing and inspecting. The militiamen were shocked at what they had done. The road was littered with pools of blood and disjointed corpses. Some of the militiamen broke down and wept, knowing that it was eternally too late.

Lee and a couple of the other leaders ordered the bodies be quickly interred, while the wagon with the youngest children and babies was driven several miles north and given into the hands of a shocked Rachel Hamblin, who did her best to calm and clean the terrified children, feeding them whatever she could find. The story was not completely divulged to her, allowing her confusion to conjure the nightmarish episode.

The grisly work of burying the dead stained the murderers for the rest of their lives. Scraping shallow pits for the bodies, they dragged, then covered them with dirt and rocks. Some of the men mindlessly kicked dirt over the pools of blood and splatters that formed on the road. Pieces of shattered skulls were trailing lines of hair. Torn shirts and skirts were also littering the ground, crying voicelessly for their owners.

The Paiutes were culturally removed from the settlers and emigrants, never realizing the impact such a massacre would have, reverberating down through generations. After robbing the dead of their choicest baubles, the natives went back south to inspect and claim the cattle and other livestock they wanted.

For the Mormon militiamen, the work was finished all too soon and they began trudging back towards Cedar City. The silence was deafening in their ears. There were no more outlines of the moving, active people from Arkansas. All had been hacked down to the dust. Lungs no longer breathed the warm air, muscles no longer lifted or leveraged the skeletons wrapped in unique skin patterns. A host of spirits fled their earthly tabernacles of clay, speeding to the sacred courts on high. Gone was the laughter of the children, bright eyes dancing in the sunlight as they ran and played and laughed. Hair pulled smartly into ponytails had been covered with earth. Dolls and dishes, colorful string and tin cups, piles of empty clothing, and dusty shoes were inspected, the choicest objects being then kept aside by the criminals. The balance of the desecrated stores was sent to be used by the local population.

The spectacle of genocide was complete. Filth and memories were scraped together and buried, some within human minds. Predators came during the night to feed and fight over the dead. Nothing would erase the visions of fear and confusion and surprise and disloyalty and slaughter. The massacre was as complete as men could deconstruct it, stamping the quiet Mountain Meadows with the life-blood and gore of 120 victims. *How could it ever be justified? How could the families and relations ever be reknit? How could the atrocities be undone? How could the beastial workings of enlightened people be forgotten? Could the screams of those whose voices were crying from the dust ever be silenced? Could the ghastly images of murder ever be washed away? Could the hopes and dreams of the unfortunate emigrant party from Arkansas, whose heartfelt anticipations of a better, more abundant life, be flushed away? Driven forth by dry, erratic winds?*

God is the sole mediator, the sole Savior.

Chapter 56

"The angels are ministering spirits; they are not governing spirits." John Brown

The road back south felt shorter than he remembered but Shep heard his heart thumping deeply within his chest. It was a life-changing motivation. Brigham hadn't said it in so many words but there was an urgency in his message. As if blessed from on high, his mount sped quickly along the road, seldom stumbling. Passing by several farms, he recognized many people he had recently passed. The questions on their faces spoke their curiosity as to why he was again riding so swiftly by them. Important business, no doubt.

The trip from Cedar City required three days for a fast rider, then three days again to return. Silva's dash reached Isaac Haight's office in two days.

Stomping the dust from his pants, he tied his horse to a post and trotted inside the building. Haight's face registered both surprise and regret with the Brazilian's appearance. He accepted the letter with trembling hands and read its contents as quickly as he could. It was as though he was searching for something that might ease his aching heart.

He shook his head violently and tossed the letter onto his desk, then turned and stared out his office window.

"I'm headed right back Brother Haight. Do you have another message for the Governor?"

"Oh, God, no. Too late. It's too late," he moaned.

Haight was a militia major and somewhat trained. He also was a stake president of the church, as well as the mayor of Cedar City. William Dame was another militia commander who lived in Parowan but never seemed to be far away from Isaac Haight.

He wasn't sure if it came with the job or perhaps his growing sensitivity or age or what, but Shep found himself looking closely at several young men in town as he was riding north and picking up speed. These men were militiamen under Haight's command ultimately or perhaps Higbee's or Lee's. None displayed any positive aspects. Rather, they appeared otherwise occupied with the ground, looking into the dust. No one was whistling or smiling or making eye contact with him. There seemed to be an almost universal focus on something else and it didn't feel uplifting. Shep thought long and hard about it. What could it be that was occupying these folks' thoughts, especially of the militiamen? It was odd, to say the least.

Shep's pony started to limp noticeably just before he reached Corn Creek, allowing a reason for him to stop at the Pahvant village, looking to trade for another cayuse and exchange a few words with the venerable Chief Kanosh.

"*Ay problemas?*"

Kanosh enjoyed speaking Spanish, especially with Shep Silva. "No por aqui, mas talvez mas para bajo. Perto de Cedar."

The words concerned Silva. "*Luchando?*"

"*Si.*"

"*Verdad? Sus guerrillas?*"

"*No. Aval mucho matando.*"

Of course, he heard it said. Kanosh always had his ear to the ground. His people reported everything to him. They were the cream of informants. The Mormons were less focused. If Mormons had died, Shep knew Haight would have said something to him. Brigham needed to know these kinds of things. He had remained deathly quiet.

"*Los Mormones?*"

Kanosh shook his head vehemently. "*Mericats.*"

The thought brought Shep up short. *A fight dealing with the emigrants? Had it been another tribe? The Paiutes? Were some of the people of Cedar City involved? Why wouldn't Haight have said something?* Even though he looked like hell, he didn't say anything to Silva nor did he mention anything about other messengers heading for Salt Lake City.

A man arrived with his new mount, having already saddled him. Shep checked the horse over quickly, then mounted. Chief Kanosh also appeared to have run out of things to say.

"*Mas nada?*"

Chief Kanosh smiled weakly, his eyes looking old, and shook his head slowly. "*Nada mas.*"

Silva vaulted into his saddle and reined his mount to leave. "*Muchas gracias, amigo,*" he said with a sincere smile. Reaching down, Shep grasped his friend's arm in a solid exchange, and for a moment felt the years and experiences the man had been through, course into his soul.

"*Un placer a ver-lo.*"

Shep's head was spinning, trying to fathom what had happened. Something big enough to have reached Kanosh at Corn Creek. It also had affected a score of Cedar's militiamen. He finally decided that he would have to wait for more information. That was another nice thing about his position as a deputy marshal. He usually came across pertinent information sooner than others. Hopefully, this time would be the same.

He tried removing the worries from his mind, spurring his horse to greater speed. The animal was impressive, having powerful legs, sure footwork, and lasting endurance. Shep didn't sleep well that night, tossing and turning in his blanket. He assigned it to his extended journey and his aging frame.

Shep arose early while it was yet dark, galloping past sleepy Nephi and then morning chores in Payson. The road he chose was down closer to the lake than up along the foothills and nearer to Provo. The towns kept increasing in size. He let his thoughts wander and wondered how things would resolve between territory officials and the soldiers. It could be a trial. If there were a fire, it could spread dangerously engulfing the populace. His mind reverted to the emigrant party. Was there a connection to the soldiers? He had not heard the slightest rumor about that. Rumors were always rife given the hysteria that had permeated the desert territory since the announcement of the oncoming troops.

The road was more congested in these parts. Wagons and horses and cattle crowded the way, crawling around the point of the mountain, the Jordan Narrows. Interaction between the Great Salt Lake City and the towns in the valley just south stayed busy. He glanced longingly to the west and wondered about the state of affairs in Tooele. He would get over that way soon enough.

And Yasmin? Would she have had the baby by now? She appeared quite ready when he had checked in with Harriett. What a wonder is childbirth. What a blessing for both Aaron and Yasmin, two people who had been brought together most miraculously. It would do Aaron a world of good to have a child. *Boy or girl?* Aaron would make an excellent father. *And what would they name the child?* Shep was quite confident something had already been decided.

An hour later Silva galloped up to the front of the Beehive House. It was a striking form of architecture. Shep's panting horse was flecked with sweat. His bones felt stiffer than normal, creaking from his head to his feet when he stepped carefully from the saddle and plopped onto the earth. He sighed and gazed west to the setting sun. How beautiful was that? And then he thought once more about Brother Haight. He had sent nothing specific with him to share with Brigham. Too bad. The loss of an opportunity. And then a thought struck him.

What if something awful had taken place? Something big? Something too horrible? What if Haight were vying for time to come up with a story or an excuse? What did Kanosh mean when he mentioned the fighting and killing? It had to do with the Mericats, a name the Indians used to discern between the Mormons and other white emigrants.

Shep wracked his brain but could not remember seeing any evidence of the emigrants in Cedar City. And then. Then he remembered seeing several head of Texas long-horned cattle. The cattle the emigrants had with them. *What were they doing in the town?* He doubted they had been traded. He looked back towards the setting sun when a sickening realization washed over him. *Had the militia fought with the emigrants? But there was no rejoicing, no chest-beating. If the militia had won or lost there would certainly have been some sign. Luchando. Matando. The listless looks on the young men's faces in Cedar City. Could there have been a massacre?* The idea suddenly answered his questions over the previous two days. *What better could account for the strange way folks had been acting? No one wanted to talk. It had been quite disconcerting.*

Angry Indians and overzealous Mormons?

He quickly tied his horse and started for the side door but gagged. He stopped suddenly and then bent over and wretched into the flower garden. The heaving of his stomach didn't stop for several minutes. It was paralyzing for a moment. No, he decided. That would be preposterous. He straightened up and knocked on the door. He was surprised to see Brigham was the one who answered. The Governor sized up his rider, then took a couple of sniffs.

"What is that smell?" he asked Shep, screwing up his face and plugging his nose.

"Vomit."

Chapter 57

"I am prepared for the worst, but hope for the best." Benjamin Disraeli

The pioneers had proceeded on using handcarts and on September 11th the sixth handcart company of the experiment arrived in Salt Lake City, led by Israel Evans. It had 149 individuals and left Florence on June 20, 1857. No one died in this crossing. They had arrived in Boston on the ship named George Washington, March 27, 1857. From there they took the rail to Iowa City on April 30th and left on May 22nd for Florence.

Two days later, on September 13th the seventh handcart company arrived in Salt Lake City, led by Christian Christiansen, and was composed of 330 individuals, a majority coming from Denmark. 6 individuals in this company had died. They sailed on the L.N. Hvidt, leaving Copenhagen to Britain, then took the Westmoreland to Philadelphia and arrived on April 25th. Arriving in Iowa City on June 9th, they left the handcart hub on June 13th and arrived in Florence on 7 July 1857.

****

Dr. John Bernhisel wasn't looking forward to his long trip back to Washington. Having Van Vliet traveling with him would make things a little better. At least he would have someone of diverse background to talk with and that would make the miles go by swifter. Usually, when he made the trip, Brigham would arrange it so that he at least traveled with missionaries.

The two left on Monday, September 14th, before Shep Silva had returned from Cedar City and they headed up Emigration Canyon. Captain Van Vliet cut an imposing figure, riding in their light carriage. He looked quite official in his sparkling uniform. Their four mules were happy to be away from the corral and were strong and young and eager to get out of town and up into the canyon. The afternoon air was warm and scented. Even though the creeks had almost dried up, the one by the roadside was still running, making a pleasing sound as it danced down towards the valley.

"How do you rate your visit to Great Salt Lake City?"

The captain was pensive. The doctor was a good man. He could be jovial or also serious as the mood directed.

"Quite well. I enjoyed being with you and was given free rein these past few days and encountered many things I didn't know about the city. It surprised me in many respects, John. First, I think that's the way Brigham wanted it. He's quite proud of everything the people have accomplished."

"For good reason?"

"Yes, of course. On the other hand, I was hoping he would be more conciliatory towards me and the soldiers, and the government. He isn't ready to bend."

"You expected him to be different?"

The Captain shook his head. "No. I guess not. I've known him for more than ten years, back when I was in Iowa. He has always championed his people. He is quite sensitive about the number of times the Mormons have been kicked from their homes. I just think he won't get far with Buchanan or Johnston. They're hard men and are used to having their orders followed. An upstart governor in the territory will not gain their favor by fighting with them, whether religious or not."

"Brigham's hardly an upstart. He's been around."

Captain Van Vliet agreed.

The road wound up Little Mountain, then down and then up again over Big Mountain. Van Vliet had their driver stop at the top of the knoll, long enough for him to look back at the quiet valley. He was starting to fret about the future. The military was designed to break and blow things up and took its job seriously.

"I don't think Johnston's arrived with the column yet. He's the one who's in charge. I can talk to Colonel Alexander all I want but he has no authority to change plans. I'm sure he'll just wait and turn things over to Johnston. That could be tricky."

Their light carriage rode down the hill easily, the men being jostled naturally. They camped for the night, preparing for the 25-mile trek up the narrow Echo Canyon the next day. As the road turned and they began to start up the canyon, they saw three horsemen in their way, apparently awaiting them. Drawing closer, Bernhisel could see that one was Porter Rockwell.

"Nice morning for a jaunt," he drawled.

"You boys lost?" Dr. Bernhisel replied.

Rockwell shook his head. "Brig just wanted to make sure you get to Bridger without any trouble. I guess we're the troubleshooters." He laughed at his joke and patted the six-shooter he kept in his coat pocket.

The escort was thoughtful but Van Vliet couldn't help but wonder if Governor Young didn't also send them along to keep an eye on them as well. Again, Van Vliet could see the men along the route and ridges working on several enterprises: breastworks were going up, trenches were being dug, numerous caves fortified, rocks piled in strategic places where they could be pulled down on anyone wanting to use the road without permission. The road continued climbing higher. The captain could see why it had been chosen. It was a prime defensive location.

"You ever wonder," he asked Porter, "what might happen if the army chooses another canyon to enter the territory? Might not be so simple then."

Porter just smiled. "It's a cat and mouse game, Captain. We'll just do the best we know how." He waved at one of the men above them on the ridge.

"After talking with Colonel Alexander, the two of you both headed for Washington?"

John Bernhisel nodded after pulling a letter he had in his vest and pointed at it. "This is a letter Governor Young has written for Thomas Kane. I'm supposed to deliver it before I get back to Washington."

"Think he'll want to jump into the fire again?"

"He's our best ally. If anyone can help our cause back east and in Washington, it's him."

"And I'm just going to make a report to President Buchanan," Van Vliet joined in. "He'll be wanting to know about my visit with Governor Young and what we might expect as the column moves into the valley."

"What you going to tell him?"

"I was hoping for a better response from Brigham. Unfortunately, he had just spoken with a couple of women, British nurses during the Crimean War, and they told him about some of the Russian tactics. The scorched earth policy. They were quite convincing in their presentation and now that seems to be the way Brigham is thinking. He is not wanting to back down."

"Was one the Rost woman?"

Bernhisel nodded affirmatively. "Matter of fact, she just gave birth to her first baby a couple days ago. A girl they named Esther."

"You think Buchanan will listen, given the threats?"

Van Vliet threw his hands up in the air. "Maybe if we had the telegraph out this way. But communication is too slow. I'm afraid the die might be cast. Johnston is a hothead military man from way back. Then again, if I have the chance, maybe I will talk with Lt. Colonel Cooke. He's one of the officers with the 2nd Dragoons who are coming out to support the infantry. The federal folks, like Governor Cumming, will be traveling with him. He spent a while in Crimea as a military observer during the war. Perhaps he could sway Johnston better than me."

"Do I know him?" Dr. Bernhisel asked.

"I don't think so," Van Vliet replied. "Lt. Colonel Philip St. George Cooke took the 2nd Dragoons into Bleeding Kansas to help staunch the trouble there. But he's also a military man, mind you. He thinks every problem can be answered with soldiers and guns."

"All I can say," Bernhisel added, "is that Governor Young has been quite adamant. As of today, he is forbidding any outside military presence, any foreign armed forces whatsoever, from entering the territory, no matter what the pretense."

"See? And that's exactly what I've been concerned about," Captain Van Vliet answered.

The second counselor to Brigham Young and now the leader of the Utah Territory's defenses, Daniel Wells set out the position of the settlers: "*In such time, when anarchy takes place of orderly government and mobocratic tyranny usurps the power of rulers, the people of the Territory have left their inalienable right to defend themselves against all aggression upon their* constitutional privileges. It is enough that for successive years they have witnessed the desolation of their homes, the barbarous wrath of mobs poured upon their unoffending brothers and sisters. They are not willing to endure longer these unceasing outrages, but if an exterminating war be purposed against them and blood alone can cleanse pollution from the Nation's bulwarks to the God of our fathers let the appeal be made.

"You are instructed to hold your command in readiness to march at the shortest possible notice to any part of the Territory. See that the law is strictly enforced in regard to arms and ammunition, and as far as practicable that each Ten be provided with a good wagon and four horses or mules, as well as the necessary clothing, etc., for a winter campaign."

On August 28th Colonel Albert Sydney Johnston was ordered to replace General William S. Harney for the Utah Expedition. He was ordered to take his dragoons and follow after Colonel Alexander. President Buchanan thought Harney's services could be better used in Bleeding Kansas. It was the first part of July when President Buchanan appointed Alfred Cumming to be the new governor of the Utah Territory, replacing Brigham Young.

On September 16th, Lt. Colonel Philip St. George Cooke, commanding a group of dragoons, left Fort Leavenworth, escorting Alfred Cumming and his wife, Elizabeth, along with several federal attorneys, all geared towards taking control of the territory and making sure that the federal wishes were carried out. Colonel Johnston left the following day with his dragoons. The mounted forces moved much quicker than the infantry. Their goal was to meet up with the 5th and 10th Army Infantries being led by Colonel Alexander and then head into Great Salt Lake City at the end of October.

It did not work out that way.

On September 15th, Brigham Young officially mobilized the Nauvoo Legion, more of a decorative step than anything substantial. The second counselor in the church's first presidency, Daniel Wells, was the de facto military leader of the Legion. On his staff, he had Generals George Grant, William Kimball, James Ferguson, and Hiram Clawson. Reporting to them were Colonels Robert Burton, Nathaniel Jones, James Cummings, Chauncey West, Thomas Callister, William Pace, Warren Snow, Joseph Young, and Albert Rockwood. Guerrilla commanders, the real movers, and shakers of the organization were Lot Smith, William Hickman, and Porter Rockwell.

Daniel Wells put out the marching orders: "On ascertaining the locality or route of the troops, proceed at once to annoy them in every possible way. Use every exertion to stampede their animals and set fire to their trains. Burn the whole country before them and on their flanks. Keep them from sleeping, by night surprises; blockade the road by felling trees or destroying the river fords where you can. Watch for opportunities to set fire to the grass on their windward, so as, if possible, to envelope their trains. Leave no grass before them that can be burned. Keep your men concealed as much as possible, and guard against surprise."

Alfred Cumming made sure to find Lt. Colonel Cooke one evening after camp had been set and dinners were being cooked.

"May I have a few minutes, Colonel?"

The cavalry commander nodded and pointed to a campaign chair for Cumming to sit.

"I understand that you know this Brigham Young. Is that correct?"

"Ten years ago, I led the Mormon Battalion across the southwest during the war with Mexico. As a consequence, I was able to meet with Governor Young then and get to know him somewhat. I guess I didn't spend much time with him, but I know some about his concern relating to the men of the battalion. It was a ploy he hatched to get some funds from the government to help with their move west. It worked out fine. The men I led in the battalion were the very best. Not being trained with military proficiency, I was quite impressed with how regimented or disciplined they all were. I believe we marched farther than any other US military group in history. It was a difficult campaign. Fortunately, we were spared any direct conflicts with Mexico, but had we been called upon to fight, I have no doubts the men would have responded just as well to my orders as they did all during the march."

"Are they a fighting force?"

Cooke shook his head. "I don't think the Mormons in the territory have any artillery. Few have ever participated in field maneuvers, from what I understand. But their backs are against the wall. I know they are tired of being driven and having their constitutional rights trashed. We could be in for a serious scrap."

"Do you think they are seriously attempting to secede?"

"I think Judge Drummond has just been stirring the pot. He had some bad experiences with the folks in the territory, and this is the way he's paying them back. Once he got President Buchanan's attention, I believed he pressed it for all he was worth. Mr. Buchanan has ordered us to quell any insurrection and we certainly will. I'm a bit worried about how we're going about it, sending the infantry and cattle out first without any cavalry support. The Mormons could very well make mincemeat of our men before we ever arrive. That and or make off with our livestock."

"But we could get them back, right?"

Cooke shrugged his shoulders.

Cumming continued on. "Were you part of Delafield's Observation Commission in the Crimea a couple years ago?"

"Not really. I was over there as part of a military observation assignment, but I wasn't wined and dined like those three. I had some serious work to do. We traded posts, spending some time with the Allies and some with the Russians."

"And?"

"I was there for a year, the same time as the Commission. We learned a lot. Mostly we saw a bunch of blunders made and large numbers of dead. The armies are quite close to each other, and they pick up ideas from each other quickly. Then again there is a lot to be said about democracy versus what Russia has going on. It's a time-proven mess and will doubtless fall. Modern warfare has escalated to be much more destructive than it once was. The artillery simply blows folks up. The bombs interfere with cavalry charges, making great divots in the ground. We witnessed great courage on both sides. We also saw some of the stupidest mistakes ever, that cost the lives of many men and lost vast stores of supplies."

"Do you think our military learned what they were supposed to?"

"Time will tell, Governor."

Captain Stewart Van Vliet and Dr. John Bernhisel kept their escort of Porter Rockwell and his comrades until they reached Ham's Fork. After that, they were left on their own, picking up their military escorts, and allowed to proceed at their speed, moving eastward along the emigration trail and looking for the 5th and 10th Infantry Regiments being led by Colonel Edmund Alexander. This portion of the army was also accompanied by two battalions of artillery, dragging four six-pound and two twelve-pound howitzers. Miles and miles of wagons carrying their supplies stretched out on the trail. Large herds of cattle and horses were also being driven alongside the military columns.

Van Vliet passed Devil's Gate and Independence Rock, then the northeastern expanse of road that separated the Sweetwater before finally meeting up with the North Platte River. Up until the time he got that far away, Captain Van Vliet was under constant surveillance by spies from the Mormon forces. He worked and reworked his presentation for Colonel Alexander, practicing his best to describe the time in Salt Lake City, as well as the mood of Brigham Young and the exercises that were being invoked, preparing the mobilization of the defenders, the Nauvoo Legion.

For all his effort, Van Vliet got nowhere. Colonel Alexander was not happy. He felt he had been waiting long enough already for Colonel Johnston's arrival. He wanted Johnston to make the necessary corrections regarding an invasion of the main city of the Utah Territory. He now knew that fortifications were being made in the Echo Canyon as well as the Weber Canyon. These were the two easiest canyons leading into the Salt Lake Valley. But they were both narrow and easily defensible. Perhaps moving north along the Oregon Trail, they could descend on the territory from that direction but it would cost time, a luxury that didn't enjoy.

Alexander was also aware that it was late in the season and his forces and supplies were sitting ducks for the mounted guerrilla forces that opposed him.

After spending as much time as he thought necessary, and getting nowhere, Captain Van Vliet gave up. He and Dr. Bernhisel took their buggy and continued to Fort Laramie, then crossed the Nebraska plains to Florence. From there, they traveled to Iowa City, caught the rail across the northern States to

Washington where they both could pursue their efforts with leaders of the nation, along with Thomas Kane, regarding the army that was plodding blindly into the Utah Territory. It also gave them another concerted effort to mold or stamp the territory into the State of Deseret.

Chapter 58

"I had reasoned this out in my mind, there was one of two things I had a right to, liberty or death; if I could not have one, I would have the other." Harriett Tubman

Caching has been used to store goods since time immemorial, to safeguard, protect supplies for a future date. The method allows to keep things dry from flooding, below the frost line during the cold, stores were buried to preserve the necessities to sustain life. Sometimes cache sites were marked and the supplies were used by anyone in need. At other times, the caches were secreted, marked with code when meant for specific persons. Food, fuel, clothing, bedding, ammunition were the frequent things hidden away, providing relief and assistance for others at another time.

On Monday, 21 September 1857, Colonel Robert Burton was at Devil's Gate, inspecting the area, especially at Fort Seminoe, and then the 70 Legionnaires who were with him began caching stores around the immediate location, in the event of a future need. It was the next morning when one of Burton's outriders reached the camp to inform him that the US Army's Fifth and Tenth Infantry Regiments could be seen approaching Independence Rock. Wagons filled with supplies and livestock were spread out over the flat trail for miles. Teamsters and herders were also scattered in the mix.

The contest regarding the sovereignty of the Utah Territory was set to begin.

Riders were sent racing overland to inform General Dan Wells whose office was temporarily set up at Fort Bridger, of the oncoming force, giving him time to begin collecting his supplies for relocation to another spot.

At the northern end of Echo Canyon stood a well-known cave that had been discovered years earlier by Jackson Redden. It was located on the northwestern side of a hill about two-thirds of the way up. From the outside, it looked like a large oven. Its oval mouth was high enough to allow a man to walk in without stooping. From there it proceeded like a tunnel, its smooth walls and ceiling acting very well like a chapel. It was the first place that acted as a church for the Mormons when they came into the Utah Territory. It could easily hold fifty people.

Now it was called Cache Cave and was the backup location of the Legion's military staff. General Wells relocated his headquarters there. All of the riders knew how best to find it, to pass along important or sensitive information.

Under Colonel Burton's orders, the Legionnaires crept stealthily towards the army camp, setting up their post one-half mile away from the soldiers. This ghost encampment mirrored the movements of the army. From here, they would continue to monitor the soldiers' movements, gathering whatever kernels of information they could, by listening to conversations or ascertaining orders. Riders kept up a constant flow to inform Wells and his staff.

The infantry marched past Devil's Gate, not suspecting the Legion's caches, and on to Pacific Springs, arriving late on the 24th. By the time their tents were pitched, the soldiers were dead tired, wanting only to crawl into their beds and get some sleep.

Colonel Edmund Alexander thought it would be best for them to move to Ham's Fork, twenty miles northeast of Fort Bridger and about fifteen miles away from where Black's Fork entered the Green River, and there await the arrival of Colonel Albert Johnston and Lt. Colonel Cooke with their cavalry. Forage for the cattle and other animals was in rich abundance. Water was also plentiful.

This was an exciting time for Shep Silva, being with Porter and four other Legionnaires. They had been shadowing Alexander's troops for several days. It was now time to give them a taste of what they had signed up for.

"We'll go in at 2:00 a.m. The boys should be exhausted and snoring by then," Porter said, chuckling with glee.

Shep thought he sounded like a playful youth engaged in a game of kick the can or hide and go seek.

"Remember to do your best to keep between the tents. The boys won't be shooting at us if they're worried about hitting their own. You four, drive the mules out as fast and far as you can. We'll get them back here to the Big Sandy and cross the creek before the army knows what hit them."

Porter divided the other four. "Me and Shep will bring up the rear. We'll see just how far the boys can drag their wagons without mules."

The plan was perfect. It was unsuspected. The results would devastate the soldiers. The six Mormons crept up to the camp, where everyone, including the sentries, was fast asleep. The corral was quietly dismantled, pole by pole. Then all hell broke loose, as the Mormon raiders began clanging their oversized brass clapper cowbells, whistling, shouting, and shooting their six-shooters into the air. The mules were not expecting the attack either, and they stampeded directly as the mounted men wanted, charging off into the sagebrush, while dazed and confused soldiers piled from their tents in various forms of undress. Horses ran among them, snorting and blowing snot and frozen air across the campgrounds, carrying ghostly forms of wild, screaming banshees, who yelled, waved, and fired weapons. Herders stumbled about trying to orient themselves. One cried, "Soldiers! Turn out! We are attacked!" The night air rang with war whoops as the successful raiders charged from the army's midst and off into the blackness, chasing the wild-eyed mules, running pall-mall away from the encampment.

A flummoxed Colonel Alexander waved and yelled for the regimental bugler to start sounding Stable Call. It was a frantic bid to turn the tide. And as happens in battle, an unforeseen event fell into the army's lap. The bell mule had been running with the herd, when the rope around his neck caught in sagebrush, bringing him to an immediate stop. Bucking and kicking, he was unable to extricate himself from the brush, but the sound of his bell together with the familiar-sounding of Stable Call from the bugler brought the crazed mules to their senses. Understanding that it was time for them to return to their stables where they would receive their portion of grain. The mules wheeled in a large arc and charged back to where they had started. By this time, the bell mule had also released himself from the ornery brush and joined in the stampede. It was a wild fiasco that terminated again at the corral.

Porter and Shep had dismounted and were prepared to begin driving the mules across the Big Sandy, while the other four were also afoot trying to scare the mules in the proper direction. The plan didn't work. The six Mormon horses decided to join in the rush for grain, leaving the stunned raiders watching impotently from behind, standing in a cloud of dust.

All was over within a few minutes. The mules and additional horses were corralled and captured. Frantic soldiers were relieved and grained the animals, nervously peering each direction into the darkness, wondering what more they might expect.

Located on a small knoll yards beyond the camp, the six raiders gawked at the outcome of their plan. Silva began chuckling and shaking his head. This promised to be a long campaign.

"I'll be damned!" Porter muttered, also shaking his head. "Let's get out of here."

The six defeated raiders trotted over the hill, out of sight of the army.

Despite the disaster, Shep felt exhilarated. The temporary setback was a learning opportunity. Had the large-scale plan worked as designed, the army would have been seriously impaired. This got his mind running with the possibilities. He was confident they would pull off other such plans.

Porter wasn't feeling as positive, kicking small rocks and cussing. He didn't want his first salvo against the army to be remembered as a fiasco, a defeat, a loss. "All I have to say is that I'll not be going back to our main camp on the Little Sandy walking. I'll either be in the saddle or dead."

He insisted that they keep their camp dark that night. No fire. Finding their wagon, they dragged their blankets out from the box and were soon fast asleep, except Rockwell who was intent on figuring out another plan that might resolve him of his first failure.

The next day, Colonel Alexander and his men continued their march toward Ham's Fork, shadowed again by Porter Rockwell and his raiders, drooling for another chance at revenge. They didn't have to wait long. The army camped along Little Sandy Creek. That night after the fires of the camp had dwindled to smoldering coals, the raiders again snuck into camp, keeping close to the small creek in case they were discovered. A horse nickered, alerting them to a string of fifteen horses. They carefully untied them and led them away, "borrowing" them for the remainder of their campaign. It felt good to have at least a semblance of victory under their belts. Saddling up, the raiders rode west to the Big Sandy where a larger group of Mormon Legionnaires was camped. Smiles etched on the raiders' faces seeing the arrival of Porter and his men's new mounts.

With the gathering of the men, Lot Smith felt it a perfect time to address them about the army. "This is an example of what can happen if we are careful," he said. "No doubt God was looking after our men. We have a good chance to demoralize the men, steal their beef, burn their wagons and scorch the earth. It's up to us to keep these troops from our valley. We're blessed that their cavalry hasn't shown up yet to support the infantry, but they'll be along before we know it. We need to slow them and encourage them to winter out here. It'll give Brig and the boys a chance to decide what to do. One more thing. As much as we might not like these troops from Leavenworth, them being pro-slavers and wot not, don't forget that they're southern boys and know how to shoot. Let's do our best to stay out of their sights."

The first camp on Ham's Fork was named Camp Winfield. Colonel Alexander reached Ham's Fork on Monday, September 26, and began setting up a more permanent camp, calling it Camp Winfield after the army's commanding general, the seventy-year-old, Winfield Scott. The General was referred to as the Grand Old Man of the Army or Old Fuss and Feathers. He had run unsuccessfully against Pierce in the 1852 presidential election but the Whig Party was badly divided over the Compromise of 1850. He didn't know how pleased the old general would be about the status of the approaching conflict. Alexander was tired and frustrated, wondering where his backup was. He was ready to turn the command over to Johnston. The two-and-a-half-month march had been draining. Indians had made off with some of their livestock but now that they were in the mountains, it was the Mormon raiders' turn to steal and pilfer their stores. Fortunately, the weather had cooperated thus far. He hoped their luck would remain. The west was rife with tales of early and lingering and freezing winter weather. Colonel Alexander followed the orders of Colonel Johnston four weeks later and had his men move to begin the establishment of another camp, in between Fort Bridger and Fort Supply, calling it Camp Scott.

Porter, Smith, and Hickman were in their element. And they were the motivated leaders who inspired their men to great efforts. They ranged across the high plains, picking off stray animals or sneaking up on the larger, slower-moving columns, trying to collect around Camp Winfield. Once they were settled all were fair game, herders, teamsters, soldiers or artillerymen, officers, enlisted men, or civilians.

One of the good things Colonel Alexander found as he reached Ham's Fork was that he overtook a large wagon train with his supplies, as well as some cattle. Along with another train just in front of them, they were headed for Fort Bridger. Alexander was feeling bloated with supplies. Something that Lot Smith also noticed. His rangers moved quickly, attacking the wagons and driving off the cattle. The teamsters and herders were allowed to gather some of their most needed items from the wagons before the Mormons gathered the captured 50 plus wagons and put them to the torch. The huge bonfire was visible for miles. Smith's men galloped off to herd the sixty cattle down the range, leaving the stunned teamsters and herders to wonder what they should now do.

The raid was a major blow for Colonel Alexander and his men, deflating the soldiers and encouraging the Mormons. 500,000 pounds of provisions were destroyed

Hosea Stout, who was engaged in the hostilities wrote *"Learned last night that Capt. Lott Smith had captured six wagons of our enemies...in conformity with the orders to annoy and harass our enemies and break them down but not to kill any of them. He has since taken and burned 52 more wagons on Green River and took the oxen. These wagons had some 5000 lbs. each lading of the most choice and costly supplies but he before burning them caused the teamsters to take out their own property and such supplies as they needed to furnish them to the states."*

On Thursday morning, Porter and some of his men rode to Fort Supply, ten miles southeast of Fort Bridger. It had been started as a competition for the mountain man's settlement. After a few years, the Mormons bought the fort from Jim Bridger anyway. The folks manning Fort Supply understood the precarious situation they were facing with the advent of the army. After moving the livestock out of the corrals and loading their wagons full of their things from the cabins, the people moved off towards Echo Canyon. Then it was Porter's turn. He and his men carefully set fire to Fort Supply and watched while the historic post burned to the ground, removing it as a possible haven for the incoming army.

"We're under the gun," Porter told his men. "Living on borrowed time. We got to fix things up so the army has to winter out here. They keep trying to move towards Bridger. From there, it'd be an easy jaunt into Salt Lake."

"Maybe they'll just hunker down at Ham's Fork or Bridger."

"Is that what you'd like to do?"

The man shook his head.

"Me either. General Wells wants to fire Fort Bridger today, just like Fort Supply. Let's get over there."

The men jumped on their horses and thundered after their leader but pulled up when they saw plumes of smoke rising in the air from the fort. Bill Hickman had beat them to the prize. He and his rangers were first to reach the fort. There, as they explained the need to burn the facility, the merchants asked that they be allowed to apply the match. It was their way to help in the defensive effort.

Porter and his men arrived in time to see the last of the fort's wooden gates fall into a burning pile. The walls of the fort had been constructed of stone and were all that didn't burn. The destruction of the fort made the mountain man Jim Bridger rattle off a string of curses directed at Brigham and the Mormons a month later when he heard about it. It had been a monument to his memory. He resented the current custodians of the place burning it down, regardless of the threat of oncoming US forces.

Another group of refugees began their exodus towards Echo Canyon and from there to the Salt Lake Valley beyond. This time they noticed the men working to fortify the canyon had finished building their series of dams along the creek, creating a bunch of ponds. In the event of the army's invasion through the canyon, the dams would be destroyed, sending huge waves of water rushing down the narrow gorge, flooding the road located close to the creek. General Wells and his staff, located above the canyon in the Cache Cave nodded approvingly of the plan.

Rockwell borrowed several raiders from McAllister's group long enough to siphon off more cattle from the army. Wells wanted the cattle stampeded at Ham's Fork or else the forage needed to be burned. It would be the orders they followed for the balance of the campaign. They left the weaker animals for the soldiers' supplies, then drove their confiscated spoils down towards the Weber River and on through the canyon, where they would emerge close to the city.

Being a smaller man but especially strong and resourceful, Shep Silva was a preferred messenger of the guerrilla leaders. The Brazilian was an expert covering the territory in record time. Even though the US Army struggled with its logistical challenges, the structure of the Nauvoo Legion was also lacking, not possessing the professional organization of their opponents. As a result, some stronger personalities emerged. Bill Hickman was rough and could be mean, to the point of cruel. Porter enjoyed a long career as a lawman and consequently had built quite a daunting reputation. He had been a confidant and bodyguard of Joseph Smith's and then an associate of Brigham's. Major Lot Smith was younger than the other two, about the same age as Shep himself, but outranking them all, he was a firebrand and anxious to prove his abilities. He was sure that Porter spent most of his time damning him. They didn't agree with one another but when aligned against a common enemy, they were the best of allies. That's what Shep enjoyed but when they were not marshaled against their opponents, the Brazilian enjoyed not being in the crossfire. He liked all three leaders, although he chose to keep Hickman at an arm's distance. These were brave, wise, determined men, who collectively knew far more than others of the era. In combination, Shep couldn't see how the US Army could ever stand a chance.

On October 5 the Mormons left Big Sandy and went on to the road where they found 24 wagons belonging to the army. They burned 22 of them and took 7 mules and 2 saddles. It was a productive day and the news getting back to the camp didn't make Colonel Alexander happy.

The Legion men continued to stay close to the soldiers, watching and disturbing their camp. On the 6th they thought about driving off their cattle but they were scattered 8 miles up and down the creek, with the poorer animals at the end of the herd. The next day they began firing up the grass, scorching it to make foraging a chore. Porter stood on a hill observing the soldiers and when they finally came out to chase the raiders off, he simply signaled his men and they rode safely back into the mountains. After the soldiers returned to camp, the raiders returned and continued burning the grass until it turned dark and the dew kept the grass from burning. It was a cat and mouse game that infuriated Colonel Alexander.

The next day the burning of grass continued until noon when the soldiers began shooting their cannons to scare them away. The Legionnaires retreated long enough for things to die down, then returned and started their fires again.

Rockwell kept watch on the camp for a week. His men were careful not to engage the soldiers, giving them some distance. At night, the raiders chose to creep as close to the camp as possible, to listen in on the conversations. It was becoming clear that their tactics were affecting the soldiers.

"How we doing?" Shep asked Porter one evening as they left their dark camp and rode for the Cache Cave. It was a considerable distance. Silva was happy to have the company and Rockwell seemed to enjoy opening up to him.

"Right on the money, I'd say."

"Any word about the cavalry?"

"We just know they're headed this way. Don't know how long they'll take. That's why we need to push our work, keep scorching the feed, and making off with as much of their livestock as we can. The soldiers are already on rations. It will be a long winter for them."

Both of their horses were surefooted, giving neither man a reason to worry. The rolling hills began to drop in elevation, leading them towards the opening of Echo Canyon. The light emanating from the oval opening of the cave could be seen for miles. There was little worry of a military foray in their direction. Besides that, a bevy of sharp sentries watched the trails night and day. They would provide all the warnings Wells and his staff might need.

Rockwell and Silva could feel that they were being watched. Still, the sentries stayed out of sight. Leaving the creek bed, they climbed the last number of yards up the hill, then dismounted and turned their horses over to some stable hands to feed and water them.

It was late at night but several men were awake, hunched around tables glowing from the candlelight, talking in low voices and scanning maps. Some of the staff were stretched out on cots, beneath heavy blankets and snoring merrily. With the arrival of Rockwell and Silva, orderlies awakened the officers and escorted them to their large main table.

"Good ride, brethren?" Wells asked as they began pulling up their chairs and looking into one another's faces across the table, the flickering light caused the lines on their faces to dance.

"No problems."

"Hickman and Smith have been chasing off a number of the cattle every day. How's the scorching going?"

"Right as rain."

Shep liked visiting with these men. They gave him an added sense of wellbeing. He also had no trouble asking them questions. "Burning the grass sets us up as targets. The troops have begun firing their cannons at us. How long are we going to be doing this? The cattle are already feeling the effects of less food."

438

"One of the best sources of information for this kind of warfare came from Harriet Matthews or da Silva, I should say." General Wells was a smart man who seemed to know everyone. "Your wife was the one who spent a couple years in Turkey. She was aware of the Russian tactics of scorching the earth. She shared with us how devastating it could be to remove the forage from the animals. The work destroys any logistics that are mounted or attempted. This is a ploy we want to invoke as well. We are entirely outnumbered. Our resources are limited but we have the advantage, being smaller, faster, and knowing the terrain as we do. We don't mean to harm the animals," he said, nodding at Silva, knowing the Brazilian's sensitivity towards them. Shep nodded back, gratefully. "Still, their health and well-being goes a long way towards the health and well-being of the troops. As we remove them, we also remove strength and ability from our foes. Hopefully, we'll be able to continue to siphon off their herds and burn their wagons and isolate them in time to face a harsh winter."

"Any news of their reinforcements? Their dragoons?" Porter asked.

"Thankfully, they're bringing Alfred Cumming and his wife, along with some other politicians and their wives. These folks are slowing the column down substantially. I don't think we'll see them before November."

"That's how long we've got to get their cattle out of here?"

"Maybe. Maybe not. That depends on how long the storms stay away. We also know Colonel Alexander is thinking about taking the Oregon Trail route to circumvent Echo and Weber Canyons, to get around our defenses. I don't think they've got the moxie or the time. Certainly not as long as our boys keep them off balance."

"What about the southern route?"

"We're not worried about the Old Spanish Trail. We have people coming from San Bernardino keeping an eye on things for us there."

"What about the river?"

"The Colorado? We've heard some upstarts are wanting to come at us from that direction but they have neither the manpower, resources, or organization. They've been fighting with one another more than anything else. I don't even think President Buchanan knows anything about them. I think they've just been wanting to scrap but the winter will chase those thoughts away quick enough."

"One last thing, General," Porter said, pausing as he stood. "Our men are running powerful low on victuals."

Wells nodded. "I'll have Burton and his boys send a wagon your way."

It was a good update. More than they needed but enough to keep their raiders up to speed. Porter and Shep gathered up their things and started for the cave opening in time to greet another rider just arriving from Hickman's troop.

On October 9th, US Infantry Captain Jess Gove wrote his wife: "*Ere this reaches you, you will doubtless hear of battles and engagements, but this will all be unreliable...Three supply trains have been destroyed, two on Green River and one on Big Sandy, 10 miles before or on the other side of Green River.*"

The next day, Hosea Stout wrote *"Like for a Storm this morning. 149 head of the captured oxen passed, look well. The deserter, a long slab-sided Dutchman reports that many of the soldiers would desert if they believed they would be well treated here, also that they are dissatisfied with their officers and that the officers were divided in their councils what to do."*

On Sunday, October 11th, Bill Hickman reported having seen a huge herd of cattle near Camp Winfield on Ham's Fork. It was the news Smith and Rockwell had been hoping for. Gathering up their men, they reconnoitered and found everything just as Hickman said. Quickly checking to make sure it wasn't a trap put out by Colonel Alexander, 100 armed and mounted Mormon raiders charged up and over the hill, descending on the terrified infantry sentinels, terrifying the men and causing the cattle to stampede. Within minutes fourteen hundred head of cattle were chased across the creek and divided up into smaller, more manageable groups, then herded away. The Legionnaires left twenty of the weaker animals for the soldiers, knowing their rations had been severely depleted. The winter promised to be long indeed.

On Tuesday, October 13th Captain Jesse Gove again wrote to his wife:

"Tomorrow we strike the Oregon road which, I am told, is very good. It takes the Mormons perfectly by surprise that we have avoided their strongholds, Echo Canyon and Emigrant Canyon, Fort Bridger and Fort Supply. Our distance this way is nearly double than through the canyons, but our progress cannot be stayed this way by any natural defenses. If the Lord gives us 25 days of good weather, we have them very tight."

On Thursday morning Captain Marcy decided to try a new tack against the mounted Legionnaires. He picked 100 of his infantrymen, had them saddle mules, then after mounting, they attacked Lot Smith's men. The Mormons dashed away, trying their best to avoid a shootout. The soldiers were able to get within 150 yards of the fleet raiders and discharged 30 bullets at them. A bullet went through the hat of one of the raiders, while another grazed a horse's leg. The chase was exhilarating but over too soon. The soldiers were dubbed the jackass cavalry by their compatriots and the raiders.

Colonel Alexander was frustrated at not hearing from Colonel Johnston and decided to take his troops and move on to winter at Fort Hall in Oregon, but he never made the push. It snowed four days later, bringing a halt to all movement of the army. Unfortunately for him and his men and their supply trains and herds, the raiding and burning of their wagons as well as the "liberating" of their necessary beef continued in ever-growing numbers. Inclement weather didn't cause the depredations to cease. On Saturday, October 17th Porter left the battle, driving 624 steers and 4 mules to Salt Lake Valley. He took with him two deserting teamsters from the army to help him with the herd. This was also the day it snowed in the mountains and high plains. The temperatures plunged dramatically.

Arriving in Great Salt Lake City on Monday, Porter had his two new associates board with Mother Taylor, the mother of Apostle John Taylor, insisting that her rooms were much better than any of the Townsend House, the only hotel in Salt Lake City.

As tensions continued to rise among the people of the Utah Territory, the men, now formally considered part of the Nauvoo Legion, were trained more systematically in the arts of warfare. Trenches were dug, bullets were cast, rifles were cleaned and upgraded, food was conserved, essentials were packed, wagons readied, roads prepared for a large evacuation. Communications became more evident as riders charged up and down the Wasatch Front carrying messages and warning of changes.

Replying to his critics, on Sunday, October 25th, Brigham Young said, "Colonel Alexander accuses us of what he terms a very uncivilized method of warfare. If we are to do as they do, we shall have to get drunk, to swear, to quarrel, to lie and believe in lies and indulge in many other like traits of civilization for us to get as they do."

Chapter 59

"It is wise for us to forget our trouble, there are always new ones to replace them." Brigham Young

Leaving their homestead in the capable hands of the Wetoyous when Shep left for the mountains, Harriett packed up and moved to Salt Lake City to be with Yasmin, the baby, and Aaron. She told them it was to allow Aaron time to spend at his store, while in reality, she buried her dubious scheme.

"Everything is just fine," she assured them, mostly wanting the chance to spend time with the infant.

"I didn't realize being a deputy marshal meant that your husband was also a guerrilla."

Harriett sighed. "He wears a number of hats and does the bidding of a number of folks. It keeps him busy and away from the house far too frequently."

Aaron decided to quiz Harriett. "Have you heard from Brigham since you arrived in the city?"

She shook her head. "I doubt he even knows I'm around."

"Oh, he knows you're around, believe me," Aaron assured. "Maybe he's just waiting for his deputy to finish his business on the hill with the army. I think the two of you can expect a bid to visit with him in his office."

Washington DC was dreary. The brilliant fall leaves on the broad-leafed trees had given way to the blustery winds of an early cold front and lowering gray clouds. Migratory birds were readying to fly south, while scavenging squirrels scurried about the trees and grass, gathering their supplies. The scent of moist earth hung in the morning air, the steeped ground was wet enough to encourage worms to crawl out of their holes, then lie helplessly on the trails and lawns, exposed to the depredations of hungry winged predators.

Smoke billowed out of countless chimneys, carried away by the cold gusts, and not allowed to pocket above the city. Too bad. There were many days of the year when the skies were clear, the temperatures were warm, the waters of the Potomac reflected the blue of the heavens. People strolled peacefully along the walks and streets. Not today. There were few people outside. Those who were caught in the cold, hurriedly sought houses or offices where inside they could escape the dank and foreboding climate.

The darkness of the day invited the use of lamps, many of which stood lit in the windows. Such was the office of Dr. John Bernhisel. He was happy to have finally arrived in the capital, safe and sound. He missed the sociality of Salt Lake City. He enjoyed the hospitality of friends there, as well as the kindness of his wives. These women were all past their childbearing years, but they appreciated his willingness to open his home to them, to give them a status of importance, that of a plural wife of a very dignified man. The women were all well matched, one with another, and they got along famously. When Dr. Bernhisel was absent from the city because of his ponderous assignments in the States, their activities continued unabated. Frequently they would stop and write him to let him know of any curious happenings or their feelings and affection for him.

He left earlier than normal this season and had yet to receive the inspiring letters. He did possess a letter, however, that was important and doubtless would carry long-reaching import. It was a letter from Brigham Young that he and Captain Van Vliet had carried with them from the Utah Territory. It was addressed to Colonel Thomas Kane.

The poor man was always called upon by Governor Young whenever assistance was hoped for or required. Bernhisel wondered how his young wife was able to put up with the pulling on her husband's time and talents. Perhaps she didn't handle it well behind closed doors but from an outsider's perspective, all seemed normal. Elizabeth was a tender and young mother who doted on both of her children as well as Thomas and his parents. She was the perfect match.

As expected, a knock came on his door and a servant quietly opened it and ushered Captain Van Vliet into the office. The smiling officer was impressed with the room's décor and he looked quickly around at the pictures and accouterments ornamenting the room. The two had not seen one another for a week since arriving in Washington.

"Is it good to be back?" the captain asked the doctor.

"All right, I suppose. Anything's better than that hard wagon bench. I'm getting way too old for all this running to and fro across the continent. The old bones just aren't what they used to be."

"You'll get no argument from me. I feel exactly the same."

The men found their chairs and situated them around Dr. Bernhisel's oversized wooden desk and traded the usual gossip and news, waiting for the arrival of Colonel Thomas Kane.

"Has he been in town long?" Van Vliet asked.

"A couple days. There are times he spends a lot more time here than in Philadelphia. He's got his own apartment a few blocks away that he shares with his father when he's down here working."

"You mind?" Van Vliet asked, removing a cigar from his vest pocket, then lit up before receiving an answer from the doctor. He puffed energetically, then watched the smoke waft towards the ceiling. "I know you don't appreciate the smoke," he said, "but it really helps me to relax. And I want to be relaxed when the colonel gets here."

John Bernhisel waved his nonchalance. The smoking didn't bother him as much as the blatant use of tobacco without saying something about his aversion to it. Most were aware that Mormons didn't care for tobacco, even though some smoked or drank coffee and tea or even liquor or wine once in a while. "It's just not in keeping with the teachings of the gospel," he explained to his inquisitive guests. Dr. Bernhisel was a complete teetotaler.

The cool dampness of the office pushed the warm smoke upwards, allowing the doctor more comfort as he breathed.

They both spotted Kane out the window, as he ran across the lawn, splashing as he went. By now the windows of heaven had once again opened up and it was raining. A few moments later and the colonel was announced and led into the office. Smiles were all around and hands were shaken. Bernhisel introduced Van Vliet to Kane, who confessed to having known some about his exploits after West Point, especially in the Mexican-American conflict. He was pleased that Van Vliet had made the effort to meet with Governor Young before the arrival of the rest of the troops.

"Besides being wise," he said, "it shows the respect due to Brigham, giving him a heads up before his territory is teeming with a bunch of angry or drunk troops."

"It really was the least I could do. The Governor gave me free rein around the city. I tell you that they impress me. Quite an industrious bunch. The city is a wonder, very modern and pleasing in every aspect."

Kane nodded appreciatively. "I wouldn't expect anything different. So, any news?"

"Well, besides my getting to know Dr. Bernhisel, I had several good interviews with the Honorable Governor Young. Very pleasant fellow, except when it comes down to dealing with soldiers and an unexpected invasion of his territory."

"If he hasn't recounted their history already, the doctor here could enlighten you as to the number of times the Mormons have been driven and denied over the years."

"We had a rather instructive conversation during our ride back to the States. Like I told Governor Young, I believe the Mormons have been lied about the worst of any people I ever saw. One thing though, I wasn't too happy about Brigham's responses to the approaching army, ordered out by President Buchanan. He was none too repentant and promised that the Nauvoo Legion will fight a delaying action against our men. I heard him preach one Sunday an emotional speech when he had all the Saints raise unanimous hands who were ready to guard against any invaders."

"I don't think I would expect anything different from him. His people look to him for guidance and protection, something I think he's done rather well, until now."

The three stopped speaking for a few minutes, giving them time to process their thoughts. It was Kane who finally broke the silence.

"All right, doctor, I'm here. You told the messenger that you had something of importance for me."

John Bernhisel opened his top desk drawer and removed a letter, then handed it over to Kane. "A letter to you from Brigham," he said.

The colonel took a letter opener from the desk and sliced the envelope open, removed the contents, and scanned the note, while the others waited expectantly. He read carefully and when they thought he had finished, he returned to a couple of sentences, then placed his hands on his beard.

"Any news you care to share with us?" Dr. Bernhisel asked.

Kane smiled, then chuckled. "Just the regular trouble. The world's coming to an end and my help is wanted in the worst way. Brigham wants me to talk things over with President Buchanan before it gets too late. He thinks it could help. Also, time is of the essence."

The men began reflecting again.

Bernhisel spoke up. "I remember Brig telling me once that if we could keep the peace through the winter, something would turn up that would save the shedding of blood. Think he's right?"

Kane took a deep breath and exhaled, then stood to leave. "Certainly hope so. I'll get an appointment with Jim Buchanan before it gets too late. First, I'll have a chat with Jeremiah Black, the Attorney General, and see if he doesn't have any ideas. I've been corresponding regularly with him ever since Judger Drummond began stirring the pot earlier this year. After I visit with President Buchanan, then I guess I'll need to get back to Philadelphia and let Bessie in on my plans, at least the ones that I have up here," he tapped his head, "before I get too drawn into this mess."

All mirth had disappeared from John Bernhisel's face as he said, "You are doing us a great service, sir."

"It's my pleasure, doctor." A few steps took him to the door, where he paused long enough to turn and look back. "Didn't you graduate with Tecumseh Sherman?"

Van Vliet smiled. "One of my best friends."

"Give him my best." Colonel Thomas Kane pulled his coat around to button it and disappeared into the hallway.

****

The barren hills around Green River continued to witness the dangerous game of tag and hide and seek between the army and the territory irregulars. Several times the Legion troops became too cocky and were nearly captured. Wagons of supplies and livestock were pilfered and driven beyond the army's reach. The rolling hills provided very little cover for the raiders during daylight hours but at night the twisting draws were well used to keep the mounted riders out of the infantry's sight, as well as allowed the renegades to work themselves right up next to Camp Winfield pitched next to Ham's Fork of the Green River.

Friday, October 30th, Newton Tuttle reported: "*In the morning our spy discovered 5 wagons and 2 men on horseback ahead of them towards us. From the Green River, we left 25 men with the pack animals. Lot took 25 men and went out to them and told them to go back to the States or we would burn their wagons. We then went on to the Green River and camped 1 mile below the road. There was a large camp of soldiers up by the road but we could not get a chance to stampede their animals.*"

Finally, on Tuesday, November 3rd, Colonel Albert Johnston arrived with his dragoons. In crisp military fashion, he removed Colonel Alexander as commander of the column. He instantly took into account the dire situation faced by his men and ordered them to give up Camp Winfield and relocate all their resources to Fort Bridger, ordering them to stand down and settle in for a long winter stay, that they would not be going into the Salt Lake Valley until the spring. It came as bittersweet news.

November 4th, Captain Jesse Gove wrote: "*What Col. J. intends to do no one knows. It is rumored, however, that he is going to Salt Lake City if it is a possibility. I hope so.*" And Legionnaire Henry Ballard, penned: "*In camp it was very cold. News came that our boys had taken some more cattle, and the soldiers had moved 4 miles up Blacks Fork toward Bridger.*"

On Thursday, November 5th, following the European model of inviting newsmen to embed themselves with the troops, the New York Times correspondent in the Army Camp recorded: "*There is but one alternative. Either the laws of the United States are to be subverted and its Territory appropriated by a gang of traitorous lechers, who have declared themselves to constitute a 'free and independent State' or Salt Lake City must be entered at the point of the bayonet, and the ringleaders of the Mormon rebellion seized and hung. Whether the entrance can be affected this year is a matter of great uncertainty. My own opinion is that it cannot.*"

The trek was becoming more treacherous for Lt. Colonel Cooke, who wrote: "*The air seemed turned to frozen fog. Nothing could be seen. We were struggling in a frozen cloud.*"

In the same blizzard, Johnston's column began marching southwest along Black's Fork toward Fort Bridger, 35 miles away. This trek was the major ordeal of the campaign. Draft horses and mules died of starvation and thirst. Wagons had to be abandoned for later retrieval. Sagebrush, sparse and buried in the snow and ice, was the only fuel.

Johnston had his troops solidify and establish a perimeter for their tents and the growing compound close to Fort Bridger that was called Camp Scott.

Lt. Colonel Cooke arrived with his dragoons a couple of days after, still escorting his bevy of civilians who were anxious to begin governing. The journey had taken its toll. The weather was extremely cold and adverse. They were disappointed with the news that they would be remaining close to Fort Bridger for the next months. Near Camp Scott, Ecklesville, named after the new chief justice of Utah Territory Delana Eckels, was established for the civilians, including the supply trains not burned by the Mormons.

November 10th, Captain Jesse Gove wrote: "*The 5th Regiment came up last night. It is very cold. I nearly froze in my tent last night. Animals died last night by fifties.*" Two days later he added: "*Thermometer 14 degrees F. Horribly cold. By this time, Col. Johnston had caught up with the troops at Ham's Fork and ordered them to Fort Bridger. This march was accompanied by constant blizzard and cold. It is amazing there were no deaths among the soldiers during this march.*"

Saturday, November 14th, the New York Times correspondent wrote: "*We reached Fort Bridger on the 14th, and we shall remain here, in camp, this winter. The wall of the Fort is built of cobblestone, laid in mortar, four feet thick at the bottom about two feet thick at the top, and twenty feet in height. Adjoining this wall is a large corral. These improvements were found uninjured, but the wooden gates, which were very strong, were almost entirely consumed by fire; all the buildings which surrounded the Fort were also burned to the ground.*"

On their November 17th arrival at Fort Bridger, which had been burned and abandoned by the Mormons six weeks earlier. Moving slightly apart from the fort, Johnston ordered the completion of Camp Scott, including cabins to be used as residences for Governor Cumming and his federal associates.

Soldiers were changed into carpenters and woodmen, chopping trees, splitting logs, framing cabins for the newcomers, who were not used to spending long nights in tents. Within a very short amount of time, despite the frigid weather, some cabins began to take shape, encouraging the wistful eyes of the Honorable Alfred and Mrs. Elizabeth Cumming, who were hoping to change their lodging soon. Elizabeth Cumming was a dutiful wife who wrote her observations conscientiously.

On Friday, November 28th, Elizabeth Cumming described the last few days of their journey. "*Thermometer below zero in the day—at night not only cold, but wind. We left 200 animals dead; we loosed the harness and they fell on the road.*"

On Monday, November 30th, two men arrived at Camp Scott from Salt Lake Valley with 800 pounds of salt and a letter from Brigham Young, mentioning that he knew the entire company was out of salt. Young also assured Johnston that his gift was not poisoned.

Colonel Johnston, who indeed had no salt, had ordered some from Fort Laramie about three weeks before. He refused all 800 pounds because he would "not accept a present from an enemy of my government."

Camp life turned out to be much easier than the journey, despite reduced provisions. On Sunday, December 13th, Elizabeth Cumming wrote, "*Though the hills around us are very bleak and windy, we are encamped in a basin, so surrounded by hills, that the winds reach us very gently. A most rigid economy in the distribution of provisions is necessarily observed, to give us some assurance of being fed till spring.*"

The Cummings had additional private food stores, but the common soldiers lived on 10 ounces of flour and 4 ounces of fat pork per day, and coffee once a week. On these rations, they had to cut firewood and haul the loaded wagons, part of their regular camp duties.

Alfred Cumming and the other Buchanan appointees administered the Utah Territorial government as best they could, in a tent 75 miles from its capital, as did Johnston and his staff at Camp Scott.

****

Responding to a sharp knock on his front door, Aaron quickly glanced out the front window to see who it was, checked the time registering on the clock on the wall, then turned and said to his wife and Harriett, "What did I tell you?" He opened the door and invited the three men inside.

It was evening in Salt Lake and the Rost home was well lit by several lamps, a benefit for one who deals with the sale of kerosene. A potbellied stove was doing more than its share of work heating the house.

Brigham Young entered, carrying a cane and leading Heber Kimball and Dan Wells.

Aaron shook the men's hands and offered them the couch to sit, while Yasmin and Harriett shuffled their chairs to better face the visitors. "What an auspicious evening to have the First Presidency to come calling."

Brigham chuckled. "Out making some visits and Brother Dan reminded me that Sister Harriett was here for a spell, while Shep's up playing war games with the Legion. So, we decided to come and give our best."

"I thought you were at Cache Cave keeping an eye on affairs?"

"Back and forth, now and then," Wells replied.

"Where's the baby?" Kimball asked.

"She's sleeping, thank goodness," Yasmin said. "So, I trust there'll be no raucous laughter."

The men heeded her warning, instantly lowering their voices. Wells chuckled slightly.

Brigham got straight to the point. "We're mostly here to see you, Sister Silva. Lots of things flying around these parts. We're doing our best to keep the lid on the pot. The government has suspended our mail service making it quite difficult to find out what's happening in the States. When Dr. Bernhisel and Captain Van Vliet left, I gave them a letter for Colonel Kane asking for help, especially with any negotiations. Communications being as poor as it is, I'm nevertheless expecting him sometime in the coming months. I think he'll be getting to San Francisco about the same time as Elder Joseph F. Smith's return from the Hawaiian Islands. The passes over the Sierras should be socked in. I would expect them to go south to San Pedro and Los Angeles, then San Bernardino, and come this way using the Old Spanish Trail. What I'm wondering is if you and Brother Shep might think about making a trip down that way to welcome them and escort them home? I believe the colonel will be traveling incognito. We don't want to expose our hands before its time. But you know him, am I right?"

Harriett's mind raced. "Oh, yes, sir. I do know Colonel Kane. Both he and his young wife, Elizabeth."

"Then you could introduce him to your husband and see that he gets back up here without too much trouble?"

"But Shep's with the Legion."

448

"General Wells here will see to it that he's released promptly, and you can make your plans."

"Then we are willing to do whatever is necessary."

Days later, a tired and worn Shep Silva reined his horse on the street outside of Aaron Rost's. The saddle seemed to be a part of his lower backside and he winced gingerly as he swung his right leg over the horse and settled it onto the ground. It required several moments to regain his balance. He sighed. Riding so hard and for so long was not meant for the aging. And he should know because he had just passed his twenty-seventh birthday.

Carrying the reins gently, he began trudging around the back of the house to where Aaron had built a comfortable outbuilding for livestock and his chickens. He was grateful that his friend always kept his trough filled with water. His horse agreed and began drinking greedily, while Shep undid the cinch and slid the saddle from his back, then hung it haphazardly against a post.

Rost appeared out of nowhere, having heard his arrival. He clapped Shep's back heartily and pointed him towards the house. "Long day?"

"You don't know the half of it," he groaned.

"Dinner's ready. Stay here tonight. I think Harriett's ready to go back to Tooele. Mostly I think she's just glad to have you home."

"That makes two of us."

The reunion was joyful. Harriett kissed her husband more than was normally appropriate for an Englishwoman. "It's because I've missed you so!" she exclaimed, beaming with happiness. She also could hardly wait to show off baby Esther, whose growth and development were carefully noted by Uncle Shep.

Shep was pleased to see that the baby's arrival also marked a shortening in the Rost's schedule. They seemed to want to retire earlier. He also noted that they arose later, but this had to be because of the lack of sleep a fussy baby withheld from them during the night stretches.

A crude straw mattress on the floor was provided for their guests, as the Rosts extinguished the lamps and made for their bed. Shep was tired down to his bones. He could not care less about the mattress. But to lie so closely again to Harriett. How he had missed the quiet motion of her breathing or gazing upon her flaxen locks after she had taken her hair down. Hugging each other close, Shep felt himself drifting off to sleep.

Harriett had other ideas. "Brigham came by the other day. He spoke just to me, suggesting that you and I make a trip to lower California. Doesn't that sound fun?"

"What?"

A week later, the Silvas had loaded a wagon and were pulling out of Tooele, heading south. The weather in the valleys was decent. Most of the snow had melted. The idea of riding to California sounded slightly better after Shep had a week to recuperate. The Wetoyous also found the idea to be wonderful and began pleading with them from the first minute it was revealed, to make the trip with them.

"You will need someone to spell you with the drive," Herman announced. "And I have become quite good."

"The animals will need caring and watching," Zeenyo added. "The Hansens have already agreed to care for the farm and our animals."

"There are scores of folks in San Bernardino I haven't seen for months," Linda G said. "It really would be a shame for you to travel all that distance without taking us along. And I hear that Ina Coolbrith is engaged to marry Bob Carsley. In April."

It was too much to fight. Shep dutifully acquiesced. Harriett was already in favor of the plan. She and Linda G were becoming fast friends. They looked forward to sharing the female intimacies only they could appreciate, just how much she missed being away from Shep and how tall and rugged looking the oldest Hansen boy was.

Chapter 60

"Were there none who were discontented with what they have, the world would never reach anything better." Florence Nightingale

December had seen the return of Porter Rockwell to the front lines around Fort Bridger, Camp Scott, and Ecklesville. By this time of the season, most of the Legionnaires had been dismissed and allowed to go home. For now, most of the activity was keeping a close eye on the comings and goings of the army and those they protected. General Wells continued to encourage close observation. Especially at night, spies infiltrated the areas and listened to the conversations. As a result, Wells was kept up with many of the thoughts and plans.

Porter split his time between the mountains and the valley where he lived. When he learned of Shep's call to find and escort Thomas Kane to Salt Lake City from lower California, he packed an extra horse and headed south to intercept Silva's wagon.

"Do you know who that might be?" Harriett asked when she spotted the horseman, stopped at the side of the road, still a distance from their wagon. It looked as if he were waiting for them.

"Not sure. Maybe Porter."

Drawing closer they saw that they were right. The Marshal smiled and waved as the wagon moved closer. "Headed for California, I hear."

"Yep."

Addressing the others in the wagon, he asked, "Mind if I borrow Shep for a few minutes. Won't hold you up none. Herman, you can just keep on driving."

This sounded like an interesting development. Shep hopped down from the wagon and mounted Porter's second horse, then following his boss's lead, they set off south, keeping in front of the wagon. Before long they had pulled away to some distance.

"I just wanted to have a word with you, Shep. There have been some goings-on in these parts, dealing with Tom and John Aiken, so-called businessmen from California. They had some intentions of linking up with the soldiers, then setting things up for the men once they reach the valley. Have you heard?"

"Nothing. It's been quiet in Tooele."

"Well, there was a run-in or two and the men from the party turned up dead. Blame has been set squarely on me. I just wanted to be the first to assure you that I did nothing wrong. I followed my assignment as best as I know how.

451

Despite all their finery, the men were pukes, but I didn't murder them. No doubt, you'll be hearing plenty about it in the coming months but there really is nothing to it. They were shady folks dealing with shady plans that got the best of them."

"All right." Shep thought for a few moments. "And you dragged me away from Ett and the Wetoyous. Why?"

"Just hoping to let things lie. No use stirring the pot if they haven't already heard. But now, if they say something, you can set them straight. Nothing underhanded is going on. Mostly, I want you as a deputy to feel confident about my actions. We are all still above board."

"Why the extra cayuse?"

"An excuse. You want him?"

"I don't think we'll be needing him."

"Good enough for me."

Shep dismounted and handed the reins back to Porter. He saluted to the approaching wagon, then turned and rode off towards the east.

"What was all that about?" Herman asked.

"Just law stuff," Shep replied, climbing back onto the buckboard and seating himself as close as he could to Harriett.

The road that had grown on top of the Old Spanish Trail was fairly clean and well kept. Most of the towns through which it ran did their best to keep it cleared of debris or dug runoff routes for the water, not wanting them to develop large ruts. Because of the efforts, travel was easier and markedly quicker than it had been even a year earlier.

Some citizens from the towns scrambled to talk with them as they were passing through. Many recognized Shep. All wanted an update on what was happening with Johnston and his soldiers or plans that Brigham might be concocting. Shep didn't have much news and that helped calm residents more than he thought. It was a pleasant trip.

Days later, upon reaching Corn Creek, they stopped for the evening to allow Shep a chance to introduce his wife and the Wetoyous. The latter were intrigued by the Pahvant town and their methods of cooking and farming. The Pahvants were equally impressed with their Hopi brethren and they immediately began trying their best to communicate, waving and signing and laughing good-naturedly.

Chief Kanosh was more than hospitable when meeting Harriett and Linda G. The additions to Shep made him see his friend with another dimension. It appeared the Brazilian was making a home for himself. He was surprised that Shep was headed back towards lower California, having recently returned from the state. Once again he parried any questions relating to Cedar City, choosing instead to talk about Harriett and the Wetoyous. His questions carried late into the night, not allowing Shep any of his own. He finally determined that the old chief did not care to discuss events from the previous September.

Two days later they rode through Cedar City. Once again the citizens seemed quiet. Unlike other towns, Shep was not flooded with questions. He spotted Isaac Haight coming out of a livery stable with someone who looked to be John Lee but they didn't pay him any mind and certainly didn't care to converse with them. Not at that time.

As they left the town, Shep made sure to skirt the road leading to Mountain Meadows. There remained too many questions. He would take it up with Governor Young once they returned.

After Cedar City, the road began to drop down from the plateau, depositing them on a broad, dusty plain. The change that pleased the travelers was the immediate rise in temperatures. Even deserts could have their good sides. They were now about 100 miles from Las Vegas. Shep wondered if anyone was even still manning the place.

****

Elder Joseph F. Smith was happy to once again be on the mainland, even though he was just getting ready to leave San Francisco and steam southward to San Pedro and Los Angeles. He wanted to cross the Sierras on his way back to Salt Lake City but was not disappointed when he was told the snow was too deep on the pass to allow the trip. This meant he would need to go the southern route and that went right through San Bernardino. The thought of seeing Ina once again excited him. Of all his friends and relatives, she was the most consistent in writing. He hoped that he wouldn't be too late to see her before she got married. And he knew that was what she intended to do. He at least wanted to add his two cents into the mix.

When the steamer started boarding, he found a place for his suitcase, then returned to the railing to watch as the boat shoved off and moved into the bay. Steamers were so much faster than sailing ships and they could travel in any direction, not depending on the captain and crew to adjust and readjust the sails. Thankfully, there was usually a breeze blowing from the ocean.

The boat wasn't as crowded as he thought it might be, so he started to look at the other passengers, most of whom were going to the lower California as well. After several minutes he noticed a middle-aged man of slight build. Like most, he had a beard and was also intent at watching the passing shoreline.

One thing Joseph F was not, was shy, especially after spending nearly four years as a missionary in Hawaii. "Excuse me, sir, it looks like you're going south. To lower California?"

"Indeed."

"Do you have family there? Oh, and please excuse my manners. My name is Joseph. Joseph Smith."

"Ah, so it is," the man smiled. "You wouldn't hail from the States would you?"

"Yes, sir. I was born in Missouri. But these past years I have been serving as a missionary in the Sandwich Isles."

"You're a might young for that, don't you think?"

"I'm certainly younger than most. I think my guardians sent me out there to keep me out of trouble."

"That's hard to believe, son. My name is Dr. Osborne." He extended his hand to shake, which Joseph grabbed quickly. "I'm from Philadelphia."

"And headed for Los Angeles?"

"We'll see. And you?"

"I live in Deseret. Most folks call it Utah Territory. Great Salt Lake City."

"And you like your home there?"

"I've missed it something powerful but now that I'm headed back, I'm starting to miss the islands and my friends there."

"Naturally."

"I don't mean to pry, sir, but you really do look familiar. I want to say that I've seen you before. Maybe you spent some time around the Mississippi River?"

"I have. Some years ago."

"Yes!" Joseph exclaimed exultantly. "And were you a soldier? An officer, perhaps? I seem to remember an officer who looked just as you do. Maybe a tad younger. He helped us a great deal. Do you know anything about my people? The Church of Jesus Christ of Latter-day Saints?"

"The Mormons? Yes, as a matter of fact, son, I know a fair amount."

Now it was Joseph F's turn to slow down. He realized that he had stumbled upon someone who knew much more about history than he did. "You knew some of the problems we had back in 1846?"

"That's when I was visiting from the east."

It was more than ten years earlier. Joseph wasn't quite eight years old. But he seemed to recall just this man, astride a horse and conversing with Brigham Young at Council Bluffs. They had just been expelled from Nauvoo, kicked out of the United States, denied their constitutional rights, treated as refugees, foreigners.

Joseph's demeanor quieted down somewhat. He nodded. "Then you know Brigham Young?"

"I do," he answered matter of factly, pleased with the young man's deductive abilities and memory. "I had the opportunity to visit your Nauvoo just after the expulsion."

Joseph was leaning hard against the railing, deep in thought. After several minutes he finally turned and confessed. "I'm sorry, sir, but I just can't recall a Dr. Osborne. I was quite young," he hurried to add.

"That's quite all right, son. Most people know me by another name. That of Thomas Kane. I was a colonel."

The recognition was immediate and Joseph's face lit up. "Yes! Colonel Kane! Yes! I remember you helping to muster the Mormon Battalion. And I remember you visiting with our people and encouraging us. It was something we really needed." He stopped momentarily. "But why Dr. Osborne?"

Thomas Kane felt comfortable that there were very few people near them on the railing. "I am traveling under disguise at the request of very important

454

people. I am involved in a very sensitive mission, myself. And it has to do with the Utah Territory."

With that said, Joseph was all in. He had heard very little about the political trouble facing the people in the territory. He had heard that Almon Babbitt had been killed on the plains and that Dr. Bernhisel was spending great amounts of his time in Washington. He knew that John Taylor was managing a newspaper in New York called *The Mormon* and most recently, that Elder Parley Pratt had been killed in Arkansas. Talk of the territory seceding was new to him as were some of the policies implemented by the new president, James Buchanan.

"So, you don't want folks to know you are heading to Great Salt Lake City?"

"There are plenty of people who would just as rather I not go to help with negotiations. I guess it could be dangerous."

"Who doesn't want you there? Mormons or Gentiles?"

"Don't know. It's just best I travel without folks knowing who I am or what my business might be. I am glad to meet a young man of your abilities."

The compliment pleased Joseph F. He also felt a special connection to "Dr. Osborne" and was determined to do whatever he could to help. He also wanted to know about the secret mission, how he had come to this place and his plans for getting to Great Salt Lake City. Kane had sailed from Philadelphia on January 4th and traveling more than 3000 miles to the Isthmus of Panama, then taking the newly completed Panama Railroad over the following 40 plus miles, catching another steamer for San Francisco, landing on the west coast, and San Francisco, January 29th. Once there, he was also informed of the snows in the Sierras and decided to travel south. They left the city early enough to reach San Pedro the next day.

"I am connecting with some Saints who are bound for San Bernardino and then Salt Lake City. I am sure you would be a welcome guest and of course, nothing will be said about your true identity."

They docked at San Pedro and the two friends took a carriage north to Los Angeles. From there they joined a wagon train that was headed for the town of San Bernardino, which because of the exodus of members going back to the Utah Territory, had lost much of its Mormon influence, but still boasted more than 3000 inhabitants, nearly equaling Los Angeles.

"Dr. Osborne" was not overly physical and most of the emigrants were pleased just to have a man of his caliber, a doctor, in their train. Joseph F earned his keep by fetching wood and keeping the fires going as well as the livestock fed.

One evening, shortly after leaving the still bustling city of Los Angeles, their camp was invaded by several ruffians, looking for some sport and easy pickings. They had decided to focus on the Mormons and arrived screaming, cursing, and shooting into the air. With their foul language, they promised to kill any Mormon they found. Their attitudes confirmed their intentions. It was enough to scare most of the Saints in the party and they ducked under wagons or hid out in the sagebrush or looked for cover down by the creek.

Joseph F had been collecting wood and wasn't aware of the intruders until it was too late. His clean-cut appearance was a dead give-away and some of the men grabbed him. One drunken assailant waved his pistol in the young man's face and scowled.

"You one of them dammed Mormons?" he roared, virtually spitting in Joseph's face.

Elder Smith was scared. He also knew he was caught and had nowhere to run, so he straightened up and looking directly into the drunkard's face, replied, "Yessiree! Dyed in the wool. True blue, through and through!"

The ruffian was shocked by the answer. He backed away, lowering his pistol and thought. "By God! If you ain't the bravest man I've ever laid eyes on!" he admitted loudly. "And you're the pleasantest man I ever saw. Shake!" he bellowed, extending his hand to the Mormon missionary. Joseph was only too grateful to comply. "I'm glad to see a fellow stand for his convictions!"

With that, the desperadoes caught their horses, mounted up, and rode away into the darkening desert, still quite drunk and still firing off their pistols. But a serious incident had been averted by the young missionary, something the others were very appreciative of and would not allow him to forget his bravery.

"That was very impressive," Kane remarked that night as they were laying down to sleep. "Perhaps you have the same moxie that your people do. The moxie that is concerning one and all back east. It's the moxie that has many folks calling the president's move to send troops to the territory, 'Buchanan's Blunder'."

They reached San Bernardino the following day. It was a delightful time of reunions. At first glance, Kane was pleased to see Ina Coolbrith run into her cousin's arms. When he was introduced, he was slightly saddened to learn they were not seriously involved. But she was sparkling and literate and possessed a trunkload of poetry to her credit. He was also impressed to learn she had published several works with the Los Angeles Star. These same poems had also been picked up by more papers up north. She was a woman of serious consideration. Her name was Ina and she reminded him of his own Bessie, talented and mature beyond her years.

Kane didn't have long to watch Joseph's reunion or regret missing his welcoming party. Harriett Matthews Silva appeared from behind the throng and rushed to throw her arms about his neck. He instantly recalled her. He was then introduced to Shep Silva and the Wetoyous. It was one of the best homecoming experiences he had ever encountered.

Kane's identity and mission were quickly disseminated among the necessary handful and he slipped back into being the frail Dr. Osborne.

He also was pleased to make the connection between them and his friend, Aaron Rost. "He's been an acquaintance for some time now," Kane explained. "He told me about his Brazilian friend who is turning into quite the marksman. That's you, I take it?"

"I'm far from being a marksman but I do enjoy shooting. Aaron got me a Sharp's carbine and that is one beautiful shooter."

"That's one of the points I have heard often enough around Washington. The military would like to adopt the use of the Sharp's rifles."

'Dr. Osborne' was pleased. If these were to be his companions for the trip to Great Salt Lake City, he felt there would be a series of topics that could be explored. He looked forward to finding out more about these people.

Ina was in seventh heaven. Joseph looked better than she remembered. He had grown taller and filled out, looking more like a man. His voice was deeper and he had a more confident air about him that was also an attractive characteristic. Taking him by the hand, she pulled him from the group, stopping long enough to inform Shep that she would return Joseph F after a while.

Joseph sighed, wishing Ina were not his cousin. Then again, he knew that even cousins married, and things worked out. Why, even Thomas Kane had married his cousin, Elizabeth. Well, Bessie was almost his cousin, and they seemed to be more than fine. *And just look at this charming person on my arm. What does the future hold for her? What would the future hold for her if she were living in Deseret?*

"I want you to meet Bob," she said, now holding onto his arm. "I just know you're going to like him. It is so nice to have you back on the mainland. We've missed you incredibly. I've missed you incredibly."

Joseph wasn't quite as sure. As good as it was to see her again, he found himself slightly relieved that their train was planning to start for the territory in the morning. They walked several blocks, with Joseph not being able to recall any of the structures. A lot of construction had taken place since he was in San Bernardino but even though these buildings were newer, they were also shabby, looking like shanties.

"Where does Bob live?"

"Right there," she said, pointing to a low lean-to built up against a store. It had a single window and he could see a faint light peeking through the glass.

They knocked on the flimsy door. Joseph could feel Ina's grip on his arm tightening with anticipation. When the door opened, Joseph could see a man of medium height and build, dark-complected. There was also the unmistakable odor of alcohol coming from within.

"Bob!" she exclaimed and jumped into his arms as if she hadn't seen him for months. "I brought my cousin over to introduce to you. He just got into town!"

Joseph felt he was slowly being sized up by the other.

"Ah. This is the famous missionary to the islands, huh?" Bob stood aside and waved him in. "What's your name again, son?" he asked. The usage of the word son was used derisively. Bob was only slightly older.

"Joseph. Joseph Smith."

"Oh, yes," Carsley chuckled. "Like the famous one." He laughed again, thinking his emphasis on the name was a clever ploy. "You a religious fanatic too?"

Joseph was uncomfortable and didn't care where the exchange was heading.

"Guess so."

Seeing her dreams beginning to sink, Ina jumped into the middle. "I wanted Joseph to meet the man I've promised to marry," she squealed slightly. "I've told you both about each other in my letters and thought it was high time you met."

Carsley nodded and motioned to a chair for Smith to sit. "Want a drink?" The offer was made more as a challenge.

"Thank you. No. As a matter of fact, I need to be getting back to the wagons. I have a couple of chores to finish up before turning in."

"Suit yourself, boy." Bob slouched back to his chair and poured himself another drink, this time filling the glass nearly to the brim as if compensating for what Joseph would not be drinking.

Ina was starting to feel frantic. This was not how the reunion was to have played out. She had seen it numerous times in her mind. But she was quite aware that neither cared for the other. Perhaps they were jealous. Or perhaps Bob should not have started drinking so early. The 'religious fanatic' jab was meant to be snide. It was uncalled for and she promised that she would bring it up with Bob in the morning.

Ina and Joseph both smiled and shrugged at Bob, then walked back outside and started their way back to the encampment. For several blocks, they walked in silence.

"He really is a nice man."

"I can tell."

"Oh, stop. He's just possessive and seeing me on your arm has lit his fuse."

"Undoubtedly."

"Please, Joseph. Don't be so judgmental. So he drinks now and then. It doesn't make him a bad person."

"I never said it did."

"Maybe not with words but your tone sure did."

"Ina. I'm sorry. I did not mean to be such a rube. I came fully expecting to meet the man of your dreams. And yes, you have mentioned him in your letters. But what I found was quite different. He doesn't even seem to be a polite man. Certainly not a gentleman. He came across as a callus bore. I'm glad I'm not marrying him."

The sentence caused Ina to giggle, almost like a little girl. She quickly regrouped, trying to assert a more mature manner. "Well, I'm happy to be the one marrying him. And we will have a beautiful life and a beautiful family. I was going to insist that you return for the ceremony but I've decided that you will obviously be too busy preaching to the hapless folks of the territory, folks you don't even know, weaving a fairytale for them as the only way to keep them from leaving and moving on to better climes and taking their tithes with them." Once she had spoken, she was shocked at herself. But it was true. She had also thought about it over and over again, as well. *Why would Joseph allow himself to be backed into such a corner? Where was the future in that?*

Her words angered him but he chose to resist firing back. "I want you to be happy," he said. "And if Bob truly is the man of your dreams. I wish you both well." There. He was pleased with himself, having taken the high road.

They walked again in silence, grimacing at each block they passed, knowing it was bringing them inevitably back to the wagon train, and Joseph's departure.

"He wasn't wrong, you know," Ina finally said. "There really is a touch of fanaticism surrounding Mormons."

"Ina, Joseph was your uncle too. Do you think he was duped and that he duped the rest of the family? He was a simple farm boy, for goodness' sake. Where would we all be without the Book of Mormon?"

"It's a story. That's all. A fairytale. Life is much too serious to be banking on the ramblings of a New York farm boy."

"But he's not alone, Ina. Thousands have left hearth and home in order to follow the promptings of the Holy Ghost."

"The imaginings of frenzied minds. Idle wishes of the poor and underclass."

Joseph was starting to feel more than frustrated. *Why couldn't she see how important this message was? Life-altering. World-changing.* Even the Hawaiians backed off when he would get excited or begin thumping the pulpit.

"I believe it, Ina. Lock, stock, and barrel. Uncle Joseph was a prophet of God. He certainly was a man, complete with foibles and shortcomings, but when he spoke as a prophet, he was always spot on. My pa and your pa would not have stood by and been duped, letting their families wallow through poverty, assault, and the cold, if the Lord was not in it."

Ina shook her head with concern. "The church, with its pitifully small numbers of missionaries, thinks it will convert the world? None of the missionaries are as bright and good as you, Joseph, yet tell me, how many people joined after your preaching? A score? A hundred, perhaps? Did King Kamehameha dive into the water wanting to become a member of your church? Did you need to stand font duty because of the lines of prospects waiting to be baptized?"

Joseph F sighed deeply. He knew that he had lost the contest. On the one hand, he was pleased to know that Ina was thinking for herself, drawing her conclusions, making her own decisions. On the other hand, he felt she was slipping away, being seduced by the world, seeking fame and fortune at the altar of popularity.

"I know the waters seem cloudy at times, even muddy. But I also know the Book of Mormon is true. It's a book preserved for us in these end times. Following its teachings, we can grow closer to the Lord and be better Christians."

"So says the Mormon missionary."

Smith remained undaunted. "It's a relic. It's tangible. You can heft it, look into its pages, read its teachings. It's a second testimony of the Savior, following the Bible."

"Didn't that just fit into the dialogue?"

"I don't think so. There were multiple people who saw the gold plates. They testified that Uncle Joseph really had them. There are eleven other men, besides him, who gave their names and honor, to confirm the truthfulness of his claims. My pa and his pa, Joseph Senior. They all stood and testified of these things. Eleven good men. And you know, not all of them remained faithful. A number fell away and accused Joseph of unspeakable crimes. Yet none of them, not one, ever denied his testimony of the plates and the Book of Mormon. Eleven men, Ina."

The poetess wasn't convinced.

"The plates were taken from a hill, where they had lain in a stone box. Then, just like Jesus, it rose up out of the ground, leaving its cold, stone box, and like the Savior. Remember, there were eleven men who saw the risen Lord. They touched him and testified that he had returned from the dead. His witnesses went forth proclaiming the gospel. These poor, uneducated fishermen, changed the world. Well, my dear, the Book of Mormon has come forth in these latter days as another witness of Christ. There are many witnesses to its truthfulness, but even if we only see the eleven right now, and the Prophet Joseph, I happily and willingly add my own witness to theirs. The Holy Ghost has spoken to my heart. I know that it is true from the crown of my head down to the tips of my toes." Joseph realized that he had been dominating the talk. Lecturing, mostly. He also knew that no one's mind was ever changed through an argument. He stopped. "Didn't mean to run on so long," he said apologetically. "Sorry."

Ina smiled and bowed gently. "*Touché.*"

> Then hail to Deseret! A refuge for the good,
> And safety for the great, if they but understood.
> That God with plagues will shake the world
> Till all its thrones shall down be hurled.

Chapter 61

"I can't die but once." Harriett Tubman

Arriving the day before was perfect timing for Joseph F and 'Dr. Osborne', as the planned wagon train set to leave for the Utah Territory, was upon them. Shep and his party had arrived several days earlier and were planning to travel on to Los Angeles to look for 'Dr. Osborne' until a wired message informed them of his landing in San Pedro, giving him and the Wetoyous a couple of extra days to reconnect with friends in the Inland Empire.

The Wetoyous could see the changes in the town just over the previous year since they had left and Shep could see other changes since he had been only months earlier. Most of the faithful Saints had chosen to follow Brigham's counsel and left. trying to stir up the people to bloodshed and every wicked thing.

The void was being filled by less than pleasant folks. One missionary from San Bernardino bitterly recorded that the Saints are, "selling out, or rather sacrificing their property to their enemies. The apostates and mobocrats are prowling around trying to raise a row, trying to stir up the people to bloodshed and every wicked thing." The situation was becoming desperate: "O, is it not Hell to live in the midst of such spirits? They first thirst for and covet our property, our goods, and our chattels, then they thirst for our blood. I think I shall feel like I had been released from Hell when I shall have got away from here."

Kane was counting his good fortune, having run into Joseph F. They shared their wagon and were careful to get in line behind Shep, allowing Herman and Zeenyo to trade places and renew their friendship with the young returning missionary. They commented to each other how serious Joseph had become, especially in regards to the gospel. But it was nice. He gave them a lot to think about as he told his stories. Joseph F's influence continued further, especially at night, as they were making camp, cooking, and getting ready for bed. He shared a series of experiences with people Shep knew from when he lived in the islands. Harriett thought it sounded so exotic and warm, much different than her chilly island of Britain.

Being able to spell the drivers, as well as having more mules to change out to pull the wagons, allowed the train to move faster and longer. Crossing the Mojave was easier and wetter thanks to the season. Shep asked both Harriett and Thomas to pay close attention to the mood and personality of folks in Cedar City. Both commented on the dismal feelings. Shep didn't care to explain but appreciated their added testimony. Once again, he was glad they chose not to stay there but continued moving north.

During one of the short exchanges of drivers, Shep found Thomas Kane sitting next to him, giving him the chance he wanted to ask more about the goings-on back in Washington. He found Kane to be a wealth of information, exactly as Harriett had told him.

"I think it's amazing that you know this Jeremiah Black and that he's Buchanan's attorney general."

"Mostly it's my father who has been his friend. But yes, it has proven to be a great help in getting an audience with President Buchanan. A lot of people, mostly politicians right now, are ganging up on him for sending troops to the Utah Territory. They have termed the mistake, 'Buchanan's Blunder' and rightly so, I suppose. Why he would go off half-cocked with nothing more than the accusations of a disgruntled federal judge, is a mystery."

Shep nodded. "Bill Drummond. We have had several run-ins."

"But to have our commander in chief prosecute such an invasion before doing his due diligence, investigating the charges, is preposterous. The only redeeming grace I suppose is his directing me to travel out here to see if I can't be of assistance in reconciling Brigham Young with Alfred Cumming."

"Think it will take?"

"I do. They're both reasonable men. Neither wants bloodshed. I'm hoping that Cumming and his wife aren't frozen to death before we can't get them into the valley and have an audience with Governor Young."

"My sources seem to think Governor Cumming and his entourage are well enough situated."

"My greatest concerns lie with Colonel Johnston. He is a hothead, a typical military man. He resents anyone trying to pull the wool over the eyes of the nation. The Mormons in this case. I don't think he'd allow his soldiers to run rough-shod over the people of the territory but who knows? After an extended encampment in the snow and frost maybe his patience will wear thin."

"I don't think the Legion is any match for trained soldiers. We are outgunned and outmanned. On the other hand, we are tired of being driven, not allowed to enjoy the peace we seek, not allowed the rights promised by the constitution. I hope that no fiery officer decides to lead a charge down Echo Canyon without permission. That could be a real trial."

Kane agreed. "And that's exactly what the president is worried about. He's convinced that under the right circumstances, the Mormons could beat Johnston's army, regardless of weapons or ordnance. After suffering a lingering winter, our troops will not be in a position to fight. That's the worry with Colonel Johnston. I'm not sure he'll take the status of his troops into account before ordering an attack. Captain Van Vliet agrees. He's seen the defenses going up and knows somewhat of the strength of the Legion. This promises not to be the rag-tag mobbing of Missouri or Illinois. The president is certain such actions would be devastating for his political career."

"Placing lots of trust on you."

"Unofficially."

"Enough to make Johnston back off?"

"And then give me some clout, some inroads to negotiate with Cumming and then Brigham."

"We'll get you to Salt Lake City as quickly as we can. And we'll blame all the need for hurrying on Joseph F."

"Sounds good to me."

The speed of the wagons was faster than usual. The animals and the axels held out, while teamsters chuckled and nodded knowingly at the returning missionary. Four years is a long time for anyone to be absent from home and friends.

It was a huge feeling of relief and accomplishment for Shep when the wagons rolled into the blossoming city on Thursday, February 25, 1858. Governor Young was overjoyed to see both Joseph and Colonel Kane. He had a lot riding on his friend's arrival and now everything was beginning to line up. Instead of having Kane stay at the Townsend House, Brigham arranged to have the colonel stay with William Staines. Staines was a close friend of Young's, an all-around Renaissance man, who loved music and gardening and dabbled in politics. Staines built the first mansion in Salt Lake City. It was a luxurious, palatial house with plenty of room. And Staines, being an Englishman, was keen on having a man of Kane's reputation stay with him.

Also, now that Thomas Kane had officially arrived in the city, the pretense of 'Dr. Osborne' was thrown out. He instantly became the man about town, invited to endless dances and dinners. The busy schedule wore him down considerably, but he did his best to keep all entertained and happy with his attention.

During the following days, Governor Young held a series of councils with Kimball and Wells and the other community and ecclesiastical leaders of the area. But Dan Wells was the one who had most of the news Kane was interested in: the defensive posture of Deseret.

Shep took his wife and the Wetoyous back to Tooele. It was feeling like home. The Hansens were happy to see them as well as pass off the chores again to Zeenyo. Benson's grist mill was more than excited to have the strapping Herman Wetoyou back and shouldering his load. All in Tooele did their best to corner one or the other to quiz them about their trip. California seemed like a million miles away and exotic, warm and rich in both soil and gold. They were also pleased that Shep and Harriett had advertised the wealth and abundance in Tooele and a number of the emigrating Saints chose the area for their new home.

Returning just over a week later, Shep reported to the governor's office in the Beehive House, finding both Kane and the Governor there and visiting about the city and the territory.

"Has your stay helped solidify any of your ideas?" Shep asked Kane.

"It has been a good visit. Matter of fact I spent a couple days with Aaron and Yasmin and Esther. It has been relaxing and informative. I think Aaron told me everything there is to know about kerosene and the advancement of rifles, while Yasmin shared a number of stories from her past but especially the war in Crimea. Then there was the baby, of course. She makes me a trifle homesick for my children."

"So? What's the plan?"

Brigham clapped his hands and smiled. "I think Mr. Kane will talk the Honorable Alfred Cumming and his wife into coming down into the city and we'll have an exchange of authority. He will become the new governor. I will step aside. And I think Governor Cumming will direct Colonel Johnston to keep his troops far away from the city. Anyway, that's my wish. And I think Governor Cumming will then take up his new residence at Brother Staine's place. I can't think of anyplace better, and both Brother Staines and Colonel Kane here agree."

"All right then, are you ready to leave?"

Colonel Kane nodded. "Just have to grab my stuff and get it into your wagon. I've already said my goodbyes to the Rosts and the others about town."

The meeting was over and the men stood and shook hands.

"We're counting on you, Colonel," Brigham said seriously.

"The Lord has heard your prayers, Brigham. How can I fail?"

The two young mules Shep had harnessed to the wagon were strong and anxious to get moving. They pulled the wagon easily up the bench and towards the mouth of Emigration Canyon, while Kane and Silva basked in the sunlight. It would officially be spring in another two weeks but already the warmth of the days was coaxing the buds forth on the trees, as they started up the canyon.

"Did Brigham say anything to you about any other escort to Camp Scott?"

"Rockwell is set to meet us at the beginning of Echo Canyon and will have a horse for me to take into camp and use until I return."

They met the territory marshal a couple days later. Porter was in good spirits and had a beautiful bay horse in tow for Kane to transfer to as they neared Camp Scott. Mormons were still not wanted close to the compound and Porter and Shep agreed that it would not be good to push their luck.

Halfway up the canyon, they were joined by another company from the Legion. That night they bunked in the Cache Cave. Colonel Kane liked the natural enclosure and the view it gave of the surrounding country. He was also impressed by the amount of information the Legion had collected as well as the use of maps and messengers. They were confident in their abilities but not cocky.

Two days later, after guiding the attorney close to the area, the Mormons bid adieu to Colonel Thomas Kane and watched as he rode down into the basin where Fort Bridger was located. Very soon, sentries spotted him, and cavalry riders surrounded him for the remainder of his journey. He would spend the night there and then go to Camp Scott the following morning.

Artillery officer for the Expedition, Captain John Phelps wrote:

"Saturday, March 13- A man calling himself Mr. Kane of Philadelphia, bearer of dispatches from Washington arrived. I happened to be at

headquarters when he rode in from Bridger's Fort. He was a short, dark-complected young man and well mounted. Without looking right or left he moved straight forward to the commanding officer's tent and seemed as if he wished to ride into it instead of stopping outside, so near did he urge his horse to the opening. Someone—prob a servant—knocked and informed the Colonel that someone wished to see him. The Col was engaged in conversation and did not come out immediately, and this delay when compared with the man's forwardness seemed to look and be felt as a check. Presently the Col came partly out, but stopped apparently by the man's horse whose head was nearly in the opening, and looking up in a crouched attitude, his own head being near the horse's head, said, "Who are you?"

"Are you Colonel Johnston?"

"Yes."

"I am Mr. Kane from Philadelphia and bear some dispatches from Washington. I ask your permission to see Governor Cumming first. I'll see you afterwards." Kane's tone displayed his disregard for the commander.

"You got it." Col Johnston turned away and stepped back into his tent.

"I'll see you again, Col," he said. "Come on, Sergeant. Take me to the Governor's."

They crossed the short distance to the cabin where Alfred Cumming lived. It was immediately apparent that a woman was also present, as the house was neatly kept and decorated. Colonel Kane was introduced by the sergeant and let into the house.

Both Alfred and Elizabeth Cumming were impressed with Kane, especially that he had gone to such an extent to reach them. It was also not lost on them that he was an official herald of President James Buchanan. His valet was full of official documents describing the duties of the federal officers as well as warning them of the sensitivity of the mission.

Governor Cumming remained unconvinced with Kane's mission. It took a week of careful negotiations before Colonel Thomas Kane was able to persuade Cumming of the necessity of his going to Salt Lake City to meet Brigham Young, without an army escort. His only companion would be Thomas Kane.

After days of scouring the papers, then questioning and requestioning Kane, Governor Cumming finally decided that he was right. This was the most proper way to proceed. "But I want to bring Elizabeth," he insisted.

****

On Sunday, March 21st, Brigham Young announced the policy that the people of the territory would begin to implement to counter the arrival of the federal troops. It was termed the *Sevastopol Policy* and related, as nearly as he could tell, after having interrogated both Harriett and Yasmin, about the Russian tactics at the close of the siege of the city in 1855. Brigham stated:

"You may ask whether I am willing to burn up my houses? Yes, and to be the first man that will put a torch to my dwelling. I am for letting them come and take 'Sebastopol'." Young believed that Kane would be able to persuade Cumming to come to the city but as an extra caution, he encouraged the Saints to prepare their homes and farms to be burned. If the US Army were to enter the city without invitation, the policy detailing further scorched earth would begin. All the buildings would be razed, along with the gardens and fields. The enemy would have no claim to the labors of the Mormons.

On Temple Square, the foundation trenches were covered and filled in and then the ground plowed over, hiding any hint of the massive construction that had been taking place.

The word was quickly spread throughout to nearby communities that the people were to ready themselves, their wagons and teams, for a quick relocation south by the end of June, should the need arise. Families were prepared, bishops worked hard to make sure that everyone was able to comply. Fiery speeches were delivered from the pulpit, denouncing the treachery of the federal government, while proclaiming God's willingness to support the sacrifice and obedience of the Saints.

In Washington, President Buchanan had his hands full with the Congress.

Senator Sam Houston of Texas stated that a war against the Mormons would be "one of the most fearful calamities that has befallen this country, from its inception to the present moment. I deprecate it as an intolerable evil. I am satisfied that the Executive has not had the information he ought to have had on this subject before making such a movement as he has directed to be made."

On April 1st, Senator Simon Cameron of Pennsylvania declared that he would support a bill to authorize volunteers to fight in Utah and other parts of the frontier only because,

"This war is a war of the Administration; and I desire that the responsibility of it shall be on the Administration. I have no faith in their ability to conduct it; and I believe that before a year has passed over it will be evident to every citizen of the country that they have committed a great blunder."

Five days later, on April 6th, President James Buchanan issued a proclamation detailing the reasons for his decision, most of which he had received from Judge William Drummond and had not investigated further. Nevertheless, he pushed forward and wrote the following proclamation:

But being anxious to save the effusion of blood and to avoid the indiscriminate punishment of a whole people for crimes of which it is not probable that all are equally guilty, I offer now a free and full pardon to all who will submit themselves to the just authority of the Federal Government. If you refuse to accept it, let the consequences fall upon your own heads. But I conjure you to pause deliberately and reflect well before you reject this tender of peace and good will.

466

Now, therefore, I, James Buchanan, President of the United States, have thought proper to issue this, my proclamation, enjoining upon all public officers in the Territory of Utah to be diligent and faithful, to the full extent of their power, in the execution of the laws; commanding all citizens of the United States in said Territory to aid and assist the officers in the performance of their duties; offering to the inhabitants of Utah who shall submit to the laws a free pardon for the seditions and treasons heretofore by them committed; warning those who shall persist, after notice of this proclamation, in the present rebellion against the United States that they must expect no further lenity, but look to be rigorously dealt with according to their deserts; and declaring that the military forces now in Utah and hereafter to be sent there will not be withdrawn until the inhabitants of that Territory shall manifest a proper sense of the duty which they owe to this Government.

April 7th, Governor Alfred Cumming, assisted by his wife, Elizabeth, and accompanied by Colonel Thomas Kane, climbed into their light carriage, in contradiction to the wishes of the US Army, Colonel Johnston, and the three hardline federal judges who had arrived with them, started on their trip, unescorted, to the Salt Lake Valley. Porter Rockwell and four other Legionnaires joined them at the head of Echo Canyon, to insure they traveled in peace and comfort and that they would arrive without any complications. Dan Wells made sure Governor and Mrs. Cumming could see the troops lining the ridges, leading them to think there were many more than existed. It was wonderful for the Cummings to leave the cabin and be out in the fresh mountain air. The stormy weather had finally moved on. Morning temperatures were chilly, but the sun soon burned off any lingering dew and warmed the air considerably by noon. Their escorts were silent, allowing Governor and Mrs. Cumming all the time they wanted to visit with Colonel Kane while trying to get a lay of the land.

Early Sunday morning, Porter sent one of the men ahead to alert Brigham of their pending arrival. It was evening when the wagon and its escort arrived in the city. Being the Sabbath, it was quiet. Porter took them to William Staines' mansion, where the owner politely introduced himself and gave them a tour of the house, letting them know where things were and that he would be living just across the street should they need anything in particular. He then gave them the keys to the doors, informed them and Rockwell that Governor Young wanted to meet with them at 9:00 in the morning, and he left.

The next morning, Porter took the pair to the government office building where they were cordially received by Governor Brigham Young and a room full of territory leadership. Governor Cumming was introduced as the new governor, succeeding Governor Young, who then delivered the territorial records and seal to the Honorable Governor Alfred Cumming. After several impromptu meetings with Young, Governor Cumming felt well placed and respected. It was a dream position.

Carrying a white flag, Porter and Shep rode back to Camp Scott with news of the successful installation of Governor Cumming and to retrieve the balance of their belongings. They also left strict orders from Cumming that the troops remain put until they received his orders to leave the Fort Bridger area.

After another week the rest of the government officials and their families were ushered from Camp Scott, brought down into the valley, and welcomed. It was a pleasant way to finish up their winter stay on the prairie.

Another blessing that followed the lifting of sanctions, was the reopening of the mail from the States. People flocked to the post office to collect even the most outdated letters.

Thomas Kane was in his glory, watching the arms of government coalesce. Despite the suspicions that plagued the early days after the arrival of the balance of the government employees, feelings soon began to warm, and people began to see each other mostly as friends and allies, citizens of the same nation, rather than opponents and enemies.

Colonel Kane had finally given in to the pleadings of Yasmin and Aaron, deciding to live in their home during his stay in Great Salt Lake City. Esther was charming and crawling all around the house, daring the Colonel to chase her as she squealed with delight. The home setting was just what Kane needed. He felt a comfort and peace that had eluded him for months. Yasmin's cooking also helped to ease any worries He started to regain his weight and his strength. And although Governor and Mrs. Cumming had a maid and a cook to tend to their needs, Kane knew they also were quite satisfied with their new home and work assignments. Keeping his ear to the ground, that was also what he heard from the other Washington transplants.

Chapter 62

"We should never permit ourselves to do anything that we are not willing to see our children do." Brigham Young

Even though mail from the States had been suspended for several months, letters sent within the territory were frequent and delivered in a timely fashion. In Tooele, Harriett received a perky letter from Yasmin, detailing the growth of Esther and also of Aaron's schedule. She also spoke about Colonel Kane, the pleasure of having him in their home but then the reality of his needing to get back to Washington and his family in Philadelphia.

"I close, dear Harriett, letting you know that it is one of his greatest desires to come and visit you and your family before his departure. Would that be possible?"

Harriett dashed off a positive response the minute she received Yasmin's letter.

"Visitors?" Shep asked. He was dog-tired. He and Zeenyo had been fencing all day. Driving the posts into the rocky ground was man's work and it wore him out. He tried having Zeenyo spell him, but it never lasted very long. As the day drew on, the heat of the sun began to loosen the wire he needed to unwrap and tie to the posts. He was happy to have a new pair of leather gloves protecting his hands. At times he would get angry with some of the poles or his hammer or of the wire and he would grip tight and bear down on the project in his hands and the effort would peel the skin from his palms regardless of calluses. He would then have to remove the torn skin, leaving large and painful divots. These required a week to heal. "Did Ett say anything to you about visitors?"

"Nope."

As they neared their house, Shep recognized the carriage as the one belonging to the Rosts. It had seen better days. Aaron needed to add a coat of paint. Shep and Zeenyo stomped on the porch to loosen the mud from their boots before entering the house. They were both surprised to see that Tom Kane had accompanied the Rosts on their trip.

Hands were shaken. Shep pretended not to feel pain, choosing to smile instead. Yasmin had taken the baby into the kitchen to visit with Harriett and Linda G.

"Things going well enough in the city? Governor Cumming happy?"

"As good as can be hoped for, I think," Kane replied.

"I haven't heard anything from Brother Wells so I'm thinking things are still quiet as far as the troops are concerned. Our Legion boys haven't been called up this season."

Aaron chuckled. "I'm glad I'm no longer a young man. War games are a young man's playground." Looking over at Kane, he added, "Or men who enjoy dressing in uniforms, no matter the age. Am I right, Tom?"

The Philadelphian only smiled and nodded. "Brigham's still worried about Johnston's proximity. He's mobilizing the folks in the territory for an evacuation. It looks exactly like a military operation."

"Our bishop hasn't said anything lately."

Kane continued. "I think Brig thought about the Bitterroot Mountains up north but has finally decided the Saints should go south. He's notified the people down south to prepare their wagons and start sending them north for the people in the city to use. Brigham wants to avoid any conflict with the army if at all possible and do that by getting out of the way. He held a war council and wants to be as prepared as possible. He's also ready to burn everything, following the Russian example at Sevastopol."

"Does Staines feel the same? He's the reason Brigham's even got the gardens and orchards he does." Shep laughed.

"Speaking of the military, Brigham has divided the Church into three groups. The folks in the south are sending their wagons and supplies to the city. Up north, the families are packing up and leaving, moving south, past Provo. They are leaving some of their young men at home to keep irrigating and watching the fields. They are also the ones assigned to burn things should the army show up. If anything, Brigham is acting like a military officer. He's dividing the wards into groups of tens, fifties, and hundreds, with overseers to help and guide. Quite impressive. The last group is more than 30,000 in the valley who are to get set to leave and move south, again leaving their houses, gardens, and fields prepared to burn. That also includes the other buildings in the city."

"Lots of anger has been brewing. The soldiers want to destroy the valley and the city, especially Colonel Johnston. He's upset at having been so successfully put off for the winter. He wants to use the cannons and everything."

The next morning, after the Rosts had left, Shep took Kane out to see his horses and the pastures he was struggling to enclose. Harriett had already given him a tour of the farm.

"I'm impressed, dear fellow," Kane noted as they rode their carriage beyond the fields. Looking south and west they could see Rush Lake and the Rush Valley, where the previous soldiers with Steptoe had grazed their herds.

"What's your thoughts, Colonel? You think Johnston's going to behave himself?"

"I do. Either that or Governor Cumming will give him a solid boot." He stopped speaking for a moment and eyed Shep. "There's something I've been meaning to tell you and didn't want to drag it out so long. Mostly, I've wanted some time for myself to think it over."

"All right."

He pulled a letter from his vest pocket. It had been addressed by a woman's hand. "I just received this on the 24th from Bessie, my wife. It was held up because of the mail from the States being suspended. Anyway, she wrote to inform me that my father passed away, back in February when we were making our way up here from lower California."

Shep's eye swept the far horizon slowly. "I am truly sorry, *meu amigo*. I know the two of you were very close. Ett has told me some about your very colorful family. You are truly blessed."

"And your father?"

Shep shrugged. "I never knew him. I don't know who he was. My mother never spoke of him."

"Sorry."

"Not a problem, Colonel. All of us are given our own special circumstances. Some are kings and some are paupers. What took me from Brazil to the islands and finally here to America, more than the geography has been the people I have met, so wonderful, so varied."

"And what of Linda G?"

"The Hansen boy has finally asked her to marry him."

"And so God continues to work his wonders within your sphere. You are a blessed man."

"I really have no idea where I would be without Ett. She is so deep and beautiful. And not without your influence, I might add." Shep took a deep breath, smelling the fragrance of the sage and feeling the warmth of the sun on his face. "This country is so large and possesses so many different climes. But here, Colonel, here is where I feel the happiest."

"I get hay fever."

Shep Silva laughed good-naturedly. "I guess we all have our challenges. I still wish everyone knew how to speak Portuguese."

"The world would definitely be a better place."

For the next two weeks, Colonel Thomas Kane was invited to help around the house, in the barnyard, evening plowing, and planting. Shep had him help with the horses and cattle. They visited Benson's grist mill and got some pointers from Herman. On Sundays, the Colonel dutifully attended church with the ward. The bishop gave some heads up about the current status with the soldiers at Fort Bridger and what the members could do to prepare.

The time passed more quickly than anyone around Colonel Thomas Kane wanted. He was pleased with the experiences. He was anxious to return to Washington and report to President Buchanan. He missed Bessie and his children. He also figured that this was his last hurrah among these charming people, members of the Church of Jesus Christ of Latter-day Saints. Like a sponge, he hoped to have soaked up as many sights and memories as he could, knowing they would color his life for the balance of his years.

On May 12th the Silvas rode with Colonel Kane back to Salt Lake City where he gave his final good-byes to President Young, Governor Cumming, some other local leaders, and the Rosts. Under a guard of Legionnaires, he left the valley, climbing Emigration Canyon. Looking back, he wondered about the future. Would Deseret remain the defense and refuge from the whirlwind Brigham Young claimed it would be? Riding east, he looked forward to his chance to bring his report to President James Buchanan.

Before Colonel Kane and Governor Cumming arrived in Salt Lake City, Church leaders had decided that the Saints in northern Utah would need to evacuate their homes and move south to avoid conflict with the United States army when Colonel Johnston arrived later in the season. Brigham Young vowed, "Rather than see my wives and daughters ravished and polluted, and the seeds of corruption sown in the hearts of my sons by a brutal soldiery, I would leave my home in ashes, my gardens and orchards a waste, and subsist upon roots and herbs, a wanderer through these mountains for the remainder of my natural life."

By the time Governor Cumming arrived, the once teeming city was already becoming depopulated, following Brigham Young's direction. Cumming tried to have them cease but was unsuccessful.

For this "move south," the Church was divided into three groups, each with a specific mission: Those living in southern Utah were not to move but were instructed to send wagons, teams, and teamsters to northern Utah to assist in the move. The young and vigorous Saints living in northern Utah would remain behind to irrigate crops and gardens, guard property, and set fire to the straw-filled homes if need be. And some thirty-five thousand Saints living north of Utah Valley were to make the move. Each ward was allotted a strip of land in one of four counties south of Salt Lake County. Provisions were to be moved first and then families.

The move was carried out in strict military order, each ward being organized into tens, fifties, and hundreds, with a captain over each. Families were expected to transport their furniture, in addition to food and clothing.

One pioneer teenager recorded, "We packed all we had into father's one wagon and waited for the command to leave. At night we lay down to sleep, not knowing when word would come of the army which we thought was coming to destroy us.

"One morning father told us that we should leave with a large company in the evening.

"Along in the middle of the day father scattered leaves and straw in all the rooms and I heard him say: 'Never mind, little daughter, this house has sheltered us, it shall never shelter them.'"

Hulda Cordelia Thurston, a young girl living in Centerville, Utah, recalled the difficulty of the move: "*In the spring of 1858 we moved at the time of the great Mormon exodus. We went as far south as Spanish Fork, and on the Spanish Fork bottoms there was good feed for our stock and plenty of fish in the river. At that time all the people living north of Utah Valley moved south leaving their homes with furniture, farming implements, in fact their all, not knowing where they were going nor what their destiny. ...*

"During that exodus I shall never forget the distress and poverty of the people. I have seen men wearing trousers made of carpet, their feet wrapped in burlap or rags. Women sewed cloth together and made moccasins for their feet. Many women and children were barefoot. One good sister, a neighbor who had a family of seven, told my mother that aside from the clothing on their bodies, she could tie up in a common bandanna handkerchief every article of clothing they possessed. She would put the children to bed early Saturday night and repair and wash and iron their clothing preparatory for Sunday. The people were practically all poor for we had had several years of great scarcity of crops because of the grasshoppers."

Upon arriving at their destination, families lived either in the boxes of their heavy-covered wagons, canvas tents, dugouts, or in temporary board shanties and cabins.

Church records and assets were removed or cached by the public works department. One group hid all the stone that had been cut for the Salt Lake Temple and leveled and covered over its foundation so that the plot would resemble a plowed field and remain unmolested. Another group boxed all of the <u>tithing</u> grain in bins and transported twenty thousand bushels to specially erected granaries in Provo. Additional wagon trains carried machinery and equipment to be housed in hastily constructed warehouses and sheds.

The move south occupied almost two months. It was completed by mid-May. A daily average of six hundred wagons passed through Salt Lake City during the first two weeks of the month. An estimated thirty thousand Saints left their homes in Salt Lake and the northern settlements.

Governor Cumming and his wife pleaded with Church members not to leave their homes, but the Saints chose to heed their prophet. The exodus of such a large body of people drew national and international attention to the Church.

The London Times reported: *"We are told that they have embarked for a voyage over five hundred miles of untracked desert."*

The New York Times declared: *"We think it would be unwise to treat Mormonism as a nuisance to be abated by a posse comitatus."*

The move placed the United States government in an unfavorable light as a persecutor of innocent people and demonstrated the leadership ability of Brigham Young. The title and accusation of Buchanan's Blunder again reared its head. Fortunately, negotiations between the government and the Church kept the army from invading. Early in 1858, President Buchanan decided to send a peace commission to Utah. In early June two commissioners, Ben McCulloch and Lazarus Powell, arrived in Salt Lake City, carrying President Buchanan's proclamation, his offer of pardon for the Saints if they would reaffirm their loyalty to the government. Church leaders were indignant at the idea of a pardon. Once again, they reiterated that they had never been disloyal. Nevertheless, after several negotiation sessions, it was accepted. Church leaders felt they could accept the pardon because of the raiding activities of the Nauvoo Legion. One of the agreements between the peace commission and Church leaders was that the army would quietly enter the capital city and then establish a federal military post at least forty miles away from both Salt Lake City and Provo.

On June 19th the New York Herald reported the end to the Utah War, stating: "*Thus was peace made—thus was ended the 'Mormon War' which may be thus historicized, Killed, none; wounded, none; fooled, everybody.*"

Unfortunately, the reporter wasn't quite right. The Utah War claimed about 150 lives, including 120 from Mountain Meadows, and that was about the same number as were killed in the seven-year contemporaneous Bloody Kansas.

One of the issues that worried Brigham Young was the finding, arresting, and prosecution of the murderers at Mountain Meadows. The horrid specter haunted the ex-governor. He brought up the idea several times to Governor Cumming. The latter dragged his feet, thinking Buchanan's proclamation would cover the guilty and allow them to go free. He decided to leave the topic alone and perhaps visit it later and after emotions had calmed.

****

For the talented, young, charming Ina Coolbrith, California's southland was perfect for a woman in love. The spring was vibrant, singing with rebirth and newness of life. Colors, once pale and uncertain, were blossoming forth, resplendent with dazzling hues and aromas.

Despite the unusual interaction between Bob and Joseph F, Ina felt comfortable and sure in her decision to get married. It was a tale as old as time, the meeting of the fair maiden and the powerful young knight. All things were coming together, blending as hearts beat and eyes looked heavenward, counting the stars and wishing upon meteors. Her life was coming to fruition. Legions of prosperous folk applauded her work, adored her choices. Bob Carsley was such a pick. Handsome, hardworking, ambitious. He wasn't afraid to memorize his lines, to act out on stage, to travel for the betterment of the troop, and yet stay founded in the reality of making money, performing a service for the community. His work being an ironmonger was well known and respected. His future looked as bright as Ina's.

They should get married and what day would be better than April 21st. They chose to speak their nuptials in San Gabriel, the region's most pleasant garden spot.

To sing and shout in the fields about
In the balm and the blossoming!
Sing loud, O bird in the tree;
O bird, sing loud in the sky,
And honey-bees blacken the clover bed
There is none of you glad as I.

It was the event of the year. People from all over southern California came to the home of Dr. Hall near the San Gabriel Mission. The darling of the Los Angeles Star was being wed to an honorable man of many untapped talents. Ina was at the pinnacle of her life. All her dreams were coming true. Of course, some personalities were not able to make the festivities, but all would go forward as prescribed. Life was a journey, and all would be encountered again.

The leaves laugh low in the wind,
Laugh low with the wind at play;
And the odorous call of the flowers all
Entices my soul away!

The editor of the Star wrote after the wedding: "*Cupid, the sly archer, has been winging his shafts pretty freely of late, in this locality. Among his conquests, as will be seen elsewhere today, we find enrolled our young friend and highly esteemed correspondent, Miss Josephine Smith, whose compositions, over the signature of "Ina," have frequently delighted our readers. Entering now on the serious duties of life, we may be permitted to wish her all felicity, and that her future may be as happy as her past has been and full of promise.*"

The young couple moved into a small, adobe house on a treeless street, not far from her sister, Charlotte, where she could find advice for domestic issues. Bob was proud of his wife and proud of the fact that he had captured the most radiant young woman in all of lower California. He was charming and witty. Both of them enjoyed flattery, that was what drew them together.

"But there's more to it," her sister warned. "Bob has an artist's temperament. He needs to be given his space as well as his adorations."

"Does he see my poetry as competition?"

"Perhaps. It would be good to talk with him about your intentions. Where you see yourself going. You definitely have made an impact on people here in Los Angeles."

"And I love our home. It's a perfect bungalow but it gets hot in the afternoon. I'm not sure, but I think I will give my pen a rest. At least for the near future."

"That could be all Bob needs. Some more time and attention from you."

"Or maybe a baby."

"What?" Charlotte asked.

"I think I'm pregnant."

Chapter 63

"Prayer keeps man from sin, and sin keeps man from prayer." Brigham Young

As I was sittin' by the fire,
eatin spuds and a drinkin' porter
suddenly a thought came into my head
I'd like to marry Old Reilly's daughter
Old Reilly played on a big bass drum
Reilly had a mind for murder and slaughter
Reilly had a big red glistenin' eye
and he kept that eye on his lovely daughter

One-Eyed Reilley was a long-treasured and lusty ditty from the barracks the soldiers enjoyed singing as they marched. The stanzas of the tune were virtually unlimited in length as well as their bawdy content, each company vying to make the verse filthier than the previous. On Saturday morning, June 26, 1858, Colonel Johnston led his troops from the mouth of Emigration Canyon and into the valley of the Great Salt Lake. The capital city of the territory was mostly deserted. There were no animals. The wide streets were quiet. Storefronts were vacant. There were only a few young men, who watched carefully behind walls or around corners, ready to burn the city at a moment's notice.

Her hair was black and her eyes were blue
the major and the corporal and the captain saught her
the sergeant and the piper and the drummer boy too
they never had a chance with Reilly's daughter

Well I got me a ring and a parson too
I got me a scratch in a merry quarter
settled me down to a peaceful life
happy as a king with Reilly's daughter

The band had to be commanded to stop and serenade Governor Cumming at his new residence. William Staines and his wife were conspicuously absent. By this time the soldiers believed Cumming to be sympathetic to the Latter-day Saints, so they were less than enthusiastic in their performance.

An embittered Colonel Albert Johnston commented, "I would give my plantation in China Grove, Texas, for the chance to bombard this city for just fifteen minutes."

His backup, Lt. Colonel Charles Ferguson Smith, ranted, "I do not give a damn who might hear me. I'd like to see every damned Mormon hung by the neck."

The one exception among the officers was Lt. Colonel Philip St. George Cooke, who had led in the long, nearly two-thousand-mile march of the Mormon Battalion eleven years earlier. In US Army circles he came to be known as the father of the cavalry. At this time, he simply took off his hat and held it over his heart as a symbol of respect to the disenfranchised.

Captain Jesse Gove wrote: "*Left camp early. I am rear guard of our own regiment. We found the city evacuated. All had gone to Provo except a few men left to burn the city if ordered. The city is 50% better in structure and situation than I expected. It is beautifully laid out and watered at every street. Brigham's palace is a magnificent structure. His apartment for his wives is attached. It is said that the inside is furnished in the most elaborate style, furniture imported, two or three pianos, etc.*"

General Burton of the Nauvoo Legion recorded: "*At 10 a.m. troops commenced passing through until 12:30 when those in the rear halted. At 2 p.m. again commenced to pass through until 5:30 p.m. There are reported to be 600 wagons, 6000 head of animals and 3000 men. They camped over Jordan, west of the city.*"

Only a few Latter-day Saints had been left behind to set the torch to the city if the army did not respect its pledge to leave the property alone. These serious men watched closely the antics of the US soldiers. Hearing the raucous verses of the song failed to impress them.

> *Well five big knocks come knockin' at the door*
> *who should it be but Reilly after slaughter*
> *with two pistols in his hand*
> *lookin' for the man what had married his daughter*
> *I grabbed Old Reilly by the hair*
> *I rammed his head in a pail of water*
> *shot his pistols into the air*
> *a damn sight quicker than I married his daughter*

The army moved down North Temple Street and west to the Jordan River. They followed the river south for several miles where they set up a temporary camp. Johnston finally decided they would move to Cedar Valley, forty miles to the south. It was east of the Rush Valley and west of Provo but shielded from the number two city in the territory and Utah Lake by a decent mountain. But it was only separated from the town of Fairfield by a small ditch. The camp was named Camp Floyd after the Secretary of War, John Floyd. It was set on 100 acres. The US government pumped $200,000 into the local economy for the construction of the camp. During its three-year tenure, the camp grew to 7000 inhabitants, making it the third-largest community in the territory, smaller only than Salt Lake City and Provo. Camp Floyd also boasted one-third of all the soldiers in the US Army. The soldiers were shunned from the Mormon communities. Whenever the soldiers wandered away, Salt Lake City averaged a murder every week. Soldiers held competitions as to who could be the worst in the Mormon eyes, who could break the most commandments. Finally, the army set up its theater, temperance society, circus, and brought in the first Masonic Lodge of the territory. The army made forays into the west desert to fight Indians or to survey new overland routes to California. Two of their new roads cut off 254 and 283 miles to Carson Valley. A new and safer road was opened up from Fort Bridger, bypassing Emigration Canyon and going through the Provo Canyon to Camp Floyd. Under Colonel Johnston's watch, the soldiers gathered up the seventeen orphans created by the Mountain Meadows Massacre and took them back to family members in Arkansas by way of Fort Leavenworth.

Of early concern to church leaders, Fairfield, a satellite town of Camp Floyd, was viewed as bringing moral decay to the area. Termed "Frogtown" by the Saints and army alike, it became a den of gambling houses, dance halls, brothels, and saloons, frequented by soldiers, teamsters, emigrants, and local settlers. Theft, prostitution, and murder filled the streets and back halls. Church leaders mourned the spread of moral and social deterioration throughout the valley. One member said, "Camp Floyd and Fairfield was full of rottenness and evil of every description and I'm sorry to say our people of both sexes mixed up with them largely and of how bad it did look to see young ladies whose parents were faithful."

The army's livestock grazed west of the camp and toward Rush Valley but finally needed to be expanded to pastures in nearby counties.

More than 300 buildings were erected, most of them being made from adobe brick. Lumber was in great demand and the Mormons took advantage of the market, being already in place and up to speed. Grains and feed were also needed. Men were needed to complete the construction of the camp. The local economy was flush with currency, something that wasn't expected. The advent of Johnston's Army following the Utah War signaled the end of Mormon society's isolation from the rest of the United States.

Johnston's soldiers lived in tents through most of the summer. The construction of Camp Floyd was started on Tuesday, August 24th and amid gunfire and patriotic music, it was finished on Tuesday, November 9, 1858. Brigham Young had insisted that the camp be built at least forty miles from Salt Lake City so that if there were any troubles and the army was sent, he would have some time to muster his forces.

On July 1st, Brigham Young authorized the return of the Saints to their homes. It was an uncanny sight, seeing thousands of Mormons in wagons and driving livestock, headed north to their abandoned homes and farms, while on the other side of the river, miles of soldiers were making their way south to the land designated for Camp Floyd. There was an uneasy association between the government troops and the local population. By sad experience, the church leaders had learned not to trust unregulated soldiers. Evils of the army influence were preached weekly over the pulpits, and except for necessary work details, the people were warned to stay away.

The sudden growth of Camp Floyd and Fairfield proved to be a windfall for kerosene sales. Aaron Rost made several trips to the area peddling his oil and keeping the area lit well into the night, sparkling jewels. He was also quick to learn of the building of an infirmary in the camp and the desperate need for qualified nurses and laundresses. The information was disseminated among people in Salt Lake City as well as Tooele and Provo.

There was a great and unforeseen result of burying the foundation stones of the temple. Upon digging them back up, workers discovered cracks in the sandstone. This would never do, not since Brigham had prophesied that the edifice was to last through the millennium. The sandstone was switched to a much harder granite. It was more to cut and farther away as well as heavier but that was the direction the workers and artisans and President Brigham pursued.

"The camp looks to be in good shape," Shep said truthfully to Lt. Colonel Cooke who was giving him the private tour.

"It's hard to believe all the work that's gone into the project," Cooke replied. "I was surprised at how well your people here in the territory are at building. I guess I shouldn't be. Everything I have seen around the valleys looks quite professional. Very upscale. The carpenters aren't even all British."

"They've been at it for years, especially working with adobe. It's amazing how warm the houses stay in the winter and how cool they are in the summer. I think the troops will be pleased."

"Anything's better than tents."

Shep smiled but didn't say anything. He felt justified having the soldiers spend the previous winter in tents and living on starvation rations. Riding around the facilities, he recognized some troops that he had come across during the conflict of a year earlier. "You want to graze towards the Rush Valley?"

"We have quite a few horses and oxen and mules, too. We'll end up shipping some off to nearby counties for forage and to get through the winter. We have been spending a lot of cash for hay and grain. It makes the locals quite happy, but we need to change business around. What we want to do is avoid fighting over grazing rights. There's already some squatters we'll need to deal with."

"We're doing the best we can but it's a challenge."

"And you're willing to provide horses should we need some quick?"

Shep was pleased. "I have a thousand I can bring you. Many are mine. Some belong to the folks in Tooele. We've already talked it over and everyone is fine with the dragoons using them should the need arise."

"That's a relief. One more problem off my plate."

"Oh, that all our problems could be fixed so easily."

"Amen, brother."

"So, let me ask you, what's the biggest problem you're facing?"

"Really? You're interested in the goings-on in Camp Floyd?"

"I am still a deputy, Colonel Cooke."

George Cooke nodded and spit into the frozen ground. "Not enough women. The good kind, mind you. Too much drinking and gambling. Letters are slow to get here. Our water tastes like mud. The troops pass around sicknesses way too quickly. What else or is that enough?"

"Aren't you glad you're still not camping out around Fort Bridger?" The Brazilian's laugh was melodic, masking how dangerous he could be if the conditions warranted. Cooke was fully aware of some of the antics he had been involved with while the troops were in Camp Scott. He also knew of Shep's connection with Lot Smith and Porter Rockwell. The names evoked nasty memories and frustrating episodes. The US military had been backed into a corner by the mounted Mormon guerrillas.

"I'm okay with it Shep but there are plenty of folks around here who have long memories. I don't think you ever want to spend much time alone with Colonel Johnston."

"He's an ass."

"You'll get no argument from me. But he's still out of sorts over the way he thinks the Mormons have treated the government, meaning him and his troops."

"He asked for it."

Lt. Colonel Cooke nodded and decided to change the subject. "Want to know the real problem we've got here? Trying to get a chaplain. The men have been bawling about the lack of religion. You'd never guess it, but they want to hear about God's word. A lot."

"That's not what we usually hear around these parts. At least, not from folks not belonging to the church. Most seem to think the area oozes religion. Some think it's steeped into the sagebrush. Most who are passing through want to get through as quick as they can. Course they've heard their fill about the Danites and whatnot."

"The soldiers are scared of the Mormon preachers. I think they're afraid of getting caught in the web or the snare or whatever. So, we contracted to get a chaplain out here. At first, the men were happy until they learned that he's Catholic. Then all hell broke loose. Listening to them whine, you'd think they were all leaders in the Reformation. They despise Catholics almost as much as Mormons."

Shep laughed out loud. "Let's take a ride and I'll show you the area you can have your herders bring your animals. We'll work out some other plans to keep them safe and fed for the next while."

****

Colonel Johnston jumped up from his desk and met Harriet Silva halfway across his office. He was smiling and kindly took her arm and led her to an

480

overstuffed chair. "Miss Harriett, I'm happy to greet you. I understand that your husband is showing Lt. Colonel Cooke some of the range for the animals to graze. I also understand that you are a trained nurse and have inquiries about our infirmary?"

"Yes, quite."

"Fortunately, we are not involved with a shooting war, something you already have plenty of experience with. No, I'm happy to admit that our men are dealing mostly with colds and seasonal sickness. It would be a feather in our cap to have someone of your abilities to watch over our sick and afflicted. I don't know your schedule, but I believe we could use your services at least a couple of times a week."

"I know several other women who are qualified to care for the infirm, as well. They live just up the road from us and would also be interested in some form of employment."

"I see." Colonel Johnston furrowed his brow as if he were deep in thought. "I believe something can be worked out. I certainly want you to be content with our offerings. We have been pleasantly surprised with the quality of work given to us by the locals. Of course, we have paid handsomely for these services."

Harriett nodded her understanding.

"And it's good when people have more than one area of expertise. Are some of your acquaintances also capable of doing laundry or cooking?"

"I was led to believe that you simply needed nursing staff, colonel."

"Oh, please. When we're alone in my office, you may call me by my name. Albert. And yes, I can understand any confusion. During the winter our level of illness is higher but as things continue to warm up the sickness lessens. Does that make a difference?"

"The women I know are simply looking for a couple of days labor and to gain more experience. They seem to have enough cooking and laundry in their homes."

"I believe I understand clearly enough." Colonel Johnston was a charming, southern officer, sporting a heavy mustache. "I'm sure we can work something out that will be to the satisfaction of all involved." His standing seemed to indicate that the interview was over. He walked to the door and quietly closed it, leaving him and Harriett isolated from others in the building. "Please, Miss Harriett, I want you to understand that I am more than a little attracted to you. I am flattered to find you here in my office speaking with me. I have been wanting someone, a woman, to talk with, someone to share more intimate thoughts. Would you be interested in knowing me better?"

"No, sir." Harriett tried to step around him to reach the door, but he blocked her path.

"Would you at least consider my offer? Together, I know we can reach a number of pleasant conclusions, regarding your friends, or one another."

"No, sir. I want nothing to do with you, intimately or otherwise." Again, she tried stepping around him, suddenly aware of the disparity in their sizes. Colonel Johnston was aging but still bulky and built like a warrior.

"I'm not suggesting that you be a prostitute," he said in a low, quiet voice that was turning husky. "We have enough whores around here. I don't care to smear your reputation. Everything could be kept under wraps."

Harriett shook her head and once again tried stepping around the colonel. "Do you not understand my position, sir? I have made myself crystal clear."

"Oh, my dear. Please…" Albert slid his hands around her waist and pulled her close, bending down to kiss her lips. He was surprised when her arms lifted and wrapped around his neck.

Then her hands grasped the back of his head and jerked it forcefully downward, smashing his face onto the top of her head, sending a flash of pain from his nose out onto his cheeks. Before he could gasp, Harriett's knee shot up and connected solidly with the colonel's crotch. Albert Johnston bent over and staggered backward, then slowly dropped to the ground. Blood spurted from his discolored nose. One hand reached to cover his face, while the other moved underneath his belt and lower, all the while a deep groaning emitted from his distorted mouth.

No longer having the burly obstacle blocking her path, Harriett hopped over the dazed soldier and opened the door. She stopped and looked down at Colonel Johnston. "I told you in no uncertain terms, multiple times, sir. I trust this will never happen again. Not with me or any of my associates. I will make sure that none of our women are ever alone with you and we will do our future business with Lt. Colonel Cooke."

The door slammed behind her with finality, as Harriett walked from the officers' building.

****

Shep and Harriett, Aaron, and Yasmin were happy to have been invited to the wedding of the twenty-year-old Joseph F. The young man had been active with the Legion the year before after his release from his mission until the hostilities ceased. He was a serious but pleasant man. All who knew him could see the importance the gospel played in his life. More than anything, he wanted to pursue the plan the Lord had for him. He fit in well with the society of Salt Lake City.

After his stint with the Legion, he began to search seriously for a wife and came across the sixteen-year-old Levira Annette Smith. She also was his cousin, the daughter of Samuel Smith, Joseph's brother, who had died tragically a month after the Prophet's murder. Some markers might have been raised but they were young and quite taken with one another.

The Endowment House had more people than usual to witness the sealing. Hearing once more the precise words of the covenant brought back sweet memories for the Rosts and the Silvas. Shep and Harriett were satisfied with the life they were living. Aaron and Yasmin were expecting their second baby in a few months. Business was good. Both couples were settling into the roles of responsibility in their respective communities.

Joseph F was tall and skinny. Levira was short and petite. April 5th would be a day etched into their lives together.

Each week, Latter-day Saints partook of the sacrament, emblems of the body and blood of the Savior. It was a time also for them to renew the covenants they had made before God. These covenants were sacred and personal, whether baptism or endowments, the people remembered the promises. The sacrament was not taken to demonstrate fidelity to the church, success in keeping commandments before the bishop, or curious parents. The sacrament was eaten and sipped, witnessing to God, that the covenants entered into remained forefront in their minds and lives.

As he watched the young couple, Shep couldn't help but think of Ina and Bob Carsley. They had been married almost a year earlier. He hadn't heard of any baby's birth but then again, they were living in Los Angeles. That remained a long distance from the territory and the dissemination of news was slow. He understood that correspondence remained open between Joseph F and Ina. Family relations.

He also knew that many frontier people chose to marry closer kin.

On June 22nd, Henry Comstock discovered the silver lode in Nevada at Gold Hill and Virginia City, starting another rush of prospectors. This time, people came from California as well as the eastern states.

Harriett started going to Camp Floyd several times a week, always accompanied by Linda G or one other sister from Tooele, attending to the sick and infirm soldiers. Besides seeing that they had clean bedding and good food, they made sure that the soldiers were exposed to fresh air and sunshine. Harriett and her associates were never bothered by Colonel Johnston, who made sure to keep his distance from the infirmary.

Crime in the area was rising, due in part to the influence of the soldiers or people preying on them. Shep stayed busy, while Porter was trying to establish his inn and saloon at the point of the mountain or the river narrows, where the Jordan River left Utah Valley and ran into the Great Salt Lake Valley.

As the weeks, then months dragged along the numbers of criminal infractions began to diminish and Shep found himself spending more time with his horses.

Chapter 64

"Slavery is the next thing to hell." Harriett Tubman

The Rosts had been good taking turns driving to Tooele to visit until Yasmin's growing belly precluded it. Then, the Silvas took their turn, riding into Salt Lake City to visit their friends and tend little Esther.

"I have a proposition for you," Aaron told Shep one day late in July. "I need to make a trip back east to check on some kerosene orders and also buy some carbines for the Legion. I'll be carrying some serious currency and I think it would be prudent to have someone with me, especially someone who is able to handle a weapon, if need be. You're my first thought. Want to go?"

It was intriguing. Shep had wanted to make the trip for quite some time. "Let me clear it with Ett."

"I already did. She can stay here and keep an eye on Yasmin. Linda G can handle things at the infirmary."

"Aren't there rifles you can buy from the armory at Camp Floyd?"

"They have some rifles but they're not the Sharps carbines. But I also need to get to New York. It would give you a chance to see Kane in Philadelphia. It's been a year. What do you think?"

Aaron had made the trip a number of times. It wouldn't be like he would be just wandering off into the States. "Isn't it getting late in the year?"

"We'll return on the southern route, Panama and Los Angeles and San Bernardino. Snow won't be a big thing until we get past Cedar City. We'll be back before you know it," Aaron promised. "It would be a big favor for me."

Aaron had a light carriage and two mules ready that whisked them out of town and up the canyons at a good clip a few days later. Echo Canyon seemed deserted since Shep had been there last. The breastworks were abandoned, the dams that were built across the creek had worn away. Cache Cave was an empty shell. Continuing, they cruised past Fort Bridger which was starting to come to life again. They could also make out the deteriorating remnants of Camp Scott. They followed the Green River then crossed South Pass and started towards the Sweetwater and Devil's Gate and Independence Rock. The sights and smells brought back the memories.

"How much better would it have been to cross during the summer?"

"I could always do without the snow."

"And the cold and wind?"

"Yep. That too."

Fort Laramie was the gateway down into the plains of Nebraska. It was the furthest east Shep had ever traveled in America. Chimney Rock and then Ash

484

Hollow. The journey had been infinitely quicker than climbing with the handcarts three years earlier. The Platte River was a natural roadway. A herd of buffalo blanketed the grasslands. Images of mounted Indians could be seen far in the distance, circling a portion of the beasts.

Several days later they rode into Florence. It had become an even more bustling city, its streets crowded with anxious pioneers. Several days earlier, they had passed a handcart company led by George Rowley headed for the Great Salt Lake City. It consisted of 235 people and had left Florence early in July. Their trip into Zion was bound to be better than what Shep and Aaron had experienced. The handcart idea was a good one as long as the leaders obeyed the directives. Despite the horrors of 1856, two more handcart companies had successfully arrived in Salt Lake City in 1857. None had traveled in 1858 because of the tension with the government.

The travelers Shep and Aaron saw were headed for the Oregon Trail and Territory, also being cautious about the approaching end of the year for starting their travels.

Shep and Aaron crossed the Missouri River. The road leading to Iowa City was clear and dry, making their ride easier and swifter. After reaching the city, they passed their mules and carriage into the hands of some Mormons who were set there as guides for other emigrants, either from the eastern states or from Europe and Britain. Like everywhere else along the trail, the season was winding down. The missionaries were willing to take control of the carriage and mules without a charge, but Aaron knew better and paid them for their efforts.

Tickets were purchased for the east coast. Shep remained surprised at how easily they traveled. Contrary to Aaron's concerns, Shep's skills and weaponry were never needed. His time was spent looking at the vast countryside and the growing cities and farms. The land was fertile and broad. Shep heard that the population was exploding but from his perspective, it appeared the land could absorb many more. Many of the hardwood forests were being cut down and replaced by towns and villages. Roads ran in every direction.

What was conspicuously absent from the landscape was the Indian villages. The natives were invisible once they climbed onto the railroad. Perhaps some were camouflaged because they were wearing white men's clothing. Nevertheless, it was a somber awakening, like a spreading sickness. And it was heading westward.

The waterways were jammed with traffic. Coal, timber, iron, and passengers were using the rivers to build their mini-empires. Northern cities were expanding quickly, as the society did its best to keep up with the Industrial Revolution that had started a decade earlier.

Making the switches, they rolled into Washington. Shep was impressed by the size and activity swirling around the capital. Then again, this was the head of the United States of America.

The Potomac was beautiful, making Shep chuckle as he recalled how piddly the Jordan River or the Humbolt or even the largest river of the Great

485

Basin, the Truckee, appeared in contrast. He was familiar with the American and Feather Rivers in northern California but even these were small when compared to the Ohio, Mississippi, and the Susquehanna rivers. These waterways had a great deal to do with the expansion and vibrancy of the States. From multiple sources, he had heard that the southern states were far behind the industrialized north. But that was how they wanted it. They were more agrarian, hence the greater need for slaves to work the plantations.

Shep couldn't understand the tradition. He was glad to have never come into close contact with slavery. He had seen how Judge Drummond treated Cuffy. The slave could have easily drubbed his master and escaped but for some reason he didn't. The Judge saw to it that Cuffy was educated and literate. Even in the north, there was a budding need for 'servants' to help with the growing homesteads and burgeoning wallets.

The two men found Dr. John Bernhisel scrambling to finish his packing. "I'm hoping to get back to the territory before winter hits," he explained.

"You gonna make it?"

"That's what prayer and hope are for," he answered.

Bernhisel was a breath of familiar air. Shep was impressed with how well he negotiated the halls of power. Numerous men greeted him warmly, almost kindly, while knowing where he was from and whom he represented. He was a sincere man of integrity, a polygamist, a characteristic that cut through artificial boundaries and partisan politics. The United States continued to be a young nation working through a series of processes.

"I'll be taking the rail tomorrow, but you are welcome to use my apartment," he told them. "It might do you good to familiarize yourselves with the city. There really are some decent folks hereabouts."

Living on his own, Dr. Bernhisel kept a Spartan existence, a fact that impressed both Aaron and Shep.

"Not many around here left to sway," Aaron commented after seeing him off in his cab the next day.

"He's beyond that, *amigo*."

"Think so?"

"Some folks are just plain good."

"Will that make his travels back home more bearable?"

Shep just smiled.

It took three days of serious riding for Shep and Aaron to travel from Washington to Philadelphia. The men were tired when they reached the home of Thomas and Elizabeth Kane. The couple was excited to have the visitors and even more so after the two newcomers fussed and played with their children.

"Strong and beautiful," Shep announced. "Better pack them up for the territory as quickly as possible."

Aaron nodded in agreement. "God knows we could use such an infusion."

Bessie grinned merrily. The newspapers were rife with descriptions of how homely and ragged the plural wives of the Utah Territory were. Some columnists said the Mormon men were doing God a favor by grabbing up such unattractive denizens of the desert. Thomas knew better.

It was difficult to imagine that Kane had been gone from the valley for more than a year. He continued to pace until Rost and Silva assured him of the direction things were going.

"Governor Cumming is doing well with Brigham and the boys?"

"Like he's died and gone to heaven," Shep noted.

"Things have calmed down quite a bit," Aaron said. "I could never have pried Shep away if he were still busy arresting all of Johnston's men."

The idea made both the Kanes laugh.

"I think Johnston's a short-timer anyway," Thomas added. "I heard that he's being breveted to a general and sent back to Kentucky for bit."

"He'll be ready," Shep said.

"Then who? Lt. Colonel Smith?"

"Maybe for a short while. But I think President Buchanan is convinced that Lt. Colonel Cooke is a better fit. He gets along well enough with both Cumming and Young."

Aaron decided to change the topic. "You think it will be all right for me to leave Shep here for a while when I'm in New York?"

"Bessie?"

Kane's wife gave them a beautiful smile. "Anyone wise enough to marry the fetching Harriett Matthews is always welcome."

The reminder pleased Shep.

"If he'll agree to teach me more about the carbine. I want to become just half the marksman he."

Shep shrugged and motioned with his head. "It's stashed in my stuff."

"Fine!" Colonel Kane announced and clapped his hands. "I need to see you boys in my office for a minute. Would that be all right with you, my dear?"

Bessie was already collecting her children from the floor and shooing them to their rooms.

"So mysterious," Shep said as they entered his heavily paneled office.

Kane picked up a letter that was lying on his desk. "I just got this from a friend in Washington. It was sent to the Secretary of War, John Floyd, the namesake of your military camp." He handed the document over and watched as Shep and Aaron began reading it together.

"I thought especially about you Aaron. I'm not sure how close you have remained with John Brown, since the time you spent in Kansas. The letter was sent to Secretary Floyd and is anonymous, but we think it came from Dave Gue of Iowa. Brown spent some time there."

Cincinnati, Aug. 20, 1859. SIR: I have lately received information of a movement of so great importance that I feel it to be my duty to impart it to you without delay.

I have discovered the existence of a secret association, having for its object the liberation of the slaves of the South, by a general insurrection. The leader of the movement is "Old John Brown," late of Kansas. He has been in Canada during the winter, drilling the negroes there, and they are only waiting his word to start for the South to assist the slaves. They have one of their leading men (a white man) in an armory in Maryland; where it is situated I am not enabled to learn.

As soon as everything is ready, those of their number who are in the Northern States and Canada are to come in small companies to their rendezvous, which is in the mountains of Virginia. They will pass down through Pennsylvania and Maryland, and enter Virginia at Harper's Ferry. Brown left the North about three or four weeks ago and will arm the negroes and strike a blow in a few weeks, so that whatever is done must be done at once. They have a large quantity of arms at their rendezvous and are probably distributing them already. I am not fully in their confidence. This is all the information I can give you.

I dare not sign my name to this, but trust that you will not disregard this warning on that account.

Shep and Aaron finished at the same time and traded glances.

"You haven't said much about him."

Aaron furrowed his brow. "It's no big deal. I haven't been in the abolitionist camps for a while." He thought deeply for a couple of moments. "But Brown's my connection. He's the one I'm getting the Sharps from. He knows folks in the armory there in Harper's Ferry."

Kane drew a deep breath. "You'll want to be careful. Secretary Floyd has blown off the threat. Thinks it's a hoax. He hasn't put the pieces together about Gue's associate named Brown in Iowa and the revolutionary in Kansas. Too common, I guess. Anyway, there could be something serious afoot. Bessie and I have been involved plenty with women's suffrage and of course, there's my involvement with your folks in the Utah Territory. But there are easily more concerns and money backing the anti-slavery movement. It has become a North versus South issue. Brown seems to be a master at stirring the pot. The last time I was in Washington I had a visit from Fredrick Douglass. He's aware of Brown and has distanced himself somewhat. He thinks Brown might be planning some sort of insurrection or uprising of the slaves. This is just what the nation doesn't need right now. Anyway, Douglass thinks it's suicide. I pass it along merely for your consideration, my friends."

"Certainly. I appreciate your information."

That night as the two Mormons were turning down the lamp in their room, Aaron nudged Shep. "You saying your prayers?"

"Soon."

"I haven't said anything about Brown because I'm just planning on scooting up to the kerosene office and plant. I shouldn't be too long. Then again, Brown has agents all about and I'm a marked man. Like I said, he's the one I'm getting the carbines from."

"Wells thinks we need them?"

"Don't you?"

Shep decided the question was rhetorical.

"I'll be careful."

Aaron Rost got up early and caught his coach for New York. Shep couldn't help but be proud of the manner his friend attended to his business. Singlehandedly he had changed the lifestyle of countless people in the west. He had also established a good business in Salt Lake City that provided a decent home for Yasmin and Esther. And they were also expecting a second baby in the spring.

Kane had a marvelous rifle range set up on his farm. Various shaped targets were propped up at assorted distances. He also had a series of presses to create bullets, along with enough lead and gunpowder to keep the two men busy for a long time.

Colonel Kane was fascinated with the breechloading rifle. And even though it was a .52 caliber bullet, its accuracy was lethal. The sights were simple but being a carbine, it was easy to carry on a saddle. Trained soldiers would be able to lay down a deadly sheet of lead.

"Most of our soldiers carry these P1853 rifles," he explained needlessly to Shep. "The weapons proved their worth in the Crimea. Then again, they are bulky and slower to reload. This Sharps can shoot just as far but for every mini-ball that can be loaded into one of our regular rifles, a carbine could fire five or six. Don't let our Indian tribes get a hold of these," he added cautiously. Again, Shep thought Kane was preaching to the choir.

Tom Kane was especially interested in the sights of the carbine. He noted several ways they could be improved. Shep kept quiet and nodded.

Tom shot incessantly over the next few days until his bruised shoulder encouraged him to find another pastime. At least for a while. "Soldiers, but especially cavalry armed with these carbines could be a guerrilla force to be reckoned with." He gazed at Shep then chuckled. "Look who's telling who, what."

Both Bessie and Tom's mother, Jane, were intrigued by Shep's Brazilian accent. He did his best to entertain them with tales from South America, although most were fabricated.

Escravos de Jo'
Jogavam caxingar.
Tira! Bota! Deixa ficar!
Guerreiros com guerreiros jogam zigue zigue-zag.
Guerreiros com guerreiros jogam zigue zigue-zag

Job's slaves playing caxingar, picking up, putting down and leaving alone, Warriors playing this silly game.

He couldn't recall much from his childhood. Some of his tales were infused with lore from the islands. They were always colored green. It didn't seem to matter. They were happy to have his attention, especially when Thomas had business that needed tending, leaving them alone. Shep was always capable of coming up with a reason to remain on the home front. Colonel Kane had sacrificed more than his share in the protection of the Utah Territory. And he was a real friend. And his father had died during his most recent trip to the west. The least Shep could do was be as charming and focused on these women who had given so much for him and his associates.

Aaron's trip to New York was lucrative and informative as well. He signed half a dozen contracts for large amounts of kerosene. He also went on multiple tours of processing plants that were producing the valuable liquid. It was a life-changer. He had seen the difference in the short years he had worked with the whalers and then spent time in San Francisco, San Bernardino, and finally Salt Lake City. Folks no longer needed to go to bed with the sun. Industry could continue long after dark. Students could study later into the night. Streets were better lit and far more secure.

His visit was productive and educational. Business-wise, he had done extremely well. Briefly, he forgot other activities revolving in his life until a knock came on his hotel room door. He opened it to see Owen Brown, son of the abolitionist. Owen was four years younger than Aaron. Of John's sons, he was probably the most level-headed. Years before he had injured his right arm, leaving him somewhat debilitated.

"You still looking for those carbines?" he asked after Aaron invited him into his room.

"Now what do you think?"

"I've been watching you and your kerosene. Looks like you've found a good niche for business."

"I suppose."

"Well, Pa wants you to stop by his place before you pick up the guns and head west."

"I can do that."

"He's looking for all the help he can get. Big things are brewing."

"Does he have plenty of money?"

"Money's not the problem, Aaron. It's getting folks to line up."

Following Owen's directions, Aaron made his way south several days later into Maryland, to a safe house on a two-acre parcel, originally belonging to a Dr. Kennedy, who had died the year before. The house was being rented by Brown just across the Potomac and two miles north of the Harper's Ferry armory. Brown was calling himself Isaac Smith.

The older man greeted Aaron like a long-lost friend. He invited him into the humble dwelling, smiling and clapping him happily on the back. Kansas seemed like ages earlier.

"Owen tells me that you're telling everyone in the neighborhood that you're a prospector."

Brown was proud of the subterfuge. "Gets the job done. Then folks don't come around as often looking for food or to visit."

"Well, what about this name? Isaac Smith? Does it mean you're a Jew or simply deciding to follow the Prophet Joseph Smith?"

Brown broke out in a horse laugh. "By God, I never even thought about that," he laughed. "And which direction would you suggest?"

"I didn't choose to be Jewish but from my experience, they seem to be good folks. The Mormons are the ones I'd lean on or else be wary of."

"How would that look on the rolls of your church? John Brown and Joseph Smith? The church could be called the Church of Common Named Folks."

"Common names aside, you both have done your best to stir the pot."

"I'm here shaking the tree in the east and old Brigham has taken hold and is doing all the shaking in the west." John brought Aaron into the kitchen and got him seated, then proceeded to fill him in on things since the summer of 1856 in Kansas.

John Brown had been anxiously engaged with the abolitionist movement for thirty years. Since Rost left Osawatomie, Brown spent time in Kansas and then Iowa, going up to Canada to speak with the free slaves who had made their escape from the US. He also stumped in New England for more financial assistance. He was successful in garnering help from a handful of prominent people, especially the Secret Six. Gerrit Smith and George Luther Stearns were the wealthy donors, Franklin Benjamin Sanborn was a teacher, Theodore Parker and Thomas Wentworth Higginson were both Unitarian ministers, and Samuel Gridley Howe was a doctor. The Secret Six were free with their resources, although they wanted their names kept quiet to keep them from the knowledge of the governor of Massachusetts. Never in the same room together, the six combined to help Brown with his plans. Stearns and Smith were wealthy, the others were well placed socially. All had come to the opinion that slavery could only be dissolved through violence. Besides these, several others were willing to help but on a lesser scale. Brown had also contracted with Hugh Forbes, an English mercenary who had fought under Giuseppe Garibaldi in Italy and was paid $100 a month as a drillmaster for his forces.

John Brown's first plans had to do with training and positioning five squads of five men each, having them work along a twenty-five-mile stretch in the Maryland mountains. They would patrol and be responsible for their five miles of the territory.

Frederick Douglass had been a frequent visitor at Brown's, where they talked over and debated the best tactics to be used. As things began to narrow and Brown finally decided to attack the armory and arsenal at Harper's Ferry, Douglass' support waned. It had little chance of success and he opted not to join.

Harriet Tubman was another of Brown's favorite contacts. He called her "General Tubman" and found her to be an invaluable resource for runaway slaves to Ontario and the logistics surrounding the underground railroad. She had a high profile and was all in as far as the attack and hostage-taking were concerned. The problem she was currently experiencing, however, was a severe illness.

"Join us, Aaron. You're just what the doctor ordered. You are smart and capable. Who knows the Sharp's carbine better than you? And you know, as well as I do, that slavery is a moral abomination. It has to be stopped. Our nation will not be able to withstand the depravity for much longer."

Rost shook his head thoughtfully. "Give me the night. I'll have something to run by you in the morning."

The farmhouse was Spartan, housing a score of white abolitionists and a handful of ex-slaves. During the daylight, they stayed inside and out of sight and spoke very little. At night, they would range over the neighborhood in small groups, trying not to attract attention. They would also use the evening hours to drill and do target practice. A couple of women from Brown's household acted as cooks and did the laundry, with varying success.

John Brown rousted Aaron before the sun rose, anxious for his decision. "And? What's it to be?"

"I can't join you, John," the Prussian said somberly. "The timing doesn't work for me. I have a small girl back home. My wife is expecting our second baby. My first allegiance, after God, is to them. I've prayed about it a lot, John, and I think my talents would be better put to use making sure slavery doesn't get a toe-hold in the territory. That, and arming our boys in the event of another scuffle with the feds."

Brown lowered his head and nodded slowly. "I figured as much, Aaron. I prayed about it, too. I've always known that you have other preconditions, things that need your attention first. But you can't fault me for trying." Brown stood and walked across the small room, then back again. "By the by, your carbines are crated and ready to ship. Of course, they're stenciled as Beecher's Bibles, especially since they will be used on those Godless, anti-Christ, Mormons, living in the Rockies. Where do I ship them?"

"Baltimore. We'll be sailing in a week or so to Los Angeles and then Old Spanish Trail north."

"Sure wish you were staying here."

"You're on God's errand, John."

"From your mouth to God's ears, my friend."

492

Chapter 65

"And they also of the tribe of Judah, after their pain, shall be sanctified in holiness before the Lord, to dwell in his presence day and night, forever and ever." Doctrine and Covenants

Half a week later, a tired Aaron Rost was deposited before the Kane home in Philadelphia.

"I was starting to think you were lost!" Shep said happily. "Yet here you stand!"

"Was the trip worth your while?" Thomas asked.

"Better than I expected."

Leaving the Kane home proved to be more involved than anticipated. Bessie and Jane both started crying, as Shep and Aaron walked to their waiting cab.

"It's good to get the two of you out of here," Kane said as they carried their luggage to the carriage and began storing it. "If Shep had stayed much longer, I think Bessie would have thrown me over for him. My ma was definitely thinking of ways to keep both of you around."

"Philadelphia would never be the same."

"The Kanes would never be the same," Aaron added.

After handshakes, the two were off for the shipyards in Baltimore.

"You never mentioned anything about the carbines."

"The less Colonel Kane knows, the better. Everything is set. They are crated for shipping and awaiting us in a locker on the docks."

"And now, with more of your silence, you're telling me you didn't meet up with any of your abolitionist pals?"

Aaron Rost smiled, then leaned over the side of the carriage and spit into the dirt. "What is it with God using men of such plain, common names? Got an any answers, Mahonri-Moriancumer?"

"You got me, Maher-shalal-hash-baz."

The ride through the countryside leading to Baltimore was heavily ladened with broad-leafed trees that were turning colors in the fall air. The temperature was brisk as was the wind against their faces. Both men were deep in thought, wondering about their activities and friendships and whether or not they would ever see the Kanes again. Philadelphia remained far away from Deseret.

"Do you ever wonder about the reality of the scriptures?"

Until this time, the two men had been riding in relative silence, both caught up with the things of their lives. Aaron's opening alerted Shep of his friend's lining things up for a discussion. He wanted to embark on a dialogue and was looking for Shep's participation. It was how he maneuvered his topics. But they were still quite a distance from Baltimore. The interaction would help the time go by.

"What do you mean?"

"I mean the humanity, the earthy actions of the players. When I read about Abraham and Sarah and Isaac and Rebekah and Jacob and Rachel, they all sound quite regular. There doesn't seem to be any supernatural occurrences. It's not quite like the Apocrypha. The folks all seem to be normal. They are caught up with emotions and frustrations. I believe them to be good people but also short-sighted, quite human. Know what I mean?"

Shep chuckled. "I guess. Where'd this come from?"

"I've been thinking about the reality of the scriptures. They are wonderful and down to earth. Even though there are plenty of miraculous events, they aren't presented as anything that can't be attained by regular, normal folks. Like you and me."

Shep Silva shook his head. "I'm thinking you need to spend more time selling kerosene. Or maybe, keeping your nose away from the fumes. They might be having an effect on your brain."

"No, really, Shep. Look at how real folks are. Abraham lies to the Pharoah about Sarah. Did Abraham even tell Sarah when he was going to sacrifice Isaac? Maybe. Maybe not. But it must have killed her, because the next thing we read in the story after Abraham and Isaac return from Mount Moriah is about the death and burial of Sarah. Then Isaac tells the same lies to the Canaanite king about his wife Rebekah. Jacob listens to his ma, and lies to Isaac in order to sneak away after swindling the blessing of the primogeniture."

"Big word, that."

"Ah."

"Like Ma-her-sha-lal-hash-baz."

Shep chuckled and countered. "Ma-hon-ri-Mo-ri-an-cu-mer. You have adroitly pointed out that both these long names have the same number of characters. Also, Mahonri-Moriancumer, the name given by Joseph Smith to the baby. wasn't Reynolds' first born."

Rost didn't pay attention. "Primogeniture. It means blessings go to the firstborn."

"Speaking of that, the importance of the firstborn, it never worked for Abraham, whose firstborn was Ishmael, or Isaac, whose firstborn was Esau, or Jacob, whose firstborn was Reuben, or then Joseph, whose firstborn was Manasseh. What's with that?"

"Eighteen."

"What's that?"

"Eighteen. The number of letters in both of these long names. Same length. Interesting, *nicht wahr*?"

"*Ne'*. I think the days have been dragging on you, Aaron."

"Or what about *Rosh HaShannah* in 1827? September 22nd, the day Moroni finally gave the Gold Plates to the Prophet Joseph. It was the Feast of

Trumpets. What better symbol for the trumpeting of the truth throughout the world with the Book of Mormon?"

"Imagine that."

Rost pretended not to have heard. "And in the New Testament, Joseph, Mary's husband. He entertained angels and they protected him and his family from Herod and got them down into Egypt. Joseph accepted Jesus and raised him as his own son and then was married to Mary. He sired kids with her. These snots didn't cotton to their big brother being the Son of God, not until after his resurrection. What would that have been like? Can you imagine trying to fulfill a mission like Jesus' without your family's support? Even Joseph Smith's family believed him. But it was different for Jesus and his step-father."

There was no getting around the fact that Aaron had plenty of time to think.

"He was raised as his son and the people of the town thought Joseph was his pa and referred to him as the carpenter's son. And do you think Satan left this good man, Joseph, alone? Not on your life. Yasmin told me about a story she had from Syria. Very old, from folks who were a mix of Jews and Christians. They said that Satan chased Joseph around his whole life, tempting him, causing him to question the truthfulness of the virginity of Mary, that maybe she wasn't as pure as he thought. That instead of God being Jesus' father, it was a German mercenary named Panthera and that's why Jesus had lighter colored hair and blue eyes."

"Jesus had blue eyes?"

"Hell if I know. That's just what some of these people were telling my wife when she was little. These are just some old stories. But some taste like real-life tales. I'm just saying, I think it sounds right. Don't you think Old Scratch would be after Joseph, always challenging him about the life of Jesus and Mary's chastity?"

"All I know is that they all made it through this life. Now we're the ones on deck."

"Of course. Of course. But the scriptures, don't you find them dealing with real folks? No fairytales here."

"Yeah, I guess so. I've never worried too much about it."

"But it's good. Look at how the Jewish Bible, the Old Testament is woven into these latter days. Folks in this country like new things. New is a good word to Americans. Old is just the opposite. Christians shy away from the Old Testament because it's old. They like talking about the new covenant, although they still name most of their children after Old Testament people. Anyway, look. When Moroni showed up to Joseph Smith, what did he quote? Stuff from the Old Testament."

Shep stopped and thought for a bit, then shook his head. "Nope. Moroni also quoted Peter from the New Testament."

"Yeah, I know, but Peter's quote was just quoting something from the Old Testament."

Shep shook his head. He was already tiring of the exercise. "Excuse me, Aaron, but where's this all going?"

"I'm just trying to show you some of the connections that exist between the Bible or beliefs of our folks and the scriptures of the Restoration. I will say that I appreciate the idea of Passover better than the Latter-day Saints' Pass By."

"What the hell you talking about, Aaron? What's this 'pass by'?"

"In the Word of Wisdom, the scriptures simply say that all who keep these commandments shall have health in their navels and marrow in their bones and run and not be weary, other specific Old Testament blessings, and that the Destroying Angel shall 'pass by' them as the Children of Israel, and not slay them. Now that's Old Testament."

"Sorry, Aaron. I think you've sailed over the waterfalls."

"It's all true, Shep. The Restoration uses some good words but not always to the stature of the Old Testament. Look at what the Prophet wrote from the Liberty jail. He said 'and not many years hence, that they and their posterity shall be swept from under heaven, saith God, that not one of them is left to stand by the wall'. Get it? Does that sound familiar, or what?"

"I don't know what the hell you're talking about. You're starting to sound like a crazy Prussian."

"Stand by the wall? See? It's the Old Testament phrase used in the histories, Samuel and Kings, about six or seven times say that God will cut off from Baasha or Ahab or whoever and not leave him one that pisseth against the wall."

"What?"

"Yep. But the Passover's better. Back in 1836, just after the Prophet had dedicated the Kirtland Temple, the first day of Passover was on Saturday the 2nd of April. All the Jewish kids in the world were gathered around in their homes asking their grandpas why that night was different from all others and then during the *seder* the children would be watching the Cup of Elijah to see if his spirit was there, drinking the wine, making it drop down lower and lower. And the children would all go to the door and open it and bid the Prophet Elijah to enter their home. It's a sign of God and the end of the world, quoting the last two verses of the Old Testament. This coming of Elijah before the end of the world so he can turn the hearts of the children to their fathers so the earth isn't destroyed by the Lord's coming. Well, that year, 1836, on the very next day after Passover was Easter Sunday. It was the very day Joseph and Oliver were in the Kirtland Temple praying and they had their vision of the Savior. It was also when Elijah showed up to them and gave them the keys for the sealing of the children to their fathers. The day after the Jews had been waiting and watching. See? So the earth wouldn't be destroyed at the Second Coming. The earth had been set up as a school for us, where we could come down from God's presence and receive bodies and be exposed to good and evil, and where we could be sealed together as couples and families by the power of the priesthood, fulfilling the reasons God even created the earth. See? The Creation. The Fall, and the Atonement."

Shep nodded his agreement, hoping it would silence Rost. He then looked at his friend closely. "I feel bad for John Brown. All the while he was jabbering at you, trying to win you over to his side, to get you to join the abolitionists, you were busy stirring your own concoction, coming up with your own ideas about the Restoration."

"Don't forget that the scriptures tell us to learn from good books, words of wisdom and stuff. We're supposed to get it by study and by faith. Study, my good fellow. God's given us curiosity and a brain to pursue it. The answers are there. We just need to be diligent in our search."

"You're making my point, Aaron, as to why I like spending time with my horses. They never dump stuff like this into my lap."

Again, Aaron did not seem to hear. "One other good connection, since we're talking about the turning of the hearts of the children. Speaking through the Prophet, God told the early saints to avoid war, renounce it, and proclaim peace, and then to turn the hearts of the children to their fathers and the hearts of the fathers to the children. Paraphrasing those same last verses of the Old Testament. And then he says this: *'and again, the hearts of the Jews unto the prophets, and the prophets unto the Jews; lest I come and smite the whole eareth with a curse, and all flesh be consumed before me.'* What do you think about that?"

"Maybe Jews need to read their scriptures more?"

Rost flopped his hands with exasperation. "Have you even been listening to a word I've been saying? The Jews! The Jews need to turn their hearts to the prophets. Moses said that he wished his whole nation was a nation of prophets. God knows the Jews read their scriptures. They love reading and quoting the prophets from the Bible. But the prophets He's talking about here are living, breathing folks. Joseph Smith quoted from John's Revelation and said that anyone who has a testimony of Jesus, that he is the Savior, the Son of God, says it by the spirit of prophecy, and having the spirit of prophecy makes him a prophet. So, the Jews need to be turning their hearts to us, the Latter-day Saints. We have the testimony of Jesus. We are the prophets and we need to be turning our hearts to the Jews. See? And it will bless the earth and help it to fill its mission as well."

"So, is this what you do when you're traveling alone? You come up with all these puzzles and games, labyrinths to trick your mind? Wanting to get things in order for you? Or at least the way you see things?"

"I do my best."

"How does Yasmin ever put up with it?"

"She's the one who encourages it."

"And I say you're a bald-faced liar." Shep chuckled, pleased with himself at not having been drawn in by Aaron's musings.

Baltimore was a bustling seaport. Fort McHenry was a five-pointed bastion, situated at the water's edge, watching and protecting all of the maritime comings and goings. A large flag of the United States always flew over the battlements, reminding one and all of the British bombardment in

1814, when the attorney and slaveholder, Francis Scott Key, penned the words of his Star-Spangled Banner. That was another era. The young nation now was rich and vibrant, inviting ships from all over the world to come calling. Baltimore remained a favorite port.

Due in large part to the role of the Baltimore and Ohio Railroad, commerce was active. Tobacco and grain had been the city's first exports, going to sustain colonies in the Caribbean. Both tobacco and sugar cane were labor-intensive, calling for the heavy use of slave labor and making Maryland a stronghold for the slave market in the north. Industry and sawmills began changing the complexion of the city. Also, Baltimore had the first telegraph linking to Washington and making it even more important on the national scene. Gaslighting was a big part of the city, giving a serious market to kerosene.

Aaron and Shep checked for their crates in the harbor locker area. They had not arrived yet. Although Rost was only able to acquire 150 carbines, John Brown wrangled 200 for his supporters.

"He wailed a lot more for them than I did, I guess," he surmised.

"I expect the shipment anytime," the shipping clerk told the men. "We just got the telegram informing of it being sent from Harper's Ferry. I guess that's a problem with the telegraph. We find out about things being shipped much sooner than it takes for them to arrive." He thought for a moment. "I wasn't aware that Maryland and certainly Harper's Ferry, was such a center for publishing."

"What do you mean?" Aaron asked.

"Well, the manifest states that these crates are filled with Bibles to be sent along to the Utah Territory."

"Right you are. The Beechers are big evangelizers, doing their very best to get those godless Mormons back on track with the word of God."

The clerk knew exactly what he meant. "Something has to be done to keep them from wandering too far out into the desert."

"That's our job, sir."

Later that evening, a runner was sent to the hotel room where Aaron and Shep were staying. On the piece of paper was scrawled a quick message informing them that their crates had arrived and that any help they could offer getting them offloaded and accounting for their receipt would be appreciated.

It took just minutes for them to reach the docks where the clerk pointed them to a low riding wagon with a beige canvas cover draped over the bow and two slaves were just beginning to untie the load. The smaller man noted their arrival and carried a bill of lading to give to Aaron for his signature.

"Mr. Isaac wanted to make sure you received this in time for you to sail, sir," he said, watching Rost scribble his name.

"Good for you to get it here so quickly," he replied, handing the papers back. He couldn't help but notice the poor quality of clothing the man wore. And his shoes were coming apart. The young man didn't seem bothered.

"But I take exception," the other slave said to Rost.

Aaron had yet to look at the man, but Shep had already sized the larger man up. Rost glanced over and immediately recognized Cuffy Cato. "Well, I'll be damned," he said, suddenly smiling and waiting to see how his nemesis from bygone days would react to his presence. "It's been a while, Mr. Cato."

The oversized man hopped down catlike from the wagon and approached the taller, slender Rost. The two Mormons briefly held their breath, until Cuffy extended a huge open hand for Aaron to shake. The tension of the moment evaporated.

"Good to see you again, Mr. Rost."

Aaron took his hand, noting the hard calluses on his palms. He nodded pleasantly. "It's been a while, Cuffy. I must say that I almost didn't recognize you without your whip or your scowl."

"Just doing my job, Mr. Rost." Turning to Shep, he said, "I see you're still armed."

"Caught me, again."

"So, Mr. Cato, what brings you here to Baltimore, if you don't mind me asking?"

"John Brown."

The answer startled Rost and caused him to take a step back and ponder. "The abolitionist?"

"That's him."

"And what?"

Cuffy decided to explain. "I was with Judge Drummond visiting Washington a while back and had the chance to meet Frederick Douglass. He didn't care much for the judge, but he had some great ideas for me. So, I just left. I ran away from Judge Drummond. The underground railroad had me up in Pennsylvania before I knew it. That's where I met John Brown. Mr. Douglass had told me about him. So, I just listened to what he had to say. I can't fault him at all. When he moved down to Harper's Ferry, I followed him."

"You were there when I was?"

Cuffy nodded slyly. "And you didn't even know." He smiled at his own subterfuge.

"So, you know my position?"

"Mr. Brown wouldn't let any of us forget it. He crowed about you and your work in Kansas and your desire to help the poor, picked on Mormons and he wished we had ten more just like you to help us."

The compliment made Aaron beam. Shep was still looking a bit confused.

"How much time did you spend with Brown?" he asked.

Aaron waved off the question. "Not important. But enough, I hope."

With the awkwardness of the introduction past, the men removed the tarp from the wagon. The other man had retrieved a flatbed cart to load and then wheel to another building for storage. The crates were quite heavy, but the four men made short work of the chore, although the effort caused all of them to breathe heavier. The work finished, Cuffy and his associate, Jeremy, folded up the canvas tarp, stowed it in the wagon box, and prepared to leave.

"One moment, please," Aaron said. "It's getting late. You staying the night anywhere close by?"

"Just over there by the docks," Cuffy replied, pointing across the wharf.

Rost nodded. "Shep and I need something to eat. Mind joining us? Both of you?"

The meal was plain but filling. It tasted extra good because of their work and the fact that none of the four had eaten since daybreak. Most of the extended meal was spent listening to Cuffy and Aaron exchange stories about their lives and especially their interactions in the territory with Drummond and Ada.

"Have to admit, you had me plenty worried sometimes," Cuffy said.

"You and me, both. I didn't know if I was coming or going. And that Miss Ada is such a beautiful woman. What's she doing? Still with the judge?"

"Nope. She got tired of him and threw him over. She's from these parts. I think she's worried that her charms might be slipping. A couple years back she was married to some old schoolteacher here in the city. Charles Fletcher. She might be trying to get back with him."

"Will it work?"

"You tell me. I'm just a slave."

The statement caught both Shep and Aaron by surprise. "You're no slave, Cuffy. You're one of the best men I have ever seen and not just because you're so damned strong. Black or white. You're loyal to a fault. And I am a much richer man because of your friendship."

Cuffy Cato smiled appreciatively. He was still trying to get used to having white people speak openly with him.

Rost pulled the pocket watch from his vest and checked the time. "It's late. Time to get some shut-eye," he said and pushed back from the table.

Shep claimed that he would settle their account while Aaron and Jeremy and Cuffy left the inn. Cuffy ran around behind the building to relieve himself, while Jeremy and Rost waited. Three white men sat idly in front of the inn, a few feet away. Dockworkers. It was obvious they had been drinking. They began making derogatory remarks about anyone socializing with niggers.

Aaron took Jeremy's arm and they started across the street, wanting to put some distance between them and the malcontents.

The other three jumped up and ran after them, stepping directly in front of them.

"Where the hell you sonsofbitches going?" one asked, slurring his words.

Jeremy was nervous and began looking for a direction to run. One of the men grabbed his coat and slammed his fist into the side of his head, knocking him forcefully to the ground. Always the peacemaker, Aaron held up his hands. "Gentlemen, please." He bent down to take Jeremy's arms and hoist him to his feet. A solid blow to the back of his head sent bolts of lightning ricocheting through his eyes, dropping him next to his associate. The men quickly circled the two on the ground and began kicking them mercilessly. The beating knocked the two on the ground senseless. They were only able to grunt when the blows landed.

And then Cuffy arrived. His large fists felled two of the assailants in quick succession. Then he picked up the third by his neck and crotch, pile-driving him headfirst into the packed dirt and rocks of the road, putting him out of commission.

One of the assailants stood, wiping the blood from his mouth, and drew a six-shooter from his coat and aimed. Cuffy saw the movement and lunged at the man just as he tripped the trigger. The pistol rocked back as Cuffy closed, crumpling the man again to the earth. But the bullet that had been aimed at Cuffy's face, struck him in the throat, just below his chin, killing him instantly. The villain scrambled to extricate himself from beneath Cuffy Cato's body. He stood long enough to shoot a bullet into Jeremy and Aaron, then turned and fled into the night, not caring to check on the well-being or status of his partners.

Lacking control, Aaron turned his broken head around, eyes frantically searching for a horizon, when through his bloodstained lips, he struggled to utter a simple phrase, tainted by ancient melody: "*Shemai Yisroel, Adonai, Eloheinu. Adonai, echaaad...*"

The altercation was over. Shep, leaving the inn, suddenly found himself facing his friends on the ground and a growing crowd of onlookers. The pooling blood on the hard earth looked black in the night, spreading over the road, steaming with warmth. A couple of bystanders noted curiously how the mixing blood of the slaves and the white man looked to be exactly alike.

A quick check by Silva told him that Cuffy was dead. He turned Aaron over and also found a bullet had pierced his chest, killing him. Jeremy was seriously wounded in the torso.

The life-altering event lasted seconds but would reverberate through generations.

Heavying a deep sigh, Shep sat down next to the trio. *How many times had he joked with Aaron? The quintessential businessman from Prussia. The charming kerosene salesman. The devout member of the church. The proud husband and father. The loyal friend. And Cuffy Cato. How many times had he seen him walking obediently behind Judge Drummond? Or saying prayers over his meager food? Or carrying himself like a prince in chains?*

Shep knew that his life was richer because of the influence of these two men, so different and yet so much alike. A treasure trove of memories could be examined.

And he knew that if Jeremy were to survive his wounds, he needed to get medical help as soon as possible, cutting down on his feelings of sorrow and reverie.

The telegram sent by Shep spurred Thomas Kane into action. He saddled a horse and rode for Baltimore to be of assistance, arriving a day and a half later. The sorrow caused by the deaths was palpable. Colonel Kane saw to it that Jeremy was given the best hospital bed. He also arranged to have Cuffy and Aaron taken back to Philadelphia, where he and Shep oversaw the funerals.

"I know Harriett Tubman," he told Shep. "I've sent word to her, and she will take care of Jeremy. Money has been forthcoming for the lad's recovery."

"Your kindness is appreciated, sir."

"Ma and Bessie wouldn't have it any other way, my friend. Now, what about you?"

The weight of the moment finally descended on the Brazilian. He had been surrounded by friends. Concerned neighbors of the Kanes' wished him well and offered money to help in his travels. But with the prospects of traveling back to the territory, he stood quite alone.

"I'll be fine," he said, wistfully.

"There is some other news I've waited to share with you," Kane said. "John Brown and his men took over the arsenal at Harper's Ferry a few days back. I figured we had enough to keep us busy with the funerals. But I thought you should know."

Shep registered surprise. "Was he successful?"

Kane shook his head. "They ran into some Marines and had a short battle. Brown had 22 people helping him take hostages and then fight. Some folks were killed."

"Including Brown?"

Kane shook his head. "Just wounded. They'll be wanting to hang him quick enough. Two of his boys were killed in the action, though."

"How's all this going to end?"

"Your guess is better than mine. I spend too much time in Washington, listening to politicians. The real people, the farmers, and merchants, they are going to want to be heard. Lines are being drawn and citizens on both sides are angry. Like I said, North versus South. Pro and anti-slavery. It really doesn't look good."

A week later saw Tom and Bessie and Jane Kane standing on the dock, with their two children, waving goodbye. His steamship slipped from its moorings and moved into the deeper waters of the Chesapeake Bay. Shep smiled and waved and wondered how he would ever break the news to Harriett and then the young mother, Yasmin Rost. Had she even had their second baby, yet?

Clouds hung low, being blown by the approaching winter storm. The seas were colored gray and were choppy, capped by foamy white crests.

Silva watched the Kanes' figures growing smaller, as the ship pushed into the turbulent waters. The steamboat would sail down the eastern seaboard of the United States, then cross the Caribbean to Panama, where he would catch the rail trip across the isthmus to the Pacific. In Panama City, he would catch another ship up the coast to the harbor of San Pedro and Los Angeles. It promised to be a long journey.

Several days later they docked at Charleston, South Carolina. Shep picked up a newspaper carrying the proceedings of the trial for John Brown emblazoned across its pages. It was of profound interest to people of the South. He found particular interest in the statement ascribed to Brown.

Given the chance, John Brown's last words were poignant and well publicized.

The law demanded that a guilty person could not be hanged for 30 days after his conviction, so John Brown was hanged on December 2, 1859, before a bevy of onlookers.

Victor Hugo wrote the same day: *Politically speaking, the murder of John Brown would be an uncorrectable sin. It would create in the Union a latent fissure that would in the long run dislocate it. Brown's agony might perhaps consolidate slavery in Virginia, but it would certainly shake the whole American democracy. You save your shame, but you kill your glory. Morally speaking, it seems a part of the human light would put itself out, that the very notion of justice and injustice would hide itself in darkness, on that day where one would see the assassination of Emancipation by Liberty itself. Let America know and ponder on this: there is something more frightening than Cain killing Abel, and that is Washington killing Spartacus.*

On the day of his death, John Brown wrote: *I, John Brown, am now quite certain that the crimes of this guilty land will never be purged away but with blood. I had, as I now think, vainly flattered myself that without very much bloodshed it might be done.*

Chapter 66

"The difference between us is very marked. Most that I have done and suffered in the service of our cause has been in public, and I have received much encouragement at every step of the way. You, on the other hand, have labored in a private way. I have wrought in the day – you in the night...The midnight sky and the silent stars have been the witnesses of your devotion to freedom and of your heroism. Excepting John Brown—of sacred memory—I know of no one who has willingly encountered more perils and hardships to serve our enslaved people than you have." Frederick Douglass' writing about Harriett Tubman

Ocean travel had changed a lot since Shep left Hawaii in December 1851. At that time, most of the travel was accomplished by sailing ships. They were sleek and quick when the sailors understood how to set the sails. They were wooden and used time-tested methods to cut through the waves. But beginning in the early 19th century, the use of steam power was coming into its own. Steamboats were widely used for travel up and down the American rivers early in the century but by the 1840s, steamships were becoming more common on the high seas, as the ships were more frequently being built using metal. Steamships were faster and more reliable than sailing ships and they could carry larger cargo. Steamships could leave New York City, transfer their mail onto the transcontinental railroad in Panama, and have their products in San Francisco, within 40 days. Travel by wagon, in season, would easily take 100 days longer. Many of the Forty-niners reached the goldfields by traveling on steamships around the Cape Horn, but this route, although cheaper, was much longer. The California gold was shipped to the East Coast using this route, but after the sinking of the SS Central America in September 1857, leading to the Panic of 1857, shipping switched to the Panama route, which was much safer and faster once the rail was completed in 1855.

The steamships were larger, noisier, and dirtier than their older counterparts. The romance was gone, traded for speed and utilitarian usage. Gone were the days of the swarthy seadog captains and the multitasking seamen. Now men sweated, shoveling coal into the furnaces that generated vast amounts of steam needed to propel the vessels.

Silva's ship swung past Cuba, not choosing to stop in Havana, reminding him of the loss Tom Kane had experienced less than three years earlier, when his brother, Elisha died. This served to remind one and all that human bodies are meant to withstand only so much. Even the young and stalwart can succumb to the vicissitudes of the elements.

Reaching Panama, the Beecher's Bibles cargo was offloaded and placed onto a railcar whose route wound through the tropical forest of the isthmus. The trip by rail to Panama City was a breeze. The crates were then loaded onto the SS California, setting out for the north. Shep had no reason to visit the city or spend the night on shore. His cabin was more than adequate. The ship stayed within sight of the coast, giving Shep a sense of the speed the ship was able to employ. The long, heavily forested shores of Central America slowly gave way to the rocky and brown coast of Mexico, as the steamship continued its journey towards California.

They docked for the day once they reached San Diego. Small cliffs were visible, but the terrain looked flat and dry. The anxiety Shep had experienced when he was leaving Baltimore had calmed considerably. Reaching California was a milestone. He relaxed the final leg of the journey until they docked in the unfinished harbor of San Pedro, serving the city of Los Angeles.

In a few days, it would be 1860. When Aaron had been killed, Shep found himself the recipient of his friend's considerable stash of currency. It was a prospect he had never encountered. Even when he left the islands, he needed to be cautious with his funds. Now, he had much more. He had no trouble arranging a wagon and eight mules to transport him and the carbines to Los Angeles. From there he would ride to San Bernardino and finally up the Old Spanish Trail and the Great Salt Lake City.

By the time he reached the City of Angels, Shep was ready to sleep. He considered spending the night in the new camp next to San Pedro, named after Colonel Richard Coulter Drum, Assistant Adjunct General of the Army's Dept of the Pacific. It promised to bloom into much more than the several huts and tents it currently sported. But it was not appealing.

Los Angeles had grown. It was much more than the pueblo of 1852. Still, it was small enough that he didn't have any trouble locating a stable for his animals and a place where his crates would be carefully guarded. He was also able to get some easy directions.

The late-night knock on the door was unexpected, causing both Ina and Bob Carsley to jump from their bed. Checking on their baby, they saw that he had not awakened. Bob opened the door carefully, while Ina peeked over his shoulder to ascertain their visitor. The streetlamp was weak and not very close. Shep also knew the community was a good customer of Aaron's. The dancing light barely illuminated Shep's features. Still, it was enough to bring an excited scream of glee from Ina, as she pushed past her husband and ran into the Brazilian's arms. She hugged him tightly, then kissed his cheek.

"Shep Silva! You bless my eyes! How wonderful it is to see you!" She grabbed his arm and pulled him into their small home.

Bob Carsley was relieved to see his wife's response. He began to smile and lit a lamp in their parlor, throwing light on the interior of their still sparsely furnished, newlywed dwelling.

"Bob, this is my friend, Shep Silva. He showed up with Marshal Rockwell when we were visiting the Ousleys in Santa Clara. Remember when Ma got so sick and lost all her hair and the marshal cut off all his locks to have a wig made for her. Remember me telling you?"

Carsley slowly nodded as his memory returned. He smiled again to show his appreciation.

The Carsleys were happy to have Shep spend the night. The following morning, despite their begging, Silva insisted that he needed to get back to his home. It was pleasant to sit in their home and visit and observe their interactions. Shep was hoping they would keep working together and build a strong family.

With the dawning, he was able to see their beautiful little boy, Bobby. Just over a year old, the precocious child was walking, while trying to run, keeping his mother at wit's end. The curly-haired toddler was independent, keeping the adults at arm's length unless he got hurt or was hungry or frightened and then he snuggled closely into Ina's embrace. Protective arms assured him of safety and warmth. Bobby was also a talker, jabbering incessantly to one and all, knowing that everyone secretly understood his lyrical ramblings.

Shep wanted to put off his travels, but seeing the growing child reminded him of his need to return to Yasmin and relay to her the tragedy that had befallen Aaron. After hugging Ina and Bobby once more, he shook Robert Bruce Carsley's hand, then tried to close the door as he left their quaint home. Ina stepped in and kept the door open. Shep had acquired memories to tide him over during the balance of his journey, many dealing with the charming Ina and her budding family.

"Come back and see us," Ina pleaded, waving bravely and smiling from her door. She presented a lovely picture.

Shep continued to sense his Brazilian roots. He was open to different lifestyles and people. He never worried about judging others or cursing parents because of the way children turned out.

Were there cracks in the relationship between Bob and Ina? Was there an underlying tension? Every relationship experienced growing pains. These needed to be dealt with sooner or later. How carefully God has placed his children on the earth. Far too many were never exposed to a loving set of parents, food, and security, warmth, and acceptance. Satan did his best to insert violence and fear and depression among all peoples, regardless of color or clime. God's children were resilient. They choose happiness.

Shep decided that acquisition was the damning doctrine infecting far too many. The desire to own things, education, homes, clothing, power, beauty, keeping these talents or stewardships to themselves or using them in a fashion that would elevate them above their brethren, dividing the family or tribe or community or nation into castes or levels of prosperity. Modern societies chose to ignore the poor and unfortunate, thinking that man prospered in life according to the management of the creature.

The New Testament referred to it as the love of money. Money, wealth, and resources were good and necessary. But all were not bequeathed equally. That's where Christ's admonition to love one's neighbor as himself came into play. *How could someone profess to love his neighbor who is starving, while feasting sumptuously? And these were the common, everyday perversions. What about the more nuanced problems?* Ina had access to her sister for a listening ear or advice. But Bob's family lived far away in New England. The influence of his mother and father lessened with the distance and time.

Bob did not drink while Shep was in their home, but he noticed an array of liquor on the shelves and the bottles had been opened. *How would the effects of alcohol impact the family and his relationship with his wife?* Often, the use of alcohol manifested itself in abuse, but Shep did not notice any bruising on Ina or Bobby. A growing sense of worry regarding the Carsleys dogged him during the balance of his journey.

In San Bernardino, Shep picked up several more families wanting to travel to Salt Lake City. They had their modes of transportation but having someone who had made the trip numerous times lessened their concerns. Silva was happy to be of service and did his best to instruct about the workings of the wagons, care of the animals, and outdoor lore. It didn't take long to realize his small party stood in awe of his knowledge.

The small wagon train snaked across the Mojave Desert, gratefully reaching Las Vegas, before marching again across the wide, arid landscape, then beginning the climb up the plateau.

Folks in Cedar City had relaxed since the last time Shep had visited. Still, the citizens were standoffish, keeping to themselves. They were happy to sell necessities to the incoming emigrants but did not encourage their looking into land and farm opportunities in the area. This disparity became even more apparent as they left the town and entered Beaver, then Parowan, Fillmore, and Nephi. By the time they reached the Utah Valley and Provo most of the folks they passed showed great interest in them and their plans for settling in the northern portion of the territory, spending much of their time detailing the advantages of becoming a part of their community. Smiles were abundant. Accents and a variety of languages were exhibited. People did their best to speak English, whether it was easy or not. They saw literacy with the language as being a symbol of their belonging to the nation on multiple levels.

Two of the families chose to leave the small train in Provo and inspect the environs for themselves.

The trip took less than a month. Rolling up the broad avenues of Salt Lake City brought a feeling of relief and satisfaction to Shep Silva. He had apprised the people of various stables and shops for their comfort. Most already knew people living in the city and made their way to find them.

As he expected, Shep found his wife still living with Yasmin in the Rost home. Countenances were raised with his arrival and before any news could be distributed, Aaron and Yasmin's new baby boy, Isaac, was presented for his inspection.

"He has so much hair. It's dark enough for him to be a Brazilian," he blurted, before remembering the somber tale he had yet to share.

"Where's Aaron?" Yasmin asked, standing on her toes to see past Shep.

Harriett quickly reacted to Shep's pause and rushed to her friend's side.

Shep took a deep breath and paused. "Aaron was killed by some criminals in Baltimore," he said simply, then felt a lump swelling in his throat.

Yasmin's face instantly responded. The smile was replaced by a look of sheer horror. *Her husband? Her Aaron? Her best friend? The father of their children? Dead? Gone? Never again to darken their door? His voice never again to tell his stories or jokes?*

As the strength left her legs, Harriett caught her and carried her to a chair. "There's no such thing as 'never'!" she cried with inspired instinct into Yasmin's ear. "'Never' has no place in God's economy. He knows exactly where your sweetheart is." Harriett lowered her friend gently down. "Aaron is being cradled in a loving embrace by celestial parents. God's promises are sure, my dear. And our sweet Aaron waits intrepidly for his reunion with you."

Tears burst from Yasmin's eyes as she began screaming her disbelief, not in words but sobs and gasps. Harriett hugged her and began rocking her, while Shep carefully took baby Isaac from her arms.

Minutes passed without anyone moving more than a step. Yasmin's plaintive wails grew softer as Harriett's shoulder caught most of her tears. The reality of frontier life had warned her of such a possibility. But now? With so much to live for? The cries turned into softer moans. Her frantic mental searching was soothed by Harriett's consoling words and the warmth of her embrace.

Little Isaac's sleep was unbothered by his mother's outbursts. He remained calm, sleeping, breathing quietly. Shep took him to his crib and carefully placed him within. At that moment, he was grateful that Esther was playing with her friends next door. He conscientiously returned to the parlor and stoked the pot-bellied stove to keep the cold from the room, while trying to be invisible.

The hours dragged by slowly, with Harriett hovering next to Yasmin, cooing encouragement and strength. When Isaac finally awoke, his mother took her into their bedroom to nurse, followed closely by Harriett. Shep walked next door to bring Esther home.

He had experienced several times during his life, the healing powers of time. He knew that the hurt and confusion and loneliness would endure. In the meantime, it was his and Harriett's role not to allow Yasmin to be by herself unless that was what she chose. But with each tick of the clock upon the mantle, with each crackle of the fire as the wood was consuming, with each setting and rising of the sun, the nightmare of Aaron's sudden absence would lessen and fade. So very slowly, at first, but fade it would. Death remained the equalizer. Death's cold hand would visit every person, eventually, rich or poor, old or young, male or female, all would come face to face with the monster known as death.

And that was precisely why Yasmin had grasped the gospel of Christ so fiercely. It was contrary to the traditions of her family but the desperation that

508

etched itself upon so many people in so many places around the world and in so many ways needed to be answered.

And so it was, several nights after Shep's advent, Yasmin awoke suddenly from her slumbers. Her heart was pounding and her chest heaving. Her eyes sought recognition in the darkness. Harriet, sleeping next to her, bolted upright and reached out to clasp her friend.

"It is all right, Harriett," Yasmin said in a whisper. "I know very well now the path that lies before me. The Lord has ushered Aaron back into his heavenly courts but not before giving me two beautiful children, whose very existence will constantly remind me of the love I share with Aaron Rost. And after this short separation, we will be together again, forever."

Shep Silva noticed the change in Yasmin the next morning, as he rolled from his blankets on the floor. She was up and scrubbing in the kitchen while Harriet and Esther played with the baby. The darkness of sorrow had somehow slipped away. He looked inquisitively at Harriett, who only smiled.

A warm breakfast of porridge was soon ready. Yasmin insisted on saying grace over the food. No specific mention was made about Aaron, just thankfulness for life and friendship and access to a healthy meal.

After allowing what he thought was enough time to pass in relative quiet, although, not by Esther or Isaac, Shep finally asked Yasmin about the change in her mood.

"The scriptures term the Holy Ghost as the Comforter. For years I have wondered about this aspect of our religion. Why would the Prophet Joseph have been so emphatic about its presence and importance? Why would Heavenly Father see to it that every one of his children who chose to follow the Savior into the waters of baptism, then be given this supernal gift? Because that's what it is. It is the most wonderful gift conceivable to us here in mortality. As we are born again, this time into the family of Christ, God gives us the birthday gift beyond comprehension. It will abide with us through our lives as we keep the commandments and as we are still, listening to his guidance." Yasmin shook her head and smiled. "I am sorry. I apologize for the lack of faith I have shown, especially after having seen such great feats demonstrated on the frozen prairies by the most humble of folks. They were on their way to Zion. They didn't expect death and privation, yet after seeing what so many of them lost, why should I complain? Why should I not also expect to be given such a crucible to try me? I love God. I love the gospel. I love my husband. I do not expect the challenges to dissipate. I don't expect things to always be rosy and pleasant. But God has given me the strength of purpose. I know in whom I trust. All will be well with Yasmin bint Manara Rost and the two cherished children we have called down from heaven by our love and devotion. They are my living bridge into eternity."

Shep took the next couple of days knocking about the Great Salt Lake City. He ran into Porter Rockwell and reported his findings about Ina and her family. His experience with Yasmin put some things into perspective, and he was much quieter and slower to react when faced with a drunk soldier or a crying, lost child. After several assurances from his peers, he decided it was time to return to Tooele.

Aaron Rost had trained several men to run his store before ever leaving the territory. It did not require much deliberation on Yasmin's part to take her children and accompany the Silvas back to their farm.

Shep sat alone on the buckboard, driving the mules. The two women situated themselves with the two little children in the wagon box, stuffing blankets around them for warmth and comfort. Esther napped and Harriett and Yasmin spoke in quiet tones about the future and their beliefs in God's planning.

The valley was filling up with cabins and farms. Fences lined the roads. An abundance of young trees was standing stalwart in orchards or as designed windbreaks. It was noon but the sun was far to the south, the direction they were traveling, its rays having little effect warming the landscape or its denizens. The latest storm had come through the valley two weeks earlier but now there were only small patches of dirty snow littering the ground.

The cold air was not conducive for hawks to soar. Shep felt the absence of the feathered predators and found himself hoping the spring and warmer weather would hurry and arrive. Winter was fine for some things but with the rebirth of spring, the world seemed to open up and stay that way for months.

Concern over Yasmin and her children had vanished from Shep's mind. He watched how carefully Harriett had pulled her friend and the children into her embrace. It was normal and natural. The friendship burned as brightly as ever. He never worried about Yasmin stepping away from her responsibilities as a mother or friend. She had proven herself over and over again. She was devoted to her children. She clung to Harriett for support but looking only for assurance of her love and affection.

There were times when Shep felt out of place, like a foreigner. He refrained from invading their space or intruding when their discussions were guarded, being shared just between them. On the other hand, Yasmin was not a wallflower. She happily spoke with Shep. She enjoyed recalling memories of Aaron and thirsted for any that Shep could think of, experiences she was not fully aware of. She enjoyed hearing of the friendships they made, especially the time they spent together when Shep left Hawaii or their most recent trip back east. Topics of their discussions enlivened her. She was pleased to know the extent of the Kanes' affection for them and the closeness Aaron felt to John Brown and his commitment to freeing the slaves.

"You're sure Porter has room for us?"

"That's what he told me, Ett. I think he's been expecting us for a while. I guarantee that he'd be hurt if we didn't stop in."

"Does he get many soldiers at his place?"

"That's why he keeps the liquor. They keep him on his toes and drink up his stock as quick as he can get it. And that's good because if he didn't have to worry about their drinking, I'm afraid he might drink it up. All by himself."

The thought caused Yasmin to laugh. "Porter Rockwell is such a legend. It's funny thinking of him as a regular man. And a man who enjoys drinking, at that."

Shep sighed. "We all have our crosses to bear. I just hope he's not drinking when I need his help. That would be a scary thing. But when his eyes are clear, he sees everything."

The road sloped down towards the river near the narrows, marking the southern point of the Great Salt Lake Valley. It was a treacherous place during winter storms. Clouds and winds collected frequently, blinding teamsters and animals with blowing snow. Accidents were commonplace in the winter. The river was running high and fast. Happily, Rockwell had built an inn up and away from the matrix of desolation. But not too far.

Soldiers from Camp Floyd could ride to his saloon and back within a day. And they did. Merchants in Frogtown worried Rockwell's liquor sales might hurt their own but the lawman was careful not to overdo it, not to encroach on the main businesses in the town adjacent to Camp Floyd. Rockwell's main interest was to keep an eye on the comings and goings of people throughout the territory. His inn was well placed for a gathering of emigrants and rumors.

The return to Tooele signaled joy as endless neighbors came to leave tasty offerings, mementos of their appreciation and value. These mementos were quickly gobbled up by Herman and Zeenyo. The fetching Linda G had married the strapping Jared Hansen and lived scarcely a few blocks away and she was expecting their first baby, Ole and Georgina Hansen's first grandchild.

Mark and Martha Sweeney had settled well into the society of the town, their precocious children melded successfully into the population and before long, no one could remember what life was like without their presence. Brigham Young had called Mark to be the new bishop in Tooele, just more responsibilities for the tired and worn priesthood holder, but nothing he was afraid of. He grabbed onto the calling with gusto and shepherded his flock with all the attention, humility, and devotion of St. Francis of Assisi.

"You got time to take a walk with me?" Bishop Sweeney asked Shep at his front door.

"Of course." He poked his head into the kitchen and informed Harriett that he would be taking a walk with the bishop, then grabbing his hat, headed outside. The lane at the side of his home had several saplings planted to act as a windbreak as they grew bigger. They were already starting to bud.

The bishop got straight to the point. "I got a message for you from the Prophet. He thinks you should take a plural wife." Mark Sweeney knew whereof he spoke. He and Martha had also been called to enter into a plural marriage the year before and the new, younger wife, Karen, was now expecting a baby.

The news was not unexpected. Over the years Shep had toyed with the idea several times but each left him feeling empty and concerned. He thought he understood the doctrine as well as anyone. He had also observed how different relationships handled the call. For some the adjustment was simple. For others,

511

it was complicated. Most polygamist members of the church consisted of one man and two wives and they were structured for the bearing and rearing of children. But other men were called to take multiple wives, many of whom were past their childbearing age. Still, a vast majority of men were never called upon to practice 'the Principle'. Scratching a living out of desert soil and raising faithful children was sacrifice and work enough for most couples. And embarking on plural marriage was totally under the purview of the president of the church, Brigham Young. It had nothing to do with lust or libido but everything to do with acceptance, forgiveness, and charity.

About half of the plural marriages flourished, another quarter of them fought hard to maintain their relationships and were somewhat successful. The last quarter was a dismal failure and lives were shattered.

Selection of candidates for a plural marriage had a lot to do with the need, the local bishop and the Prophet, very little had to do with the husband but most with the first wife. It was up to her whether or not the marriage was entered into. She carried the weight of the relationship and veto. If the marriage worked well or utterly failed rested heavily upon her.

Entering into a plural marriage did not equate to eternal sex for the husband. Many relationships were strictly Platonic, especially when the women were past childbearing age. Physical intimacy was generally reserved for the production of children.

These relationships were not viewed in sordid, back-alley connections. Families, with their attendant responsibilities and obligations, were merely expanded.

Since the death of Aaron Rost, Shep could read the writing on the wall. During his return trip, he had pondered the possibility. Yasmin was a beautiful woman and a fine mother. She was also a long-time friend and associate of Harriett's. But these were not motivating factors. He did not want to invite Yasmin, the wife of his friend Aaron, into his bed to satisfy his lust or for breeding purposes. Nor did he think Yasmin's presence and friendship with Harriett would turn a plural marriage into an easy fit.

"You know where this is headed?"

Shep nodded somberly. "I'll speak with Ett."

Since his return from Baltimore, Shep had touched bases with his wife about the possibility of helping Yasmin and her two children, Esther and Isaac. They agreed that bringing them to live in Tooele to be closer, would be advantageous. But when Shep breached the subject of expanding their family, inviting Yasmin and her children to be a part of them, Harriett was ecstatic, both shocking and concerning him.

"I cannot think of a better solution, my dear!" she exclaimed. "Oh, Shep! This is an answer to my prayers. But will you be up to dealing with both of us? I don't mean in the bedroom. That is something we can talk over. But Yasmin and I have a long history together, and a good head start on you."

Chapter 67

"The biggest labor problem is tomorrow." Brigham Young

Two days later, Bishop Sweeney and Martha rode in their wagon, in front of Shep, Harriett, and Yasmin. Esther and Isaac were staying at home, being watched by Linda G.

President Brigham Young met them at the Endowment House in Salt Lake City. After visiting individually and collectively, he too was convinced of the rightness of their decision. Entering into the sealing room, he then, using the authority of his office and priesthood, joined the three of them together as husband and wives. In this situation, because Yasmin had previously been sealed to Aaron forever, instead of using the words 'for time and all eternity,' Brigham simply used 'time', indicating that the relationship was meant only to endure for mortality. In the eternities, Yasmin would be joined again with Aaron.

All of this was conducted by strict adherence to the women's agency. They had free will to give themselves according to the dictates of their hearts.

After the ceremony, they bundled up in their wagons and made the return trip to Tooele. The three Silvas knew that their marriage was just budding. No one was anxious to contemplate the idea of marital consummation. If and when that ever took place, would come up at another time and place. For now, Yasmin and her babies were sheltered beneath the loving embrace of Harriett and Shep Silva.

That evening Mark Sweeney was surprised to find Shep at his door. "I wasn't expecting anything quite this fast," he confessed, pulling on his coat and stepping outside.

"It's nothing of the sort, Bishop. But I have some questions that have been eating at me for quite a while. And bringing it up with Brigham today certainly didn't feel right."

"Okay." Mark was at attention.

"What can you tell me about the goings-on at Mountain Meadows?"

"Ah, yes," Mark answered. "A lot is still just rumor. I don't know everything about it, but I have visited with President Young several times regarding the issue. Brother Haight gave the go-ahead to the militia and the local Indians to attack the Fancher wagon train. This was back in September of '57. I understand there was a horrible massacre and only the youngest of the children were spared. Jake Hamblin got back from Salt Lake soon afterward. It happened close to his ranch. He says it was awful. Nothing could describe the horror and depravity. The children were scooped up and taken away but

513

everything else was left helter-skelter. Animals scattered the people's remains all over the valley."

Shep nodded. "President Young had me return with a letter for President Haight. I could sense it, Mark. The whole town of Cedar, the whole area was weighed down with a terrible spirit. I knew something had gone wrong but just couldn't guess. Until I did and the thought made me puke. That, and we were in a mess with the Army invading the territory."

"Doesn't make it right."

"Nope."

Sweeney sighed deeply. "I don't know what will ever come from an investigation or who will be fingered. Colonel Johnston finally gathered up the 17 children and returned them to their surviving families in Arkansas last year. I know Brigham spoke with Governor Cumming about it several times, trying to get something going to find out the extent of the massacre but Governor Cumming was right cautious, thinking he could never get anything going, especially after President Buchanan had issued his proclamation, forgiving one and all about involvement with the Utah War. And he didn't want to stir things up with the Indians. It's a mess."

Shep agreed. "And it'll get messier the longer it goes without answers and accountability." He sighed and the two men sat on the Sweeney's porch, each immersed in their thoughts.

After a few minutes, Silva was the first to break their silence. "So, Johnston's gone?"

The bishop nodded. "Couldn't happen soon enough. I know he's happy. He never cared for folks around here nor the whole territory. He's gone back to Kentucky for a bit. That's what I hear. Colonel Smith took over Camp Floyd but that didn't last long either. Lt. Colonel Cooke now is the one in charge."

"That's a plus for us. He has always been a man of honor."

"If you don't have any plans, why not go with me to General Conference on the first of April? It would get us out of town and maybe give the women a chance to visit."

"Just tell me when."

****

Businessmen William Hepburn Russell, Alexander Majors, and William Bradford Waddell had worked together since 1855, moving freight and mail across the west. They called their company Central Overland California and Pike's Peak Express Company, competing directly with Governor Young's YX or Young's Express Company, along with several others. Russell, Majors, and Waddell also contracted with the Army to provide wagons, animals, and supplies for the troops. They were heavily involved with the Army when they left Fort Leavenworth in the summer of 1857 and marched towards the Utah Territory to quash any thoughts of rebellion or secession. As a consequence, the company suffered severe setbacks when the Mormon guerrillas burned and pillaged their wagons, then made off with large numbers of their cattle, mules, and horses. As a direct result of the fiasco experienced on the high plains during the winter of 1857-58 and to recoup some of their losses and keep them from falling into bankruptcy, the men decided to start another audacious business. They called it the Pony Express.

It started April 3, 1860, and stretched from St. Joseph in Missouri to Sacramento, California. On that date, a rider left St. Joseph, heading west and another rider left Sacramento, heading east and they crossed each other in route, both arriving at their destinations at the opposite ends on April 14th. It called for the hiring of strong, yet small, young men. They couldn't weigh more than 125 pounds. The young men who would ride between stations set every 5 to 10 miles, changing horses and setting off again. They rode day and night. Each carrier would be expected to cover about 100 miles before being switched out for another rider. The 186 Express Stations were small and mostly set up to hold extra horses for the company. Some of the stations were just farms that were already established. It was the barest of existence and the people who ran the stations worked long hours.

It took the Pony Express 10 days to cover the 1900-mile route, greatly reducing the time it took for mail to travel from the west coast to the east. The company had 400 horses for the effort. Most of these were horses raised in the west and capable of the rough trip. Besides being wary of Indians and marauders, the riders also had to be on the lookout for tainted water from which they could contract cholera, predators, or bad weather.

Swing stations were meant only to allow the exchange of horses while the home stations would provide room and board to the exhausted riders.

The route across central Nevada had been blazed by Captain James Simpson and his survey team, from Camp Floyd, in 1859, drastically cutting the distance. Before then, mail going from Salt Lake City, went north to Tremonton then dropped down to the Humbolt River and followed the road to Carson Valley, then it was up and over the Sierras to Sacramento. But this was only when the weather was moderate. In the winter the mail was carried south along the Old Spanish Trail into lower California, then routed north to Sacramento. The Butterfield Overland Mail Company was also contracted to carry mail down the southern route, using the old Mormon Battalion trail, then up and into Missouri and places east.

Each of the riders was expected to swear an oath: "*I...do hereby swear, before the Great and Living God, that during my engagement, and while I am an employee of Russell, Majors, and Waddell, I will, under no circumstances, use profane language, that I will drink no intoxicating liquors, that I will not quarrel or fight with any other employee of the firm, and that in every respect I will conduct myself honestly, be faithful to my duties, and so direct all my acts as to win the confidence of my employers, so help me God.*"

The 84 riders earned $100 a month carrying the *mochila* stuffed with letters. The company also hired 400 people to man the various stations.

It could also be very dangerous.

In April, several Bannock and Shoshone arrived at Pyramid Lake to discuss with their brothers the encroachments being made by the settlers, especially as a result of the 1859 discovery of the silver in the Comstock Lode. Rumor spread that some whites had kidnapped two Indian women and were holding them at the William's Station on the Carson River. Some of the warriors went to investigate and shooting erupted, ending in the deaths of five white men.

The Indian leaders, including Chief Winnemucca, felt war was warranted. Chief Numaga tried restraining the others but after the Williams Station incident, he gave up. "There is no longer any use for counsel. We must prepare for war, for the soldiers will now come here to fight us."

William Ormsby, who had been attending to the education of Sarah Winnemucca, gathered 105 volunteers from Virginia City, Carson, and Genoa and rode towards Pyramid Lake to punish the offenders. Thinking the Indians would be primarily armed with bows and arrows, the white men were armed with pistols.

A small group of natives lured Ormsby's party up the gulch made by the Truckee River, leading to the lake. Once the party was far enough in, the Paiutes closed the circle, having successfully surrounded their attackers. And most of the Indians were armed with rifles. Ormsby was killed, along with 76 of his militiamen. The few survivors were barely able to escape.

The engagement enraged the whites and they mounted another assault against the Paiutes, this time they drew a larger number of soldiers from Nevada as well as troops from California. Wanting to teach the Paiutes a lesson, they attacked again but with only limited success. Three soldiers and 25 Indians lost their lives, bringing the Paiute War to a close.

The next month a regular contingent of soldiers began the construction of a fort, dubbed Fort Churchill, named after the Inspector General of the US Army, Sylvester Churchill. Construction of the fort finished up the following year and Fort Churchill also became a station for the Pony Express.

For eighteen months, the heroic efforts of the pony express riders and station workers moved important mail back and forth across these great distances. The federal government wanted to join the company with the Butterfield Overland Mail Company that worked across the southern route from California and into New Mexico. It wasn't successful.

Zeenyo Wetoyou held out a scrap of paper for Shep to read.

"Wanted: Young, skinny, wiry fellows not over eighteen. Must be expert riders, willing to risk death daily. Orphans preferred."

"What do you think?" he asked almost breathlessly. "I could make $100 a month and would probably only be riding between Willow Springs out west, then up to the head of Echo Canyon on the east."

"That's it?"

"Yep. About 100 miles a day. Stations are set pretty close together for me to change mounts."

"You'd go on Simpson's road?"

Again, he nodded. "I'd come out by Rush Lake and through Camp Floyd, then over to Rockwell's and up Emigration Canyon. Not all in the same day, mind you."

"No further?"

The question made Zeenyo pause. "Well. I could be asked to go further west at times. There's a need, I guess. But I was told, probably not. Not for most of the time. I'd be right here, close by. How's that?"

Shep looked at Zeenyo hard, and probably for the first time in his life, he saw that he too, was becoming a man. So good. So kind. So responsible. So willing to help others. And now, so resourceful.

"Sounds great, Zeenyo. I almost wish I were ten years younger."

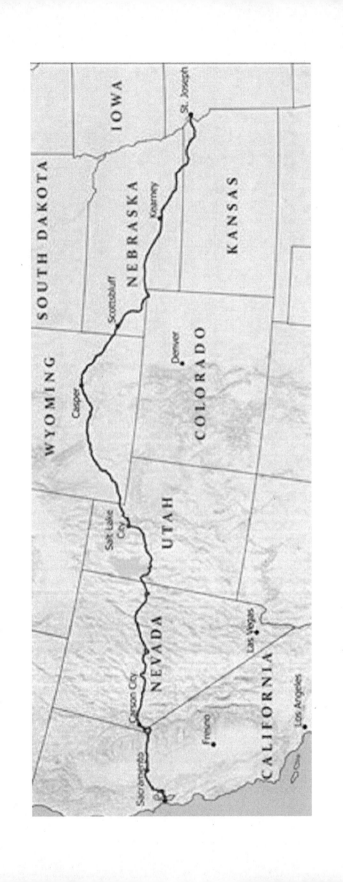

April 1860

My dearest Ina,

I apologize for waiting this long before writing to you. I know that you married Bob and have been quite busy, especially with your move to Los Angeles. Also, Shep Silva informed me of his visit and how wonderful it was seeing your little boy, Bobby.

I also wish to express my congratulations about your marriage and the birth of your first child. That he is so active and happy is a testament to you as his mother and of course to Bob. I wish you all the best.

I also got married last year. It was my good fortune to find our cousin Levira, daughter of Uncle Samuel. Do you remember her? Like yourself, she is young, perhaps too young to know better. Anyway, she is my wife, and she makes me happy. I hope to be following in your parental footsteps soon but so far there's no news that we are expecting a baby.

We have a small home in Salt Lake City, where I do most of my work. Levira's mother is also close by and helps a lot with any concerns, worries, or whatnot. I think she's tiring of the valley. Doesn't care for sagebrush much. She's talking about moving to California. That wouldn't make my wife too happy. Not just yet, anyway.

I just learned that our age-old enemy, Gov Lilburn Boggs died. Right there in California. I will let you know that it doesn't make Porter too awfully sad. Me either, to be perfectly truthful. He passed the 14th of last month.

Things this way are calming down, especially after the near-war, we got into with the government. Col Cooke is now in command of Fort Floyd and he's doing a fine job. It makes things a lot easier when he and Governor Cumming are getting along with President Young.

The big news I have is that President Young has called me to serve another mission. This one will be in Britain. I'm sure that island is not as beautiful as the Sandwich Islands. It won't be near as warm, either. At least the people speak about the same language as us. I should get over there sometime around the end of July.

Please write and tell me how you are doing. I so enjoyed your letters when I was in Hawaii. I am sending you the address in England where you can write. I hope you will use it.

Love you and to all your family and friends. As ever,
Joseph F. Smith

July 1860

Dear Joseph,

I received your letter in a quick manner. I have not responded as soon as I ought for several reasons, which I promise to detail you later.

I am pleased to know that you are now in Great Britain. You continue on as a hero. You honor me with your service and conviction.

My family is doing as well as can be expected.

But, my dearest Joseph, I am devastated. My heart has been wracked with unspeakable sorrow and I will attempt to inform you of the details.

Our child, our firstborn, our pride and joy, has died. There was no reason. There was no explanation. Everything had been moving along as best we could expect. Then one morning, as I went into his room to awaken him, I found him lying lifeless in his bed.

The horror of that moment returns over and over again, seizing my heart with cold, clammy fear and pain. I have not been able to ascertain the reason for Bobby's death. The doctors do not seem to know. They simply wag their heads with ignorance. It is not that they should know every last thing but surely, they must know more than I. Yet, they continue to act surprised and unable to assist. It is like they retreat into a shell for protection, waiting for the sorrow to wane.

I am bereft, Joseph. I know not where to turn or what to do. A silence has descended upon me. I no longer care to speak. I do not wish to visit with friends or family. An overpowering ache has me in its grasp, threatening to end my own existence.

I have cried repeatedly until no more tears would emerge from my eyes. My face is puffy. I am forlorn. No one cares to be near me when all I care to do is bewail my motherhood.

You spoke of your own sweet wife, as yet unable to bear you children. Forgive me when I applaud your heaven-sent blessing. Levira's womb has yet to feel the growing within her. The pangs of labor and childbirth. And finally, the inexpressible joy of nursing her very own baby. Memories of infant fingers clutching your hair. Sweet childhood expressions mean so very much more than concocted words. Gone forever, my dear Joseph. I am at a loss to know how best to describe the depths of my sorrow. I wander through the house, searching for the lost babblings of my child. I seek once more, for the sun's light to glisten in his hair as he plays in our garden.

I am lost and forlorn, Joseph. And Robert, my soulmate. Where is he? Does he dote upon my suffering? He does not. Does he try and comfort me with soothing words? No. Does he clasp me into his embrace, combing my hair with his fingers? Forbid the thought. Instead, he has chosen to find release at the bottom of a bottle of liquor. He drinks when he comes home from his labors. He drinks into the evening, hardly touching his food. He refuses to talk and when he does, no one is able to decipher is slurring, spittle-connected phrases.

Bob drinks through the night and again begins another day with the aspiration that forgetfulness will come with inebriation.

With Bobby's death has also come the death of my love for his father. It too was once vital and living. Is there a resurrection in store for these fleeting hopes? Past seasons when I naively reached for a combined future? My mother and sister are beside themselves. I am waiting daily for them to come and have me declared insane. I crane my ears, hoping against hope to once more capture the image or voice of my child, in the white clouds or the frothy waves. Where do I go, Joseph?

I write you particularly at this stage because you are a man of God. You cleave unto that religion that was brought forth by our uncle, who people still refer to as the Prophet Joseph. I seek for your advice. Where can I go to find solace for my beating heart or my sharp gasps of pain? Would you, so cavalierly, push my face into the Bible or suggest I forget myself and work to elevate other downtrodden? Do I disguise abject wrenching of my soul in manufactured trivia?

Now, dear heart, understand that I know that by the time you receive this missive, the gauntlet I am now going through will have ceased somewhat. I know that this is true. On the other hand, I reject the fact, not caring to have my heartache mellowed by the passing of time. This heartache testifies of what I once possessed. Therefore, I am not in a hurry for it to flee. Just know, that now, at this moment, I continue to roar and tear within this poor tabernacle of clay, wishing for a reunion. Either that he would be returned to me or that I might go to him.

I also choose not to advertise this defining moment in my life. Sharing such devastation is inconsiderate. Most will never understand, and I am a poor communicator, trying to translate the darkest woe. Very few are worthy to know of this brilliant light that once illumined my soul. Bobby has been a prize well beyond my merit and yet he was mine and I held him securely and still could not keep him from slipping away.

I cherish your love. I need you now more than ever. Our relationship is sacred. It is holy. It is the one remaining hope I claim as a bridge to the celestial courts on high.

I will love you always,
Josephina Donna Smith Coolbrith Carsley.

Chapter 68

"In the heavens are parents single? No, the thought makes reason stare. Truth is reason, truth eternal, tells me, I've a mother there."
Eliza R. Snow

Judge Stephen Arnold Douglas was a political powerhouse from the state of Illinois. Beginning his vocation early on in Illinois, he championed the rights of people on the frontier, including the Mormons. After they left, he continued for years speaking and fighting for and representing frontier ideas in Washington that resonated with many. He was a careful politician who considered his steps seriously.

He championed the 1850 Compromise and the Nebraska-Kansas Act, especially promoting the idea of popular sovereignty. He felt the writers of the Constitution intended the United States to be organized and governed by white, Anglo-Saxon peoples, that the Constitutional rights and privileges did not extend to slaves, Indians, or others, not of the majority ethnicity.

Being a spokesperson for the Democratic Party, Douglas butted heads numerous times with the rising popularity of Whig member, Abraham Lincoln. The latter then assisted in the formation of the Republican Party in 1856. In 1858, these two politicians held a series of seven debates, vying for control of the Illinois General Assembly. Douglas squeaked out the victory, gaining more seats for his party than Lincoln, winning the battle but eventually losing the war.

Politically speaking, 1860 was a year of decision and folly. Northern Democrats and Republicans were split into a variety of factions. That year Democratic Convention was held in Charleston, South Carolina from April 23rd to May 3rd. Vote after vote was held trying to determine the party's candidate, with Stephen Douglas consistently winning the majority. It wasn't enough. The Democrats reconvened a couple of months later in Baltimore, on June 18th. This time, Stephen Douglas was finally awarded the nomination, but Southern Democrats boycotted the convention and decided to hold their own, pro-slavery meeting. The Southern States, felt they were being pressed by anti-slavery forces. As a response, they nominated John Breckinridge along with a radical pro-slavery platform. The Constitutional Union Party then popped up and nominated John Bell. This effectively split the southern vote. The South began threatening to secede from the Union. Meanwhile, the Republican Convention was held in Chicago, Illinois on May 16-18 and ended up selecting hometown hero and rail-splitter, Abraham Lincoln to be their candidate of choice. The lethal split in the Democratic Party virtually assured the election of Abraham Lincoln on November 6, 1860.

After the election, Stephen Douglas limped away but then threw his support behind Lincoln, thinking erroneously, that Lincoln's strength would somehow keep the Union together. It didn't.

The last two Mormon handcart companies commissioned by Brigham Young, arrived in Salt Lake City in the fall of 1860. Daniel Robison led the ninth company into the valley, having 233 emigrants. One person died during the crossing. They arrived on August 27, 1860. The tenth and final handcart company of the Latter-day Saint experience was led by Oscar Stoddard and consisted of 124 emigrants, arriving in the Great Salt Lake Valley on September 24th. Not a single one of their company perished during the journey.

October 1860

Dearest Ina,

I am completely incontinent. There is nothing I can do or say that might lift you from your desperate circumstances. You have heard it all before from your friends and neighbors. But not from me. So, belatedly, I send my own condolences. Having never experienced what is facing you, I simply tell you that I am eternally sorry. I cannot conceive of what you are going through. Dreadful. I wish I possessed a fraction of your talent to enable me to express myself. Woe is me, for I am undone.

Since I received your letter ultimate, my heart has been wrenched. From afar and on this fair isle, I roar within my soul, God knowing my feelings that I do not consider you ever meriting such a blow.

Certainly, you feel abandoned. When those dearest to you remain aloof and away, how can you not just feel alone and rejected by all upon the earth and in the heavens?

You are quite right in your assessment of me. I want to write you a list of things to do, hoping my poor additions might in someway help fill the gaping hole that you find in your heart and soul. I am incapable. My hand is unable to lift the quill and sketch out the letters and phrases that might carry comfort.

Just know this, my dearest Ina. I pray multiple times each day for your release from this awful situation. In my heart, in my soul of souls, I know that God hears and answers prayers. My sincere yearning is that you too have applied for this comfort, then just as quickly, I realize that there isn't a stone in your existence that you have left unturned. I do not question your abilities or sincerities. I question my own. As I preach the reality of the gospel to these benighted folks in Britain, I hear my own words returning to condemn me, asking me why I haven't done more or cannot seem to do more to help you.

As far away from you as I am, as slow as the letters take to post, please believe me when I tell you of my love and concern. Little Bobby has gone home, to be with his heavenly parents. They cherish his embrace, while these same celestial beings know and love you as well, and long to feel the closeness of your embrace again.

This next year starts a new decade. I am wishing you every aspect of relief and joy. I am troubled by my lame attempt to cheer you, knowing full well of my own shortsightedness. I can only move forward faithfully, doing what I have been called upon to do, knowing that the God of us all, somehow and someway, loves you even more than I do. I wrestle to see how this is possible, yet the Holy Ghost has told me repeatedly that it is so.

Again, dearest Josephina, hear me as I plead that you always know of my love and affection for you.

As the eternal waves of emotions striking your shores finally begin to ebb, think of me, your champion. I will never desert you. Rather, I intend to see you and our decidedly wonderful family again, together forever, in the gleaming courts on high.

Forever, I remain yours,
Joseph Fielding Smith

****

On November 27, 1860, Judge Orson Hyde of the Utah Territory, feeling vindicated by the polls, penned a letter to the defeated 'Little Giant'.

Judge Douglas,

Will the Judge now acknowledge that Joseph Smith was a true Prophet? If he will not, does he recollect a certain conversation had with Mr. Smith, at the house of Sheriff Backenstos, in Carthage, Illinois, in the year 1843, in which Mr. Smith said to him: "You will yet aspire to the Presidency of the United States. But if you ever raise your hand, or your voice against the Latter-day Saints, you shall never be President of the United States."

Does Judge Douglas recollect that in a public speech delivered by him in the year 1857 at Springfield, IL, of comparing the Mormon community, then constituting the inhabitants of Utah Territory, to a "loathsome ulcer in the body politic;" and of recommending the knife be applied to cut it out?

Among other things the Judge will doubtless recollect that I was present and heard the conversation between him and Joseph Smith, at Mr. Backenstos' residence, before alluded to.

Now, Judge, what think you about Joseph Smith and Mormonism?

Orson Hyde

A Deseret News reporter asked Lincoln about his intentions concerning the Mormon situation. Lincoln responded: "Sir, when I was a boy on the farm in Illinois there was a great deal of timber on the farm which we had to clear away. Occasionally we would come to a log that had fallen. It was too hard to split, too wet to burn, and too heavy to move, so we plowed around it. That's what I intend to do with the Mormons. You go back and tell Brigham Young that if he will let me alone, I will let him alone."

****

"What got into our women last night?" Bishop Sweeney asked Shep the next morning as they were walking toward their common pasture to check on some cattle.

"What do you mean?"

"Did they talk to you at all?"

Shep thought for a bit. "About what?"

"Oh, I guess they said lots of things before Martha and Sarah left. The power and gift of the Holy Ghost. Men, women, old, young, Easterners and Westerners, Northerners, Southerners, pro and anti-slavers, Indians, religions, Poles, Russians, English, Hawaiians, Hopi, Utes and Shoshone. All of us becoming one. Now, what does that mean? Becoming one? They came home quite pleased with themselves, thinking they had solved all the world's ills. They also both took out the scriptures and read until quite late into the night."

"And that's a bad thing?"

"Listen Shep, I've been after Martha to read her scriptures more seriously for years. I've been after the whole ward to read their scriptures more seriously. What happens if now they really start? I'll need to drag out the scriptures myself just to stay up with them. They might start pestering me with doctrinal questions. Then what?"

"I guess that's when you finally get what you've wanted."

Chapter 69

"Freedom is a road seldom traveled by the multitude." Frederick Douglass

Dec 1860

Dearest Ina,

My heart is broken. I can only imagine the grief you have gone through.

Here in Britain, we have recently learned of the election of Abraham Lincoln. I applaud the wisdom of the American people here. It will bring a swift end to the misery known as slavery. But I'm also afraid it will be messy, if not bloody before all is said and done. In the turmoil of our nation, I also see a reflection of your own life. Challenges lie before you. I am confident that you will find the resolve to overcome the Adversary. Power emanating from your heart will wash away the sorrow brought on by the terrible loss of Bobby and also the filth and degradation you have been presented with from he who should have known better.

I am so sorry for you. The winter solstice will be coming soon. It means the days will grow longer. Flowers will bloom and buds put forth blossoms and then leaves. The earth will be renewed and it's my hope that you will feel the added strength.

I love you, dear heart. I don't mean to wallow. I merely want you to know that it is on my mind and dwells in my heart.

I am grateful for the work here. It keeps me sane and engaged. I am learning quickly again that all of us have problems. Not as serious as what you have gone through, mind you, but problems that worry and rob us of sleep. I remain thankful for the gospel of Jesus Christ that orients me in my life and decisions.

I love you and am concerned about you. I apologize for this small letter but I wanted to get something sent your way before too much time had passed.

Always and forever yours,
Joseph F. Smith

****

From December 20th to February 1, 1861, seven southern states chose to secede, South Carolina, Mississippi, Florida, Alabama, Georgia, Louisiana, and Texas. Many of the citizens thought they were following the example set by the Utah Territory in 1857. On January 29ᵗʰ Kansas was admitted to the Union as a free state.

The coalition of southern states elected Jeff Davis as president of the newly formed Confederate States of America. Secession as a word and theory had been used in the United States as early as 1776.

Jefferson Davis was an energetic and high-profile man and being a champion of the South, had been elected president of the Provisional Government of the Confederacy on February 9, 1861—as a compromise between southern moderates and radicals—was confirmed by the voters for a full six-year term. By the time of his inauguration as full president on February 22, 1862, the Confederate capital, which had originally been in Montgomery, Alabama, had been moved to Richmond, Virginia, in part to defend the strategically important Tredegar Ironworks.

A graduate of the U.S. Military Academy at West Point, Davis was a celebrated veteran of the Mexican War. He served as secretary of war under Franklin Pierce and as a longtime U.S. senator from Mississippi. His first wife, Sarah Knox, was the daughter of President Zachary Taylor. Although a strong advocate of states' rights, Davis tried to temper the antagonism between North and South in the tense days leading up to the war, opposing secession even after South Carolina left the Union in December 1860. However, when Mississippi seceded in January 1861, the slave-holding planter cast his lot with the Confederacy.

Immediately after his February 18, 1861, inauguration as provisional president, Davis sent a peace commission to Washington. Abraham Lincoln, committed to preserving the Union at any cost, refused to see the emissaries of the Confederacy. In early April, Lincoln dispatched armed ships to resupply the federal garrison at Fort Sumter under the command of Major Robert Anderson. In response, Davis ordered the April 12ᵗʰ bombardment of the fort. The attack marked the beginning of the Civil War. The Union forces surrendered the next day on the 13ᵗʰ.

It was at that time that the border states of Virginia, Arkansas, Tennessee, and North Carolina joined the secession.

General Albert Sidney Johnston spent most of 1860 in his home state of Kentucky. Towards the end of the year, he was given command of the Pacific and on December 21ˢᵗ he sailed for San Francisco but then when his new home state of Texas seceded in January 1861, he resigned his new commission but stayed in place until his replacement/relief arrived in California, on April 10, 1861.

After a short interim when Colonel Smith succeeded Colonel Johnston as camp commander, Colonel Philip St. George Cooke became Camp Floyd's final commander. On February 6, 1861, Cooke was ordered to change the name of the camp to Fort Crittenden, in honor of Senator J. J. Crittenden of Kentucky. The change was made because of the strong anti-Union tendencies that were then openly manifested by the U.S. Secretary of War, John Floyd.

Then, acting under orders from the War Department, Colonel George Cooke cut the post complement down to 700 men.

On March 2, 1861, the organization of the Nevada Territory took place, claiming the Carson Valley and the property that butted up against California, then east to the 116th meridian. The following year this line was moved farther east to the 115th meridian and finally to the 114th.

Lincoln's first inaugural was held in Washington DC on March 4, 1861. Security was tight. Proceeding to the podium the president was surrounded by soldiers, making it impossible for onlookers to see Lincoln. Security had been arranged by the Old Man of the Army, General Winfield Scott. More people expected an attempt on the president's life at this time than on any other.

March 1861

My dear Joseph,

Let me say at the outset that I am doing much better. I am healing from the nightmare. It is a chapter in my life I wish to leave buried, carefully in the past. My memories belong to me. I will always cherish them. I loved him fiercely and he gave in return, so unselfishly, unknowingly, really. I do not wish to ever pull him back into this realm of sorrow and fear, something I feel I would be doing by simply mentioning his sacred name.

Of course, at a future date, I will be open to discussing him with you because of your importance in my life. However, I will not speak of my son with anybody who is not extremely close, as I would find that dishonorable. I hope you understand. I am not trying to forget this glorious chapter in my life. Rather, I am wanting to hide it away from the mundane. It will always remain with me. I will select with whom I should share it. My parents and sister and you but beyond that will require a special dispensation.

I am still married to Bob Carsley, as shameful as that makes me feel. My husband is an abusive man, mentally and spiritually. He has not lifted his hand in anger against me but I am confident that this is only a matter of time. Yet, when he is drinking, all semblance of kindness flees. Whore is his favorite epithet that he throws repeatedly at me, usually screaming at the top of his voice.

If I were charitable, I would see that perhaps liquor and coarse language are a symptom of his misery and sorrow after the death of our child. I have not written much since I was married but have somehow maintained an air of celebrity. Unfortunately, this is a card that Robert has chosen to play, at my expense. The volume in his accusations and the sordid manner in which he portrays me attracts the most degraded denizens of the bars and saloons. I must admit that some of these very fellows are drawn to my husband, who through his own blurry and fogged vision, embraces them as being well met.

The local newspapers have clutched at the misery of our marriage. They find it titillating to pontificate about our position or the future of our lives together.

I am beginning to think more about my writing. It brings me such release and joy. I find that I still maintain some readers who would appreciate hearing from me, so my pen should be busy for a while.

You continue to be my knight in shining armor. You are my hero. You are my champion. Please do not let this status offend you. I promise to keep you solidly fixed on this pedestal until perhaps someday in the future, I might find another worthy of my heart and love.

I cherish the Spanish phrase, hasta la vista. I dream of la vista, with you in my mind's eye.

Again, thank you for your sympathy, loyalty, and charity.

I love you, dear heart, sincerely,
Ina

On May 17, 1861, the War Department ordered Colonel George Cooke to take the rest of his troops and leave Fort Crittenden. Before leaving, Cooke was ordered to dispose of everything on the post to the best advantage of the government.

At the sales which followed this order, $4 million worth of supplies sold for $100,000. One of the principal buyers was Brigham Young who, through his agent and son-in-law H. B. Clawson, paid $40,000 for the things which he obtained.

The effect of this windfall may be gauged from the fact that the value of goods sold amounted to approximately $400 per Utah family.

Before the departure of the Expedition, Cooke disposed of everything which could not be sold. The Army took surplus munitions from the fort and blew them up, while they razed houses and buildings. When the last of the troops left Utah, on July 27, 1861, Colonel George Cooke presented the camp flagpole to Brigham Young.

In May, Judge Stephen Douglas had become sick. Family and friends thought he would fight it off, get better and return to work. Instead, on June 3rd Douglas died, unexpectedly. It occurred on the same day as the first official battle of the Civil War called the Battle of Philippi. Overwhelming Union troops, both in numbers and weapons, chased the Confederate soldiers down the road, leaving some to rename the battle the Philippi Races because of the fleeing soldiers. The skirmish also opened up the way for West Virginia to be split away from its mother territory.

The final day for Camp Floyd was July 27th. The soldiers pulled back and headed for the States where they would then be siphoned off to their respective states. This had a direct effect on the town of Fairfield. By September 2nd only 18 families were left.

Even though Colonel Philip St. George Cooke had been born and raised in Virginia, his allegiance was with the North, causing him long-term problems in his family. One of his sons-in-law was J.E.B. Stuart, who promised to never again speak with Cooke.

In October 1861, Brigham Young sent 309 families to establish a colony south of Cedar City, off the plateau, and into the desert. The intention was to grown cotton but that didn't work very well. The town was named St. George. Some heard it was given this name after Joseph Smith's cousin, now an apostle, George Smith, who at the time was encouraging the Saints to eat raw potatoes to stave off scurvy. The name might have come from honoring Colonel Philip St. George Cooke, who saw that the Saints were given splendid deals during the dismantling and destruction of Camp Crittenden and the sale of its contents.

Zeenyo Wetoyou worked hard for the Pony Express earning far more money than he had anticipated. His normal run was from the Simpson Ranch in western Tooele County and would run up through Salt Lake City to the top of Echo Canyon when he was riding east. This would require two days and the distance was divided to allow for another rider. The return trip was just the opposite. The horses provided for the company were mostly Shep's and were grain-fed western mustangs. These tended to be stronger and faster, more durable than other horses. They could easily outrun the horses used by the Paiutes and Shoshones in the middle of the basin. These were the tribes that gave the express riders the most trouble.

Many of the boys started off carrying a rifle and a six-shooter but the rifles were cumbersome. Zeenyo was different. Besides his pistol, he used a Sharp's carbine that gave him greater distance and power and was relatively short and light. A scabbard on the saddle carried the carbine well. The tribes across the desert knew who he was and stayed away. Zeenyo had also proven himself to be an excellent marksman.

Those managing the stations and the horses appreciated these young men, their strength and courage. Many of them carried horns to signal the station of their approach. Most of the time they simply jumped off the horse, grabbed the *mochila* filled with letters, threw it onto the next horse, mounted, and rode off again. There wasn't much time for socializing.

The Express riders traveled 24 hours a day, moving the mail across the continent much quicker than it had ever gone before. Mail usually took ten days in summer to deliver and sixteen days in winter. Lincoln's first inaugural address made the trip in a record seven days and seventeen hours.

Russell, Majors, and Waddell were generating plenty of money, from the riders' point of view but overall, the pony Express was losing money and they had a lot to gain back. Mormon guerrillas during the winter of 1857-58 on the high plains had damaged a number of their wagons and made off with substantial amounts of cattle. These debts had been forgiven by President Buchanan. But then the three businessmen had suffered the loss of another huge herd of oxen, pulling cargo in the Ruby Valley when they were frozen by a blizzard.

The Federal Government thought they could help with the mail by assigning some to the Butterfield Overland Mail Company that traveled the southern route, from St. Joseph's down to Santa Fe then Tucson, Yuma, and over to Los Angeles. From there it could be easily transported up to San

Francisco and Sacramento. They used many of the Wells-Fargo stagecoaches. But these became a target for the Apache, Kiowa, and Comanche tribes. Also, once the shooting during the Civil War started, the Confederates took their turn at spoiling the mail runs. It was looking bleak.

Chapter 70

"To learn is to be young, however old." Aeschylus

The idea of having a telegraph line between the major cities in California made the people of the state realize how isolated the Pacific Coast was from the rest of the nation. The telegraph plans agitated the planners and financiers in the country. It had been considered by the Congress as the western territories were acquired.

But the hope of a telegraph system didn't die. The contract was awarded to the Western Union Company. There had been talk about setting up telegraph poles from Omaha, Nebraska, overland to Salt Lake City. Then from the west, stringing poles from Carson City, which already had a connection over into California, telegraph poles would be set up closely following the shorter Pony Express Trail that had been surveyed out in 1859 by Simpson. The trouble with this plan was that the high plains from Omaha until nearly Salt Lake City were void of pine trees. The same was true coming from the west. This meant that poles would need to be cut and transported by wagon to be used. The glass insulators for the western side of the line along with the wire needed to be shipped from the East Coast around to San Francisco.

President Lincoln was not convinced that the project would ever work, even if given 10 years. The architects of the idea didn't agree, thinking they could get things done in swift order.

If all the California lines would consolidate, calling themselves the Overland Telegraph Company, they would build the line from the Pacific to Salt Lake City, while the Western Union Company would build from Omaha west to Salt Lake City. This company later consolidated with Western Union, then owning and controlling all the lines from San Francisco to Salt Lake City to Omaha.

****

Zeenyo Wetoyou galloped north along Tooele's Main Street, then turned off and rode up the lane to where Shep's house stood, next to the Hansen's.

"Finally got some time?" Shep asked, watching as the young man dismounted and tied up his horse.

"About time, says me."

Shep chuckled and opened the door, bidding him enter. Smells of a tasty stew wafted in the air, making his mouth water. "Smells so good."

"Can you stay long?" Harriett asked, wiping her hands on her apron and stepping up to Zeenyo, she hugged him and kissed his cheek.

"Till the morning," he announced victoriously.

"Dinner will be ready shortly if you want to wash up."

"Thanks. Got a wire scrub brush?" he joked.

Harriet didn't miss a step. "It's out in the barn. Make sure to get between your toes."

It was so good to be back home. Knowing his brother was home, Herman also came by. The food was wonderful and filling. Sitting around the table brought him happy memories. Esther didn't like to stay in her chair, insisting on sitting in her mother's lap or else with Harriett. As the time-worn on, her shyness worn away and she started climbing on Zeenyo. Yasmin's prayer was simple and perfect. The food was gone all too quickly.

"I was hoping to take some back on the trail with me," he said.

"Yasmin has already packed you a bag that should keep you full for a while."

Turning to Shep, he said, "You said Brig has some plans for you?"

"There's a real push to get a telegraph line stretched out across the country. Western Union is starting to put up poles from Omaha, coming this way, and stringing wire to the Great Salt Lake City. Then over west, the Overland Telegraph Company is ready to start the same thing, coming this way from Carson Valley. The telegraph wires should meet up in Salt Lake City before too awful long. It will be a game-changer."

"Will they be using the Pony Express route?"

Shep nodded his head. "Best as I can tell. The trail's still new and kind of rocky. But it shaves a lot of miles off from the California-Humbolt road."

"So what's Brigham got for you?"

"Cutting and collecting poles. There's really not much timber along the trail. He wants me to find and cut enough to help."

"He's helping with the wagons?"

"All set. It should be quite the undertaking."

"Did Brig clear things with you?" Zeenyo asked both women. They smiled and nodded.

"They'll be glad just getting me and Herman out of the house."

"How long?"

"I think it'll go fast. By the end of the year."

"And the Shoshones and Paiutes?"

"I think that's why Brigham is having Herman go along. He has a special knack."

"Doesn't hurt that he's a Lamanite, as well."

"They think he's funny speaking Paiute or Shoshone while sounding Hopi."

Things were set for the western part of the telegraph. Wire and insulators had arrived and were placed at the proper locales. Wagons carrying pine logs were coming down from the Sierras and starting their trek eastward across the desert. Shep and his teams began arriving on the south end of the Tooele Valley, after having deposited a substantial amount of the poles at the bottom end of the Oquirrh Mountains that would be enough to finish the work, carrying the line into Salt Lake City. Just west of Camp Floyd, they began working southwestward, dropping the logs, moving across Skull Valley, and then onto Deep Creek.

Some of the empty wagons began making their way to the south and the north, after crossing the desert, searching for pine forests and cutting more logs, then laying more down towards the northern end of the Ruby Valley, where the only settlement existed of soldiers.

Jim Street had met with Brigham Young and received his willingness to help. Street had shown up early in the spring to speak with Brigham and arranged the necessary poles from Salt Lake City, west to the Ruby Mountains. Shep Silva was also asked to help, along with several other crews. Even with this help, it remained a mystery as to how they would complete the work in the given time.

Street's contacts with the Mormons were for three hundred miles of poles from Salt Lake City, stretching west, taking them past the Ruby Valley. In this central portion of the line, some local trappers and frontiersmen had been contracted to fill in. It was a concern with the men working on the telegraph line since they hadn't seen any trees large enough for the poles, but these trappers living in the central portion of the area knew what they were talking about and found the needed trees for the project up distant canyons.

Beginning in Carson City in the west and Omaha in the east, the work began in earnest. From Omaha the route selected moved up the South Platte River, past Fort Kearney, then Fort Laramie, over to the Sweetwater and through South Pass then down into Salt Lake City. Going east from Carson City the route ran straight to the Ruby Valley, then over to Egan Canyon, Deep Creek, and then Camp Floyd and Salt Lake City. The only settlement between Carson and Camp Floyd was a run-down military encampment on the southern end of Ruby Valley, where a few soldiers were stationed.

A healthy competition emerged between the two companies stringing the wires. Bets were made and the work moved forward faster than anticipated. The line was first measured and staked off, then the hole diggers followed, and then the pole setters, and finally the wiring party. The men averaged between three to eight miles a day. An advance telegraph station kept everyone aware of the current status quo and this was passed along to San Francisco as well as sent overland by the Pony Express. Hard work and endurance helped the men to push through the trials and finish their work before the winter of 1861 set in.

****

Herman Wetoyou was happy to get back to his home in Tooele. Benson's grist mill never looked so good. His friends greeted him warmly and were full of questions about the transcontinental telegraph line. They all felt its importance, the connecting of the East Coast to the West Coast, and in a manner that would make the Pony Express unnecessary.

It was especially pleasant for Herman to be greeted so warmly by Bishop and Martha Sweeney's eighteen-year-old daughter, Sharon. *Had she always been so comely? Had she always paid such attention to him?* Herman wasn't sure but he was willing to find out.

Harriett and Yasmin quickly whipped up a wonderful supper for Herman, setting the table with their finest plates, cups, and silver utensils. It seemed that he had been gone an extra-long time.

"Done for now?" Shep asked after the hungry edge had been taken from Herman's stomach.

"All done," he said with satisfaction. "It'll just be a day or two before the Western Union guys make it down to Salt Lake City and we'll be ready for the grand unveiling. Brigham Young has been asked to send a message to Mr. Carpentier. He's the president of the Overland Telegraph Company in San Francisco. It's quite the honor and should bring lots of satisfaction to lots of folks." Herman smiled, then picked some food from his teeth. "What about here? Anything new going on?"

"Colonel Cooke closed Camp Floyd," Harriett said. "His soldiers are needed back east. I guess the war is starting to really get going."

"Fort Sumter wasn't a fluke?"

"Doesn't seem to be."

Yasmin sat down cradling Isaac. "I am happy we don't live around water. The battleships are powerful and frightening. I'm glad we're far from them."

"I'm just glad the war isn't going on here in the mountains."

"There have been some skirmishes, we've heard," Shep noted. "The South didn't seem to be ready. But we just heard that there was quite the battle outside of Washington beck in July."

Harriett couldn't wait for Shep to unroll the tale. "It was called the Battle of Manassas and the southern boys whooped the North quite handily. Some folks left the capital and took their stroll out to watch the fireworks thinking it would be a walk in the park. That's not how it turned out."

"It was a horrible slaughter," Yasmin added. "I don't miss terrible days like those at all."

"Colonel Cooke is from Virginia. Is he siding with the South?"

"Southerner born and bred but he sides with the North. The Yankees. I guess he's been an abolitionist for years."

"His son-in-law is Jeb Stuart and I hear he's also related to Stonewall Jackson, both southern leaders of ability. He's afraid his family will no longer speak with him."

The table was silent for a bit.

"Did you learn much?" Shep finally asked.

"Keeping the wires up and running, especially over the Sierras during winter will be a problem. But it's been working for several years so far.

Mountain men are lined up and well paid to make sure the wires stay up and running. Even when the snow comes down in feet."

"How do the men travel through that kind of weather? Doesn't the snow just shut things down?"

"You would think but the men have been watching the likes of Snowshoe Thompson for a while. Norwegian snowshoes have become quite popular. They are long pieces of flat wood, like slats, twelve or fourteen feet, that are curved up on the front tips. People can travel fast down the mountains. When going up the hills, pieces of cloth are tied around the boards, keeping the men from slipping backward. Anyway, these men have been quite successful at keeping the telegraph wires clear and working, even during the most dangerous winters. I'm certain they will continue with the national telegraph and keeping the East Coast connected with the West."

"I'm impressed with folks' bravery. There is a cause that has called up some folks, whether they are trekking through the mountain snows to keep the telegraph working or riding night and day to deliver mail across this broad land. There seems to be quite the effort to keep the two ends of the country connected."

"Anything else you learned?"

Herman shrugged. "When I started, I always kept a pistol on my hip. I just knew I was going to be coming face to face with a highwayman or agent or a contrary Indian. But it never really happened. I ended up keeping my pistol in my coat pocket. Good thing I didn't need to get at it too quick."

"You said the wiring was almost done. When are we going to know?"

Shep smiled. "You'd be surprised at these two women. They both have been practicing their Morse code. Both are pretty fast and accurate."

"The telegraph station in town has already offered us work," Harriett added with a smile. "It's good practice and good pay. And it helps keep us posted on what is happening in the city."

"And it's much easier and closer than Camp Floyd's infirmary," Yasmin said. "Putting a telegraph up and stringing it around the Utah Territory won't come for a while. It's still too expensive. But we want to be ready when it happens."

"Porter's coming by in the morning. He always has interesting news."

The overland telegraph was a completed fact. A few years earlier news from the States' side was semi-monthly, and from twenty-five to thirty days old. Then came the semi-weekly mail by the overland route. This news took on an average from eighteen to twenty days. After that came the Pony Express. The latter was a vast improvement over the first two methods but only made it clearer that something had to be done to bring California within the sphere of the civilized countries of the world. The telegraph accomplished this with its first click.

With the advent of a transcontinental telegraph, the feeling of isolation the people of the Pacific Coast had worked under, vanished. San Francisco was in instant communication with New York and the other great cities of the Atlantic seaboard. It was a great change but one which the folks were more than ready to adapt to, having waited for so long. At that moment California was brought into the circle of States. The ring was complete. The state was no longer beyond the pale of the United States and civilization. They had renewed assurances of prosperity and peace, linked by electrical wires to the rest of the union.

All along, Lincoln doubted the project, thinking it would take 10 years to complete, if at all. But he was encouraged to do all possible to make sure that California stayed with the Union. It was also important from his point of view to keep the Nevada and Utah Territories, with their people and resources, on the side of the North. The Transcontinental Telegraph project was completed in 4 months. It started July 4, 1861, and was officially finished November 15th, but the line from the east reached Salt Lake City first and a message was sent by Brigham Young on October 18th.

Hon. J. H. Wade, President of the Pacific Telegraph Company, Cleveland, Ohio;

Sir:--permit me to congratulate you on the completion of the overland telegraph line west to this city; to comment the energy displayed by yourself and associates in the rapid and successful prosecution of a work so beneficial; and to express the wish that its use may ever tend to promote the true interest of the dwellers upon both the Atlantic and Pacific slopes of our continent. Utah has not seceded, but is firm for the Constitution and Laws of our once happy country, and is warmly interested in such useful enterprises as the one so far completed.

Brigham Young.

On the same day the first message was sent, Acting Governor Frank Fuller wired President Abraham Lincoln and received the following two days later:

Hon. Frank Fuller, Acting Governor, Utah Territory;

Sir:--The completion of the telegraph to Great Salt Lake City is auspicious of the stability and union of the Republic. The Government reciprocated your congratulations.

Abraham Lincoln.

On the same day, the first message was sent, Acting Governor Frank Fuller wired President Lincoln.

On October 24, 1861, Western Union Telegraph Company linked east and west in Salt Lake City; telegraphs had crisscrossed the eastern states in the 1830s and 1840s. California became a state in 1850 and the telegraph went all over it. 1841 when President Harrison died it took 110 days for the information to reach Los Angeles. There was now a connection from Carson City to Salt Lake City to Omaha. It was then an instantaneous communication from east to west. Brigham Young was the first to send a message from Salt Lake City to San Francisco with the 1861 completion.

Two days later, on October 26, 1861, the famed Pony Express came to a halt.

Zeenyo Wetoyou collected his pay and rode thoughtfully back to Tooele. *What was the meaning of that name? Was it Goshute? It meant 'bear'.* The world was changing. The war between the states was becoming more serious with the passing of each day. Battles and skirmishes were quite active in Missouri and Arkansas and Kansas, but these were ominously spreading eastward to the more populous areas.

Chapter 71

"The greatest fear I have is that the people of this Church will accept what we say as the will of the Lord without first praying about it and getting the witness within their own hearts that what we say is the word of the Lord." Brigham Young

September 1861

Dear Ina,

Thank you for giving so freely of your time. I cannot imagine any worse trial than what you have gone through these past months. It is my belief that God has not abandoned you. Rather, he has extended his hand to you and pulled you into an eternal, parental embrace. On your part, you have waited, hoped, cried and endured. You are the real hero in this tale. Having very limited resources, you have extolled strength and resilience.

I have had the opportunity to travel all about this isle. I have seen the results of the great war that took place between the British and their allies and the Russians.

I am hoping that you and the people of California are also somewhat protected from the war, that your mother and father, brothers, and family are insulated from the anger and hatred that even now resides in the breasts of so many.

To you, my sweet Ina, I am reminded of several scriptures that seem to capture your position in life. First: "ye are the children of the prophets; and ye are of the house of Israel; and ye are the covenant which the Father made with your fathers, saying unto Abraham: And in thy seed shall all the kindreds of the earth be blessed."

I remember reading this one time and instantly thinking of you because you are a child of the prophets, so intimately. Then it broadens out because of your talents and wisdom, sharing your thoughts and feelings with people all around the world. Do you see yourself in this verse?'

The second is extremely personal for me and found in Isaiah 41: "For can a woman forget her sucking child, that she should not have compassion on the son of her womb? Yea, they may forget, yet will I not forget thee, O house of Israel."

There has never been one doubt in my mind and heart that you are the quintessential mother. No one could have loved Bobby more. You loved, nurtured, and sang to him. Only our all-knowing Father understands the

reasons for Bobby's brief life. There exists no question regarding your devotion and all-encompassing love.

These scriptures are written now in the fleshy tables of my heart with your name gently etched on top. I love you, dearest cousin.

Be careful in your choices and relationships. You continue to have so much to give, so much to offer all the rest of us. Go with God, my beautiful Ina.

Forever, I remain your adoring servant,
Joseph F. Smith

The first of December 1861

Dearest Joseph,

I love the connection we both share because of our names and of course, certainly, our families. Your words come as a refreshing breath into my heart.

You, my dear Joseph, seem to have the ability to liken all scriptural verses to me. The manner in which you do this is inoffensive. It is gentle and tender. I do not feel oppressed by your desire to capture another proselyte. Of all things, I am of all people, most blessed to have you as a member of my family, someone to whom my happiness and well-being is of utmost importance.

Never feel trepidation about sharing your thoughts and testimony with me. You understand that I usually hold a completely different understanding of the cosmic universe. This, however, does not mean that I do not scour your words and feelings seriously, seeking to find the message you have inserted for me, because of your sensitivity to Deity. Please, continue to reach out and share with me. You always make me feel that I have worth.

Finally, as relates to my life with Robert Bruce Carsley: I have undergone a series of dreadful experiences. I thought Robert was going through the same things I was after Bobby's death and maybe he was, but he handled things a lot differently. As I said before, he started drinking a lot. He already struggled with liquor but with the death of our baby, Bob seemed to close off his relationship to me. He stopped speaking to me and my mother, except to yell and swear. He completely avoided Pa. More and more of his time away from work was spent at the saloon. Any extra money was quickly gambled away.

Pa finally closed down his business in San Bernardino and he and Ma moved to Los Angeles. There wasn't much for us in the city so we rented a tent in Camp Drum. We also thought we would be safer from the violent rants and fits and tirades that Bob would throw every time he returned home.

Our fights always spilled into the streets, where we would make a spectacle of ourselves. The local citizenry quickly took sides. Bets were even placed on who the real culprit might be. I had always thought that I comported myself above suspicion but apparently not.

Besides Pa, our family had several professional friends who looked after us. These men scared Bob and he would quickly back down. Some of the newspaper columnists were intent on turning our sordid lives into a public circus.

One afternoon Bob returned and immediately began calling me a whore. Ma tried to calm him down as she tried again and again to rescue me from his clutches. He wanted to take me to his tent and interrogate me.

Pa was finally summoned. When he arrived, he pulled me from Bob then demanded that they fight a duel. In the past, this form of action always caused Bob to reconsider and quiet down. Not this time. Pistols were quickly sought, then like the coward he is, Bob shot at Pa before he was ready, but his bullet went wide. Pa then calmly and coolly took a bead on Bob and shot him in the hand, causing severe damage. The surgeon was called but he could do nothing for the injured limb. He ended up amputating Bob's hand. This had a drastic effect upon Mr. Carsley, who no longer cared to stand in the way of my divorce proceedings.

Robert Bruce Carsley has left lower California and gone back to his home in New England. I believe he intends to work on fishing boats, no longer caring to act on stage or be an ironmonger.

The judge told me that all will be finished by the end of the month. An annulment will be granted, and it will be as though I had never been married in my life. This is a sad conclusion of my life with Bob Carsley. No matter how foolish or drunk he became, he was the father of our beautiful little boy. It will be a connection I will have with him forever. I am thankful that he is no longer a part of my life, but I am sorry for him and the ways he chose to grieve for our son.

I will be moving shortly back to San Francisco. There are numerous job opportunities and like-minded writers, book, and literary folks there who will help me to right my mind and calm my soul. I am tired of the desert and look forward to the fog and coolness by the bay.

Heading back up north, I am reminded of where I was ten years ago, how I was excited to enter the kingdom of California, how enchanting the landscape was, how beautiful the sea and varied the flowers. I loved the smell of the ocean and the sound of the constant lapping of the waves.

I have started writing again. The following is a very personal memento. It brought me solace as I pondered the few months I had with my son. It stands as a bookend to my work. Never will Bobby be far from my thoughts, but always will I shield his memory from the profane and worldly.

So fair the sun rose, yester-morn,
The mountain cliffs adorning!
The golden tassels of the corn
Danced in the breath of morning;
The cool, clear stream that runs before,
Such happy words was saying;
And in the open cottage door
My pretty babe was playing.

Aslant the sill a sunbeam lay;
I laughed in careless pleasure,
To see his little hand essay
To grasp the shining treasure.
Today no shafts of golden flame
Across the sill are lying;
Today I call my baby's name,
And hear no lisped replying;
Today—ah, baby mine, today-
God holds thee in His keeping!
And yet I weep, as one pale ray
Breaks in upon thy sleeping;
I weep to see its shining bands
Reach, with a fond endeavor,
To where the little restless hands
Are crossed in rest forever!

I love you, dear Joseph. I am grateful for the time and thoughts we have shared. I am thankful for your unswerving kindness amidst the scandal of my life. I will write you as long as you so desire.

Sincerely and lovingly, I remain yours,
Ina

Chapter 72

"...and he denieth none that come unto him, black and white, bond and free, male and female; and he remembereth the heathen; and all are alike unto God, both Jew and Gentile." Nephi

It was a cold, wintry day. Work had gone on as usual for most people. It was mid-week. Then again, despite it being a Wednesday, it was also Christmas Day, 1861. Six inches of snow on the ground insured that it was a white Christmas. Businesses continued, stores were open, and commerce throughout the Great Salt Lake City was active. Gray clouds hung low, overhead, hiding the sun and giving the day a gray, subdued color. Winds from the west, gusting over the Great Salt Lake, carried humidity through the valley, encouraging most people who were outside, to tighten up their coats and cloaks. Even though it was still early afternoon, windows of the houses lining the broad boulevards were lighted in contrast to the darkening day.

62 years old, Dr. John Milton Bernhisel just finished seeing his last patient of the day and closed up his office, not caring to lock the door behind him. There had been sporadic thefts through the area but not enough to cause him alarm. He also didn't think there was anything in his rooms that might attract the curious or scoundrel.

Julia and Elizabeth would be preparing supper within a couple of hours. He enjoyed returning home to the greetings of his fifteen-year-old son, John Jr. When he had married Julia sixteen years earlier, she was the recent widow of William Van Orden. They had five children. Bernhisel helped with the raising and rearing of these children. John Jr. made six. The family made his somewhat quiet, bachelor's life much livelier. Following Brigham's suggestions, he entered into the law of plural marriage, joining with six other women but no more children were sired. Dr. Bernhisel was content to dwell with the women, providing them with a hearth and home and sociality. Besides that, he was a very busy professional. His service and attention were needed in numerous areas.

He had spent the past several years raising the profile of his medical office. He had attended the University of Pennsylvania School of Medicine, graduating in 1827. He joined the Church of Jesus Christ of Latter-day Saints and spent several years living in Nauvoo. At one time, Bernhisel even lived with the Prophet Joseph and delivered a couple of his and Emma's children, also tending to the family's ills. Being a close friend of Smith's, Dr. Bernhisel accompanied the small group of the Nauvoo city council to the county seat of Carthage in June 1844, where Joseph and Hyrum were incarcerated and later murdered. Dr. Bernhisel regretted not having been present during the time of the assault on the jail. He wondered if his presence might have deterred the violence.

Because of his extensive education, Dr. John Bernhisel was an active politician and had been called to represent the Territory of Deseret as they had sought for statehood. The name was later changed to Utah but Bernhisel continued to travel to Washington each year, debating and arguing and pleading with other representatives from the states and territories but always protecting and defending the rights of the citizens of Utah, most of whom were also members of his faith.

In March he had once again been elected, this time to the 37th Congress of the United States for another two-year term. These were trying times. A month later, the confederate forces in South Carolina had followed Jeff Davis' directive to bomb Fort Sumter. The secession of southern states followed. Conflicts and skirmishes began with the summer. Lincoln's Union troops overestimated their power and abilities, losing spectacularly to the Confederacy at the Battle of Manassas in July. Battle lines were being drawn. Hopes were that the war could be deflated but with the death of every soldier, opinions became that much more entrenched. Although there was much talk about abolitionism and the freeing of the slaves, there was also much posturing about the importance of a solid union versus the rights of individual states.

On top of his medical concerns and political responsibilities, Dr. John Bernhisel had been appointed by President Young to be on the board of regents of the University of Deseret. The school had been established in 1850 and despite the challenges of funding and location and instruction, the institution moved forward, growing in enrollment and popularity. Professors were being sought out and hired, bringing higher education into the valleys of the mountains. Having the multifaceted Dr. Bernhisel on the school's board of regents was a feather in their cap.

The wind whipped around him, sending Dr. Bernhisel scurrying down the street, heading for the stately government building.

"Dr. Bernhisel."

"Brother Bernhisel," came the several calls of an acknowledgment as he passed people on the boardwalks.

He replied with a smile. "Madame," or "Sister." Or "Good afternoon, brother."

It was a short walk from his medical office to the corner of Main Street and South Temple Street to the Council House. It was also referred to as the State House. The stone building was finished in 1852 and was used for many government and church functions, most notably for temple endowments until the 1855 completion of the Endowment House located on Temple Square. Originally the building had been built to house the government of the provisional State of Deseret. Deseret was never officially recognized by the United States Government. Instead, they organized the Utah Territory. During the first legislative session held in Fillmore, legislators complained about the lack of housing and adequate facilities in that city, so Salt Lake City was again designated Utah's capital.

Once the capital returned to Salt Lake City, the Council House again was used as territorial offices and also housed several other entities such as the University of Deseret, the Deseret News, and Deseret Boarding House. The building was also used as a meeting place by the leadership of The Church of Jesus Christ of Latter-day Saints.

Looking out over the city he was once again amazed at what he saw. Less than fifteen years earlier this had been a desolate, forlorn desert valley. Beautiful houses, mercantile buildings, and theaters spread throughout the city center. Well-used livestock barns, corrals, and auditoriums were located on the outskirts of town. Saints embraced the obligation of labor, sometimes for money but frequently as a service, viewing service to their fellowman simply as service to God.

Stepping into the warm building, Dr. Bernhisel nodded to several couples who were leaving the edifice. He thought he noticed that at least one of the women was pregnant, most likely. It was hard to tell these days, since the population in the city was fairly strict in following the Victorian fashions quite closely, not wanting to advertise a growing child within the womb. Still, the Utah Territory remained a fertile place and not just because of plural marriage. Following the teachings of the scriptures, along with the admonitions of apostles and prophets, the birthrate was significantly higher than any other place in the nation. The women maintained their responsibilities by bringing children into this life and then nourishing and nurturing them, while the men tried to provide and teach the best they could. The importance of good examples was never brushed aside.

Walking up the hallway, Bernhisel was surprised and pleased at the same time to recognize the form of William Staines. He was about twenty years younger than the doctor. He had also built a beautiful house, the first mansion in the city. Bernhisel liked Staines a lot. He was not known for his place in governing councils, or church hierarchy. He did not have more than a single wife, nor did he claim a huge posterity. He didn't pioneer any new settlements, didn't burn any enemy wagons, or pilfer their livestock. He hadn't killed outlaws. William Staines remained a solid citizen of the city. He was pleasant, educated, patient, and not self-serving.

"Doctor."

"Brother Staines. Do you have a moment? Could you visit with me in my office? I won't keep you long."

"Of course." He turned around and followed Dr. Bernhisel into his small, cluttered office. "You and the misses going to socialize this evening?"

"That's the plan," John replied while collecting a series of papers from a chair for his guest. "There's a dinner and dance scheduled across the street from the Beehive House."

Staines was surprised. "Brig putting it on?"

"Not that I know. He might show up. Mostly I'm looking for a chance to relax and get Julia out of the house. Shep Silva is coming into town with his family and wants us to tag along with them."

Staines nodded and took the seat. "We've had some nice dances of late. We have another we are attending tonight. I'm pleased there are such talented orchestras. They could compete with any I'm aware of. And choirs! Thank goodness for the Welsh."

Bernhisel smiled. Most Englishmen weren't as charitable as the Welsh. "You staying busy during these short days?"

"I'm very happy the winter solstice has passed. It's always good to look forward to the days lengthening and the arrival of spring. You have to admit, there's something heavenly about preparing the soil then planting and raising flowers or gardens or crops or fruit. Will you be going back east anytime soon? Washington calling?"

The doctor sighed and slumped into his chair. "I guess so. As soon as your days get long enough to melt the snow. Of course, a lot depends on the state of the union. Folks are shooting up the countryside. I hear."

"Me, as well."

"I really want to stop in and see the Kanes."

"You'd be doing all of us a favor."

"You always do all of us a favor, Bill. You flavor this whole valley with your goodness."

The comment caught Staines by surprise and made him blush. They were saved from a further remark by the knock on the door. Staines was closest and answered it. It was Shep and Harriett.

"Saved again," Dr. Bernhisel said quietly. Changing his focus he rose, "Come in, come in!" and took their hands. "This will only take a moment. Please find a place to sit."

The Silvas appreciated that he was less formal with them.

Bernhisel started rummaging through his desk drawers looking for something. "My friends here asked about the conflict several days ago," he explained. "I told them that I had something that might interest them."

"Oh?"

"The Prophet's prophecy about war."

Staines shook his head. "I may have heard something, but no."

"Twenty-nine years ago on Christmas Day, Joseph said he received a revelation," his voice trailed off as he kept looking, then dropped down to another drawer.

"Shep and Harriett."

"Brother Bill."

"Found it!" John announced victoriously, drawing several pages from the drawer and waving them exultantly through the air. "You asked about the rebellion and I remembered something the Prophet Joseph had said in 1832. And I remembered it was on Christmas Day. That's why I asked you to stop by today. At the time there had been a series of disputes in the country about slavery and South Carolina's nullification of tariffs. Things were tense in the States. On the other hand, things in Europe had been fairly quiet. Industry was booming, lots were being displaced but as far as war is concerned things had been quiet since the days of Napoleon. And then Joseph came up with this." He handed the pages to Shep, who held them far enough away to allow both Harriett and Staines to read.: "*Verily, thus saith the Lord concerning the wars that will shortly come to pass, beginning at the rebellion of South Carolina, which will eventually terminate in the death and misery of many souls;*

"*And the time will come that war will be poured out upon all nations, beginning at this place.*

"*For behold, the Southern States shall be divided against the Northern States, and the Southern States will call on other nations, even the nation of Great Britain, as it is called, and they shall also call upon other nations, to defend themselves against other nations; and then war shall be poured out upon all nations.*

"*And it shall come to pass, after many days, slaves shall rise up against their masters, who shall be marshaled and disciplined for war.*"

"See? And he goes on to declare that war is ready to be poured out upon all nations. He says this trouble beginning with South Carolina will be the commencement. So, no, I don't have much confidence in the direction we're headed."

Harriett looked closer. "Joseph was saying that there was the appearance of troubles among the nations and that these appearances were becoming more visible as the church was coming out of obscurity."

Staines said, "This was when he was in Kirtland, Ohio? Yes? Wasn't there a north-south conflict then?"

"I think there's been a long history of trouble between the northern states and the pro-slavery south."

Shep began thumbing through a couple of other pages and scanning the words. "Here's another," he said.

"*I prophesy, in the name of the Lord God, that the commencement of the difficulties which will cause much bloodshed previous to the coming of the Son of Man will be in South Carolina.*

"*It may probably arise through the slave question. This a voice declared to me, while I was praying earnestly on the subject, December 25, 1832.*"

"You see this as what we're going through?" Shep asked Dr. Bernhisel.

"Merry Christmas!"

Staines excused himself, shaking hands and walking from the office, explaining that he was going to find his wife and promising they would try and meet at the dance hall in an hour.

"Where's Yasmin?"

"She wanted to stay home with Esther and Isaac."

"How's she doing? Things still too raw?"

Harriett and Shep nodded at the same time.

"Sorry. Please tell her that we love her and missed seeing her." He nodded graciously. "Can you let yourselves out? I need to run home before the party."

Sitting in the office, Shep and Harriett had a chance to reflect on the year. Long and hard. Even though war was starting to boil over, there were plenty of politicians and people back East who wanted to see polygamy stomped out with the same finality as slavery. At least for now there were hundreds of miles separating the States from Deseret. The moat was comprised of miles of sand and sagebrush. General Dan Wells had volunteered to use the Nauvoo Legion to protect the transcontinental telegraph wires. That was the extent of Utah Territory's involvement in the war. For the last time in their lives, the feeling of isolation from the States meant something more as fratricide continued to build and bleed, as members of the same congregations, the same genealogies, the same traditions, and language began killing one another in greater numbers. The fractured refugees from Nauvoo, Illinois, and the incoming converts were able to shelter themselves from the storm in the valleys of Deseret, finding a defense and a refuge from the carnage, bloodshed, fury, and despair of the Civil War. The conflict would end more American lives than any other, leaving multitudes of physically and mentally wounded in its awful wake.

"A penny for your thoughts?"

Shep smiled. He loved how important his opinions were to Harriett. "Ready to leave?" He helped his wife into her coat, and they closed the door behind them and began walking toward the front door. "Plain and precious things," he said. "Certainly, doctrines and beliefs and prayers have been tinkered with." Shep was grateful to have time to think.

"Who is more 'plain and precious' than the Wetoyous? Or Yasmin? The Brazilians are fine people. And the folks in Hawaii and Africa and the Chinese. Are the slaves, with their inspiring gospel hymns, not as precious and plain and choice as any of the rest of us? They sing, even as their families are broken apart and shattered by people who think they are their masters."

Whenever Harriett got Shep speaking his mind, she found herself being carried to a higher mountain where the view was broader, not nearly as provincial and myopic as was frequently forced by day-to-day life. Shep's kisses were tender and heartfelt. His arms were strong. He was a man of integrity and sincere in everything he did. Whenever he thought, his mind delved into delightful aspects of the gospel. His prayers were frequent and many times accompanied by tears. It was obvious that he had been told, within his heart, of other dimensions of the gospel.

"You're right, Giuseppe," she said almost in a whisper. "I think that perhaps the plain and precious things, the things we are praying for, the restoration, might also include the House of Israel."

Giuseppe Mercedes da Silva nodded, feeling a knot grow in his throat and tears begin to well in his eyes. "Brazilians might not run roughshod over the earth, but we cry a lot."

"It is one of the most endearing aspects you possess."

548

"We're not Zion yet, my dear, but I think we're on the right track. We just need to stay out of God's way, forgive and love each other, and he'll take care of things. Do you believe that, Ett?"

The dance hall was brightly lit, and people were entering the doors. Lilting music could be heard coming from within and graceful forms seen through the windows, as they danced carefully to the melody.

"Do you remember what you asked me when we were married?"

"May I be yours, forever?"

Harriett nodded.

Shep smiled, happy that what he had said was remembered. "I didn't want to be overbearing."

"You are a gift to me. A gift from the Lord."

"A gift? Not the gift?"

"Of course. You, Giuseppe Mercedes da Silva. You are the embodiment of God's blessings in my life. You love me as I am, with all my scars and wounds. It doesn't bother you that my hands are rough and cracked."

Shep pulled on her arm to stop walking, as he gazed deeply into her eyes. "You, Harriett. You are the fount of my joy. My happiness comes through you. God will see to it that we receive our just due. For now, I wish only that you will let me be yours."

The couple opened the doors to the hall and were greeted by innumerable smiles and waves. The lamps gleamed brilliantly, reflecting on the faces and forms of their friends. Conversations were pleasant at the small tables, where folks ate and listened. Others strolled away and floated across the dancefloor. Even those who had no ability or understanding of the steps or turns, held their partners closely, exchanging the nearness and warmth of the moment.

Lyrical voices and laughter blended mystically with the orchestra. Tonight they were remembering the birth of the Savior of the world, the Redeemer Jesus Christ. The pioneers sought to draw the presence of God downward into their midst.

All knew that change would come with the morning. The world would continue to spin. People would die, others would be born. Life would become enriched and impoverished. They would face the future with faith.

This night was a time of rejoicing, a time of remembering, a time of rest and relaxation. It was a time of joy, knowing how close God was. The work would go on, individually and collectively. Taking strength from moments like these, these people, the outcasts of nations, knew the atonement of Christ meant exactly that: the at-one-ment of God's children.

Harriett leaned forward and kissed Shep's cheek, ever so gently. "God loves you, my dear. And I love you." Touching his cheek, she repeated ever so carefully, "*Deus te ama, meu bem. E eu te amo.*"

Appendix

"That thy church may come forth out of the wilderness of darkness, and shine forth fair as the moon, clear as the sun, and terrible as an army with banners." Doctrine and Covenants

Tsar Nicholas I 1798-1855 "I regard human life as service because everybody must serve."

Wakara, chief of the Timpanogos 1808-1855 Leader of Los Chaguanosos, April 1840, stole 3000 horses from California; slave runner, brutal leader and baptized member of the church. "There are bad Mormons as well as bad Indians."

Parley Parker Pratt 1807-1857 (Thankful, Mary Ann, Elizabeth, Mary, Hannahette, Belinda, Sarah, Phoebe, Martha, Ann, Keziah, Eleanor; 30 children) "There is one only living and true God, without body, parts, or passions; consisting of three persons—the Father, Son, and Holy Ghost. It is painful to the human mind to be compelled to admit, that such wonderful inconsistencies of language or ideas, have ever found place in any human creed. Yet so it is."

Elisha Kent Kane 1820-1857 adventurer, died in Havana after rescuing several explorers

John Kintzing Kane 1795-1858 21st Attorney General of Pennsylvania 1845-46; Father to Thomas and Elisha and Elizabeth, died while Thomas was traveling in the territory to help with the Utah War. "Public interest is best served by the free exchange of ideas."

John Brown 1800-1859 abolitionist; hanged after the Harpers Ferry attack "I acknowledge no master in human form."

Lilburn Williams Boggs 1796-1860 Sixth governor of Missouri 1836-1840; died in Sonoma, California

Truckee, Paiute holy man, and chief died Oct 1860—fluent in Spanish and learned to read and write English; father of Winnemucca and grandfather of Sarah Winnemucca

Lola Montez (Eliza Rosanna Gilbert) 1821-1861, Irish-born dancer and actress, mistress of King Ludwig I of Bavaria who made her Countess of Landsfeld; emigrated to the United States.

Stephen Arnold Douglas 1813-1861, Known as the Little Giant, Illinois politician and opponent of Abraham Lincoln's in the 1850s. Candidate for the US presidency in 1860.

1862 The Morrill Anti-Bigamy Act, focusing on the practice of Utah's plural marriage was passed by the US Congress

General Albert Sydney Johnston 1803-1862, leader of the expedition of US Army during the Utah War 1857-58; killed at the Battle of Shiloh, the highest-ranking military man to die from wounds during the war, on either side.

Dan Jones 1810-1862 (Jane, Elizabeth, Mary; 6 children—his first wife had 8 children that died young) convert from Wales, a friend of Joseph Smith, the final prophecy of Joseph Smith said that he would complete a mission to Wales, which he did.

1863- Emancipation Proclamation January 1, 1863- freeing the slaves living in the southern states.

On January 29th, the Bear River Massacre between 270 and 400 Shoshone men, women, and children were killed by US forces near Preston in the Utah Territory.

On Friday, August 21st, In Lawrence, Kansas there was a massacre by Quantrill's Raiders, killing 150 men and boys.

Howard Stansbury 1806-1863 military surveyor in Utah Territory in 1850

Chief Juan Antonio 1783-1863 Cooswootna, Yampoochee- He Gets Mad Quickly- leader of the Cahuilla tribe near San Bernardino.

1865- The Courthouse at Appomatox.

President Abraham Lincoln shot was shot at Ford's Theater in Washington DC.

The Black Hawk War starts in Utah

Lt. Colonel Edward Jenner Steptoe 1815-1865 was sent by President Pierce in 1854 to investigate the murder of Captain John Gunnison.

Isaac Morley 1786-1865 (Lucy, Leonora, Hannah, Harriet, Hannah, Nancy, Hannah; 7 children with his first wife) was a lifelong participant in the church. "There is not time nor circumstances through which we may be passing but there is opportunity for improvement."

Thomas Long "Pegleg" Smith 1801-1866 trapper, Mexican horse rustler, a friend of Wakara and Jim Beckwourth

1867- After being disbanded shortly after Joseph Smith's death in 1844, the Relief Society was reorganized

Hector Hugh McClean 1816-1867 Scottish-born murderer of Parley P. Pratt, and first husband of Eleanor McComb.

James Pierson Beckwourth 1800-1867 famous American trapper, fur trader, scout, guide, adventurer.

1868- Zion's Cooperative Mercantile Institution was started by Brigham Young on October 15th. Some in the state referred to it as Zion's Collection of Mormon Idiots.

Heber Chase Kimball 1801-1868 (Vilate, he married a total of 43 wives but some were for caretaking. 17 wives bore him 66 children). "My Father and God is a cheerful, pleasant, lively and good-natured being."

Christopher Houston "Kit" Carson 1809-1868 American explorer; "The cowards never start and the weak die along the way."

1869- The Transcontinental Rail Road was completed with the driving of the Golden Spike at Promontory Point, Utah on May 10th.

Antonga or Black Hawk 1830-1870, he was shot near Richfield in 1860, the wound never healed and finally caused his demise. The 1865 Black Hawk War in Utah was named after him.

Sylvester Mowry 1833-1871

Numaga, Little Winnemucca 1830-1871 "In appearance he is all that romance could desire, deep-chested and strong-limbed, with a watchful, earnest expression of countenance, indicative of graver thought and study that is common to the aboriginal race."

1872- Elizabeth and Thomas Kane rode the rail to Utah and spent 3 months visiting Brigham Young and the people of Utah. It was their final visit before Young's death.

Alfred Cumming 1802-1873 governor of the Utah Territory from 1858-1861

Agnes Charlotte Coolbrith Smith Peterson 1836-1873, the oldest daughter of Don Carlos Smith and Agnes Coolbrith.

1874- the Poland Act- facilitates prosecutions under the Morrill Anti-Bigamy Act

Eleanor Jane McComb 1817-1874 Parley Pratt's final wife, mother of Fitzroy, Albert, and Ann McLean.

John A. "Snowshoe" Thompson 1827-1876 lived the last of his life in Carson Valley, carried mail over the Sierras during the winters between Genoa and Placerville.

Agnes Moulton Coolbrith Smith Pickett 1811-1876 mother of Ina. Married to Don Carlos Smith and then William Pickett.

George Davis Grant 1812-1876 LDS leader during the rescue of the handcart pioneers in 1856 and during the Utah War 1857-58. Grantsville was named after him.

1877 St. George Temple dedicated; the first temple finished since the Nauvoo Temple in 1846; temple work begins in earnest

John Doyle Lee 1812-1877 (Agatha, Nancy, Louisa, Sarah, Rachel, Polly Ann, Martha, Delethia, Nancy, Emoline, Nancy, Mary, Lavina, Mary, Mary, Emma, Terresaa, Ann; 56 children) Indian agent and militia leader in southern Utah during the Utah War. Involved with the Mountain Meadows Massacre. He was the only one executed for the deed, killed by a firing squad, some felt like a scapegoat for the murders.

Amasa Mason Lyman 1813-1877 (Louisa, Diontha, Caroline, Eliza, Paulina, Priscilla, Cornelia, Lydia; 38 children) apostle, frontiersman, first mayor of San Bernardino, and missionary.

Brigham Young 1801-1877 (Miriam and then Mary Ann, Lucy Ann Decker was his first plural wife; 55 wives, 56 children) The second leader of the Church of Jesus Christ of Latter-day Saints. As he lay dying, his final words were, "Joseph, Joseph." The first governor of the Utah Territory. "I feel like shouting hallelujah, all the time, when I think that I ever knew Joseph Smith, the Prophet whom the Lord raised up and ordained."

1878 Reynolds vs. the United States; polygamy is declared unconstitutional.

William Z. "W.Z." Angney 1817-1878 American soldier and settler in California.

Orrin Porter Rockwell 1813-1878 (Luana, Mary Ann, Christina; 7 children). Friend of the Smiths and marshal of the Utah Territory. When he died, he was the longest living member of the Church.

Orson Hyde 1805-1878 (Marinda and 7 more wives, 32 children) Member of the original Quorum of the Twelve Apostles of the Church of Jesus Christ of Latter-day Saints. Dedicated Jerusalem for the return of the House of Judah. Missionary and judge.

Jemima McClenahan Drummond 1816-1879 the wife of Judge William Drummond, mother of five, and claimed never to have been divorced from the judge

Mary Seacole 1805-1881 Jamaican-born, a British nurse, sets up British Hotel behind lines during Crimean War. "Beside the nettle, ever grows the cure for its sting."

Tsar Alexander II 1818-1881 "It is not difficult to rule Russia, but it is useless."

Orson Pratt 1811-1881 (Sarah, Charlotte, Adelia, Mary Ann, Louisa, Sarah, Juliet, Marian, Eliza, Margaret; 45 children) "The greatest desire of my heart was for the Lord to manifest His will concerning me."

John Milton Bernhisel 1799-1881 (Julia, Elizabeth, and 5 more wives— didn't marry until he was 46; one child) Educated at University of Pennsylvania, physician, and politician. "A contented mind is a continual feast."

Edward Griffin Beckwith 1818-1881 Explorer of the Central Rockies in the 1850s.

William Carter Staines 1818-1881 from England- English Gentleman of refinement and culture; built the first mansion in SLC and donated it for Governor Cumming's use; agriculturalist and inventor. Stressed the necessity of having the Spirit to guide us in whatever we do. "Some argue that it is too expensive to fence and raise fruit but it is my business to decorate and beautify Zion, it is part of my religion as much as going to meeting, praying or singing."

Benjamin Disraeli 1804-1881 British politician, twice Prime Minister and member of the Conservative Party. "Never apologize for showing feeling. When you do so, you apologize for the truth." "Courage is fire and bullying is smoke." "Never complain and never explain." "Justice is truth in action."

James "Jim" Bridger 1804-1881 Mountain man, trapper, scout, and guide "Be thankful for every mountain because it's the mountain top that will give you the best view of the world."

1882- The Edmunds Anti-Bigamy Act declares polygamy to be a felony

Giuseppe Maria Garibaldi 1807-1882 Italian freedom fighter. "Give me the ready hand rather than the ready tongue." "The priest is the personification of falsehood." "Bacchus has drowned more men than Neptune."

Jan Jozef Ignacy Lukassiewicz 1822-1882 kerosene in 1850s Poland- first street lamps 1853

Anna Murray Douglass 1813-1882 first wife of Frederick; they had four children, Rosetta, Lewis Henry, Charles Remond, and Frederick Jr.

Winnemucca, 1820-1882 northern Paiute leader

Thomas Leiper Kane 1822-1883- Elizabeth said his last words to the Mormons: To George Q. Cannon of the First Presidency- "*My dear Mr. Cannon:*

"*Your friend suffered intensely until a few hours of his release, and his mind was wandering from the outset of the attack. Yet in the intervals of consciousness he was fully persuaded of the approach of death, and made efforts to give us counsel and to bid us farewell. In one of these lucid moments, he said: 'My mind is too heavy, but do send the sweetest message you can make up to my Mormon friends—to all my dear Mormon friends.'*

"*Nothing I could make up could be sweeter to you than this evidence that you were in his latest thoughts.*"

"*The name of Colonel Thomas L. Kane stands most prominent...an instrument, in the hands of God, and inspired by him, to turn away, in 1858, the edge of the sword, and save the effusion of much blood, performing what the combined wisdom of the nation could not accomplish, and changing the whole face of affairs, the effects of which will remain forever. Your name will of necessity stand associated with the history of this people for years to come, whatever may be their destiny.*" Wilford Woodruff

Charles Coulson Rich 1809-1883 (Sarah, Eliza, Harriet, Sarah, Mary, Emeline; 51 children) Military lear in Nauvoo, apostle, and missionary, second mayor of San Bernardino.

William Adams "Wild Bill" Hickman 1815-1883 (Bernetta, Sarah, Minerva, Sarah, Hannah, Sarah, Mary, Martha, Mary Jane; 36 children) gunman, guerrilla leader in the Utah War.

1884 Logan Temple dedication

Elijah Abel 1808-1884 lifelong African-American member of the church. Missionary and ordained to the priesthood but during the administration of Brigham Young was denied its use. Joseph Smith was referring to Elijah when he said, "Go into Cincinnati where you will see a man who has risen by the powers of his own mind to his exalted state of respectability."

1887 the Edmunds-Tucker Act strengthened the previous act

Eliza Roxcy Snow 1804-1887 "It is the duty of each one of us to be a holy woman. We shall have elevated aims, if we are holy women. I will go forward...I will smile at the rage of the tempest, and ride fearlessly and triumphantly across the boisterous ocean of circumstance...And the 'testimony of Jesus' will light up a lamp that will guide my vision through the portals of immortality and communicate to my understanding the glories of the Celestial kingdom."

Alexander William Doniphan 1808-1887 military officer and attorney, a friend of the Mormons, especially when they were being driven in Missouri.

John Taylor 1808-1887 (Leonora, Elizabeth, Jane, Mary Ann, Sophia, Harriet, Margaret, Josephine; 34 children) friend of Jmith Smith and present when he was killed, apostle and third president of the Church of Jesus Christ of Latter-day Saints

1888 Manti Temple dedication

William Wormer Drummond 1818-1888 spoils system federal judge in Utah Territory, appointed by President Buchanan. Accused the people of Utah of seceding from the Union. Supporter of Stephen Douglas. Roamed the low saloons on Chicago's west side at the end of his life and died in a cheap lodging house. Ada or Mary G. Carroll was born about 1830. Married to Baltimore school teacher, Charles Fletcher; became a consort of Judge William Drummond and accompanied him to the Utah Territory. Cuffy (Coffee) Cato was from Virginia, literate, and Drummond's slave.

Mahonri-Moriancumer Cahoon 1834-1888, son of Reynolds, was given a name and a blessing by Joseph Smith in Kirtland, Ohio. It was the first time the name of the Book of Ether's Brother of Jared was revealed.

1889- Endowment House was razed because of rumors surrounding unauthorized sealings.

Samuel Brannan 1819-1889 Sailed to California from New York City aboard the Brooklyn. Settled in the state and became its first millionaire because of the gold rush and real estate. He left the church and died a pauper.

Albert Carrington 1813-1889 (Rhoda, Mary; 15 children) an apostle and leader of the church.

Hosea Stout 1810-1889 (Samantha and 5 other wives, 19 children) Nauvoo policeman, one of the first to take the Utah bar examination, frontiersman and politician, journalist, and the oldest man to participate in the rescue of the handcart pioneers in 1856.

1890 Manifesto- declaring the recension of plural marriage because of federal law.

John Charles Fremont 1813-1890- Free Soil, Free Men and Fremont; first Republican presidential candidate, 1856. Military officer, explorer, cartographer, politician.

Daniel Hanmer Wells 1814-1891 (Hannah, Lydia, Hannah, Susan, Louisa, Martha, Emmeline; 37 children) church leader, Nauvoo Legion general during the Utah War. "It is not the great things of the kingdom that cause men to fall away and go to destruction. It is the small things of life—matters of traffic and deal, upon which people stumble. Large mountains are magnified from small molehills, and they loom greater and greater the longer the persons travel in that."

William Pickett 1816-1891 new settler in Nauvoo, Illinois. Married Agnes Coolbrith Smith and they had twin boys, William and Don Carlos. Trekked to California during the gold rush. Settled in Southern California.

Sarah Winnemucca 1844-1891. "Be kind to bad and good, for you don't know your own heart. For shame! For shame! You dare cry out Liberty, when you hold us in places against our will, driving us from place to place as if we were beasts."

Lot Smith 1830-1892 (Lydia, Jane, Julia, Laura, Alice, Alice, Mary, Diantha; 52 children) along with Rockwell and Hickman, a Mormon guerrilla leader known as The Horseman during the Utah War. Colonizer.

1893- Salt Lake Temple dedicated- 40 years in its construction

Frederick (Augustus Washington Bailey) Douglass 1818-1895. Abolitionist, hero in the fight to end slavery, and vocal defender of human rights. Emancipated slave and proponent for slaves and women's suffrage. "Knowledge makes a man unfit to be a slave." "Without a struggle, there can be no progress." "The white man's happiness cannot be purchased by the black man's misery."

Colonel Philip St. George Cooke 1809-1895 leader of the Mormon Battalion. Military observer during the Crimean War. Known as the father of the cavalry. Participated in the Utah War and was the last commandant of Camp Floyd.

1896- Utah admitted to the Union as a state.

Ephraim Knowlton Hanks 1826-1896 (Harriet, Jane, Thisbe, Hannah; 26 children) "Temporary defeat is just opportunity in disguise."

Dr. Harriett Amelia Kane 1855-1896 Child of Tom and Bessie Kane.

Wilford Woodruff 1807-1898 (Phebe, Mary Ann, Sarah, Mary, Mary, Emma, Sarah, Sarah, Eudora; 34 children) fourth president of the Church of Jesus Christ of Latter-day Saints. "No obstacles are insurmountable when God commands and we obey." "My advice to the Latter-day Saints is to refrain from contracting any marriage forbidden by the law of the land." "The Lord will never permit me or any other man who stands as President of this Church to lead you astray. It is not in the programme. It is not in the mind of God. If I were to attempt that, the Lord would remove me out of my place, and so He will any other man who attempts to lead the children of men astray from the oracles of God and from their duty."

Martha Deloney Gunnison 1823-1898 widow of Captain John Gunnison, lived in Grand Rapids, Michigan

Franklin D. Richards 1821-1899 (Jane and 10 other wives, 29 children) apostle, missionary, and Mission President of the British Mission.

Washakie 1808-1900 Shoshone Indian chief. "I fought to keep our land, our water, and our hunting grounds. Today, education is the weapon my people will need to protect them."

Electa Rockwell Ousley 1816-1900 sister of Porter Rockwell, moved west and lived out the balance of her life in Santa Clara, California

Stewart Leonard Van Vliet 1815-1901 During the Utah War, he was the first US officer into Salt Lake City and conferenced with Brigham Young. A supporter of the Mormon people, he returned Young's letter to President Buchanan.

Queen Victoria 1819-1901 (Alexandrina Victoria) one John Brown, a Scottish servant, became her closest confidant after her husband's death. She

Instituted the Victoria Cross medal after the Crimean War. It remains the highest award for gallantry in the British armed forces.

Lorenzo Snow 1814-1901, brother of Eliza and 5th president of the church (Charlotte, Mary Adaline, Sarah Ann, Harriet Amelie, Eleanor, Caroline, Mary Elizabeth, Phoebe, Sarah Minnie; 42 children). "Be better today than you were yesterday, and be better tomorrow than you are today." "As man now is, God once was; as God is now man may be."

Honorable Judge John Fitch Kinney 1816-1902 Chief Justice of the Supreme Court of Utah Territory, appointed by President Pierce 1854-1857, left just before the hostilities of the Utah War commenced.

Melissa Burton Coray (Kimball) 1828-1903 Married to Sergeant William Coray of the Mormon Battalion. One of three women to accompany the march. Her husband died in March 1849. She later married William H. Kimball (Heber's eldest) in 1851. A California mountain peak is named after her.

Green Flake 1828-1903 (Hark Lay and Oscar Crosby) A hard-working African-American member of the church who trekked early to the Utah Territory.

Robert Bruce Carsley 1833-1905 (married Ina Coolbrith, 21 April 1858- divorced, 26 December 1861). Ironmonger and fisherman. He returned to the New England area.

Jane Manning James 1822-1908 Dynamic African-American woman, member of the church for life. She started by knowing the Prophet Joseph and Emma Smith.

Elizabeth Dennistoun Wood Kane 1836-1909 (m. 1853 at 16 years) Wife of Thomas Kane. Very literate writer and advocate of women's rights. Finally became a medical doctor. She accompanied Tom to Utah in 1872, spending 3 months among the Saints and getting an up-close look at plural marriage, changing her opinions substantially.

Florence Nightingale 1820-1910- "I attribute my success to this—I never gave or took any excuse." "The world is out back by the death of every one who has to sacrifice the development of his or her peculiar gifts to conventionality." "Women have no sympathy and my experience of women is almost as large as Europe."

Leo Tolstoy 1828-1910 (Count Lev Nikolayevich Tolstoy) Military officer in Crimean War, writer, and philosopher. With his correspondence with Susa Young Gates, he received a copy of the Book of Mormon and the story of Joseph Smith.

"The Mormon people teach the American religion. Their principles teach the people not only of Heaven and its attendant glories, but how to live so that their social and economic relations with each other are placed on a sound basis. If the people follow the teachings of this Church, nothing can stop their progress—it will be limitless. There have been great movements started in the past, but they have died or been modified before they reached maturity. If Mormonism is able to endure, unmodified, until it reaches the third and fourth generation, it is destined to become the greatest power the world has ever known."; "I've always loved you, and when you love someone, you love the whole person, just as he or she is, and not as you would like them to be."; "Wrong does not cease to be wrong because the majority share in it."; "Nothing is so necessary for young men as the company of intelligent women."; "Is it really possible to tell someone else what one feels?"

Harriett Tubman 1822-1913 Abolitionist, and an instigator of the underground railroad, liberating scores of slaves. She was nicknamed Moses. John Brown adored her, calling her the General.

Joseph Fielding Smith Sr. 1838-1918 (Levira, Julina, Sarah, Edna, Alice, Mary; 45 children, adopted 5 more) He was the son of Hyrum Smith, who was killed in Carthage, Illinois with his brother Joseph, June 1844. He was the 6th president of the Church of Jesus Christ of Latter-day Saints (1901-1918). Apostle, missionary, and church leader. Thirteen of his biological children and one adopted son preceded him in death. Julina Lambson was his second wife and their first child was named Mercy Josephine, born in 1867.

Ina Coolbrith was the name used by Josephina Donna Smith Coolbrith (Carsley) 1841-1926. Ina was born in Nauvoo, the daughter of Don Carlos Smith, brother of Joseph Smith. Her mother, Agnes, was frightened by the violence that followed her husband's family and after leaving Nauvoo, gave her daughters her maiden name, asking that they never make their connection with the Church public knowledge. It was a promise that was kept, although Ina always kept in touch with her cousin, Joseph F, and considered him a close friend. After her divorce from Robert Carsley, she never married. She was a librarian in Oakland and lived in San Francisco. An important figure on the literary scene, she was well acquainted with other literary greats of the time, Joaquim Miller, Mark Twain, and Jack London. Her home was destroyed in the 1906 San Francisco earthquake. On 30 June 1915, Ina was given the prestigious title of the first poet laureate of the State of California and the peak immediately south of Jim Beckwourth's Pass was named Mount Ina Coolbrith. "Were I to write what I know, the book would be too sensational to print but were I to write what I think proper, it would be too dull to read. Where is the peace that should with thee abide, O Earth?"

Deseret - Deshret/Dsrt - In Egyptian, it signifies Red Land, the sign of the bee, holy land; crown; desert or red land on either side of the Nile Delta. The Bee was the symbol of the Egyptian king of Lower Egypt.

In Deseret doth truth rear up its royal head;
Though nations may oppose, still wider it shall spread;
Yes, truth and justice, love and grace,
In Deseret find ample place.